Elizabeth Waite was born in Tooting, south London and lived there until she was thirty-four years old. During the war she worked as a bus conductress at Merton Garage. In 1956 she and her husband moved to Devon and bought their first guesthouse. The author of many novels, Elizabeth started writing when she retired. She now lives in Pevensey Bay, Sussex.

ELIZABETH WAITE OMNIBUS

Wheeling and Dealing

Life's for Living

SPHERE

This omnibus edition first published in Great Britain by Sphere in 2009
Elizabeth Waite Omnibus copyright © Elizabeth Waite 2009

Previously published separately:
Wheeling and Dealing first published in Great Britain by
Time Warner Books in 2006
Published by Sphere in 2006
Copyright © Elizabeth Waite 2006

Life's for Living first published in Great Britain by
Time Warner Books in 2005
Copyright © Elizabeth Waite 2005

The moral right of the author has been asserted.

A CIP catalogue record for this book is available from the British Library.

ISBN 978-0-7515-4154-0

Printed and bound in Great Britain by
Mackays of Chatham Ltd, Chatham, Kent

Sphere
An imprint of
Little, Brown Book Group
100 Victoria Embankment
London EC4Y 0DY

An Hachette UK Company
www.hachette.co.uk

www.littlebrown.co.uk

Wheeling and Dealing

PART ONE

1952
Going Upmarket

Chapter One

DENNIS DRYDEN DROVE HIS Jaguar along the tree-lined avenue and into the drive, which was bathed in brilliant sunshine. He turned the key in the ignition but it was a few minutes before he got out of the car. When he did, instead of walking straight up the flight of stone steps, he stood still and surveyed the front of this lovely old house. Who in hell's name would have thought that he, a lad from the East End of London, would ever have ended up owning a place such as this?

In Epsom in Surrey of all places.

The steps leading up to the house ran straight on to a veranda which stretched the whole length of the front part of the building. Four tall upright pillars supported the roof of the porch, and the massive oak front door had to be seen to be believed.

Still, he hadn't bought this property for the look of it from the outside, had he? It was the inside that had knocked him for six, and what was more, with a bit of ducking and diving and because he had the readies available, no mucking about with bank managers or mortgage companies, he'd got it for a knockdown price.

Mind you, he was well aware that he owed a great deal to his old man. A man who lived by the code of the East End and expected everyone he did a deal with to do the same. And woe betide anyone who didn't adhere to that code of honour.

When Ted, his father, had first asked if he wanted to come and have a butcher's at a country mansion, he thought the old man had gone bananas. A place that belonged to a real lady; her husband had died some years ago, she was eighty-six and lately had become very frail. Sheltered housing seemed to be the only answer.

How come his father was on such intimate terms with her ladyship?

Trust. Right from the beginning. Through the grapevine Ted Dryden had heard that what with death duties and debts of one sort and another the old lady was desperate. The truth was, he had known the old girl for years through meeting her at various racecourses.

A few years ago Ted had been running a book at Cheltenham. Her ladyship had backed a rank outsider, and as the leading horses galloped towards the line the crowd had erupted in cheers and shouts. As Ted was paying her out she had got so excited.

'God, I've won a whole lot of money, haven't I?'

With that remark she had swayed on her feet and would have fallen to the ground had Ted not caught her in his brawny arms. A couple of brandies in the clubhouse and he had driven her home.

You could say these two people were as different as chalk and cheese, but for all that they had become good friends. Each of them was lonely, she having lost her husband and never having had any children, while Ted's wife had been dead for twelve years. They had become good friends, with Ted visiting her at least once a month.

Money-wise, and health-wise, matters for her ladyship

had gone from bad to worse. With the exception of Dorothy Sheldon, her paid companion, who was herself in her late sixties, she had no one, having long since paid off the rest of her staff.

With his father doing the business, Derek had bought the place for a knockdown price. That was what happened when you dealt direct with folk. No agents slicing the cream off the top, and as Dennis had the ready cash to cover the whole house as it stood, lock, stock and barrel, except for the family heirlooms and a few of her lady-ship's favourite items, it had all been plain sailing.

There had been another bit of luck, proving that it wasn't what you knew but who you knew in this life: his father had managed to secure a marvellous roomy apart-ment in leafy Chelsea for the old lady. The place was well run, with staff, including a warden, on duty twenty-four hours a day, a lift to all floors, a restaurant on the premises which would serve meals to residents' rooms should they not wish to come downstairs to eat, and several well-heated and nicely furnished public rooms if residents felt the need to socialise.

Dennis had no misgivings that Lady Margaret had been done down. If he hadn't bought the place someone else would have, and while he knew he had got a good deal, he also knew that his father had been fair, seeing, as far as he could, that her ladyship's move went as smoothly as possible. She had made it clear from the start that she wanted not only enough money to clear her debts and live comfortably for what remained of her life, but also, apparently, to get away from this big, lonely house as quickly as possible, taking with her only what would fit into her new home.

He placed the key into the lock of the heavily built front door, but it was all of half a minute before he managed to turn it and was able to open the door. The large, high-ceilinged hall smelt damp and dusty. After closing the door, he stood with his back to it for a few seconds before walking towards the middle of the hall, to stand on a large Persian rug and gaze up the high-panelled staircase.

Well, now he had some sorting out to do and no mistake.

Ella, his wife, was right about two things. One, this time he might have bitten off more than he could chew! And two, she and their two children were never going to agree to come and live in this gloomy, dark house. On the second count he knew his Elly would be unmovable. She was an East Ender born and bred, and wild horses wouldn't make her move from her beloved London.

Slowly he climbed the stairs and on reaching the first landing stared down at the grounds that surrounded the house. The state of the lawns, flowerbeds, trees and shrubs cried out that it was many a long day since a gardener had worked there. Poor old soul. Seemed like most of her ladyship's friends must have deserted her. Or even more likely, most of them were already dead.

The fact that she had turned to a man like his father for help spoke volumes.

Ted Dryden was a good man at heart, but a rough diamond at the best of times. Though born and bred in the East End of London, he could polish himself up when the need arose. He was the sort that had come from nothing without any privileges and had made it to the top by sheer undeniable guts and determination. He had the confident manner of a successful bookmaker without any airs or graces. A damn good friend who always made sure he repaid a favour.

But you wouldn't want him as an enemy!

And I'm his son, Dennis thought, allowing himself a wry smile.

Dennis was fifty but looked younger, in a rough-and-ready kind of way. A boyish face and a way with the ladies; intense bright blue eyes with lots of lines across his forehead. A thick mop of dark hair, his sideboards going a bit grey, though unlike his father he had never grown a moustache. He did match his dad in height, each of them standing six foot three in their stockinged feet.

He turned away from staring down at the overgrown grounds, walked a few yards down the corridor, pushed through a heavy door and stepped into a deep-carpeted small lounge. Dust-sheets covered three armchairs, probably thoughtfully placed there by Dorothy Sheldon. Apart from that there was no other furniture and basically the room looked awful. The decor hadn't been touched for years: the once expensive wallpaper had faded and the ceiling, which should have been white, was now a dirty brownish colour.

Going further into the room he stared at the large open fireplace. Great log fires must have burnt there at one time was his immediate thought. It was then that his gaze fell on a small footstool on which lay two old racing programmes, one for the Derby and one for the Oaks. Alongside was a pair of ladies' spectacles, still attached to a long silver chain.

He had always considered himself a hard man, but at that moment he felt utterly gutted, and the lump that had formed in his throat was threatening to choke him.

There must have been a time when racing was a great part of her ladyship's life. Especially with the glorious downs of Epsom and the great racecourse right on her doorstep. Maybe she and her husband had even owned their own horses.

How had Lady Margaret sunk to such a low level?

Folk still talked about her husband as being a thorough gentleman.

Some gent! He'd left his wife almost penniless, with a

huge house that she could not afford to keep in good repair. If tales told were true, in his lifetime the house had had a host of servants, and he had employed a coachman who drove his horse-drawn carriage even after he had acquired two motor-cars. And naturally he went to shooting parties and rode with the local hunt.

Dennis hadn't known him, and neither had Ted, but they'd had many a discussion about this gentleman in the last six months and they were both of the same mind. A gentleman looks after his family and makes provision for them when he's called to meet his Maker. No decent man lives so much beyond his means that when he dies his poor wife struggles on a pittance until it comes to the crunch and she is forced to sell not only her house, but almost every stick and stone inside it.

Dennis sighed heavily and walked slowly back across the room, closing the door softly behind him. As he descended the stairs he was shaking his head. His face was thoughtful and his eyes were sad. What a way to end one's life.

Poor Lady Margaret! Poor soul!

Chapter Two

ELLA DRYDEN WRIGGLED HER plump bottom more comfortably into her armchair.

By God, her old man had done a damn silly thing this time. He had actually signed the contracts and everything had been completed legally, and now he was the proud owner of that musty old house miles away from London.

What in the name of God was he going to do with it?

He had been full of it when he took her down to see that place. But Ella had made it quite clear it wasn't for her. There and then she'd sworn to him that that was the first and last time she'd set foot in the place!

Dennis didn't need any telling what his Ella was thinking, but just got on with eating his dinner. Damn good cook was Ella. Steak and kidney pie today, with masses of vegetables and a jug of gravy the likes of which nobody else he knew could make. As for her pastry! Light as a feather. And he'd take a bet that she'd been to at least two other houses today and delivered a good hot meal to an old soul that was living alone. Always cooking and feeding half the blinking street was his wife. Talk about being lady bountiful. Old Mr Parsons loved her cheese scones, Ma Bristow's delight was Ella's fruitcake, while poor Mary Marsh and her two fatherless kids always got a free dinner every Saturday, and they were only the ones he knew about. More than likely there was half a dozen more that he was helping to keep.

Ella just couldn't keep her thoughts to herself any longer.

'You've really done it this time, Dennis.' She spoke sharply. 'I never thought you'd go through with it.'

'You said you liked the 'ouse,' he said, munching on a well-salted roast potato.

'Yeah, well, some of the inside I did.'

'Well, if I could persuade you to move you'd be living in the inside, you daft woman, not on the outside.'

'You're the daft one, Den. No matter what yer do with the place yer can't pick it up and put it down 'ere in London, can yer?'

'I thought you'd be glad to be rid of all the dirt and squalor around 'ere. All the local council and the landlords are intent on doing is knocking down these old streets of houses and building high-rise flats. See how you feel about moving when it comes to that.'

'When! It ain't 'appened yet. No need t' meet trouble 'alfway. Besides, Babs and Teddy don't think much of moving. Got their mates and their school and they like it fine. Come to that, you'd 'ave to drag them screaming to get them away from their gran, an' you know it.'

'You've just been sitting there thinking up excuses. You could persuade yer mother t' come with us if you went the right way about it.'

'Not a chance in hell, Denny boy. You've 'eard Mum say often enough that she was born in that 'ouse an' she'll go out of it in 'er box.'

'Well, if that's the case, you'd better start looking for an old folk's 'ome for her, 'cos it's a dead cert that sooner or later they'll demolish all the houses in these back streets.'

'Oh yeah?' Ella now twisted her body round and faced him. 'The day will never dawn when I stand by and see my mother go into a home. You ought t' know by now you don't get my mother to go anywhere she doesn't want to. You get away with bullying me most of the time, but nothing you say or do this time will coax me into moving from London to live in the back of beyond.'

She lowered her voice a little and, changing her tone, said, 'Why do you always 'ave t' play the big I am? If you wanted us to move, why not buy a place near here? Buying an 'ouse out in the country won't make you into a country gentleman. Or is it that you've got yerself another young bit of stuff that you want to show off to?'

'Oh, you're not going to start off on that track again, are you?' Dennis said, sighing heavily.

Ella shook her head sadly as she added, 'I know I'm not growing old gracefully, I'm nothing like the young, slim girl you married, but then you're no oil painting. But you flash money around and that's the only reason the young women flatter you.'

'You finished?'

'Yeah, we'll leave it for the present, but there's lots more I could say. Just don't ever play me for too big a fool, Den. I can smell cheap scent, and it's me what scrubs the lipstick off yer shirts. Perhaps you should stock up with some of that new kiss-proof lipstick they've got in Woolworth's.'

'Oh, we're going to 'ave all the old rigmarole today, are we?' Dennis said, reaching for the crusty end of the loaf of bread, which he used to wipe his plate clean.

Ella was about to tell him a few more home truths when the sound of another war of words cut her short. Babs and Teddy were at it again! It was bad enough when

11

they were just bickering, but from the sound of the noise now coming from upstairs it had gone beyond that stage.

'I'd better go an' see what they're up to,' she exclaimed impatiently.

Dennis laughed. 'Leave 'em to it. You were about to tell me what a rotter you really think I am.'

'You don't need me t' tell you. Try looking into yer own conscience once in a while.'

And with that she pulled herself up from the depths of her armchair and marched out of the room, shouting, 'Teddy! And you, Babs!'

She was halfway up the stairs when her twelve-year-old son, Edward, named after his grandfather, stuck his head over the banisters and called down to her, 'Mum, can't you keep this blinking sister of mine out of my bedroom?'

Ella paused for a moment and looked up at him, saying, 'Whatever she's done, do you have to make such a racket? You'd better not have laid into her, or your father will tan your backside.'

Teddy drew back and she went quickly up the remaining stairs, calling, 'Babs, are you all right?'

On the narrow landing she pushed open the door to her son's bedroom to see her young daughter, just eight years old, deliberately tearing pages from a book and adding them to a pile of screwed-up ones that lay beside her. She couldn't believe her eyes, and yelled at the top of her voice, 'Good God, girl! What on earth do you think you are doing? If there is one thing I've taught you in your short life, it's to treat books with respect.'

Babs let go of the torn page she was holding and turned her face towards her mother, crying, 'I'm getting my own back. He's pulled all the lovely curls off my best doll's head, the big china one that Gran bought me. I'm going t' get Dad to kill him, I am.'

'Shut up! You are both as bad as one another.'

Ella now looked at her son. He was a big lad for his age, well built, with bright blue eyes and a thick mop of curly hair. Oh yes, he was the image of his father. She glared at him as she said, 'One of these days you're gonna go too far. I'm warning you, even yer father won't give in t' you for ever. Why did you do it?'

Teddy's lips tightened now as he said bitterly, 'She sneaked in here an' she's torn up at least six of my fag-cards. I only left them out of the box 'cos I was going to exchange them with Johnny Riley. You wanna tell her to keep her hands off my belongings. Besides, she thinks she knows everything. Teacher's pet 'cos she can do adding-up in her head. But she knows nothing about sport.'

'All right, all right, so you're both different, which is a good thing.'

'She's spiteful an' horrible,' Teddy screamed. 'Just what did she get out of destroying my cards?'

'That's enough!' Ella was shaking. 'Whatever the reason, boys should never hurt little girls. You've been told that often enough.'

'She's not a little girl. She's nearly as big as me and she kicks me often enough.'

Ella turned round now, took hold of her daughter by her shoulders and shook her, saying, 'That was a horrible thing to do. You know how much his collection means to him. Why did you do it?'

There was a sulky look on Babs's face now as she said bitterly, 'Because he's such a know-all and a big-head and he's Dad's favourite. Dad gets him all those cards and he knows the names of all the cricketers and footballers, but when it comes to school work he's almost bottom of the class.'

'Oh God above, give me strength,' Ella muttered. Then, pointing to the door, she said, 'Come on, Babs. Out! This

13

is his room and each of you should thank yer lucky stars that you've got a room of yer own. There's a great number of kids that have never known that luxury.'

Babs got off the bed and walked out. Her long dark curls swinging, she went across the landing, thrust open the door to her own bedroom and went in, shutting the door firmly behind her.

Little madam, her mother said to herself, a fact that she partly blamed her own mother for. Babs could do no wrong in the eyes of her grandmother.

She turned to her son and stared hard at him for a moment before she said, 'Don't look at me like that, Teddy. It's only right that yer father and grandfather take yer to football matches and help you to keep up with all forms of sport, but it won't 'elp yer to know all the famous names when it comes to earning your own living. Girls won't like you either if all you ever think and talk about is sport.'

'Who cares about girls, they're all dead soppy,' he answered defiantly.

Ella changed the tone of her voice. 'Why do you do it, son? Why must you always be fighting with yer sister? And I know for a fact that when you're at school, you want to boss everybody.'

'Because I want to be like me dad an' me grandad. They're their own bosses an' nobody gives them any stick.'

The words sounded so much like a challenge, they startled Ella. Teddy was only twelve, and he was speaking as a man. She hadn't imagined that her son was already thinking that he wanted his life to run as his father's did.

When it came to their physical needs, Dennis was a good father and a good husband. He saw to it that Ella always had enough money to feed the children well and put good clothes on their backs, and he made sure they

14

went to school. No wagging off like a lot of the young lads round here did. For a moment she pondered. It was great that Teddy had been taught to be interested in sport and to stand up for himself, but had these two things become an obsession with both his father and his grandfather?

She didn't need any telling that Edward Dryden had had a hand in her Denny buying this big house out at Epsom. It was near a racecourse for one thing, and what with Ted being a bookie, horse-racing had become an obsession with both her father-in-law and his son. And now she had to face the fact that Teddy had the urge to be like them.

Oh, life was difficult.

Ella chewed on her lip as she went slowly back down the stairs.

When all was said and done, she hadn't married Dennis with her eyes blinkered. She had known from the beginning he was a Jack-the-lad. A good many girls had had their eyes on him, and she had been proud that he had looked her way.

She sighed and told herself she might have done better, but watching some of the goings-on round these parts, she wondered. There were young women living with men who had never married them, and others with husbands who knocked them about unmercifully or gave the bulk of their wages to the local pub owners. It was the plight of the children of these families that sparked pity in her and caused her to readily admit that she could have done worse than marry Dennis Dryden.

Oh yes, much worse. A whole lot worse.

Chapter Three

'YOU'VE GOT YOUR WAY over the Epsom house. I've put two applications in to the council, one for turning the whole place into flats and the second one for renovating the place and maybe using it as a hotel.' Dennis Dryden's voice was harsh as he told his wife what his options were. She was still dead set against moving. No matter how hard he had tried to persuade her, she was absolutely determined that she was not going to live anywhere but London.

Ella nodded, but did not reply. She sensed that Dennis had more to say. She stared out of the kitchen window at the small cobblestoned back yard and watched her two lines of washing blowing in the breeze. At last she said, 'It would be nice to live in the country, just for a while now and again, to be able to keep your house and your clothes so much cleaner, but by God I'd miss the shops, the markets and most of all me neighbours.'

'Oh yeah,' Dennis agreed, 'we'd all miss the bloody neighbours!'

His sarcasm ruffled her feathers and she went on, 'You probably wouldn't, but could yer live without yer local pubs and yer dad's betting shop? An' another thing, what about all the blokes you've got working for you on yer dodgy deals? Would they be willing to travel out into the sticks every day to get their orders from you?'

Stifling his anger, Dennis nodded dumbly. Ella's current life was pretty hard; she took such good care of their two kids and her mother. His father too, come to that, 'cos there weren't many Sunday dinnertimes that he wasn't round here with his feet under their table. Dennis made sure he didn't keep her short of money, yet her whole life seemed to be one long struggle against the dirt and grime of these back streets of London. He sighed as he did his best to smile at his wife.

'Trouble with you, Ella, is fear of the unknown. You've never known anything different and you don't particularly want to, do yer?' he said resentfully.

Ella lifted her hands in a helpless gesture. 'I was born here and we've all survived the war, so why should we up and leave it all behind now just to satisfy your ego?'

He stared at her for a moment before picking up his coat and thrusting his arms into the sleeves. He walked slowly across the room towards her, then stopped within an arm's length of her. In a low voice, now, he said, 'You're very fond of calling me a big-head, aren't you, Ella? In the past you've called me brash, and on one occasion you even said I'd stop at nothing to pull off a deal. That's right isn't it?'

'Suppose it is, if you say so.'

Dennis lowered his head and thrust his face closer to hers. 'You don't like the deals I do, but all the same you and the kids benefit every which way there is. I supply the wherewithal so that you can be the kind-hearted woman who is generous to the needy. Well, my dear wife, here's something for you to think about. Whichever plan the council gives their approval to, I shall be employing

17

a darn sight more men than I do now. Bricklayers, carpenters, plumbers, you name them, and I'll have no difficulty in finding them. Why? Because it will be steady work and they know that I will pay them well. So it won't be just me that makes money, will it?'

Ella's large bosom rose and she let out a long breath before she said, 'So according to you, everyone is 'appy to go along with whatever you decide except me.'

'That's the message I'm getting, far too often if you want me to be blunt. Tell me straight, Ella, just what is keeping you here?' He was dismayed by her dull tone of voice and her lack of enthusiasm.

Ella pursed her lips. That was the big question. She had always considered herself ordinary, contented with her lot, and she wanted her two children to be the same, but not Dennis.

Oh no, not him!

He'd been fighting his way all his life, ambition driving him, determined that he was going to move his family up the scale. She was no fool; she knew Dennis regarded her as a hindrance, thwarting him at every turn. She was well aware that although she was twelve years younger than him, she hadn't worn so well. She had borne two children and from then on had become plump, and that was putting it kindly. She was always clean and tidy and so was her house, yet he was forever telling her she had no style, whereas the type of women he took out could wear old sacks and still appear attractive, because he always chose younger women who were very slim. When Dennis had a few beers inside him and was admiring the ladies who happened to be in the pub, he would look at Ella and say unkindly, 'Can't stop me from looking.'

More often than not, she would cast her eye over the bunch of girls sitting near the bar and her reaction would be, 'Skinny lot, a damn good meal would do them good.'

18

Dennis would laugh loudly and say something along the lines of 'The nearer the bone, the sweeter the meat.'

Sadly, these days that didn't apply to her.

She looked down at herself, her baggy, shapeless dress covering her wide hips and fat legs. Could she move away from London? Live out in Epsom? She doubted it. She'd be like a fish out of water!

This house might be old-fashioned, with none of the mod cons the youngsters were always on about, but it was clean, comfortable and more to the point it was her home. Apart from cracks in one wall, a few slates off the roof and every window having been smashed, it had withstood all of Hitler's air raids. There were parts of London where whole streets had been destroyed, and if the German bombers hadn't driven her out of her home in those awful years, she saw no good reason why she should move away now.

What Dennis wanted was to get away from this colourful, noisy working-class area. He hated the back-to-back houses and long, narrow streets hemmed in by factories, and the street markets where men shouted their wares from early morning until as late as ten at night, when huge paraffin lamps would still light up their stalls. Of course all that had stopped during the war, what with the blackout and the food shortages, not to mention the fact that all fit and well men had been sent to foreign shores to fight for their country.

Things were getting better, though. The Government had set up a special committee to ensure that all houses which were still standing had the glass replaced in every window and all structural faults put right.

The men who had been lucky enough to come home had discarded their uniforms. They mostly wore overalls during the week, but on Sundays they wore trousers and jackets or their demob suits. And for the lads who were still single, a trilby hat worn jauntily to one side was an absolute must.

On the whole, life was getting back to normal. And now Dennis was asking her to pack up and move away to live an entirely different life. Mix with different people, be a bit more upper-class. Could she do it?

'No! No! Never!' She had shouted the words out loud.

From the look on Dennis's face, she thought he was going to blow a gasket.

Ella stood in the middle of the room, eyes cast down, looking at the floor.

'Yeah, take a good look. How many other houses in this street 'ave got carpet on the floor?' he raged at her. 'You, Ella, when it comes to me, are a bleeder! You bleed me dry. I provide and pay for every last damn thing that comes into this house, but what do I get in return? Sod all. Well, you've gone too far this time, but don't for a minute think you'll put the kibosh on my plans. Not this time you won't. Stay here with the kids, live yer dreary life. I'll see you don't starve but I don't 'ave t' let you drag me down with yer.' Dennis had hissed the last words at her.

Ella was frightened. He had never threatened her like this before. 'I didn't mean that you shouldn't have bought the house.'

'Didn't you?' with a scornful look. He was glad that he had raged at her; it had given her something to think about. He was fed up to the teeth with her never wanting to do anything worthwhile. Stuck in a rut, her and her bloody mother. There was simply no pleasing either of them.

Ella sank down on to a chair as Dennis stormed out of the room. She listened to his footsteps go along the passage, and when the front door slammed, tears trickled down her plump cheeks.

He was right. He was a damn good provider.

When the going was good, that is. At times Dennis had a convenient memory. How about the times when things weren't going the way he wanted them to? Then anything and everything he could lay his hands on was taken out of the house and sold. It was no joke. One week he'd had a radiogram delivered to the house, and then, to the sheer delight of both Babs and Teddy, their father had taken them out and allowed them to choose at least two dozen records. For days on end they played music and sang along with the records. Never before nor since had Ella seen her children so happy.

Then one morning the kids had come down for their breakfast and found the whole caboodle had gone. In fact the front room had been stripped bare. For a mere five and a half weeks the children had thoroughly enjoyed that radiogram. Oh, good old trustworthy Dennis had replaced it, but not until seven weeks later, and the presentation hadn't seemed the same the second time around.

That was only one incident.

Most worrying of all was that Dennis would disappear for days on end. Why did she worry herself at such times? Because how was she to know that he hadn't had an accident? But voice her concern and Dennis would laugh and just say that every businessman had to be away from home at times. Quite so, but without telling his family where he was?

The erratic behaviour of their father took away a feeling of security the kids should have. Not just for worldly goods, but for a steady, permanent way of life with a dad who could be relied on to always be there.

Ella busied herself clearing the breakfast table. Going through to the scullery, she stacked the dirty dishes on the wooden draining board, then filled the kettle from the cold tap, placed it over one of the gas rings, struck a match and lit a low flame beneath it.

Talking aloud to herself she said, 'While the kettle's boiling I may as well go up and make the beds.'

It was dead on the stroke of eleven when she came downstairs, arms full of more dirty washing. She smiled to herself as she heard the front door open and her mother calling out loudly, 'It's only me, luv.' Regular as clockwork, Winnie Paige arrived at her daughter's house at the same time Monday to Thursday. Fridays she came earlier because the two of them went to the market, while Saturdays and Sundays she kept herself to herself in case Dennis was around. They had never exactly seen eye to eye.

For as long as Ella could remember, her mother had been the local flower-seller. On weekdays she had sat outside the underground station with her basket of blooms. She had long since given up working during the week, but although she was in her late seventies, she still worked on a Sunday, getting one of her neighbours who was a totter to trundle her wheelbarrow up to the London Hospital, where she did a roaring trade.

Ella said, 'Hallo, Mum, you look smart this morning. You off out somewhere?'

It was true, Winnie did look good, and Ella sighed, wishing she could look more like her mother. Winnie Paige was only five foot four, and slim in build. She dressed smartly although her face was florid and weatherbeaten. Her motto was 'God helps those that help themselves', and so she did her best using a little make-up and a lot of face-powder. Her hair was marcel-waved and peeped out from her smart hat to cover her ears. She wore a brown costume that had seen better days but still showed signs of having been an expensive outfit when first made. She wouldn't thank you for telling anyone that she bought her clothes from a second-hand stall run by a middle-aged couple who often acquired garments from well-to-do ladies.

Ella had now reached the bottom of the stairs and she gave her mother a look that went from top to toe. You never look like that on Sundays, she grinned to herself. And that was true. Come Sunday, a black shawl and an old felt hat was Winnie's uniform; she wanted her customers to feel that she needed them to buy her flowers.

'I feel a bit fed up this morning,' Winnie said frankly as she walked into her daughter's kitchen. 'Sarah Brown from Brady Street died yesterday. She had been ill for a long time, but she was a good friend and I need cheering up a bit. I thought you and I might go out somewhere.'

'Nice idea, Mum, as long as we're back in time t' meet the kids from school.'

'Course we will be, an' we'll take them into Joey Lyons, buy them hot chocolate and a cupcake.'

'I'm nowhere near ready yet, though. I haven't washed up, and there's all this laundry,' Ella moaned.

'Oh Ella, for God's sake. I'll wash the pots while you get changed, and the laundry can wait till tomorrow. Go on, and wrap up warm. These last few days of March are very cold and damp. I'm glad Easter is late this year. Let's 'ope the weather improves before the kids break up.'

Ella knew she would get nowhere arguing with her mother, so she smiled at her affectionately and did as she was told.

Winnie looked serious as she watched her daughter shrug her arms into her long coat. How she wished she could do something about Ella's image. Some mornings when she arrived, Ella was sloshing about in her nightdress and dressing gown. Why didn't she wash and dress herself as soon as she got up; perhaps even walk the children to school? There was so much Winnie wanted to say, but she knew things weren't that good between Ella and Dennis so she had to tread carefully.

'Ella,' she began as they walked arm in arm to the tram stop, 'would you let me buy you a new outfit?'

'Oh 'ere we go, Mum. You always have to start. You're not saying that I need new clothes, you're telling me, as you always do, that I'm too fat.'

'Well, luv, it's only because I hate to see you slouching about. You don't make the best of yourself, now do you?'

'You've always said I'm like me dad was, and he was a great heavy brute, wasn't he? So I guess it was how I was born.'

'Yes, I suppose you do have a lot of your father in you,' sighed Winnie. 'But I still say you don't make the best of yourself. Will you let me sort a few things out for you today?'

Loath as she was, Ella gave in. 'All right, but can we have something to eat before we go to the shops or up the market?'

'Course we can, but then . . . Well, we'll wait and see, but by the time I've finished with you, that 'usband of yours will be seeing you in a different light.'

As the day wore on, Ella began to think her mother had gone over the top. They were weighed down with bags. Most of the items they had found on Winnie's favourite stall, but a couple had come from a select shop in the London Road. Looking at herself in a full-length mirror and listening to the complimentary remarks not only from the sales ladies but also from Winnie, Ella had to admit her mother knew what she was talking about when it came to clothes, and today she had given Ella a magnificent boost.

She began to feel grateful to her mother. She knew she

had let herself slide, and that fact alone had played a big part in spoiling things between her and Dennis. She would make an effort, she promised herself, perhaps even have her hair shampooed and set, wear one of her new outfits.

Would Dennis look at her in a different light?

Hopefully he would. She was willing to meet him halfway over lots of things, but there was still that problem about moving out of London. She just could not give way on that.

Then a bright thought came to mind. Whatever Dennis decided to do with that property, when everything was completed to his satisfaction, he'd be able to sell it at a huge profit.

She smiled to herself. There was nothing in this world that her husband loved more than making money.

When his pockets were full, life was great. Times when he was broke, it was a question of God help them all.

Chapter Four

ELLA HAD LAIN AWAKE half the night listening for Dennis to come in. Now she laid her arm across the bed to where he should be lying, yet she already knew he wasn't there. She wished she hadn't had so much to say: why oh why had she had to rub him up the wrong way? She could just as easily have gone back to Epsom with him and given the house another look over. Made suggestions, aired her views, even gone along with his plans. That wouldn't have meant she had to move there; she could have gone on stalling. But no, she'd jumped in with both feet, adamant she wasn't moving come what may, and Dennis wasn't going to forget it.

He hadn't come home last night, and God alone knew when he would make an appearance again.

She struggled to sit up, threw the thick patchwork quilt and the blankets to the end of the bed and swung her legs round until her feet touched the thick bedside rug. Feeling under the bed, she brought forth her slippers and slid them on: at this time in the morning the oilcloth that covered the floor of the bedroom always felt icy cold. She crossed to the window and drew the curtains back. It was already light, and she gazed over the back yards and the slate-covered rooftops. The tall chimneys of the factories were already smoking, and soon the shrill sirens would blast the air, signalling to the workers that the morning shift was about to start.

When she'd given the children their breakfast and seen them off to school, it would seem a long morning until her mother came in. Dennis hardly ever left the house before ten.

Oh well, she'd stated her case firmly enough; she wasn't moving from here and so she'd just have to grin and bear it.

Three weeks later and still Ella hadn't seen sight nor sound of her husband.

Her mother kept saying, 'Stop worrying, he's got it made. From what I hear down at the King's Head, your Dennis is doing all right for himself, got workmen swarming all over that place he bought out at Epsom.'

Ella was silently wondering where he was living. Surely he wasn't sleeping in that huge house while all that work was going on? She might not admit it, but she missed her Den, very much, especially now that Teddy had joined the Boys' Brigade and Babs went to the Brownies and she had some evenings on her own. She wasn't worried about money; she knew Den would turn up sooner or later, if only for his clothes. Besides, she had been going through his wardrobe, brushing the shoulders of his tailored suits and checking his pockets, and had found a leather wallet that held one hundred pounds in small notes, winnings from horse-racing as well as dogs, she had no doubt, and she felt no qualms about carefully using it for housekeeping money. She folded his pile of shirts more neatly and hung his flashy ties on the rail that was fixed to the inside of the wardrobe door.

Ted, her father-in-law, still came round, sometimes for

a meal, other times just long enough to have a cup of tea. He never left without leaving at least a couple of pound notes on the table.

Saturday morning, Babs and Teddy were playing out in the street with a lot of other children. Ella had warned them to stay out of trouble, Teddy especially, because he was in danger of becoming a real terror now his father wasn't around.

Ella and her mother were just about to set out to do their shopping when Ted Dryden pulled his car into the kerb, lowered the window and called out, 'How about you two joining me for a drink in the Globe tonight? I'll pick you up about 'alf seven.' Without waiting for a reply, he put the car in gear and drove away.

Mother and daughter looked at each other in amazement. The Globe was a posh pub, quite a way from this area, but it was also known as a meeting place where crafty crooks did dodgy deals.

'What d'yer reckon?' Winnie asked as the pair of them exchanged meaningful glances.

'You go,' Ella urged her mother. 'I can't leave the kids on their own.'

'Don't make excuses. You know darn well Janey Brown from next door t' you will willingly come into your place and stay with them. She's sixteen, so she knows what she's doing, and I'll give her 'alf a dollar.'

Ella shifted her shopping basket to the other hand and linked arms with her mum. Laughingly she said, '*You* want to go, don't you?'

'Well, it's not every Saturday night that we get asked out, is it?'

'No, you're right there. So we're going, are we?'

'Yes, we are, an' for once do me a favour, try dressing yerself up. I'll come round early and heat the tongs up and see what we can do with your hair.'

'I'll wash my hair when we get back and give it a jolly good brushing. Isn't that good enough?' Ella said.

'No it isn't.' Winnie patted her own permanent-waved hair theatrically. 'You won't know yourself by the time I've finished with you. You've let yerself go for far too long, but today I'm taking you in hand.'

Ella knew her mother was speaking the truth, so she just squeezed Winnie's arm and kept silent.

The weather during March had been really depressing, the gale force winds beating against the old houses, feeling almost as if they were penetrating the walls, and howling down the chimney pots, sending clouds of smoke into the kitchen and making it nigh on impossible to keep a good fire going. But today everything was much calmer: the wind had died down, the streets were dry, and a weak sun was doing its best to shine through the fluffy clouds. This change in the weather had brought the world and his wife out, and everywhere you looked there were crowds.

Ella and Winnie took the bus to Bishopsgate. As they stepped down on to the pavement they smiled at each other. The atmosphere was different, real East End; people smiled and had a bright word as they passed. Across the road, on the corner of Middlesex Street, stood one of London's most famous pubs, known far and wide as Dirty Dick's. Of course that wasn't the name that appeared on the justice's licence. The real name of the delightful old-fashioned pub was actually The Old Jerusalem.

Winnie suggested they should pop in and have a drink. The pub was full, noisy and bustling, as was to be expected on a Saturday, but today it was even busier than usual, and there wasn't an empty seat to be seen. Winnie pushed her way into the snug and ordered two glasses of the house speciality beer served straight from giant hogshead barrels. It was a strong but refreshing drink. They had almost drained their glasses when someone's elbow caught Ella in the back and she said, 'Let's get out of here, Mum.'

They made their way out through the rear entrance, through the alley, and into Middlesex Street. Real cockneys called this street 'The Lane'. In reality, there were several streets, narrow and cluttered by stalls and impassable to all but pedestrians. On Saturdays this great street market sold mostly china, household goods and food. Fruit and vegetables, meat, fish, home-made bread and cakes. Ella loved the different smells, and listening to the totters shouting that the china tea services on their stalls were pure English bone china and at the prices they were asking they were practically giving them away.

They were not without competition. A father and son were flogging bed linen, and their ribald comments as to what would happen if you were to put their sexy sheets and eiderdowns on your bed were beyond belief.

As for the meat van! Two brothers owned it, and there was always a wide choice of meat for sale both for roasting and stewing, as well as bacon, sausages and chickens which, although dead, still had their feathers on and needed to be plucked when you got them home. The brothers would skin rabbits for you and hold on to the skins because a dealer in fur would pay a good price for them. These two young men were using a microphone and their saucy jokes were a bit near the mark.

It was jolly good free entertainment to visit these London markets.

'Are we going to have something to eat before we do our shopping?' asked Winnie.

'I 'ope so,' was Ella's reply, walking more quickly towards the café.

Winnie looked irritated when they found the café to be as busy as the pub had been, but a familiar voice shouted out, 'Come over 'ere, Win, there's a couple of empty seats at our table.'

Ella elbowed her way to the counter. The café was stuffy and the windows were steamed up, but it was a good meeting place. Customers mostly knew each other so there was plenty of gossip going on, and you always got damn good food and a decent hot drink.

Ella came back with a tray that held two large mugs of tea and a plate piled high with hot buttered toast. She plonked her backside down on the only empty chair, smiled and said hello to Pam and Bill Edwards, who were old friends of her mother. She also nodded to an elderly man with grey hair and a moustache who was sitting with them. Bill merely said, 'This is Boris Lindsey, a neighbour of ours; this is Win's daughter, Ella Dryden.'

Ella gratefully grasped her huge mug in both hands, sipped her tea and then began to munch at a slice of toast while her mum and Pam chatted away nineteen to the dozen, but she felt a little uneasy. This Boris hadn't taken his eyes off her.

Suddenly he reached out and touched her arm. 'You ain't Dennis Dryden's wife, are you?'

'Yes, I am,' she replied with surprise, looking into the man's bright eyes.

'I'm glad t' meet yer,' he exclaimed, 'I've 'eard a lot about you lately. Got two kiddies, ain't yer?'

'Yes, I have,' Ella said quietly.

The man shook his head. 'That makes it worse. I'm ever so sorry, luv. Wasn't much I could do about it, though.'

'Would you mind telling me what you're talking about?' Ella said, puckering her forehead.

'I suppose I 'ave t' come straight out with it now.' The man's face showed shock and he sucked his lips. Then, taking a deep breath, he blurted out, 'The minute Bill said yer name was Dryden I put two an' two together.

31

Your 'usband has been taking my granddaughter out. She brought him round t' my place the other night 'cos her mother wouldn't 'ave him in the 'ouse. I didn't let him in neither, told him to wait in that big flashy car of his. I couldn't 'elp but think he were dodgy. My Anne's barely half his age.'

Ella leant her elbows on the table and said quietly, 'Don't let it worry you, Boris. Your Anne's not the first an' it's a dead cert she won't be the last.'

She was doing her best to put a brave face on but she was finding it hard. It was no surprise, but it was hurtful if she admitted the truth. To be told something like this by a total stranger, and worst of all to know that he was sitting there feeling sorry for her. She felt awkward to say the least, and breathed a sigh of relief when her mum looked over at her and suggested that it was about time they started their shopping.

'Goodbye, luv, take care,' was shouted back and forth, and they were back outside in the cold fresh air.

An hour later, loaded down with bags of shopping, Ella would have been more than pleased to go straight home. Her mother had other plans.

Head held high, and a look of determination on her face, Winnie led the way through side streets that would bring them out into a different kind of market. Here all the stalls were covered in on three sides with sheets of canvas, giving customers a sense of privacy. The goods on offer for sale were also very different. Some sold rings, bracelets and necklaces. One stall had a wonderful display of timepieces: clocks of all shapes and sizes, pocket watches with chains for gentlemen, and for the ladies not only wristwatches but some very ornate fob watches which Ella glanced at with envy.

The owners of the last stall in the row were also the

proprietors of the glass-fronted shop which stood directly opposite on the pavement.

Winnie Paige had become acquainted with this family some years ago and had benefited greatly from the friendship inasmuch as she was able to wear really good clothes that had not cost her a fortune.

Mother and daughter were still walking when Isaac Cohan stepped in front of them and blocked their passage. Arms flung wide, he spoke loudly. ''Allo, Winifred, where the 'ell 'ave yer been? Sight nor sound of you we 'ave not seen. Come 'ere.'

A flush of pleasure rose in Winnie's cheeks as she looked at this short man with the broad smile on his face. He was wearing a smart pinstriped suit with narrow lapels, a sparkling white shirt and a dark blue tie.

She dumped her shopping bags at her feet and willingly went into this portly old man's arms.

Even passers-by paused to look, and Ella watched with pleasure as these two old friends greeted each other. It was a show of warmth and affection. When they broke free, Ella was surprised to see that her mother's eyes were brimming with tears, and it came to her that although her dad had been dead for years, her mum must still miss him. It was then that she told herself that in future she mustn't take Winnie for granted so much, and must remember not only to tell her that she loved her, but to show her that she did.

'And how is our Elly?' Isaac asked. Without waiting for a reply, he herded both of them towards the shop, shouting through the open doorway, 'Wally, come and see to the stall.'

A tall young man appeared, and as soon as he spotted Winnie he said, 'Winifred Paige, how nice to see you. My mother will be pleased.'

'And this is her daughter Ella. I don't think you have

met each other before, but we have known her since she was a little toddler, though we haven't seen her for years, not since she married and got a family of her own.'

Isaac's son shook hands with Ella and told her he was pleased to meet her, then he crossed the road and went to stand behind their stall. Ella turned her head; she had to give this young man a second look.

Walter Cohan was a lot taller than his father, and in his early forties, Ella guessed. He had deep dark brown eyes, a handsome tanned face and a head of thick black wavy hair. Ella couldn't have said why, but despite the short acquaintance, she liked him and the friendly way in which he had treated her and her mother.

The inside of the shop was much larger than it had appeared from the outside. Ella looked about, her eyes darting from side to side with unconcealed curiosity. There were blouses, jumpers and cardigans expertly displayed in glass-fronted cabinets. Two waxwork dummies stood against a wall, one dressed in a businesslike navy-blue two-piece costume, the other one attired more modestly in a perfectly plain high-necked, long-sleeved black dress that fell to just about calf length. What made the garment look so glamorous was that the last six inches of the dress was covered with an adornment of heavy black silk fringe.

Ella's imagination was running riot. Imagine dancing, wearing a frock like that! Get real, she scolded herself, you'd have to starve for six months to even get into it.

Sadie Cohan put down the pen with which she had been writing and came round from behind the counter. She was not very tall, and her dark hair was fastened back and secured into a neat twirl at the nape of her neck. She was wearing a beautiful tailored suit in a worsted material of soft brown with a beige silk blouse beneath the jacket. She was an attractive woman, with fine black

34

eyebrows, her face lightly powdered, her features outlined by lipstick and a hint of rouge.

She grasped both of Winnie's hands in her own, squeezing them tightly. 'At last, at last you come to see us. Please come through to the sitting room. So much shopping you have done. I must make you some refreshment. You will take a glass of lemon tea with Isaac and me?'

Then, realising that she had not greeted Ella, she smiled at her with genuine pleasure and spoke to her in a warm tone. 'Please, come, sit down. You must be Winifred's daughter of whom I have heard so much, though it is many a long year since I have seen you. It is nice that you visit us now.'

'It is nice to meet you too,' Ella said politely.

It was then that they heard voices coming from the shop. 'I will attend to the customers. You stay, my dear, and chat with our friends.' Isaac looked at Winnie. 'Please excuse me, duty calls.' He inclined his head with that grave courtesy of his and went through to the shop.

Sadie crossed to the stove and within a few minutes had returned with three glasses on a small tray. She handed one to Winnie and then, giving one to Ella, said, 'You have not had lemon tea before, I think, but you will like it. I hope you both enjoy it.'

Ella sipped the hot drink and to her amazement found she really liked it. Black tea, lemon-flavoured, with pieces of real lemon and herbs floating in it, and it was sweet and hot. She had never tasted anything like it before, though she didn't feel that she should mention this.

When Winnie had drunk half of her tea she set the glass down on a coffee table and took the bull by the horns. 'Sadie, I need you to do me a favour. It's for my Ella really.'

Poor Ella, she wished that the floor would open up and

swallow her as she listened to Winnie telling Sadie Cohan how her daughter had let herself go, only dressed in loose, flowing dresses, old cardigans and coats that had seen better days, and never bothered to use a bit of paint and powder. There was so much conversation going on between these two old friends and it was all about her, Ella was on the point of leaving. She stood up, feeling gutted that her mother should say such things about her, and more so to this total stranger.

'Where d'yer think you're going?' Winnie asked crossly.

'Well I'm not staying 'ere to listen to you describe me as a fat, blowzy old woman. I'm going home,' she said miserably.

Total silence descended and two pairs of eyes stared at Ella.

It was Sadie who broke the silence. 'I am so sorry. You are absolutely right. We talked as if you were not here and that is unforgivable.'

Ella was thunderstruck.

Winnie's cheeks had flushed a deep red, but she got up and came over and patted Ella's arm. 'I was only doing it for your good, Elly, please. You're far too young to dress the way you do, and it's only because Dennis doesn't pay you much attention these days and all your time and money is spent on the kids. What about your own life? You should be allowed to live a little as well, as other people do.'

Ella was so surprised that her mother hadn't yelled at her, she was speechless.

Sadie gave her a sweet, understanding smile and said, 'If you will let me, I can really help you. Has your mother told you we buy clothes that have been worn by high-class women? We also buy from theatrical wardrobes. Our stock is not new but we have home-workers who do repairs and every article is cleaned before we offer it for sale.'

Ella couldn't think of an answer; she just looked at her mother, who nodded her head and solemnly gave her a thumbs-up sign.

'Ella . . . do you prefer to be called Ella or Elly?' Sadie asked.

'I don't mind. It was Elly when I was at school, but since I've got older I seem to be more of an Ella.'

'Well,' Sadie laughed, 'sit down and I am going to give you your first lesson. You are not to be offended, because what I am going to tell you about is what you wear under your clothes. Have you ever heard of a corselet?'

'Well, yes, but I've never seen one,' Ella stammered.

'I am wearing one and I'd guess your mother is also. It is a modified corset combined with an uplifting brassiere. We sell them and they are brand new.'

The three women looked at each other and their combined laughter filled the air.

It was a moment or two before Sadie turned to Winnie and said, 'I think it better if you disappear for a little while, leave Ella and me to work a few things out.'

'All right,' Winnie said with a shrug. 'Maybe I'll go over to your stall, see what Wally is getting up to.'

Sadie closed the sitting room door behind Winnie and turned to Ella.

Ella felt a lot more comfortable with her mother out of the way. 'Why do you have a shop and a market stall?' she asked.

Sadie grinned. 'Because the men of my family are so well organized. Clothes on the stall are cheaper, within the reach of poorer folk, and the turnover is faster. In the latter years the shop has always been Wally's domain, though he doesn't let on: Isaac still regards everything as his territory. Wally is young, such ideas he has, this son of ours,' she murmured, shaking her head. 'But first I go to our stock room while you take off your clothes down to your underwear. Nobody will come in; you will not be disturbed.'

Left alone, Ella was flustered. *Take her clothes off!* Finally she did as she had been told, then, catching a glimpse of herself in a tall cheval mirror which stood in the corner of the room, she gasped and hastily put her coat on to cover herself.

Sadie's arms were full when she re-entered the room. One look at Ella and her heart was filled with sympathy. Without appearing to even notice that Ella was wearing an outdoor coat, she put the pile of clothing down and held up a long brassiere-type article. Smiling broadly, she looked straight at Ella and said, 'Believe me, pet, this is a girl's best friend, so come on, no shyness with me. I fit women every day.'

Ella's top half was soon laid bare, and she slipped her arms through the shoulder straps while Sadie, standing behind her, did up the long line of hooks and eyes.

'Lift your bosoms into the cups and fiddle them around until you feel comfortable,' Sadie suggested. Then, coming round to stand in front of Ella, she gasped in admiration. She had guessed well at what size to bring.

'Come, look into the mirror and see for yourself the transformation,' Sadie said in a soft voice.

Ella could not believe it! She had been wearing a bra, but it hadn't done much for her. This corselet had at least five inches of material below what would be a normal brassiere, and its lining was finely boned, which held her ribs in. She found that if she stood up straight, shoulders back and tummy in, her figure certainly looked a darn sight better.

Sadie slipped a dress over her head and Ella was suddenly transformed.

It was a soft woollen dress with a full skirt, long sleeves, pearl buttons down the front and a large white linen collar, and although it had been darned a little way along the hemline, its simplicity and the rich colour, which could be likened to that of port wine, added to the impression of elegance. This young woman could be quite beautiful, Sadie thought, intrigued by the difference an undergarment and a second-hand dress had made. Her hair needed attention, yet the colour, dark copper, was real enough, and if washed and treated it could be shimmering. Her features were also good if only she weren't quite so plump, and she seemed such a nice, unassuming woman. Sadie badly wanted to help her.

She was not wrong in these assumptions. In her younger days, Ella Paige, as she was then, had been something special, only a slip of a girl but a real beauty.

'You're very quiet, Ella,' Sadie said. 'Do you not like the dress?'

'Like it!' Ella had been turning this way and that, seeing herself in the long mirror from every angle. 'Doesn't it make a difference to me?'

'Yes, it does, but remember, a lot of that is down to your corselet. Now, slip the dress off. I have a skirt for you to try, and two tunic blouses that will both tone in so that you will be able to alternate your outfits.'

'Sadie, how much are all these clothes going to cost?' Ella asked suspiciously, her heart thumping wildly.

'No more than you can afford,' Sadie said, then she whispered, 'Besides, your mother insisted to me that the cost was to be her treat.'

'Oh, I'm not going to let her do that,' Ella said rather sulkily. 'It's kind of me mum to offer, but I can pay me own way.'

'Let's get sorted what you are going to buy first,' Sadie insisted as she helped Ella to take off the dress. As Ella bent her head and leant forward, her hair, her thick, dark auburn hair, fell across her outstretched arms.

'Tell me why you have neglected yourself so much,' Sadie said.

'You wouldn't understand.'

Sadie shook her head. 'Try me. It might help just to talk.'

Ella sat down, now wearing only her stockings, big bloomers and this lovely silky-feeling corselet. Her vest with its wide shoulder straps lay on the floor with her coat, tweed skirt and thick woollen jumper.

'It didn't seem worth while getting dressed up,' she sighed. 'I only went out shopping or to meet the kids from school. I suppose I've got slovenly. Dennis is only interested in younger, slim girls. He tired of me a long time ago.'

'Men! They think they know so much and they yearn for their youth. Sadly, we all grow old, but you are nowhere near that stage in your life yet, Ella.'

Having said these wise words, Sadie picked up two skirts from the pile of clothing she had fetched from the stock room, asked Ella to stand up and held each one in turn up against her. She cocked her head to one side and screwed up her eyes, looking at the skirts carefully and critically. Both were well tailored and had originally been expensive.

'What do you think?' she asked Ella.

'The black one is a bit fussy, too many pleats, but I do like the dark green one, if yer don't mind me saying so.'

Sadie smiled faintly. 'You don't need much teaching. You are perfectly right. The green one is the ideal colour for you. It will show off the glints in your hair once you get it washed and tamed.'

Ella frowned. 'I have let it get matted. I'll buy some shampoo on the way home.'

'Buy some conditioner as well. It will make all the difference.'

'Mum said that later on she will curl it with the hot tongs for me.'

Sadie stared at her, stupefied with horror. 'Is that what she does?' She croaked the words.

'Sometimes. I think it makes it look nice,' Ella admitted sheepishly.

'Well, Ella, my dear, dear girl, Winifred is doing you no favours. Hot tongs will eventually ruin your gorgeous hair. Learn to wash it regularly, comb it well and leave it to dry naturally, and then practise putting it in different styles. Just a touch of oil rubbed between the palms of your hands and gently smoothed over your head will give your hair an even better gloss.'

Ella seemed doubtful, and was frowning and biting her lip as Sadie slid the green skirt over her head.

'It could have been made for you,' Sadie declared. 'A little tight around your waist, I think, but we can move the button nearer to the edge, and when you lose a little weight you can move it back or . . .' Sadie stopped talking for a moment and grinned. 'Leave the original button in place, sew a second one on, and when you can fasten the skirt on the first one comfortably you will know your figure is more trim.'

'Yeah, when!' Ella said crossly.

'Keep the skirt on, I've two overblouses for you to try,' Sadie said firmly, ignoring Ella's small burst of bad temper.

The first top Ella tried on was a creamy beige in colour, long-sleeved, soft to the touch and had a neat collar and lapels which were edged with a satin ribbon of the same colour and fastened with shiny crystal buttons down the front. It fitted very well across the shoulders, but as Ella made to tuck the blouse inside the waistband of the skirt, Sadie cried out in horror.

'No, no, that you never do, not unless you are very slim and can wear a wide belt. You leave the blouse hanging outside your skirt, look, see, it has slits up the side which are very fashionable, and hanging loose it hides a multitude of sins.'

Once again Ella twisted and turned in front of the cheval mirror. Suddenly her emotions got the better of her and the backs of her eyes stung with unshed tears. She wouldn't have believed that she could look so different, neater and a good deal smarter. She turned to thank Sadie Cohan, but the words wouldn't come, and she stood still and just stared at this kind Jewish lady, wide-eyed. Eventually she said, 'How do you do it?'

Sadie smiled. 'It's easy when you know how.'

Ella swallowed hard. 'I thought I was a bit old to keep up with fashion.'

Sadie raised her eyebrows. 'If you are too old, what does that make me? Would you mind, Ella, if I ask how old you are?'

Ella hung her head. 'I'm thirty-eight, thirty-nine this year.'

Sadie was shocked. This poor overweight young woman looked at least forty-five. She did her best to hide her astonishment, but Ella said quietly, 'I know what you are thinking.' Then, very bravely, she said, 'My husband is twelve years older than me, and more often than not he looks younger than me.'

Sadie answered kindly with a smile, 'That's men for you.'

Ella felt she could confide in Sadie and she quickly said, 'We were married for six years before I had my first child, and during those early years our marriage was great. Dennis was proud to show me off because then I looked good.'

'And you will again,' Sadie was quick to reassure Ella. 'You do know how to dress, you just haven't bothered. It's time you showed that husband of yours that you aren't going to be left behind. Anyway, this second top is exactly the same as the cream one, so you have no need to try it on.'

She tossed a garment to Ella, who immediately held it up and gasped with pleasure.

The material was a much paler green than the skirt that Ella was still wearing, and was perfectly plain apart from a dark green motif embroidered on the breast pocket.

'A perfect match, I'd say,' Sadie remarked, looking at Ella's smiling face. 'So, one dress, one skirt, two blouses and your friendly uplift, will that do for today?'

'Oh, yes please, Sadie. I don't know how to thank you.'

'Then don't try.'

While Ella was putting her own clothes back on, Sadie was taking great care over the packing of Ella's new garments. Each article was wrapped in tissue paper and all were placed in an elegant carrier bag which was embossed with just one word raised in capital letters: *COHAN'S*.

Winnie had a short conversation with Isaac and Sadie, but she had her back to Ella and therefore Ella had no idea how much money her mother had spent on her this afternoon. It did help her to see the wide, beaming smile on her mother's face as she put her purse away in her handbag, picked up the carrier bag and said, 'I can't wait for us to get home. You can give me and the kids a fashion show.'

'Hmm, Babs might think it's great fun, but can you see Teddy sitting still long enough to watch?' Ella said with laughter in her voice.

Sadie hugged them both and kissed them each on both cheeks. Isaac, gentleman as always, wrapped his arms around Winnie, giving her a big bear-hug, then he actually kissed Ella's hand, a gesture which in most men she

43

would have found rather queer, but somehow it was part of Isaac's old-world charm.

'Say goodbye to Wally as you go out,' he said, then, wagging a forefinger at Winifred, he said, 'Not so long you leave it before you visit again.'

Sadie had to have the last word. To Ella she said, 'You have the beginning of a new wardrobe, and you have a very smart mother. Listen to her and heed her. Meantime I know your size now and have a good idea of what you like, so I shall be putting aside any article that I think for you would be good. Be sure you come again soon.'

Ella thanked Sadie again for all her kindness and for the lemon tea.

Outside, Wally asked a customer to excuse him for a moment and came over to them. He gripped Winnie's hand firmly. 'Goodbye, Winifred. Thank you for coming to see my parents. Nothing gives them greater pleasure than to see old friends.'

Turning to Ella, he said, 'I think we shall become friends too.'

Ella's face was serious as she nodded and murmured, 'Goodbye, Wally.'

Loaded down with shopping bags, mother and daughter struggled to board the tram. Once seated, Winnie said, 'Are you pleased with yer new clothes?'

'Am I pleased? More than that, I can't wait to show you everything.'

'I knew I was doing the right thing, taking you to see Sadie. I trust her judgement, she has such good taste,' her mother said with a satisfied smile on her face.

'By the way, Mum, I want to stop at the corner shop and get some shampoo. I'm gonna wash my hair if we're going out tonight.'

'Not so much of the if. We *are* going out and you're going to be done up to the nines.'

Winnie wasn't about to listen to any excuses. The invitation from Ted Dryden to take them both to the Globe for a drink had been on her mind all day. There had to be more to it than he was saying, else why had he driven off without giving either of them a chance to ask any questions? It had taken a bit of thought on her part, but she felt sure she'd got it right. Nice as Ted was, and always good to Ella and the kids, he was still Dennis's father. Dennis was going to be in the pub, Winnie would lay a pound to a penny. Those two men had got some scheme going.

Well, when they set eyes on my Ella tonight, they're in for a real surprise, she thought, knowing that she was being vindictive but not caring one jot.

Chapter Five

AN ASTONISHING AMOUNT OF time had been spent on getting Ella ready to go out for the evening. 'Anyone would think we were going to a royal do,' Winnie muttered as Ella stooped down to pull on the pair of black court shoes that her mum had lent her.

'I'll never be able to walk in these blinking shoes,' she groaned. 'One's all right, but the right one is pinching my toes.'

'Well, thank yer lucky stars that you ain't got t' walk anywhere tonight. Ted is picking us up and as soon as we're in the pub you can kick my shoes off and keep yer feet tucked underneath the table.'

'All this fuss an' bother, I'll end up looking like a dog's dinner,' Ella said ungratefully.

Winnie had also given her daughter a pair of nylons, one of the best things to have come over with the Yanks during the war. Even the worst pair of legs looked better clad in silky, shimmering nylons than in the thick lisle stockings that were the only hose which had been available for years.

Eyeing Ella from top to toe, Winnie was well chuffed.

Her daughter really and truly did look totally different. Her hair especially.

Ella had washed it twice, put conditioner on and left it for five minutes to soak into the roots. When it was towel dry, she had alternately brushed and combed it until it gleamed. It had taken ages before she had got the style right. Eventually she had taken some of the long strands and slowly began to coil them on top of her head, pushing a great many hairpins into the coil to keep it in place and letting the rest of her hair hang free down on to her shoulders.

To tell the truth, she had got the idea from taking notice of Sadie Cohan's rich dark hair, and though she had not managed to achieve the exact same result, for a first attempt she was more than pleased with herself.

Teddy was staring at her, not quite able to work out what all the fuss was about. 'You look ever so different,' was all he said.

Babs was jumping up and down and running round Ella until Winnie was driven to shout, 'Babs, will you please sit down and stop running around like a blue-arsed fly.'

'Well, Mum looks like a real posh lady and I want to know why me and Teddy can't come out with you,' Babs moaned.

Janey from next door pacified Babs by showing her a huge jigsaw puzzle she had brought in with her, then whispered to Teddy, 'I've got quite a few sweets, and I've brought you in one of my brother's books of true adventure stories.'

'Oh good-o, thanks, Janey.' Teddy sounded as pleased as Punch.

The sound of a honking motor-horn told them that Ted was waiting outside. Winnie, dressed elegantly herself, reached for her fur-collared black coat, but as Ella put out a hand to take her own coat down from where it

47

hung on a hook on the wall her mother cried, 'You don't imagine I'm going to let you ruin everything by wearing that old coat.'

Ella looked down at herself. She was wearing the soft woollen dress that Sadie had so kindly advised would suit her. The wide white collar lay high and flat around her neck and emphasized the make-up that her mother had insisted she put on her face. Winnie had told her she could keep the lipstick and Ella was thrilled. It was in a flashy gilt case and the colour was called Russet Rose.

Winnie had come by it when working in the cloakroom of a London hotel. A guest had handed her coat over the counter and the lipstick had fallen out of the pocket. Winnie had gone down on all fours to retrieve it and popped it into her own handbag. Later, when the lady came for her coat, she hadn't mentioned it and Winnie had told herself that by the look of her fur coat she could well afford to buy herself another lipstick.

'If I can't wear my coat I'm going to freeze,' Ella said, looking bewildered.

'You should learn to trust me more,' her mum said. 'I have thought of everything.'

From her old shopping bag Winnie produced a white shawl. It had been hand-crocheted in the finest of wool and edged with a heavy knotted silk fringe. Ella was struck dumb as she watched her mother fold the shawl into a triangle and then drape it around her shoulders, crossing it over her chest. Ella nestled her cheek into the softness. It felt so luxurious.

'Oh Mum, I don't deserve you,' she murmured with a sob in her voice.

'There's days when I would agree with you,' Winnie laughed. 'But right now we are going to have a night out, so goodbye, kids, and if tomorrow Janey tells me you have both been good, I will give you a tanner each.'

'Cor, thanks, Gran,' Babs cried, well pleased.

But Teddy grinned and said, 'Make it a shilling, Gran, an' I'll be a saint.'

Winnie did her best to hide her smile as she answered, 'You, my old son, will get more than you bargained for if Janey tells me you've so much as said a word out of place. Yer mother doesn't 'ardly ever go out. She deserves this treat and she don't want to be bothering her head about you all night. You got that?'

'Yes, ma'am.' Teddy struggled to keep a straight face while giving his gran a mock salute.

'Cheeky little sod, he gets more like his father every day,' Winnie muttered to Ella as they closed the kitchen door and made their way down the passage.

'Blimey! What's got into him?' Ella muttered, when they saw her father-in-law standing on the pavement and holding the rear door of his car open for them.

'Looking forward to a night out then, girls?' Ted chirped as Winnie got in the near-side door and Ella walked round the back of the car and settled herself comfortably beside her mother in the back passenger seat.

It was a clear night, no rain, no fog and no wind, a fact that Ella was grateful for. This shawl was beautiful around her shoulders but it wouldn't keep the cold out, and she hoped the pub, once they got there, would be nice and warm.

Luckily enough there was a vacant space only yards from the front door of the Globe, so Ted had no bother in parking his car.

The public bar was crowded as usual, but Ted ushered them both through into the saloon. A few couples were chatting noisily at tables on the far side of the room, and a young couple were gazing dreamily at each other over their glasses at a corner table.

'Ain't love grand,' Winnie murmured enviously as Ted

indicated a large round table that was not occupied. Once seated, Ted asked, 'What would you gals like to drink?'

'I'll have a gin an' it,' Winnie said with no hesitation.

Ella pondered for a moment before saying, 'I think I'll have a milk stout.'

'No you won't,' her mother contradicted her.

Ella felt her cheeks burn and for one awful moment she thought her mum was going to tell her that was what made her fat.

Ted felt the tension. 'How about a Southern Comfort, Ella? Nice drink that is.'

'OK, thanks, Ted,' Ella quietly agreed, cheeks still flaming.

Ted left them to go to the bar. Winnie took her coat off and laid it across an empty chair, and Ella undid her wrap and let it lie loosely around her shoulders.

Conversation was sparse between mother and daughter until Winnie let out a yelp.

'I knew it, I damn well knew Ted hadn't brought us for a drink out of the goodness of his heart.'

The look of outrage on her mother's face and the ferocious sound of her voice made Ella turn her head and look in the direction that Winnie was gazing in so savagely.

'Oh no, I should have known it was too good to be true,' Ella whispered sadly.

The colour had drained from her cheeks and her hands were trembling. Her first thought was to get out of this place and go back home. Her husband was standing by the bar talking to two men, and the three of them were surrounded by smartly dressed, good-looking young women.

Ted brought their drinks over, smiled at them, then turned on his heel and without saying one word returned to stand at the bar with his son.

Ella took a sip of her drink and sat there listening to

her mother rant and rave on about how crafty and sly Ted Dryden was. She finished her long, angry, aggressive speech by adding, 'What I want to know is why the pair of them have gone to such lengths to get us here tonight.'

Ella couldn't bring herself to answer. Her heart was heavy. Dressing in her new clothes and taking so much trouble over her hair had been a sheer waste of time. She sat there staring at the mat on which her glass was placed, not really seeing the advertisement that was printed on it. When her mother at last calmed down, Ella forced herself to raise her head and look towards the bar.

The girls that surrounded Dennis and his mates were not only much younger than herself, they were also a darn sight slimmer. Ella's eyes filled with tears as she watched her husband place his arms around the shoulders of a pretty blonde-haired girl and draw her close until her slim body was leaning against his huge frame. Then he lifted her up and seated her on a bar stool. Once settled, she pointed the toes of her high-heeled shoes downwards to the floor and began to swing her silk-clad legs in a very suggestive way.

He must know by now that I am here, Ella told herself angrily. More than likely it had all been prearranged between himself and his father. Like her mother had said, she would give a lot to know the reason why they had been set up.

She sighed heavily as she gazed at her husband's big frame, his broad shoulders and dark good looks. Why was it that men didn't go to seed as quickly as women did? Because they didn't have to bear children or grapple with the day-to-day troubles that came with bringing them up, she supposed.

Once folk had said that she and Den were the ideal couple. He hadn't altered much; he still reached for the sky and invariably got it. It was she who had become shabby and disappointed with his expectations of how life should be led.

As if he was aware of her watching him, Dennis turned and met her eyes, a slight smile playing at the corners of his mouth. She lowered her gaze first, and confused and hurt looked down, gripping her hands tightly together in her lap.

Little did she know that Dennis was asking himself if he was seeing straight.

He just could not believe the difference in his wife and was wondering how and when it had come about. And more to the point, why? Who the hell was she trying to impress? Not for one moment did the thought enter his head that it might be for his benefit.

He wasn't the only one to have noticed Ella and her mother.

One of Dennis's associates, Stan Wilson, grinned. 'The sooner you unwind yourself from that tart who is wheedling up to you, Den, and get over to talk t' your missus, the better, I'd say.'

'Yes,' Pete Jarvis, the third man in the group, agreed. 'Your missus is looking pretty sharp tonight.'

'Makes yer wonder what's going on there.' Stan put his oar in again.

'Good Lord Almighty!' Dennis roughly pulled the arms of the platinum-blonde from around his shoulders and moved a step nearer to Stan. His temper was boiling over. 'Anybody ever tell you you're a nosy git, Stan?' he hissed, his blue eyes glinting angrily.

'We were working out a good deal 'ere, but just you remember, Stan, business is one thing! My family life is down t' me and sod all t' do with you.' Then, turning his head, he said, 'You wanna remember that an' all, Pete.'

Stan Wilson nodded. He wanted to laugh at the absurdity of this daft situation but had a feeling that right now wasn't the time for joking. Indeed, it was Ella Dryden that he felt sorry for, but as Dennis was pointing his finger into his face, Stan Wilson knew when to back off. Dennis was not only far bigger than he was, he had a reputation for going utterly crazy when annoyed.

'I was paying a compliment to your Ella,' Pete said quickly, doing his best to play the peacemaker.

Dennis sniffed loudly and, ignoring the question of his wife, said, 'We gonna settle this deal tonight or not?'

The three men closed ranks. One look at their faces and the good-time girls knew when to take the hint. They picked up their glasses and moved to the far end of the bar.

Even Ted, who was standing to one side sipping Scotch, looked warily at the three men and decided they were best left alone for a while.

As he walked to the men's toilet he was thinking about his daughter-in-law. There certainly was a change in her tonight. And very much for the better was his decision. He had been bowled over at the sight of Ella; she really was done up to the nines. He had his own idea as to why his son had asked him to bring Ella and her mother here tonight, but he wasn't dead sure. In fact he was hoping that he was wrong. He needed no telling that his son played his cards very close to his chest, and just lately he was beginning to wonder whether Dennis had any conscience or real feelings. All married couples had their tiffs, and men the world over strayed after a fresh bit of skirt, but to walk off and leave yer wife and kids, no, that wasn't on. He was certainly baffled by the fact that both Ella and her mother had turned themselves out as if they were going to a dinner and dance. There was tension in the air, you didn't need to be able to read the tea-leaves to be aware of that much. What the bloody hell is going on? Ted wondered for the umpteenth time.

The answer he came up with was that a lot more than Dennis had admitted was being sorted here tonight, and Ella did not deserve to be brought into it.

Ted felt awful knowing he couldn't trust his own son, at least not a hundred per cent. He ran his hands through his hair, feeling his face burning with embarrassment. The truth as Dennis told it was that Ella was being awkward, refusing to move out of the East End, but there were two sides to every story. Not in a million years could he see Ella and her kids fitting into that big house in Surrey. In fact in his opinion it would take dynamite to shift Ella from the East End.

But that didn't give Dennis the right to treat her like dirt.

Dennis drained his drink in one gulp as his father rejoined them at the bar and looked straight into Ted's eyes. He felt sure he knew exactly what his father was thinking.

And he was right.

Taking big strides, he crossed the bar and sat down on the empty chair opposite his wife. He nodded his head at his mother-in-law, who drained her glass and gulped down the strong gin before saying, 'I know when I'm not wanted.'

Taking her empty glass with her, she went straight to where Ted stood and said loudly, 'Do you expect one drink to last me all night?'

Dennis and Ella stared at each other, each reluctant to make the first move. Then, taking a thick envelope from the inside pocket of his jacket, Dennis slid the packet across the table saying, 'That should keep you and the kids going for a while.'

If he expected a thank you from Ella, he was in for a long wait.

Quickly he said, 'You know I would never see you and the kids skint. How are Teddy and Babs?'

Ella stared at the floor. It was as if she was deaf.

'I have a right to know.' He looked at his wife, really looked at her, and sighed.

Ella shook her head. 'Suddenly you're concerned? All these weeks and what 'ave you cared? You've always said Babs was your golden girl, the apple of yer eye, your precious favourite. What is she supposed to do now?'

Dennis felt a moment's pang of guilt and it showed.

Ella was glad. It proved he had a streak of humanity in him after all. Once started, she felt she was fully entitled to rub salt into his wounds.

'They come 'ome from school telling me their friends' dads 'ave taken them to the zoo or to the pictures. What am I supposed to say? Daddy's too busy doing up a big posh 'ouse out in the country which in the end will make him a load of money?'

That is, she thought, if he doesn't end up getting caught buying building materials and tins of paint that have fallen off the backs of lorries.

'Teddy says he likes Grandad better than you 'cos at least he takes him to watch the football on Saturdays.'

Dennis laughed. 'He don't mean it, does he? He knows I 'ave to work. I didn't think he'd miss me living at home.'

'Course you didn't. That's your trouble, you never think about anything except making money.'

He looked at her and sneered.

'Well, luv, I don't see you refusing what's on the table, and I know for a fact you had what was in one of my suits. You an' the kids ain't been living on fresh air.'

Ella looked at her empty glass and said in a sad voice, 'Teddy and Babs need new shoes, and I've kept up the rent so far, but . . .'

'There's more than enough in there to keep you going for a while.' Using one finger, Dennis edged the package nearer to Ella, and this time she picked it up and put it into her handbag.

'I'll get us both another drink,' he said, reaching for Ella's empty glass.

'That's right, Den, money and booze will cheer us both up.'

He shook his head in despair as he walked slowly back to the bar.

His mind was in a whirl. Never had he seen Ella look so smart; nor had he heard her sound so cocksure of herself. He had asked his father to bring her here tonight to let her see that he was doing all right. Coping well on his own. Yet really hoping that she would plead with him to return home.

He didn't want to be the one to climb down. That would mean losing face and give Ella the upper hand, but he missed his family and he missed Ella's cooking. Sad but true, things hadn't turned out at all as he had planned.

In fact he was in two minds as to whether or not she had already turned the tables on him.

In the Globe that Saturday evening the landlord felt uneasy. Jack Riley had been in the business a long time and he had a nose for trouble. He had seen more than his fair share of bar brawls, and right now he could sense one brewing.

At first he paid no attention to Dennis Dryden and his mates, drinking hard and fast in the corner of the saloon bar. It was the scantily dressed young women who were playing up to them that bothered him. It wasn't unusual for women to go for well-dressed men, knowing that they would be bought a good many drinks. The situation did not often get out of hand, mostly being good-humoured banter with the men taking just a few liberties.

Tonight it was different. Dryden's wife and his mother-in-law were in the bar. Dennis had left the group and gone over to talk to his missus; whatever it was that had been said had left him with a thunderous look on his face. He had soon rejoined the others back at the bar.

He picked his glass up and took a gulp, then wiped his wet mouth with the back of his hand.

'You know what, Dad? I've lived in that poky little 'ouse ever since me an' Ella got spliced, an' both our kids were born in that upstairs bedroom. Yer could say I've managed to keep the wolf from the door one way or another, couldn't yer?'

His father nodded, wondering what Dennis was getting at.

'I don't treat Ella badly, the odd slap now an' again but only when she's out of order. Neither she nor our kids 'ave ever gone hungry. I might 'ave strayed a bit now an' again, but what man can put his 'and on his heart and swear he's never played away from 'ome? Besides, take one look at my Ella sitting over there. When did you last see her looking like she does tonight? A bloody long time ago if ever! You know darn well I'm only speaking the truth. She's run t' seed and that's a fact. Wearing tent-like dresses and flip-flop slippers is how I see her when I get home, an' in the bedroom, well, if she ain't got an 'eadache it's like mounting a camel, only even the humps are flabby.'

Ted was getting worried. Winnie was still standing at the bar and her face had turned white with temper. Suddenly she pushed aside Stan Wilson's restraining hands and made for Dennis. She pulled her arm back and then swung it, hitting him full in the face.

Dennis staggered back, blood streaming from his nose.

Winnie wasn't finished. She gave him a mighty shove and he fell in a heap on the floor, but still she wouldn't leave him alone, slapping him round his head with her handbag, kicking his legs, and all the while shouting abuse.

Ted came up behind her and lifted her away from his son as though she were a baby.

Stan and Pete hoisted Dennis to his feet as Winnie struggled to free herself from Ted's vice-like grip.

'Put me down, you rotten sod. You're as much t' blame as he is, letting him talk about my daughter as if she were dirt beneath his feet. Just let me get at 'im! I'll swing for 'im!'

'Stop it, Win, you're old enough to know better. You shouldn't go losing yer temper at your age, it's bloody stupid.' Ted looked over to where Ella was still sitting. 'Look at your gal, she's going potty. Go on, go over and sit with 'er and I'll bring a brandy over for each of yer.'

Winnie grinned sheepishly and dusted her skirt down. 'It's not fair the way Den goes on about her. Heart of gold that girl 'as and he don't give a damn for her.'

Dennis was on his feet now, gingerly leaning on the counter still holding a blood-stained handkerchief to his nose.

Ted looked at the empty glasses. 'What yer all 'aving? Same again, or d'you want a short?'

'I dunno as I wanna drink 'ere while that hell-cat an' my bloody missus is still 'ere,' Dennis said.

Ted grabbed his son's arm. 'Look, Den, you were out of order, went a bit over the top. I take it that yer talk with Ella didn't go down so well. Didn't she go down on her knees an' beg yer to come 'ome?' he asked sarcastically. 'Forget it, son. 'Ave anuvver drink and keep quiet fer Gawd's sake.'

Dennis was embarrassed that his father had hit the nail right on the head.

'I ain't gonna plead, no way. I'll get at her through the kids; she'll come round, you'll see.'

Ted laughed, and called to the landlord, 'Come on, Jack, fill 'em up.'

Digging in his back pocket for his wallet, he added, 'I'm gonna take a brandy over to Ella and her mum an' then I'll take them home.'

''Ope it chokes the pair of them,' Dennis muttered.

Ted did his best not to smile. He was only sorry that his son might soon come to realize what he had lost.

The way things were looking tonight, Ella might just stand her ground this time and refuse to dance to his tune.

Chapter Six

JUNE HAD BROUGHT THE promise of a good summer. So far there had been days of constant sunshine and clear blue skies. Ella kept telling herself that she would get out more, and that as soon as the children broke up from school for their six-week summer holiday she would make picnics and take them to various places; maybe Battersea Park, anywhere out in the fresh air.

Promises were one thing; keeping them was an entirely different matter.

She didn't have the inclination to do much these days, and if it weren't for her mother's perpetual nagging she more than likely wouldn't have kept herself looking as neat and tidy as she did. Winnie made sure that she watched her figure, kept her copper-coloured hair glossy and smooth and wore decent clothes.

Ella knew she meant well, because she'd overheard her mum say to a neighbour, 'Anything to avoid my poor Ella falling into a fit of depression.'

Three months had passed and Dennis had not returned home to live. He had cut her adrift and she had no one to blame but herself.

Surprisingly, he had remained friendly, often dropping in, mostly on the off chance. Some Sundays he'd turn up with his father for his midday roast dinner. Her mum always went on about how daft she was to feed him, but Ella looked at it from a different angle. It made the kids happy to sit round a table and enjoy a family meal with their dad and grandad rather than just her.

It also kept Dennis in touch with his children, and money-wise he had been fair, coughing up seven pounds a week; well, most weeks! She could never totally rely on him.

Ella was never completely relaxed when Dennis was around. She always felt that she had to be on her guard. If he should arrive and find his mother-in-law there he would turn tail and make a hasty retreat, but not before he had let them know exactly what he thought of the pair of them.

One wrong word from Ella or one complaint about the shortage of money and he would blow his top, grab her roughly, push her to the floor and storm out into the street.

Dennis hadn't changed; he still had a short fuse.

Teddy teased his sister something rotten because their father often took him out, mostly to watch a football match on a Saturday afternoon, but he never took Babs anywhere. Whether from a feeling of guilt it was hard to say, but after one of what he and Teddy called their 'men-only outings' he always brought back a decent present for Babs. Secretly Ella thought that the reason Dennis made sure his young son still favoured him was because she had told him, that night in the pub, that Teddy thought more of his grandfather than he did of his father.

Neighbours had stopped asking awkward questions and by and large they looked out for Ella and her two children. Always willing to give her a hand if and when she needed help.

Yet to Ella, each day was so monotonous. Every morning she was up bright and early. She laid out the children's

61

clean clothes, did a bit of housework, and then put the porridge on to simmer while she got the children out of bed. All washed and dressed, the three of them sat round the table and ate breakfast, chatting like they always did.

'On Wednesday, Mum, can I have some flour, sugar, margarine and a few currants or sultanas, oh, and two eggs if you can spare them, please.' Proudly, Babs puffed out her chest. 'Teacher said we're going to start cooking lessons an' we can bring the cake home what we're gonna make.'

'Well I've been doing woodwork classes for a long time and I'm making something special for you, Mum.' Teddy wasn't about to be outshone.

'I think you're both getting on ever so well at school,' Ella said as she sprinkled spoonfuls of sugar over their porridge.

With time to spare, Ella cleared away the breakfast things while the children packed their books into their satchels and got ready for school. At half past eight they were ready for the off, both of them looking neat and tidy in their uniform. Several children came out of the line of terraced houses and they all joined up, chattering away nineteen to the dozen. Ella stood at her doorway and watched until they had turned the corner, then went back indoors mumbling to herself, 'Another long, miserable day. Still, I've got a great pile of ironing to do, that will pass the morning away.'

It was not to be.

Hardly had she got a blanket spread over the kitchen table and an old sheet that had a good few scorch marks on it laid over the top and the two flat irons set on to the top of the hob to heat up, than there was a rattle of her letter-box and a voice called out, 'It's only me, Ella.'

Ella didn't need any telling to know to whom that voice belonged, and in a way she was glad of the distraction.

Ah well, she sighed as she went up the passage to open

the front door, even Miss Turner had to be better than having no one to talk to.

Putting a smile on, she said, 'Good morning, Miss Turner, have you come for a chat or are you in a hurry?'

'Now, now, Ella, how many times have I asked you to call me Nellie? It ain't everyone gets that liberty but you are different,' Nellie Turner said, pushing her way past Ella and walking towards the living room.

Ella had to laugh to herself as she looked at this middle-aged woman. She certainly was a character. She was scarcely taller than five foot two, dressed in a blue frock that looked as if it had come out of the Ark, and her navy blue cardigan had seen better days. Her greying hair was pinned tightly in a bun and the glasses she wore were plain and steel-rimmed.

This woman let everyone know that she was *Miss* Turner because she had never been married. Very kindly she had devotedly looked after her elderly parents until they had died, which had been within three months of each other. She missed them terribly but would be the first to say that they had left her comfortably off. Now she was the proud owner of their very nice house, which they had bought and paid for years ago. Alone and often lonely, with time on her hands, Nellie Turner lived her life by poking her nose into other folk's business. There was still a lot of good in this sad lady. She'd do anything for someone in trouble but she spread gossip faster than a forest fire took hold.

Seeing that Nellie had settled herself comfortably in what had been Dennis's armchair and was undoing the buttons of her cardigan, Ella said, 'I'll make us a cup of tea as soon as I've folded all these bits an' pieces.'

Nellie was up on her feet in an instant. 'You put that iron back on the hob an' see t' the tea and I'll fold the ironing,' she insisted.

With the table cleared and a cup of tea and a plate of

biscuits set out, they sat drinking their tea in comfortable silence until Nellie sat her cup down on her saucer with a clatter and her face suddenly became serious.

'Ella,' she said quietly, 'there is something I think you ought t' know. You won't get upset if I tell yer, will you?'

'Try me,' was all that Ella said.

'Well, I don't want yer mum to find out that you 'eard it from me, but Connie Baldwin reckons she's 'aving a baby.'

'What, young Connie Baldwin whose mum an' dad live over the paper shop?' Ella asked, frowning.

'Yes, that's the one.'

'Do her parents know about it? She's not sixteen yet, is she?'

'Sorry, luv, but it's no t' both of those questions as far as I know, and what her mum an' dad are gonna say when they find out, the Lord only knows. Won't be long before they do, though, mark my words. Half the street knows already.'

Ella stared in disbelief, thinking to herself that Nellie was enjoying telling folk about a young girl's misfortune. Aloud she said, 'Wonder if the fella will be man enough t' marry her?'

'He won't,' Nellie said smugly.

Ella was watching her closely and she couldn't fathom what the look on Nellie's face was supposed to mean.

'How the 'ell can you be so sure?' Ella sat up straight and her body was rigid as she looked directly into Nellie's eyes. She didn't like what she was seeing, and she leant across the table and stabbed her forefinger into Nellie's chest.

'I'm not daft, yer know, Nellie! You've come 'ere this morning t' tell me something. Something I ain't gonna like. I've got it in one, 'aven't I?' Without waiting for an answer, Ella stood up, prodded Nellie again and said, 'Well, say yer piece. I'm warning you, I'm not the most patient person in the world.'

Nellie was shocked. She hadn't expected Ella to react in such a nasty manner. She met the younger woman's eyes and could see that she had pushed her further than she should have.

Ella grew tired of waiting. 'I'm warning you, Nellie, for the last time, whatever it is you think I should know, spit it out. Don't make me lose me temper.'

All the colour had drained from Nellie's face and it took a great effort for her to get the words out, but eventually she croaked, 'According to Connie's friends, your Dennis is the father.'

'Hmm, some friends! Poor little cow, she sure as hell don't need any enemies,' Ella murmured sadly.

She plonked herself down. All the wind had gone out of her sails.

Dennis, Dennis, Dennis, she was saying over and over inside her head, have you really sunk so low?

She sighed deeply. At times he could be so charming and the trouble was he knew it. He would look straight into a young girl's face, smile at her with those big blue eyes and know straight off that he could lead her on like a lamb to the slaughter.

He was well aware of his good looks. He had a decent, trim body with broad shoulders, and his height seemed to fascinate females both young and old. But to put such a young girl in the family way must be a new experience for him. Surely it couldn't be true.

Please God don't let it be true, she prayed silently. If it were, she would lay her last penny that the day would come when he'd live to really regret it. If that day hadn't already dawned.

Nellie drained her teacup to the dregs and hastily began to button up her cardigan. She hadn't got the reaction from Ella that she'd hoped for and it would be just her luck for that mother of hers to turn up, and then she

65

would be for it. She knew Winnie Paige didn't like her much; she'd called her a nosy old gossip to her face on more than one occasion. All the same, I came here in good faith, she told herself, hoping against hope that she could get out quickly.

Too late! The sound of the front door opening and then being slammed shut had Nellie trembling in her shoes.

'Ella, you there, luv? Come an' give me an 'and with this load of shopping. Sorry I had to kick the door shut.' Winnie sounded as bright as a button.

Ella stared at Nellie as if she was something the cat had dragged in. 'Sit down again an' stay where you are,' she ordered as she went to meet her mother in the passage.

Nellie's expression froze. Stay there, Ella had said. Don't look as if I've got much choice now. She knew she'd dropped a clanger. Telling tales about Dennis Dryden to Ella was bad enough; now with her mother to face as well she'd have to do some hard thinking to wriggle out of this one.

Winnie poked her head round the door. ''Allo, Nellie,' she greeted her daughter's visitor. 'I only went in t' the greengrocer for a bag of spuds and two women told me you was 'ere visiting my Ella. Don't suppose you were the bearer of good news, were you?' Sarcasm was clear in her voice and she was smiling broadly.

That fact alone threw Nellie. 'I 'ave t' get back home. Your Ella can tell you all about it. I've told her all that I know.'

'I bet you 'ave,' Winnie said, looking at her with contempt.

'OK, Nellie, you get off now. By the look on my mum's face she's already been told all there is t' tell.' Ella's voice was hard now, as were her eyes. 'But just one thing: try keeping yer tongue between yer teeth, 'cos if my kids come 'ome crying that someone has taunted them about their dad, I'll come after you. I mean it, I will, Nellie.'

Winnie had taken all of the shopping through to the scullery. Now she stood dead in front of Nellie Turner and stared at her coldly.

'I will see you later, Nellie, and you can tell me the whole story and explain to *me* how you come to know so much. And believe me, it had better be bloody good.'

Nellie Turner held her breath as she slid past mother and daughter, thinking what a fool she'd been. She wished she hadn't got out of bed this morning, let alone come along here to tell Ella Dryden that her husband had been playing around with a very young girl.

When she was finally out in the street she felt faint with relief.

She decided there and then that she would steer clear of both those women from now on. At least she'd do her best to.

Not a word was said until they heard the front door close. Then, suddenly, Ella went to pieces. Choking on the words she said, 'Mum, I take it that you've 'eard about Den and Connie Baldwin.'

With an aching heart Winnie nodded her head.

'What about Babs and Teddy, Mum? I've done my best to keep them happy, their lives normal, that's why I've never minded when Den comes in for a meal. Folk will talk, their kids will listen to what their parents are saying, and before you know it they'll be jeering at my two that Den is going to be father to another child.'

Winnie couldn't find words to say that would do any good, so she murmured, 'I'll go and put the kettle on.'

Ella sat down, covered her face with her hands and began to cry softly. Her temper, for the time being, had run its course.

Her mother took her time, but finally she came in from the scullery carrying a tray which held two steaming cups

67

of tea, two china side plates and a jam sponge sprinkled with icing sugar.

'Come on, Ella,' she urged. 'A nice cuppa and a piece of cake will do us both good.'

'Don't be so daft, Mum, how the 'ell will eating and drinking solve the ruddy mess we're in?'

Her mother rolled her eyes in exasperation. 'Ella, listen t' me. We 'aven't got much to go on yet, so let's wait and cross our bridges as we come t' them. I don't know why you let that silly spinster come in t' yer house, though I suppose it was better to hear the news while you were indoors.'

Winnie stopped talking suddenly, threw back her head and let out a great belly laugh. Ella was so startled that she took her hands from her face and stared at her mother.

'Oh, luv! If someone, anyone, 'ad come up t' you in the street and told you that your Dennis had put a slip of a girl in the family way, you wouldn't have stopped to think whether it were true or not. You'd 'ave punched them in the mouth so hard they'd 'ave been knocked into the middle of next week. And more than likely they would 'ave needed to see a dentist.'

Much as she didn't want to, Ella saw the funny side of what her mother was saying. Tears still brimming from her eyes, she got to her feet and hugged the slight figure of her mother close.

'Thanks, Mum. You're marvellous. Always there when I need you.'

Winnie used her handkerchief to wipe her daughter's face before saying, 'When I was told about it in the green-grocer's I thought even Den wouldn't go that far and I was hoping it wasn't true.'

'So was I,' Ella murmured sadly. 'So was I. But if it *is* true, Den has showed me up good an' proper this time, ain't he?'

Winnie decided it was better not to answer that one.

Chapter Seven

ELLA WAS FINDING EACH day a sad and worrying time. She was almost afraid to go out. Neighbours were so ready to stop her and sympathize, and that was exactly what she did not want. Some were just being inquisitive.

She was well aware that it had to be even worse for Mr and Mrs Baldwin and their poor young lass, not that she had had any contact with them. There was nothing she could do or say that would make matters any better, and more than likely any attempt on her part would end up making matters a damn sight worse.

Connie Baldwin was the youngest of her parents' four daughters. Why in God's name had Den had to pick on her? Probably to prove to himself that he was still man enough to pull young girls.

Ella gave a wry little smile as her mother came down the stairs, having been up to say goodnight to the children. She was shaking her head and talking to herself, but quite loud enough for Ella to hear every word.

'Those kids miss their dad, I know they do, and it's only natural that they should.'

Ella knew only too well the truth of what her mum

was saying, but she was at a loss to know which way to turn.

Winnie made straight for the dresser and picked up a bottle of sherry. 'I bought this while I was out shopping this morning, thought a glass or two might cheer us both up.' Taking down two glasses from a shelf, she filled each one almost to the brim with the rich dark cream sherry. Passing one to Ella, she pulled an armchair round and sat down facing her daughter.

'Den not been round?' Winnie started the conversation with a question.

'Mum, you know darn well he 'asn't. Don't suppose he's proud of himself; more likely he's afraid t' show his face, though I did think he would have kept in touch with the children.'

'Yeah, I thought that, especially Teddy. He so looks forward to Saturday with his dad, doesn't he?'

'Used to, you mean! I think he's given up now. Can't blame the boy. For the first few Saturdays he got himself ready and nearly wore the mats out walking from the front-room window to the gate, watching for his dad to come down the road. He don't bother now.'

'Selfish bastard Den is, always was and always will be if you ask me.'

Ella wasn't surprised at her mother's comments. She had never had a good word to say about Dennis from the day Ella had brought him home. For the first six months of their married life they had lived with her parents, and Dennis had got on really well with her father. Not so with her mother! Life had been anything but easy. They only had what had been Ella's bedroom, and the walls were paper thin. Ella had longed for a sister to talk to, but she only had two brothers. Since her dad had died, they came round about once a year to see their mum. Winnie's fault: she didn't like either of her daughters-in-law, so she was only running true to form by disliking her one and only son-in-law.

Ella sighed and told herself to be fair. The relationship between herself and her mother had always been good, and there wasn't anything that Winnie wouldn't do for Teddy and Babs. It was true she often had a go at her daughter, but Ella knew that it was always for her own good.

The trouble was, once her mum got started on airing her views as to what a bounder Den was, Ella knew there would be no stopping her, and for once she decided that Dennis was not *all* bad.

The early years of their marriage had been happy enough and she had always felt quite special because, of all the girls that were around at the time, he had chosen her. And she could say, hand on heart, that he had never overstepped the mark sexually before he put a wedding ring on her finger. Inwardly she laughed; not that they hadn't come pretty close on more than one occasion!

To begin with Dennis had worked for his father, going off to various racecourses and often being away two or three days at a time. Always great when he came home! It was after Teddy was born that he had become involved in dodgy deals. It was almost unbelievable that he had never got caught. Several of his so-called mates had been sent to prison, but Den, together with whoever else had got off scot-free, had made it his business to see that the families of the men who were locked up for long stretches were well taken care of.

Dennis never told Ella any details; she wasn't sure she wanted to know what he got up to anyway. Perhaps she was a coward. But the less she knew, the better, as far as she was concerned.

Still thinking back, Ella remembered how, when she had first found out that Dennis had been taking other

71

women out, she had been so hurt she had just given up and let herself go. It was only recently, since her mother had taken her to visit the Cohans' shop, that she had made a great effort to keep her appearance up to scratch. Sadly, it would seem she had left it far too late.

As Winnie saw the hurt in her daughter's eyes, she felt the urge to really do some serious harm to Dennis Dryden.

'Let it go, Ella. He's not worth worrying over,' she urged.

Ella was baffled for a moment, felt her temper rising. She told herself to relax and to try and calm down, but instead she got to her feet and stood facing her mother. Big fat tears were rolling down her face as she shouted, 'You've never had one good word to say about Dennis, but you wanna think on. There hasn't been a Christmas since Dad died that you ain't spent under his roof. OK, right now he's broken my world in two, but remember, Mum, having a baby takes two. Does he face up to his responsibilities? No, I'll agree with you on that point. He disappears, where to, God only knows. All I do know is that he ain't got the guts to come an' tell me about it himself.'

Winnie's mouth gaped open at Ella's sudden outburst.

Once started, Ella decided it was time she stood her own ground for once.

'I've spent a long time scraping together pieces of information that others have been only too willing to tell me, and by now I think I've gathered most of the facts bit by bit. I've come to the conclusion that in more ways than one Dennis is a bounder, but when it comes to this business with Connie Baldwin, my 'usband is not entirely t' blame.'

It was a very long time since Winnie Paige had felt she was being chastised. This angry outburst had come out of the blue. She decided her best option was to keep her mouth closed tight.

72

Staring at the shocked look on her mother's face, Ella let out a great sigh and looked upwards. 'Dear God, give me strength.' For a moment she hesitated, in two minds as to what to do. But somehow, despite her regrets and doubts, her instincts remained strong. For too long she had turned a blind eye to whatever Dennis got up to, and now, simply because she had refused to move out of London and live deep in the country, he had left her and the children. At least that was what she had believed, until this matter of Connie Baldwin had been brought to the surface.

During the past few weeks she had dithered and been frightened to even think of a life without Dennis around. For too long she had done nothing but sit around feeling sorry for herself. Now that she had made her decision, she was going to face all her troubles head on.

It was in this fighting mood that she made up her mind that it was time her mother stopped thinking that Dennis was all bad.

Taking a deep breath, she began.

'Connie Baldwin's always been aware of her own good looks and slinky figure. She was apparently known as something of a flirt and at fifteen developed a crush on Dennis. It doesn't take a great deal of imagination to believe that she was flattered that a smart man like Den paid her attention. Then again, all things being equal, I suspect that the fact he had a big car and flashed his money about went a long way when she was boasting to her friends about where he was taking her and what he was buying for her. I don't think Dennis would have had to twist her arm, do you, Mum?'

'Hmm!' For what seemed an age, Winnie looked grumpily at her daughter. Eventually she said warily, 'It's a devil of a mess whichever way you look at it.'

Ella gave a small, bitter laugh. 'One minute we were

jogging along, coping with the ups and downs of everyday life as married couples do and then I find the bottom has dropped out of my world.'

'Yeah, well, you're not the first wife to find out that her 'usband has got a young girl into trouble, and it's a dead cert you'll not be the last. But you will have to deal with it.'

And though she made no further comment, Ella knew her mother spoke the truth.

There was no getting away from it. Trouble lay ahead, and she already had the feeling that it would be big trouble.

Chapter Eight

WHETHER IT WAS BECAUSE Teddy had played her up all evening, as good as saying outright that it was her fault that their dad didn't live with them any more, or because she had run out of money and was going to have to go cap in hand to her father-in-law because she hadn't set eyes on Dennis for weeks, Ella didn't know. Whatever the reason, she had slept badly, dreaming a lot and waking in a cold sweat. Now, having given the children their breakfast and seen them off to school, she stood in front of the mirror combing her hair and telling herself she looked like something the cat had dragged in.

Deciding she would make a fresh brew, she turned towards the scullery. As she held the kettle underneath the cold tap she heard the front door open and footsteps coming down the passage. Oh God, not me mother this early in the day, she moaned softly to herself.

She turned towards the living room and was shocked to see her husband standing there, still as a statue. She felt the colour drain from her face.

'What the 'ell . . .'

'Hallo, Ella, long time no see.'

His voice sounded different. She felt nervous of him. It was weird, unnerving, seeing him standing there.

'I see you were about to put the kettle on. Don't let me stop you, I could murder a cuppa.'

Ella laughed, she couldn't help herself. 'My, you've got some nerve, Den, walking in bold as bloody brass as if you've never been away.'

With all the confidence in the world he pulled out a chair and sat down. 'Watch what yer saying, Ella my love, this is still my 'ouse.'

'Is that so? Well, I 'ope yer wallet is bulging, 'cos I 'aven't been able to pay the rent for the last two weeks and me and the kids ain't been living it up like lords either.'

As Ella had been stating her case she had been studying him. She hated to admit it even to herself, but he did look good. He had always dressed well, but today he looked elegant. He also looked very sure of himself, a fact that made Ella aware that things were going well for him.

Dennis gave her a saucy grin. 'Go on, gal, make us that brew. You know full well I'm here to give you some dosh. Come what may, I'd never see my family starve.'

Ella was really rattled now. 'No, you'd shut yer blinking eyes and carry on buying drinks for all the scroungers in the pubs.'

She banged about out in the scullery as she made the tea, deliberately giving Dennis a big chipped mug, and was on her way back with it when she felt she couldn't keep her mouth shut. He was in the wrong, not her.

Setting his tea down in front of him, she sat herself down opposite, making sure that she could look him straight in the eye as she spoke.

'You weren't man enough to face me with the truth, were you? It were the neighbours and yer so-called friends

76

that made sure I was kept well informed. The one good person in all of this rotten mess 'as been yer father. He filled all the blanks in for me, and when he says something at least I know it's the truth.'

Dennis leant across the table and would have taken hold of her hand. Ella wasn't having any of his soft soap. She drew her hands back like a scalded cat and sat with them tightly clenched in her lap.

'Oh, Ella!' he sighed as if he were the one being wronged. 'I would have preferred t' tell yer meself, but I 'eard that you'd been got at. Who was it that came t' you with a likely tale?'

'As if you didn't know! Who would it 'ave been other than the street gossip, Nellie Turner? I warned her that if our kids got t' know they were gonna have a brother or a sister, I'd swing for 'er.'

'My God! What a bitch that Nellie can be. Teddy and Babs don't know, do they?' Dennis sounded so concerned, and yet Ella knew it was an act he was putting on.

'Come off it, Den, you ain't even asked how the kids are. Remember what they look like, do you? Even you can't convince anyone that you live in cloud-cuckoo-land. I told Teddy and Babs straight that what people were only too willing to tell me might be the truth, but until you had the guts to face me and tell me outright that you'd been with a young girl and made her pregnant, we couldn't be sure.'

'What did you 'ave to tell the kids for?' He was getting more angry by the minute.

'Don't be so stupid, Den. Teddy 'eard everything from the kids at school, and Babs came 'ome in tears because some of the girls taunted her that her dad was going to 'ave a new baby that wouldn't be part of our family. How the hell do yer think that made me feel? What was I supposed to say to her?'

'I'm sorry, Ella. Honest to God, if I could turn the clock back . . .'

'Yeah, yeah, you're sorry now, but not 'alf as much as me and the kids are. As to that little word *if*, what was it you used to say to me? If yer aunt 'ad balls she'd be yer uncle.'

Dennis was fighting to defend himself but damned if he was going to crawl.

'I was drunk, you know how these young girls come on to us men, and they're half-naked when they walk into the pub. Connie Baldwin was asking for it.'

'You know what, Den? You're unbelievable. You sit there and tell me that you couldn't 'elp yerself. Next you'll be asking me to believe that you haven't been taking that girl out, showing her a good time and having an affair with her, that it was all just a one-off.'

Tears were stinging the backs of her eyes now and she was annoyed at herself for letting him upset her so much.

Dennis clenched his fists. 'Trust you t' believe the worst of everybody. Boiling it all down, you can't exactly blame me for looking elsewhere. You're always such a bloody miserable mare, and all the years we lived together you walked about looking like a rag-bag, and a fat old bag to boot.'

'Listen here, Dennis, I'll give way on some of what you say. I did get fat, a lot of women do when they've had two kids, and of course I didn't exactly dress meself in the latest fashion. How could I, even if I had wanted to? I never knew where I stood with you. Some weeks you were really generous, buying God knows what for the kids, but lose on the gee-gees or do a deal that went down the pan and you'd storm in and sell everything you could lay yer hands on. It was those weeks that always frightened me. You'd give me barely enough to buy food, let alone put shoes on the kids' feet and clothes on their backs.'

Dennis took an envelope from his pocket and laid it on the table between them. Ella lifted the flap and stared at the thick wad of notes in disbelief.

She sighed as she said, 'While you're about it, you'd better settle up with your father. It's only what he's been handing me that has kept us going.'

He didn't answer her.

She shook her head. 'All you really care about, Dennis, is number one. You've made that pretty obvious. Look at you. New suit, and the shoes on yer feet must 'ave cost a pretty penny. Suppose you've been staying in some posh 'otel. I ain't even had the money for Teddy to go on his school trip. Time an' time again your son has said, "I bet my dad will pay for me to go," but you've never bothered to come near nor by. The pity of it is for weeks on end he waited every Saturday for you to come and take him to football, 'cos he said over and over again, he didn't care what *anyone* said, you were *his* dad. That's why I get so cross when I 'ave to tell the kids that they can't have things 'cos you haven't sent us any money.'

Now Den was really angry and for a moment she thought he was going to hit her.

'You know where an' when t' hurt a man when he's down, don't you, Ella?'

'Hmm! You are neither down nor out, you're just bloody mad that the son you're supposed to think so much of is beginning to realize what you are really like.'

Dennis sighed and gritted his teeth. 'Ella, listen to me. I had to get away for a time. I had business that needed sorting, but as you so rightly say I am not down and out and I won't leave you without funds again. You shouldn't believe all the gossip nosy folk round here tell you. Young Connie Baldwin is a right little flirt. *If* she is carrying a baby, it could belong to anybody.'

'Oh, she's carrying a baby all right!' Ella's voice was

rising, though she was trying as hard as she could to control it and her temper. 'That girl passes my front window five mornings a week and I ain't blind. This affair has been going on for a lot longer than I've known about it. Though you'd 'ave me believe different.'

Dennis sniffed. His whole face was red as he stared at her hard.

'If what you're claiming is true, then it's like I've said before, you've only got yerself to blame,' he said, punching his clenched fist down heavily on to the table, making his now empty mug fall over on to its side.

'My fault! All the pain and aggro you've caused me and the kids, and now you've got the cheek to suggest it's all my fault . . .' Her voice trailed off as she had to stop and draw a deep breath.

'Yeah, a marriage is supposed to work both ways. You, Ella, are a taker, never willing even to meet me halfway. I had plans, big plans. My old man did me a favour when he asked me if I wanted to buy that house at a knockdown price. Most women would have been over the moon having a deal like that dropped in their lap. But oh no. Not you. You'd rather stay in this dingy little 'ouse that is damp an' 'asn't seen a lick of paint since before the war. Why? 'Cos you're dead lazy. Couldn't get off yer backside and come an' see if there was anything you could do t' help. You'd rather sit drinking tea all day, or chatting over fences to women like yerself what ain't got no ambition. Is it any wonder that I turned to another woman? I'll tell yer again, 'cos it doesn't seem to have sunk into that thick 'ead of yours, you make no effort. Dead scruffy, that's what you are most days when I come home.'

Ella gave a sarcastic laugh.

'Oh, it's easy to blame me, helps t' ease yer conscience, does it? I might be a lot of things, Den, but soft in the 'ead I ain't. You're making a big mistake if you think you can get away with coming out with these old woman's tales. First off, Connie Baldwin is not a woman, she is a young girl who is at least five or six months pregnant, I'd say, and I don't for one moment think that she conceived the very first time you ever took her out. No, you had to butter her up first, show 'er what a great man you was, big car, plenty of money, knew yer way around London. I reckon the first time you got in that young girl's knickers was way before you or your father knew that old lady was thinking of moving from her big 'ouse. Me refusing to uproot our two kids and live out in the back of beyond had nothing whatsoever to do with you 'aving your filthy way with Connie Baldwin. You 'ad the sweets, Den, and now you 'ave to put up with the sours. Just a pity that your own kids 'ave to suffer in the process.'

Dennis closed his eyes. He had never seen Ella in this kind of mood before. Her moaning he was used to, but today she was being a right pain. He leant towards her and whacked her full force in the face.

It felt as if her face was on fire as her head rocked backwards.

Pushing the table until it was resting hard against Ella's chest, Dennis stood up and pointed to the envelope that still lay on the table between them.

'Will that lot keep you going for a while?'

Ella nodded her head slowly.

'Never let it be said that I keep you or the kids short of money.'

She couldn't bring herself to answer.

'Did you hear what I just said?' Dennis bellowed menacingly.

'Yes,' Ella said reluctantly.

'Well, don't go telling folk that me not living 'ere is a hardship for you,' he shouted back over his shoulder as he made for the door. Then, grinning, he said, 'Tell Teddy and Babs that I'll be seeing them soon.'

After she'd heard the front door slam, Ella sat still for a good five minutes, just staring into space. She didn't know which hurt the most: her painful cheek, the thudding in her head, or the fact that she hadn't been able to throw his money back into his face. Sad but true, she needed the money to feed and clothe her children, never mind pay the rent.

That was the moment when she decided she was going to get herself a job.

Chapter Nine

ELLA HAD GIVEN A young lad a threepenny bit to take a note around to her mother. All she had written was that she had an errand to run and would call in on her way back. That had been an hour and a half ago, and Winnie was curious. For the umpteenth time she went into her front room and walked over to the window, and now she watched as her daughter walked down the street, her shoulders stooped as if they carried the weight of the world. 'Now what's happened?' Winnie murmured thoughtfully. 'Poor Ella, life can't throw much more at her.'

Shaking her head, she straightened her lace curtain and hurried to the kitchen to put the kettle on. 'It has t' be something more to do with Dennis,' she said to herself. 'That man is a right selfish sod.' From her shopping bag she took out a bag of six jam doughnuts and set them one by one on a plate, which she placed on a small table covered with a pretty tablecloth.

'You timed that well, Ella,' she called out as she heard the front door open and Ella walking down the passage. 'The kettle has boiled an' I'm just about to make the tea.'

First glance told her something wasn't right. Ella looked terrible. Her copper-coloured hair that she had been taking such good care of lately straggled across her face.

Winnie walked across the living room to her. Ella put her hands up to her face and tried to turn her face away from her mother.

'You all right, luv?' Winnie asked, knowing full well it was a daft question.

Ella nodded her head.

Very gently her mother took hold of her chin with one hand and used the other to uncover her face. Ella flinched.

The very look of her made her mother's blood boil, because despite the fact that Ella had powdered her face, it hadn't covered the ugly bruise that ran across her cheekbone.

'Bloody men! I don't need to be told who done that to you,' Winnie said, and Ella could tell she was bristling with anger. 'Come on, luv, sit yer down an' I promise yer one thing. I'll make damn sure that 'usband of yours will live to regret the day he laid a finger on you. It was Dennis, wasn't it?'

'Yes,' Ella admitted quietly.

'I guessed as much, but let's have our tea and a doughnut and then you can tell me what's 'appened to make him lose his rag.'

What she really wanted to do was ask a load of questions. But she knew better. Wait, and Ella would tell her all in her own good time.

'I'll fetch the tray. They're nice jam doughnuts. I got 'em from Bloomers, the posh bakers. Still warm they were when he 'anded me the bag.'

Returning with the tea tray and two fancy plates, Winnie would have gone on chatting, but something about the way Ella was sitting hunched up and quiet made her pause.

'Ella, luv, what's really up?' She came nearer. 'Don't

tell me that ol' man of yours whacked yer one 'cos you asked him for some money? What the 'ell does he think you and the kids are living on, bloody fresh air?'

When Ella raised her head, her mother saw tears rolling down her swollen cheeks and knew there was something very wrong. Quickly moving the tea tray out of harm's way, she knelt down beside her.

'You don't 'ave t' tell me your Den has put in an appearance. I can see that for meself, but what I want t' know is what he had t' say for himself, 'cos it couldn't 'ave been very nice seeing the state he's left you in.'

Not yet able to open her heart to her mother, Ella bowed her head again and looked away.

Carefully Winnie wrapped both arms about her. 'Something big 'as upset you, I can tell.' Laying her face on Ella's head, she murmured, 'I'm here, luv, I always will be. Just think about it, you can tell me. I might even be able to help.'

A moment passed. Feeling loved and safe in her mum's arms, Ella sobbed quietly.

Winnie released her hold, saying, 'I'll pour the tea out. Don't know why, but a cuppa always seems to help.'

They each sipped their tea, and the everyday sounds of the street coming through the open window made Ella realize that life had to go on. Winnie got up and pulled a coarse linen tea-towel from a drawer in the dresser. Handing it to Ella, she said, 'Wipe yer face and try an' eat a jam doughnut.'

Ella looked into her mum's face and managed to smile. 'And that will make me feel better, will it?'

'Course it will, but don't go getting sugar all over me best tablecloth.'

Winnie grinned as she watched her daughter pick up a sugary doughnut and take a big bite. If only I could sort out her problems as easily! she thought.

Some time later, Ella actually did start to feel better. She gave her face, and especially her lips, which were smeared with jam, another good rub with the towel, then took a deep breath, looked at Winnie and said, 'How am I supposed to cope with all this, Mum? Dennis didn't deny that he was the father of Connie Baldwin's baby, but according to him everyone else is responsible for the mess we're in; none of it is his fault. First off he went mad 'cos Nellie Turner had told me about the affair, called her every wicked name under the sun. Then he pleaded with me not to tell Teddy and Babs, and when I told him that I'd already had to tell them the truth because the kids at school were 'aving a field day, well, that was like adding fuel to the flames. I thought he was going to burst a blood vessel.

'Then, well, you wouldn't believe it. Accusations were coming from all corners. He was drunk at the time, couldn't help himself. Young girls come into the pubs half-naked just asking for it. When I told him there was no way I was going to believe it had been a one-off, and that I was well aware he had been taking Connie out and buying her things for months . . . that was when he stuck his face close to mine and—'

'He put his fist in yer face?' Winnie screamed the words.

'No, Mum. Not at that point. What he did do made me feel a darn sight worse.'

'Lord Almighty!' Winnie jumped up fast, nearly knocking the teapot flying. 'Sorry, luv, carry on, I'm listening, but the more I hear, the more I'm sure Dennis Dryden was born bad.'

He told me *I* drove him to it. Said I was a miserable mare, a fat, lazy old bag, and the clothes I wore weren't fit to put in the rag-bag. Without thinking, Mum, I needled him. Told him he was selfish. Always buying himself good clothes, real leather shoes, and riding around in a flash car, while his kids and I had to wear whatever we could get. That really rattled him. But still I hadn't the sense to leave it there. I had to push me luck.'

'No one could blame yer, gal,' Winnie cut in. 'About time somebody told that bloke a few home truths.'

'You ain't heard the worst of what I said yet.' Ella's voice was low.

'Well, go on, let's 'ave it all out in the open,' Winnie urged.

Ella put her hands to her head. It was aching like mad, and her cheek felt as if it was on fire.

'I told him I might be scruffy and miserable, but at least I did me best to bring the kids up well and I led a far more decent life than he ever did. He wanted to know how I worked that out. I told him outright it was him that was turning schoolgirls into whores and young Connie Baldwin into an unmarried mum.'

Ella's voice was rising in panic and Winnie's temper was almost out of control.

'That was when he grabbed my chin with his hand and pulled my face towards him and told me I needed to watch my mouth 'cos he could always take the kids away from me. I tried desperately to pull away from him, and that's when he pulled his right arm back and slapped me in the face.'

'Some slap!' Winnie murmured.

'That's not all, Mum. He punched me in the stomach just as I stood up, and I got the full force of his fist. I don't know what hurts the most, me stomach or me face or me head.'

Winnie stood up and started to pace the floor. 'Oh, you poor luv. I'll see Ted gets to know what his son is really like, but you've got to calm down and start thinking. There's more than one way to skin a rabbit. First question, did he leave you any money?'

'Yeah, he did, but t' be honest, Mum, I would have given anything to be able to tell him to stuff it. Teddy needs new shoes, though, an' I'm behind with the rent, so . . .'

'You could talk to me more. You know I can manage a little every week.'

'You shouldn't have to, Mum, and you buy far too much for me and the kids as it is. But there is something else I haven't told you yet.'

Winnie raised her eyebrows and sighed heavily.

'Go on then, we might as well get it all out in the open.'

Ella tried, unsuccessfully, to sound optimistic. 'I've made up my mind. I'm going to do my best to get a job. However, I still feel really shattered, so I thought I'd leave the job-hunting for a few days.'

'You're doing the right thing.' Her mother grinned, showing her good white teeth; she was very proud that at her age she still had no false teeth. 'But before you even start thinking about looking for work, you and I are going to pay a visit to Sadie and Isaac Cohan's shop. Sadie will sort you out a couple of smart outfits, my treat, and that Dennis of yours will regret the fact that he called you a rag-bag. You'll see. And I think getting a job is a jolly good idea, shows you've still got some go in yer. You'll find a decent job, I know you will. It'll give you a bit of independence, and get you out an' mixing with other people.

'But for now, you take yerself upstairs and have a lie-down while I wash these cups and plates and make myself presentable.'

'Well, if you're gonna do yer face and dress up to the nines, that will be the day gone.' Ella really smiled for the first time since she had come into the house.

'Why, you cheeky moo! I can see Dennis hasn't completely knocked the stuffing out of you. Anyway, I think we both deserve a break. How about we do a bit of shopping, then 'ave pie an' mash or fish an' chips if the fancy takes yer, then we'll go an' meet the kids from school and buy them a treat. How does that sound?'

'Mum, what would I do without you? You wanna know something? You're better than any tonic. Far, far better. You might get on me nerves sometimes with yer nagging, but I love yer t' bits.'

Ella laughed loudly and swiftly ducked as her mother picked up a cushion and threw it at her.

Chapter Ten

'WELL, ELLY, ARE YOU feeling any better?'

Sitting side by side on the low wall that fronted the school, Winnie had lapsed into using her daughter's pet name, that had suited her so well when she was a child.

'No lies, mind,' she warned. 'I'll know if you're not telling me the truth, though I still think I should have taken you up to the hospital.'

'Mum, Mr Greenway cleaned up my cheek and forehead all right, and the witch hazel he gave me will ease the burning and help the bruising, he said, so stop yer worrying.'

'Yes, old Mr Greenway is a marvellous chemist. Folk 'ave been going t' him for years. He's just as good as any doctor an' a damn sight cheaper too.'

'Also, Mum, I felt so sick all the while we were out until we had our pie an' mash, but since then I've felt much better.'

'It's like I'm always telling you, keep the inner man fed well an' you can cope with anything. Now, no brooding tonight, and bright an' early in the morning we're off to see what Sadie can do about some decent everyday clothes for you.'

Ella didn't bother to answer. School was out and she could see her two children surrounded by their mates running across the playground.

'I can't believe how fast Teddy is growing. It seems only last week that I bought those long trousers, and look at them now, they're up round his ankles.'

'Makes yer feel proud just looking at him,' Winnie declared, a grandmother's love shining in her eyes.

'He's so like his dad,' Ella remarked sadly.

'Only in looks,' his gran quickly commented.

Teddy was very tall for his age, with long, lean limbs and a thick, wild shock of unruly dark hair exactly the same as Dennis's; he also had his father's bright blue eyes.

As he drew nearer, Winnie said, 'The lad does seem to 'ave shot up all of a sudden. But then, so has Babs. A few more years and she's going to be a real beauty, an' no mistake. I tell yer, gal, with that long chestnut-coloured hair, and those big brown eyes, both of which she gets from you, she'll drive the fellers up the wall.'

She pointed to Teddy, who had stopped running and was waiting for his sister. As she drew near, he held out an arm and she put her hand into his.

'See that, he knows we're watching, but I'm sure one way an' another he'll always look out for her.'

Both mother and daughter chuckled and Ella added, 'I'll try and remember that next time they're going for each other like two tom cats.'

Both children came bounding up and were greeted with hugs and kisses from their mum and their gran. Teddy was busy telling his mother how he was going to be sent up to the senior school, and that he had put his name down for woodwork classes. Winnie was cuddling Babs, telling her how she thought she must be the prettiest little girl in the whole school. 'Did you do all right today?' she asked.

'Yes, why?' Babs's smile was as bright as ever.

'Just wondered, that's all.'

'Well, I did my best, at least I think I did, but . . .'

'But what?'

Babs shrugged. 'Nothing really. Just some nosy kid thinks she knows more about my dad than I do. Gran, I'll always love my dad.'

Winnie closed her eyes in distress. Her grandchildren meant the world to her.

'Of course you will, darlin'. Of course you will.'

As she put her arms around Babs again, inwardly she wanted to cry. Why should it be that when families ran into trouble, it was always the kids who suffered the most?

Although Ella's attention had been taken up with Teddy, who had asked what had happened to her face – 'My own fault,' she lied, 'I didn't look where I was going' – she had heard what Babs had said and it hurt her to the quick. She forced herself to keep her voice soft and calm as she said, 'Who wants to choose where we go for a treat?'

She was doing her best, acting like this was a special day.

Teddy pulled a face. 'That depends on whether we're going to get something to eat first. I'm starving, Mum.'

'Me too,' Babs declared.

Even Winnie grinned. You couldn't help laughing at Teddy. Food always came first with him.

Ella smiled as she said, 'Going for something more like an ice-cream was what I had in mind.'

Quickly Winnie cut in. 'You two kids choose where you would like t' go and what you fancy to eat, an' we'll say it's my treat this time. That's if yer mum says it's all right.'

Teddy and Babs both grinned and in agreement said, 'Hot dog and a milkshake, please, Gran.'

Ella smiled once more. 'OK. You two could charm the hind legs off a donkey.'

Babs and Teddy were sitting on high stools, noisily sucking through straws at their strawberry milkshakes and waiting for their hot dogs to be cooked. Ella and her mother were seated at a corner table in this cosy café with a toasted teacake and a pot of tea in front of them.

'Have you decided what you're going to do about Connie Baldwin?' Winnie asked cautiously.

Ella thought it was hardly surprising that her mother had once again brought this subject up.

'What do you suggest I do, Mum?'

'Time's getting on; that baby will be born before you know it.' Winnie sighed.

'I know what you're trying to say, Mum, and I think I know what you want me to do.'

'Oh yeah, and what's that?'

'You think I should see a solicitor and go for a divorce, don't you?'

'That's for you to decide, Ella luv. There's nobody on this earth who can make your mind up for you where that's concerned. But while you're deciding, think on this. That young girl is gonna be walking up and down your street wheeling a pram with your Dennis's baby in it, and she ain't going to make no secret of it. I reckon you should ask someone to tell you whether or not she is going to keep the baby.'

'Thanks for the advice, Mum. God knows I need it at the moment, but who the hell do you reckon that someone should be?'

Winnie looked at her daughter. 'By rights it should be your Dennis, but it don't seem like you're going to get much joy from him. So then, Ella, you tell me what you are thinking of doing.'

93

The tone of her mother's voice made Ella aware that she was fast losing patience with her.

'What I wish is that Dennis would take the flipping girl as far away as possible, live with her and her baby and leave me and my children alone.'

'Is that what you really want, Ella? For Den t' go miles away? What about Teddy and Babs? They're his children as well, you know.'

That was the nagging worry at the back of Ella's mind. Whichever way she turned, it seemed likely that she would be depriving her children of their father. Hadn't she heard her own little girl tell her gran that she would always love her dad?

Pushing these thoughts impatiently away, she nodded warily. 'I'm not sure what I want any more. I only know it would take a miracle for our lives to go back to being what they were before.'

She leant forward in her chair and covered her face with her hands. Gingerly, she felt the swollen side of her face. Earlier on the pain had been so bad she had thought Dennis had broken her cheekbone, but thankfully Mr Greenway had assured her it was just bruised.

Winnie scowled at her. 'It's a pity, but nothing will really get sorted until one of us has a talk with Connie's parents.'

'Well it's not going to be me.' Ella bristled slightly. 'I'm not going anywhere near them.'

'Did you ask Dennis if he had discussed the matter with the girl's father?'

Taken aback, Ella stared at her mother for a moment. 'You're 'aving a laugh, aren't you? Den face Mr Baldwin! That would be some meeting, that would. Probably end up with murder being done. More than likely, all he's done is tell the girl to get rid of it.'

For a while they sat silently eating their teacake and

sipping their tea. Finally Ella changed the subject and asked, 'Mum, do you think I drove Dennis away? Was I so lazy and scruffy all the time?'

Her mother took a long, deep sigh. Reaching out her hand, she held Ella's, and the look she gave her was soft and loving. 'I'd never lie to you and I would never willingly hurt you,' she said. 'Never in a million years. But you don't need me to remind you that Connie Baldwin is not the first girl that your Den has gone astray with.'

'You think I don't know that?'

'All right, Ella, but you have to face the facts, hard as the truth is to bear. Dennis is and always will be a ladies' man. The younger they are, the more attracted he is. Since you ask, yes, maybe you did let yerself go a bit, but he hasn't been the perfect husband by any means. A few weeks of the year he'd be rolling in money, treating you like a queen and buying the kids God knows what. The rest of the time you never knew where yer next shilling was coming from half the time. So do me a favour, stop taking his guilt on your shoulders.'

Seeing the look on her daughter's face, and sensing the uncertainty, the misery and the loneliness that Dennis had brought down on her, Winnie decided she would have to interfere.

Doing her best to smile, but feeling embarrassed, she said, 'I'll tell you what I'm going to do. I'm going to arrange to meet Ted Dryden and try and get some answers. Just him and me, we'll meet somewhere quiet and I'll tell him straight that if his son can't or won't sort things out, then he had better get to the truth of the matter himself. I'll also remind him that his son already has a wife and two children, and that those two children are his grandchildren.'

'But, Mum, Ted has been like you, good t' me and the kids. I don't want to start quarrelling with him. At the

95

moment, without his grandad there would be no men in our Teddy's life, an' that wouldn't be good for him. But I am grateful and I do agree that if anyone can sort this mess out it will be Den's father.'

Having said that, Ella gave a soft sigh of relief. For too long they had done nothing but listen to gossip. Now perhaps her father-in-law would face Connie and her parents dead on and some kind of solution might be found.

Seeing that Ella had faith in her and had agreed to accept her offer, Winnie half wished she hadn't been so brave.

I only hope I'm doing the right thing, she said to herself.

Chapter Eleven

ELLA AWOKE TO SEE the sun was streaming in at the window of her bedroom. She lay for a while staring at the thin flowered curtains. How many times had she washed and ironed them? They were getting so threadbare, it was about time she had some new ones.

Then she remembered, and she was so thrilled that she swung her legs around to the side of the bed, got up, flung the curtains back as far as they would go and opened the top of the window.

It was going to be a glorious summer's day. It had to be. She had a job; or rather, she was going in Thursday morning for a couple of hours just to be shown the ropes, then a trial run starting this coming Friday at six thirty. It was only Tuesday, plenty of time to get her hair done and do something about her clothes.

Talk about coincidence, or was it fate?

She and her mother had been coming down the street yesterday, both loaded with shopping, when they almost crashed into Mike Murray.

'You wanna watch where you're going, Mickey, dashing about like a madman. Skiving off for a few hours, are yer?'

Mike was brought up sharp by the sound of Winnie's voice.

'Oh, hallo, Win, Ella, sorry, me mind was miles away. In me head I'm trying to piece together an advert to put into the *Borough News* and if I don't get it in today it won't be in Friday's edition.'

'What's so important? What's the ad for?' Winnie couldn't help being nosy. After all, Mike Murray was the manager of the British Legion working men's club and they'd all spent many a great night in that place, especially when her Alf was alive. Different when your husband dies and you're left on your own, she thought. Don't get out and about so much. A woman on her own was always regarded suspiciously by married women.

'I don't know, Win, gal, don't seem t' be able t' keep staff five minutes these days. Half the young men have their fingers in the till and the bits of girls yer get t' work behind the bar would turn the place into a knocking shop if they 'ad their way. Pull a pint, they can't pull their own knickers up, 'alf of them.'

'Sounds rough, Mickey. Perhaps you ain't treating your staff all that good.'

Mickey looked amazed. 'Thought you knew me better than that, gal.' He was watching Winnie's face and suddenly he said, 'You wouldn't wanna job, would yer?'

Winnie groaned. 'What, me, stand on me feet all them ruddy hours? Not on yer Nellie.'

'I've never worked behind a bar, but I could wash glasses.' Ella's voice was quiet but she sounded desperate.

'Well, well,' was all her mother said.

Mike turned to face Ella and looked at her with respect. 'If you mean it, Ella, I'll start you on whenever you say. You'd be quick to learn, I know yer would, and I'd make sure the other staff gave you a bit of help.'

Ella was astounded. She felt herself blushing furiously. What on earth had made her jump in like that?

'I couldn't do all day, Mike, especially now when me kids are soon gonna break up from school. Summer holidays are about six weeks, yer know.'

'That's all right, luv, we'll sort something out. Evenings and weekends is when I'd need yer most. Thirty bob a session to start with, but five quid if yer do two sessions on a Saturday.'

'I'll come to your place and look after the kids.' Winnie had sounded really enthusiastic.

Now, in her excitement, Ella couldn't believe all that had really happened. She ran down the stairs, not bothering to put her dressing gown on, but as she waited for the kettle to boil, doubts began to creep into her mind. Would she be able to hold down a job? Busy place was the Legion.

The back door opened and her mother came in, smiling bright as a button and really smartly dressed.

'Morning, my luv, thought I'd get round here before the kids go off to school, then I can clear up while you're seeing t' yerself.'

'What's the hurry, Mum?'

'I wanna get you over to Sadie's nice an' early so you an' she can take yer time sorting through whatever gear she has in stock. Got t' 'ave you well turned out when you start yer first day down at the Legion, ain't we?'

'Mum . . .'

'You don't need t' tell me, luv, you're 'aving a fit of the collie-wobbles.'

'Well, yes, I did kind of jump in with both feet, an' now I'm not so sure I'm up to being a barmaid.'

Her mother stared hard at her. 'Don't put yerself down, Ella. Being with Den all these years has sucked away a lot of your confidence, but you just listen t' me, gal. You're good enough to work anywhere. Yer brain might be a bit rusty, but you're certainly not dim, not by a long chalk you're not. A few days and you'll take to serving behind that bar like a duck takes t' water.'

She moved closer and laid her hands reassuringly on Ella's shoulders.

'It's only natural for yer t' be a bit scared at the thought of facing all them customers. But you'll be fine. Think of all the people you'll meet. I bet there'll be a good many you know already, and you'll make new friends 'cos there's always a good social life down at the Legion.'

Ella stared at her mother thoughtfully. Winnie was right. This job could be a turning point in her life. It would certainly make Dennis sit up and take notice. And she liked the sound of a social life.

Winnie could imagine what was going through her daughter's mind and she quickly said, 'You never know, luv, this might lead to a whole new way of life for you.'

That did set Ella thinking, and suddenly a feeling of excitement stirred within her and for the first time in God knows how long she began to take a lively interest in the future.

'You're right, Mum,' she said, grinning. 'When I woke up this morning I wasn't sure that I hadn't dreamt that Mike had offered me a job. Now talking to you I'm OK. Mike said two weeks' trial, so if I get through that all right I shall stay on, do me best and see where it leads.'

'That's the spirit, gal, an' you'll feel even better after our visit t' Sadie. Now you get yerself upstairs an' get yerself dressed. I'll see t' the kids. I'll even walk them t' school.'

'Mum, d'yer mind holding yer horses for a bit? I'd just put the kettle on when you arrived and I ain't even got round to making a pot of tea yet. Sorry, but I can't pull meself together until I've had at least two cups of tea of a morning.'

'You waste 'alf the day, you do,' her mother muttered.

Ella heard what she'd said and laughed.

'Just 'cos you get up at the crack of dawn 'cos you're too wicked t' sleep.'

'Get on with yer, you saucy hussy, and pour that blinking tea out if you're going to.'

It was a quarter to ten when they got off the bus opposite Dirty Dick's pub and began to walk down the side streets that would lead them to Cohans' shop. There were no stalls set out today.

Ella pushed the glass door, holding it open for her mother to step into the shop first. She was right behind her, and for a moment she felt envious. The shop and the clothes on display were even better than she had remembered. But envious was the wrong way to feel. From what her mum had told her, she knew the Cohan family had worked extremely hard to get their business up and running.

Having heard the ping of the bell as the shop door had opened, Sadie came through from their living room. Seeing Winnie, she ran towards her, wrapped her arms around her and kissed her on each cheek. Releasing her hold she said, 'It's so good to see you. And you too, Ella,' she added before kissing her as well. 'You listened to what I said.' Sadie was nodding her head and smiling.

Ella looked a bit bewildered.

'Your hair, it looks gorgeous. In fact you look different altogether. If I didn't know your mother so well, I'd say there was a new man in your life.'

Winnie laughed, but Ella didn't.

'You couldn't be more wrong,' Winnie said. 'The man in my daughter's life ain't worth the air he breathes and he puts my Ella down at every turn. If he had his way he'd live the life of old Riley while she'd spend her whole time scrubbing, cleaning, doing the weekly wash and making sure a damn good dinner was put in front of him every night. Well, between us we've decided it's pay-back time. Ella is going to have a life of her own. That's why we're here: she's got a job, starts on Friday, and she needs some everyday good clothes.'

'You come to the right place, I'm pleased to say.' Isaac was standing in the doorway that led from their private quarters. His voice was so full of pleasure that it made Winnie feel glad they were here.

He was wearing Prince of Wales check trousers, and a fawn shirt open at the neck with the sleeves rolled up to his elbows. As he embraced Winnie he apologized. 'If I had known you two ladies were coming, I would have worn a suit.'

A flush of pleasure rose to Winnie's cheeks, as it always did when she came face to face with this dear old friend.

He held out his arms to Ella and she gladly went into them for a warm and welcoming hug. 'So our little Elly is going out into the big world to earn her own living. I heard right, did I not?'

'Well, I'm going to try.' Ella looked briefly at her mother, who nodded her encouragement.

Isaac rubbed his hands together. 'Now then, best that your mother and I disappear and leave you in the capable hands of my beloved Sadie, but we shall be kind to both of you.' He paused and winked at Winnie. 'We shall make each of you a glass of lemon tea and bring it through to here.'

'Good,' Sadie said happily. 'Ella and I can manage quite well without help from either of you, but the tea will be much appreciated.'

Sadie was a good-looking woman and she knew it. Why? Because she worked at it. She had lovely dark eyes, long dark hair that had a sheen to it, and her styling was different from time to time. In fact there was nothing about Sadie Cohan that one could take for granted. As on the first occasion they had met, she was wearing an immaculate worsted suit, which should by rights make her look businesslike. Ella decided it must be the way that she did her make-up and her hair, because Sadie looked sexy. Then again, maybe it was the way that she held herself and the way that she walked, full of confidence. Ella sighed. She was sure she herself would never be able to acquire such self-assurance.

They sipped their hot lemon tea and talked about everyday life. Yes, both of Ella's children were doing well at school, though they both missed their dad.

'I gathered from what your mother said that you were having marital problems,' Sadie said with feeling.

'That's putting it mildly,' Ella exclaimed.

'Well, in that case, let's get on to happier things, find out if I have any clothes that take your fancy, shall we?'

'You are joking.' Ella looked around the shop and raised her eyebrows. 'Anyone would 'ave t' be really picky if they couldn't find several things they would die for in this shop.'

'If only that were true,' Sadie murmured. 'Some days I get more than one customer there is no pleasing, no matter how hard I try.'

'I promise I won't be like that,' Ella said quickly.

Sadie patted her shoulder. 'First things first, strip off to your underwear.'

Ella couldn't help it: she still felt embarrassed, even though this time she had come prepared.

As she removed her cardigan and undid the buttons of her blouse, Sadie clapped her hands. 'Oh good,' she cried. 'You are wearing your long bust bodice.'

Ella kept quiet. She wasn't going to tell Sadie that she only ever wore it when she was going out. Around the house it felt restricting, but she knew she would buy another one today, because if she really did get the job at the Legion, she would wear this type of brassiere every day to work. So it would have to be one on and one in the wash.

It was as if Sadie read Ella's mind.

'Do you find it very uncomfortable?' she asked.

'Not now I've got used to it, and since my mum has encouraged me to lose a bit of weight, it does seem to minimize my bosoms.'

Sadie eyed Ella's still large but quite shapely breasts as she slipped a simple black linen dress over her head. Ella did up the line of buttons that fronted the dress while Sadie moved backwards and eyed her from top to toe.

Winnie had helped her daughter a lot. Ella did look a good deal thinner, much smarter, younger even.

Ella was smiling at her image in the three-cornered looking glass. 'I've never had a black dress before.'

With a businesslike air Sadie examined her. 'Well, it suits you to a tee. Black always looks smart.'

It was true: the design was simple, seeming to reduce her tummy and skimming over her hips.

'Maybe with your first week's wages you might buy yourself a nice pair of black shoes that would go with any outfit,' Sadie suggested.

'Wouldn't I need a touch of colour with a dress like this? I don't have any what you'd call good jewellery.'

Sadie turned her back on Ella, walked to a glass-fronted cabinet and from a drawer withdrew two silk scarves, one emerald green and one red, each with a delicate, intricate pattern woven down both sides. First she draped the green scarf around the neck of the dress, tossing one long end over Ella's left shoulder.

Ella gasped in surprise. The difference the scarf made was dramatic.

Laughing at the expression on Ella's face, Sadie

104

removed the green scarf, replacing it with the red one, only this time she allowed both ends of the silk to dangle to the front of the dress, tying a loose knot to keep it in place.

'See, two different outfits. And there are many more ways one may wear a scarf. You just need to practise.'

Ella considered this. Would she ever be able to adapt clothes to make herself look as elegant as Sadie did? She doubted it, but by God she was going to have a damn good try. She half turned to gaze at herself in the mirror again. She was more than pleased with her reflection.

'What you need now is a basic good skirt with which you can wear blouses or jumpers. I suggest navy blue. What do you think, Ella?'

Ella considered for a moment. She would much rather leave the choice to Sadie but she didn't want to appear to be too dim. 'Yes please, Sadie, I think navy blue would suit me fine.'

Sadie produced three skirts. The first one Ella did not like; the material was good but it was a pinstripe. Hesitantly she looked at Sadie. 'If you don't mind, I think that one is too mannish.'

Sadie roared with laughter. 'Oh, Ella my dear, I am thrilled to hear that you have an opinion of your own.'

'Then you are not going to put me down as an awkward customer who has ruined your day?'

'Certainly not. How about this one?' Sadie took a skirt by its waistband and flung it neatly so that the all-round pleats spread over the carpet.

'Beautiful,' Ella said quietly, 'but not for me. Sadie, can you see those pleats fitting over my hips?'

'You are not only getting bolder, you are acquiring more dress sense by the minute! However, my stock of skirts is pretty low at the moment, so it is this third one or wait until your next visit.'

Having taken off the black dress, which Sadie carefully folded, placing both scarves on the top, Ella sat down on the gilt chair and pulled the tailored skirt up over her hips. The waistband was fine, and she was able to do the top button up without any difficulty. She stood up and ran her hands down her sides. The skirt felt slinky, and as she looked into the mirror and noticed there was a slit to the side which reached nearly up to her knee, she turned to Sadie and they both laughed.

'Go on, say what you're thinking,' Sadie urged.

'Sexy,' Ella said, drawing herself up to her full height.

'Exactly. Now all I have to do is find you two or three decent tops and you'll be fit and ready to become part of the business world.'

One long-sleeved white blouse was added to the pile; also a very pale blue twinset, and when Ella protested that she wouldn't be able to afford so much, Sadie told her to be quiet. Fully dressed now, Ella asked if she might buy another long-line brassiere and Sadie said she had to go upstairs to fetch that.

Ella sat shaking her head in disbelief. She was so lucky, and if her mother would pay half of the amount she had spent today, hopefully she would be able to pay her back in weekly instalments out of her wages. With that thought in mind she started to silently pray. Dear Lord, let me be good at this job, please don't let me end up a complete failure, the kind of useless slag that Dennis has come to believe I am.

Sadie came back holding not only the bra she had gone for, but also a pink blouse.

'This is my present to you, a good-luck omen for you to wear at your new job.' She was holding the blouse up high for Ella to see, and only one word came to her mind: exquisite. 'It will tone perfectly with the navy skirt,' Sadie assured her.

'But redheads can't wear pink,' Ella protested.

'Whoever called you a redhead? Deep copper-coloured hair such as you have is a rarity, and don't let anyone tell you any different. Take a good look at that blouse and tell me you don't want it.'

Ella took the blouse and looked at the workmanship on the collar and cuffs. It was the most delicate and intricate that she had ever seen.

'Hold it up against you and look in the mirror.'

Ella did. 'Brilliant,' she said softly. 'Sadie, how can I ever thank you?'

'By enjoying your job and making a new happy life for yourself.'

Ella couldn't answer. Tears were choking her, her eyes glittering.

After a friendly argument as to who was going to pay for what, mother and daughter said their goodbyes, promising to come back soon and let Isaac and Sadie know how Ella was doing.

'Happy?' Winnie asked as they walked to the bus stop.

'Absolutely, Mum.'

'Well, it's still early. What say we get the bus and go up West for a change?'

'All right with me,' Ella agreed happily.

It wasn't long before they were standing at a coffee stall on the corner of Hyde Park, eating what could only be described as wonderful bacon rolls, and sipping strong tea served in thick white china mugs.

The sun had brought out the smell of the grass and the flowers, which looked a picture. Their lunch finished, they decided they would sit by the Serpentine for a while.

Late afternoon found two very tired but happy women trudging their way home.

Chapter Twelve

'SO HOW'S THAT THEN, Mike?'

Placing a brimming pint of old ale on the bar next to a pint of Guinness, which had a creamy head about half an inch deep from the rim of the glass, Ella grinned.

Mike seated himself on one of the bar stools and eyed her with satisfaction. 'Told yer, practice makes perfect.'

'You're just being kind. Took me four goes before I got that Guinness right.'

'Ella, slow but sure. That is one of the most difficult pints to pull. In one afternoon and with not much waste in the slop trays, you've learnt how to change an optic, and attaching that device to an upside-down bottle of spirits is no easy task. You know you have to keep the ashtrays emptied and cleaned whenever you have any spare time. You've also been down the cellar with me and watched me change a barrel, not that there will ever be the need for you to have to do that, I hope. We've a couple of good potmen who also know their way around a pub cellar. Yes, looking at those two pints, all in all I'd say you've proved yer worth this afternoon. How do you feel about taking the job on?'

'Well, Mike, I'll admit I was scared t' bits when I walked in here, but yeah, if you're willing to give me a chance, I'd like to try an' do the job.'

'You'll be fine, Ella. I knew you would be. Of course it will be different in here at the weekend, what with the entertainers an' what have you. It can get pretty noisy. Just don't ever let yerself get flustered. Myself or one of the bouncers will always be within earshot. Anyway, there's a whistle beneath the bar; one blast from that and the whole place will go silent.' He grinned broadly. 'You only blow that on very rare occasions. Most arguments can be dealt with easy enough. Blokes know that once chucked out they stay out, and as the prices in here are far cheaper than the pubs, none of them want that.'

Mike turned from looking at Ella to watch Sam Richardson sliding on to the stool next to him.

'Hallo, Sam, you're early. What's brought you here at this time of the day? Oh, by the way, this is Ella Dryden. She's going to start working here tomorrow night.'

Ella smiled knowingly at Sam, and he smiled back and said, 'Long time no see, Ella. You all right?'

'Yes thanks, Sam, I'm fine.'

'I take it you two know each other then,' Mike said, nodding from one to the other.

'You could say that,' Sam smiled sadly. 'Ella and my Lottie went to the same school, were in the same class for years, great friends, weren't you?'

'The best,' Ella answered quietly.

Mike Murray was well aware that Sam had been on his own for years. Only twelve months after he had married Charlotte Fuller, she had suffered a miscarriage, and lost so much blood she herself had died. As far as Mike knew, Sam had never looked at another woman.

'So, Ella, you're going to be a working woman?' Sam remarked.

'Hopefully. Mike has been kind enough to offer me a two-week trial. How about you, Sam, you don't work 'ere, do you?'

'No, I'm a partner in a firm of accountants, Hirst and Richardson. I'm here because we do the books for the Legion.'

'Always knew you would do well, Sam, but you moved away after Charlotte . . . Oh God, what 'ave I said?' Ella flushed with embarrassment.

'Please.' Sam reached out and touched her hand. 'Don't upset yourself. It was a long time ago and it's nice to meet someone who was so friendly with Lottie. Another time perhaps we'll have a chat about old times. All right if I go through to the office, Mike?'

'Yeah, course, mate. I'll bring yer a drink through when I've finished talking to Ella.'

'Probably be seeing something of you then,' Sam said, smiling at Ella as he bent down, picked up his briefcase and walked away.

Mike came round the bar to stand beside Ella. 'You can get off home now if you like. I hope you feel confident enough to come back tomorrow to really start work.'

'Yes, I do, and thanks, Mike, I promise I'll do me best.'

'That'll be good enough for me then, Ella.' He leant his back against the edge of the bar and folded his arms. 'Strange that, ain't it? You and Sam Richardson meeting up again like that.'

Taking a deep, calming breath, Ella said, 'I hope I didn't upset him talking about his wife. Has he never married again?'

'No, not t' my knowledge. I don't think he's the type to be pushed into anything.'

'I wasn't pushing nor prying,' Ella retorted sharply. 'There was a time when him, Charlotte, my Den and me used to go around as a foursome, but like a good many more, Sam found out that a little of my Dennis went a long way. Den would keep bragging about whatever it was he was up to.'

'I know what yer mean.' Mike's voice was all concern. 'Oh, by the way, while we're on the subject, Ella, you do know that your Dennis is a member here, don't you?'

'Yes, I've been here with him an' me family many a time, though it was a while ago.'

Mike smiled warmly. 'Yer right, it's ages since he has drunk in here, but you never know. When word gets around that you're working 'ere he may just saunter in for the hell of it. But don't let it bother you. Just remember, any trouble, I'll deal with it.'

Ella laughed. 'Oh, he won't upset me. I'm rather hoping Den does come in for a drink. I'd dearly love to serve him just t' prove that I can do something worthwhile when I put me mind to it,' she said defensively. Then added quickly, 'Mike, I am grateful t' you for this chance.'

'You don't have to be, Ella, it works both ways.'

As Mike Murray let Ella out of the side door, he was thinking how she had smartened herself up and a smirk twitched at the corners of his mouth. He wouldn't mind seeing Dennis Dryden walk in while Ella was around.

He'd lay odds she'd be able to hold her own.

Chapter Thirteen

ELLA DRYDEN WAS AS happy as a lark as she pushed open the side door of the Legion. It was not yet six o'clock in the evening and her shift didn't start until six thirty. Her mother had taken Teddy and Babs to the pictures, so she had thought she might just as well come to work as stay at home on her own. She had been working here for a month now and she loved the job. To begin with there had been endless gossip, and some queer reactions from members.

She smiled as she recalled the first weekend that she had been behind the bar, when Mrs Baldwin had fronted her, stating loudly that she was not going to be served by the likes of Ella Dryden.

Mike had been fantastic.

'Give me one good reason as to why you do not wish to be served by Mrs Dryden, and I will sack her immediately.' His voice had been quiet but menacing. The whole bar had suddenly gone silent.

Alf Baldwin had stuttered and stammered, doing his best to calm his wife and persuade her to keep her voice down. She paid no heed to him, yelling loud enough for everyone to hear. 'You know damn well what 'er old man has done to our Connie.'

Mike had remained quite calm and in a firm voice had said to Kate Baldwin, 'Would you care to explain to this crowd exactly what Mr Dryden and your daughter's affairs have to do with Mrs Dryden? Apart from the fact that I would say it is her and her children who have been sadly wronged.'

'Aye, that's right.' Many heads were nodding and the mumblings seemed to reverberate around the hall.

Kate Baldwin had been stunned. She had anticipated an entirely different reaction from her neighbours. She looked up into Mike's face first and then turned her gaze on Ella, and what she saw there made her flinch.

She lost her temper again, this time having a go at her husband.

'You silly old sod, I told yer we shouldn't come in 'ere tonight. Everyone has been only too willing to tell me that Ella Dryden was working at the Legion.'

Alf Baldwin was dying for a pint and he decided it was time he got one.

'You, Kate, can do what yer like an' go where yer like, but my throat is parched and I'm staying right where I am. As Mike has just pointed out, what's going on in our family had nought to do with Ella. I for one admire her. She ain't sat on her backside and moaned, she ain't come to our 'ouse spoiling for a fight with our Connie; she's picked 'erself up an' got 'erself a job, and if Mickey's satisfied with her that's good enough for me. If you don't like it, then sod off 'ome an' I'll follow you when I'm good and ready.'

For a short moment Ella had felt quite sorry for Mrs Baldwin, who had sheepishly made her way to the nearest empty table and sat herself down without saying a word. Alf had looked at Ella but stopped short of saying he was sorry. Instead he said, 'Gis a pint of best bitter, a gin an' tonic and take one for yourself, Ella.'

With a straight face she had served him and then said, 'Thanks, Mr Baldwin, I'll 'ave half of shandy.'

From that day onwards everyone had not only shown Ella a bit of respect but had let her know that they were on her side.

She had got herself into a routine and in fact looked forward to coming to work. There was many an evening when she thought it was better than going to the Hippodrome. Fridays and Saturdays were a laugh a minute. Several of the male comedians told jokes that were near the mark and some were downright blue, but the customers, all adults, loved them, and as long as the money kept coming into the tills, Mike was happy.

There were two well-built men, Tom and Derrick, both in their early forties, serving behind the bar besides herself and Molly Riley. By the time Mike called last orders both Molly and Ella were ready to drop, feet hot and sweaty, legs aching like billy-o, and there was still all the clearing-up to do.

Cleaners came in every morning, even Sunday, to hoover the carpets and give the toilets a jolly good clean, but all four bar staff pitched in and left the tables cleared and wiped down and the dirty glasses stacked behind the bar.

The weekly pay packet that Mike handed each of them meant so much to Ella. It went a long way to making her feel independent but also gave her a feeling of self-respect.

The strangest thing that had happened so far was only three days ago, yet it was still vivid in her mind. She grinned. Until she had come to work at the Legion, she had never realized how the other half lived.

It was Saturday evening and Janey, her neighbour, had offered to stay with Babs and Teddy so that Winnie could

114

come to the Legion for a drink. Probably because it was a hot night and there was nowhere at the club for folk to sit outside, trade had not been so brisk.

When Mike had called time, he'd whispered to Winnie that she was welcome to stay behind and have a quiet drink with the staff, and he would put her and Ella into a taxi so that they got home safely.

The usual crowd had left the pub, and Mike closed and bolted the double front doors before settling down to a drink with all the staff, including the two potmen. They had chattered amongst themselves until Molly's Irish blood came to the fore and she had started singing. Such a sweet voice she had and one would have had to have a heart of stone not to have been moved almost to tears as she sang, one after the other, the old, dearly loved Irish ballads.

It was turned one o'clock when Ella and her mother got out of the taxi, and Winnie made no objection when her daughter insisted she stay the night at her house.

Janey was in bed with Babs, one arm around her daughter, the other flung outside the bedclothes. Both were fast asleep. Next Ella looked in on Teddy. He too was well away, and she bent and, smoothing his thick hair off his forehead, gently kissed him.

Next morning she crept quietly downstairs, filled the kettle, placed it on the stove to boil, and then, having made a pot of tea, drank her usual two cups before washing and dressing herself.

There was no sound of movement coming from upstairs and Ella decided it wouldn't hurt to leave them all to have a good lie-in. It was a gorgeous morning and she felt so much better. Today she was wearing her smart navy blue skirt teamed with a crisp cotton blouse with a high neck, long sleeves and cuffs with six buttons. Her chestnut hair was piled up into a bun on the top of her head, but she had allowed a few tendrils to fall round her face and she had used a light covering of make-up, shaping her lips with a very pale lipstick. She was proud of the fact that despite her life having been turned upside down, she had got on with it and wasn't doing too badly. Daytime mostly she could cope, especially now she had a job that kind of brought a social life with it.

Nights were still awful.

She'd be a liar if she said she didn't miss Den. She still turned over in her big double bed and reached out an arm to cuddle up to him, and all she ever found now was empty space. Also, she would never be able to forgive Den for what he had done to their two children. She knew she was partly to blame for him having a roving eye and a yearning for much younger women. She had let herself go and now she was paying the price. Babs and Teddy were a different matter altogether. Each, in their own way, adored their father and he had disdain-fully rejected them.

And for what? Although she knew she had no say in the matter as to what would happen to Connie Baldwin and her baby, it didn't stop her feeling sad. Whichever way you looked at it, that young girl's life would never be the same.

If she had the baby adopted, for many years to come she would constantly be thinking of that child. Ella hoped with all her heart that if she kept it her parents would always be there to help with the problems, because God knows problems there would be!

Would Dennis stand by Connie Baldwin?

Well, I wouldn't put my money on it, was the answer Ella gave herself. He'd practically deserted his older two kids. She smiled to herself. Dennis changing napkins and helping with a newborn baby. Well, that would certainly be a first!

As she had neared the pub later that morning, she saw that Mike was standing outside on the pavement eyeing a top-barrow that was upended in the gutter loaded with old iron and various bundles of what looked like clothes.

'Was this here when you went home?' he asked Ella.

'I dunno, it was dark and I'd 'ad a few drinks,' she laughed.

'Oh well, somebody will claim it later on, I suppose,' Mike said, turning and leading the way in.

Only Tom and Ella were going to man the bar this lunchtime, and as they set to laying out the beer mats and making sure that all the optics were in working order, Peggy Briggs, one of the cleaners, called out, 'Anyone do with a cuppa tea?'

'Not 'alf,' Tom said quickly. 'Yer must 'ave been reading my mind.'

'How about you, Ella?'

'You're a life-saver if ever there was one,' Ella told her. 'I'll just take meself into the ladies' and tidy meself up and then I'll sit down and enjoy a cup, please.'

'We ain't got round ter doing the ladies' yet; we've done the gents, though,' was Peggy's answer.

'I'll take me chance in the ladies' if you don't mind,' Ella told her as she picked up her handbag and went into the ladies' cloakroom. Two steps and she couldn't for the life of her have said what was wrong, but her every instinct told her that something was.

She looked up at the window. The curtains had gone! And the vase of flowers which sat on the windowsill was also missing. She had always greatly admired those heavy brocade curtains, and although the flowers were artificial, they had been tastefully arranged in a truly lovely heavy vase.

Suddenly there was an unearthly sound, like a grunting pig, which made Ella turn very quickly, and it was then

117

she let out a scream that had Mike running, thinking that poor Ella was being murdered.

'Where the bloody 'ell did he come from?' Mike said angrily, his hands on his hips as he stared down at the spectacle of the scruffy old man stretched out on the floor in the far corner of the cloakroom.

'I don't know,' was all Ella could manage to say as she too stared at the white-haired old man, who was struggling to sit up. His tatty overcoat and boots were caked in mud. Across his legs were draped the missing curtains and the vase of flowers stood by his feet.

Mike stepped nearer. The man's face and hands were filthy and the pong coming from him was disgusting.

'I got locked in,' he mumbled, saliva dribbling from between his thin lips. 'I'm sorry, mate.'

'Don't you "mate" me, yer bloody filthy tramp. Just tell me how yer got in here an' why you had the damn cheek to pull our bloody curtains down.'

'I didn't mean no 'arm.' He sighed heavily and leant his head back against the wall. 'I'm Sid Thomas, the totter man.'

'I know who you are right enough, but how the 'ell you got in 'ere is what's puzzling me.'

'I'd 'ad a good day an' I thought I'd treat meself to a pint 'fore I went back t' me yard, but the pub was empty when I pushed the door open, not a soul about, never did get me drink. I needed to 'ave a slash, so I came in 'ere, an' when I finished suddenly the 'ole place was plunged into darkness. I sat in 'ere an' I must 'ave fell asleep, an' . . .'

'You didn't get a drink in this pub because it must have been well after time, but any fool can see you'd had far too many pints before you landed up here.'

'Well, it was late an' I was tired out an' cold.'

'And you decided our curtains would keep yer warm?

118

Yer must 'ave yanked 'ard at them. You not only brought the curtain pole down, you've brought 'alf the bleeding wall with it.'

Ella had the urge to ask about the flowers but thought it better to keep her mouth shut.

'I checked on both sets of toilets, I know full well I did.' Mike was angry.

Ella thought it was a good job that this bloke was still down on the floor, because if he'd been standing up Mike would have knocked him down for sure.

'Then I went down t' the cellar to turn the pumps off, and that must 'ave been when he wandered in, 'cos I came straight back up, locked the side door and turned all the lights out.'

'I've 'urt me back an' I can't get up,' the totter moaned. 'A drop of brandy might do me good.'

Ella giggled.

'You got as much chance as a snowball in hell,' Mike yelled at him. 'And another thing, we ain't picking yer up, not in the state you're in. I suppose that barrowload of old junk outside in the street is yours as well.'

'Oh, fank the Lord it's still there. An 'ole day's work that was.'

Mike had had enough.

'Ella, go phone the police. I don't want him charged, I just want him out of here. It will soon be opening time and we've this place to get cleaned up. One thing I do know, the smell of him will take some getting rid of.'

Holding her handkerchief to her nose as she went to make the call, Ella was in total agreement with Mike's last remark.

In less than fifteen minutes a uniformed policeman had arrived. He stared at Sid Thomas with a murderous look in his eye. 'I'm gonna nick yer for breaking, entering and trespassing on British Legion property,' he growled. 'But

119

I ain't soiling my uniform by helping yer t' yer feet. I'll phone for the Black Maria and it wouldn't surprise me one little bit if the boys don't take yer out in the yard and put the hose on yer.'

'What about me barrow? That's me living, that is,' Sid implored.

'We'll get some lads t' push it to yer yard. I'm sure your missus will be only too pleased to give them a couple of bob.'

'A couple of bob! Cor blimey, you've got t' be 'aving me on. An' anyway, who said anyfing about bringing me missus in on this?'

'Oh don't worry, Sid lad, we'll be more than happy t' let yer missus know where you are, and if she won't come and stand bail for you, I'm sure our sergeant will find a nice cell for you.' He took a large white handkerchief from his trouser pocket and blew his nose hard before adding, 'Of course, that is, after our boys have thought of a way to really clean you up.'

During the last twenty minutes or so there had been moments when Ella had wanted to laugh. However, as two young constables led a sorry, tired and totally dejected totter man out to the black police van, she felt an enormous amount of pity for him.

It had been nearing closing time when the policeman had returned and walked into the saloon bar, where Ella was serving. She was looking forward to going home to the good Sunday roast dinner which she knew her mother would have prepared.

'Just thought you'd like t' know, our boys really cleaned your old totter up and his missus came to the station t' take him home.'

All the staff had laughed.

'Bet he wasn't very pleased to see her,' Ella remarked.

'You've hit the nail on the head there all right, miss.

First thing Mrs Thomas wanted to know was where he'd been all night. He could 'ardly admit he'd been in the ladies' toilet, could he?'

'Thanks for letting us know he's all right,' Ella said, smiling at him. 'Are yer gonna have a drink while you're here?'

'I shouldn't 'cos I've still an 'alf-hour t' go before I'm off duty, but . . . well go on, then, I'll 'ave a pint.'

Ella took a clean glass from the shelf, and as she held it under the tap and pulled on the beer pump she could feel Mike's eyes on her. She placed the filled pint glass on a towelling mat and went to pick up the half-crown that the policeman had put down.

Mike beat her to it.

He picked up the coin and returned it, saying, 'Have that one on the house. Never know when we'll need you boys in blue, and we're more than grateful that you dealt with our intruder so quickly.'

Later, as Ella had walked home in the sunshine, she had been smiling. Talk about you meet all sorts in a pub. Her day-to-day living had certainly altered, but there was one thing she'd have to admit to: life was never dull now.

Chapter Fourteen

CONNIE BALDWIN WAS TALL, blonde and very pretty, but her flirtatious manner towards any man who gave her a second look had not endeared her to other women. A few of the neighbours felt pity for her because she was only sixteen years old and heavily pregnant by Dennis Dryden, a fifty-year-old man who should have known better. By and large, though, the general opinion was that she had only got what she had asked for. Dennis had flattered and spoilt her, given her presents galore and taken her out and about to places she had never before seen the inside of.

What she was too young to have realized was that in this life everything comes with a price-tag.

Today she was dressed up to the nines. As pretty as she was, she was empty-headed when it came to common sense. One attribute she did have was dress sense, and she knew it. She was wearing a black suit, the jacket left unbuttoned, the maternity skirt of the new-look length, the white blouse she wore hanging loose to cover her bump. She wore sheer black silk stockings with fancy heels and a slender seam, and black stiletto high-heeled shoes, and was carrying a leather handbag which must have cost more than most young women earned in three months.

Her father placed her suitcase down by her feet and stood beside her. Her mother was in the front porch, leaning against the wall, her arms crossed over her skinny chest.

'Try and behave yerself, luv,' Kate called, 'and tell yer Auntie Harriet that we'll come up to bring yer home whenever she's 'ad enough of yer.'

'Don't keep on, Mum, I'll be all right,' Connie said quickly. In fact I'll be glad to get away from here for a while, she added under her breath.

'All right, Con? You're dressed up. Going somewhere nice?' Len Evans, their next-door neighbour, was leaning over the low wall.

'Only to Croydon to stay with me mum's sister,' she said as a taxi came into view and drew up outside the house.

Kate Baldwin sighed heavily as she watched her husband hand the suitcase to the driver, help Connie into the back of the cab and then climb in beside her.

'The break will do her good,' Len Evans remarked as the cab drew away from the kerb.

Kate laughed cruelly. 'A break would do me an' her father some good, but that ain't likely to 'appen.'

She looked agitated, and Len was embarrassed. He looked into his neighbour's tired eyes and felt a moment's sadness. She wasn't a bad woman nor a bad mother, and as for Alf Baldwin, he worked every hour that God Almighty sent and all he asked in return was a quiet life with a few pints of beer over the weekend.

This business of their Connie having a baby at sixteen was a hard blow, as it would be for any working-class family. Gossip from all sides, Connie getting most of the blame, and it wasn't even born yet.

Trying to help, Len Evans said, 'I know me and my wife have said it before, but we do mean it. If there is any way in which we can 'elp you only 'ave t' ask. Has Connie decided if she is going to keep the baby?'

'Neither me nor her dad 'ave got a clue, and t' be honest, I don't think our Connie has either. She day-dreams. That I do know. Always on about how that sod Dennis Dryden will marry her and take her somewhere bloody posh t' live. We all know it ain't gonna 'appen. Thanks anyway for yer offer, but you've enough on yer own plate with four young-sters to feed an' clothe, so you go indoors and do yer best to sort out your own problems and let us try and sort out ours, eh?'

Kate Baldwin gave a sharp nod in her neighbour's direction, then, head high, she turned and walked into her house, shutting the front door firmly.

The train was already in the station when they arrived, and Connie's father was grateful. At least they wouldn't have long to stand about on the platform.

Surprising himself, he suddenly said, 'You know, luv, I don't agree with yer mother sending yer away, even if it is only t' your aunt. I don't care what she says, when there's trouble, families should stick together. Yer sisters, they ain't turned against yer, and if anyone talks about you in their hearing they give them a sharp answer, that I do know.'

Connie was thinking her father was an absolute darling. He saw good in everyone, and as she stood looking into his tired eyes, tears of distress began to trickle down her face. Alf gently took hold of her hands and squeezed them.

'Oh, Dad,' she whimpered, 'what am I gonna do?'

He had no answer to give her. Putting his arms around her in a comforting hug, he longed to be able to turn the clock back. Could he have made things turn out differently? Who knows?

A guard was walking along the platform, slamming carriage doors. 'Come on, my luv, up you get.' Her dad put his hand under her elbow to assist her, then handed in her suitcase. 'Don't forget, it's only a couple of stops, so be on the lookout. East Croydon is a very busy station, so stand still until yer Uncle Jack spots you. He promised me faithfully he'd be there to meet you.'

'All right, Dad, don't worry about me so much,' Connie said tearfully.

'Do me one favour, try and get along with yer Aunt Harriet. Her bark's worse than her bite,' he grinned.

Connie sighed, a long, deep sigh. 'I'll do me best, Dad.'

'I know yer will, lass, an' don't forget you've got the telephone number of the corner shop. Mrs Taylor said she will always take a message.'

It was too late for any more talking. A shrill whistle rent the air and the train began to move.

Connie stepped back from the window and sank down in a corner seat. Early afternoon and the train wasn't full. She gave another great sigh and raised her eyes to heaven.

'Dear God, please help me to make the right decision.' Her mind was in a turmoil. When she was with Dennis, she had no trouble in believing everything he told her. Away from him, doubts crept in. Would he really divorce his wife and marry her? He said he would for the sake of the child she was carrying. Yet he already had two children, and what message did that send out to her? He said they would move away from London, that she would want for nothing and that he would always love her and the baby. What about her leaving all her own family and friends? What about his wife and their family?

Was he going to be true to her or were his promises going to turn out to be like pie-crust? For too long she

125

had dilly-dallied. Soon, very soon, she was going to have to decide just what was the right thing for her to do.

Left alone, her father didn't move straight away, but stood staring after the train long after it was out of sight. Up until now he had kept his thoughts to himself. However, he had known Dennis Dryden for a good number of years and his opinion of him had never altered. He was a horrible, sly, devious git who had always fancied his chances with the ladies.

The trouble was, Dennis had never known what it was to need anything. His father had seen to that. Spoilt him rotten, more so since his mother had died. Some would say that Ted Dryden bought his son's company, because when it came down to brass tacks, he might be a rich man – most bookies were – but all the same he was a lonely one. A decent one too by all accounts. Pity he hadn't taught his son to live by his set of rules.

As Connie walked up the steep slope from the platform at East Croydon, she felt disgusted. Her Uncle Jack looked like a tramp. His trousers and jacket were crumpled, his shirt none too clean, and he hadn't even bothered to have a shave. He had no manners either. Twice he had stopped to relight his rolled fag, and although she had placed her case at her feet and breathed a heavy sigh, he still had not made any attempt to take the case and carry it for her.

'You've been 'ere before, so yer know it's not far t' walk, but Longfellow Road ain't got any shorter.' He laughed. 'It's still a long bleeding road.'

Jack Briggs was right. It was a very long, steep road and sod's law being what it was, his house was right at the top end of it. By the time he opened the front door, Connie was sweating buckets and her breathing was slow and heavy.

'So you've arrived, young Connie.'

'Oh.' Connie stared at her aunt, thinking she must have been standing behind the door. Harriet Briggs was a big sharp-faced woman with dry frizzy brown hair, and at this moment she didn't look at all pleased to have had her niece forced upon her. It was true, she had only agreed to have Connie to stay because she felt sorry for her sister, Kate. She had never been over-fond of this girl; even as a toddler she had been nothing but trouble, right bossy, forever throwing tantrums if she didn't get her own way. Always had been pretty, though, pretty as a picture, and everyone used to say she would break many a man's heart when she got older. That prophecy had now become a reality.

'Come on through,' Harriet said more kindly than she felt. 'I've got the kettle boiling, and we can 'ave a chat over a cuppa an' you can bring me up to date as to what's been 'appening.'

Although the thought of having to spend weeks in the company of her aunt and uncle did not make Connie feel very happy, she knew the best thing she could do right now was play along and do her best to keep the pair of them sweet.

'I could murder a cup of tea, please, Aunt Harriet,' she said as she took off her jacket, hung it over the back of a chair and then sat herself down in a big squashy armchair. Glancing about her, she came to the conclusion that this front room was very nicely furnished, light and airy and very clean.

Sighing with relief, she remembered what her mother had told her. Harriet had been a nurse before she had married Jack Briggs, and during the early years of their marriage she had trained as a midwife. Apparently many of the local families had good reason to be grateful to Harriet Briggs. She had delivered many of their babies, slapping the breath of life into some of them.

127

'Tea won't be long.' Harriet half-smiled at her niece, but turning to her husband she looked him up and down. 'You dared to go an' meet our Connie looking like that?' she sneered. 'You ain't got an ounce of respect left in yer. When you called out that you were going to the station I thought you had washed and changed. I would 'ave had you back by the scruff of the neck if I'd seen yer.'

'Oh, I'm sorry,' he said mockingly. 'I thought the girl was 'ere with us 'cos she's in the pudden club and the neighbours were giving your sister a hard time 'cos she'd let 'er daughter run wild with a married man. I didn't know yer wanted me to treat 'er like royalty.'

Harriet curled her lip in contempt. 'You're such an honourable man, never put a foot wrong in yer life, is that what you'd 'ave us believe?'

Jack mimicked her voice. 'No, my dear, you're the saintly one in this family, but now I know where I stand I shall do me best to mind me p's and q's.'

'I don't want any special treatment,' Connie said, trying to lighten the situation.

Her uncle grinned nastily. 'You won't get any, at least not from me.'

Harriet felt guilty that Connie hadn't been in the house two minutes and already she had had to witness how things stood between herself and her husband.

'Jack,' she pleaded, 'go wash your hands and come an' have some tea. I've made sultana scones.'

'I don't want any tea,' he said irritably. 'I'm going for an evening paper.'

'Well, take the dog across to the park. He could do with a good run.'

'Trying to get rid of me now so you an' she,' he nodded towards Connie, 'can 'ave a good old natter about how terrible life 'as treated both of you?'

Harriet rolled her eyes to the ceiling.

Jack moved nearer to Connie and, resting a hand on each side of the armchair in which she was sitting, leant his head down until his face was only inches from hers.

'You, young lady, had better keep yerself t' yerself while you're under my roof. I don't want fellows coming knocking on my door 'cos they think my niece is an easy touch.'

She flinched away, but she wasn't going to let him think that she was frightened of him.

'You don't need to threaten me, Uncle Jack. I don't want any men, not even for company, thank you very much. Christ knows I've come unstuck with the one I've got, haven't I?'

He took hold of her chin and waggled it.

'Just remember what I've said.'

Without another word he shrugged himself into his jacket and walked out. His wife did not say goodbye to him, and neither did Connie.

Harriet brought a loaded tea tray in from the kitchen, placed it in the middle of the table and sat down, telling Connie to come and sit beside her.

'I really am sorry you had t' listen to all that,' she said. Then she grinned. 'He likes to think he's such a big man, does my Jack. Coming to meet you all scruffy-like is his only means of protest. He won't work himself, never been able to hold a job down longer than a month, and of course he doesn't like it that I do still work. He's a dog in the manger, is Jack. He doesn't want me to earn money but he doesn't mind me paying all the bills.'

Connie nibbled on a scone. It was very good, better than those her mother made. All the same, she wasn't sure that leaving home and coming here to Croydon was the right thing to have done. The way things had started off, it certainly didn't seem that they were going to settle down to play happy families!

Her whole life was an utter mess. What she felt she needed right now was a damn good weep.

However, she still had some pride left and she wasn't going to let her aunt see her cry. Why, she asked herself, did she always have to play it the hard way? Never let folk know what she was really feeling?

She reached for her cup of tea and took a long, steady drink, telling herself that God had made everyone different. Wondering once more if she had she jumped out of the frying pan into the fire by coming here.

She couldn't answer her own question, she was too uncertain. But sensing that neither her aunt nor her uncle really wanted her here had given her yet another problem to think about.

Chapter Fifteen

CONNIE WATCHED HER UNCLE closely. She detested him. His very nearness gave her the creeps. She had formed the opinion that given half a chance she wouldn't be able to trust him any further than she could throw him.

During the fortnight that she had been living in Croydon, she had come to really like her aunt, though in a funny kind of way. She felt sorry for her, despite the fact that on most occasions Harriet had proved that she could hold her own. Not only with the nasty piece of work that was her husband, but also with their weird son, who had turned up out of the blue.

Connie vaguely remembered her cousin being known as Reggie when they were all young children, but when he had arrived unexpectedly the day after Connie, he had insisted that he now went by the name of 'Duke'.

Her uncle had taken Duke's homecoming in his stride, but Connie had been shocked when all the colour had drained from her aunt's face as she stared at her son, muttering, 'Christ, where the hell 'ave you turned up from?'

'All you need to know, Mother, is that I'm home now,

at least for a while.' And that was all he had been prepared to say on the subject.

Much later, when they had been alone, Harriet had told Connie the little she knew about her own son. He was sixteen when she had last set eyes on him, and that had been three years ago. Where he had been and what he had been up to she hadn't got a clue. On the whole, these were unhappy times for Connie.

Most days her aunt was out of the house for two to three hours at least. Connie forced herself to go for a walk rather than stay in the house with her uncle. The way he looked at her, and his nasty tongue when and if he spoke to her, was more than she could take.

It was a relief to have Duke in the house, although he never got out of his bed until eleven o'clock in the morning. By midday he was all spruced up, his natty clothes cleaned and pressed, his hair shiny with Brylcreem. If her aunt was at work, Connie would prepare a light lunch, or a late breakfast as Duke called it, and they would sit in the garden to eat it. He would talk to Connie about any number of subjects which she found very interesting, but if she asked questions as to what he intended to do that day, or indeed for the rest of his life, he would close up like a clam. Regularly each evening he left the house at seven, never returning before midnight.

'May I come out with you?' Connie had been bold enough to ask him one evening.

'What! And 'ave me mates thinking I might be the father to that baby you're carrying? You have got t' be joking.' That and a great shrug of his shoulders was the only answer he'd given.

'Where *are* all yer mates?' his mother had asked one evening as he stood combing his thick jet-black hair and admiring himself in the mirror that hung on the wall over the fireplace. 'There used to be hordes of them coming round here for you and mostly I thought they were a good bunch of lads. Always polite t' me, they were.'

'Most of them are in the nick,' said Duke despondently.

His mother made no reply.

Duke looked from Connie to Harriet, and the looks on their faces had him shrieking with laughter.

Was he joking? Connie wondered.

Suddenly she felt very lonely shut away from her family. She missed her mum and dad, her sisters, and the jokes and friendly patter of her East End mates.

Harriet's mind was also working overtime. Her son had come home with some really decent clothes and he certainly didn't seem to be short of money. He hadn't been in the house five minutes when he had called her aside and given her sixty quid.

'It's a small fortune,' she had protested.

In a rare show of affection he had put his arms around her and held her close for a moment, patting her back and kissing the top of her head. 'Make sure you spend it on yourself, Mum, no handing it over to me father. You promise?'

Harriet couldn't have answered; she had been softly crying. She couldn't bring herself to question where or how he had come by the money, but she was thinking he wasn't all bad; there had to be a lot of good somewhere in this only son of hers.

Connie felt tired and irritable as she looked at the calendar. It was already the last week in August and the hot weather was getting her down. Every day seemed to be longer than the previous one, and being pregnant was no joke. She could barely walk to the park let alone down into Croydon with this heavy weight dragging her down morning, noon and night. These days her affair with Dennis Dryden did not seem so glamorous.

Where was he?

Probably miles away upcountry, doing some dodgy deal or at least finding work from councils or big offices and sub-letting the contracts to middle men for a whacking backhander. He had laughed himself silly one night when he had had more than enough to drink and opened up and told her a few details of what he actually did for a living.

'Never do for yourself what someone else is willing to do for you,' he had said was his motto, but had hastily added, 'so long as you've made sure you've creamed off your share of the profit first.'

Ducking and diving would be her term for what Dennis had openly bragged about. She shouldn't be grumbling about him really, she chided herself. She'd known what she was getting into, and although first off she had given a few thoughts to the fact that Dennis had a wife and two children, you only had to take one look at him to know that if he wasn't showing Connie a good time, it would be some other young girl. He was that sort of a man.

Besides, when he had first paid attention to her she had thought the sun shone out of his backside, as did an awful lot of people. There was no two ways about it. Dennis was a natural charmer.

When she had told him she was pregnant, he had surprised her. To be honest, he'd made no bones about it. Promised her everything, even marriage. But how long was it since she had set eyes on him?

Too long.

Facing up to the truth, Connie felt tearful, thinking of the good job she had had to give up, the dances she went to with her mates every Saturday night, the lovely smart clothes that used to fit her. All that she had lost.

Now she was fat and ugly and nobody really wanted her. With both hands she clutched the rim of the kitchen sink and began to cry.

An arm went around her shoulders and she turned quickly, shuddering as she looked into the face of her Uncle Jack.

'What's the matter, girl? What are you doing out here on your own?'

His voice sounded full of kindness, but Connie wasn't fooled; indeed, she was frightened.

He saw she had been crying.

'Has that son of mine been upsetting you?' His voice had changed and was harsh. ''Cos if he has, I'll kill the little rotter.'

'No, Uncle Jack, Duke has always been all right with me. It's just . . .' A great sob strangled her words.

'I know it can't be easy for you, but you can tell me what's troubling you an' I'll help if I can. Here, wipe your eyes,' he said, handing her a big handkerchief.

Connie found it hard to believe how nice he was being to her. Using the handkerchief, she rubbed her face and then shrugged her shoulders. 'It's just everything suddenly seemed to get on top of me.' She did her best to smile to counteract the sadness in her voice.

'Come here and give yer old uncle a hug.'

As he cuddled her, Connie was thinking of her dad. She was so glad Jack was being nice to her. She badly needed to feel someone liked her, that not everyone was against her.

'Go and sit in the front room and I'll make us a cup of tea. It shouldn't be too long before your aunt gets back, and she always knows how to cheer you up, doesn't she?'

Connie wondered briefly about this sudden change in her uncle's attitude. She leant back in the armchair, tiredness sweeping over her. It didn't ring true; her uncle was up to something, she knew he was. Eventually it would come to light. Then again, perhaps she was misjudging him.

At least she hoped she was.

It was about time somebody gave her a break.

Chapter Sixteen

'WHO WOULD HAVE BELIEVED it?' Mike Murray was almost dancing for joy as he and Sam Richardson surveyed the completed extension of the British Legion club. 'Finished well on time and it looks wonderful, well worth while.' Mike's voice held a note of admiration for both the builders and the architects, who had, each in their own way, convinced the board of directors that this venture was sorely needed.

'Brought in well within budget.' Sam, ever the accountant, smiled. 'I am more than a little impressed.'

The club's main building had always been solid and substantial but as the club membership had grown, a wooden barn of a place had been erected within the grounds. For a good many years it had certainly served its purpose. Fund-raising dances, whist drives and coffee mornings had all been held there. However, the fact had remained that although there had been a basic kitchen within the building giving provision for coffee and tea, no licence to sell alcoholic drinks had ever been granted for that part of the club, so a bar had never been installed. Therefore it had hardly been popular with the men. If they were there at a dance with their wives they had to cross the yard to the main building in order to get an alcoholic drink from the bar. This went against the grain, especially during the winter months when the snow underfoot could be treacherously icy, and certainly did not do much to encourage the men to leave the comfort and warmth of the main clubhouse and their beloved darts board and snooker tables.

Mike Murray's biggest problem had always been that this hall being separate from the bar kept the takings down.

Few had been surprised when a year ago the wooden barn had finally given up the ghost and the roof had collapsed. Even fewer had mourned its passing when the news had been announced that an extension was to be built directly on to the main building and that the extra premises were to be licensed. The suggestion had been put forward and accepted by the committee that a restaurant should also be incorporated in the plans.

A few seconds passed before Sam exclaimed, 'It's all gone much smother than I imagined. We didn't come up against too many hiccups, did we?'

Smiling, Mike nodded his agreement. 'No, we didn't, but don't let's start counting our chickens before they are all hatched. There is still quite a bit of interior decorating to do, and most important of all, we still have to obtain a licence to sell alcoholic drink within these new premises,' he said matter-of-factly.

'Oh, don't go all sober-sides on me, not now we've come this far. I can't believe even now that at every stage the Legion committee came up with the cash.'

Mike reached out and touched Sam's shoulder lightly. 'You, my old son, can take a huge chunk of the credit for that. Once you'd seen the professional plans, you worked out the cost practically to the penny.'

'Oh, come off it,' Sam exclaimed loudly. 'I like what you're saying but it's not true. There was a whole team working on this project from start to finish. Anyway, shall we leave the congratulations until the official opening night finally comes around?'

Mike grinned broadly. 'That'll be a night to remember!'

'I'm sure it will be,' Sam laughed, then quickly added, 'Have you forgotten you've a darts match on here tonight, and it's a qualifying round, isn't it?'

'Jesus wept an' well he might!' Mike shouted, showing his irritation. 'I 'ad forgotten all about it.'

'Blowing yer top won't help. Besides, I know the staff have it all in hand. I spoke to Ella and Molly this morning and they said they were snowed under with enough food to feed an army. The draymen are down in the cellars now, so I presume Tom and Derrick have everything under control.'

Molly and Ella didn't need any reminding that it was darts night.

This was the busiest night Ella had seen since she had started working at the Legion. The visiting team from the Crown and Anchor had brought quite a few supporters. Tom, Molly and Ella were serving drinks in the public bar, leaving only Derrick and Mike's wife Beryl to do a spell in the saloon. During the matches the three of them behind the public bar were kept very busy. There was little time for conversation, let alone to keep the bar wiped down. As the evening wore on and the two darts teams became more excited, both Ella and Molly thought their heads would burst with all the noise, and the air being thick with smoke didn't help. Every time a winning dart was thrown, the cheers that rang out were enough to deafen everyone. The only time there was complete hush was when the caller announced that a double top would secure the match for the home team.

No problem for Wally Stebington. He toed the line, spat on his hands and rubbed them together. A single arrow was all that he needed.

Straight and true it flew from between Wally's fingers to bed itself in the narrow space between the two wires at the top of the board.

'*YES!*' The unanimous cry rose to the roof as the regulars celebrated their victory.

The visiting team weren't quite so happy. Having stuffed their faces with quite a lot of the good food that the Legion had provided, most of them and their supporters left to get a last late drink back at the Crown and Anchor.

Both Molly and Ella sighed a huge sigh of relief as Mike called, 'Last orders, please, ladies and gentlemen.'

Glancing round the bar, Molly muttered, 'Looks as if a ruddy bomb hit this place tonight.'

'Yeah, and I feel as if I've gone ten rounds with a heavyweight boxer,' Ella answered. She wasn't feeling very good-tempered. There had been a few customers who had gone out of their way to let her know that they had seen Dennis from time to time. Mostly the gossipmongers were nosy old biddies whose biggest aim in life was to make mischief. As she poured the slops into the troughs and stacked the dirty glasses that Molly was collecting, Ella reflected on the different versions she had had to listen to over the past few weeks.

Her Dennis looked so well, was living off the fat of the land. One day he was supposedly living in a big house in Hampstead wearing well-tailored suits and expensive shoes. The next story would have him living in Windsor.

'In a royal apartment of the castle?' she was tempted to ask. Instead she had learnt to keep a straight face and her feelings well under control.

'Whenever I see your old man he's never short of female company.' One spiteful old biddy threw her twopennyworth into the conversation, not caring whether it was true or not.

But on that occasion it had been one remark too many, and Ella had thrown caution to the wind.

Leaning across the counter, she cupped the woman's chin in her hand. 'Would you like me to give you a face-lift?' Ella's voice was low, heavy with menace. As she saw the fear in the woman's eyes she felt an urge to punch her in the face.

The woman dropped her eyes and tried to back away, then she felt Ella's fingers make contact with her hair. One mighty tug and Ella was holding a few strands. She let go, shoved the woman in the chest and threw the hair into her face.

'I hear another word from you about my affairs and so 'elp me God I'll strangle yer. You got that?'

'Yes, yes,' the woman stammered, trying not to show her fear as she shifted her weight from one foot to the other. One thing was certain, she had learnt that it wasn't safe to wind Ella Dryden up.

With the darts match over, Ella and Molly set about the clearing-up like a couple of zombies. Dead tired, and longing to put her feet up, Ella suddenly noticed that Alf and Kate Baldwin were standing by the door, looking at her with some concern in their eyes. The expressions on their faces bewildered Ella, and suddenly she felt so sorry for them both. It was a shame, she thought, the disgrace their daughter had brought on them, and it wasn't over yet. Not by a long chalk it wasn't.

Suddenly she realized they had been staring at her in silence for quite a while.

'Is there something you wanted to ask me?' she found herself saying.

Alf Baldwin straightened his shoulders. 'I know we've no right to question you, Ella, you've more than enough on yer own plate, but our Connie's time is drawing nigh and we wondered if you had any idea what your Den was going to do.'

Ella leant her weight on the nearest table and sighed heavily. What in God's name could she say to these parents? When first it had become known that Connie was pregnant and that Dennis was the father of the baby, Kate Baldwin had gone more than halfway to blaming Ella. Still, it didn't do to bear grudges.

'I haven't seen my Den for some time,' she managed to say. 'As to his intentions regarding your daughter, your guess is as good as mine. I did 'ear that you'd sent her to stay with your sister. How's she been doing?'

'I don't think she's all that happy in Croydon,' Kate Baldwin said quickly. 'It's hard t' know what t' do for the best. We don't want her to end up bringing the baby up all on her own. The council will only allocate her some dirty, poky flat in a grim, tumbledown back street. We're overcrowded as it is with only three rooms over the shop.'

Ella looked at her in silence for a moment. 'I don't know what I can do.' She felt she was becoming a little too involved, but she wanted to help if only she knew how. 'Tell yer what, Dennis's dad, Ted, is coming t' dinner with me termorrow. I'll 'ave a word with him. Maybe he's been in touch with Den. Anyway, we'll see. No 'arm in asking him, though whether we'll get a straight answer is another matter altogether.'

'We've no right t' ask fer your help, Ella, but we can't think straight at the moment. Thanks anyway,' Alf Baldwin said gruffly.

Ella felt tearful then, thinking of all the trouble Dennis had caused. Not only to Connie Baldwin and her parents, but also to her own two children. It was going to take a long time before young Teddy and Babs gave up hoping that their dad would come back home and their lives would return to what they were before this storm broke over their heads.

No matter which way you looked at it, her Dennis was a devil, a selfish devil who gave no thought to anyone but his bloody self!

She shuddered and glanced back in the direction of the bar, which was by now packed high with dirty glasses. 'I'd better get back ter work or Mike will think I'm slacking.'

She turned away quickly; the look on Kate and Alf Baldwin's faces was making her stomach turn.

'I'll let you know if Ted tells me where Dennis is.'

She spoke the words softly, and the Baldwins both nodded their heads.

'Thanks for talking t' us, Ella,' Kate said as she buttoned up her coat and took hold of her husband's arm.

Ella went back behind the bar, her mind in a whirl as she found herself dwelling on the conversation she had just had with Connie Baldwin's parents. She had seen such despair in the eyes of that father and mother. None of this trouble was of her making, she knew, yet her face was flushed and her hands were shaking as she bent over the sink.

Den had had the sweets and buggered off and left everyone else to pick up the pieces. She wondered if he was sorry for all the trouble he had caused.

Of course he wasn't, she answered herself angrily, otherwise he would at least have kept in touch with his children. Babs hadn't been the same since her dad had left home. Young as she was, she knew she had been rejected. Gone from being Daddy's little sweetheart, spoilt rotten, given hugs and kisses every day of her life, to almost having no dad at all. Kids at school taunted her that her dad was going to be someone else's father. The nastiness and cruel words hurt more than blows would have done.

Teddy was only four years older, but he seemed better able to cope with the fact that his father didn't live with them any more. Maybe it was because his grandad was around and took him out and about. Teddy was tall and lean, cheeky, noisy and sometimes a bit rough, but always lovable.

Babs was totally different, which was only to be expected, a dainty little girl with long chestnut-coloured hair and big brown eyes. She took after her grandmother's side of the family and was the apple of Winnie's eye. But no one, least of all her mother, could fathom what she was thinking. It grieved Ella more than anything else that Den could have walked out of his daughter's life almost without a backward glance when previously he had been so protective of her.

Oh well, nobody had ever said that life was going to be fair, Ella told herself as she gave the long bar a final wipe-down with a towelling beer-mat.

At least she had pulled herself together and got this job, for which she was eternally grateful. This was her life from now on, and the sooner she accepted the fact that Dennis was no longer part of it, the better off she would be.

When Ella woke the next morning she could barely lift her head from the pillow. She still felt dead tired and utterly weary. Then the bedroom door opened and her mother was there holding out a steaming cup of tea.

'Oh, Mum! Whatever would I do without you? If I live to be a hundred I'll never be able to pay you back for all you've done for me over the years. Never. But one day I'll make it up to you in one way or another.'

'Of course yer will, darlin'. You do anyway just by letting me share yer life.'

Suddenly Ella sniffed and then in great haste placed

143

her now almost empty cup down on the bedside table and swung her legs over the side of the bed.

'Jesus! That's roast beef I can smell cooking, isn't it? I forgot all about Ted coming to dinner today. What time is it? How long before he turns up 'ere?'

Winnie laughed. 'Stop asking so many questions. Everything is under control; all you've got t' do is get washed and dressed. It's almost one o'clock an' Ted's been 'ere since ten. He brought loads of fresh veg with him, and took both the kids out and bought them a present. Babs has been 'elping me make pastry for the apple pie and Ted, daft as a brush, is out with all the kids from the nearby streets playing cricket in the alley. He sent Teddy to buy sticks of chalk so that he could draw stumps on the end wall. Never grow up, Ted won't.'

The dinner was a great success, with Ted declaring that Win's roast beef melted in the mouth.

'That's 'cos it's cooked on the bone; none of this boned and rolled rubbish,' Winnie declared firmly.

Ted leant across the table and said to Ella, 'I bet the butcher wants t' run and hide when he sees your mum coming!'

'I 'eard that, Ted Dryden, an' I notice you wasn't so damn cheeky until after I fed yer.'

'We 'aven't finished dinner yet, 'ave we, Gran? What about our apple pie and custard? I rolled the pastry out, didn't I?' Babs's whole attitude was full of indignation. They didn't get pudding every day of the week, so how could her gran possibly forget that they were supposed to have pie and custard?

Ella felt good as she watched everyone laugh, and at that moment she could have taken her young daughter in her arms and almost crushed her to death, such was the love she was feeling for her.

All in all she was feeling good today.

That was until Ted, having scraped his pudding bowl clean, began to talk about his son.

'I've got a message for you, Ella, from Den,' he began.

'Hang on a minute,' Winnie cried as she got to her feet and reached for her purse, which lay on the dresser. 'We grown-ups are going to 'ave a decent cup of tea, but I forgot to fetch any drinks for you two. Teddy, take Babs to the corner shop and let her choose a bottle of whatever she wants.'

'Cor, can I 'ave cream soda, Gran?'

'Course yer can, me darlin'.'

'An' can I have a bottle of Tizer?' Teddy wasn't going to be outdone.

'Yes, luv, but don't leave go of yer sister's 'and as yer cross the road. That can be a busy corner sometimes.'

'Oh, all right,' Teddy agreed, but none too happily. Boys didn't hold their sisters' hands.

'Now,' Winnie said with a sense of achievement as she watched the two little 'uns scarper, 'I'm gonna take meself off out into the scullery and you two can say what yer got t' say, but you should both know better than to discuss what is happening to their father in front of Teddy and Babs.'

Winnie expected Ted's reply and she got it.

He apologized immediately.

Alone, Ted took a good look at his daughter-in-law. He was amazed at how well she was coping with the two children. She was a good mum, and she'd put herself out and about and found herself a full-time job. Another point was she looked and acted so differently than she had when his son had been around. She certainly wore different clothes.

He was embarrassed. He didn't like being the messenger. Nothing would give him greater pleasure than to see his Den and Ella back together again, but no matter

145

how hard he tried, he wasn't able to achieve much headway. When it came to being obstinate, there wasn't much to choose between the pair of them.

Den was no saint, Ted was well aware of that, but he was a red-blooded man, and most men played away from home at some time.

Noticing Ted's hesitation, Ella spoke up sharply.

'Come on then, spit it out, this message that Dennis couldn't deliver himself.'

'Den's turned over a new leaf, you know, Ella.'

'Huh,' was all she said.

Ted wasn't pleased at her reaction and it showed.

'Try an' 'ave a little faith, gal, give way a little bit, 'cos honestly Den's doing his damnedest to lead a different life. You wanna see what he's managed to do with that property he bought at Epsom. I'll take yer t' see it if yer like, you've only got t' say the word. It's being beautifully restored, especially those great big rooms. When Den's finished with it it will be absolutely fabulous and he'll make a mint if he sells all those apartments.'

'You'll be telling me next that Den has done most of the work himself.'

'Well, he tells me he's done a fair bit of it. Why don't you let me set up a meeting for the two of yer?'

Ella was trying her best to picture Dennis in overalls with his sleeves rolled up and actually working. Doing what? He always said himself he was a Jack of all trades and master of none. Yet as she lifted her eyes to look at Ted's face, he didn't appear to be joking.

'Are you serious?' she asked, her voice cracking.

'Never more so,' he said, reaching out to take her hand in his. 'I wish for nothing more than to see you two back together and the kids bright and happy, a real family like you used to be.'

Whose fault was it that they were a broken family? And

146

if she and their children were still of such great importance to Dennis, why wasn't he sitting opposite her now instead of his father?

Her thoughts were suddenly of Connie Baldwin and her sad parents, and she felt her temper rising, but before she could decide what to say to her father-in-law, he spoke again.

'Maybe Den *is* different now. Couldn't you have him back, Ella? Give him another chance? Maybe he has changed.'

The truth was, she argued with herself, that she wanted to believe what Ted was telling her. But how many times had she had promises of changing for the better from Dennis himself?

Suddenly this was more than Ella could stand.

'Yeah!' she said loudly. 'And maybe he's still a lying, cheating bastard.'

Chapter Seventeen

'SOD IT!' JACK BRIGGS swore loudly, feeling something sharp pierce into the ball of his right foot. He leant against the wall of the kitchen and shoved his foot up on to the seat of a chair.

'It's a bloody drawing pin,' he sniffed as he wiggled the round top of the pin loose before he was able to withdraw it from his flesh. He hobbled to the one armchair which stood beside the fireplace, and once he was sitting down lifted his right leg to rest across his knees and did his best to examine the bottom of his bare foot, which stuck out below the leg of his cotton pyjama trousers.

His wife leant forward and slapped his leg, causing him to bring his sore foot down hard on to the floor. He winced. 'What did yer do that for? You can see I'm in pain,' he complained loudly.

'Serve yer right,' Harriet retaliated. 'You shouldn't be walking around the house with nothing on yer feet and half-undressed this time in the morning. Just look at yer! Yer 'aven't had a wash let alone cleaned yer teeth or combed yer hair. You're a disgrace at the best of times, but I thought you'd 'ave made an effort with our Connie staying in the house. Instead I reckon you've got steadily worse. I'm beginning to wonder whether you're doing it deliberately just to annoy me.'

Connie was sitting at the breakfast table nibbling a piece of toast.

Oh Christ! she murmured to herself. Don't let them start on at each other, not so early in the day. Mind you, the very sight of her Uncle Jack was enough to start her heaving. His pyjama jacket was unbuttoned, showing his hairy chest, he hadn't shaved for at least two days, there was enough grime beneath his fingernails to plant a pot, and his bare feet were none too clean. He just sat there oblivious of what his wife or his niece thought of him, merely watching as Harriet lifted the heavy steaming black kettle off the hob and carried it through to the scullery.

Connie heard the rattle of the big enamel bowl being lifted down from the shelf above the stone sink. As Harriet came back into the living room she threw a piece of Lifebuoy soap into her husband's lap, took an old tea-cloth from the dresser drawer, quickly ripped it in half and tossed one of the pieces at her husband saying, 'Yer can use that for a flannel. So move yerself, get out there and give yerself a good wash from top t' toe, 'cos Connie and I are going upstairs to make the beds, and when we come down I want to see you looking reasonably clean and dressed properly.'

Aunt and niece watched Jack stumble to his feet and leave the room clutching the piece of clean rag and the bar of red soap. They heard the echo of the bowl rattling in the sink and then the scalding water being poured into it. They both smiled as they heard Jack muttering.

'Bloody bossy bitch. Just 'cos she's got a job, messy one at that, delivering babies, how could anyone enjoy doing that with all the blood an' guts coming out all over the bed.'

Harriet caught hold of Connie's arm and steered her towards the stairs. 'Come on, luv, let's leave him to it. We'll do the beds then I must be away. I've two women I have to check on today, but I'll do a bit of shopping down in Croydon, see if I can find something nice to eat that will tempt you, and when I get back we'll go for a walk over the park and eat our lunch sitting on one of the benches. How's that sound?'

'Oh, Aunt Harriet, that sounds real good. I'll change into that loose cotton dress you made for me and I'll be ready and waiting. Shall I bring a bottle of cold tea?'

'No, luv, we'll 'ave a treat today. I've still got a couple of bottles of my homemade elderberry wine hidden away. We'll sneak one of those out with us.'

When they came downstairs, Harriet was dressed in what she called her everyday uniform, ready for work. Connie was wearing a loose cotton dress and carrying a book, intending to go and sit in the garden and have a quiet read.

Jack Briggs responded to the surprised look on their faces by giving them a mock salute and bending from his waist to make a regal bow.

'You don't 'ave t' bow an' scrape,' Harriet grinned, 'but I will say you don't polish up bad when you make the effort.' To herself she was thinking what a pity it was that he didn't try a bit harder every day.

'Thank you, my dear wife, for those kind words,' he mocked. 'And how about our Connie? Does she approve of her uncle today?'

'Yes, I do now,' Connie quickly answered.

Jack was wearing black shoes and socks, plain grey trousers, a blue checked shirt and even a tie. The same thought immediately came to both of the women. The tie was one of Duke's. They managed to suppress their smiles

150

as Harriet said, 'Well, I must be off. I'll be back about one o'clock.'

Connie went to the front door with her aunt and stood watching her walk down the street until she was out of sight. As she turned to go back inside the house she had a premonition that everything was not as it should be. She suddenly felt fearful. Of what, she couldn't have said.

'Got the whole place to ourselves,' her uncle leered at her. 'Shall I make us a fresh brew?' he asked, holding the big teapot in his large hands.

'Not for me, thank you, Uncle Jack, I've had enough to drink. I'm going to find a shady spot and sit out in the garden.' There was more than a little fear in Connie's voice. She didn't like the idea of being on her own with him and she wished she could slip upstairs and wake Duke up. She glanced at the big clock that stood on the mantelshelf over the fireplace. It was only just turned nine. Duke wouldn't thank her for waking him at what he would call an unearthly hour.

'Come for a walk with me, Connie. I'll buy yer a drink later when the pubs open,' he suggested, moving closer to her and stroking her bare arm.

Connie knew trouble was brewing, and she wanted to back away, yet she made herself stand still. 'Drink is the last thing I need, Uncle Jack, the very smell of it makes me feel sick, but you go, you're all spruced up and it's a lovely day. Won't get many more days like this, two more and we'll be in September.'

She knew she was talking for the sake of it. Her uncle was standing far too close; she could feel his hot breath on her face. She had to get away from him. Her every instinct told her that he was plotting something. If only she could go home. If only she hadn't been daft enough to be flattered by Den Dryden's attention. If only . . .

Connie looked out of the kitchen window, staring into

151

the peaceful garden. She could go on for ever saying to herself 'if only', but all the talking in the world wouldn't let her have her life back as it used to be.

Her uncle stepped as near to her as he could get and, with his face only inches from hers, said, 'I don't know why you're trembling. I've never laid a finger on yer, 'ave I?'

Connie clutched her hands together tightly, pressing them against her swollen belly.

'I have to sit down or I shall fall down,' she pleaded.

'So! No one's stopping yer,' he said, cupping a hand beneath her elbow and steering her towards the armchair.

'I'd rather go and sit outside in the fresh air. You come out there too, it's so hot in here.' Right now her instinct told her to get out of the house. If he tried anything on with her out in the open she could at least shout and scream and the neighbours might hear her. Here indoors he could place a hand over her mouth before she could shout loud enough for Duke to come down. Anyway, Duke would still be dead to the world. If only he would get up now and come down those stairs! Another 'if only'.

Her uncle practically pushed her down into the armchair then stood swaying above her, looking down at her with a broad smile on his face. It was then he started to talk, his words little more than a whisper, almost as if he were talking to himself.

'You come into my home, queening it over everyone. Not an ounce of shame in yer that yer carrying a baby. Don't suppose yer really know who the father is. Don't look like Dennis Dryden is gonna let you lumber him with it, does it? Ain't seen sight nor sound of him, 'ave yer? It's yer poor mum an' dad that I feel sorry for. Neighbours do love to gossip and cast stones. Life must 'ave been bad for them to turn yer out of house an' home an' dump yer on me and 'Arriet. What 'ave we ever done that we should be made to house yer an' feed yer?'

Heart thumping like mad, Connie pushed her head sideways. If she spoke quietly and stayed calm he might back off.

'Uncle Jack, listen to me. Please. You and Auntie Harriet have been so good to me, but if my being here has upset you so much, I will go home today. Maybe it's best that I should. I can't have much longer to go an' I wanna be with my mum when the baby comes.' Her voice trembled and she wasn't far from tears.

That made no different to Jack Briggs. He had set his course and he was going to have his way while he'd got the chance.

His arm shot out, his hand grasping her hair, and at the same time he was pulling her forward. She opened her mouth to scream but he had anticipated this; he fished from his pocket the rag that Harriet had given him to use as a flannel and suddenly her scream was muffled as he shoved the ball of cloth tightly into her mouth.

'I tried being the nice kindly uncle but you didn't want to know, did you? Oh no, you've been playing Lady Muck, and I was dirt beneath yer feet. Well, I'm fed up with the way you've taken over my home and the bloody way you've looked down yer nose at me. I've put up with all of that, and right now I think I'm within my rights to 'elp meself to a bit of pleasure. You've put it about a bit before you came 'ere, that's obvious, and yer know what folk say, "A slice off a cut loaf is never missed."'

Connie wriggled from side to side, trying to get her hands free so that she might take the cloth out of her mouth, but that only brought her a hefty slap across the side of her face and she felt warm, sticky blood trickle from her nose.

She saw stars and at the same time felt him grasp the front of her dress. With one violent swoop he ripped the material from the neck to the waistline.

From that moment on there was no fight left in Connie.

Time passed as her uncle bent over her swollen breasts, stroking them gently in turn. Then abruptly he pulled her bra straps from her shoulders, letting her big breasts fall free. Now he became a wild animal, sucking at her nipples, biting down hard on the first one and then doing the same to the other. Squeezing, pinching, digging his fingers into her tender flesh, and the more she winced with pain, the more excited he became.

Her nipples had been sore for weeks now, and biting them was the worst thing he could have done. The burning pain he was inflicting on her was more than she could bear. She wanted to be sick. She wanted to die.

Yet he wasn't finished yet.

Straightening himself up, he bent low, grabbed both of her ankles and pulled hard until her body slid forward and she was lying flat on the floor. It only took seconds to roll up the bottom half of her dress and petticoat, and rip the crotch of her knickers apart.

He freed himself of his clothes until he was totally naked and then he was on top of her, pinning her to the floor. Connie was past caring. She prayed to die. She did her best to close her mind to what was happening to her body. She did feel anxious about the baby, but what good would it do to cry out now?

Eyes screwed up tight as they would go, hands balled into fists, she lay there, hurting, burning, suffering pain like she had never imagined.

Still her uncle repeatedly, roughly rammed himself into her as hard as he could go. He was having what he regarded as his revenge on her.

At last! It was over.

Grunting happily, her uncle rolled away from her. He lay on his side, panting for a minute or two, before he stood up and pulled his pants and trousers back on. It wasn't enough that he had raped her. Now he lifted his foot and kicked the side of her body.

'Get up and get some clothes on, you filthy little whore! At least now you know what I think of you.'

Connie hadn't died, no matter how much she wished she had.

There was only one thought in her mind. Get up off this floor. She needed to wash and scrub herself and leave the house before her aunt got home or her cousin came downstairs.

The side of her face was sore, and as she gently touched it she could tell her cheek was swollen and that there was dried blood around her nose and on her top lip. Her aunt would know something was wrong, but how could she tell Harriet that her husband had raped her, or tell her cousin that his father had used her as he would a whore off the streets.

She staggered to her feet.

Her uncle grinned as he finished dressing himself. 'You look like a tired-out whore. Go and change yer dress an' we'll tell yer aunt yer went for a walk and bumped into a lamppost. You've only got a bit of bruising, don't look like you've been in a car crash or anything like that.'

Connie didn't answer; she was crying softly. She felt so sore, it was as if her whole body was screaming, even her insides.

'You tell yer aunt any different and by God I'll make you sorry.' He hissed the words at her.

Connie lifted her head and stared hard, and he could feel the hate beaming towards him.

'Look, it's like I said, it's not as if you were a virgin. Tell yer what, I'll make us a cuppa and something nice to eat while you're tidying yerself up.'

She nodded, resigned now that it would be pointless to argue with him.

155

The sooner she got out of this house, down to the railway station and home to her mum and dad the better. She just knew she wouldn't feel safe or even clean until her dad put his arms around her.

Chapter Eighteen

THE LONG WALK SEEMED never-ending. Her back was aching and getting worse with every step. Her swollen stomach had made her tend to throw her weight backwards, which didn't help.

Finally she arrived at East Croydon station.

With a heartfelt sigh of relief, Connie sat down on a platform bench and placed her brown paper carrier bag between her feet. There wasn't much in the bag, and she hadn't bothered to pack her case. Her one thought had been to get out of that house and on her way home. What she had just suffered at the hands of her Uncle Jack had been a nightmare she wouldn't inflict on her worst enemy. Why did her Aunt Harriet put up with him? He was downright selfish and lazy, and after what he had done to her this morning she considered he was no good to man or beast.

She had had a great deal to think about as she trudged along the roads.

Nothing in her world made sense any more; nothing could be classed in black or white. Everything she did or touched went wrong. Was it just her? She didn't think so.

No one was wholly bad, and no one person was perfect either, least of all herself. They say as you sow so shall you reap. Well, if sowing wild oats was what she was supposed to have done, then the harvest had been a sour one. Was she so bad? All she had longed for was a bit of fun, a few nice clothes and someone to take notice of her, make a fuss of her.

God knows, she'd grown up like most of the youngsters of her age. Hating the war, hating the fact that two oranges had to be shared between all of the family – that was the few times they ever saw a piece of fruit. As for sweets, a penny bar of chocolate, a few fruit drops and maybe one gobstopper and that was the ration for a month. When it came to clothes, all they ever wore were hand-me-downs. For three winters running she had worn a coat that her mother had made from an old grey army blanket. Her eldest sister had very bad feet because she had been made to wear shoes that were too small for her, because there were not enough clothing coupons to enable their mum to buy her a new pair.

Then suddenly the war had been over.

London could once more have bright lights everywhere, though not all signs of the bombing had yet disappeared: wreckage, ruined buildings and masses of debris still scarred many parts of the city. Dance halls had reopened, so had theatres and cinemas. Young women could take their pick of the new-look clothes that every shop suddenly had a good stock of. To go up to Marble Arch and Oxford Street, look around C&A and Selfridges was such a joy. The only problem now was not a shortage of clothing coupons but money. As a family they didn't do badly, but it was always sufficient, just enough, rather than extravagance.

Then Den Dryden had come into her life. Snappy dresser, loads of money and not afraid to spend it. But most of all he owned a car! Leather upholstery, walnut dashboard, oh, the very smell of the interior of Den's car had always sent shivers of delight up her spine whenever he opened the door and handed her into the front passenger seat.

Of course she had showed off, bragging to her mates about the places he had taken her to. Naturally each and every one of them had been envious, and if the truth be told there wasn't one amongst them that wouldn't have gone out with Den if they had been given the chance.

But it wasn't one of those girls that Den had chosen. It was me, Connie told herself as she placed her hands over her big belly and smiled wryly.

Was she feeling bitter now? Of course she was.

Den had promised her so much. Even when she had told him she was pregnant, he'd assured her he would cherish both her and the baby. They would want for nothing.

That was a laugh if ever there was one!

How long was it since she had set eyes on him? Even his own father didn't know where he was, or if he did he wasn't telling.

It was Connie who had been left to face the gossips and the sneers from all sides, including those coming from her so-called friends. As for money, she had less than four shillings left out of what her father had given her. For all Dennis knew, or cared it would seem, she could have starved to death.

What had happened to her today had been the last straw. Her Uncle Jack might not be a blood relative. Still, would it have hurt him to show her just a little respect? To be honest, respect was probably asking too much.

A lot of what he had said was true. She had let an older man make love to her, make her pregnant, and she *had* known from the beginning that Dennis was a married man and that he already had two children.

That still didn't give Jack Briggs the right to rape her. Especially as he had done it in such a crude, spiteful way. Even animals didn't treat each other with such brutality.

Ah well, sitting here won't get me home, Connie thought. She felt in her pocket: yes, she had her ticket safe; she had bought it at the ticket office before she had ventured down the steep slope to the platform.

What would she do when she arrived at Victoria? She hadn't got enough money for a taxi. She could telephone Mrs Taylor at the corner shop, and she'd send someone round to tell her mum and dad that she was at Victoria station. She had kept the slip of paper her dad had given her, with Mrs Taylor's number written on it, safely in her purse.

What I need, Connie told herself, is to make sure that I've got my story exactly right in my head. The first thing her parents would ask would be why she had returned home so unexpectedly. Not in a million years could she bring herself to tell them the truth.

There would be ructions! Jack Briggs would be damned lucky if her father stopped short of killing him, and that would be like adding fuel to the flames where the gossips were concerned. Her father would be arrested, and even if he only gave her uncle a good battering, he might still have to go to prison. No, she couldn't talk about it. Far better to keep her mouth shut and her thoughts to herself. She would just have to swear to her parents that she was homesick.

What was done was done and couldn't be undone, so why cause her family more heartache? Bad as she was, she didn't want to heap more trouble on her parents.

The train shuddered to a stop in front of her, and with a thankful sigh she waited whilst a well-dressed lady opened the door and stood back, allowing Connie to precede her into the carriage. With difficulty she climbed the high step and eased herself on to the nearest corner seat.

The carriage was empty apart from a working-class man who was seated in the opposite corner. He appeared to be engrossed in his copy of the *Daily Mirror*. In actual fact, he had taken his eyes away from his newspaper to cast an appreciative glance at the smartly dressed lady.

As his eyes automatically turned to Connie, he raised them heavenwards, his disapproval plainly showing.

She wasn't wearing gloves and her finger showed no wedding ring. Connie knew instinctively what he was thinking. Like a good many others, he was condemning her for being immoral. She was going home and she would have to face the gossips once more, and most of them would probably judge her to be just as evil as the look this stranger had given her. Still, it wouldn't be too long before she had her baby in her arms, and she would love it and care for it against all odds. After all, the wee mite hadn't asked to be born and things might turn out for the better once it was here.

Wasn't her mother always saying that inside every cloud there was a silver lining? She would do her best to keep that thought uppermost in her mind, though the way her life had turned out, God alone knew what a hard job it was at times to look on the bright side.

Within a few minutes a whistle blew and the train began moving along the tracks. Connie wriggled in her seat, thinking she would never feel the same again. Her whole body was sore and her thighs hurt so much she felt they must surely be black and blue with bruises. The moment she got home all she longed for was to be able to have a good long soak in a hot bath. She smiled wryly. Even that would be an impossibility. In the flat above the shop where her family lived, no one could have a bath on demand. There was a bathroom but no running hot water. A gas copper had to be filled with cold water and lit, and one had to be patient and wait for it to be heated. Even then it was a right carry-on transferring the hot water from the copper into the bath.

To arrive home unexpectedly and ask to have a bath! She would need a very good explanation.

Watching idly as the London buildings and the blocks of ugly, dirty-looking flats flicked past the window, she felt sorry for the tenants who had to live in these buildings. Rows and rows of washing were strung out on iron balconies. The thought crossed her mind that most of the washing would be dirty again by the time it was dry. What with the fumes from vans and lorries plus the sooty smoke coming from the railway lines, surely anything white would turn grey on the line.

The train was gathering speed and it sounded as if the wheels were squealing. Now, suddenly, the lady sitting opposite leant forward and held out a hand to Connie.

'Would you like a barley-sugar, my dear, they do help if you're feeling a bit queasy.'

'Thank you,' Connie smiled as she took the sweet. Unwrapping the paper, she popped the barley-sugar into her mouth, and as she sucked it she immediately felt better. Mostly because of the kind action a complete stranger had shown towards her, and also because it tasted good and had begun to make the inside of her mouth feel so much cleaner. She shuddered. For one awful moment she could actually feel the tongue of her beastly uncle being thrust into her mouth.

Good God! What was happening?

The noise was suddenly terrific, and the train seemed to be swaying from side to side. Connie wanted to steady herself and put out her hands for something to grip. She touched netting and a kind of pole and knew that it was the luggage rack, that had fallen down from overhead.

Without warning the carriage was full of thick dust and there was a smell of burning.

She was so frightened she could hardly breathe.

She tried to stand up, but before she could find her balance, there was an almighty crash and, in a moment of total horror, another line of carriages loomed in towards them. There was a crash, far worse than any clap of thunder, as tons of metal clashed together at great speed. Then, with a thunderous roar, the carriage Connie was in tipped and rolled over on its side, throwing her backwards. She was hurting everywhere as she was buffeted about amongst broken seats, shards of glass and twisted metal.

It seemed ages before the banging and clattering stopped and they were left lying in a confused state. Where was the kind lady who had befriended her? Connie reached out and they managed to just about touch each other's fingers across the twisted metal that seemed to be everywhere. Their attempt to make contact must have moved something because more shattered glass showered down on them and they heard the male occupant of their carriage scream out in agony.

The noise of grinding and crashing metal continued. It was horrific. Then the carriage gave a great shudder as it settled.

Connie felt a hard blow to the side of her head and something heavy hit her across her chest. She struggled to protect her baby. She wanted to put her hands across her swollen belly or at least lift off whatever was pinning her down. She couldn't move either arm. She felt a terrible pressure, a great weight holding her down.

Her body had felt battered and bruised when she had got on the train, but now she knew her unborn baby had been hurt because in her belly there was such awful pain, burning and throbbing.

She heard male voices urging folk to stay as still as possible. She wanted to laugh. Stay still on this filthy floor with what felt like a ton weight on top of her? Did she have any choice?

Mercifully, it wasn't long before she was drifting in and out of rational awareness. Time had lost all meaning. Then voices were calling, 'There has been a terrible train crash but help is at hand. We'll get you out, you will be all right.'

Would she? Connie didn't believe she would ever be free of this heavy weight which was pinning her down. But she didn't have the energy to voice her thoughts; she was finding it difficult to breathe, it hurt so much.

Someone had once told her that God paid his debts without money.

Lord Jesus, please, I know I have sinned over and over again, but do I deserve what is happening to me today? I just want this awful, terrible pain to go away. Please, please, make it go away. And please, I want to see me mum and me dad.

Part of her prayer was answered. She no longer felt any pain. She had lost consciousness.

Chapter Nineteen

BAD NEWS TRAVELS FAST!

Winnie Paige came into her daughter's living room so quietly that Ella immediately knew she was the bearer of bad news.

For a moment her mother remained still. The news she had just been told had been such a shock and the events of the previous weeks were crowding into her mind. Then she roused herself, and taking the large pin out of her hat, she placed the hat and her gloves on the table and then took off her coat. Moving to the range, she lifted the kettle, which was already full of water, and pushed it nearer the hot plate to boil. The kettle had been black-leaded and like everything else in Ella's kitchen was sparkling clean. Unlike most folk's ranges, Ella's had two ovens, one large and one small. The smell that was filling the room told her that Ella was roasting a joint but also had made a bread pudding, which was in the smaller oven. The smell of fruit and cinnamon was mouth-watering.

'Well, lass, you've been busy this morning. I'll make us a brew an' hope that bread pudding will be ready to eat. What time does your shift start today?'

Winnie's voice was over-bright and she certainly was acting uneasily, her movements all quick and jerky.

'Mum,' Ella set two cups and saucers down on the table and turned to face her mother, 'I'm not daft, yer know. You've got something to say, and as you're taking for ever to spit it out, I can only imagine that it's bad news. Why don't you tell me what has happened? Get it over an' done with.'

The knuckles of Winnie's hands were showing white as she gripped the edge of the kitchen table. She took a deep breath and said, 'You heard about that train crash that happened midday yesterday, didn't you?'

'Yes, bad do, wasn't it? Not far out of Croydon apparently. Everyone was talking about it in the bar last night; it made the evening papers.'

Winnie's voice was thick with emotion as she said, 'Young Connie Baldwin was on that train.'

Ella's hands flew to cover her face. After a while she shook her head from side to side murmuring, 'Oh no, oh no.' Then, 'Was she badly hurt?'

'Plenty of tales flying around but nobody seems to know the full story. Her aunt and uncle and their son Reg are over here, stayed the night with Kate and Alf Baldwin from what I hear.'

Ella shuddered. 'I feel I should go and visit Connie's parents, ask if she's been badly hurt, but I'm probably the last person they would want to see. I'll more than likely hear more news when I get to work. There's not much goes on that doesn't get discussed in the Legion.'

Winnie looked anxious as she asked, 'You know Pete Jarvis, don't you?'

'Only that he's always been pretty friendly with my Den. I don't like him much, never have. Why are you asking?'

'Most folk believe that he's a right bent old lag, sell

fridges to Eskimos he could. It figures, 'cos a man is known by the company he keeps,' Winnie stated sharply. 'None the more for that, it seems he was in the district and apparently went straight to the scene of the crash and did all he could to help.'

'Did he see Connie? Or find out if she was badly hurt?'

'Not that I've heard, but Mr Taylor said he came into the corner shop for some cigarettes just as he was closing up and he looked so awful that he took him into their back room and Mrs Taylor gave him a mug of strong tea with a drop of the hard stuff in it. Apparently he poured his heart out to them. Best thing he could 'ave done, 'cos they reckon he was in a right old state of shock.'

Ella was getting exasperated. Why did her mother have to be so long-winded in getting to the point?

'Thought you were going to make the tea. I'm going to put me washing in the copper to soak and then we'll sit down and you can tell me what you know all in one piece, because dribbling a bit of news here an' there is driving me mad.'

'All I know is hearsay,' Winnie grumbled, but she did as Ella had bid, spooning three heaped teaspoons of tea into the big brown teapot then covering them with boiling water from the black kettle, all the time wishing that there was a drop of whisky knocking about here, but Ella didn't keep spirits in the house since Dennis had left. She had listened to Mrs Taylor's version of what Pete Jarvis had had to say, and the very thought of a pregnant young girl being involved in such a disaster had made her feel sick to her stomach. I hope to God they got her out safely, poor kid, she prayed.

Now, seated round the table, tea in front of them and a plate each which held a piece of steaming hot bread pudding, they were both silent, their heads buzzing with thoughts.

167

Ella's main thought was, Shouldn't Den be contacted? Suddenly she voiced that question aloud.

'Not for us to interfere, is it, luv? I do think you're right, but whether or not the Baldwins will feel the same way is another thing entirely.'

'So you still don't know whether young Connie was hurt or not?'

'No, but according to Pete Jarvis, there couldn't have been many that escaped unharmed. He said the crash site was like nothing he had ever seen before. Coaches of one train were lying on their sides and another train had crossed into the oncoming track and been hit by a third. Wreckage was piled on either side of the second engine and two carriages had been forced on top of one another. Pete said the smells were awful, burning, oily grease everywhere, not to mention the blood. According to him it was a major alert: there were workers everywhere, firemen cutting into the smashed carriages, doctors and nurses crawling about in the wreckage helping the injured that they could manage to get to. Loads of ambulances. Policemen were guiding some of the casualties on to the sloping banks and sitting them down. Even those, Pete said, were all injured, bloodstained and covered with filth. Neighbours in the houses near by were very kind and helpful. Pete went with two other men to collect blankets that were offered. The ambulancemen did have their bright red blankets, but of course there wasn't nearly enough to cover all the folk that needed them.'

'Oh, Mother! All the things we've said about Connie, and to think she had to be caught up in an accident like this. I feel awful. Not knowing what to do is driving me mad.'

'Oh for God's sake, there's nothing you or I can do at the moment,' Winnie told her angrily. 'We just have to wait and see. If the girl has been injured she will be in hospital, and if not, please God, she'll be home with her family and then perhaps they will want to get in touch with Dennis. He has a right to know, especially if the baby has been hurt. There's one thing that Mrs Taylor told me this morning that's got me wondering. Connie's parents hadn't been expecting her home; they didn't seem to know how or why she was on that train. When Len Evans – you know, their next-door neighbour – came in the shop this morning, he didn't know what had happened to Connie, but he said Kate's sister and her husband arrived quite late, and it was nearly midnight when their son turned up, and Len said there was a hell of a ding-dong going on in there. Shouting and swearing by all accounts.'

'Ah well,' Ella sighed, 'I can't sit here all day nattering. I've got to get ready for work. Are you going to meet Babs from school this afternoon?'

'Yeah, course I am. Teddy won't come near nor by me, though. His mates call him a sissy if he walks home with his gran.'

Winnie stood up and fastened her hat securely with her hatpin, then shrugged her arms into her coat. 'I think it's more likely that you'll hear first if young Connie has been hurt; anyway, I might pop in the Legion myself at dinner time. Be great when they have the new part up and running. I'll be able to have meals in there on a regular basis then.'

Ella stood up too. 'Thanks, Mum, for coming in so early and telling me that Connie was on that train. I'd rather have heard it from you. I'll come to the door with you.'

'That's all right. Just don't get yerself worked up, no matter what you hear.'

'I won't, but I do hope somebody can contact Dennis.'

'Stop worrying over him. A bad penny always comes

169

back. I'll lay yer ten to one that his old man knows where he is.'

Ella closed the front door and leant against it, her heart beating nineteen to the dozen. She felt dreadful.

The information her mother had given her was a bit garbled and Ella was unsure of what to believe. Why had Connie Baldwin not told her folks that she was on her way home? She tried to comfort herself with the thought that no news was good news. In any case, she was bound to find out more once she was behind the bar of the Legion.

Fully dressed now, Ella glanced in the mirror. No one could describe her as plump and dowdy now. Since having been lucky enough to get herself a job that brought her into contact with people from all walks of life, she knew she was a different person. She worked hard and that had helped her to lose some weight, but the difference in her appearance was mainly down to the influence of Sadie Cohan. They had kept in touch, and Ella regarded Sadie as a true and valuable friend.

Today she was wearing a beige-coloured, plain, slim-fitting dress with a tailored coat made from matching material that hung neatly from the padded shoulders down to her calves. Her plain court shoes and her handbag were almost the same colour as her thick copper-coloured hair. She missed Dennis, of course she did, but in some ways his leaving had done her a power of good. It wasn't ambition that drove her, or the desire to have expensive things. It was the freedom to be herself, never having to be at the beck and call of Dennis when he came home in the early hours of the morning. Never having to lie awake wondering where he was and who he was with when she and the children hadn't seen him for days. Another great feeling was that having proved she could hold down a responsible job, she did not have to depend on others.

However, her insistent thoughts gave her little peace and she was relieved when it was time to leave for work.

As Ella pushed open the swing doors of the saloon bar, Mike Murray spotted her immediately and strode quickly to be by her side.

'Hallo, Ella,' he said, his voice full of sympathy. 'I take it you've heard the news?'

'Yes, pretty dreadful, isn't it? Have you heard if Connie Baldwin was hurt?'

'Yes,' he answered, and she knew he had been expecting the question. 'I'm afraid she's in hospital. Apparently they had to cut the poor lass out of the wreckage. We've just had the news on the radio. Nineteen dead and over fifty injured at the last count.'

Ella's face drained of colour. 'That's awful.'

'Yes,' Mike agreed. 'Folk 'ave been coming in telling us some ghastly stories. It must 'ave been a hell of a crash.'

'So who told you about young Connie?'

Mike sighed heavily, which told her more than any words could have done that Connie was in a bad way.

'Come on,' he said, taking hold of her elbow, 'take your coat off and I'll get you a brandy. In fact, I'll 'ave one with you.'

There were more customers than usual in the bar for this time of the day. They picked their way through to get behind the bar and soon they were leaning against the counter each with a glass between their hands.

Ella needed no telling that Mike knew something hideous had happened to Connie, but she didn't prompt him to talk about the details. He'd tell her in his own good time.

The silence between them was broken when Alf Baldwin came to the bar. The haggard look on his face had Ella expecting the worst, even though the poor man hadn't said a word.

'Just come from the hospital, 'ave yer, Alf?' Mike asked quietly.

'Yes, I've left her mum and her aunt up there sitting with Connie. We've come home to see to a few things but we'll be going back shortly. I'll 'ave a pint, please, Mike, and what will you 'ave?' he asked, turning to the tall, broad-shouldered young man standing at his side. 'This is me nephew, Reg. It's his mum an' dad that our Connie has been staying with.'

Reg was a tall, well-built young man with a head of slicked-back dark brown hair. He wore navy blue trousers and a white striped shirt with a dark tie that had been jerked loose and hung like a noose around the collar of his smart dark leather jacket.

His face seemed to tighten and he clenched his fists as he nodded at Mike before saying, 'I'll 'ave a pint and a whisky chaser.'

Ella stood where she was for a few minutes, her eyes on the young man. Something was eating away at him. Mike handed both men their drinks before asking for the latest news on Connie, and Ella felt that the question had been like putting a naked flame to a pool of petrol.

It was Reg who quickly spoke. 'If it weren't for my old man, my cousin would never 'ave been on that bloody train.' His voice was a sheer blast and every person in the bar turned to stare at him.

'Now, now, son, you had yer say t' yer father last night when you arrived. Let's leave it like that fer now. We don't want our dirty linen being washed in public, do we?'

'You can say what you damn well like, Uncle Alf, but I'm for letting the whole world know what a toerag my dad is.'

Ella drained her glass and moved further along the bar to start work.

It didn't take much working out, she thought.

Her mother had said that Reg had arrived at the

172

Baldwins' house very late last night, a while after his parents. Len Evans had said that no sooner had the son arrived than there had been a helluva bust-up. Connie apparently was on that train running away from something or someone, since neither of her parents had had any notice that she was on her way home.

Reg had downed his whisky and drunk more than half of his pint of beer, but the drink had not calmed him down. Quite the reverse.

Molly Riley stood close to Ella and quickly made the sign of the cross. 'Jesus holy Mary, will yer listen t' that young man's language?'

'Mike's letting him get away with it because you only have to look at him to see how upset he is,' Ella said.

'Our Connie was trapped in that bloody disaster for hours before the doctors and the paramedics could cut her free, and God alone knows if she's gonna make it.' Reg's voice was so full of anger that he was almost choking on his words. 'I'll tell yer what, though, Uncle Alf, if our Connie does die, then so will that lying, cheating, filthy shyster that passes for my father. I don't know for sure what it was he said or done t' Connie, but she didn't leave our house and get on a train without saying goodbye to me or me mum without some very good reason. If you hadn't pulled me off him last night I would have got the truth out of him, but the very fact that he shot out of the house the minute I accused him said it all for me.'

'Reg, will you leave it, please, people are listening to every word you're saying,' his uncle pleaded.

'OK, but sooner or later I will get the truth out of him an' then I'll 'ave the bastard, and make no mistake, I'll flatten him.'

'Sorry, Mike. I'll make sure he keeps his voice down.' Alf jerked a thumb at his nephew.

Mike leant towards Ella and whispered in her ear, 'He's

a holy terror, that young lad, but I bet he's got his facts right. Young Connie wouldn't have upped and left that house without so much as a word to anyone if something hadn't driven her away.'

'You're probably right, Mike, and I wouldn't be in 'is father's shoes when he does find out, 'cos I know him of old. That boy's got a temper. Always did 'ave, even as a child, an' I wouldn't guess it's got any better as he's got older.'

Just then the bar doors opened and two policemen came inside.

Mike came quickly from behind the bar and hurried towards them.

A quiet conversation was carried on, then Mike turned his head towards Mr Baldwin, nodded and beckoned him to come forward. The taller of the two policemen approached and he and Alf Baldwin each covered half the distance that lay between them. The quietness and patience of the constable's speech was enough to tell folk that he was the bearer of bad news. Whatever had been said had certainly sapped what little energy the poor man had left.

Dragging his feet, he returned to the bar, caught hold of his nephew's arm and very quietly said, 'Come on, Reg, we have to get back to the hospital.'

Ella shook her head in despair as she watched Alf Baldwin and his nephew follow the policemen.

Mike picked up the two dirty glasses and stared at Ella, and she raised her eyebrows at him. It was one of those rare moments that occur in everyone's life.

One of those times when there really isn't anything to say.

Chapter Twenty

ALF AND REG ARRIVED back at the hospital at two o'clock to find Connie's three sisters sitting in the corridor, empty coffee cups on a table beside them and looks of sheer misery on their faces.

'I take it there has been no change?' their father asked, not really expecting to receive a reply.

Amy, the eldest daughter, started to rise, but Reg laid a hand on her shoulder and said kindly, 'Sit where you are. I'll get us all a fresh coffee.'

The hot liquid brought a little colour to the girls' cheeks, and both Alf and Reg drank theirs gratefully.

'Who's sitting with yer sister now?' their father asked.

'Just Mum and Aunt Harriet.'

'Have yer seen anything of yer Uncle Jack?'

The three girls glanced at each other, but it was Sheila, the youngest, who answered. 'Oh yes, he turned up here all right,' she said sarcastically. 'Practically threw himself across the bed and kept muttering over and over again about how sorry he was. Two male nurses dealt with him very efficiently, told him not to come back at all today, and not even tomorrow unless he cleaned himself up and was sober.'

'See, I knew all along I was right. Something he said or did frightened the life out of Connie and made her start for home.' For a change Reg's voice was low, but that gave more emphasis to his words than if he had shouted them.

Suddenly Alf Baldwin was struggling to his feet. His chest was heaving, and he seemed unable to speak. He clutched at his chest, shaking his head slowly as tears filled his eyes. Swaying, he would have fallen if Reg hadn't wrapped his arms around his taut body and held him close.

'Sheila, go quietly, but fetch your aunt, and a doctor if you can find one. If not, bring a nurse. Be as quick as you can.'

It was Amy who took charge of the situation now. 'Reg, if I help you, shall we see if we can get my dad into the waiting room. It's only just over there.'

Within minutes Kate Baldwin had rushed into the room and dropped to her knees in front of her husband. He was sitting back in an armchair with his eyes closed, his face drained of colour.

'What's wrong, dear?' she asked, her voice trembling with concern.

Alf opened his eyes. 'It's just this sharp pain, it feels so tight right across here.' He rubbed a hand over his chest. 'I'll be all right in a minute.'

Kate was telling herself not to panic. She didn't like the look of her husband at all. His face was a terrible colour and he was having a lot of trouble breathing. She took hold of one of his hands and held it between both of hers, and using soft circular movements she massaged his fingers, which felt bitterly cold.

Suddenly there were people in white coats, and two trolleys were being pushed into the centre of the room. A male voice issued a command.

'We need to get him on to the floor, lying flat. And clear this room.'

No sooner were the words heard than all the Baldwin family and Reg Briggs were being herded out into the corridor.

Kate just succeeded in patting her husband's knee before scrambling to her feet. 'The doctors are here now, Alf, an' they'll help you.' All the while she was telling herself to stay calm, not to let her husband see how worried she really was.

Once on her feet she managed to gently kiss his forehead, but she couldn't put a smile on her face as she assured him, 'I'll be back in a minute.'

Next thing she knew, she was being led out of the room by a young nurse, and it sounded so dreadfully final as the door closed behind her.

A few whispered words and the ward sister quickly got the message.

'Come along, Mrs Baldwin, I've sent your family along to the canteen, and Mrs Briggs – your sister, isn't it? – is still sitting with your daughter, so we'll wait in my office.'

'He will be all right, won't he, Sister?'

It was such a sad question, and one that the sister could barely bring herself to answer. However, she did her best.

'Mr Baldwin couldn't be in better hands. We'll know more when the doctors have had a chance to examine him.'

'Whatever it is that's wrong with him must have caught him unawares. He didn't complain of feeling ill this morning.'

'Well, neither of you have had much sleep. All the stress and strain you've been through since the train crash has probably caught up with Mr Baldwin.' The sister put her hand on Kate's arm. 'Shall we both silently say a little prayer?'

Kate Baldwin covered her face with her handkerchief and between sobs prayed like she'd never prayed before. 'Dear God, my Alf doesn't deserve this. Please don't let him die. Not now. Our Connie needs him. I need him. Please help him.'

Brian Holmes had been a doctor at St Thomas's for almost fifteen years. He was a kindly man, tall and well built, with a shock of dark hair. Despite the fact that he had had to break bad news many times, he had never got used to doing it. Wasn't it bad enough that the Baldwins' young daughter lay lingering between life and death? Her parents had barely left the hospital since she had been brought in.

Obviously she had lost the baby she had been carrying. Her injuries were so severe he found it hard to believe that she hadn't given up the ghost herself by now. Three times she had almost died, and yet something or someone had kept her holding on.

Now, with no warning whatsoever, her father had suffered a massive heart attack and died immediately.

Some time had passed before Dr Holmes gave a light knock on the door and entered Sister's office. The doctor exchanged glances with her.

Oh dear God above! How were they supposed to break the news to Mrs Baldwin?

'Well, Doctor,' Kate spoke abruptly, 'how bad is my husband? He's never been ill in his life. You won't have to keep him here in the hospital, will you?'

Brian Holmes raised a hand to silence her.

'I am so sorry, Mrs Baldwin, there is no easy way of telling you that your husband suffered a massive heart attack and died almost instantly. There was nothing I or anyone else could have done for him. If it is any consolation to you, he didn't suffer.'

178

'No!' Kate screamed. 'You can't be telling me that my Alf is dead.'

The sister broke all the rules. She took the terrified woman into her arms and held her close, rubbing her back and speaking softly.

'You must try and be brave, Mrs Baldwin, you can't afford to break down. Connie still needs you. No one knows what's going to happen. She might regain consciousness at any time, and if you go to pieces that wouldn't help anyone.'

'First thing she'll ask for is her dad,' Kate sobbed into the sister's shoulder.

Less than one hour later a sad group were gathered around Connie's bed. Her mother, her three sisters, her Aunt Harriet and her cousin Reg.

It was as if Connie gave a gentle sigh, then passed away.

Harriet Briggs also sighed as she squeezed her sister's hand. But her sigh was one of relief. If Connie had lived she would have been crippled for life, and the fact that the baby had been crushed to death in her womb would have haunted her for ever. Keeping those thoughts to herself, Harriet whispered, 'God works in a mysterious way. Think about it, Kate. Connie is not on her own, her dad has gone with her, they'll make the journey together.'

At that point in time none of what Harriet was saying made any sense at all to Kate. She was grateful that her three other daughters were there, and they each held on to her as she bent over the bed and kissed her youngest daughter goodbye.

It was early evening by the time they all got out of the hospital.

'A drink is what we need,' Reg said loudly as he looked

at his watch. 'Yes, it's turned opening time. Let's make for the nearest pub.'

His mother was in two minds about her son. This last couple of days he had come through with flying colours. No one could have asked more of him. But she could read his thoughts as he sipped the dark whisky. She needed no telling he was not finished with his father yet.

'Come on, Auntie, drink up that Scotch,' Reg urged, 'then I'll get us a taxi. The quicker I get all of you home, the better. There's nothing we can do tonight except see you get some rest. Time enough in the morning to start to sort things out.'

Luck was still not on their side. To get a taxi to stop at that time of the day was an impossibility. Every passing cab already had a fare.

'Duke, Duke!' A large black saloon car had pulled in to the kerb a few yards up the road and a young man was calling and beckoning.

Reg took to his heels and ran. Opening the passenger-side door, he poked his head into the interior of the car and a hurried conversation took place. Running back to his family, he gasped, 'Christ, that's a bit of luck. That's Charlie Seymour, he's doing a favour for a car hire firm, picking that car up from being valeted and taking it back to the showrooms. He'll take us all home; he's got his own big van back on the site.'

'He'll never get us all in, will he?' Harriet asked.

'Come on, he can't hang about for long. There's a bench seat in the front; you, Mum, and Auntie Kate can sit there and I'll squeeze in the back with the three girls. Even if I squat down on the floor it's got to be better than getting on an' off of buses.'

Reggie's mate had kept the engine running. They piled in, and within minutes were on their way.

'The car showrooms are just off the King's Road, so

I'll let you lot out by the Albert Bridge. Wait for me there. I'll only be five or ten minutes, then I'll get you all home.'

Reg nodded. 'You're a bloody good mate, Charlie. You'll never know how glad I was t' hear yer calling me.'

'Been a bad day, 'as it?'

'You can say that again, pal, but you've turned up trumps.'

Charlie drove across London by way of Hammersmith and soon they were heading down the King's Road, then turning into Oakley Street, with the wonderful Albert Bridge at the end of it.

'Shan't be long,' Charlie shouted as they piled out.

With the five women safely on the pavement, Reg jumped into the front passenger seat and the car sped off.

'What a day,' Harriet Briggs murmured.

No one answered her.

The three girls were walking up and down, each lost in her own thoughts. To have lost a sister and their father all in the space of one afternoon was a pretty heavy blow. How the hell was their mother going to cope?

Amy suddenly realized that being the eldest, all the problems of arranging the funeral would fall on her shoulders. She felt sick to the bottom of her stomach. Would there have to be two separate funerals? God above, she wouldn't know where to begin.

Harriet had her arm around her sister's shoulders as together they leant against the brickwork and stared out at the wide, quick-flowing River Thames. All around them life was still going on in London: people were hurrying home from work, tugs were hooting, gulls were scavenging for food, and the smell was like no other.

Kate gave a deep, heavy sigh as she placed her hand on top of her sister's.

'I knew in my heart it would be better if my Connie

died, her injuries were so bad, but now . . .' Her voice trailed off.

'I know, luv, for Alf to be taken like that is a mighty shock. The only consolation is that Connie has him with her. She's not on her own.'

Kate leant forward, put her elbow on the ledge of the bridge and rested her forehead in the palm of her hand. With her other hand she clutched her sister's arm.

After a bit, 'What do you think, Harriet?' she asked.

'About what?'

'Was my Connie a real bad lot? Her carrying on with Dennis Dryden has ruined the lives of two families, and there's still so many questions to which we don't know the answers. Why do you think she upped and left your house without so much as a word to you?'

Harriet bit her lip, took a deep breath, and then spoke, her voice coming out clear and full of concern. 'We both know Connie was not a bad lot, as you put it. That Dennis Dryden could charm the birds out of the trees and Connie is not the only young girl who has been caught by the likes of him. You don't need much imagination to know what he promised her.' Her voice was tight with temper as she added, 'I bet he promised her the moon and the stars to go with it.'

Kate lifted her head high and managed a slight smile as she looked at her sister.

'How did she act while she was staying with you? Did she behave herself?'

'She was fine,' Harriet answered sadly, 'she really was.' She shook her head as tears flooded her eyes and blurred her vision. 'I'm blaming meself. I should never have left her in the house alone with Jack.'

'What are you talking about?' The implications of what her sister had just said had Kate's mind working over-time.

182

Harriet wished she hadn't said anything. She stared at Kate, guilt filling her mind, and tried to turn her head away, but Kate caught her chin with one hand and tilted it up so she had no choice but to look at her.

'Wasn't your Reg in the house when Connie left?'

'Yes,' Harriet whispered, trembling inside, 'but when I questioned him about it, he admitted he was still in bed. He hadn't seen Connie at all that morning.'

'Harriet! For Christ's sake. Am I hearing right?'

'Wait, luv, just hold yer horses. I don't really *know* anything. Honestly, Connie was a real gem while she was with me, but I saw the way Jack had been watching her.' She looked into her sister's face, pleading for understanding.

'So what your Reg has been hinting at may well be the bloody truth. Christ Almighty, I don't know what t' believe. Over these last few weeks, one minute I've been blaming my own girl for all the trouble she'd caused, an' the next minute I've been persuading meself she'd been wronged and left stranded to deal with it all on her own. My Alf didn't blame her, she was the apple of his eye, the lastborn, the baby of the family.'

The honking of Charlie's horn stopped any more speculation.

The two older women linked arms as they walked towards the roadway where Charlie had parked his white van. Never had Kate felt so heavy-hearted. What had started out as a terrible day was getting worse as the hours went by.

Reg sat up front with Charlie while the women travelled in the back of the van. No one bothered to speak, though there were plenty of questions that needed asking, and answers would have to be found at some stage.

Kate watched the different expressions flicker over her sister's face and heaved a great sigh. Harriet looked awful.

Her straggly grey hair, usually so neat, had escaped from beneath her hat, and her dear kind face was the colour of grey slate. What was she blaming herself for? If Jack Briggs had assaulted Connie, the blame couldn't be laid at Harriet's door. She was the one who went out to work, brought home the money that put food on the table and paid the rent. Kate couldn't remember when Jack Briggs had ever held down a decent, steady job.

But surely not. The very idea was unthinkable! Connie was his niece. Yet there had to be a good reason for her to leave the house and get on a train to come home without saying a word to anyone. Not even getting in touch with her father to meet her at Victoria station.

Had she had a row with her uncle and stormed off?

If half the accusations Reg had thrown at his father last night were any way near the truth, then by God the man deserved to be hung, drawn and quartered.

Why oh why did I ever send her away from her own home?

Pride! Downright stupid pride. Because neighbours talked. My Connie wasn't the first girl that got herself pregnant by a married man, and it's damn sure she won't be the last. I should have stood up for her. Kept her home where she belonged, shown her that no matter what she had done, her family loved her.

Too late now to tell her anything.

Charlie brought the van to a halt in the middle of the long row of old terraced houses. Blackshaw Road, where everyone knew their neighbours' business.

Charlie opened the back doors of his van, and he and Reg were helping the women down when suddenly Reg turned and ran towards the house. The look on Harriet's face frightened Kate half to death.

Jack Briggs was sitting on the pavement, his back

184

propped up against the wall. The very look of the man was appalling!

Reg was the first to reach him. He shook him roughly, shouting at him to get up. Then he quickly stepped back; the sour smell of Jack's breath was revolting. That was not enough to deter his son, though. Reg stared down at his father's face. Jack had not shaved or washed, and by the look of his jacket he had vomited.

'You filthy swine.' Reg's face was dark with fury. 'You couldn't even keep your rotten hands off a young girl who was a member of yer own family. I should have known why Connie was afraid of you. Because she was pregnant, you tried t' 'ave her over right under me mum's nose.' The words were emphasized by sharp kicks.

'Keep your voice down! Do you want the whole street t' know what's been going on? You wanna remember, Reggie, we've got t' go on living here.'

Reg shook his head as if to shake off his temper. 'I'm sorry, Aunt Kate. I'll get Charlie to give me a hand with him. We'll put in the back of the van and then we'll sling the bastard in the river, and don't tell me my dad can't swim, 'cos I don't give a monkey's if he dives deep down to the bloody mud.'

Kate looked at Harriet. Under different circumstances they would have had a good laugh, but right at this moment they both doubted they would ever laugh again.

'Come on, girls, it's about time we took charge,' Amy declared loudly. 'Let's leave the men to it and get ourselves inside the house. Sheila, you put the kettle on. What our mum and Aunt Harriet need is a good strong cup of tea.'

If they were ever going to get any sleep tonight, she needed to see that their tea was well laced with a good strong dose of whisky.

And she had already decided that she would make sure they got it!

Chapter Twenty-one

ELLA WAS WASHED AND dressed when the children came downstairs, the table was set for breakfast and the bread board was piled high with thick slices of bread ready for toasting. Even though it was still August, there was a bright fire burning in the grate. It paid to keep the fire going most days because the back boiler made sure there was hot water for washing, the two ovens were constantly used for cooking and the big black kettle was always simmering away on the top of the hot range.

Babs and Teddy were scrambling to sit up to the table when they heard Gran's voice calling out, 'It's only me,' as she let herself in and came down the passage.

'Morning, Mum,' Ella muttered.

'Morning, Gran,' the kids said in unison.

'You're up and about early,' Ella commented.

'Well, there wasn't any more news about Connie Baldwin, only that she was holding her own, but I did hear about Alf Baldwin from the milkman. What a shock, eh?' Winnie said, sounding really upset. 'I guess all of you at the Legion were told last night.'

'Yes, Mike had given the Legion's number to the family

and told them if they needed any help not to hesitate to ring. But nobody expected Mr Baldwin to pop off like that, did they?'

'Poor man, too many worries piled on his shoulders one after the other. Didn't expect him to have a heart attack and go as quick as that, though. Nice ordinary bloke he was; if he couldn't do you a good turn he certainly wouldn't do yer a bad one. Not a fair world, is it?'

'No one ever promised it would be, my luv,' Ella said, giving her mother a hug.

'But Mum, I feel so guilty for all the nasty things I said about young Connie.' A single tear trickled from Ella's eye, down her cheek, and she quickly brushed it away.

Winnie lifted a hand to stroke her daughter's face. 'Try not to worry, Ella, none of this is your fault.'

Ella leant over the sink and put a handful of soda crystals into the washing-up bowl. If what her mother was saying was true, then why did she feel so bad about everything?

There was a commotion at the table as the children argued over the use of the sugar-pot for their porridge, and Ella tutted with anger.

'Stop quarrelling. Get on and eat it while it's still hot,' she ordered. 'You staying for a while, Mum? If so, start making the toast for me, will yer.'

Just then Babs tugged at the milk bottle that Teddy was doing his best to hold on to, and as was bound to happen, it went flying, spraying milk all across the table.

'Behave yerselves, I've enough to cope with today without you two playing up,' their mother yelled.

'It was her fault,' Teddy grumbled.

'No it wasn't. He always wants to grab everything first.'

Ella thumped her fist on the table. 'Enough! Get on an' eat yer breakfast, else I'll whack the pair of you and then I'll know I've got the right one.'

Brother and sister glared at each other, then Teddy took advantage of the brief lull in hostilities to grab the first piece of toast his gran put on the table.

Babs tried to take it from him but he slapped her hand away. 'You're a pain in the neck, you are,' he muttered.

'Oh yeah?' Ella stood with her hands on her hips. 'You, my son, will 'ave a pain in yer arse if I whack yer backside with my shoe.'

Winnie was worried. It wasn't very often that Ella lost her temper, and certainly not with her own children. By and large she had the patience of Job.

'Come on, you two, eat up and then get yerselves ready and I'll walk to school with you. Maybe I'll even treat you both to a packet of sweets to eat in your lunchtime.'

That put a smile on the kids' faces, but Winnie was being crafty. She knew Teddy wouldn't want to be seen walking with his gran, so a bribe was necessary. Besides, the sooner she got Babs and Teddy out of the house, the sooner she might find out exactly what was niggling away at her daughter this morning, 'cos a hundred to one something very bad had upset her.

By the time Winnie returned to the house, clutching a bag of freshly baked bread rolls, she was pleased to notice that her daughter's temper, which had flared so quickly, had receded somewhat.

With a fresh pot of tea, a jar of marmalade and a full round of butter laid beside the rolls all set out on the table, mother and daughter sat themselves down facing each other.

'So, are you going to tell me what's eating you, luv, or did you just get out of bed the wrong side this morning?'

'Mum.' Ella's voice was low, and the very sound of it rang warning bells in Winnie's head.

'Mum.' She tried again. 'It's obvious you've heard that

188

poor Mr Baldwin died very suddenly, but what you don't seem to know is that his daughter died soon after he did.'

Winnie's hands flew to cover her mouth and the colour drained from her face. Some minutes ticked by before she was able to speak. Then, shaking her head slowly from side to side, she muttered, 'Dear Jesus, that poor woman, what she must be going through.'

One phrase was going through Ella's mind. Over and over again she was asking herself, Where the hell is Dennis? Surely he should be here shouldering some of the responsibility.

Last night, when the news of Alf Baldwin's sudden death had reached the club, Ted Dryden had been in the bar. Connie Baldwin was still alive when Ella had decided that she was unable to stay neutral. She had approached her father-in-law with the suggestion that at least his son should be made aware of Mr Baldwin's death and the fact that poor Mrs Baldwin was having to cope with the likelihood that Connie might also die.

Her father-in-law's voice and manner had been abrupt but not unkind. He had said he couldn't say where his son was to be found, but on the other hand he hadn't said he didn't know. Played his cards very close to his chest, did Dennis's father.

Winnie pulled herself together, poured milk into each cup and then, lifting the teapot, filled the cups to the brim. Talking as if to herself, she was saying, 'You don't expect your children to die before you do, but to lose your husband and your youngest girl both within the space of a few hours must be more than a body can take. Oh, that poor, poor woman.'

'Yeah, I know, Mum, my heart aches for Mrs Baldwin. Her Connie and my Den didn't know what they were starting, did they?'

'They didn't stop to think, Ella, none of us do. So often we let our hearts rule our heads.'

189

Ella sighed at hearing her mother's true words.

They ate their breakfast in silence, though neither of them managed more than one bread roll.

'It's a queer how-d'-yer-do,' Winnie remarked as she helped her daughter to clear the breakfast table. 'According to what his father has told you, Dennis has disappeared off the face of the earth. When yer think about it, that young Connie Baldwin got the rough end of the stick, didn't she?'

'How do you work that one out?' Ella asked.

'Well, to be shoved off to live with an aunt and uncle just 'cos her mother was feeling the shame of having a sixteen-year-old-daughter pregnant by a married man wasn't right, and by all accounts all the time Connie was away, Dennis never once made contact. Says a lot for your ol' man, don't it? Full of big talk, supposed to think the world of his children, but first sign of trouble and he scarpers, leaving everyone to fend for themselves. Still, that's always been your Den's motto. "I'm all right Jack!" Sod everyone else. He's always been a nasty piece of work. A big man with his fists when it came to keeping you in line.'

In spite of feeling as if she was drowning in sadness, Ella almost wanted to smile. There was something immensely comforting about her mother. No two ways about it, she always called a spade a spade!

'Mum, can I leave you to tidy up here and make the beds? I'd better get in to work a bit early today. You can bet your life the place will be packed this morning; half the East End will want to know all the gory details of what has been going on.'

'Yes, luv, I'll see to everything, you get yerself off.'

'Thanks, Mum,' Ella said as she slipped her jacket on. Somehow she wasn't looking forward to this coming shift.

★　　★　　★

She had only walked a few yards when Reggie Briggs came out of the corner shop.

'Off t' work, Ella?' he asked cautiously.

'Yeah, needs must,' then, feeling that she ought to say more, she added, 'I am so sorry, Reg, so . . .' but she couldn't find words to describe the way she was feeling, because although none of these terrible happenings were of her making, and certainly not her fault, she had never felt like she did now. Never in her whole life.

'I know, I know, Ella, none of us know what to say or what to think.' Then, taking hold of her arm, he said, 'I'll walk to the Legion with you. I could use a drink.'

As they walked, it was Reg who started the conversation.

'It's my Aunt Kate I feel the most sorry for, she's blaming herself for so much.'

Ella knew what he meant. 'D'you know, Reg, your aunt and uncle had the happiest marriage I've ever known. They lived for each other.'

'I know, only makes it a bloody sight worse, don't it? Me aunt won't know how to live without him.' He stood still for a moment and took a deep breath before saying, 'We can all be so damn clever after an event. It was a mistake to send me cousin to go and stay with me mum and dad. Don't get me wrong, my Aunt Kate thought she was doing it for the best. She says herself now she should have been bolder and not given a damn for the gossips, let them get on with it and say what they liked.

'My mum is a gem, though, and she really did her best to care for Connie. Up until now she's never willingly opened her eyes to what a slimy toad my dad is. By God, there are some evil so-an'-so's in this world, but he takes the biscuit. I may as well tell you now, 'cos sooner or later the whole town will get to know. He forced himself on our Connie.'

Seeing the look of shock on Ella's face, Reg quickly added, 'Oh yes he did, and when you think about it, pestering his own niece in the state she was in was really acting dirty.'

Ella stopped walking and stared at the strapping young man beside her. His eyes looked haunted and he looked far older than he was. She let him go on talking. That was all he needed at the moment, a good listener. It was the only way he would get some of this horror out of his system.

'When I was a kid, I used to have to watch my dad treating Mum so badly 'cos I knew I wasn't a match for him. I could never understand why she stayed with him. Many's the time he's knocked her black and blue. As soon as I could, I left home.' Reg's voice was very tense as he continued. 'But things are different now, and if he so much as shows his face near me again, he's gonna realize that. If he wants to bully anyone, he can 'ave a go at me, and I'll soon put him straight.'

Ella felt such pity for this lad. He might act tough and let everyone think he was streetwise and well able to take care of himself, yet what had happened had knocked him for six. He had been forced to grow up and face reality almost overnight. She didn't know what to say, and was relieved when they reached the club and Reg held the door open for her.

One foot inside the place and Ella pulled a face. There were three times the normal number of customers in the bar and the club was buzzing with a variety of different stories about what had happened to Mr Baldwin.

Ella left Reg to join his mates while she went behind the bar.

'Are we glad to see you, Ella.' Tom spoke for himself and Derrick. 'Haven't had a minute to go down and do any cellar work, an' the way things are going, both the mild and the lager barrels will need changing.'

'If nothing else, gossip about a tragedy is always good for trade.' Derrick grinned at Ella as he hung a towel over an empty pump. 'Will you be OK by yerself till Molly turns up?'

'She's just coming through the double doors now,' Ella told him. 'You two get away, we'll manage all right.'

''Allo, Molly, you're well needed here this morning, the news is all so sad.'

Molly only just managed to sound civil as she said, 'Good morning, Mrs Turner, don't need to ask you what's brought you out for a drink so early in the day.' With that she pushed by and went to join Ella behind the bar.

The two women hugged each other, both on the verge of tears.

'So hard to take it all in, isn't it?' Molly commented. 'And it's so wrong that folk don't all turn out for the best of reasons. There always has to be the street gossip like Nellie Turner.'

'You weren't on yesterday, Molly, so how did you get to hear the news?'

'I went out to do a bit of shopping in the afternoon and the whole street was shocked that Mr Baldwin had died so suddenly, but you know I live opposite the Baldwins', and earlier on I had seen Jack Briggs slumped down half on the pavement and half in what you could call their front way. Wasn't nothing t' do with me, I don't deal with drunks. Then later in the evening a big van draws up, and oh dear, it doesn't bear thinking about.

'Kate and her girls and the aunt got out of the back of the van, and then you never heard such a commotion in all your life. The noise drew me to the window, and hellish it was to see a lovely young man laying into his own father, and him on the ground as it so happened.'

'You mean you actually witnessed Reg giving his father a good hiding?'

The conversation had to be put on hold there. Customers were clamouring to be served and the two barmaids were run off their feet.

'Are there going to be any meals today?' more than one customer wanted to know.

'Do you know if there is?' Molly asked Ella.

'When I came in, Mike told me that Beryl was going to rustle up a few dishes, but so far I haven't even seen so much as a sandwich.'

Ella was concentrating on pulling a pint of Guinness when the creamy flow ceased and all she could get was a hiss and spitting. She could see the top of Mike's head where he stood at the end of the bar, and she shouted, 'Mike, will you call down and tell Tom that the draught Guinness has gone.'

With a few minutes' lull, Molly answered Ella's question.

'Yes, more's the pity, and there was me thinking he was such a nice, kind and considerate lad.'

'I think you got it right first time around, Molly. Anything that was dished out to Jack Briggs would seem to me well and truly deserved.'

'And how would you be knowing that?' Molly asked with a toss of her head.

'Well, from piecing bits of information together, it turns out that he had been making Connie's life a misery every time she was left alone in the house with him. That's why she was on that train coming home. He violently attacked her.' Ella was choked as she wiped tears from her eyes. 'If it hadn't been for that dirty old man, that young girl would never have been on that train and she would still be alive today.'

Molly made the sign of the cross and murmured, 'Holy Mary Mother of God, are you saying that her own uncle raped her?'

'It would seem so. I suppose he thought that since she was under his roof and pregnant, he was entitled to take liberties.'

'Good gracious me!' Molly was appalled. 'This goes from bad to worse.'

'You can say that again,' Ella said as she pulled hard on the pump. At least some things were going right. The Guinness was back to normal, rich and dark with a thick creamy head.

It was a long, tense morning shift and every member of the staff was more than relieved when Mike called, 'Time, gentlemen, please.'

Ella was moving amongst the tables emptying ashtrays, collecting glasses and wiping tabletops when suddenly she had a queer feeling that somebody was watching her.

She raised her head and immediately it was as if she was turned to stone. Her eyes were wide open and staring as if she was seeing a ghost.

For there, leaning against the wall, was her husband.

Chapter Twenty-two

REG BRIGGS HAD NO choice but to get down to the business of making the arrangements for the burying of his cousin and his uncle. His aunt was in no state to make any decisions.

'First off I'm going to get in touch with an undertaker,' he said whilst they were all sitting finishing breakfast.

'I'll come with you,' Amy offered.

'Thanks.' Reg accepted her offer eagerly. 'Wasn't looking forward one bit to going on me own. Before we set out, I think we should make a list, and for that we shall need your help, Aunt Kate.'

'Yes,' said Amy. 'It would be much easier, Mum, if you could let us know what you would like.'

Writing pad and pencil at the ready, the three of them sat around the table.

'Aunt Kate, which undertaker do you think? I don't know this area very well.' Reg lowered his voice every time he spoke to his aunt.

'Well, there's the Ashley brothers, they've always been known to do a decent, respectful funeral.'

'If that's what you want, Mum, though lots of people

prefer cremation these days.' Amy met her mother's angry look without flinching.

'Your father and your sister are getting a Christian burial, so we'll have no talk of cremation if you don't mind,' wailed Kate. 'It makes me feel terrified just thinking about burning people.'

'That's all right, Mum, that's why Reg is making a list, just to be sure we've got everything as you want it to be.'

A short silence followed that outburst until Reg asked, 'Next person to get hold of is a vicar, isn't it? You do want a church service for them both, I presume, and a vicar will be able to advise us on a plot in the cemetery.'

Discussing all the details and being relieved of most of the responsibility made Kate Briggs feel a little better. At least she wasn't on her own. 'Well, there is the Reverend Clifford James. He lives in the vicarage next to the big church behind the market. Can't say as how I've been a regular church-goer, except Monday afternoons for the mothers' meeting – I never miss that – and you were all christened in that church.'

'So the Reverend James knows the family?'

'Yes, slightly, but me mostly 'cos he always looks in of a Monday afternoon and has a cup of tea with us. You can talk to him about hymns, and maybe he will want to know a bit about Connie and your father.'

'That all sounds straightforward enough, Aunt Kate, but seeing as how my Uncle Alf has lived here all his life, don't you think we should put a notice in the local paper?'

'Well, we'll see. But first you've got to get a date for the funeral . . .' Kate Baldwin hesitated. 'Do you think it's necessary to have people come back to our house for a drink and a bite to eat? Some of yer dad's relations we ain't seen for ages, but people do usually travel quite a long way to attend family funerals. Besides, I think perhaps it helps, seeing old friends and relations; you can have a bit of a talk and remember old times, especially when our Connie was a baby. Somehow I think that will take the edge off all the sadness.'

The old-fashioned custom of having a wake had not occurred to Amy, but she thought it made sense. 'Yes, Mum, you're right. We'll organize something. I'm sure a couple of our neighbours will be only too pleased to help out with seeing to the food.'

'Well, that seems to be everything for now, so Amy and I will get going.' Reg got to his feet, folded his written list in half and placed it in his top pocket. 'You'll be all right, Auntie, won't you? Sheila's just put the kettle on; she's gonna make you a nice fresh cup of tea.'

Kate sat sipping her tea. She was still finding it hard to realize that she had lost two of her loved ones.

Suppose I ought to be thinking about flowers. Connie is easy, the prettiest posy that the florist can make. No wreath for her, at least not from her mum. Alf was a different matter altogether. As far as Kate could remember, he had never bought flowers for anyone in his life. Even for close family deaths the buying of the wreaths had been left to her. Alf had always been an honest, hard-working man, a good provider for the essential things in life, but buying flowers would never have entered his head.

Bless him. He shall have some beauties now. I'll go on my own to choose them, she vowed.

The final day had dawned. And that was the trouble.

They had bought two adjoining plots so that father and daughter could lie side by side. When the earth covered the coffins, what could be more final than that?

The narrow London street had never before seen anything like it.

In every house the blinds and curtains had been drawn before the hearse came slowly into view with a second one following closely behind. Each was drawn by grey horses, a black cloth draped across their backs.

All the women mourners were dressed from head to toe in black; each wore a hat stripped of any adornment and replaced by a wide black ribbon. The men had turned out in strength to pay their last respects. They walked tall and upright, smart in their dark suits, white shirts and black ties.

On the pavement men removed their hats and bowed their heads.

No one had set eyes on Jack Briggs since his son had laid into him, and the mourners were more than grateful that he had stayed away. Every member of the family knew they would need all the strength they could muster to get through today.

Kate Baldwin stepped out of her house looking very poised and dignified. As she neared the front gate she raised her head, and her eyes had to gaze on not one but two coffins.

The sad sight was too much.

Her body shook and she released great gulping sobs of pain and would have fallen to the ground had not the strong arms of two male mourners grasped her one each side and helped her into the motor-car.

There would be no harsh words of judgement against young Connie Baldwin. Not today.

Her sins had been well and truly paid for.

Dennis Dryden had suggested that both he and Ella should go to the funeral.

Ella had flatly refused. She was convinced that they would be the last people the Baldwin family would wish to see in the church.

She had sent a card of condolence, really aching inside for poor Kate Baldwin's sorrow, yet unable to find words that would truly express her sympathy.

At last it was all over. Friends had left the house first, and now all the talking between relatives was coming to an end. Reg and Amy, seeing them off, watched the last car disappear and then, with a great feeling of relief, turned and went back into the house.

For once Ella couldn't face serving behind the bar of the working men's club. Not tonight, she told herself over and over again. If some of Mr Baldwin's mates came into the club, all chewing over the facts of what had happened, airing their views out loud, never mind whether they were right or wrong, it would be more than she could stand.

'Please, Mum, go up to the corner telephone box and call Mike for me, will you?'

'And what am I supposed to say to him?'

'Tell him I'm not well, that'll do.'

'No, luv, I'm not gonna do any such thing. Go yourself, tell him the truth. You know darn well Mike will understand. He knows there's been a lot of pressure on you lately.'

Ella reluctantly made the call herself, and as usual her mother was right.

'Ella, you take a couple of days off if you like,' Mike said quickly. 'I should have thought on, it's been pretty rough on you one way and another. We'll see you when you've given yourself time to calm down.'

'Thanks, Mike, you're a good bloke.'

'You're not so bad yerself, Ella,' he said laughing as he replaced the receiver.

Heaving a sigh of relief, Ella came out of the telephone box, and was lost in thought when she saw Dennis. He

200

was standing in the middle of the pavement, blocking her way. When he had turned up in the club they had spoken only a few words to each other and she had made it perfectly clear that that was how she wanted things to remain.

'Ella, please, we need to talk,' he begged. 'Go home, see to the children and then meet me somewhere. That's not too much to ask, is it?' Then he smiled. Nothing had changed. His smile had always been amazing, and it lit up his whole face, causing his brilliant blue eyes to sparkle.

Ella wouldn't admit it even to herself, but her heart was thumping like mad as he took hold of her arm and began to walk beside her.

She felt ill at ease, agitated by this unexpected meeting. She also felt her appearance was not up to scratch. Today having been so sad, she had not bothered to really do her hair nor to put any make-up on her face. There was, however, nothing she could do about it until she got home. Her feelings were made worse because he looked every inch a very successful man. Tall, broad-shouldered, wearing a dark suit that had obviously been handmade by an excellent tailor. He hadn't altered in that respect. Nothing but the best for Den.

He said, 'Is there anywhere you'd prefer to go this evening?'

'Do you really want to talk civilly and seriously to me?' she asked him doubtfully.

'I wouldn't be here if I didn't.'

'Haven't you anything better to do?'

'Like what?'

'Some dodgy deal to fix or someone's palm to grease so that you make sure you get a contract you're after.'

'Oh, please, Ella, you're not going to start all that again, are you?'

Ella smiled at him icily. 'Why not? You're not going to

201

try and convince me that you've changed that much, surely?'

'You're determined not to give me a chance, aren't you?'

'Can you blame me?'

'No.' He shook his head, accepting this.

She said, 'I must go home. Mum will be wondering what to give the kids for their tea.'

'Will you come out for the evening if I pick you up about half seven?'

She did not reply at once, and for a long moment Dennis thought she was going to refuse.

Then she smiled. 'All right.'

'Good. I'll take you somewhere nice, we'll 'ave a slap-up meal and then we can talk. Get down to brass tacks.'

Ella laughed bitterly as she said, 'A posh invitation from my own old man; I'd better spend some time putting on the powder and the paint. We can't have folk saying you've lost yer touch, Den, taking an old bird like me out on the town.'

They looked at each other and suddenly they dissolved into laughter, and Ella felt her heart grow lighter, because it was the first time they had laughed together for a very long time.

Had she done the right thing, agreeing to go out for a meal with Dennis tonight? So much water had passed under the bridge.

While her mother cooked tea, Ella sat looking through the children's homework with them, but her heart wasn't it. When young Connie Baldwin had died she had vowed that she never wanted to see Dennis ever again, mainly because of the upheaval he had caused in the lives of their children.

Seeing him today had reminded her of just how much she had missed him.

When she got into bed at night she would read a book for quite some time. On other occasions she would lie awake and remind herself that Dennis had buggered off and left her with two young children and more often than not without a regular income. First off, life without him had been so empty, but with the help of her mother and Sadie Cohan, she had found the strength and the determination to turn her life around. She was much more independent, dressed differently, looked different, and indeed she was a wholly different person. She was proud of the fact that she had pulled herself together, got a job and become independent.

With the light out and the house quiet, the big double bed seemed so empty, and she would be lying to herself if she didn't admit that she missed Dennis. There had been some wonderful times in the early years of their marriage. Then Den had changed, become Jack-the-lad, and family life didn't matter any more.

It was a big world out there, deals were there for the taking, and Dennis had made sure he got his share of what was on offer, whether by fair means or foul.

Ella spent a great deal of time getting ready. First she rubbed her hair with a scented oil that Sadie had told her to buy, then she brushed it hard until her arm ached. By the time she had put the bulk of it up into a French pleat and left tendrils to dangle across her forehead and down over her ears, she was well pleased with the result. It was glossy and the chestnut glints shone through. She had decided to wear a plain black dress that ran straight from the shoulders down to her calves. It had a square neckline and long chiffon sleeves. To the left-hand shoulder of the dress she fixed a sparkling emerald-green brooch. Sheer silk stockings and high-heeled court shoes gave the finishing touches.

Since Ella had worked at the British Legion, she had become a dab hand at putting on her make-up, and the result this evening was almost professional.

'Mum, how do I look?' Ella gave a little twirl and Babs exclaimed, 'Smashing,' while even Teddy said, 'Wow.'

Winnie was more cautious. 'You're living dangerously, if you ask me. I just don't want to see you hurt again, but your mind is your own. You make yer own decisions.'

Ella didn't answer her mother, because if she had done, she would have said, 'That's exactly what I intend to do.'

As she stepped out of the front door, she was struck at how wintry the weather had turned. It had been a dingy, cloudy day, but at least it had stayed dry for the funeral. Now it was a cold evening, with a strong wind blowing in from the river, and she was thankful that her mother had loaned her a white cashmere stole which she was aware looked very elegant draped around her shoulders. She smiled softly to herself. This stole must have come into her mother's possession via Sadie; they both had a lot to thank the Cohan family for.

Dennis had knocked at the door and then gone back to sit in his car. The minute Ella appeared, he was out like a shot and holding the front passenger door open for her. The first thing that struck her was that he had a different car, and when thoughts began to run through her head as to why he might have decided to change cars, she immediately told herself it was none of her business. Tonight of all nights she was not going to allow herself, or Dennis for that matter, to start raking over old coals.

'You look great, Ella, so different,' said Dennis.

All the effort had been worth while. At least he had noticed.

As soon as she was seated in the car, Dennis offered a travelling rug to lay across her knees.

'Thank you, Dennis,' she said, surprised.

'On our way then,' he said, turning the key in the ignition.

Ella watched the narrow streets and soot-stained buildings disappear, and soon the car had crossed the Thames and they were driving through Fulham. Once they had passed the great power station the whole outlook changed. There were terraces of tall houses, and trees growing along the pavements.

'Where are we going?' Ella felt compelled to ask.

Dennis grinned. 'To Crystal Palace.' Then he turned his head and, seeing Ella's look of astonishment, added, 'To Norwood actually.'

The only thing that Ella knew about Norwood was that it wasn't far from Croydon.

Den looked at her, and laughed at her expression of bewilderment.

'Up an' coming place this side of the river is going to be in the near future,' Dennis said with conviction. 'Bomb damage, decaying buildings and dilapidation in general have not been dealt with quick enough. Now things are on the move, redevelopment is going ahead fast.'

Ella caught on quickly. 'And you've submitted plans, bargained with a few men in the know and grabbed some very nice contracts for yourself.'

'I wouldn't put it exactly like that,' Den said anxiously, 'but in the main you're right. I have got work permits and contracts, which means I can offer jobs to a good many blokes.'

Ella felt herself go tense. 'Good Samaritan as always,' she said sarcastically, 'but you won't be breaking yer own back, will you, Den?'

'Come now, Ella,' Den wheedled, 'the piper calls the tune, and the conductor of an orchestra is in charge of the baton. Anyway, you should feel proud. In a few minutes we shall be passing some very high hoardings enclosing a site where I have thirty men working, an' you can take it from me, they are all good craftsmen.'

'Good for you,' Ella muttered, but inside she was seething.

Not one question about Babs or Teddy. For twelve years he had been around for young Teddy, and for eight years for Babs. How could he suddenly stop loving them? Almost shutting them completely out of his life. With all that had happened, didn't he ever have feelings of guilt? Ella spent as much time with them as she could. She did feel that she was a good mother, the three of them bound tightly in a mother–child relationship, yet nothing she could say or do could compensate for them having no father around. She had to work; flush as Dennis made out he was, they hadn't set eyes on him for ages, and she could not rely on him giving her a regular income. She worried that there was less time for her to devote to her children, and every day she thanked God that her mother was around. Without her, she didn't know how she would cope.

She remembered that it wasn't so long ago that she had been fat and miserable, knowing that life was passing her by and that she was obsessive about her children. Now she had a good paid job she worried that she was neglecting them. Why did life have to be so full of problems?

In the car the silence was heavy now. Neither of them seemed to want to talk and Ella was pleased when Dennis drove into a small car park. It was well dark by now and there weren't many people about. He came quickly around to the passenger door, opened it and helped her out of the car.

Ella looked around with interest. This was a very nice-looking place, but exactly what it was was hard for her to tell. It could be a classy pub, or a smart restaurant, or even a club of sorts. The gardens surrounding the building were well tended and the building itself was lit with fancy lanterns.

Dennis held out his arm to Ella and she hooked her hand through his elbow as they walked up the steep flight of steps that led to the front entrance. Reaching the top, they had to part and enter in single file because there were revolving doors.

They went inside to a luxurious entrance hall and Ella was at once conscious of the smell of mouth-watering food. She hardly had time to loosen her stole before a giant of a man appeared from nowhere and with something of a flourish wrapped his arms around Dennis.

Ella looked on in astonishment. Next moment the two of them were slapping each other on the back. It was minutes before Dennis introduced the man as Jeff Anderson, quickly adding, 'He owns the place.' Then he winked, and both men threw back their heads and laughed. 'Even if he did only pull off the deal by the skin of his teeth.' This remark was for Ella's benefit.

Suddenly Dennis playfully punched Jeff's arm and said, 'God, you were a lucky bastard.'

'Don't I know it.' Jeff grinned. 'But you don't do so bad yourself, Den boy. Case of the devil looks after his own, eh?'

When he finally turned to Ella he said, 'Good evening, Mrs Dryden, I am so pleased that Dennis has persuaded you to accompany him tonight.' This big man had a soft, almost gentle voice, but Ella couldn't stop herself from thinking that he must be the most ugly man she had ever encountered. His bruiser's face was like that of a pug dog. At some time he had certainly broken his nose. Apart from his face, though, he looked great. He was immaculately turned out, and his huge frame suited the evening suit he was wearing down to a tee.

'Bar first or straight into the dining room?' Jeff asked.

'We'll eat first.' Dennis answered for the pair of them. 'Got some serious talking to do.'

'Fine, your table is ready,' Jeff said as he led the way.

Sliding glass doors led into the large dining room, with beamed ceiling and red flock wallpaper. The tables were set with starched white cloths and folded white serviettes. There were red candles in glass bowls and vases of fresh flowers on each table, and in a huge fireplace big logs burnt slowly, giving the room a warm glow. Most of the tables were occupied.

As Ella hesitated, Jeff snapped his fingers and a waiter appeared and led them to the one set in the bay window, which stood empty.

'Enjoy your meal, I'll see you later,' Jeff said, but Ella felt that he was only talking to Dennis, not to her.

'Thanks, mate,' Den said as Jeff slapped him heartily on the back.

When they were seated and studying the long menus, Dennis leant across the table and said to Ella, 'Don't let Jeff's looks put you off. He's a great bloke. Provided you don't upset him, of course.'

The waiter appeared again with an ice bucket from which he took a bottle. He wiped the outside and presented it so that Dennis could read the label. 'Fine,' was all that Dennis said, but Ella heard what the waiter had whispered to her husband as he took away their menus. Apparently their meal was not to be of their choice. Jeff Anderson had laid everything on for them in advance.

Ella hadn't realized just how hungry she was, and never in her whole life had she eaten such delicious food. They had got through four courses and two bottles of wine before the table was set with coffee and a cheeseboard that offered a great variety.

Ella was pouring cream into her coffee when Dennis said, 'I have a great deal of explaining to do, don't I?'

She stopped dead and stared at him coldly. 'I'd say that's putting it mildly.'

He had the guts to look guilty. 'I have a proposition to put to you. You don't have to answer me tonight, but Ella, please don't take for ever making up your mind.'

She stared at him in disbelief. Finally she said wearily, 'OK, let's hear it.'

'I want us to put the past behind us and start again, even if it is only for the sake of the kids.'

'Hmm, that's rich coming from you. You haven't given a damn about Teddy or Babs, not when things were going your way. Now when yer past has caught up with you and folk don't think of you as the great I am any more, you want to come crawling back to me.'

Dennis put his coffee cup down with a clatter.

'Hold yer bloody horses, Ella, and let me outline what I think would work a treat for all of us as a family. You've got to take up a bit of the slack as well as me, though. You've got to agree to move out of that decrepit old house where the streets are so narrow and all you women do is wage an endless struggle against the dirt and grime. I can offer you the choice of several houses, all this side of the river, where life is so much better and cleaner and there are good schools for the kids. We could make a fresh start.'

'How come you're suddenly concerned with the welfare of your own children?' she asked him coolly.

Dennis glared at her. 'Ella, I'll take you home now. We don't want a slanging match here. All I ask is that you give some thought to what I am asking of you. You can pick the house and the district, I can't say fairer than that.'

Ella rose and was about to drape her stole around her shoulders, but Den had different ideas. He settled her down in a beautifully furnished lounge and told her he would send a drink in to her. He had a bit of business to settle with Jeff and wouldn't be long.

Another drink was the last thing that Ella wanted. She left it untouched.

Sunk in the depths of a squashy, comfortable armchair, she let her thoughts run wild. Yes, she had had a wonderful evening, but it just wasn't real life. But then that was her Den. He was larger than life. He had amazing energy and ambition. She was well aware he hadn't altered.

Probably never would.

He would still be impossible to live with, still totally selfish, and when he couldn't get his own way, would he still be ruthless? She didn't have to think for long before deciding that she was not willing to take that chance. What he was suggesting was a total upheaval of her and the children's lives, and once set into motion there would be no going back. With Den's track record she would be mad to take such a chance.

It was midnight before they finally set out for home. When he drew the car to a halt outside her house he made no attempt to invite himself in, a fact for which Ella was grateful. Instead, he took her arm as they walked across the pavement and said, 'I'm going to be fairly tied up during the next two weeks, but promise me you'll think about what I've said.'

'All right, I'll think about it,' she said. Mainly because she was feeling so tired she wasn't able to think straight.

'Good, let's hope we've made a bit of headway tonight.' He put his hands on her shoulders and stooped to kiss her cheek. 'Good night, Ella, you're so much more like the girl I married now,' he whispered.

Pity I can't say the same about you, was what she was thinking as she went indoors and straight up the stairs to her bedroom. As she undressed and got into bed, she sighed. She had so much to think about.

She didn't get much sleep that night.

Chapter Twenty-three

FESTIVITIES PLANNED FOR THE opening night of the new extension of the British Legion premises had been put on hold. The death of Mr Baldwin and his daughter had affected so many people that Mike had felt it wouldn't be right. He had made his decision out of respect, and members of the club were in complete agreement.

However, life had to go on.

The first Saturday evening in November had been decided upon, and now, finally, the day had arrived.

Although the club did not open until six, every member of staff was assembled in the foyer by four o'clock in the afternoon. Mike did the honours and swung open the double doors. Looking around, he saw that there wasn't an employee who did not have a smile of satisfaction on their face.

And no wonder, the hall was really a sight to behold. Everything that they had been led to expect had been done, and more. A gleaming chandelier hung from the centre of the ceiling. There were discreet wall lights, a marvellous sprung wooden floor, rich, heavy curtains at the windows, a huge wide stage which could be enclosed by fringed velvet curtains. Many small tables each with four chairs were positioned around the walls, but for tonight only there was a head table which was set up for a party of twelve. All the bigwigs from the committee, who had had hardly anything at all to do with this venture, except perhaps sign the cheques, would be here in force.

The food would be exceptional, as would the dresses their lady wives would be wearing. Their jewellery would certainly glitter, because it was a dead cert it would be the real thing.

But all that was to come later.

Mike and Sam Richardson each opened a bottle of champagne and passed a filled glass to everyone. Then Mike broke their stunned silence by saying, 'Before we raise our glasses and toast the new future, I would like to say a few words. Thanks to everyone for their help and support during the whole time that this work has been going on. The architect did a marvellous job with the planning, but the man who has had to battle with the committee, coax and sometimes even twist their arms in order to secure enough funds for the work to be completed is Sam.'

Ella was standing next to Sam, and on hearing him praised like this, she took hold of his hand and squeezed it hard.

He rewarded her with a dazzling smile.

Mike hadn't quite finished his speech. 'I think the end has proved to justify the means. However, tonight is just the beginning. We'll let the committee have their moment of pomp and glory . . .' he paused, 'but remember, it is only a few weeks away from Christmas, and then they can say what they like. This is a working men's club, and over the holiday, we and our members will show them that good times can be had here. Right?'

'Right,' everyone chorused.

'OK.' He raised his glass. 'Here's to us who work here, our members who support us, and an enjoyable evening.'

Ella had never tasted champagne before and was unprepared for the bubbles that tickled her nose. But she soon found that she quite liked the taste and it wasn't long before she was holding out her glass to Sam for a refill.

The Legion had been granted an extension until midnight.

The place was packed, but both Molly and Ella were enjoying themselves just as much as the customers were.

Mike had booked a wonderful band, and early on in the evening they had watched the posh visitors dancing in a way they had never seen before in their lives and probably never would again. Working-class folk didn't do the tango!

The whole place was jam-packed. A lot of alcohol was being drunk and a lot of money was being spent.

'Now you've seen how the other half live,' Mike joked as he removed piles of notes and put more change into the tills which stood behind the bar.

Even with all that was going on, every now and again Ella found herself looking amongst the crowds to see if Dennis had turned up. He had said that he was going to be tied up for two weeks, but that after that he would be in touch, and that he hoped she would have given a lot of thought to the plans he had suggested. That had been more than a month ago, and no one had seen hide nor hair of him. Even his father denied knowing where he was.

Ah well, she sighed, at least he had taken her out and been charming to her for one evening. The ideas he had laid out for her to consider had been going round and round in her head. As he had talked, she had wondered, was a second chance possible? Could a family life be recaptured? According to Dennis it could be! She was doubtful. It would take some effort for her to be able to feel that she could really trust Dennis again. Part of her wanted to. Yet there were so many ifs and buts.

He had talked about setting up a new home, and how much better it would be for the children if they were together again as a family, yet not once had he asked to see Babs or Teddy. How could a father act like that?

She couldn't answer her own question.

When the band went off for their refreshment, the entertainment began. This was for adults only; the humour was a bit near the bone, but the stunts the comics pulled were side-splitting.

Members of the committee thought now was a good time for them to leave. Which was just as well. With them gone, folk could let their hair down and really start to enjoy themselves.

The top table was cleared of china and glasses, the tablecloths were folded, and the three trestle tables which had been joined together were dismantled, leaving much more space for dancing in the hall. The band came back on stage and the music altered, because the musicians caught the mood of the crowd and began to play a Latin American tune known locally as the conga.

Within minutes, women were pulling their men to their feet, insisting that they put their arms around the waist of the person in front, thus linking everybody together. A long single file was formed which moved forward in time to the music, the dancers making a series of steps and side-kicks. Up and down and round the hall they danced, like a human snake. Hardly a soul was left sitting down.

Then came the sing-song. 'My ol' man said follow the van', 'There's my gal, up in the gallery', 'She is my lily and my rose'. And of course no evening would be complete without 'Knees up Mother Brown'.

Ella couldn't stop herself from laughing as she watched her mother and most of their neighbours out there in the centre of the floor. Using both hands, they were holding their skirts up high and their legs were being nimbly worked up and down. Such high jinks had never before been seen in this club.

Come tomorrow half of them would be complaining about the aches and pains they'd all got.

Neither Molly nor Ella was entirely sorry when the lights were dimmed and the band played, 'Who's taking you home tonight?'. It was a joy to watch young and old couples alike, dancing the waltz and softly singing, 'Please let it be me.'

Then Mike called time.

Every member of staff had been worked to death, but the unanimous decision was that it had been a great night.

The place looked as if a bomb had hit it. However, everyone mucked in with the clearing-up, including Mike and Sam. Derrick said he'd run Molly home and Sam offered Ella a lift in his car, for which she was more than grateful. She couldn't wait to kick her shoes off.

When Sam stopped his car outside her house, it was almost two o'clock in the morning. He slid from the driver's seat and hurried round to open the passenger door.

'Thanks, Sam, I don't think me legs would have carried me home,' Ella said as she held out her hand to him. 'Thanks again.'

He took her hand between his own. 'It's certainly been a night to remember. It's been a long time since I've enjoyed myself so much.'

'You wanna ask Mike t' give you a job behind the bar,' Ella joked.

'I might just do that.' He laughed. 'Go in now, it's far

215

too cold to be hanging about. Got your key? I'll wait here until 'I see you safely inside.'

Oh, he's a nice man, Ella said to herself as she heard his car drive away. What a pity Charlotte had died so young.

I wonder why he never remarried.

Chapter Twenty-four

THE WORKING MEN'S CLUB was even more popular since the new hall had been added, especially at weekends, though weekdays it was used for darts matches, quizzes and board games.

Early one evening Sam Richardson came behind the bar to remove the till rolls and replace them with fresh ones. He noticed that Ella was looking despondent, most unusual for her.

'You all right, Ella? Or are things getting on top of you?' he asked.

'No, I'm managing,' she said patiently, then smiled and added, 'Well, just about.'

'Nonsense,' he replied. 'Here at the Legion everyone agrees you do the job so well you might have been born to it. Is it your children, are you coping with them all right?'

'Yes, my kids are smashing, it's their ruddy father, he must think they live on fresh air, and as for clothing and footwear, Teddy would have the arse out of his trousers and be running around bare-footed if it were left to Dennis.'

Sam felt embarrassed but he forced himself to say, 'Feeling the pinch, eh? Den should be giving you a regular allowance.'

'Dennis should be doing a lot more than he does,' she said resentfully.

'Have you given any thought to consulting a solicitor? You shouldn't have to work all the hours that you do. The courts would assess your husband's income and then stipulate how much he should be paying you each week. Naturally they would take into account that you are bringing up two children on your own.'

If Sam wasn't being so serious, Ella would have laughed out loud.

Sam Richardson lived in a different world to the rest of the folk around here. He might not realize it, but he had just made the biggest joke of the year! Whoever tried to work out what Dennis's yearly income was would have their work cut out. He never let his right hand know what his left hand was doing!

Den's whole working life had never been anything but bent. Schemes and scams, that was his life. Even if she were brave enough to get that far and a court order was made against Den, the chances of him paying regularly were nil, she thought furiously.

She had to get off this subject. Her pride wouldn't allow her to tell Sam the true state of affairs. It was bad enough that some weeks she had to accept money from her own mother, and she knew full well that when the coalman came Winnie ordered him to put an extra two hundredweight into her coal shed and paid him the difference.

Her father-in-law still came round, and he was always generous to the children regarding pocket money, but she supposed that he thought that because she was employed full time at the working men's club she had sufficient means to get by on. When he came for the odd Sunday roast dinner, that her mother cooked so well, he would always leave a couple of pound notes on the table. God knows how far he thought a couple of quid went.

Sam was looking at her, showing concern, and she hoped he wasn't able to read her thoughts.

'I'd like more time to spend with Babs and Teddy, of course I would.' She forced herself to smile. 'Without my mum to take them out and keep an eye on them, they wouldn't fare half so well. I feel guilty and I'm always telling myself it isn't possible to go out to work and still be a good mother.'

Sam felt he wanted to take her in his arms, but instantaneous actions like that weren't in his nature. Instead he said, 'Now, Ella, you know that's not true. It is defeatist talk and that is not like you.'

Ella gritted her teeth. 'It is the truth. And as for going to court to get regular money out of Dennis, I'd be banging my head up against a brick wall,' she answered with a touch of sarcasm.

Sam looked thoughtful. 'Well, any time you need to talk, you know I'm here two or three times a week and Mike has my firm's telephone number. Meanwhile you take care, Ella.'

'Careful has become my middle name,' Ella said, and Sam could hear the bitterness in her voice.

He bagged up the till rolls. 'See you soon, then,' he said.

Although Ella was not aware of it, Sam had a great respect for her and the way she was handling this different kind of life that she had been forced into through no fault of her own. There was a lot he would like to do for her, but she was another man's wife and there was always the fact that her two children needed both a father and a mother.

*   *   *

The first few days of December came in with high winds and a raw coldness that ate into a body's bones.

The first snowflakes started to fall as Ella and the children stepped out of the front door, and Babs laughed with delight. Clapping her hands, she yelled, 'Lovely, smashing, will it lie and get thick on the ground, Mum?'

'We won't know until you wake up tomorrow morning, pet.'

'I hope it does.' Babs spread out her hands, trying to catch the falling flakes. 'They look so pretty, like someone is spreading loads of duck feathers.'

'Hang on, Ella, I'm coming shopping with you.'

Ella turned her head and was not the least bit surprised to see her mother coming along the road, walking sprightly and dressed as smartly as ever. On her head she was wearing a fur hat which exactly matched the collar of her coat. Ella hadn't seen this outfit before and immediately she smiled as the thought sprang into her mind. My mother's paid another sly visit to Sadie and Isaac.

As soon as the four of them reached the market, Ella said, 'Mum, don't go buying a load of gifts. We've already got quite a lot stacked away and the children will be over the moon when they see their presents, no matter what they get.'

Ella had spoken quite sharply to her mother as they trudged between the stalls.

'All right, all right.' Winnie stopped to take a deep breath. 'You worry about yerself and leave me to do my bit. It would be nice if you told me who was going to be with us for Christmas Day.'

'Well, I've already told Ted that he's more than welcome, and he has accepted, though I did think he might have said he was going to spend the holiday with Dennis. I've also asked Mr Parsons and old Mrs Bristow just for dinner, seeing as they both live alone and don't seem to have any relatives. Then there's Mary Marsh and her two kids, Lenny and Vicky. I've had them every Christmas since Bill Marsh was killed when he crashed his lorry; can't leave them out now, can I? Besides, Vicky and Babs get on well and Lenny often plays football with our Teddy, so they'll be good company for each other.'

Winnie heaved a sigh. 'You know what, Ella, you're a glutton for punishment. I make that about ten that'll be sitting round your table again this Christmas.'

'Better than being sad and lonely, ain't it, Mum?'

'Course it is, luv, and don't for a moment think that I'm knocking you, 'cos I'm not. If you really want to know what I think, you're a saint, and I know everyone you invite will appreciate it.' To herself she was saying, Pity that bloody husband of hers doesn't wake himself up a bit and realize what a good woman my Ella is.

'So you approve of our guest list then?' Ella was smiling broadly.

'Yes, just glad that you've told me. I must get a little gift for everyone, wouldn't want to leave anyone out when handing out the presents, especially Mary Marsh's two little 'uns.'

They shopped for the week's food but also added quite a few items that would end up being gaily wrapped and given as gifts.

'How about we go into the café by the bus garage an' 'ave a cuppa now. Babs and Teddy might like a bowl of soup and we could have a hot meat pie,' Winnie suggested. 'Being Saturday, don't suppose you'll get much of a break later on, will you?'

'I don't think I can spare the time. I've all this shopping to put away when we get home and I mustn't be late for work,' Ella moaned.

'Oh shut up and think of yourself for once in yer life. Half an hour isn't going to make that much difference.'

221

Ella found herself laughing as her mother used her backside to push open the door to the café.

Once they were seated, Cliff, the part-owner of the place, came through carrying two great mugs of steaming tea.

'What, run out of cups and saucers, 'ave yer?' Winnie asked cheekily.

Cliff put his hands on his hips and acted as though he were offended. 'Ladies, if you hadn't noticed, the market is extra busy today with the run-up to Christmas, and me and Eddie have been run off our feet. The food is still good and the drinks are hot, but there's no time for niceties.'

Mother and daughter looked at each other but found it hard to conceal their amusement.

Winnie said, 'It's all right, Cliff, you know I was only kidding.'

Clifford tossed his head and brushed a strand of hair from his forehead. 'You don't really mind a mug, do you?'

'Not so long as you ain't charging us extra 'cos it's bigger than a cup,' Winnie couldn't resist teasing him.

To tell the truth, she thought the world of Clifford and his partner, Edward. They ran a good clean café, and as he said, the food was always very good. Their private lives were their own business.

Clifford turned to face Ella and raised his eyebrows. 'As if we haven't got enough on our plate today, why did you have to bring your mother in?'

''Cos we've all got a cross to bear and she sticks t' me like glue,' Ella said, giving Clifford a sly wink.

'Oh don't mind me, I'll order me food, keep me mouth shut and pretend that I didn't hear the two of you slagging me off,' Winnie said huffily.

Cliff put his arm across Winnie's shoulders and pulled her close, saying, 'You know you're one of my favourite customers. Didn't I bring you a hot drink the minute you walked through the door? Now decide what you all want to eat and I'll be back in a minute. Hot chocolate for you two, is it?'

'Yes please,' Teddy and Babs chorused. For a moment there they had been afraid their gran was going to have a go at Clifford, and had breathed out when they realized that no one was in a bad temper, it was all just a bit of a daft game. Adults seemed to like to goad one another now and again.

Minutes later, when Cliff returned to take their order, Ella was quick to say, 'Make it steak and kidney pie for all four of us, please, Cliff.'

Quietness reigned as they tucked into their meals. Winnie was the first to clear her plate and for a few minutes she was quiet as she drank the remainder of her tea. Then, looking across at her daughter, she asked, 'So is ten the final number that's going to be sitting round your table for Christmas dinner?'

Ella looked puzzled. 'Do you think that I've left somebody off my list?'

'It's up to you, but I didn't think you'd be inviting Ted round this year, not taking into account the way his son's treated you.'

'Oh Mum, you can hardly blame Ted for what Dennis has done.'

Ella's face was blank for a moment. It was a hard job trying to please everyone. Having gathered her thoughts together, she decided to be straight with her mother.

'I might just as well tell you now; you'll get it out of me one way or another, you always do. The truth of the matter is, Ted has offered to pay for the turkey and to bring a good supply of drinks. I could 'ardly not invite him. Besides, the kids think the world of him, and no matter what happens between Dennis and me, Ted will always be their grandfather. There's also another point to consider: you can bet your life he's spent pounds on presents for them. Much more than I can afford.'

'All right, no need to get shirty with me, but I still have to ask, what about Dennis?'

Ella was thankful that the children had gone off to the toilets. She had enough to contend with without them listening to this conversation.

The silence that followed was intense until Winnie tut-tutted. 'You're on about Ted being their grandfather; Dennis is the children's father,' she stated loudly.

'It's a pity no one has thought to remind him of that fact during the months he's chosen to stay away.'

'Well, you went out with him for the evening recently, an' at this time of the year you can't ask his father and leave Dennis out in the cold.'

'Can't I? When he dropped me off he said he'd be back in two weeks. Obviously he's lost track of time.'

'Give him a little credit, Ella. I know him an' me 'ave never got on, but I think he's trying to put the past right. According to what I heard, he paid for the funeral arrange-ments for both Connie and Alf Baldwin.'

'Oh, and that makes everything all right, does it?' Sarcasm was well to the fore in Ella's voice. 'Put money on the table and it will solve everything. All can be forgiven and forgotten. Is that what you're saying, Mum? 'Cos I hardly think Mrs Baldwin will agree with you.'

'You know darn well that's not what I'm saying,' Winnie retorted angrily.

'I should hope not. He hasn't exactly come back cap in hand. Besides, explain to me how a man can walk out on his wife and two kiddies he swears he adores, never see them for weeks on end, and send only a few quid now and again when the thought occurs to him that they might need money to live on. Every man has his faults, but Dennis has enough for a regiment of soldiers. Have you forgotten Connie Baldwin and the reason he left us in the first place, Mum?'

'No, I haven't forgotten Connie, bless her heart, she was a fool to herself. I'm sorry to say, though, Ella, the beginning of all this trouble was partly yer own fault. You wouldn't move out of the East End.'

'Rubbing salt in the wounds now, are you, Mum? Anyhow, since you know so much, tell me where Dennis is living now and who he's living with, 'cos his father swears on oath that Dennis is not staying at his place,'

Winnie shook her head. 'Nobody seems to know. One of you 'as got to make the first move, but God help us I don't think it will be you, Ella, you're too stubborn.'

'You're dead right there, Mother. Dennis made the decision to leave. I was too old and too fat for his liking. He went off with what was little more than a schoolgirl, and you wanna start thinking about the heartaches that followed.'

Winnie sat there silent and gloomy until Ella decided enough was enough. Not for the world would she upset her mother, but she was not going to take the blame for her family being split up.

'Maybe Dennis did me a good turn leaving me on me own like that. Because now I'm independent, I'm slimmer, I earn my own living and I've proved I can exist without him.'

'You're pretty good at singing yer own praises, I'll give you that,' her mother said stubbornly.

'Yeah, well, since we're talking home truths, the way Den treated young Connie didn't do much for his reputation, did it? I am truly sorry that she died. She was so young. But perhaps it's just as well that the baby wasn't born. Do you think Dennis would have been a good father to it? 'Cos judging by the way he's treated his son and daughter, I wouldn't have put my money on it.'

225

It was just as well that at that moment the conversation was cut short by the return of Babs and Teddy. Both children were smiling as they licked away at orange ice lollies.

'Where did you get them from?' their mother asked.

Teddy lowered his lolly and cheekily said, 'Clifford gave them to us, 'cos he said we had been on our best behaviour.'

Their mother and grandmother looked at each other and laughed loudly. As they gathered up their bags of shopping and got ready to leave the café, Winnie patted Teddy on the head and said, 'You should have told him, Teddy, handsome is as handsome does.'

Chapter Twenty-five

ALTHOUGH THE WEATHER REMAINED bitterly cold, the snow did not settle, much to Babs's disappointment.

'Never mind,' her mother said, 'there's still time for us to have a white Christmas.'

Pulling on her long tweed coat and wrapping a long scarf twice around her neck, Ella was ready to set off for work.

'I'll probably see you later on tonight, won't I, Mum?' she said to Winnie. 'Janey is coming in as usual, and her mother has said she can sleep here tonight as I'll be late getting home. There's still room for you, though, if you come to the Legion for a drink and want t' come home with me. You know how the kids love to wake up and find you here.'

'All right, I probably will do that,' her mother said gratefully. She hated Saturday evenings if she stayed indoors on her own.

So, Ella thought now as she walked to work, my mother thinks I should try harder to find out where Dennis is and invite him for Christmas, but I don't see it that way.

Good job she didn't come out with that daft suggestion in front of the kids; they'd have been all for it and I'd never have heard the last of it. On the evening that Dennis had taken her out to dinner, she had wavered half-heartedly in her attitude towards him. For a while during their meal she had felt safe and peaceful. It had been good to have him for company, more so because he was making a great effort to be charming.

Somehow he had made himself irresistible, coaxing her into believing that there was at least half a chance they could get back together again. For all his assurances, from that day to this she hadn't heard a word from him.

He leads a good life and outwardly has all the trappings of a successful businessman, and he doesn't give a toss for me and the kids. He makes promises that he has no intention of keeping; well, I've got used to it now, and if that's what he wants, it's fine by me. Just fine. At least I know where I stand.

So intent was she on her thoughts that she didn't notice Sam standing across the other side of the road until he called her name. Then she turned and he was there in front of her. Mostly she only ever saw him in the club; outside in the street on this winter's day he looked different. He was a strikingly handsome man, and for the first time she noticed his vivid clear green eyes. He was tall, though not as tall as Dennis, and neither did he carry the weight that Dennis did. A sudden thought struck her. Why was she comparing him with Dennis? Why not? God alone knew where Dennis was, but Sam was here and now.

His dark overcoat was of good quality and his shoes were highly polished black leather, but what made her smile to herself was the fact that he was wearing a bowler hat. Den wouldn't be seen dead in a bowler!

'Morning, Ella, let's get you inside the club. You'll freeze to death standing here.' Then he paused. 'That is, unless you've got time for a coffee before you start work.'

'Isn't Mike expecting you?' she queried.

'No, I rarely come to the club on Saturdays unless there is something special on, but I will make an exception today if you don't want to go to a tearoom.'

Ella was tempted and very surprised. Why not? she asked herself. Besides, he did look forlorn, even lonely.

She had to swallow hard before she could answer. In as natural a voice as she could manage she said quickly, 'I'd love a hot drink, but could I have tea? I don't like coffee much.'

Sam chuckled as he took her hand and looped it through the crook of his arm. Suddenly he looked younger and a great deal happier.

It was a cosy little café to which he took her. Well known to Ella and her mother because from time to time they treated themselves to a toasted teacake and a pot of tea. That was exactly what Ella ordered for herself now, while Sam decided on a coffee and two rounds of toast.

Ella didn't feel exactly at ease. Talk to him, she urged herself. About anything. Don't just sit here like some dummy, for goodness' sake.

That was what her brain was telling her to do, but she was utterly tongue-tied. They had finished eating and Sam ordered another coffee for himself, but Ella insisted that there was enough tea left in her pot.

It was with some effort but not much thought that she finally said, 'Won't be long until Christmas.'

It was a stupid remark seeing that the tearoom had Christmas decorations everywhere, and outside several strings of decorative lights had been hung from one side of the road to the other.

Quickly, to cover up her embarrassment, she tried to sound interested as she asked, 'What are you doing for the holiday?'

His forehead wrinkled. 'Nothing much.' Then he added, 'I mostly remember the first and only Christmas that Lottie and I had together; that's one thing to be grateful for, no one can take your memories away from you, but I still feel guilty.'

'Why on earth should you feel guilty?'

'Because Lottie died and I'm still alive.'

Ella felt even more uncomfortable. Trust her to have put her foot in it! She and Dennis had been at Sam and Charlotte's wedding, and then Charlotte had died within the year. It all seemed so unfair, because the pair of them had been so much in love and they would have made such wonderful parents.

'Oh, Sam.' She didn't know what to say or do. Had he been blaming himself all these years? Suddenly an idea hit her and she blurted it out. 'Sam, come to me for Christmas.' The enormity of what she had just said caused her to add, 'That's if you can put up with me kids, they can be pretty noisy at the best of times. But you wouldn't be my only visitor, there will be my mum, you know her pretty well, and two other men, one is a neighbour and Ted, my father-in-law, you know, so you wouldn't be amongst strangers.' After that long declaration Ella had to stop to draw breath.

He stared at her, too taken aback to try to hide his feelings. Since they had met up again he had tried to pluck up the courage to ask Ella to go out for a meal with him. Mike had known of his intentions and had contrived to bring the pair of them together. There were several reasons why he had hung back, the main one being he had got the impression that Ella still had feelings for Den. After all, no matter what had happened, he was still her husband and the father of her two children.

Nevertheless, there weren't many days when Ella had not been in his thoughts. She was a kind and thoughtful lady. One who hadn't sat about and moaned at the bad luck that fate had thrown at her. Instead she had buckled down, got herself a steady job and taken care of her children to the best of her ability.

Sam stifled a sigh. In his book, Dennis hadn't behaved at all well. Ella was a good woman going to waste!

He was sitting perfectly still and he was grateful for the fact that Ella couldn't have the slightest idea of what he was thinking.

A couple of minutes went by before he leant forward and touched her face gently. His voice was low as he spoke.

'Ella, nothing would give me greater pleasure than to come to your house on Christmas Day, but only if you agree to let me take you out for a meal one evening this week.'

'But . . .' She stared at him, too surprised to hide her pleasure.

'No buts,' he said. 'I'm old enough to know that life is too short for regrets. Just say yes, and we shall both be gaining something that hopefully will turn out really well.'

'Thank you, Sam, I would like to go out for a meal with you.'

He answered with a smile on his face. 'And I am suddenly very much looking forward to Christmas.'

It was a long, busy shift behind the bar that evening. But time and time again Ella asked herself, was she now going to be able to put the past behind her? Was she being offered a new beginning?

She also decided there was going to be no secret whispering or gossip being passed around when it became known that she was going out for a meal with Sam Richardson and that she had invited him to spend Christmas with her and her family. Come closing time, she managed to get Mike on his own for a few minutes.

'Mike, Sam has offered to take me out for a meal on Wednesday. Would it be OK by you if I take the evening off?'

Mike grinned slyly. 'At last he's plucked up courage to ask you then. Of course you can. Silly bloody question. I've been urging him to ask you for ages.'

'I've also asked him to come to us for Christmas, me and my mum, I mean.'

Mike really was chuckling now. 'Ella, why do you feel the need to tell me all this in advance?'

Ella found she was laughing with Mike and blushing like some silly schoolgirl. ''Cos I don't want folk making more out of it than there really is. If Nellie Turner gets wind of this you know what she's like, she'll spread the news like nobody's business.'

'Nellie is one person that you don't want to worry about. She thrives on gossip, and if there's a way to make trouble then she'll find it. That woman could cause bother in an empty house. No, you go and have a nice evening together.'

'You don't think badly of me then?'

'What the hell are you talking about? Why would I ever think badly of you, Ella?'

'I'm married.'

'Yes, you're still tied to Dryden, worse luck.'

'You don't like Dennis, do you?'

'No, I don't. Never said as much because he's a member of this club and used to be a damn good customer. But a straight question deserves a straight answer. I think he's been a right bastard, a rotten husband and a rotten father. He scarcely ever shows his face around here since he behaved so disgracefully with young Connie Baldwin. How a lovely person like you came to be tied up with the likes of him is a mystery to me.'

Ella said hopelessly, 'He wasn't always like he is now.'

'Well, all I can say is you deserve better. You have a nice time on Wednesday, Sam Richardson is a real gentleman.'

'Thanks, Mike.' Ella leant forward and planted a kiss on his cheek.

'Oh for God's sake don't go all sentimental on me. Let's get these glasses out of the way and the tables wiped down, else you'll never get home tonight.'

Wednesday came round very quickly. Rather to her surprise, Ella felt really at ease sitting in the front seat of Sam's car as he drove, but she was even more surprised when he asked, 'Did you know that I live in Hampstead?'

'No, I didn't,' Ella answered quickly, 'but I hadn't really given much thought as to where you do live, Sam. Must be nice to live outside of London.'

No sooner were the words out of her mouth than she was reasoning with herself, you had your chance. Even your own mother has told you that if you'd gone along with what Dennis wanted and moved down to Epsom when he first asked you to, it would have saved a whole lot of people a helluva lot of heartache.

Sam half turned his head. 'I couldn't stay in the flat that Charlotte and I had worked so hard on, not on my own, it just didn't seem the right thing to do. After giving the matter a whole lot of thought, I decided to get right away.' He paused and smiled. 'Didn't go far, though. Hampstead is only four miles from the centre of London.'

Ella asked, 'Is that where we're going now?'

'Yes, I thought it might make a nice change for you. The actual place we are going to is South End Green.'

Ella laughed. 'Southend is a real Londoner's seaside place; d'you know, Orange Coaches run evening trips down there in the autumn just to see the lights. It only

233

costs three shillings and sixpence. Men go to have a good old booze-up but I think the women like the food. You know what Southend specializes in?'

Sam grinned. 'Can't say that I do.'

Ella soon told him. 'Real cockney food, sausages an' mash, jellied eels, cockles, winkles and whelks, that sort of thing.'

Sam looked about as thrilled as a turnip. 'Ella,' he said, 'I don't think you'll find much comparison between the place I'm taking you tonight and the Southend you have just described to me.'

Ella felt as if she had been rebuked and thought it best if she kept her mouth shut for the time being.

The journey did not take long, yet suddenly the whole scenery changed dramatically and she was wishing it wasn't so dark. There seemed to be so many open spaces with lovely views. The places that were lit up only made her want to see more.

Sam broke the ice by telling her that the huge pond they were now driving past was in an area known as the Vale of Health. When Ella made no comment he went on, 'Many, many years ago the Hampstead Water Company drained a swampy hollow and made this beautiful pond. I must bring you back another day and let you see the real beauty of it in the daylight.' Having said that, he took one hand from the steering wheel and patted her knee.

Friends again, she thought thankfully. Obviously his South End of Hampstead had nothing in common with her Southend by the sea!

When the car came to a halt and Sam came round to the passenger side of the car to open the door for her, Ella looked around and was gob-smacked. Facing her was a unique building; if asked to give a description, the only word for it that came to her mind was a mansion. 'Is this a pub?' she asked hesitantly, knowing full well she was sounding ignorant.

'No,' he said firmly. 'Well, maybe one could use that description, but its main purpose these days is a restaurant, a continental restaurant.'

Sam was troubled. He had brought Ella to Hampstead tonight to impress her, but she was already out of her depth and the evening had hardly started. He had to do something quickly to put her more at ease.

'There are still quite a few ordinary taverns and inns in Hampstead,' he said frankly, 'like the Old Bull and Bush, the Spaniards' Inn and Jack Straw's Castle, but like everything else since the end of the war they have had to somewhat change their image and move with the times. This place where we are eating tonight has kept its original name, the Prompt Corner.'

Ella tried her best to smile but it was an effort. Odd name, she was thinking. Then she noticed there was a tall red postbox to the left-hand side of the entrance; that seemed unusual so maybe it had something to do with it. She was hoping against hope that the inside of this place wouldn't be too grand.

Sam held the door open and they went inside to a flagged passageway. As they walked along they passed open archways that led into small rooms with beamed ceilings and fireplaces where burning logs sparked and flickered. Ella sighed with relief. This building had an air of welcome about it. It might be hundreds of years old, but time hadn't altered it that much. Suddenly she was comparing this restaurant to the place where Dennis had taken her for a meal a few weeks ago.

There was no comparison!

One was modern, even a bit flashy. These thick walls, if only they could talk, would tell of bygone times. Even though it had most modern comforts, including electric

235

light, Ella felt sure that she could smell paraffin lamps and newly baked bread.

As Sam slowed down, they saw an elderly man emerging from the darkness at the end of the corridor, walking into the light to join them. Ella noticed that he was dressed as a countryman, in corded trousers and a tweed jacket with leather patches at the elbows. He had a good head of hair that had probably been dark when he had been young but was now thickly white. He was tall, not far short of six foot, but thin as a rake.

'Evening, Sam,' he called jovially. 'I see you're dining with us tonight, booked a table for two, so I take it you won't be playing chess.'

Sam replied quite seriously, 'Evening, William, no, tonight I have company.' Then, turning to Ella, he made the introductions. 'Ella, this is my good friend Major William Lemington. William, this is also a good friend of mine, Mrs Ella Dryden.' They shook hands, he saying how pleased he was to meet her and she being surprised at the grip the elderly gentleman had.

Two waitresses appeared, one to take Sam's order for drinks and the other to show them to a table in a warm, cosy, old-fashioned dining room. Their drinks arrived and they were each studying a menu when footsteps sounded across the uncarpeted wooden floor.

Looking up, Ella saw a large lady, tall and well built, dressed in a cream woollen suit, an embroidered silk scarf tied loosely around her neck. 'Hello, Sam.' She held out her hand. 'William told me you were here.' Turning her head towards Ella, she added, 'My husband told me you are Sam's companion. I'm Margaret, it's nice to have you here.'

'Ella Dryden,' Sam answered for her.

'Well, Ella, enjoy your meal. I know Sam will, he's always had a good appetite.'

As Margaret Lemington left them, Ella was wishing

236

she was at home. She was out of her depth here. Almost before she could banish this awful thought from her mind, Sam was pointing to the menu again and asking her what she would like to order.

Sam decided on smoked salmon, Ella decided she was safer with the soup. For the main course he ordered for both of them, crown of lamb. Ella wasn't sure what crown meant, but lamb was one of her favourite dinners and she hoped they would serve mint sauce with it.

The meal was lovely, though she didn't like the wine that Sam had chosen. It was too sharp, almost sour to her mind. Then the sweet trolley was wheeled in. Oh my God. Ella just stared and wondered what her mother and her two kids would make of this lavish sight. There was such a wide choice and half of what was in the various glass bowls and china dishes she didn't recognize, so she played it safe and settled for sherry trifle, but her eyes nearly popped out of her head when the waitress set another bowl beside her sweet which was filled to the brim with thick cream.

Ella refused cheese and biscuits but was amazed to see Sam still tucking in to what he called a creamy, blue-veined Stilton, which he washed down with a large glass of port.

Behind Ella, quietly, three men, all bordering on old age, had come into the room. Sam, facing the archway, saw them approaching and immediately stood up.

'Oh, there you are, old boy. No chess tonight?'

'Unfortunately, no,' Sam said grimly.

That got Ella's hackles up. If he had wanted to play chess with these old fogies tonight, why the hell had he brought her along? The quicker he took her home, the better!

'Would you like a brandy to round the evening off?' Sam asked quietly.

'No thank you, Sam, I've had more than enough of everything. The meal was delicious and I do thank you for bringing me here.' She thought the least she could do was sound gracious.

'Well, I have ordered coffee.' He glanced up. 'Ah, here it comes. Let's go and sit nearer to the fire,' he suggested.

Settled in an easy chair, Ella lifted her cup of coffee from the small table and cradled it in her hands. Sam knew she much preferred tea, but she wouldn't dream of asking for that here. Coffee was obviously the after-dinner beverage. She watched Sam's face. All evening she had felt inadequate, and she was more than half regretting having invited him to spend Christmas with her. She had not been aware that his way of life was so entirely different from her own.

'Do you miss London?' she asked with a rush, already wishing she hadn't asked such a personal question.

Sam laughed. 'Hampstead is hardly a million miles away.'

Silence lay between them, until he said, 'You think I have only elderly people as companions?'

Ella made no answer, so he went on. 'When my Charlotte died I fled London because it had so many memories. For a long time I thought I had made a ghastly mistake. I missed the theatres, the cinemas, and the British Legion club. I was only renting a flat near here when I had a stroke of good luck, or maybe it would be more truthful to say, as everyone knows, that it is not what you know but *who* you know, and as it turned out, that is what happened to me. I was made an offer that was too good to refuse. To this day I do appreciate how privileged I am.'

'Now you have got me interested,' Ella told him. 'Tell me more about this wonderful offer.'

'Very well, if you're sure you want to hear this.'

Ella drained her coffee cup and set the cup and saucer back down on the table. 'I'm all ears,' she smiled.

Sam sat up straight in his armchair. 'Ten minutes' walk from here and down Fleet Road, you turn left into Quadrant Grove and you will come upon an unusual sight. There is a terrace of small cottages. Unusual type of housing, not to be found in this day and age, but then they were built a very long time ago. I was offered the freehold of the last cottage at the far end of the row.'

Ella was deep in thought. Were all men the same? It was the kind of thing that her Dennis would say. It is not what you know but *who* you know that gets you on in this world.

Sam broke into her thoughts. 'When Charlotte and I got married we had hoped to have children and we followed the advice of the firm I still work for and took out life insurance policies. When Charlotte died so tragically it seemed almost indecent to accept the company's payout. Our managing director lives in Hampstead and it was he and his wife who suggested a move might be the right thing for me. They informed me when this cottage became available and I used Charlotte's insurance money to buy my own home.'

Later, as Sam drove her home, she felt tonight had been an eye-opener in more ways than one. Several times she glanced at Sam's face and thought with grudging admiration that he had certainly made a new life for himself. Was he pleased with his day-to-day routine? One could hardly call it exciting. Work all the week, and from what she had heard, a game of chess with elderly gentlemen was the highlight of his world.

She hoped that both Babs and Teddy would still be awake when she crept in to their rooms to check on them. Even if they were fast asleep she would cuddle and kiss them each in turn and thank God, as she did every day, that she had two such great kids.

Babs and Teddy, she repeated their names inside her head.

They made her life well worth living.

As Sam brought the car to a halt he smiled at Ella and asked, 'Are you glad you came out with me tonight?'

'Of course. I've had a great time.'

'I'm so glad.'

For a moment, she thought he was going to kiss her, but instead he leant towards her and put his arms round her and hugged her. 'Goodnight, Ella. See you at the weekend.'

And that was how they parted.

Chapter Twenty-six

THREE MORE DAYS TO go and it really would be Christmas, Ella consoled herself as she clambered out of bed. She shivered, reached for her thick dressing gown, pushed her feet into her slippers and went downstairs quietly so as not to disturb the children. It was only seven o'clock and school had broken up a week ago, so there was no need for them to get up yet. In the kitchen she reached out a hand and felt the side of the kettle. The water inside was hot because the fire had been well banked up the night before. Pushing the kettle to the centre of the hob, she murmured, 'That won't take long to boil.' She had, as always, set the breakfast table the night before.

Crossing the room, she pulled the curtains open and saw that it was snowing again, not heavily, but sleety flakes driven to swirling by the bitterly cold wind. Oh, she hoped for Babs's sake that the wind might drop and the snow would settle. Bare trees and muddy playgrounds would all be transformed should that happen. The effect of thick white snow on everyday dirty, untidy buildings would make for a grand sight. The kids would be overjoyed if it were to become thick enough for them to go out and play in it.

Steam was coming from the spout of the kettle and she made a pot of tea. She always had two cups before she was ready to face a new day.

Mike had been kind enough to say she need not do the morning shift, so the whole day until six thirty tonight was hers. Shopping for food was not one of Ella's favourite occupations. It wasn't so bad when her mother went with her, because she was always so enthusiastic about getting bargains, but today Winnie was coming round to stay with the children and help them to finish putting up the decorations in the front room. Ella couldn't bear the thought of trailing around the shops on her own. The crowds would drive her mad. You'd think the shops were going to be closed for a month or more, the amount of food people were buying.

Having eaten a slice of toast, she washed in the scullery and came back into the kitchen to dress herself. She had laid her clothes out along the brass fender to get warm and it felt so good to pull on her underwear. Fully dressed now, she went back upstairs to wake Teddy.

Her son was still asleep, looking so peaceful; his hand tucked under one cheek, his wild shock of unruly dark hair tumbled on the pillow.

'Teddy.'

He stirred, turned on to his back, yawned and opened his eyes.

'Teddy, I'm going out shopping. I want you to listen for Babs to wake up. Your gran will be here soon.'

'Umm, all right.'

'Are you properly awake?'

'I am now.' Sleepily Teddy sat up, rubbing his eyes. 'Are you going to buy Christmas presents?'

'Maybe, but you are not to go round the house searching for what you think I may already have hidden.'

He grinned. 'So there are some hidden?'

'Never you mind. Stay a while longer in bed if you want to, but it is nice and warm downstairs. I will be quite a while. I've a lot to do.'

She laughed as Teddy snuggled down under the bedclothes again, then she tip-toed into Babs's bedroom. Babs was still fast asleep, curled up and looking so small, her long chestnut-coloured hair in a heap around her pretty face. Ella didn't touch her – it would be a shame to disturb her – but instead crept out of the room and back downstairs.

Wrapped up warmly, Ella boarded the bus. Fifteen minutes later the driver parked in the bus terminal as the market clock struck nine. Ella was amazed. Already the morning was well under way. Shops were open and all the stalls were set up and doing a roaring trade. From a parked van two men were unloading crates of fruit and vegetables, bunches of holly and Christmas trees both large and small. Thank God she hadn't got to carry anything like that home on the bus. Ted had got their local greengrocer to deliver them a small tree, holly and even two sprigs of mistletoe. The kids were going to start to decorate the tree while she was out, but she wasn't supposed to know that: yesterday she'd heard Babs whisper to her brother that they should do it while their mother was at work. Teddy had agreed. 'Be a smashing surprise for Mum, that will be,' he had grinned.

Ella went from stall to stall like a dose of salts, making snap decisions over some things, pondering over others. A present for her father-in-law was the most difficult decision; finally she settled on a beige waistcoat. It was very smart and the label said it was pure lamb's wool. Woolly gloves for Mrs Bristow and Mary Marsh, a long warm scarf for Mr Parsons. Two more Dinky motor-cars, one for Lenny Marsh and one for Teddy; she already had a box of small presents for him. Two skipping ropes with brightly coloured wooden handles, one for Babs and one for Vicky Marsh, and a miniature china tea service as an extra present for Babs.

Next came the sweet stall, today looking entirely different from the usual display of boiled sweets and homemade bars of fudge. There would be four children in her house on Christmas Day, so she bought four nets of goldwrapped chocolate coins, four coloured sugar mice, two white and two pink, all with long string tails which would be useful when it came to tying them on to the tree, and two chocolate Father Christmases, one each to be put in the stockings that Babs and Teddy would be hanging at the foot of their beds.

She stopped for a moment and breathed out. The only two she had to buy for now were her mum and Sam Richardson. Nothing was too good for her mother. She would go into Boots the chemist and buy her some decent perfume and a really posh lipstick. What about Sam? Well, he was writing and doing accounts all the time, wasn't he? She'd look for a fountain pen, one that was in a nice presentation box.

She had brought two large shopping bags with her and already they were bulging when she spied a really Christmassy stall. 'Don't forget yer wrapping paper,' the stall-holder was shouting, 'and yer labels, ribbons an' cards. If a job's worth doing, it's worth doing well.'

Ella just had to buy a little of everything, but the icing on the cake, so to speak, were the fairy dolls. Displayed on a large board to the rear of the stall, they looked dazzling. Tiny little dolls, all with blonde hair, wearing a white full-skirted dress of thin fine chiffon, adorned with sparkling tinsel. The tiny right hand of the doll was holding a silver wand topped by a glittering star. They were priced at half a crown.

Oh t' hell with the expense, Ella told herself, picturing in her mind's eye the way her daughter's eyes would light up when she gave it to her, and also how great it would look when fixed on the top of their small Christmas tree.

She couldn't miss the baker's stall. The smell of warm freshly baked bread and cakes defied anybody to walk by.

''Allo, Flo,' Ella greeted the rosy-faced plump woman in her spotless white apron. 'Busy today all right, eh?'

'Yer can say that again, Ella luv, but I ain't grumbling. Gotta make it while yer can. Only comes once a year.'

Ella had been to school with Flo, and her husband Pete had always been Den's mate. At least those two were still together. She couldn't help but feel a little envious; they had four children and she could imagine what a great family Christmas they would be having.

'I'll have a large bloomer, a large Hovis, 'alf a dozen jam doughnuts and a dozen mince pies.'

Flo said, 'Sorry, Ella luv, sold out of mince pies.'

'Oh Christ, an' I just ain't got the time ter make them now I'm working,' Ella said regretfully.

'I'll tell yer what, mate, my Pete an' my eldest boy will be baking all night. I'll get him to drop you in a dozen tomorrow. I'll put them in a tin for you.'

'Flo, you're a lifesaver, thanks, luv.'

Flo handed Ella a carrier bag containing the brown loaf and the white one plus the doughnuts, and then as an afterthought she popped a paper bag on top. 'There's just four mince pies there, can't sell 'em, they got a bit squashed, but you and the kids might like 'em when yer get 'ome. Give yer mum the odd one. 'Ow is she these days?'

'Fine, she'll outlive the lot of us. She's in my place minding the kids this morning.'

'Always was a goer, your mum. Tell 'er I sent me love.'

Ella paid Flo. Then she said, 'Flo, what about the mince pies Pete is going to bring me?'

245

Flo laughed. ''Ave 'em as a Christmas box.'

Ella protested, but Flo cut her short. 'Over the holiday I'll make sure Pete brings me into the Legion. I know you're closed Christmas Day, but you're open Boxing Day, ain't yer?'

'Yeah, we are.'

'Well, you can buy me a drink then.'

'You're on,' Ella said, 'I'll tell you what, ask your Pete to make it two dozen mince pies and I'll buy yer three drinks on Boxing Day,' and they parted, both of them laughing as they called, 'Merry Christmas.'

Her visit to Boots the chemist was successful. She couldn't get over the fact that the girl behind the Elizabeth Arden counter had offered to gift-wrap the bottle of perfume she had bought, and a beautiful job she had made of it. Wrapped in silver paper, the small parcel was topped by an elaborate red ribbon bow. The cheapest Parker fountain-pen was in a very nice box and the male assistant told her a diary for the new year came free with it. Good, Ella thought, she would wrap them separately. The diary could be a present for the children to give to Sam, because both she and her mum had made sure that there were at least two presents for Ted that would bear labels saying they were from the children.

Who's left now? she wondered. She reminded herself that most of today's shopping would not have been possible if it weren't for the fact that the Legion had given every member of staff an early Christmas bonus. Should she buy a present for Mike? If she did, she would have to do the same for his wife, and what about Tom and Derrick, she and Molly worked with them day in, day out. Oh dear, she sighed, there had to be an end to it somewhere. And she was pretty sure that Mike would make sure that all the staff got together for a drink sometime over the holiday.

She set off back down the street to the bus depot. She had spent enough money for today and she hoped that everybody would like what she had bought for them. She was pretty sure they would. God Almighty! The one person who by rights should have been top of her list she had forgotten. MOLLY!

Turning quickly she ran back into Boots. Quickly she made for the No 7 counter, Boots' own make. Having sought the advice of a very helpful assistant she was soon once again making her way to the bus depot. A glowing feeling of satisfaction made her smile. A gift of bath oil, talcum powder, scented soap and a very pretty nailbrush which were all neatly boxed had been the assistant's advice and once again the offer to have her purchase gift-wrapped was gratefully accepted. Molly would be really pleased with her present.

The children must have been watching for her. They came tearing down the street overexcited, yelling and tugging at her arms, urging her to hurry, there was so much they wanted her to see.

The front door was closed and Ella smiled: it was so she would notice that a wreath of holly had been nailed to the woodwork.

Once through the door, she had no option but to drop her bags of shopping in the passageway and allow herself to be pushed into the front room. Her eyes lit up as the Christmas tree was revealed in all its glory. The children, with a lot of help from their gran, Ella supposed, had done very well, and already the base of it was surrounded with brightly wrapped packages.

High up, near to the ceiling, the paper-chains that the children had made at school and so proudly brought home were looped the whole way around the room entangled here and there with balloons. All this must have taken a great effort.

247

Ella looked over the top of her children's heads and her gaze met that of her mother. Their eyes were glistening with unshed tears, but they were tears of sheer happiness.

'I'll make a pot of tea,' Winnie said softly. 'Kettle is boiling.'

Chapter Twenty-seven

'CHRISTMAS EVE, AND MIKE'S got an extension till midnight,' Ella remarked grimly to her mother. 'You can bet yer life it will be hectic in the club tonight. Are you coming back here to sleep or are you going home? Think on before you decide, 'cos the kids will probably be up and about wanting to know what Father Christmas has left them by about six o'clock in the morning.'

Her mother laughed. 'You were the same once upon a time. Anyway, I'll see you later. By the way, before you go, have you left a bit extra for Janey?'

'Yes, I've taken care of her. I gave her five pounds when I got my bonus. She said she'd rather have the money than a present 'cos she wanted to buy something nice for her mum.'

Thank God the customers were all in a festive mood. Almost every time they ordered a drink they said to the staff, 'Take one for yourself.' Molly remarked, 'Bejesus, if we drank half of what's on offer we'd never live to see Christmas Day.'

Mike had arranged that four cabs would be at the club

by twelve thirty, making sure that all members of staff had safe transport. God knows what the time was when Ella got home. She didn't know and she didn't care. Once upstairs in her bedroom she took off her clothes, let them lie where they dropped on the floor and climbed thankfully into her bed. She was asleep almost before her head touched the pillow.

The sudden noise was terrible. Ella heaved a hefty sigh and did her best to shove her head under her top pillow.

God! It only seemed like she had been in bed for a short while!

'He's been, he's been, come on, Teddy, wake up, Father Christmas has been, please Teddy, wake up, let's see what's in our stockings.'

Teddy wake up? The way Babs was going on, the whole bloody street would soon be wide awake.

Ella lay back, stretching her arms and legs, smiling as she remembered how good she and her mum had felt when filling those stockings for her children. They had both spent more on small toys and sweets than they could really afford, but the sounds of delight coming now from Teddy's room, where the two of them were comparing what Father Christmas had brought, made all the effort well worth while.

She found herself thinking back over the previous evening. It had been one hundred per cent better than anyone had anticipated. After all, Connie and Alf Baldwin's funeral hadn't been so long ago. Even Mike had said that might still have an effect amongst some of the members and that the festivities might not be so jolly this year.

Well, he'd been wrong.

Maybe the new premises and the bright decorations had all had something to do with it. Whatever, the evening had been great. Not one cross word. Drinks had flowed freely but everyone had remained friendly and jolly.

Mrs Baldwin and her daughters had not put in an appearance, but Ella supposed one couldn't expect that family to want to celebrate Christmas.

She reached an arm out of bed and yanked open the curtains. It was still dark, the streetlights were still on and she held the alarm clock near to the window. Jesus, it was only twenty minutes to six.

'All right, I give in,' she said aloud as she listened to the yells and screams and even a trumpet being blown. She couldn't tell the children to be quiet. Not today. She slipped her feet into her slippers and tied her dressing gown tightly about herself and half stumbled down the stairs.

Pushing open the kitchen door, she stared in astonishment.

'God, Mother, where do you get your energy from?'

The fire was burning merrily halfway up the chimney, almost every bit of floor space was taken up by presents and small toys which Father Christmas had supposedly filled their stockings with and the smell of roasting turkey and pork had Ella sniffing with delight.

Wiping a stray hair from her sweaty forehead, her mother smiled and said, 'Go and look in the front room, see if you approve.'

Ella did as she was told, and as she opened the door her breath caught in her throat. She cast her eyes around the room, and as she did so she muttered out loud, 'God above, this takes some believing.'

The extension leaves had been pulled out of their old dining room table, making it almost the full length of the room. A bed sheet had been used to cover the table and a sheet of red crêpe paper was set on top of that. Where on earth had her mother got it all from?

There were twelve places set. Winnie hadn't been too pleased when she was told that Sam Richardson had been invited, and had said sharply, 'Let's pray that your husband turns up as well.' Hence the twelfth setting, Ella supposed. Half-heartedly she was hoping the same thing, but there was no way she was going to admit it to her mother.

Slowly she walked the length of the long table. It was set beautifully, with lace place-mats and red candles in brass holders. There was a bowl of holly entwined with a couple of white Christmas roses in the middle of the table, and to top it all a fire had been lit in the black wrought-iron fireplace. Three strings of Christmas cards were strung across the wall above the mantelpiece.

Going back into the kitchen, Ella was at a loss to find words, so she just hugged her mum and planted a kiss on her cheek. She hoped she had conveyed just how grateful she was.

Babs and Teddy came tearing down the stairs and into the kitchen, where they plonked themselves down side by side on the hearth rug, still delving into the long stockings that Father Christmas had filled.

'Look, Mum, a London bus, and when you push it hard on the lino sparks come out of it. I've never seen one like this before, it's the bee's knees,' Teddy declared excitedly.

Not to be outdone, Babs was holding up pretty clothes that would fit a fair-size doll. She didn't know that her gran had knitted them all, and that the new doll would come later when everyone opened their presents.

Ella glanced at her mother as the children took out the various small gifts they had collected and secreted away over many weeks, all of which had been stuffed into the large stockings the children had hung at the foot of their beds. Each of them was choked. The joy on the children's faces and the way their eyes lit up was enough to make any grown-up want to cry.

Cry, yes, but not tears of sadness.

An hour later, when all the noise and laughter had died down, Ella, her mother and the two children were seated around the breakfast table.

Even breakfast was an extraordinary meal on Christmas morning. Home-cooked gammon, scrambled eggs and red pickled cabbage which Ella had salted away in screw-topped jars weeks ago. Plenty of toast with jam or marmalade to follow, because their Christmas dinner was not going to be eaten until four o'clock.

Well satisfied, Ella leant back in her chair, looked at her children and said, 'Well, are you both pleased with your presents so far?'

'Oh yes.' Babs was the first to answer. 'May I wear my new pink dress when Grandad gets here? And the silver shoes that Gran bought me?' She wanted assurance.

Gran had taken Babs with her to purchase these items. It would have been a disaster if on Christmas Day they had not fitted the child.

Teddy knew there were bigger presents to come and he was impatient.

'Why have we got to wait until everybody arrives before we open the big presents that are in the front room?'

Ella sighed. She had been expecting this. 'Because you know full well we are going to leave yer gran to get on with the cooking, and like we promised Babs's teacher, Miss Whitehead, we are going to a special church service this morning.'

'She's not my teacher, so why do I have to come?' Teddy crossly demanded to know.

'Because I said so,' his mother answered quickly in a voice that would brook no argument. 'You won't be the only boy there, I should think the whole school will attend seeing as how your headmaster wrote a letter to every parent which explained that it would be a simple thanksgiving service mainly for you youngsters. Besides, a little bird told me that you helped to make and set up the crib in the church. Don't you want me and your sister to see it?'

'Wasn't only me,' he said sulkily. 'All the boys helped, we did it in our woodwork class.'

'All the more reason for you to be there, and do you think, young man, that just this one day of the year you could do as you're told and we could have less of your backchat, please.'

Teddy's face broke into a broad grin. 'All right, Mum, but when we get back from church can we open our big presents?'

Ella playfully swiped her son around the head. 'Whenever you agree to do anything there has always got to be something in it for you. Now get yerself ready before I forget that it is Christmas Day and really swipe you one.'

While the children were putting their coats on, Ella had a few moments alone with her mother.

She said, 'Happy Christmas, Mum, and thanks for all you're doing.'

'Happy Christmas to you, my luv, now get going an' don't forget to say one for me.'

Ella felt happy and proud as she walked down the street, Babs holding one of her hands and Teddy the other one. They stopped several times to wave at their school friends and for Ella to greet her neighbours. Voices called out; other people gave one another a hug, everyone falling into step as they made their way through the huge churchyard.

'I already know what carols we are going to sing,' Babs said, tossing the end of her new long red scarf around her neck.

Teddy was horrified. 'You mean we've got to join in with the singing?'

'The choir will lead the congregation and we will all be handed hymn books.' Their mother was pouring oil on troubled waters.

As they went through the wide gates and down the path beyond which led to the wide flight of stone steps and the huge door of the church, for a moment Ella felt sadness overwhelm her. Dennis had carried each of their children into this church, wrapped in a beautiful shawl and cradled safely in his big brawny arms, and with her hand linked through the crook of his elbow they had gathered with a host of family and friends to have them christened. Where was their father today? Her mum was right: he should be sitting around the same dinner table as they were, but the last thing she could do was tell Dennis what she thought was best for him. He had a mind of his own, that had always been a well-known fact.

The children hesitated inside the church, and she gave them a gentle push. A kind lady wearing a very smart hat handed them each a hymn book. Ella thanked her and she wished them all a very happy Christmas.

'Come on, kids, see if we find somewhere to sit together.'

A great surge of sound from the organ and waves of music filled the church.

'O little town of Bethlehem, how still we see thee lie.' Ella mouthed the words

The church was already nearly filled, and they had begun to move down the centre aisle when a hand touched Ella's arm. A stout gentleman said, 'If all of us shuffle up a bit, there will be more than enough room for you and your two children.'

255

Ella said, 'Thank you,' and guided Babs and Teddy into the pew before seating herself on the end of it.

To the right of the altar steps there was a huge Christmas tree, lavishly decorated and twinkling with candles. To the left the nativity scene had been set: the three Wise Men, Mary, our Blessed Lady, and Joseph surrounded the crib which held the baby Jesus. As every year, the children who had at school helped to make the setting were being taught to commemorate the birth of Christ.

Ella squeezed Teddy's hand, letting him know that she was proud of the fact that he had been involved in setting up this festival tableau.

So far, so good. The children must all have been practising well-known carols at school, and they sang with passion, their voices filling the church. The choir sang just one hymn, and during their performance the congregation was still. The music was the only thing that mattered. If only Dennis had been there! But what was the use of if only? That was the one thought that spoilt the morning for Ella.

Walking home, Teddy asked, 'Mum, do you think Dad will turn up today?'

Oh my God! How am I supposed to answer that one?

Ella's expression was unreadable as she sought to find a suitable answer for her son.

'Maybe. But if I were you, Teddy, I wouldn't count on it.'

Chapter Twenty-eight

CHRISTMAS DINNER HAD BEEN a great success. Ella's biggest thrill was watching her own two children and Lenny and Vicky Marsh stare in wonderment as Winnie carried in the great dish that held an enormous Christmas pudding and Grandad Ted soaked the top of the pudding with brandy then set it alight. Blue flames danced merrily and the four children screamed with delight. A slice of pudding, a hot mince pie with a dollop of brandy butter, and there wasn't one amongst the eleven sitting around the table that could eat another morsel after that.

The ladies drained their one and only glass of wine while Ted poured another glass of brandy for Mr Parsons, Sam Richardson and himself. The table was strewn with the crumpled paper napkins, the remains of crackers that had been pulled and paper hats that had by now fallen off their heads.

Babs had for some time been looking longingly at the pile of fancy-wrapped parcels that still lay on the floor around the tree.

'Please may we get down from the table, and when are we going to open our big presents?' she whined.

'Right now, pet,' her mother answered lovingly. 'We'll leave all this mess until later and then your gran and I will clear it up after the parcels have all been given out.'

'Never seen such a rush in all me life,' Mrs Bristow laughed. The four children were on their knees and were reading aloud the words each label had written on it.

'This one's for you, Lenny. This one is for you, Mum, and this great big one is for me.' A delighted Teddy was already tearing at the wrapping paper. And so it went on. Even the adults were pleased to receive gifts, and the joy of watching the children was beyond description. Grandad Ted had been so generous: an exact model of a royal perambulator for Babs to wheel her dolls in, and the huge box labelled for Teddy had turned out to be the latest Meccano set.

Eventually things quietened down. Mary Marsh and Mrs Bristow had insisted on helping Ella and her mother to clear everything out from the front room and into the kitchen, and now all four were busy washing up. Ted had taken the leaves out of the table, folded it up and stood it against the wall, thereby giving the children a lot more floor space in which to play.

Teddy was looking through his Beano annual. Babs was engrossed in seeing what kind of underwear her new blonde-haired doll was wearing. Vicky too was cradling a doll in her arms and Lenny was busy assembling a wooden fort, which had twelve soldiers to go with it.

Suddenly there was a gentle tap on the front door. The women looked at each other and raised their eyebrows. A caller on Christmas afternoon? It didn't seem likely.

'I'll go,' Winnie offered, stepping over the bags of rubbish which lay in the middle of the kitchen floor.

Two minutes later she was calling loudly, 'Ella, will you come here a minute please.'

The front door was wide open, and Ella gasped sharply

258

as she stood and stared at the sight of two very expensive bicycles standing side by side on her doorstep. One was bigger than the other and bright blue in colour. It had brakes, a shiny bell on the handlebars, a crossbar and a large black leather bag strapped on the back. The other was obviously meant for a small girl. Mainly coloured silver, it had a pink basket attached to the front of the handlebars, and fixed to the back of the frame were two extra wheels which Ella knew were known as stabilizers. They could easily be removed once a child had got the experience and confidence to ride a two-wheeled bike.

Her eyes were brimming with tears as she stared at her mother.

'Yes,' Winnie said, 'there are labels on them. You don't need telling, but just look at them.'

Each tag read, 'Have a great Christmas, I love you, Dad xx'.

'No sign of him, I suppose?'

'No, I ran to the gate but he must have moved fast.'

'Bastard!' Ella couldn't help herself. 'He still thinks money buys everything.'

'I know, luv, I know. But just watch the kids' faces when they see these bikes, they'll be over the moon.'

'I'll have a damned hard job to hide them both until Christmas is over.'

'Why in hell's name would you do a daft thing like that?'

''Cos it makes what you and I have struggled week by week to buy for them look small and paltry. He either does nothing at all for them or else he goes over the top.'

'Come on, luv, at least he has tried.'

'And you don't think if he'd come into the house bearing no presents but just lifted them up in his arms and given them a great big bear hug that wouldn't have pleased them even more?' Ella's voice was very harsh.

'Don't let's go into the whys and wherefores, Ella, let's enjoy the rest of the day. Call the kids now, come on, at least their father has made an effort. Is that not good enough for you?'

'No, it's not good enough for me.' Ella pushed past her mother. 'If he really loved them he'd have wanted to see them and be with them, today of all days.'

Winnie followed her daughter down the passage without answering. She didn't blame Ella. Not after the way Dennis had treated her.

'Oh, all right.' Ella sounded cheesed off. She knew she had no choice, she would have to give in. She couldn't deprive her kids of such wonderful presents just because her temper had risen so high it was almost choking her.

Bloody Dennis, I was having a really great day from the moment I woke up until he rapped on the front door. Big-headed sod. Those two bikes must have cost him a fortune. She couldn't bear to go out front with the kids and watch them find what their father had left them. She asked Winnie to do it for her.

The squeals and screams of delight said it all, but the adults, who had by now all crowded around the front door, couldn't help feeling sorry for Lenny and Vicky Marsh. Those two children had lost their father a long time ago, and one would have to be blind not to notice the envy in their eyes as Teddy proudly exclaimed, 'Our dad bought them for us.'

Yet it was young Babs who echoed her mother's thoughts. 'Mummy, why did my daddy leave our bicycles on the doorstep?'

Then the words that her small daughter added felt like a knife being driven into Ella's heart.

'Wouldn't you let him come in?'

How was she supposed to answer that?

After a lot of persuasion, the children agreed that their

bicycles could be stored under the stairs, but only on the absolute promise that first thing in the morning they could ride them up and down the street.

With all the excitement damped down, and the fact that it was getting dark, Ella walked into the front room to pull the curtains. At the same time she slid the top of the window open a little because Ted had been smoking a cigar. She then threw two more logs on to the fire.

She was about to suggest that it was time they all had some tea: there was the Christmas cake still uncut, and plenty more mince pies that could be popped into the oven to get warm. Looking round, she had second thoughts. Sam and Ted were seated comfortably in armchairs one each side of the fireplace. Mr Parsons and Mrs Bristow were side by side on the sofa, their heads laid back on cushions, their eyes closed. Ella left the room, closing the door quietly behind her, deciding that teatime could be delayed a little longer. Then she climbed the stairs. The two boys were in Teddy's room and the two girls in Babs's. Harmony reigned; after all, they had plenty of new presents to keep them occupied today.

She came back downstairs and into the kitchen, where she reported that the kids were fine and the adults were resting. Winnie suggested that Mary, Ella and herself should stay in the kitchen and make a nice pot of tea just for themselves. This was unanimously agreed to be a good idea.

Back in the front room, Sam was fuming. Why had Dennis Dryden had to make such an expensive gesture? It wasn't at all fair on his wife, who had worked so hard to give several people a very happy Christmas, only to have all her good work undermined by him. How could Ella possibly have answered young Babs when she had challenged her mother as to why her father had not come into the house?

Sam held his temper and tried his best to sound casual

261

as he remarked to their grandfather, 'Children are thrilled with their bicycles, aren't they?'

Ted didn't answer him, and Sam quickly added, 'Pity their father didn't show his face.'

Ted had already heard the underlying anger in Sam's voice and decided it was time he spoke up.

'Don't go poking your nose in what is not your business.' He sounded friendly, but it was obvious he was sending out a warning.

'I don't think the man has any conscience, walking away and leaving Ella to cope with two young children on her own.'

'The man you're on about is my son, and Ella is not on her own. She knows I'm around if and when she or the kids need me.'

'I just think Dennis should play it a bit more straightforward, let Ella know where she stands. As it is, he comes and goes as and when he likes. It's no life for Ella or for the children. What about you, Ted? Do you agree with the way he is acting? You say you're there to help Ella, yet you deny that you know where your own son is living. Suppose one of the children were taken ill, are you saying you couldn't contact their father?'

Ted was out of his seat in a second, shouting, 'I honestly have no idea where my son is, but in the East End the jungle drums are quite effective. If I put the word out he'd be here within the hour. I hear from him daily, we have several mutual business interest, but his personal life is nothing to do with me and even less to do with you, so watch what you're saying and keep a tight rein on what you're thinking of doing, that's my advice.'

Ella, having heard Ted's raised voice, came quickly into the room, still drying her hands on a tea towel. Ted was still standing in the middle of the floor, his hands clenched into tight fists.

Ella gestured for him to sit down and then she glared at Sam.

'Whatever has been said between you two, just remember that you are in my house and it is still Christmas Day. I can't believe it. The kids are all being as good as gold and yet you grown men have to start a noisy slanging match.'

'Sorry, luv,' her father-in-law said, pulling a glass ashtray across the table and taking a cigar from the box which stood beside it. 'Sam here seems to think he has the right to interfere in your life. We all know that he'd like to—'

Ella held her hand up to interrupt him. She pointed a finger at each man in turn and then, with her voice full of irritation, said sharply, 'Strictly speaking I should be the only one dealing with Dennis, and I will in my own good time. Now, Mum is just bringing in a pot of tea and Mary and I have laid out lots more to eat. Unless the both of you want to clear off out and carry on your argument somewhere else, I suggest you make yerselves useful and put the table back up. You needn't put the leaves in, we can have our food on our laps.'

Mr Parsons looked relieved and Mrs Bristow smiled and said, 'Oh Ella, you're a saint, a cup of tea is just what the doctor ordered.'

Sam had never felt so ashamed in all his life. He knew he had overstepped the mark.

He had drunk far more than he was used to, yet he was aware that was no excuse.

Ella was staring at him, her big eyes never wavering even when she said, 'Well?'

She had no need to say more.

Sam got to his feet and held out his hand to Ted, saying, 'I apologize, really I mean it. You're right. It is none of my business.'

Ted Dryden shook his head sadly but he still put his

hand out and took Sam's. Then to Ella he said, 'For once, my gal, I think a cuppa tea will go down well.'

Peace was restored.

Despite the fact that it was less than three hours since everyone had declared they could not eat another morsel, they were now tucking into a typical Christmas tea.

Besides the cake, mince pies and a huge trifle, the table was covered with bowls of fruit, nuts, dates and chocolates.

Everyone had laughed heartily as Teddy had entered the room. He was wearing a football shirt which had been one of the presents he had received from his grandad.

'All right, is it?' Ted asked, tugging at one of the sleeves.

'Course it is, Grandad. West Ham colours, claret and blue, can't wait to show the boys at school, and the boots are smashing too. Maybe I'll get picked to play for the school team.'

Ted leant over and ruffled his grandson's hair, then said, 'I've got a surprise for you, my boy.'

'What, another one?' Teddy was bursting with excitement.

'It's not as good as I would have liked it to be, but all the same it's not bad.'

'Oh Grandad, stop teasing and tell me what it is.'

'Well, I was hoping to take you to see West Ham play tomorrow, but they haven't got a game on Boxing Day this year. They have got a match this Saturday away against Notts County, but I don't feel like travelling all the way to Nottingham. God knows what the weather will be like.'

Teddy was impatient. 'So how is that a surprise for me?'

Ted Dryden smiled. He adored his grandchildren.

'Hold yer horses, Teddy. My luck was in, I have managed to get tickets for the first Saturday in the New Year.'

'Great, Grandad.' A delighted Teddy was grinning from ear to ear. 'But where is the match, and who are West Ham playing?'

Ted couldn't hold back any longer. 'It's a home match, son. West Ham are playing Bury at the Boleyn Ground.'

Teddy shouted, 'Yippee! I'll wear this shirt and Grandad, will yer see if you can get me a big wooden rattle?'

'Course I will, lad, but you know what? If I got you the top brick off the chimney you'd want the stars out of the sky to go with it!'

Teddy was rolling about on the floor laughing, and every now and then he could be heard murmuring, 'Smashing, good old Grandad.'

Never had Ella loved her father-in-law more than she did at that moment.

Teddy used to look forward to regular visits to football matches with his father. Not that he had complained, but she knew the fact that his dad wasn't around had hurt him much more than he would openly admit.

Ella's eyes met those of her father-in-law and she mouthed silently, 'Thanks, Ted.' For a ridiculous moment she felt a bit weepy, but instead she crossed to where Ted was sitting, put her arms around him and hugged him tightly.

It hadn't been a bad day.

PART TWO

1953
A New Year

Chapter Twenty-nine

NEW YEAR'S EVE HAD been a great event in the British Legion. Mike had applied for and been granted an extension to stay open until half an hour after midnight. As Big Ben had struck twelve, the Thames had been lit up by the setting off of hundreds of fireworks, and every tug and ship on the river had answered with a forcible blast from their hooters. People had danced in the streets and sung their hearts out. The blackout and the shortages of the war years were forgotten. This was a different new world, everyone was optimistic.

Try telling that to the wounded soldiers, many of whom were still in Roehampton Hospital and other such places up and down the country. Still, one could not begrudge the public going mad on a night like this.

Tomorrow would be the start of a new year, and most folk were hoping for a new start. Everyday life would be a different matter. Ella was feeling a little despondent. Since the war, they had been told often enough how in future it would be a world fit for heroes. Oh yeah? How many men were unemployed? How many soldiers, sailors and airmen had lost their lives?

Customers were streaming back into the club, having seen the firework display. They all wanted a last drink, and as Ella pulled pints and held glasses under the optics, she reminded herself that 1952 hadn't been a great year for her.

She crossed her fingers. This year she would have a lot of decisions to make, but one thing was for certain: she had to make them herself, act as a capable adult and not be persuaded when other people thought they knew what was best for her.

Ted Dryden wore his Crombie overcoat, which made him look very successful – which he certainly was. Young Teddy was wearing long trousers, a shirt and two jumpers. Over the top of that lot he had pulled on his claret and blue football shirt, and to make his supporter's gear complete, his gran had bought him a hat and a long scarf in the West Ham colours.

Ella stood at the gate to wave them off.

Teddy turned, grinned at his mother and held his rattle high. Then he began to swing it round and round as he walked.

'That bloody awful racket,' Ella muttered. Thank God they were on their way. The sound of that football rattle being constantly swung this morning had her nerves in shreds. Still, going to a football match with his grandad was a wonderful way for Teddy to spend the first Saturday in the new year. Her young son was the happiest she had seen him for a long time, and for that reason alone she felt so grateful to her father-in-law.

Ella watched until Ted and young Teddy had turned the corner then she went back inside the house suddenly feeling very lonely. Her mother had taken Babs to the cinema; they were going to see Gene Kelly in *Singin' in the Rain* to compensate for Teddy going to see West Ham play.

It was her own fault that she was on her own. Sam had asked her if she would like to go up West with him, have a meal and maybe go to the theatre in the evening. She had made an excuse and refused.

Ever since Christmas afternoon when Ted and Sam had had a go at each other, she had felt she had to tread warily where Sam was concerned. Not that it was any of her father-in-law's business whether or not she went out with Sam, but she did feel, albeit half-heartedly, that Ted was right. Sam was acting a little bit overprotective. After all, she had only been out with him the once and she wouldn't have put that evening down in her book as a one hundred per cent success.

'I'll make meself a cup of tea and get on with the ironing,' she murmured, looking dolefully at the pile of crumpled clothes on the chair.

She had barely drunk her tea and was setting the ironing blanket to cover the kitchen table when there was a loud knock on the front door. She took her time walking down the passage, and as she opened the door her eyes widened with shock and she frowned deeply. There was a policeman standing on her doorstep.

'I wonder, is Mr Dennis Dryden here?' a gruff voice enquired. 'I'm Constable Didby.'

'No, no, I'm afraid he's not,' Ella stammered.

The constable nodded his head thoughtfully before saying, 'Is Mr Dryden any relation to you, ma'am?'

Ella was tempted to tell him to mind his own business, but looking at his uniform she decided she had better answer his question.

'Yes, yes, he's my husband.'

'Ahh,' he said, sounding as if he were clearing his throat. 'In that case, would you kindly ask him to contact me or any officer at the local station as soon as possible, please.'

'May I ask what this is about?' Ella had decided a bit more politeness might be in order.

'Of course, though I'm afraid it is sad news. Miss Dorothy Sheldon died two days ago and the hospital have been unable to trace any relatives. However, a firm of solicitors who were acting for Miss Sheldon had been given your husband's name as next-of-kin.'

Ella's mind was racing nineteen to the dozen. Dorothy Sheldon? As far as she could remember, she had never heard the name before. She found herself struggling to think of something to say.

All she could come up with was, 'I see.'

The policeman turned to go, then paused. 'Apparently her death was peaceful. A quiet end but the lady was all on her own.'

Ella felt guilty, but as to why she should, she had no idea.

She managed to speak calmly. 'Thank you for letting us know. I will ask my husband to get in touch with you as soon as possible.'

'Thank you, Mrs Dryden. Goodbye.'

'Goodbye, Constable Didby.'

Ella closed the door. All at once she needed to sit down. She perched herself on the bottom stair. Who the hell was Dorothy Sheldon? What had her death to do with Dennis? And another thing, how come Dennis had been named as her next-of-kin? There were certainly a whole lot of questions that needed answers.

She couldn't wait for Ted to get back from the match. Now maybe he could *prove* that he could get in touch with his son at any time.

He'd boasted about it often enough.

Ella had finished the ironing and still a lot of time stretched in front of her before her family would arrive home. She decided egg and chips would please both of her children for their tea. Meanwhile she opened the door to her big cupboard, took the flour jar down from the shelf and placed it on the table. To that she added margarine, lard, dried fruit and a two-pound jar of blackberry and apple jam. Having tied a bibbed white apron around her waist, she set to. A session of baking – a jam sponge and a few jam tarts – would keep her mind occupied.

Three hours later the front door almost came off its hinges as Teddy burst in yelling at the top of his voice, 'We won, we won! Great result, Mum, West Ham 3, Bury 2.' As he was reliving the excitement of the last goal that had decided the game for his team, he had taken a jam tart from the plate on top of the hob.

'Golly, that's blooming hot, it's burnt me mouth,' he moaned.

'Serve you right for helping yerself and not asking if you could have one,' his mother laughed. Then, making sure that Teddy was not watching, Ella gestured to her father-in-law that she wanted him to follow her into the front room.

With the door firmly closed, Ella told Ted of the visit from the policeman and did her best to explain why it was necessary for him to get in touch with Dennis.

Ted's face paled. He wasn't about to inform Ella that Dennis was at present in a police cell following a blazing row with builders who were working for him and were not only well behind schedule but were fiddling the cost of materials. He had been told the full story late last night but as usual had kept the matter to himself.

Stan Wilson, a long-term mate of Dennis, was in charge of the Wandsworth building project, and it went without saying that he was no fool. Duplicates of receipts for very large amounts of supplies had been slipped into the office.

Stan had had a word with Tom Cooke, the foreman. 'You must have been barmy, man, if you thought you could get away with it.'

'It wasn't only for my benefit. The whole gang thought a bit extra on top of their wages wouldn't be missed.'

'Well, me old mate, we live and learn, don't we? Now you're about to learn that you'd have t' get up early in the morning to put one over on Dennis.'

Dennis Dryden came leisurely out of the big shed that served as an office and walked across the site towards them. From his briefcase he took a pouch that held the wage packets of each of the workmen. Instead of handing it to Tom Cooke, as he normally would, he gave it to Stan.

'Hand these out, mate, and tell the men to be on site seven thirty sharp on Monday morning, when I'll 'ave something to say to them.'

Tom Cooke stood beside Dennis and watched silently as each man accepted his wage packet and cleared off faster than you could say Jack Robinson.

'And where's mine?' he said, trying to sound jocular.

Dennis gave him a blinding look. 'You've paid yerself twice over for the last two weeks. That wasn't very nice, Tom, I thought I was treating you well, paying you well over the odds.' Dennis's voice dripped with sarcasm. 'And another thing, duplicating invoices, that didn't impress me, that's kid's play. Thought you would have realized by now that I wasn't born yesterday.'

Then, without warning, Tom was knocked off his feet as Dennis lunged at him. Stan was trying to drag Dennis back by holding on to his overcoat, talking to him sensibly, willing him to calm down. Dennis pushed him out of the way. Using his feet to press home his point, he kicked Tom in the ribs, and as he lifted his head his face came into contact with Dennis's fist.

'Nobody robs me and gets away with it. Do you hear me?'

The workmen had needed no telling that their foreman was in for a beating, and one of them had phoned the police.

A police car roared on to the site. Slamming on the brakes, it skidded to a halt. Two uniformed policemen got out and stood in front of Dennis. Tom Cooke had staggered to his feet by now. Dennis pushed one policeman out of the way and smashed his fist once more into the side of Tom's head, saying, 'And that's yer bonus!'

The policemen took in the situation at a glance. One of them spoke to Stan.

'Do that bloke on the ground a favour and get him to a hospital. He looks like he could do with a bit of TLC.'

As the other officer pushed Dennis towards the police car, he said, 'You're nicked.'

Dennis's face was dark with temper as he lowered his head to get into the back of the police car.

He hadn't been given much choice. Still, he'd made his point.

Ted shook his head. Ella was still waiting for an explanation.

'I remember Dorothy Sheldon, of course I do, a really nice lady. So she's died, shame. She was younger than Lady Margaret, never thought Margaret would outlive her. Just goes to show, we never know.'

'How come I've never heard of her, and what's all this about Dennis being her next-of-kin?' Ella was confused, and couldn't wait to get to the bottom of the matter.

'Can't say that I know what all this solicitor business is about myself,' Ted answered warily. 'But I do remember the first time we all met; it was at Cheltenham racecourse. Officially Dorothy Sheldon was Lady Margaret's paid companion, but in all truth they were dear faithful friends.

'I need to get on the blower to contact my Den – what a pity you're not on the phone here, we'll have t' get that sorted – and I'll go with him to see this copper. Constable Didby you said, yes?'

'That's right,' Ella agreed, wondering as usual why Ted always denied that he knew where Dennis lived, yet he always knew how to get hold of him when he was needed.

Within twenty minutes Ted was walking through the front betting hall and on into the office of his main bookmaker. He owned three such businesses where bets were accepted and winnings were paid out, and nothing that went on in any of them got past his notice.

Being Saturday, business was brisk. Horse-racing might be finished for the day, but men were still placing bets. At three stadiums there would be dog-racing tonight.

Ted looked up the number for the local cop-shop, and as he waited he hoped for the best but prepared himself for the worst. Nobody seemed to know where his son was banged up.

'Elephant an' Castle police,' a quick, sharp voice answered.

'Oh, my name is Edward Dryden. I wonder, could I speak to Constable Didby?'

'Hold on, I know he's been out, I'll see if he's back in the station yet.'

Ted's heart sank. Hold on, that could mean a bloody long wait. But his fears were unfounded as a gruff voice came on the line almost at once.

'Constable Didby speaking, what can I do for you?'

'I'm Mr Dryden Senior, you visited my daughter-in-law this afternoon looking for my son, Dennis Dryden.'

'Yes, I had to deliver sad news, I'm sorry.'

'You said my son has been named as next-of-kin to Miss Sheldon. He wasn't related to her at all.'

The constable didn't speak for a moment, and when he did he sounded thoughtful.

'Probably the lady didn't have any family. Were she and your son friends? If so, perhaps he agreed to take on the duty of seeing to her affairs. He should contact her solicitor straight away.'

'Bit difficult,' Ted muttered down the line.

'How come?' Constable Didby was interested.

'Your lot has him banged up. I don't know where, but I'm told he was arrested in Wandsworth. Can I stand bail for him?'

'Depends.'

'On what?'

'Whether the magistrate agrees. When was he picked up and what for?'

'Yesterday evening . . . for brawling.'

'Pity it was the weekend. He won't be brought before a magistrate before Monday morning. You can attend the court and offer to stand bail but there is no guarantee that the judge will grant it. Then again, he might get off scot free or with just a fine, if he's lucky.'

'Oh, like that, is it? Anyway, thanks for your help.'

Ted replaced the telephone on its hook, put his elbows on the edge of his desk and cupped his face in his hands.

So there wasn't anything he could do over the weekend. He made a quick decision. He wasn't going to go anywhere near Ella, she'd be asking too many questions. Instead he would pay a long-overdue visit to Lady Margaret. It wouldn't take him long to get to Chelsea.

It had been a wise choice, Ted was saying to himself as he drove up the tree-lined avenue to the rest home.

Once inside, he introduced himself to a tall, smartly dressed lady with threads of grey in her brown hair.

Smiling, she said, 'Anne Riley, I'm the matron here.

Lady Margaret speaks of you so often, Mr Dryden, all the staff feel they know you. I'm so sorry I haven't been available on your previous visits. Lady Margaret still reads the sports pages of the newspapers and she greatly appreciates the fact that you always send her your race-card from the major meetings. It seems you keep her well informed where horse-racing is concerned.'

Ted smiled at the compliment. More than likely, Lady Margaret was still interested in horse-racing even if it was only from her armchair, and she would always associate him with the sport of kings.

Matron rode up in the lift with Ted and ushered him into a large bed-sitting room. His first impression was that it was old-fashioned but elegant. It was a much larger room and had a better view than the one that Lady Margaret had occupied on his previous visits.

His long-term friend was sitting in a deep armchair which was positioned so that she could see the beautiful gardens beyond the bay window. She turned her head as Ted stepped forward and blinked twice before saying, 'Edward, what a wonderful surprise, how well you look.'

Ted took her slender, bony hand between both of his. 'How well *you* look,' he replied. 'You haven't aged a day and you sound so happy.'

'That is because I am happy. The staff here have helped me make this my home.' Then, slowly, it was as if a cloud passed over her face. 'Dorothy's death has brought you here today, hasn't it?'

Ted nodded, for the moment too bewildered to speak.

'Sit down, Mr Dryden,' Matron said, indicating an armchair near to her ladyship. 'Would you like some tea or coffee, both of you?'

Lady Margaret answered. 'Your lovely milky coffee would be fine, please, Matron. I'm sure Edward will enjoy a cup.'

When Matron left the room the questions began and Ted started the ball rolling.

'Why has my son been named as Dorothy's next-of-kin?'

Such a deep sigh before Ted got an answer. 'Dorothy had no family, but I never thought I would outlive her. Because she was that much younger I even took out an endowment policy for her because I knew the small allowance I made her would cease with my death. When I had to move, your son was so kind and considerate to Dorothy. Having turned my big old house into four splendid apartments, he made it possible for her to purchase one. She was forever grateful to him for that. She loved living there. She used to visit me a lot until her health started to fail. However, we wrote to each other regularly.'

Lady Margaret stopped talking and a worried look crossed her face.

Quickly Ted asked, 'Is there something wrong?'

'Well, I suppose not, not now, since poor Dorothy is no longer with us, but . . .'

'But what?' Ted was quick to ask.

Lady Margaret sighed gently. 'Edward, within the last four months I have had the feeling that a gentleman, a resident in the same apartments, had been causing Dorothy some distress. She had a pet, a lovely old cat called Misty – actually it was my pet to begin with. She had to have it put down because it was so badly injured when it became entangled in some barbed wire. Dorothy couldn't prove anything, but Misty always used to make for the same patch of undergrowth whenever she let her out. She thinks the man, Mr Packard, hid that wire there deliberately.'

Ted felt he had to ask. 'Why would any man be so evil?'

'That was only one thing in a long list of nasty occurrences. Dorothy said he approached her soon after she moved in and asked her to sell her apartment to him. Naturally she refused. He pestered her time and time again to sell. Never giving her time to settle in. The Lord only knows why.'

Ted was seething with rage, and he vowed that he and Dennis would find out what had been going on.

He quickly changed the subject. 'Do you know who is going to make the arrangements for Dorothy's funeral?'

'All that will be left to our solicitor, Mr Trent, Mr James Trent. Dorothy and I made our wills a long time ago.'

A long pause while Lady Margaret gathered her thoughts. Then sadly she said, 'I don't suppose she will be buried until sometime next week. Shouldn't think many people will attend. Mr Trent will also arrange for light refreshments afterwards, perhaps in the lounge of a hotel in Epsom. I shall do my best to be there, though I rarely go out.'

Ted quickly offered, 'I will arrange for a car to take you and bring you back if you feel that you would like to attend.'

'Oh, Edward, that is so kind of you. I'll decide later on.'

'Are there any other details that my son should deal with?'

'No, I don't think so. Mr Trent will see to probate, the bank and whatever your son decides about her apartment. Everything including her personal possessions goes to him.'

Lady Margaret stared at Ted's blank face. 'Don't look so shocked. When Dorothy made her last journey up here to visit me, she told me that she had changed her will. Previously I think most of her belongings were to go to charity, but I truly believe that your son has been a good friend to her in her last months. I also have reason to believe that she knew she was very ill – not that she said a word to me.'

At that point Matron entered the room together with a maid pushing a small tea trolley.

'Oh,' Lady Margaret exclaimed delightedly, 'we are honoured, lovely savouries and a fruit cake to go with our coffee. Thank you, Matron.'

'You are both more than welcome,' Matron answered as she and the maid left the two old friends to help themselves.

Chapter Thirty

DENNIS HAD NEVER FELT such a fool in his life. He had been placed high up in the enclosure used for the accused. The magistrate was glancing through a folder which had been set in front of him, and as Dennis watched he thanked God he didn't have a record. He had listened to the policeman's version of what had happened and then to the testimony of Stanley Wilson as to his good character and how well he treated his workmen.

The magistrate was now conferring with his colleagues who sat on either side of him. They were murmuring and nodding their heads in agreement.

Dennis turned his head and looked across at his father, but Ted wouldn't or couldn't meet his eyes.

At that point Dennis would have freely admitted that he was scared. He had never been to prison. He had been in trouble enough times when he was younger, but somehow his dad had always managed to smooth things over. Now he felt he was entirely on his own. A film of perspiration was covering his good-looking face and his thick mop of hair was also damp.

Somebody was prodding him in the back, telling him

to stand up. Now he could hear the magistrate's voice loud and clear.

'Mr Dryden, this matter appears to have stemmed from a misuse of your business funds, and while the court does not take lightly the fact that you took matters into your own hands, the bench is of the opinion that you were severely provoked. Your site manager, Mr Cooke, has refused to press charges. However, you did cause an affray which led to a breach of the peace. You are therefore fined the sum of fifty pounds, but I add a warning that, should you appear before this court in the future, we shall not be of the same mind. Do you understand?'

Dennis quietly answered, 'Yes,' and then added, 'Thank you, sir.'

It was as if a burden had been lifted from his shoulders.

The experience of spending the weekend in a police cell had left him with an instinctive wish to avoid the police in future.

Two big men, both well over six foot tall, walked out of the court and into the nearest pub, where Edward Dryden ordered two large brandies. As they each tossed them back, it would have been hard to say which one of the men felt the more relieved.

'You'd better come home with me, have a wash and tidy-up before you go and see your wife, and don't forget that sometime today you have to contact that Mr Trent.' Ted's voice was low but firm.

'Thanks, Dad.' Dennis had no intention of paying Ella a visit. The less she knew about him having spent the weekend in a police cell, the better for everyone concerned. Instead he suggested, 'How about we go to Covent Garden first, get ourselves a slap-up breakfast? I'm starving; they didn't exactly feed me in the lock-up.'

His father grinned. 'Then you can thank yer lucky stars that they didn't bang yer up properly, 'cos I'll take bets you'd have lost a whole lot of weight before you came out.'

With a huge fry-up and two large mugs of tea beneath his belt, Dennis felt a whole lot better as he sat behind his father's desk in order to use his telephone.

'Gurney and Trent.' A young lady's voice answered his call.

'Oh good morning, I understand Mr Trent has been trying to get in touch with me.'

'Who shall I say is calling?'

'Oh, I'm sorry, Dennis Dryden, in connection with the death of Miss Sheldon.'

'Hold on a minute, please.'

Almost at once Mr Trent came on the line. 'Mr Dryden, so glad we have been able to contact you. Sorry about the sad news, but not totally unexpected.'

A good voice, strong and businesslike. Dennis felt better already.

'I've been told that I have been listed as Miss Sheldon's next-of-kin. Do I have to do anything in particular?'

'Oh no, Mr Dryden, you inherit, but Miss Sheldon asked that this firm be her executor. No other person is involved.'

'My father has been in touch with Lady Margaret; she told him you would be seeing to all the funeral arrangements and—'

Mr Trent intervened. 'All finalized. The first thing is that Miss Sheldon left instructions with my office that she wished to be buried with her parents. The family own a plot so that makes everything much easier. It is in Lambeth Cemetery in Tooting. Unfortunately quite a journey from Epsom. As for an undertaker, that has been dealt with, and as it stands, all documents being ready, the burial should take place next Tuesday, that's a week tomorrow. Not sure how many cars will be needed. Lady Margaret has promised to telephone or write to their few friends, and perhaps you could let me know if you will be attending and if anyone else will be accompanying you. Naturally myself and one colleague will attend and a booking has been made for the function room in the Spread Eagle Hotel in Epsom for a small get-together afterwards.

'By the way, have we got your telephone number?'

Dennis hesitated. 'I'm travelling a lot at the moment; best I give you my father's number, would that be all right?'

'No problem, we can always leave a message for you.'

Dennis gave him the number. 'Thank you again, goodbye for—'

'Mr Dryden?'

'Yes?'

'Don't ring off. Miss Sheldon was not a lady of great wealth, but you are the sole beneficiary. She had some savings, and her endowment policy will more than cover any outstanding bills and the funeral expenses. Her main asset is of course her apartment. I have to tell you we have already received an offer on this property, should you wish to sell.'

Warning bells went off in Dennis's head. His father had rattled on about another tenant, a Mr Claude Packard, who had been pestering Miss Sheldon to sell. Probably the same bloke; he sounded like a nasty piece of work.

'No way,' Dennis answered without stopping to think. 'We'll let the dust settle before we think about disposing of anything that belonged to Miss Sheldon.'

'A very wise decision, Mr Dryden. It is not a substantial legacy, but Miss Sheldon was anxious that you should know how much she appreciated your kindness to her, especially because you negotiated terms that enabled her to live in what had been her home for a good many years.'

Dennis was embarrassed. 'I wasn't kind. I was just able to cut the price a bit on that remaining flat.'

Mr Trent chose to ignore that admission. Instead he said knowingly, 'I did the conveyancing when Miss Sheldon bought it from you.'

In other words he knows I knocked quite a bit off the price for her! 'I never thought . . . I didn't expect . . .' Dennis was embarrassed. The last thing he wanted was to be thought of as a do-gooder, or a gold-digger.

Oh, what the hell, it has nothing to do with anyone but me.

'Thank you,' Dennis couldn't think of anything more to say.

'A pleasure to be of help, though sorry it has to be under such sad circumstances. Goodbye for now, Mr Dryden, we'll probably meet at the funeral.'

Mr Trent rang off and Dennis slowly replaced the receiver.

Now he had to go and face his wife.

Bonus, though, he'd get to see his kids today.

Winnie Paige was alone in her daughter's house when a tap on the door followed by footsteps coming down the passage broke into her thoughts, and she called, 'Who is it?' and Dennis Dryden marched into the kitchen.

'Oh God above, it's enough to freeze the brass balls off a pawn shop out there! Probably gonna get some real snow this time, didn't have much before Christmas.' Dennis walked towards the hearth and, taking his gloves off and shoving them into his coat pocket, held out his hands to the blazing fire.

'It hasn't started to snow again, surely?' his mother-in-law asked.

'Not yet, Win, but it won't be long. Where's Ella and the kids?'

Winnie moaned to herself: why is it left t' me to tell this bloke where his wife is?

'Sit down and get yerself warm. I'll make a brew and I've made some pies if you fancy a bite to eat.'

'Win, I'd love a cuppa, I'm chilled to the bone, but first of all, remember, I asked you a question!'

Winnie pulled a face. 'They've all gone to a party 'cos Sam Richardson's firm didn't give one at Christmas, for what reason I don't know.'

'Where the hell does Sam Richardson come into this?'

'Sam is a kind of partner, I think, in a firm called Hirst and Richardson.'

'I know all that, don't I? Known Sam from years back, but that still doesn't answer my question.'

'All right, all right. At first Sam said he'd take Babs and Teddy, then he asked if Ella would like to go with them. He said it's always a good do and the kids get given lovely presents.'

'I can buy my kids all the presents they need,' Dennis said, sounding really churlish.

Winnie decided to give as much to Dennis as he was throwing at her.

'Yeah, and leave 'em on the doorstep and run away. Hadn't even got the guts to come into the house and see yer kids on Christmas Day, never mind the other three hundred an' odd days in the year.'

One look at Dennis's face and Winnie was having second thoughts. Perhaps she should have kept her mouth shut.

'Is Sam Richardson trying it on with my wife?' Dennis asked, letting his anger get the better of him.

'I don't know, an' if I did I wouldn't tell yer. You're such a big man, why don't you ask him yerself?'

This situation had suddenly become awkward and

neither of them spoke for a while. Then a surge of relief came over Winnie as Dennis got to his feet, went to the stove and lifted the big black kettle to the centre of the range. 'Thought you said we were gonna have a bite to eat and a cuppa,' he muttered.

Jesus, it was unbelievable!

This great big bloke was sitting here in his own kitchen, and she'd lay a penny to a pound that he was wishing it was him and not Sam Richardson that had taken his wife and kids out for the afternoon.

Oh, the madness of it all!

It was Dennis who made the pot of tea while Winnie took the cups, saucers and plates down from the dresser and set them out on the table.

'Only got cold pie, veal, ham an' egg, but I did make it meself, none of that shop rubbish. Got a big stew on the go back of the hob but it's nowhere near ready yet.'

'Thanks, Winnie.' He spoke softly now as she passed him a plate on which she had laid two thick slices of the pie. 'This will do me fine.'

She also put in front of him a plate of crusty new bread and a dish of butter. 'I've got plenty of salad or some pickles if you fancy some.' She was pouring the tea out as she spoke.

'Still pushing the rabbit food, Win? Sunday tea always included salad when we all used to come t' your place. No thanks to the salad but I will have some of that Branston pickle if you'd pass the jar, please.'

He had drunk his tea and Winnie was refilling his cup before he ventured to ask, 'Are the children all right?'

Without looking at him she said, 'Young Ted is the image of you, as you are the image of your father. Three peas from the same pod and no mistake. As for Babs, she's growing fast. A really nice little girl but she gets that beautiful copper-coloured hair and soft skin from our side of the family. I don't think she's in a hurry to grow up, though. She's . . . well, she's just Babs. Everybody loves her.'

Now Winnie did look at her son-in-law and she smiled, a small understanding smile. He smiled back at her, and they continued eating in silence.

Soon he was putting his coat, scarf and gloves on. Taking hold of her hand gently, he said, 'Perhaps it might be better if you didn't tell Ella or the kids that I've been here.' When she didn't answer, he shook his head slowly and said, 'I'm an ignorant fool, and I'm ashamed of so many things that I let happen.'

'Oh, Dennis, you don't need—'

He stopped her. 'Yes, I do need. And Winnie, nobody knows that better than you do.'

His remorse brought tears to her eyes, and she murmured something indistinct.

'What?'

'Well, do something about it,' she repeated.

'Such as?'

'Tell Ella, not me.'

The funeral was over. A quiet, dignified affair attended by just six women and five men.

Lady Margaret had decided against attending, and Matron had assured Edward on the telephone that it was a wise decision, with the weather being as bad as it was.

When each mourner had thrown a handful of the cold earth down on to the coffin and the priest had shaken hands with each of them, they all moved away and left the grave-diggers to get on with their work. Dennis shook hands with both Mr Trent and his partner. However, when Ted said that they would not be making the journey to Epsom, Mr Trent indicated that he needed a moment of Dennis's time.

'I have to go down to Epsom – these ladies and gentlemen who so kindly came to Miss Sheldon's funeral deserve the little get-together that I have arranged – but you and I do need to talk. There are a few matters that require your attention.'

Dennis looked thoughtful for a moment, then said, 'I can't make it tomorrow, but how would Thursday fit in with your plans?'

'You state the time and I'll make sure that I am free.'

'Ten o'clock, your office,' Dennis said without hesitation.

Mr Trent said, 'Good,' and, as though he were sealing their agreement, he covered Dennis's hand with his own.

Ted and his son stood silently watching the cars move down towards the cemetery gates. Then, heads sunk into the collars of their expensive overcoats, they walked away towards where Ted had parked his car.

Dennis was totally unaware that the death of Dorothy Sheldon and the events which were yet to unfold would have such a shattering effect on his future life.

Thursday morning, and Dennis was listening intently to what Mr Trent had to say. So far it was pretty much as his father had suspected, having listened to Lady Margaret air her fears as to the way her friend Dorothy had been treated. Now Dennis was beginning to form his own opinion as to why this Mr Packard was so anxious to purchase her apartment.

All legalities regarding the estate of Miss Sheldon had been dealt with and Dennis now knew exactly where he stood.

'Now, Mr Dryden, shall we move on to your actual property?'

Having got a nod from Dennis, Mr Trent leant across

his desk and said, 'I take it that when you had that beautiful old house turned into four apartments, which you then sold individually, you retained the freehold of the property?'

Dennis smiled. 'How did I know you were going to ask me that?'

It was Mr Trent who now smiled. 'How do I know that your answer to my question is yes?'

'To be honest, it was my father who steered me that way.'

'A real man of the world is your father. So, we can move on. We have established that you sold one apartment to a Mr Claude Packard, another to a young man . . .' Mr Trent paused and consulted his notes. 'Ah yes, Mr Alfred Marshall. He took out a mortgage in order to purchase, but after only two months his firm moved its business to Leicester. Having been offered an all-expenses-paid move, Mr Marshall wanted to sell in a hurry. Mr Packard applied for a mortgage and bought Mr Marshall's apartment. With that move Mr Packard became the owner of two of the apartments. From then on it would seem that a series of unpleasant happenings started to occur which made life very difficult for Miss Sheldon, and to a lesser degree the fourth owner also experienced unexplained accidents.' He paused again, turned over some pages and then carried on speaking. 'A widow lady, Mrs Hines, you met her at Miss Sheldon's funeral. Apparently she also has been approached by Mr Packard as to the prospect of her selling her apartment.'

'Thinks he's clever, this Mr Packard,' Dennis said with what was almost a sneer. 'We all know the property market is rising fast, but what he doesn't know is that anything and everything that goes on or around the area of a racecourse has always been a matter of great interest to my father. Packard has been putting feelers out to members of the local council as to what the chances are of obtaining planning permission.'

'I'm with you, Mr Dryden,' the solicitor murmured. 'There are a good many acres of prime land that go with your property. By the way, are you still using the original name?'

'Yes, Lady Margaret wanted it still to be known as Maple House.'

'Should Mr Packard be successful in securing both the flat that Miss Sheldon owned, which now belongs to you, and also Mrs Hines's apartment, it would mean that he owned the whole building.'

But not the freehold, Dennis was thinking, not by a long chalk.

'So,' he asked Dennis, 'if I were to agree to sell him what was Miss Sheldon's place, has this Mr Packard got the readies?'

Mr Trent had to think for a moment; readies was not a word with which he was familiar.

Finally he said, 'I wouldn't have thought so. Scraping the barrel more like! I've been given to understand that if and when he can say he has persuaded the owners of the two remaining apartments to sell, he would be seeking to take out a legal charge using the property as security for one huge loan.'

Dennis smiled, a truly wicked smile. 'Would he now! I would really like some concrete evidence as to why this Mr Packard can't wait to be the sole owner of all four apartments. Any chance you can put some feelers out?'

Mr Trent could not quite suppress a smile. 'Given your instructions, Mr Dryden, I can make discreet enquiries.'

'Please do that, Mr Trent.'

Chapter Thirty-one

EDWARD DRYDEN WAS TRYING to catch up on a backlog of ledger work and he was fast losing his patience.

'Why on earth do you want us both to go down to Epsom?' he asked Dennis, who was leaning up against the counter.

'Hard to know where to begin really, Dad, but before the funeral you were saying that you suspected that Mr Packard was giving Miss Sheldon a load of trouble; well, now I've got a problem with this geezer and the funny thing is I just can't put my finger on the cause. Dorothy was barely cold before he had telephoned her solicitor saying he wanted to put an offer in to buy her flat. Naturally, Mr Trent wouldn't or couldn't confirm in so many words that the offer came from the same bloke that was pestering her to sell. Not a bad guy, though, that Mr Trent; he has agreed to put the feelers out and let me know if he comes up with anything.'

'So why not wait until he gets in touch with you?'

'Because I have this feeling that if he gets Miss Sheldon's flat he'll go for Mrs Hines. He won't play fair, he'll make her life a misery same as he did Miss Sheldon's. He thinks if he's clever enough he'll end up owning the whole caboodle.'

'Don't you ever stop to think, you nuthead? How can he get hold of Dorothy's flat? You own it now and sure as hell he can't make you do anything you've no mind t' do.'

'Dad, I've got a plan hatching in my head, but I'm beginning to think Packard might be a little too dangerous for me to have dealings with.'

'Son, has that couple of nights in a cell turned your grey matter to yellow? Come on through and outline what you're trying to come up with.' He lifted the flap of the counter and led Dennis through into his private office.

It was a bit long-winded, but in the end Dennis managed to outline his idea clearly enough to make his father roar with laughter.

'Nice one, my son, a really nice one, we'll drink to that, 'cos if what we suspect turns out to be the truth, then it will be a case of the biter got bit. If anybody ever deserved to be brought down to earth it's that scumbag. Only the lowest of the low picks on defenceless women, especially when he knows they've got no man behind them.'

'I'm glad you agree, Dad. But what about Mrs Hines? How the hell do we explain to her that we want to sell her place over her head yet also assure her that she can remain living there if that's what she wants t' do?'

'Tough one, my boy, I'll give yer that. Then again, as you've heard me say often enough, never trouble trouble till trouble troubles you. So we'll sort that problem when we come to it. Meanwhile I think you're right. A little reassuring talk with Mrs Hines is in order and there's no better time than right now.'

Dennis was more than pleased. If his father agreed to be involved with his plan then there would be no question of anything going wrong. It might be complicated, but Edward Dryden had a habit of always coming out of a tricky situation smelling of roses.

Edward took his car. The roads were wet but the hard ice had gone, and the overcast sky was slowly lightening.

It was about an hour and a half later when he turned in to the long private drive that led up to Maple House. During the night the wind had dropped somewhat and the two men saw that in places the snow had melted and almost seeped away, revealing patches of rough, tufty grass each side of the driveway. Dennis lowered his side window and there was the fresh smell of moss and damp earth.

Not a bad place to live, he was thinking. If only his Ella had agreed to move out of London when he had first suggested it, who knows where they'd be today. As his father brought the car to a halt and Dennis made to get out he was mumbling, 'Life's full of bloody ifs.'

When Mrs Hines opened her front door in answer to the ringing of her bell, she was fully dressed but walking with two sticks.

'Hello. What have you been doing? You weren't using sticks when you attended Dorothy's funeral.' Edward spoke kindly.

'Hello, Mr Dryden and son I suppose I should say,' Mrs Hines said laughingly. 'Come in, you're more than welcome. I was just about to have coffee. You will join me, say yes, please do, I'm that thrilled to have company.'

She hobbled back into her magnificent lounge and bade them both to sit down. 'I have just put milk in the saucepan but haven't yet put it on to boil. I'll add some more to it and then I'll make the coffee.'

'You'll do no such thing,' Dennis ordered, guiding her safely to the chair with a foot-rest in front of it where she had obviously been sitting.

Having seen her settled and left his father there to talk

295

to her, Dennis made for the luxurious kitchen. There was a tray neatly laid, one cup and saucer, one teaspoon and a small plate with two biscuits. It was an expensive tray and the delicate bone china hadn't come from Woolworth's; nevertheless, the sight brought a lump to his throat. It spelt lonely.

He found a larger tray, added two extra cups and saucers, took more milk out of the refrigerator and poured some into the saucepan, then put the pan on to the electric plate. The milk came to a boil at the same time as the coffee percolator began to steam. Finding a pretty jug, he poured the hot milk into it and set it down on the tray, unplugged the percolator, added more biscuits from a tin and all was ready.

If Ella had been there, she wouldn't have believed Dennis was capable of such an achievement. Though she would probably be the first to admit that when he lived at home she had encouraged him to be lazy by waiting on him hand, foot and finger.

Entering the lounge, Dennis grinned. 'Since I made it, I suppose the job of pouring it into the cups falls to me,' he said as he tackled the tricky job.

When they each had a lovely milky coffee in front of them, it was Ted who asked what Dennis was dying to know.

'So, why *are* you walking with two sticks, Mrs Hines? Have you had a fall?'

'Not exactly. I was careless, I suppose.'

'Now then, Mrs Hines, you leave us to draw our own conclusions,' Ted said, sounding really serious. 'Just tell us what happened.'

'I had been to our Friday night Bible class and the members of the group always stay on for a hot drink, then usually the vicar drives me home. It takes less than ten minutes in the car. Last week, as the roads were so bad, Mrs Taylor's son came for his mother and he said he had to pass my door almost and it would save the vicar a journey if he brought me home at the same time. He was so kind, he insisted on getting out of his car and seeing me safely inside the house to where the hall light was on. I thanked him and closed the front door, but as I was coming up the few stairs to my front door the light went out and I missed my footing and tripped.'

'Did anyone pick you up?' Dennis was quick to ask.

'No, there wasn't anyone around. I stayed still for a moment or two, then I managed to make it all right. I did have a restless night, quite a bit of pain, so in the morning I telephoned my doctor, who kindly came out to me within half an hour. I've bruised the shin bone on my left leg and sprained my right ankle. A nurse has called each day since, so I am fine. Funny thing, though . . .'

'Go on, finish what you were going to say,' Ted said, leaning forward and taking one of the old lady's hands between his own.

Mrs Hines looked perplexed. 'When the doctor came, he offered to replace the dead lightbulb. A kind thought, for which I was very grateful. However, he switched on the light and it worked, the bulb had not gone. It must have been a power cut.'

'Mrs Hines, think back,' Ted pleaded. 'When you finally managed to get into your apartment, was the electricity on or off?'

'Oh, it was on in here,' she said without hesitation. 'As soon as I got the front door open I remember I felt for the switch without thinking and my hall was flooded with light. Maybe the entrance is on a different circuit.'

And maybe pigs could fly if they had wings, Dennis was thinking.

The look that passed between father and son said they were both having the same thought.

There was unbroken silence while the three of them drank their coffee and nibbled at digestive biscuits. During this time Ted was casting his eyes all over the place. He had to hand it to his son, he might not do much manual work himself, but by God the men he employed were never amateurs or dabblers. Each man had to be an expert in his own trade. Dennis paid top wages and he expected only the best. It was a code he had long stood by and it certainly paid off. This apartment was proof of that. Everything about it was perfection personified.

Ted smiled to himself. Dennis was fond of saying, 'If you pay peanuts, your workmen must be monkeys.' He might cut corners in order to obtain contracts, but whether he got them by fair means or by giving out backhanders when a job was finished, he seldom received complaints. Quite the reverse.

Dennis had finished his coffee and the look his father gave him said it was time to take the bull by the horns.

'Mrs Hines, are you happy living here?' Ted gently asked the first question.

'Well, who wouldn't be, it is such a beautiful place.'

'That was not what I asked you. Please try and tell me and my son exactly how you feel. Can you do that?'

'I'll try.' Mrs Hines sighed softly and took a minute or two to collect her thoughts. 'For years I envied Dorothy and Lady Margaret, they had such a wonderful friendship, but they always had time for me when we met at church. On many an occasion they would bring me back here to have lunch with them. Of course this building was a whole house then, and the interior was rather old-fashioned but graceful. It was Dorothy who suggested I have an apartment here after you,' she nodded her head towards Dennis, 'did the alterations. I thought it was God's will because Lady Margaret decided to go into a care home and Dorothy and I would have each other for company.'

Mrs Hines paused and from a small handbag that hung from the arm of her chair she took out a lace-edged handkerchief and wiped the corner of her eye.

Father and son remained silent, letting her take her time.

'Everything was going so well to begin with. Young Mr Marshall was such a gentleman and helped us both in so many ways. We had grown quite fond of him. Slowly she shook her head. 'It wasn't to be. He was only here a matter of weeks when his firm promoted him and he moved away, and Mr Packard bought his apartment. I can't think why a married couple would want two flats.'

Dennis jumped in. 'Mr Packard has a wife?'

'Yes, yes, he does, though I don't think they are exactly amicable, nor even cordial to each other on some days.' Then, in a very childlike voice Mrs Hines added, 'I like her much better than him and so did Dorothy. Now Dorothy has gone and it doesn't seem right for me to be living here.'

Dennis looked at his father, and when he got the nod from him he began.

'Mrs Hines, I am going to tell you some interesting facts and I would like you to listen very carefully. Is that all right with you?'

'Perfectly all right,' she said, and nodded her head just once.

'Once the war was over, there was much rebuilding to be done and repair work was being carried out by men that my father and I would look upon as cowboys. They were causing a lot of unessential reconstruction to listed buildings. Therefore, the powers that be decided that every building, including dwellings, had to be registered at Somerset House. From then on, the Town and Country Planning Act became law. For example, if the title deeds of a property have been lost, new ones have to be applied for. On all such registrations, stamp duty has to be paid.

'As you know, my father and Lady Margaret were friends, mainly because of their mutual interest in horse-racing, and when she decided that this property was far too big for her to manage, she turned to my father for advice.'

Dennis stopped talking, and after a suitable interval during which Mrs Hines assured them she was all right, even saying that she was very interested, Ted took over.

'Over the years, maintenance of this property had not been kept up and matters such as the roof, to name only one item, needed urgent costly repairs. Lady Margaret decided to sell, and she and I between us negotiated a fair price and my son was able to go ahead with the deal. Dennis will tell you what happened from then on.'

'It was a lengthy business.' Dennis smiled at this genteel, white-haired old lady. 'I wanted to come and live here, bring my wife and two children, but it wasn't to be. My wife has her roots in London and no amount of persuasion from me would get her to move. So I decided to go down another road.

'Three times I put in an application and plans to Surrey County Council and each time they were turned down. The council were right, I realize that now. So was my wife,' Dennis quietly confessed. 'If my Ella had come to live in the original house she would have been like a fish out of water.' He paused, looking very thoughtful, before continuing. 'The municipal council were adamant. No outside structural alterations whatsoever to this building would be allowed.

'Then I had a brainwave! This property is detached, double-fronted and on two floors. All it really needed was for a good architect to draw up plans for the inside of the building to be split into four equal parts. Two downstairs and two on the first floor. Costly, mind you, and maybe I was a bit extravagant when it came to the fittings, but in hardly any time at all I had good craftsmen crawling all over the place, and hey presto we had these four luxurious apartments. All registered and all legal. Maybe I did boast a bit,' Dennis admitted, looking shamefaced at his father. 'I told my wife I had built a block of flats but only because I was narked because she wouldn't come to live here.'

'Now,' Ted butted in, 'having told you the basics, I think we need a proper drink before my son sets his plan before you. What do you think, Mrs Hines? A little drop of brandy?' he suggested, pulling his briefcase nearer to his feet and bending down to take out a bottle.

'I am going to put a proposition to you, Mrs Hines, and I want you to think about it very carefully.' Dennis spoke slowly and clearly.

'I will.' Having taken a sip of the brandy that Ted had poured for her, Mrs Hines sounded quite chirpy.

'I want to purchase this apartment from you.'

'You mean buy me out, you don't want me here?'

'Oh, Mrs Hines, please don't sound so horrified. Just hear me out. There is a lot I want to tell you and I did ask you to think about it carefully. That means that you make your own decision and in your own time. It doesn't matter how long you take. Now, shall I continue?'

Mrs Hines let out a deep breath which could have been a sigh of relief. 'Yes, I am listening.'

'Claude Packard wants to buy what was Dorothy's place and he also wants to purchase your apartment. As he already owns the other two apartments, doesn't that say something to you? It does to both my father and myself, something rather fishy, I'm afraid. I know at first you loved it here, and you had Dorothy close at hand, but now she had gone and you are alone again.'

Dennis could not give Mrs Hines a complete picture of his intentions, so what he was about to suggest to her

301

would require as careful an approach as would the other matter of dispensing with Claude Packard. If only he could see that life was made hard for this rotter, get a few London heavies to give him a good beating, get rid of him even, he thought wryly.

But it was far more complicated than that.

'What I am hoping to do is get our own back on Mr Packard for all the torment he put Miss Sheldon through and what we fear he might try to do to you should you refuse to sell your apartment to him.'

'Poor Dorothy,' Mrs Hines murmured. 'She was really afraid of him towards the end. She left her home to you, didn't she, Mr Dryden?'

'Yes she did.'

'Did she really have no other family? No relations?'

'Nobody, it seems.'

'Poor soul, Dorothy was such a sweet person. I think she felt it very badly when Lady Margaret left here. Though she did visit her and I went with her on a couple of occasions, and we both agreed Lady Margaret was so happy it was a good move. We all get so lonely as we get older and our friends and family have mainly passed on. We wonder why we are left.'

'If I did sell this apartment, where would I go? I have means but I wouldn't be mad enough to sink more money into making another expensive move.'

This was just the opening that Dennis was looking for.

'My father and I were thinking that if you sold this place back to us, you might like to go into the same care home in Chelsea as Lady Margaret.'

Dennis saw the doubt in her eyes and said quickly, 'I won't go into detail as to why I need to buy your property – the circumstances are too complicated – but both myself and my father will give you our solemn word that you would not lose out, not by one penny. If I buy your place, I would ask you to move out for the time that it would take us to sort out Mr Packard, and when we have done that you shall have two choices. One, we return the deeds back over to you for a very reasonable sum and you would once again become the owner of this apartment. The alternative you must consider long and hard: you could stay in the care home as a permanent resident. You say you have visited Lady Margaret, so you have seen the conditions, and we could have a word with Anne Riley, the matron. I'm sure she could find you a very comfortable large room where you could stay, kind of test-drive the place, give everything the once-over and see if you think you would be happier there. And if not, there will be nothing to stop you coming back to Epsom once we have sorted this nasty matter out.'

Ted felt he had to give this kind lady a bit of confidence, so it was he that added, 'And we promise there will be no Mr Packard on the scene by then.'

'I don't have any idea how much it costs to stay in that beautiful place where Lady Margaret is. I only know it would be a lot.'

'To begin with, all that would be taken care of by my father.' Dennis also sought to reassure her.

Mrs Hines, quite firmly for an old lady, said, 'No. I can't say that I haven't given the same idea a great deal of thought since Dorothy died, but I cannot understand why you should want to go to such lengths to sort my affairs out.'

'Because we feel responsible for you. We should have checked Mr Packard's credentials before selling him an apartment. With hindsight, we should have sought buyers of the same age group and qualities. It is an old saying but a very true one, you have to live with someone to really know them. What we have learnt from Lady Margaret has led us to believe that Mr Packard is not a true gentleman.'

Dennis would have liked to have used words that were much stronger when referring to Claude Packard, but this was a frail old lady they were talking to.

'You are not to make a rash decision, you are to take your time. The wheels of justice grind slowly but we'll get there, never fear we shall get there.'

'If I decide to go along with your plans, Mr Dryden, I wouldn't own any bricks and mortar, would I?'

'You would if you decided that your stay in Chelsea was only going to be a temporary one. If that was the case, we would sell you back your own apartment and it would be like the move that Mr Marshall made, all expenses paid.'

Dennis felt he couldn't say any more because he didn't want to be accused of badgering Mrs Hines. Ted, however, couldn't leave things so up in the air. He stood up, moved his chair much closer to where Mrs Hines was sitting and gave her a very straightforward look.

'I endorse every word my son has said to you, and whatever you decide, that will be all right by us. Should you decide to stay here, that also will be OK. If you want to go with one of the options my son has offered you, we shall insist that everything is done legally and above board. Naturally you will use your own solicitor at every stage of the proceedings.

'Now,' he stood up, looked down at her and said, smiling, 'Dennis will wash our coffee cups and then we'll be off, because I think we have given you more than enough to think about for one day.'

With Dennis out in the kitchen doing what for him was a very unusual chore, Mrs Hines spoke softly to Ted.

'Lady Margaret often talked about you to me. I know she was quite content to leave her affairs in your hands when it came to selling this house. Therefore I do know that I may trust you, but if you don't mind I shall consult

304

my own solicitor and take a little while before making any big decision.'

'Very wise, my dear. You are a very competent lady, of that I have no doubt. I have put one of my business cards on your coffee table. Should you at any time feel the need to talk to me, or ask any questions, please ring my number. Should I be out of the office, just say who it is ringing and I will get back to you quite quickly.'

'Thank you, Mr Dryden,' she said, attempting to rise.

Ted gently pressed her back down into her chair. 'It has been a pleasure talking to you, we will see you again soon.'

'I hope so,' she said sadly, 'I hope so.'

It was a very thoughtful father and son who drove back to London.

Chapter Thirty-two

'COME AWAY WITH ME for the weekend,' Sam said to Ella one morning halfway through February.

Ella was busy changing an optic behind the bar and was certain she must have misheard what Sam had just said.

'Sorry, what did you say?'

'You heard me right the first time,' he said, smiling broadly. 'I think a few days away on our own would do us both good.'

Ella was still unwilling to believe that she was hearing right. Out of the blue, just like that, he wanted them to spend a whole weekend together.

'How can I, Sam?'

'Just ask Mike for some time off. The club isn't that busy at this time of year.'

He was incredible! 'What about my children?'

'Get your mother to move into your house to look after Babs and Teddy, she won't mind.'

The cheek of the man. He obviously had it all planned out in his mind.

Ella was worried. Not about what Dennis might think

if she went off for the weekend with another man. She hadn't set eyes on her husband since he had taken her out to dinner, and that was way before Christmas. He wasn't in a position to criticize how she led her life. But what about her mother? What would her reaction be?

She was tempted, that much she had to admit. Life at the moment was all work and no play, not that she was complaining. She counted herself lucky to have found herself such a good job and she really liked the people she worked with.

Sam was a nice man, and so far he hadn't taken any liberties, though that little spat he had had with her father-in-law on Christmas Day still rankled.

Ella took a deep breath before asking, 'Where would you be taking me?'

'To Brighton, well Hove, actually, it adjoins Brighton though it is a lot quieter and considered more upmarket. It will be really quiet at this time of the year.'

'So, have you taken a lady there before?'

Sam's face flushed bright red.

'No, I haven't.' His denial came out in a hoarse whisper. 'It's a detached bungalow, out in the wilds a bit. I first discovered it when my firm used a hotel on Hove seafront two years ago for our annual conference. One evening I went for a walk and it had a "For Rent" sign in the front garden. I told my sister and her husband about it and they rented it for two weeks. I went down and stayed three days with them and their two children, and we had a great time.'

'I'll think about it,' said Ella cautiously. To herself she was saying, he hasn't suggested that we take *my* two children with us.

Sam walked away without saying another word and Ella decided he could be very aggravating at times.

There was still the question of Dennis niggling away

in her head. Did he have the right to object? No, he had no right whatsoever, she thought bitterly.

So it was more or less to spite Dennis that three days later she said dubiously to Sam, 'A weekend by the sea sounds just what I need. But Sam, could we make it in a couple of weeks' time, because this Sunday is Babs's birthday.'

Sam didn't delay in making a decision. 'That's fine. It will give me time to contact the estate agent and to book a car.'

'What's wrong with your own car?'

'Nothing, it's just due for a thorough overall and I thought this would be an ideal time.'

Ella was pleased that Sam had agreed so readily to delay their little holiday.

She and her mother were planning a party, though Babs didn't want any boys to be there. That suited Teddy, who declared with a huge grin on his face that he would go and spend Saturday and Sunday with his grandad. Who wanted to hang around with a load of silly little girls when more than likely Grandad would take him to watch a football match?

To Babs a birthday meant presents. This year she had taken great pains to explain to her gran and her mother that she was no longer interested in dolls!

After breakfast, she sat on the rug in front of the front-room fire and opened her parcels, watched with some amusement by her mother and adoringly by her gran. She was not disappointed. Winnie had given her a cream-coloured coat which Babs had tried on in the shop a week ago and declared that she really, really liked. At the time Winnie had insisted it was far too expensive. The very next day, unbeknown to her granddaughter, she had gone back and bought it.

There was a huge jigsaw puzzle from Mike Murray and his wife, a real fountain pen and propelling pencil set together with a diary that had a lock on it from her mother, and a pretty card with a ten-shilling book token inside from Sam Richardson. But Babs's best present came from her father, in a large box that had been delivered by hand yesterday and which Ella had hastily hidden under the stairs.

Babs tore frantically at the brown paper. Then the lid of the box was lifted, showing layers of tissue paper which were quickly torn away, and finally Babs gasped with delight. A party dress. Baby-blue sateen, the skirt of the dress had a top layer of white organdie, the neckline was trimmed with lace, and pearly buttons were sewn down from the neck to the waist. The short puff sleeves had organdie cuffs.

Nothing could have given Babs more delight.

'I want to put it on now, please, Mum, can I?'

'No, sweetheart, it is a party dress. You can wear it this afternoon and show it off to all your friends. What you can do is clear up all this paper and take your presents up to your room. We've got to have the party in here, and we'll need the space to play games.'

Ella was deep in thought, thanking God that Ted had come and collected her son yesterday morning. What would Teddy think about his father sending such a wonderful present to his sister? It was Christmas all over again! Spend money on his children but too much of a coward to put in an appearance. A birthday hug and a few kisses from her dad would have had Babs dancing on the tabletop.

Babs's school friends arrived at four o'clock, and for an exhausting couple of hours Ella and her mother were in charge. At least they tried to be. Each child had brought a small present for Babs, which had to be opened. One child wept when a bigger girl tugged at her ringlets. Another girl asked if there was going to be a magician who would pull rabbits out of his top hat. Ella quickly told her there wasn't.

Games were played, with Pass the Parcel seeming to be the favourite, though every time Winnie lifted the needle from the gramophone record to stop the music there was an argument as to who was rightly holding the parcel.

Mother and daughter looked at the clock and couldn't believe that it was only a quarter to five.

'Tea time,' Ella shouted above the din. The games were thankfully abandoned and they all trooped out into the kitchen.

The scrubbed table was covered by a chenille cloth and then a really pretty cloth had been laid diagonally over that. The curtains were drawn, and the fire was burning brightly.

Winnie and Ella had gone to great lengths to please: there were dainty sandwiches, ham, egg and cheese, all with the crusts cut off. Lemonade, orange squash and cream soda were supplied with straws. There was a huge fruit trifle with a jug of pouring cream, jam tarts that Winnie had made, and, of course, the cake.

The girls took their places at the table, and for a little while all was silent. Of course there were accidents and squabbles, drinks spilt, the last egg sandwich two girls both wanted, a jam tart dropped on the floor, all speedily dealt with.

Winnie came in from the scullery bearing an enormous glass plate on which stood the cake. Ella, having cleared a space, said to her mother, 'Put it down here, all we need is for you to drop it.'

Winnie did as she was bid, then reached over and turned off the centre light.

Finally Ella lit the nine candles. The old kitchen became a magic place, the dancing flames reflected in the wide eyes of the little girls who sat around the table while Babs stood beside her mother and helped her to cut the cake.

The guests had all gone home, and suddenly the whole place was quiet.

'Cup of tea, Ella?'

'Oh Mum, you are a mind-reader,' Ella said as she looked around at all the mess. 'By the way, when it's Teddy's birthday, and in fact all future birthdays, remind me to give the children sixpence each and send them all to the pictures!'

'Get on! You loved every minute of it,' her mother said as she pushed the kettle to the centre of the hob.

While Winnie set about making that most welcome cup of tea, Ella hesitated for a moment, needing time to collect her flying thoughts. This time next week, *if* all went according to plan, she should be in Hove with Sam. She shook her head. A lot could happen in a week. Finally she found a tray, and started on the tedious business of clearing up the remains of Babs's party.

She was in the kitchen washing up when her mother joined her.

'Leave all that and come and have this tea that I've made. I couldn't get Babs to take her new dress off, she'll probably want to go to bed in it tonight.' Winnie sighed and added, 'I'm bushed, I thought that party was never going to end. You'd have thought that Dennis might have shown his face, wouldn't you?'

Ella flicked a towel from the rail, and dried her hands. 'Just pour the tea out, Mother, and stop wishing for miracles.'

Each settled comfortably, the hot tea working wonders.

'Thought Sam might have popped in,' Winnie remarked casually.

'There's no reason why he should, but since you've brought the subject up, I may as well tell you he has asked me to go away with him for the weekend.'

'Well, don't sound so miserable about it. Nothing to be ashamed of, having a fling with a good-looking chap like Sam Richardson, good luck to you.'

'Don't know what you're talking about. I am not having a fling. I like him a lot but I'm certainly not in love with him.'

'Well, a weekend away together might help you to make up your mind.'

Ella turned her head and stared at her mother. Their eyes met, and it occurred to her, at that moment, that they had a remarkable relationship. What she would have done without Winnie over all these years she had no idea. Shared responsibilities, sorrows, frustrations, heartaches and laughter. Oh yes, they had had many a good laugh together and shed many tears. When Dennis had first walked out on her and she hadn't had a penny to bless herself with, her father-in-law had been a great help but it was always her mother to whom she and the children knew they could turn.

Hasn't she really and truly turned my life around? Ella asked herself. It was me who decided to find a job, but who was it who had encouraged me to slim down, wear different clothes, wash and set my hair more often? Just the fact that her mum had introduced her to Sadie and Isaac Cohan had gone a long way to giving her more confidence in herself. There was no way she could have afforded the kind of clothes she wore now if it weren't for them. In fact, as much as any person could be, her mum was practical, worldly and infinitely kind. She would share her last penny with anyone that needed it.

'So you are going to go, aren't you?' Winnie broke into her thoughts.

'I don't know. Dennis would go mad if he found out.'

'Bugger Dennis,' said Winnie. 'Did he ask your opinion when he went off the rails?'

'Two wrongs don't make a right.'

'Oh for Christ's sake, don't go all sanctimonious on me. Go, have a good time, Lord above knows you deserve it.'

'I'm married.'

'Yes, you're married, worse luck.'

'Mum, did you ever like Dennis?'

'Yes, I did, when you first started to go out with him, but like your father kept on about at the time, Dennis was twelve years older than you and you could have had the pick of so many young men. I have to say, though, that you both seemed to be so happy for the first six years before Teddy and Babs came along, and while they were still babies Dennis worked hard, even if he was always pulling dodgy deals. You didn't want for much, he was a good provider and he loved his children.'

'And now?'

'Well, a straight question deserves a straight answer. As the years passed he changed, got too big for his boots. He became a rotten husband and a rotten father.'

Having said that, Winnie felt she was between a rock and a hard place. When Dennis had called in to see her the other Saturday when Ella and the children were out with Sam Richardson, she had found it in her heart to feel very sorry for her son-in-law. He had done some diabolical things, but my God she knew he was paying for them now. Not financially, no, not by any means, but emotionally he was drained. And the thought crossed her mind that he was lonely.

That he deeply regretted his affair with Connie Baldwin and the tragic final outcome went without saying.

None of this could she speak about to Ella because she had given her word that she wouldn't say he had visited.

Ella smiled weakly. 'I never thought you would encourage me to go off with another man.'

'What do you think I am? Some sort of saint? I wouldn't expect you to spend the rest of your life in a state of chastity.'

'Then you won't disapprove if I go?'

'No, I won't. Sam Richardson is a nice fellow, been on his own for years, so why shouldn't the pair of you have a good time? God knows, life's been a big strain for you this last year, just one thing after another, but you've coped.'

Despite everything, Ella started to laugh. 'Mum, you are an absolute wonder. You're urging me to go away with Sam and I haven't even asked you yet if you will move in here and look after Teddy and Babs.'

'Because you know full well you have no need to ask me. It will be my pleasure. Now, we'll have another cup of tea, then we'd better finish clearing up and get all the dirty dishes out of the way before Ted brings young Teddy back and it's time to start cooking the supper.'

It was Wednesday before Ella saw Sam.

'Everything is fixed up,' he said, smiling at her. 'How about you? Was your mother OK about having the children?'

'Yes, she was. Actually she was all for it, said we both deserved a break. Though there is one question I would like to ask you, Sam. Why rent a bungalow for only two or three days? Surely the owners will charge you for a full week. Why not book into a hotel?'

Sam laughed. 'I've never know such a woman as you for raising difficulties. Besides, if we stayed in a hotel, we would either have to book ourselves in as Mr and Mrs

314

or have two single rooms and make sure that at all times we were really discreet. In a bungalow those sort of problems will not arise.'

Ella scowled. 'I'm not raising difficulties. I'm being practical.'

Ella's mind was in a whirl. Now she knew exactly what he had in mind and her imagination flew ahead. Seconds later she was rebuking herself. Wake up, Ella, you're no spring chicken and neither is Sam. He's too much of a gentleman to come right out with it, and you wouldn't let yourself face the truth, but now you've heard it. Face to face, head on. Call it a little holiday, or anything else you like, but if you go to Hove with Sam you are going on a dirty weekend.

'If your mother is all right about having the children, there's nothing to stop us. Get your skates on and go and ask Mike for the weekend off. Go on,' Sam urged.

Mike was a man of few words but swift action. She'd told him the true reason why she would like the time off. He put his arms around her and kissed her. 'Good on yer, me darling, you certainly deserve a break, and come t' that so does Sam. Strait-laced and sober-sides is our Sam; let's hope you bring him back with a smile on his face.'

'Oh Mike, don't let on to the staff, will yer?'

He promised he wouldn't. But all morning he was smiling to himself. When those two come back, if all goes as it should, we'll all be able to tell!

They didn't want to set the neighbours' tongues wagging, so come Saturday morning Sam picked Ella up outside the British Legion. Ever the gentleman, he took her small suitcase and, having stowed it away in the boot, came round to the passenger side of his rented black Humber to make sure that Ella was comfortably settled before they set off.

Ella felt like pinching herself as London was left behind and Sam was soon driving down the fairly new Kingston bypass, where all the signs indicated that they were en route to Brighton in Sussex.

The main approach to Brighton was so fresh and green, with great parks, greenery and healthy shrubs and trees. Sam began to give her a running commentary, which led her to believe that he was no stranger to this journey. The Pavilion was like no other building that Ella had ever seen. Standing majestically in beautiful grounds, every corner of its roof was adorned by an onion-shaped dome. 'It was built by George IV when he was Prince Regent,' Sam informed her knowledgeably.

Suddenly they could see the sea, and almost immediately Sam was driving along the sea front. It was a cold, blustery day, but still a great many people were walking along the promenade. Ella knew what a pier was, she had been to Southend quite a few times. Brighton had two of them!

Hove seemed to be an extension of Brighton, but even at first glance it was vastly different. Sam told her that while Brighton had a railway station, large shops and theatres, Hove had other attractions nearby such as a racecourse and several golf-links.

Even though Sam had stayed at this bungalow before, it took him a while to find it. From the road it was invisible, protected from all eyes by trees and a rutted driveway, bordered by high banks of shrubs.

Not much to look at from the outside, the bungalow was squat and square. They got out of the car together, and while Sam was fetching the two small cases that they had brought with them, Ella had a walk around. In front the small garden was neatly cultivated and she thought that when the spring finally arrived and the flowers came into bloom it would probably look very pretty. Walking around the back, she got a surprise. There were a great number of outbuildings. Old stables which hadn't housed a horse for years was her guess. The whole large area was paved with cobbles and flagstones all protected by high flint walls. Maybe a century or more ago a rich gentleman had had this place built, but it had to have been someone who cherished their privacy.

'Are you going to stand there staring for much longer? Or are you coming inside?' Sam's voice calling brought Ella back to the present.

Her eyes widened when she saw provisions stacked on the table which stood in the middle of the big kitchen. 'Did you bring all that with you?' she asked in disbelief.

'Of course not,' Sam laughed. 'When you rent a furnished cottage, either the estate agent or the owner always provide the essentials. Some folk might have travelled a long way, and the last thing they want to do is find a shop and go out to buy groceries. There is even a small refrigerator over in that corner,' he pointed, 'that's bound to have milk and maybe eggs.'

Sure enough he was right. Ella opened the door; inside there were six eggs, a half-pound pack of butter and two pints of milk.

'Shall we make a pot of tea and rustle up something to eat now, or investigate the rest of the rooms first?'

Ella hadn't stayed to hear the rest of his question; she had gone to explore the bungalow.

The front room cum dining room was very cosy-looking, a fawn tweed three-piece suite grouped around an open fireplace in which a fire was laid, and there and then Ella decided that Sam's first job was to put a match to the kindling wood and get that fire going. It was like an ice-well in here. Beneath the window was an oak dining table and six chairs, four high-backed and two carvers, one each end.

On the opposite side of the hall was a very large bedroom, with big windows that looked out on to a beautiful view, but it wasn't that which had Ella sending up a silent thank you. Someone had been thoughtful enough to lay out on top of the eiderdown which covered the double bed two very large rubber hot-water bottles. She'd fill them straight away, she decided, 'cos it was odds on the bed would be damp. Next door was a neat but slightly smaller bedroom. At the end of the hall she found a bathroom and a lavatory.

Sam made her jump as she turned around quickly and almost knocked into him.

'Everything all right?' he asked.

'Spotlessly clean,' she said. 'Nothing wrong, other than the whole place is absolutely freezing cold.'

Sam put his arms around her and held her close. 'I've already lit the fire in the sitting room and I've also turned the gas oven full on and left the door wide open so that the kitchen will get warm.' He released his firm hold on her but kept his arm around her waist. 'Why don't we go straight out? There is a nice high street down in Hove which has a car park near by. We can either find a decent restaurant or even have a pub lunch. What do you say?'

'Oh, yes please, Sam, but first I must boil a kettle, probably twice. I need enough hot water to fill two bottles. Can't risk that bed being damp. And another thing, before we go out will you please make sure that there's logs or coal somewhere here so that we can keep the fire going.'

'I have done that already. There is a bunker on the left-hand side of the bungalow which is well stocked with coal, and also a small shed housing a pile of logs. I've brought in a basketful of the logs. By the time we get back, the whole place should be feeling a whole lot warmer. I am sorry you're so cold, I should have asked the agent to come in and light the fire before we arrived. If that's all, let's go then and get some warm food inside you.'

Rather than unlock the front door again, they decided to go out through the back door and at the same time give Sam a chance to look at the outbuildings.

'At one time this must have been a vegetable garden,' was Sam's first comment. 'I don't remember it being as bad as this when my sister and her family were here, but then again the weather was hot and we spent most of the time on the beach.'

What they were staring at now was a sagging greenhouse and a cucumber frame. Every pane of glass of both was broken. However, there was a gorgeous smell, and for just one moment Ella couldn't work out where it was coming from. She sniffed a couple of times, then laughed and looked down at their feet. They were standing on an overgrown carpet of mint, the scent of which filled the sharp cold air.

Ella thought it was sad to see so much neglect. 'Shame,' she said to Sam, 'they've let the outside of this bungalow go to rack and ruin. Once it must have been a lovely home.'

She tugged the belt of her camel coat tighter around her waist, turned up the collar and began to run towards the car. The ground was uneven, and she tripped and would have fallen had not Sam been right behind her. His arms stretched out and caught her safely, and holding on to her he guided her to the car. Once inside, she watched as he tucked a car rug around her lap, tucking the ends about her legs. Then he walked around the car and got into the driver's seat.

Once he was seated, Ella said, 'You're taking great care of me today, aren't you?'

'Any reason why I shouldn't?'

Ella just shrugged her shoulders.

Sam had already turned the key in the ignition, but now he turned it off again and twisted round so that he was half facing her.

'Sometimes I get the impression that you ended your life the day Dennis walked out on you. You work hard, you pay your way and you take such good care of your two children, but you have no life of your own. I was like that when Charlotte died but I soon came to realize that life has to go on.'

'Oh, and now you lead such an exciting life?'

'I wouldn't altogether agree that my own life is exciting, but I was quite content until I met up with you again.'

Ella needed reassurance. 'Do you still think it was a good idea to bring me here?'

'Yes, yes, I do.' He leant towards her and laid his hand over hers. His touch was warm on her cold flesh, and she closed her fingers around his wrist, needing his heat.

Suddenly he said, 'I love you.'

She looked up into his eyes. 'At this moment you may mean what you've just said, Sam, but in reality you don't know me.'

'I love you,' he repeated. 'I think I began to love you the first time I met up with you again in the Legion. You were standing behind the bar, beside Mike, being taught how to pull a decent pint. You looked terrified.'

'I *was* terrified. I needed that job so badly, not only for the money but to prove to myself that I wasn't entirely useless.'

Sam sounded dead serious as he said, 'And although I knew you were married and Dennis and I had known each other for years, it made no difference at all. I couldn't get you out of my mind and that's when I started to make excuses to come to the Legion more than was necessary.'

'Sam, have you thought that the attraction was, maybe still is, that through me you still have a link to Charlotte?'

'I didn't try to analyse my feelings. I only know that I felt so much better when you were around.'

'That's understandable, because in all these years you haven't bothered much with female company, have you?'

Sam didn't make any reply and Ella felt bound to add, 'I was someone from the past; you knew I had gone to school with Charlotte and that we were the best of friends. And later, when you met and married her, Dennis and I and you two paired up and we had some good times together. Then Mike gave me a job and you met me again, but a lot of water had gone under the bridge. I was someone from the past.'

'Are you saying you're sorry you have come away with me?' he asked, his face a picture of sadness.

'No, not at all. But I do think it's a bit early for you to start saying that you love me.'

'Don't you have any feelings for me at all?'

'Now that is not what I'm saying. I like you a lot, Sam. It has been great to meet up with you again, and the attention you have paid me has done me the world of good.'

'I haven't paid you attention out of pity,' Sam was quick to reassure her.

He put his arms around her, pulling her close to him, and emboldened by the fact that she didn't pull away, he kissed the top of her head.

They stayed there, arms wrapped around each other, for a long time, both silent and thoughtful, until Sam asked quietly, 'Shall we go back inside? We can go out to eat tonight.'

'Oh, Sam . . .' It was a whisper; she felt like a young girl unable to say more.

'Come on, the fire should be burning well by now.'

She looked up into his face and knew what he was saying, and at that moment what he wanted was what she wanted too.

It had been a very long time since she had experienced

sexual instincts, and even longer since a man had found her sexually attractive.

She smiled, and his lips came down to cover hers and words became all at once totally unnecessary.

The fire was burning really well; even so, Sam added two large nobs of coal and placed a thick log on top of the coal.

Ella sat down on the worn carpet and stared into the dancing flames. Sam, meanwhile, was removing the large cushions from the settee. Having placed them edge to edge on the floor, he lifted her on to them, saying, 'We might as well be comfortable as well as warm.'

Afterwards, in the tranquil peace of passion spent, they lay quiet, entwined in each other's arms.

That evening they did make it into Hove and had a wonderful intimate dinner for two in an elegant hotel.

Come bedtime, Ella wore a beautiful nightdress that she hadn't been aware was in her case. In fact she had never before set eyes on this flimsy peach-coloured article of clothing that was little more than gossamer and lace sewn together with the finest thread. Her mother was more than a matchmaker!

Ella grinned to herself as she slipped this sexy nightdress over her head. Winnie might be old, but she certainly hadn't forgotten her memories!

Ella glanced at herself in the cheval-glass mirror which stood in the corner of the room and slowly slid her hands down over her hips. The feel of that thin material against her skin was fabulous; it was certainly something she wasn't used to. Slowly, before Sam came out of the bathroom, she climbed into bed and was sitting propped up with pillows when he entered the bedroom.

By the look on his face and the way his eyes lit up, he

approved of her night attire. Not that it was long before he was helping her to take it off again.

It was the early hours of the morning before they slept, but when they did they slept well and it was half past nine on Sunday morning when Ella opened one eye to see Sam standing beside the bed holding a tray.

Tea in bed! Now that was a luxury!

Having had a nice hot bath, Ella emerged to find that not only was the table laid for breakfast, but Sam was in the process of making toast and gave her a promise that scrambled eggs would be ready in five minutes.

He was well accomplished in taking care of himself and immediately the thought came to her that Dennis would be useless at scrambling eggs.

Straight off she rebuked herself. Why the hell was she comparing Sam with Dennis?

Later, with the dirty dishes piled in the sink, which was filled with hot soapy water, they donned their heavy coats, hats, scarves and gloves and set off to walk along the beach.

It was a glorious morning, still very cold, but sharp and crisp with the winter sunshine doing its best to light up the sky. The sea was calm and shimmering as the gentle waves lapped regularly against the sand.

Lots of people were out with the same idea of exercise before partaking of Sunday lunch. Quite a few had their dogs with them, and it gave Sam a good laugh when a big German Shepherd dog came bounding up to them and dropped a long thick stick at his feet. Ella was terrified, but not Sam. He stroked the dog's head and told him what a good boy he was. Then he walked to the water's edge, the dog still bounding beside him. Jerking his arm back as far as he could, Sam flung the stick far out to sea. He and Ella watched the strong way that the big dog could swim, and then they started to walk on.

Within minutes the dog had caught up with them and again dropped the stick at Sam's feet, but this time he repeatedly shook himself, jerking his head towards Sam all the time.

Ella thought it was hilarious and got out of the way. Sam, unable to avoid a fast showering of salt water and wet sand, was not so happy.

They came up off the beach, and outside the nearest pub Ella stood back and watched with much amusement as Sam scraped his shoes on the outside iron grid and brushed vigorously at his overcoat. Once inside, however, the atmosphere was so congenial that they stayed for more than one drink.

When they parted from their new-found friends, a table for eight persons had been booked for dinner that evening in the pub's dining room. Ella had never before made friends with strangers so quickly or so easily.

But that Sunday afternoon was perhaps the best of all. With the curtains drawn and the fire blazing, they took their clothes off and lay on a pile of cushions which Sam had again set out on the floor. The sexual activities that Sam indulged in Ella found attractive if not exciting, and no sooner had he rolled away from her than he was sound asleep.

Ella was the first to rise. Wearing only her dressing gown, she drew up a low table and set about laying it with knives, plates and cups and saucers. In the kitchen she made a pot of tea and cut thin slices of bread and butter, and together they ate in front of the fire.

Outside, they could hear the roar of the sea, which meant two things: the tide was coming in and the wind had become more fierce, causing the old windows of the bungalow to rattle noisily. The weather did not worry either of them; if anything, it served to emphasize their own seclusion, their snugness and their undisturbed solitude.

Much later, Sam stirred and suggested they have a nice hot bath and get ready to go out for their prearranged dinner.

Because of the wind, Sam insisted that they drive to the pub. From the moment they walked into the bar, Ella started to enjoy herself, and she even began to see a slightly different side to Sam, proving that he did not act like a dull sober-sides all the time. The meal was great, but it was the good fellowship and the intimacy of comradeship which Ella was enjoying. She felt glad that they had made the effort to dress up, come out and meet up again with these nice people. Somehow, though, that made her feel guilty. Why? Because part of her mind was saying that she and Sam had just spent from lunchtime until seven o'clock alone in the bungalow and there hadn't been a lot of conversation. If they had stayed in for the rest of the evening, would they have been bored?

It was eleven thirty when they said their final goodbyes.

'Our last evening together,' Sam remarked as they made ready for bed, and he sighed. 'So little time, I don't want it to end. How about you, Ella, are you glad that I persuaded you to come?'

'Oh yes, Sam. Really I am.'

'Well, it's not over yet, my lovely Ella.' He smiled. 'We've still got all night.'

Chapter Thirty-three

'WOULD YOU SAY THE weekend was a success?' Winnie asked her daughter as she watched her get ready to do the evening shift.

'Yes, Mum, of course it was.'

'But?'

'I missed the kids, that's all.'

'Ella, don't give me all that old rubbish. You were only away for two nights.'

'I know, but look how they rushed to hug me the minute I came through the door.'

'Course they did, because you're their mum, but they had a great time. Ted took us all to the pictures on Saturday night, *and* we 'ad fish an' chips on the way home. Sam never even came in to see us when you got back, did he?'

'No. He was in a hurry, said he was booked to play in a chess match.'

'Oh my Gawd! That says it all. A weekend quickie and he dashes back to play chess.'

'Mum, it wasn't like that at all. We had a really good time. Now will you please leave it at that?'

And mind my own bloody business is what's she's really

telling me, Winnie said sadly to herself, because Ella was hardly full of the joys of spring. And it was me that encouraged her to go. Ah well, can't win them all!

Once back behind the bar on Monday evening, Ella was glad to hear that there was to be a darts match. She felt really unsettled, not sure if she was glad she had spent the weekend with Sam or not. Such was the restless mood she was in, she got stuck into doing needless jobs, just waiting for trade to pick up, because for once she was hoping that the bar would be packed and they would be really busy.

Molly Riley watched as Ella swept everything off a glass shelf that was fixed to the wall over a mirror, then, with a lot more vigour than was needed, cleaned the shelf, swiping a damp cloth back and forth several times.

She was about to tell Ella that she herself had cleaned all this side of the bar that morning, but instead she bit her lip and waited a moment before saying, 'Ella, shall we have a drink while it's quiet? Have one on me. I missed you over the weekend.'

'I missed you too, yes please, good idea, I'll have a Southern Comfort.' Ella smiled, steering Molly away from the subject of where she had been, and why.

Side by side, the two barmaids sipped at their drinks, probably the only bit of free time they would have during the evening.

Ella knew she had been short with her mother before she came to work and she wasn't being her usual happy-go-lucky self right now. She couldn't help it. Her mind was in a whirl.

Sam had been a considerate, gentle lover, but apart from that very first attempt, which had been done in such haste on both sides, she would not have considered his actions to be passionate. He had just quietly taken her,

327

almost as if he were grateful. It had been such a long time since she had experienced sex. Perhaps it was the same for him. She had loved being held, being kissed, snuggling up to a man's warm body in bed, so in a way you could say that it was she who was grateful.

Being made love to by Dennis, well, there was no comparison.

With Dennis, it had always been because he wanted her, not just needed her. He was her husband. He took her knowing it was his right, and by God he had always known how to arouse her. He only had to run his hands over her body, lingering in places, holding her close, and she would be longing for him to take her.

Now she was getting annoyed with herself. She had left all these thoughts behind a long time ago. Why, after all the bad things that had happened between her and Dennis, was she holding on to these kind of memories?

The next two weeks Ella would have described as humdrum. She went to work, saw the children were well fed, did the washing and the ironing and made sure she took the children out on her day off. Sam Richardson came in only once a week, to collect the till rolls and to talk business to Mike Murray. He did make a point of finding Ella, saying hello and asking after her health. All very civilized and polite. Their weekend together was never mentioned. It was as if it had never happened.

Then came the morning when the postman brought two letters.

One was a very official-looking brown envelope addressed to Mr Dennis Edward Dryden the back of which was endorsed with the signification LCC which told her it was from the London County Council. Ella turned the letter over in her hands several times, pondering on whether or not she should open it. Curiosity got the

328

better of her and taking a blunt knife she slit the top of the envelope.

She was only halfway through reading the typed page when she found she was trembling, and she had to grope for a chair and sit herself down. She didn't have to get to the end of the page nor yet begin to read the second page; she had already grasped the fact that the sole purpose of the letter was to inform all residents in this area that their homes were due to be demolished.

Could the council do that? Ella asked herself, knowing full well it was a silly question. People in authority could do whatever suited them, never mind who got hurt in the process.

It was only after she had drunk a very strong cup of tea that she remembered the second letter.

It was addressed in handwriting to Mrs Ella Dryden, and was short and to the point. As she slowly read it, she was aware that it was not totally unexpected. Despite that, by the time she had read the few short lines, her blood was boiling and her temper was enough to choke her.

The writer was Sam Richardson.

It was not an unkind letter; in fact for just one minute it had her feeling sorry for Sam, though for a bag of gold she could not have said why.

Sam thanked her for her friendship (was that what the weekend had been about, friendship!) and said that he would always remember her fondly, but that he did not think they were compatible. In future his firm, Hirst and Richardson, would appoint another member of staff to be responsible for the accounts of the British Legion. He had already advised Mike Murray of this decision. He wished her well for the future.

Ella got to her feet and without a second thought picked up the poker and used it to lift the top of the hob and threw the letter right into the middle of the fire.

'Pompous git,' she muttered angrily.

As she was replacing the top of the hob, she heard her front door open and her mother calling, 'It's only me.'

Ella took the deepest breath she could manage and told herself to calm down.

Winnie came in slowly, looking thoroughly dejected. Ella was by her side in a flash and had her arms around her.

'I take it you've had a letter from the LCC, but you mustn't worry about it, Mum.'

'Mustn't I? Just 'ad a word with the milkman, and he said we'll all be rehoused in those great hideous blocks of flats that the council have built near the Elephant and Castle. Then the coalman called out that the rehousing programme had already started. I bet the landlords are none too pleased; all their properties will have had a compulsory purchase order slapped on them.'

'Take yer coat off, Mum, sit down and we'll 'ave a bit of breakfast. I'm just as upset as you are but, whatever happens it's not going to take place for some time, so we'll just 'ave t' put our heads together and see what we can come up with.'

They ate bacon, eggs and toast in silence, mother and daughter each deep in thought. With a fresh cup of tea in front of them, it was Winnie that started the ball rolling.

'Can you see me living twenty floors up? That's supposing the landlord even speaks up on my behalf, otherwise I don't suppose the council will be willing to give one of their flats to an old woman like me living on her own. More than likely they'll shove me and a good many more like me into some gloomy, dreary old folk's home. I dread the thought.'

'Oh Mum! Mum, don't keep on.'

'I'm not keeping on, Ella, I'm merely telling it as it is.'

'Yeah, I know. I'm thinking now what a fool I was to

tell Dennis that I wouldn't move out of London, and when he offered for you to move with us, I said you'd never, ever leave your house. If I'd known then as much as I know now, maybe I'd 'ave given his offer a lot more thought.'

'Easy with hindsight, ain't it, gal? If we all 'ad crystal balls we'd lead our lives differently.'

Ella didn't know what to do or say to cheer her mother up. The plain truth was there wasn't much that anyone could do. More than half of London needed to be rebuilt because of the damage caused by German bombs and land mines exploding over all parts of the city. It was inevitable that in the process folk were going to be made homeless. But then when you came to think about it, thousands of homes were bombed during the war and the tenants hadn't had to worry about being rehoused because they had been killed. At least we are alive, Ella thought, and somehow the problems will be solved.

One thing was for sure: she wasn't going to mention the letter that she had had from Sam Richardson. That was an episode in her life that was best forgotten.

Instead she said, 'I've tidied up and made the beds and I've not got to be at work until six tonight, so where would you like to go? We could look round the shops first, then shall we go to that place just off the market and treat ourselves to brown bread and mussels or eels and a nice milk stout?'

'Oh yes, Ella, yes, I'd like that.'

'Then come on, Mum, put yer coat back on and let's get going.'

Bad news travels fast.

It was just half past eight the next morning and Ella was standing on her front doorstep seeing her two children off to school. 'Have yer both got yer dinner money and yer apple an' a clean handkerchief?' she asked as she did every morning.

Teddy looked at his sister and in unison they both grinned and said, 'Yes, Mum.'

They had hardly taken a couple of steps along the pavement when Teddy let out a whoop of joy and fled down the street as if he were being chased by the devil himself.

Ella walked down the short front path and stared up the road. Dennis was standing beside a shiny black car, his arms held wide. As she watched, a lump which felt as big as a walnut got stuck in her throat.

Dennis had swept his young son up into a great bear hug and was turning round and round, never loosening his grip on his boy.

Now Babs was running. She dropped her school bag and left it where it had fallen on the pavement. 'Daddy, Daddy,' she was screaming, and Ella could tell from the tone of her voice that she was crying.

Dennis kept hold of his son with one arm but scooped up his little daughter with the other, and to Ella it was as if time stood still as he held them both close, his head bent down to rest on top of his children's heads.

Ella walked forward and picked up Babs's school bag, then a few more steps and she was silently holding it out to Dennis.

'I'll take the kids to school and then I'll be back, I won't be long,' was all he said.

Jesus wept and well he might! What was she supposed to make of this?

Dennis was helping Teddy and Babs into the back of his car, and then suddenly the car was moving slowly and the two smiling children waved to her as they went past.

Was she dreaming? She certainly had a feeling of relief. It was so good for the children to see their father.

Now that she had had a minute or two to think about

it, she thought she could guess the reason for him being here.

He had heard about the letters from the council, and say what you like about him, there was no way that he would stand by and see his family or his mother-in-law turfed out into the streets or housed in a high-rise block of flats. No way at all. Dennis wouldn't stand for that.

But it was the way he'd turned up! Out of the blue, as if nothing had happened. He might just have got up from the breakfast table and offered to take the children to school. In actual fact, as far as she knew, he hadn't set eyes on either of them for months. Certainly it was the very first time this year that the kids had seen their dad.

She stood still in the street for a moment because suddenly she felt tired, drained, and she wanted to cry buckets, but she checked herself, muttering aloud, 'None of that, come on, pull yourself together. You've coped so far and you'll go on coping.'

Although at one time Ella had vowed she would never forgive Dennis for what had happened to Connie Baldwin, nor for the way he had neglected his two children, she was prepared to be civil to him this morning, because if she were honest she was really pleased to see him. He was the one person who would be able to sort this housing problem out.

He looked completely at home sitting at the kitchen table, almost as if he had never left.

'Would you like some breakfast?' she felt compelled to ask.

'A bacon sarnie would go down well,' he grinned. But he had seen the worried frown on his wife's face, and at that moment he was wishing with all his heart that he could turn back the clock. Just taking his kids to school had tugged at his heart strings. Twice Babs had run back to ask if he were going to be there when she came out this afternoon, and while young Ted had not come straight out with an accusation, he had hinted that his father should look after their mother a bit more. The final rub had been when Teddy had told him he could only go to see a football match when his grandad took him.

'You used to take me every week,' had been his parting shot.

Ella put a plate in front of him and the sandwich smelt good. He'd missed her cooking and a darn sight more things besides. He'd been so stretched out by Connie's death that his whole attitude to life had altered. He would never be a saint, that went without saying, but if any lesson had been learnt it was that family was the one and only thing that mattered in this life. Looking at Ella, and realizing the hurt he had caused, he knew full well that he had left it a bit late in life to appreciate that fact.

Ella couldn't understand her own feelings. She only knew that she needed someone to lean on, to tell her what to do and to sort out where she, the children and her mother were going to live. She no longer wanted to have to cope on her own with all these everyday problems.

As if reading her thoughts, Dennis asked, 'Ella, would you sit down and listen to me for a while?'

'Not if you're going to tell me a pack of lies or make me a load of promises which you have no intention of keeping.' She spoke quite spitefully.

'I deserve that and more,' he said sheepishly, 'but please, let me try. Do you remember the house at Epsom where our problems first began, mainly because I was so big-headed.'

'And I was so obstinate,' she admitted. 'All past history now, though.'

'Not quite,' Dennis told her with a flicker of a smile.

'Beautiful house, which my builders turned into four fantastic apartments, yet the tenants haven't been happy there. I sold one place to a greedy man who thought he could manipulate lonely old women into doing what he wanted them to do. In other words, he was after their money. I'd be the first to admit that I've pulled a few fast deals in my time, but I've never stooped that low. My father and I only heard about this through Lady Margaret, the original owner from whom I purchased the property. Since then we've worked closely with a solicitor, all legal and above board I promise you . . .'

Dennis paused, and Ella found herself smiling at the fact that he was assuring her that his dealings were all legitimate.

Well, there had to be a first time for everything.

She got up and went to stand at the window, her arms folded tightly under her breasts. In one way it felt so comfortable to have Dennis sitting here in the kitchen, but on the other hand a lot of horrible thoughts were going round and round in her head. Even last November, or was it December, when he had taken her out for a meal, hadn't he said he had a few building contracts to see through but then he would be free, and they would meet and talk things through. Yet here they were in March, and it was the first time since that meal that she had set eyes on him. Recently she had tried to play his game, get her own back if she were truthful, and had gone off with Sam Richardson for that weekend. With that thought she hated herself and she hated him.

Dennis glanced at Ella and asked, 'Have I said something to upset you?'

'No, but I can't see why this ruddy house at Epsom is still occupying your life. When you took me out to eat somewhere near Crystal Palace you pointed out what a great contract you had going on there. Yet me, my mother

335

and all our neighbours have notices stating that every house in these streets is to be demolished. If you're so big in property, why don't you see about finding accommodation for your own family?'

He came to stand beside her and, his voice low, said, 'That is exactly why I came here this morning. You shall have the pick of where you live, and so shall your mother. I swear to you that never, while I can prevent it, will you and my kids live in those concrete blocks of flats that are being thrown up. Please, Ella, believe me, I will look after you, just try and trust me. And before you mock me, I know only too well that you have no reason to believe a word I say, never mind trust me.'

Ella remained silent. What could she say?

Dennis sighed heavily. 'I have to go. My father and I have another meeting with the solicitor, but I promised Babs I would be here when she comes home this afternoon, and I will be if that is all right with you.'

Softly but sharply Ella said, 'If you promised your daughter then you *had* better be here. Letting me down is one thing, but our kids have taken enough knocks.'

Dennis had the grace to look and sound sheepish as he said, 'Bye for now, see you about four.'

Chapter Thirty-four

THAT MORNING, AT TEN thirty, Dennis found himself once more in the offices of Gurney and Trent, but now his father was sitting beside him. Suddenly Dennis was filled with apprehension. What they were about to do was a very tricky business, and to be honest, he was worried sick.

He cleared his throat and looked at his father, and when Ted nodded his head, Dennis began.

'Thank you for the letters you have sent me, Mr Trent, you have kept me well informed. You certainly seemed to have gathered quite a lot of information about this Claude Packard.'

'Yes, though he is a very difficult man to deal with; he doesn't want his left hand to know what his right hand is doing. I have met with Mr Packard twice, and against all my advice he is still determined to do his best to purchase what was Miss Sheldon's flat, and he is also hoping that the remaining tenant is going to decide that she will be better off in a care home rather than living on her own. Should that turn out to be the case, he is aiming to purchase that remaining apartment.'

'Mr Trent, can you see that happening?' Ted asked a direct question and he expected a straight answer.

'Hmm . . .' Mr Trent hesitated. He was in a position to charge a hefty fee for the work he was doing for this pair, but all the same he had to tread very carefully.

'To my knowledge Mr Packard has approached two banks and a mortgage broker for a loan, and on all three attempts he has been unsuccessful.'

Ted had a deep thought that he was keeping to himself at least for the moment. It hadn't been hard for him to discover that Claude Packard was a gambling man, and not a very successful one at that. But he himself liked to cover his back, and when his son had told him of this scheme to beat Packard at his own game, he had made it his business to buy up Packard's gambling debts. Should one idea fail, it always paid to have another up one's sleeve.

This hedging wasn't getting them anywhere. 'Have you made any progress on offering the man a loan?' Dennis asked impatiently.

'Yes, I made an appointment with him to come to this office and I put your proposal to him.'

Dennis cut in far too quickly. 'You didn't name names, did you?'

Poor Mr Trent looked totally shocked. 'There was nothing illegal in the proposition that I put forward. As per your instructions, Mr Dryden, I informed Claude Packard that I was in touch with two wealthy businessmen who had money to invest and were willing to take a risk.'

'And he has no idea who might be putting up the money?'

'No, definitely not, those were your instructions. I set the facts out very straight,' Mr Trent continued. 'I informed Mr Packard that should Mrs Hines decide to give up her residence in Maple House, my two clients

338

would be willing to loan enough to cover the purchase price of both apartments. He was extremely happy with that agreement until I disclosed the fact that my clients would want Maple House as a whole to be put up as security against the loan. Needless to say, he was very dubious about that clause being part of the contract.'

Now it was Ted who almost blew his top.

'If that devious bloke wants to borrow our money t' buy both of those flats, the terms are non-negotiable. Other than that he can go to hell.'

Mr Trent stood up and held out his hand. 'I think we have gone as far as we can at the moment, but I would point out one thing. I think Mr Packard's interest in the flats is only marginal. I'm pretty sure he is more interested in the grounds that Maple House stands in.'

Neither father nor son made any reply. They both shook the hand of their solicitor, and it wasn't until they were in the safety of Ted's car that they allowed themselves to have a good laugh.

'Packard doesn't know us, does he, son?' Ted said. 'We can see him dreaming about how many dwellings he can get a builder to stack up in those grounds if he greases enough palms and gets planning permission, can't we?'

'What he doesn't know, Dad, is that you taught me well. He'd have to get up early in the morning to put one over on us. Anyway, he has got t' be soft in the bloody head not to even give a thought to the fact that owning the whole building doesn't mean that he will ever own the freehold.'

'Nice one, son.' Ted laughed loudly. Then he became serious and said quietly, 'I'm pretty sure that Mr Trent has an inkling of what we are about, but at this point in time it pays him to turn a deaf ear. He can't prove anything and I don't somehow think he would want to. Whatever happens to Claude Packard is nothing more than his just deserts. Picking on lonely women, and for what? Nothing more than sheer greed.'

'He hasn't taken the bait yet,' Dennis reminded his father.

'Well, we'll wait an' see, but greed will get the better of him, that's a dead cert.'

It was the second Saturday morning in March. The sun was shining and in the few pots that Ella had planted in the back yard the daffodils and primulas had opened up, their lovely colours brightening the yard up no end. It had been a strange time, with Ella just plodding along from day to day with not much to look forward to as far as she could see. Wherever she went and whoever she spoke to, the whole conversation revolved around the fact that within the very near future their houses were going to be razed to the ground. Oh, there had been tenants' meetings, council meetings and even a meeting chaired by the local vicar. A lot of questions had been asked, yet not one satisfactory answer from those in charge had been forthcoming. Men, and women also, lost their tempers, but as always shouting and hollering never got anyone anywhere.

Whole families were at a loss as to where to turn. Some folk had been born in these streets of terraced houses and had not even been driven away during the horrific years of the war. They had stood together, sweeping up broken glass as their windows were smashed during the air raids, visiting the badly injured in hospital, and attending so many funerals of long-standing friends and neighbours whose bodies had had to be dug out from beneath ruined buildings and great piles of rough masonry. Now those who had survived all that were worried as to where they were all going to live.

Ella was afraid to pin her hopes on Dennis.

He had said that she and her mother would have a choice as to where their future home would be.

Was that too good to be true? So many promises Dennis had made had never been kept.

Now, having seen Dennis's car draw up outside the house, Ella opened the back door and called to Babs and Teddy, who were bouncing a ball up against the back wall, 'Don't look now, but your father is here again.'

They both came racing in, and Teddy's mouth fell open with surprise as his father walked into the kitchen waving three tickets for West Ham's match that afternoon.

'We'll take Grandad with us,' he said, grinning.

'I haven't forgotten you, sweetheart,' Dennis told Babs, sweeping her up into his arms. 'I've brought you a real grown-up present.' Setting her safely down on her feet, he drew from his pocket a dark red velvet box. Inside was a silver chain from which hung a tiny heart, shaped in silver.

Babs was thrilled, and when her mother had fastened it around her neck, both her brother and her father said how pretty it looked on her.

'Go get yerself ready, son, we'll pick Grandad up and have something to eat before the match.' Then, turning to Ella, he said, 'I want a word with you.'

As Teddy flew upstairs to get himself ready, Ella said to her daughter, 'Walk down t' yer Gran's, will you, pet? Ask her if she's coming out with us this afternoon.'

'Oh Mum, you know she is, she always does.'

'Yes, I do know, but it will give you a chance to show off the lovely necklace yer dad has bought for you.'

Babs's face brightened at the thought and she was out of the door before Ella could tell her to put a coat on.

With both children out of the way, she turned to Dennis, raised her eyebrows and said, 'Well?'

His lightness of mood changed and his voice was quite

firm as he said, 'Let me know which day you can have off in a couple of weeks' time and by then I should have two or three houses which you might like to give the once-over. Better if you don't bring yer mother first time around; too much walking. Wait and see which district you think you might like and what the school situation is for the kids. A lot to sort out, but then you know that, don't you?'

Before she had time to form a reply of any sort, Teddy was back in the room, tugging at his father's arm, eager to be gone.

'Boy, oh boy!' Dennis Dryden muttered aloud as he replaced the telephone receiver in his father's office.

'Is that a cry of triumph?' Ted asked.

'To be honest, Dad, I'm not sure. I just cannot believe what lengths some folk will go to to get what they want. Packard must know the risks he is taking and yet he has jumped in with both feet and grabbed the offer of our enormous loan. I bet he hasn't given a thought as to how he is going to keep up the repayments, given that he already has one if not two mortgages to repay.'

'You almost sound as if you feel sorry for him, son. Are you having feelings of regret?'

'Oh no, Dad. He walked into this with his eyes wide open. True, we laid the bait, but nobody forced him to take it. I've only to remind myself how he made Dorothy Sheldon's life a misery and was well set to do the same to old Mrs Hines. I'm glad we were able to step in and help her. Whatever mess Packard sinks into is of his own making.'

'Mrs Hines is well set for the moment,' Ted remarked thoughtfully. 'We saw to it that her furniture was packed well and safely stored, and if she should decide to make her stay with Lady Margaret a permanent one, we can always make sure that she gets the best price possible for her goods.'

'Yes, you did well by her, Dad, and I wouldn't be at all surprised if she does stay put. Best thing, probably. Company when she wants it, good food, and all her needs attended to.'

'Well, if everything is done and dusted, we'd better get over to Trent's office and add our signatures to the documents.'

Within half an hour, they were once again sitting across from Mr Trent's desk.

'You will be pleased to know that we tied it all up this morning,' was Mr Trent's opening statement.

'What?' Dennis sounded really surprised. 'Mr Packard has signed already, has he?'

'Oh yes, he's signed, and I would say at this moment he is eagerly awaiting the arrival of a large cheque.'

Mr Trent watched the look that passed between father and son, and his own thought was that Mr Packard had at the very least acted recklessly. He banished the thought quickly from his mind and merely said, 'I have the papers here.' He just couldn't leave the matter there, however. Slowly and deliberately he added, 'I wouldn't say you own the man body and soul, but he certainly owes you both a considerable amount of money. However, as you stipulated, the loan is secured against the whole building. So let's hope for Mr Packard's sake that his proposed business deals go ahead.'

Dennis took the file of documents that Mr Trent had handed across the desk and passed them to his father, and Ted handed a cheque over to Mr Trent.

Edward Dryden would this very morning lock these papers away in his safety deposit box at the bank, with the knowledge that the good wishes that Mr Trent had hoped for Mr Packard was never going to happen.

Men, real men, didn't treat old ladies the way Packard

had treated Dorothy Sheldon. Ted and Dennis could bide their time in the full knowledge that payback time would come when they were ready.

As the old saying went, give a scoundrel enough rope and he'll hang himself!

Chapter Thirty-five

ELLA FELT HEARTSORE AND weary as she tried to turn the mattress on her double bed. Nothing was going right for her at the moment and she felt really washed out, aching from head to foot before she'd halfway finished her shift at the Legion.

Most of her neighbours had already been to inspect the flats which were on offer from the council, but both she and her mother were holding out, hoping against hope that Dennis was going to come up with an alternative. This time she wouldn't be so fussy, nor so dogmatic in her determination to stay in this part of London. No matter how hard she tried, she just could not see herself cooped up with her two children in a high-rise flat.

What about during the summer holidays? Their back yard might not be much to write home about, but at least she could put a table and chairs out there and they could eat their meal in the fresh air. Teddy had gone through a phase when he wanted to keep rabbits, and Dennis had built him a double hutch. What fun he'd had letting them out and chasing them around the yard, and he'd been pretty good about feeding them and keeping the hutch clean. In a flat, who knows how she would keep the pair of them amused. Or what trouble they would get up to. One nightmare thought she'd had lately was what if they were allocated a flat several floors up and one day Teddy decided to climb out of the window and fell?

It didn't bear thinking about.

Dennis was quite a frequent visitor these days: once a week, and sometimes twice. Was she glad about that?

She didn't let herself dwell on that question. Certainly the kids were a darn sight happier when their dad was around, which didn't seem quite fair to her. Both Teddy and Babs were so excited each time his car pulled to a stop outside the house, rushing to greet him excitedly because they knew darn well he never came empty-handed. It was like he was buying their love. If his visits should suddenly cease, what would they do then? Ella knew what she would do. She'd sort out where he'd got to this time and she would kill him. 'I would,' she muttered aloud. No way was he going to get away with messing up his children's lives again.

It had been ages since he had mentioned finding them a decent house, and she had felt so under the weather that she couldn't face another hostile argument.

Having struggled to put two clean pillowcases on, she plumped up the pillows and propped them against the brass head-rail at the top of the bed. Thank God she was finished in here. She had changed Teddy's bed first thing this morning, and now her own, so she would leave Babs's room until tomorrow. Time she put her feet up and had a cup of tea.

She had barely sat down when her mother was to be heard calling, 'Cooee!'

'I swear you smell the pot.' Ella grinned at Winnie as she came through the kitchen door. 'Be a love and get yerself a cup. There's plenty of tea in the pot and I did put the cosy over it.'

They were seated opposite each other, sipping their tea, and Ella felt a bit guilty. Getting to her feet, she collected two plates, knives, butter and jam, all of which she set out on the table. Then from the dresser she brought a huge round tin, and lifting the lid said, 'I made these scones yesterday. D'you fancy one?'

Ella didn't have to ask twice. Already her mother had a scone on her plate, had cut it through the middle and was busy spreading both butter and jam on it.

'Mum, at what age would you say a woman starts the menopause?'

Ella had asked the question quietly, but Winnie was startled. She could tell that her daughter was more than a little worried.

'Normally somewhere around forty, but it can differ. Some start much earlier and some much later. Why? Are you having hot flushes? To be honest, I have noticed that you've been under the weather lately but I put it down to all this bother about us being compelled to move out of our homes.'

'No, not hot flushes, but I don't feel right. Any strong smell seems to make me feel sick. Molly and I were making cheese sandwiches yesterday and suddenly I just had to get out into the open air. I couldn't breathe.'

As Ella was speaking, her mother's eyes did not leave her face, and she was clenching her hands together in her lap to stop them trembling. There was a moment of silence that hung heavily between them until Winnie knew she had to ask that one vital question.

'You haven't missed any periods, 'ave you?' she said.

Ella's face had gone pale and she was twitching. At last she managed to murmur, 'Haven't seen anything for two months. I thought I was going through the change.'

'Oh my God!' her mother cried. 'I thought you 'ad more sense than that. Menopause in a pig's ear! Sounds to me that more than likely you're pregnant.'

Ella was astounded. Of course she had suspected it, but so far she had been able to convince herself it couldn't be true.

She bit her lip, eyeing her mother, trying to assess if she was being serious. Then Winnie's lips began to tremble and with utter disbelief Ella realized that it wasn't just a possibility; her mother was serious and it was ten to one she was carrying a baby.

'Jesus Christ!' she cried, anxiety showing plainly in her eyes. Everything in the room was moving; she couldn't breathe. She was weak with horror, anger and guilt.

Winnie was beside her in a flash, pushing her head down between her knees. The sickening feeling passed and her mother insisted that she lean back in the chair and stay still while she fetched her a glass of cold water. Eventually the dizziness passed and she stared at Winnie, her eyes wide with apprehension. She was very scared. Yes, I'm a grown woman, she chastised herself, yet I'm scared stiff.

'What will Dennis say, he'll kill me,' she gasped

'Sod Dennis.' Winnie gave Ella a swift but knowing glance. 'He's hardly in a position to 'ave a go at you, and if he so much as tries he'll 'ave me to answer to,' she informed her daughter bluntly, her voice harsh with anger.

'What in God's name am I going to do?' Ella asked.

'Well, yer could tell the father, for a start.'

'Never, not in a million years! According to him we are not compatible. Besides, he doesn't come near the club now. I got the impression that I didn't come up to his expectations.'

Winnie loved her daughter dearly, and at this moment in time she could cheerfully have killed Sam Richardson. Instead she just sat there staring into space, not knowing whether to laugh or to cry. The fact was that it was she who had encouraged Ella to go off for the weekend, thinking that her daughter richly deserved a break, someone to make a fuss of her, let her know that she had changed from being an overweight slob into an elegant-looking woman who combined a full-time job with being a really good mother.

'I'm too old to have another baby, I'll be thirty-nine this year, but I can't be that far gone. I suppose one of our neighbours would know what I could do to bring on a miscarriage.' It had taken all of Ella's self-control to speak normally, for she was shaking with anger.

'For Christ's sake, gal! Give yerself time to think.' Winnie was in danger of losing her temper. 'You don't mean a word of what you've just said. We'll 'ave no more talk about going to a neighbour nor to some quack.'

Her mother did her best to ease the tension by laughing lightly, but it was a cynical laugh because her thoughts were well and truly dwelling on Sam Richardson. If she didn't have a go at him, given half a chance Dennis would.

Ella broke into her thoughts. 'Please, Mum, tell me what to do. I suppose at the back of my mind I've known for a couple of weeks that I was pregnant. I just wouldn't let myself admit the fact. I've been dying t' tell you. I couldn't tell anybody else. It's been awful for me, it really has, especially when Dennis has been here. I 'aven't been able to look him in the face.'

Winnie was racking her brains. Eventually she cleared her throat and her voice was firm as she put forward her point of view.

'The first thing we've got to get settled is this housing business. When Dennis next appears, send one of the kids to fetch me and I'll tell him straight that it's about time he kept his promise and took you to see a couple of places. God knows he's bragged loud enough that no way was his family going to live in those council flats.'

349

'But, Mum, he might not even want to know me when he finds out about the baby, never mind helping to get me a house.'

'All the more reason why you don't tell him yet. Are you sure, really sure, that you don't want to contact Sam Richardson?'

Ella straightened her back and her head flew up sharply. She was shaking with anger, feeling really hurt as she thought of that curt, unkind letter that he had written to her, and it took all of her self-control to speak normally.

'Mum, I don't care what I have to go through, nothing on this earth would make me go to Sam for help. We didn't have a bad weekend, and OK, he decided that I wasn't what he wanted in his life. That's fair enough, but there are ways of saying things without hurting folk. It wasn't as if I expected him to marry me. No, I think me having two children put him off. Children would be a hindrance in the kind of life that he leads.'

She paused for a moment and actually smiled. 'I think he'd run a mile at the thought of having to cope with a newborn baby. It would disturb the pattern of his safe, dull life.'

Winnie sniffed. 'He knew about Teddy and Babs from the beginning, but what about taking precautions?' Sighing heavily, she added, 'I suppose it's a bit late now to pursue that subject. Just remember, not a word to Dennis until he sorts something out about where you're going to live.'

'Where *we're* going to live, Mum? What about you?'

'Don't start worrying about me, you've more than enough on your plate. The council wouldn't dare put me in a high-rise flat. I'd be straight on to the papers. Can't you just see the headlines, "Old age pensioner with bad legs and a heart problem has twelve flights of stairs to climb".'

'Mum! Since when did you have bad legs? Or a heart problem, come to that?'

Winnie adopted a hurt look. 'Since the council put a compulsory purchase order on my house just so that they can bulldoze the whole street.'

'Mum, you're dead wicked,' Ella managed to say as they both fell about laughing.

Two days after Ella had talked to her mother, Dennis appeared. The front door was wide open because the weather was pushing towards spring and it was so nice to see the sunshine. In he walked, like he'd never left home, picked up a magazine and last night's evening paper from the seat of what had always been his armchair, tidily placed them on the dresser and sat himself down, his long legs stretched out right across the hearth rug which lay in front of the kitchen range.

'Kids at school?' he asked.

Ella looked at him and raised her eyebrows. 'No, they've both got jobs down on the docks.' She let her sarcasm come out with a sneer.

'Oh, you're on good form this morning, aren't you, my luv.'

'Wrong on both points,' she shot back at him. 'How the hell can I be in good form? Day and night all I can think about is that me and the kids will probably be thrown out into the street if we don't accept the council's offer to rehouse us soon. And as for being your luv, I thought you dispensed with me a long time ago.'

'Touchy, eh? Can't say as I blame yer. Got a bit of news for you, though. Couple of houses I can take yer t' see. Mind, the mood you're in today, I'll be lucky if you decide that you like either of them.'

'Thanks. Like I've got a choice now.'

In spite of all her cares and woes, Ella found that she was smiling. Like it or not, Dennis was a sight for sore eyes. Lazily stretched out, he did look great. He'd probably come here straight from the barber's shop: his thick mop of dark hair was neat and tidy, his face freshly shaved. He had nice teeth, even and straight, and although he wore an expensive suit he still had that boyish look and his intense bright blue eyes twinkled as he exchanged gibes with her.

No wonder the women fall for him, Ella said mournfully to herself.

She stood at the door to the scullery and said seriously, 'Do you want me to make you a pot of tea? Or are you taking me to see these houses right now?'

'No thanks to the tea. Yes to your second question, just as soon as you're ready to go. I might even treat you to a slap-up lunch if you're not too stroppy.'

God, this fellow could drive a person to drink. He comes here looking like a million dollars with no warning whatsoever and expects me to get myself ready within minutes.

Her beautiful glossy hair had been rolled into a secure French pleat with enough strands left loose to pile into curls around her forehead. She had selected a sage-green suit that Sadie Cohan had sold to her about a month ago; this would be the first time that she had worn it, and with it she had teamed a dark green high-necked blouse. Time taken over her make-up had been well worth while. Black high-heeled court shoes, handbag and gloves and she was ready.

When she had a final look in the mirror she checked that the seams of her stockings were straight and she was pleased with herself.

In all it had taken her twenty minutes.

As she came down the stairs her husband let out a low whistle of approval.

Ella couldn't have said why, but she was feeling extremely nervous as she sat beside her husband as he drove them to view the first of the two houses. When they had started out he had kept up a running commentary on the first place he was taking her to view. Ella felt that she had to give him a great deal of credit. He had left nothing to chance, really toured the areas and had the facts ready on the tip of his tongue.

It wasn't too long before Dennis was saying, 'This is Sydenham, and we're looking for Langham Avenue. I've already done a recce so I'm pretty sure if I take a left down here the first on the right will be the road we are looking for.'

It was.

He pulled the car in to the kerb and asked Ella to look up at the number of the house which they were parked outside.

Lowering the window, she poked her head out, looked up and said, 'This house is number twenty-two. What number are we looking for?'

'Forty-seven,' he replied. 'Must be on the other side of the road. The property is empty, but the agent let me have the keys. We'll get out and walk, shall we?'

He came round to the passenger side and helped his wife to get out of the car. It was little things like this that made her realize how much she had missed him. Not that he had often taken her out in his car, or even in the old van he drove in those early days when they were first married. Stop comparing how things used to be, she chided herself. After all, when the kiddies had been small she'd be the first to admit that she'd always put them first. More than likely Dennis had felt that he hadn't been getting enough attention at home. That could be part of why he had looked elsewhere, that and the fact that she knew now that she had lost interest in how she looked.

Dennis took her hand and linked it through the crook of his arm as they walked. It felt good.

'God Almighty! What a long road,' he remarked, adding, 'It's never-ending.'

'I thought you said you had looked the place over,' Ella reminded him.

'I did, late at night, an' I was more interested as to where it was than how it looked.'

'To me it looks a long, cold road. Not much different to where we live now. The houses are still terraced; the only difference is they are much bigger and there are more of them.' Ella was watching the numbers: 43, 45. 'Here's forty-seven.'

Dennis went ahead up the short flight of stone steps, but before he put the key in the front door lock he leant over the metal hand-rail and looked down. Then he straightened himself up, took a sheaf of papers from his inside pocket and quickly scanned the details. 'I thought not,' he muttered angrily. 'There's no mention of basement rooms on these estate agent's details.' He half turned to go, but Ella put out a restraining hand.

'We're here now, Dennis, we might as well go inside. At least it will give us something to compare other properties with.'

'All right, if you say so,' he agreed somewhat reluctantly, standing back to allow her to enter first.

Ella didn't like the house and that fact showed on her face. The place smelt musty, as if it hadn't been occupied for years.

Front room, back room, kitchen and scullery downstairs, rooms bigger than she was used to, higher ceilings and much larger windows. First floor, three bedrooms, one double, two singles, both looking out over a long, untidy, overgrown garden.

Up a flight of just five stairs and there was one huge

room which had a sloping ceiling. On this floor there was a bathroom and a separate lavatory. Ella wrinkled her nose. Both could do with a damn good cleaning.

'Almost a dormitory,' she said.

'Could fill it up with lodgers,' Dennis chuckled.

'On yer bike, mate, I'm not thinking of catering for the masses. By the way, you told me you would enquire about schools for the children and about a place for me mum.'

'I did both. The nearest school is a huge place, mixed scholars, about half a mile away, and there are no flats or small houses near that would be suitable for Winnie. Course, we could always shoot my mother-in-law, take the kids and move abroad.'

Ella turned her head so fast she stumbled, then she saw the laughter in Dennis's eyes and she laughed with him.

'You don't really dislike my mum at all, do you?'

'Course I don't, and I really did enquire about accommodation for the elderly but the agent was a hundred per cent sure there wasn't anything suitable in the area.'

'Why the hell did we come here then?'

Dennis thought it best if he counted to ten before he answered.

'The air raids reduced the number of houses in London and in fact all major cities by a very great deal; plus the fact that when the solders, sailors and airmen were demobbed they wanted to set up home with their wives. Many had had war-time weddings and had never had the joy of actually living with their wives and children. Hence the shortage of houses to rent. We are lucky we can afford to buy a house . . .' Under his breath he added, That's if we ever find one that is to your taste, then quickly went on. 'At the moment the only choice for most people is the high-rise flats that have been thrown up or the corrugated-iron huts known as Nissen huts which the

Government are placing on every available open space and charging ten shillings and sixpence every week for the privilege of living in them.'

The fact that Dennis had said '*we* can afford to buy a house' affected Ella in different ways. It was kind of him not to rub it in that she had asked for his help in finding them somewhere to live, and she had to feel grateful that apparently he could afford it. But there again, Teddy and Babs were his children as much as hers and it was a long time since he had recognized his responsibility.

In the hallway Dennis opened what he thought was a door to a cupboard; instead he found himself looking at a rickety flight of dusty steps. 'I think we'll skip the basement,' he said.

Ella took a quick look and agreed.

She hadn't meant to ask, but it came out without her thinking. 'How much is this large house?'

'Four thousand six hundred pounds. Freehold, but there's no garage.'

Ella looked at him in amazement. 'And you can afford that much?'

Straight-faced, Dennis replied, 'Money begets money and it talks all languages.'

Then suddenly they were both laughing fit to bust and he had her in his arms.

When their laughter had subsided he said quietly, 'Remember the times when I sold almost everything in the house that was movable just to give you enough to pay the rent?'

Ella wasn't having that! She still had both feet firmly on the ground where Dennis was concerned, and her voice was harsh as she gave him her answer.

'I well remember! Also I can recall the times you pawned or sold everything we owned that was worth anything just so you had the money to back a horse.'

'True,' he admitted sheepishly, 'but we're both older and a darn sight wiser now, aren't we?'

'Are we?'

At that moment Ella almost blurted out that she had made the biggest mistake of her life and was carrying Sam Richardson's baby.

Coming quickly to her senses, she broke free from Dennis's arms and told herself that now was certainly not the time for confessions.

Back in the car, Dennis turned to face her and said, 'The second house is in West Dulwich, which is actually quite near Camberwell. A gentleman is still living there but we have an appointment to view the property at two o'clock. We've plenty of time to eat first, so what shall it be? Posh restaurant or pub lunch?'

Without hesitation Ella said, 'I'd like a ploughman's, only ham not cheese, if that's all right by you.' She was hungry, but she remembered that the smell of strong cheese made her feel sick and there was no way she wanted to show herself up.

Matters between herself and her husband were going so well today, not one argument. She didn't want to spoil the situation at this stage.

It was a public house frequented by businessmen at lunchtime and the food was good. Dennis ordered rump steak for himself, asking that it be thick and rare. The ham that came with Ella's ploughman's was really tasty home-cooked gammon, and Dennis made no comment when she said she would prefer just a tonic water to drink. He ordered Scotch for himself.

It wanted just ten minutes to two o'clock when Dennis pulled into the drive of Zenith House.

No idea what Zenith is supposed to mean, Ella was

thinking, yet already she had decided that this was a nice residential area, and she certainly liked the look of this detached property which was situated in Court Lane, West Dulwich SE21.

For a start the road was tree-lined, and most of the trees were just about to burst with pink blossom.

From the moment the elderly gentleman opened the door in answer to Dennis's knock, shook hands with each of them and introduced himself as Mr Hamilton, Ella knew that she liked him. He had been tall in his younger days, but now his shoulders stooped and his brown hair was thin on top. He wore trousers with a Prince of Wales check, a fawn shirt, a tie embossed with a regimental badge and a beige woolly cardigan.

'Come in, come in, I had my cleaning lady come in an extra morning today just to make sure everything was neat and tidy, but would you mind showing yourselves around the house? I find the stairs a bit trying these days.' As he turned to go back into the front sitting room, Ella noticed that he walked with a stick.

Dennis and Ella went straight up the stairs to the bedrooms. Almost unable to believe her eyes, she asked, 'Do you have the agent's particulars on this property?'

He smiled to himself; he could tell Ella was smitten. 'Yes,' he said, giving her two printed pages but keeping hold of the third.

The landing was big and wide with two bedrooms on each side. Large double rooms to the front; the other two only slightly smaller looking out over a large, well-kept garden which had a wooded area at the far end.

'Does that piece of ground come with the house?' Ella queried.

'According to the agent's survey, yes, it does.'

'Marvellous. Imagine Teddy climbing trees in his own back garden.' Ella stopped short. 'Just a minute. There are four bedrooms and they are all wonderful. We haven't even seen the rest of the house, not even the bathroom, but would you mind telling me how much the asking price for this house is, 'cos I can't for one moment believe that we can afford to buy it.'

'Ella, let's just continue, and when we have seen the whole house I will give you this third page of the details to read.'

With that she had to be satisfied, because Dennis had already opened two doors which were set back at the top of the stairs. One was a walk-in airing cupboard and housed what Dennis told her was a boiler which gave constant hot water.

The second door led to a bathroom. Ella was dreaming. A huge white bath set on iron claw legs dominated the room. Oh, to fill that bath even half full with scented hot water and just lie there! A toilet *and* a wash basin.

On the landing Ella stood staring through a small window which gave her a great view of the tree-lined road in which this house stood. Daydreaming wasn't in it. Fancy even thinking that she and her family could ever come to live in a place like this. Dennis was cruel to have brought her here. It was like looking into a palace and being told that normal people didn't get to live in such places.

Dennis broke into her thoughts. 'Ella,' he touched her arm, 'come on, we haven't seen the downstairs yet.'

She shook herself, not at all sure that she wanted to do as he was suggesting. It would only make her feel even more envious than she did now.

Mr Hamilton was standing at the foot of the stairs, smiling up at them. 'I have laid a tray and made a pot of tea but am unable to safely carry it through into the lounge. Would you mind having it in the kitchen? Or perhaps you, Mr Dryden, would be kind enough to take the tray through.'

It was Ella who quickly said, 'The kitchen will be fine,

it is very kind of you to have gone to so much trouble.'

'No trouble at all, Mrs Dryden,' he answered, leading the way.

Oh, bless the man! Ella was saying to herself. The tray even had a lace cloth and the cups and saucers were so delicate that she thought Dennis's big fingers would never manage the handles of the cups.

'Shall I be mother?' she asked, as the three of them seated themselves around the large table.

Conversation was a bit difficult until Mr Hamilton started to speak and then there was no stopping him.

'This has always been a family home. My wife and I were blessed with four boys. One served in the Royal Navy and we lost him early on in the war. He was serving on HMS *Hood* which was sunk by the *Bismarck* off Greenland in 1941. Another son was in the RAF and he was shot down during a bomber raid over Cologne in 1942.'

He paused and smiled at Ella. 'I think living alone makes me talk too much when I have visitors.'

'How long since you lost your wife?' Ella asked, showing great concern.

'Only two years. We had a great life. My other two boys see that I want for nothing, and I have three grand-children. They all visit as often as they can, but they have their own lives to lead.'

'So are you going to live with one of your sons? Is that why you have put your house up for sale?' Dennis asked.

'Oh, no, no, actually things could not have turned out better. On the corner of the road behind this one there is a very beautiful large old house which the elderly owners left in their will to some charity organization. It has taken some years to sort things out but I think their wishes have finally come to fruition. The building is to remain but some restoration has been carried out, a warden has been installed and it has become sheltered accommodation under the umbrella of the British Legion. Their aim is to assist ex-service men and women. Some tenants will pay rent, some will buy a lease, but those who are not financially well placed will receive help. The funds for this and many more such good causes are derived largely from the sale of poppies on Armistice Day.

'I am lucky to have secured a lease on a one-bedroom apartment there; or at least I have put down a deposit. Now I have to find a buyer for this house.'

Ella almost blurted out that she was employed as a barmaid in a British Legion working men's club; instead she asked, 'Will you mind very much moving?'

'Not at all, Mrs Dryden. I shall still be in the same vicinity, able to visit friends and neighbours. But look, I should stop my ramblings and allow you to finish your tour of the house, that is if what you have seen already drives you to continue.'

'It certainly does.' Ella got to her feet quickly. She had already noticed all the main features of the kitchen: white tiled to halfway up each wall, though some of the tiles were cracked and needed replacing; loads of cupboards; deep white sink; huge wooden draining board with a large wooden plate-rack above. No wiping up of plates and dishes here, just leave them to drain. But it was the spaciousness of the room that she liked so much. The whole family could eat in here.

Stop it, she scolded herself. What family?

That was a question she couldn't bring herself to think about.

'Stop daydreaming, Ella, and come and see the lounge and the dining room,' Dennis was calling her from the hallway.

Lounge? Dining room? What would she do with rooms like that?

Goodness gracious me! This front room looks more like a hotel. No it doesn't, Ella chided herself, it is far more cosy and comfortable than that. And what about the dining room? Even if, and it was a great big if, Dennis did buy this property for her, when on earth would she ever use this room? The table was enormous, with six chairs arranged around it, and Dennis was down on his knees looking beneath it. 'Thought so,' he said, looking up at her and grinning. 'There's a leaf here that pulls out so that more people can get round it.'

More people? What was he imagining? That she was going to feed the five thousand?

From the dining room French doors led into the garden. Dennis undid the bolts and flung them open wide. This was a different world. Ella had never known anything other than a small back yard. Having lived in the East End of London all her life, a place like this seemed impossible, and it was wicked of Dennis to tantalize her so.

Thank God the children weren't with them. To see all of this and then be told it would cost far more than they could afford would be a cruel joke.

But just supposing Dennis did have the money and was willing to buy this lovely house. What then?

From the moment they had left the house this morning, she had shoved the thought that she was pregnant by another man right out of her mind. Be realistic, she told herself now. You have to tell him sometime and then sit back and watch him explode!

Dennis had gone back inside the house and she could see the two men sitting in the dining room talking to each other.

Ella walked towards the wooded area at the bottom of the garden, her eyes brimming with tears as she told herself what a fool she had been to think that an educated man such as Sam Richardson would really have been interested in her. They came from two different worlds. Perhaps he had just wanted to find out if he was still able to perform the sex act.

Now she was being really nasty!

She hoped with all her heart that he would never find out that he had made her pregnant. Bit one-sided to put all the blame on him, she rebuked herself. She had been up for it; she had had the sweets and now by golly she was having to put up with the sours.

'Ella, Ella, where are you? Time for us to go.'

Hearing Dennis calling her brought her back sharply to the present. For the moment she had to try not to think about the predicament she was in. Hastily she rubbed at her eyes with her handkerchief, buttoned up her jacket and came out from between the trees with a smile on her lips.

At the front door she shook hands with Mr Hamilton and thanked him for allowing them to see his lovely home.

'My pleasure, Mrs Dryden, my pleasure,' he assured her.

'Thanks, Mr Hamilton.' Dennis held the old gentleman's hand longer than was necessary. 'We've a lot to discuss but I will be in touch with you in a day or two.'

On hearing this, a faint hope flickered deep inside Ella. Maybe, just maybe, Dennis would end up buying this lovely house.

It was a silent drive home, but not strained, Dennis looked very thoughtful, while Ella remained hopeful.

'Are you coming in?' she asked as he brought the car to a halt.

'No, I've a lot to do, but I'll leave the last page of the estate agent's details with you. Yer might like to show them t' yer mother.'

Ella was flabbergasted as she stood on the narrow pavement and watched him drive away.

Why did he have to have a dig at her mother?

Another thing, why was he grinning from ear to ear when she closed the car door?

Chapter Thirty-six

BY THE TIME ELLA had seen her two children off to school, her heart was pounding and her head ached.

Having spent the previous evening going over and over the estate agent's details that Dennis had left for her to read, she had had a restless night. She didn't know what she was going to do.

It wasn't so much the particulars of the property that had inspired her to want to move heaven and earth to make things right. It was the few lines that Dennis had written in pencil on the bottom of the last page.

She wished her mother would hurry up and arrive; she could usually come up with a sensible solution to any of her daughter's problems. Though not this time, Ella sighed. If only she could 'disappear' this troublesome pregnancy.

She had never looked at another man since the day that she married Dennis, though the Lord above knew that he had given her enough cause to. Then along came Sam Richardson, and to be honest she had felt flattered. But now it was as if a whole new life was being offered to her on a plate. A proper family life, not one where she had to make all the decisions and some weeks do her best to make ten shillings do the work of a pound. She had blown all her chances. When she did get around to telling Dennis that she was pregnant, it would be goodbye to all the dreams that had only yesterday started to form.

'Something tells me that all is not right in your world.' Her mother had not received any answer to her usual 'Cooee!' and had been standing in the doorway to the kitchen, but now she walked over to the black-leaded range, reaching for the big black kettle. After checking that there was enough water in it, she pushed it to the centre of the hot plate, then, before even taking her coat off, delved into her shopping bag and produced a half bottle of Bell's whisky.

'Nothing like a drop of the hard stuff in a nice cup of tea when you don't know if you're coming or going,' she said cheerfully. 'Two questions an' then I might know what is causing you to look as though you've lost half a crown an' found a tanner.

'First, how did the house hunting go? And second, did you tell Dennis about the baby?'

'Oh Mum, one of the houses we saw was a place to die for. As for telling Dennis that I'm pregnant, I just couldn't bring meself to do it.'

'But during the day, how were things between the pair of you?'

'That's just it, Mum, they couldn't have been better. He was Dennis as he was years ago. Kind and considerate. Didn't try to play the big hard man, not even once.'

'And did you both like this house, or was it just your choice?'

'Mum, I'll make the tea; you read these details that Dennis got from the estate agent, and when you come to the last page, prepare yourself for a shock.'

Ella passed over the three typewritten pages, got to her

feet and busied herself laying out cups. As the steam started to spurt from the kettle, she poured the boiling water on to the tea leaves which she had ladled into the pot. Waiting for the tea to draw, she watched her mother's reaction. So far it was delightful to see such a happy smile on that well-worn face.

Thank you, God, for my mum, Ella prayed silently. If anyone had the knack of putting everything on a level footing again, it would be dear old Winnie.

She poured out two cups of tea and placed one near to her mum's elbow.

Winnie looked up. 'Where's the whisky? I didn't bring it to sit on your dresser, and by all accounts we are both going to need more than one tipple.'

'So you've reached the last page! What are your thoughts?'

Winnie didn't hesitate. 'I expect I've made the same assumption that you have.'

'Pass me that last sheet, Mum, I'll read out loud what Dennis has scribbled and see if we are both of the same mind.

'"Ella, you obviously like this house a lot. It has four bedrooms, so why not ask your mother to come with us?"'

Ella's voice wavered and it was a moment or two before she could continue.

'Can't be all bad, can he?' Winnie Paige had not felt so emotional in a very long time.

Ella made no reply, but continued to read.

'"Winnie could have her own bedroom, and the dining room, that you said you would never use, we could turn into a private sitting room for her. Naturally she'd have all her meals with us. Ask her to give it a try. If she decides after a while that she can't live with me we'll take our time and find her something nice nearby."'

Winnie was the first to say what was staring them both in the face.

'Dennis is expecting you to take him back. All of you move in together and become one big happy family again. Isn't that the impression you got?'

Ella couldn't stop the tears from rolling down her cheeks. 'Course he is. A blind bat could see that. Oh Mum, please, tell me what to do.'

Winnie reached for the whisky bottle and topped their cups up before saying, 'Ella, luv, you don't need me to tell you. You know full well what you have to do. Tell him. And the quicker the better.'

'But Mum, what if—'

Winnie cut her short. 'No ifs or buts. He has to be told now. No good putting it off. You'll be starting to show before you know where you are.'

'Supposing he goes mad and walks away?'

'Are you saying that you want Dennis back in your life, or is it just this house you want?'

'Christ, Mum, that's a bit below the belt.'

'No it's not. You have to decide. Course, there's always the chance that he will buy the house, let us have it and walk away,' she laughed, and added, 'But I can't see Dennis Dryden doing that. He may well 'ave changed quite a bit, but seeing him as a saint doesn't work for me. By the way, I got another letter from the council this morning.'

Ella looked up sharply. 'Does it give a date for when the demolition is going to start?'

'No, but it does say they can offer me a flat in Hackney, a first-floor flat apparently.'

'You're going to turn it down, aren't you? You don't want to live in Hackney of all places, do you?'

'Of course not. I'd much rather come with all of you to Dulwich.'

The look Ella gave her mother was cynical. 'And you

think any of us stand a chance of living in that big house?'

Her mother didn't have an answer to that!

The next hour was spent at the kitchen table with more cups of tea and a huge dish of well-buttered toasted teacakes.

There were several times during the course of this hour that Ella wanted to throw her arms around her mum and hug her hard. She knew that Winnie was blaming herself for having encouraged her to go off with Sam Richardson for that weekend, and that wasn't fair. Ella was a grown-up woman, albeit a neglected one, and she should have thought harder about what she was doing.

'Let's go over those estate agent's details together and you can describe the house as we go so that I'll be able to see it in my mind's eye,' Winnie suggested, doing her best to lift Ella's spirits.

Slowly Ella began to read. '"Double-fronted detached house. First floor: four bedrooms, bathroom and lavatory, linen cupboard which houses boiler. Ground floor: large half-tiled kitchen, spacious dining room with French doors leading to the garden and a woodland area at the far end which is also owned by the owner of the property, sitting room with tiled fire surround and bow-fronted window. The hallway is ten feet wide and to the left of the front door there is a second lavatory and a small wash-hand basin. A garage stands to the right of the property but is not adjoining.

'"Dulwich College, which also has a prep school for younger children, is within close proximity. The oldest part of Dulwich is known as Dulwich Village and boasts a beautiful public park.

'"The asking price for this freehold property is £5,995."'

When Ella stopped reading you could have heard a pin drop. Then Winnie rose from her seat, walked round to her daughter and put her arm across her shoulders.

'Look, luv, Dennis Dryden almost destroyed you, and for a while he didn't give a toss for his children. Even today I can't bear to look Mrs Baldwin in the eye. He hurt that family more than you or I can imagine. Worse than that, he destroyed that family.' She spoke quietly, her voice shaking with the depth of her feeling.

Ella nodded.

Her mother began again. 'It might be asking too much of him to accept another man's child; on the other hand, if he's suggesting that you try to make a fresh start, then there has got to be give and take on both sides. I understand more than you think, but you must do what seems best to you. First things first, though. He has to be told that you are having a baby. There is no other way I can think of.'

'What about Teddy and Babs?' said Ella sullenly. 'Their reaction won't be pleasant, I bet.'

'And who's going to tell them that their baby sister or brother has a different father than they do? I'll lay odds that Dennis never will.'

'Mum! What you're suggesting is that we all live a lie.'

'Oh for God's sake. Dennis won't be the first husband to pass another man's baby off as his own. Have yer never heard the saying, it's a wise man that knows his own father?'

Ella shrugged off-handedly as though she hadn't also been considering the fact that Dennis might decide to accept the baby as his own. Whether he agreed or not, she was going to stick to her guns over this. One way or another she was going to make sure that he provided a decent place for them to live.

She and the kids at least deserved that much.

Later that same evening, after having seen the children into bed, Ella was sitting darning Teddy's socks when she thought she heard the front door open. Glancing at the clock on the mantelpiece, she saw that it was twenty minutes past nine. Who the hell was coming in at this time of night?

She dropped her work on to the floor and got to her feet. Hardly had she got the kitchen door opened when Dennis came striding down the passage calling, 'It's only me.'

Once inside and seated opposite her, Dennis apologized.

'Sorry, luv, for coming so late, but I've had a helluva day. Still, this evening has made up for it. I've been on the phone to Mr Hamilton, and guess what, I told him we were interested in buying his house. He asked how much my offer was going to be, and I told him that I was willing to pay him the full asking price. Apparently the estate agent had said that he would have to accept a slightly lower price. Anyway, he was that pleased that he went on an' on about what furniture he was going to take with him, reminding me that he was only having a one-bedroom apartment, ended up by telling me that anything he did not require he would leave in the house at no extra cost, including all the carpets and curtains, though not the rugs he said, those he would make good use of.'

Ella's eyes lit up. He'd be leaving most of the bedrooms fully furnished! Unbelievable.

Then, like a bolt out of the blue, it struck her. No longer could she keep this pretence going.

'Dennis, will you listen to me for a minute? You haven't once attempted to make your position clear to me. Are you intending to move into this new house, or is it just for me, the kids and my mother? By the way, Mum was over the moon that you had given a thought to her. Only this morning the council had offered her a place. In Hackney, would you believe!'

All the time Ella had been speaking, her eyes had not left his face and now she saw his cheeks flush up.

For a moment he hesitated. 'I . . . I,' he stammered at last, 'took it for granted that we'd make a new life for the kids. You and me together. It was what I wanted right from the moment that I bought the place out at Epsom, but you would have none of it. You wanted to live an' die in the East End. Now you and I are getting on so well, aren't we?' He leant forward and touched her shoulder gently.

Impatiently she shook his arm away and in the moment of silence which followed Ella was not able to control her temper.

'You take too much for granted,' she cried loudly. 'And don't you dare try to lay the blame on me for all the bad things that have happened.'

'You've every right to be angry,' Dennis agreed.

'Humph! Too true I have. Besides, Dennis, I'm going to have a baby!'

She had blurted the last sentence out really harshly, not knowing how to tell him more gently. She was past caring now she couldn't keep this awful secret to herself any longer.

She clenched her hands together so tightly the knuckles showed white. She had given him a shock, but at least it was out in the open now.

She watched as Dennis moved so that he was sitting up ramrod straight in the chair. The colour of his cheeks heightened and his look of disbelief was incredible. That piece of news had quickly wiped the smile off his face. His hands clutched at his stomach. It was almost as if somebody had dealt him a violent and crippling blow. He looked utterly devastated.

At last he managed to speak. 'Ella, why? Who with?'

She wasn't sorry for him; in fact she almost spat her

371

answer at him. 'Dennis, ask yourself how many times I have wanted to ask you those very same questions.'

'Oh my God!' he cried. 'I knew that bloody Sam Richardson was sniffing around you. He was here in my house over Christmas. Just like him to go for another man's wife.'

'At least he chose a woman and not a girl barely out of school.' Ella was shaking, and her anger, hurt and disgust were choking her.

She hadn't meant to retaliate so fiercely. This was getting out of hand. She bit her lip and moved her chair further away from his. Any moment he might let fly with his fists.

'Jesus bloody Christ! I thought better of you,' Dennis muttered, before clenching his teeth.

'Yes, and I've wished better of you so many times that I've lost count. I made one mistake. I let Sam take me away for two days, but what you need to remember is that you left me a long time ago. I was on my own, not knowing how to cope, while you did exactly what you wanted to do and with every girl that happened to take your fancy.'

Then she added spitefully, 'But two wrongs don't make a right, do they?'

Dennis had the sense to realize that what his wife was saying was the truth, and so he swallowed hard and said sadly, 'I didn't do right by Connie. I stood by and let her mother send her away, and then that rotten sod of an uncle raped her. If it wasn't for him, I keep telling myself, she would never have been on that train. I hadn't even got the guts to go to her funeral. I should never have left you. I should have stayed but still stood by Connie. I didn't do either. I cleared off when I should have damn well stayed. You know it, I know it, and everybody knows it. But I didn't . . . and it's too late now for me to put things right. I made a bloody mess of so many lives and I'll spend the rest of my life paying for it.'

It was then that Ella began to calm down, and as she watched the emotions pass across his face she realized she could find it in her heart to feel sorry for him.

Anger on both sides had subsided, and now there was this ominous silence. Dennis had played by his own rules, but never in his life had he thought that his wife might be tempted to do the same.

He thought of her as his. She belonged to him, joined at the hip almost. Since the sad death of Connie Baldwin he had always intended to come back home and make a good life. He'd really missed his wife and seeing his kids grow up.

Now he'd left it too long and he needed no telling that he only had himself to blame for what had happened between Ella and Sam Richardson.

Sam had been there for her. He hadn't.

'Do you want this baby?' Dennis asked, his voice little more than a whisper.

'I didn't,' Ella answered truthfully, 'but then at first I wouldn't let myself believe that it was true. Then I dallied with the idea of having an abortion, but that I could not bring myself to do.'

'Does Sam know that you're pregnant?' he asked awkwardly, not meeting her eyes.

'No, he does not. And he is never going to find out, if I have my way. Since we spent our weekend together I 'aven't seen hair nor hide of him. I don't want to neither.'

Ella felt she had every right to keep secret the matter of the letter that Sam had written to her. If she were to tell Dennis that Sam had practically said she wasn't good enough for him, it would be like giving him a big stick with which to beat her.

Dennis stood up and went to the dresser. 'Since when 'ave you taken to drinking whisky?' he asked.

Ella gave him a tight smile. 'Mum brought it in.'

'There's still some left. Shall we have a drink? I think we could both do with one.'

Ella stayed silent as she watched him pour the same amount into each glass before handing one to her.

He remained standing, watching as she took the first sip.

Ella raised her head. 'I wish things hadn't gone so wrong,' she said, her beautiful eyes brimming with tears.

He tossed half of his measure of whisky back in one gulp. Then he said, 'You're right, Ella. With my record I'm 'ardly in a position to condemn you, am I? Are you sure you don't want an abortion?'

'Definitely not.'

'Why not?'

'Partly because I'm too scared, and partly because it would be taking a life.'

Dennis took a deep breath, walked across the floor and stood with his back against the door, putting the widest possible space between them. 'Ella, would you consider letting me take care of you?'

By now Ella was spent, unable to lift her head, let alone give him an answer. She was sitting hunched up in her chair, softly crying.

The very sight of her was tugging at Dennis's heart-strings. How could I have been such a fool? he was asking himself. I threw so much away, and for what? In so many ways I couldn't have been more lucky; every deal I've pulled off has made me a small fortune, but with no one to share it with it's worthless. This room, this house might not be much, but it was our home, my children upstairs in bed, and I jeopardized everything. He was almost praying, and that, he knew, would be a first for him.

'Ella, will you hear me out?'

She nodded her head slightly.

'Long ago I started to look back and I began to realize exactly what a selfish man I had become. When I left you and the children in the lurch it was a cruel thing to do. I'm not proud of my past, I only wish that I could turn the clock back, but no one gets that chance. I will buy this house in Dulwich, but whether you decide that I can become part of your life, of this family, will be up to you. If you decide that I am not to put a foot inside the door, you have my word that the house will still be yours and all necessary payments will be made by me. You will have no worries and you will not be getting another job. You will have three children to look after and I will do my utmost to treat the baby you are carrying as if it were my own.'

He hadn't moved, he'd still kept his distance, but all the time he was speaking Ella listened carefully, and she had the feeling that for once in his life her husband was speaking from the heart. Yet somehow she felt she had lost control. It seemed that both of them were experiencing a sense of terrible guilt.

'Ella?' His voice was softer now. 'Please, look at me.'

Ella didn't want to look up. God knows, every fibre of her being wanted to trust him. To have her whole family, even her old mum, all safely under one roof, with Dennis coming home every night to sit and share their evening meal round one table. Teddy and Babs would be over the moon. But there would be another child to consider. Would Dennis really accept this one as his own? He had painted a picture that said it would happen. Could she really trust him?

'Ella?' It was unbelievable but it was true: there were tears in the voice, and such sadness. 'Please . . . look at me.'

Ella raised her eyes, and what she saw tore at her heart. Her husband was crying. 'I'm sorry,' she murmured.

Most of this was not her fault, but at that moment it felt as if it was.

'I do still love you, Ella. And you know my feeling for our kids. Is there even a slight chance that we might put the past behind us?'

Ella blinked away her own tears and said quietly, 'We both know that what's done is done and can't be undone, more's the pity, so it's no use us laying the blame on each other.'

She forced herself to look up, and somehow Dennis was standing directly in front of her. Without warning he bent his head and gently kissed her. When she made no attempt to push him away, he pulled her to her feet, and this time his kiss was a long, slow, lingering one. When finally they broke apart, he had the look on his face of a schoolboy who had been caught out doing something that he shouldn't.

Ella grinned. Suddenly it was as if a great weight had been lifted from her shoulders.

Dennis remained holding her close within his arms and whispered against her hair, 'God above knows how long I've been longing to do that.'

'Really?' Ella asked.

'Yes, it's true, I've been longing to kiss my own wife.'

Epilogue
1958

ELLA AND DENNIS SAT in the well-padded swinging hammock out in the garden of Zenith House, Court Lane, West Dulwich.

They both looked sun-tanned, fit and well, and their friends and relations only had to look at them to see how settled and happy they were. They both loved these summer Sunday afternoons. Having had family and friends to midday dinner, they could relax in the hot August sunshine.

'Who would ever have thought things could have changed so much for the better since we moved from the East End of London,' Ella reflected aloud to her husband, as they watched the antics of their children and their friends.

'I know.' Dennis reached along and took hold of his wife's hand. 'It's almost unbelievable, isn't it?'

Their thoughts were running along similar lines.

Young Ted was down in the overgrown wooded area with his two German Shepherd dogs and three of his mates. All four were privileged young men, attending Dulwich College, and it was so hard to believe that their son would be eighteen years old this autumn.

Ella's eyes moved and settled on her two daughters. Babs was fourteen and into the stage where fashion and make-up was beginning to be a big item in her life, though she did take her studies seriously.

As Ella lazily let her mind wander back over the last five years she knew she had a great deal to be thankful for.

Their children were being given so many advantages that she herself and Dennis could never have dreamt of. But then again, five years ago would they have imagined that their own lives would have changed so drastically?

Suddenly Claire let out a scream. One of the other girls had pushed the swing too high and just for a moment Claire had been afraid. Dennis was on his feet in a second, running down the garden, making sure that their youngest child wasn't hurt.

Ella allowed herself a happy, grateful smile. In three months' time Claire would be five years old.

There wasn't a more loved child anywhere in the country, on that she would stake her life. Also, never a day went by that Ella did not thank the Lord for all his blessings. It had always been a known fact that Teddy was the image of his father and Babs favoured Ella's side of the family. If you saw the two girls together, you would have to assume they were sisters. Claire had the same long chestnut-coloured hair, the big brown eyes and the angelical look that came from the Paige side of the family. If the truth be known, it was a fact that both Dennis and Ella were extremely grateful for.

If she had been born with different colouring, however, it was doubtful that it would have made the slightest difference. From the day she had been born she had brought love with her. And to the whole family it was a lasting love.

★   ★   ★

'Tea's coming!' the cry rang out, and children and adults came from all directions.

Winnie Paige and Ellen Hines each came carrying a tray loaded with fruit scones, jam and cream plus at least four very large home-made cakes.

Bringing up the rear were Edward Dryden and Mr Hamilton, now lovingly known as the Major. All four adults were, as usual on these occasions, in charge of the china and the two huge teapots.

Mrs Hines had enjoyed her stay in Chelsea in the company of Lady Margaret, but after a year she had decided that she would prefer to return to her own apartment.

No problem. Dennis and his father had asked the bank to send out the official documents calling in the loan on the apartment that had previously belonged to Ellen Hines. To his own detriment, Claude Packard had ignored the warning from the bank. This had resulted in a visit from the Drydens. Very reluctantly Mr Packard had allowed them to enter his flat.

Dennis had made the initial move by saying, 'Mr Packard, you should not take out loans that you are unable to pay back.'

Then Ted had quickly chipped in, 'Another lesson you need to learn is that you shouldn't gamble if you cannot pay up when your horse doesn't win the race.'

Ted had almost found it in his heart to feel sorry for the man as he spluttered, 'What the hell have my gambling debts got to do with you?'

'Everything, Mr Packard. It is to me that you owe the money! I own three bookmakers and I bought your debts.'

It had been a joy to both father and son to watch the man squirm.

They had reminded Packard of his dirty tricks when Miss Sheldon had been alive, and warned him it was payback time, though actually they let him off lightly, reclaiming only the apartment for Mrs Hines. However, they did remind him that should he fall short in just one mortgage payment in the future, they would send the bailiffs in and he would be homeless.

'The same applies if you pester Mrs Hines in any way whatsoever. Have we made ourselves clear?' Ted asked loudly.

Mr Packard had nodded his head.

'I would like a verbal answer if you don't mind, just so that I know we have made ourselves clear,' Ted had insisted.

Quickly enough Claude Packard had said, 'Yes.'

'He's got the picture,' Dennis said, loud enough for Claude to hear as they left.

So Mrs Hines's furniture had come out of store, she was back home in Epsom and the family had remained friends. Once a fortnight Winnie Paige went to spend the day with her. Then the next fortnight Ted would drive to Epsom and fetch Ellen to spend the day in Dulwich with the Drydens.

Another turn-up for the books was the fact that Mr Hamilton had revealed that he was a great lover of horse-racing, and so Ted had befriended him and made a point of inviting him to attend all the main races of the season.

'The Major' was a frequent visitor and a great favourite with all the family.

As Ella took the hot cup of tea that her mother was holding out for her, they exchanged happy smiles.

The fact that Mr and Mrs Dryden and their children had moved to West Dulwich had been of great benefit to a lot of people.

Life's for Living

Bob

There is never a day
that I don't miss your love,
your companionship and all the ups
and downs that make a marriage.

Human beings can live for quite a while
without water or food, but they cannot
withstand loneliness.

It is the worst of all sufferings.

Chapter One

SOUTH LONDON, 1926

MR GILBY, THE RENT COLLECTOR, was having a bad day. He was smartly dressed: dark suit, the trousers pressed to perfection, worn with a sparkling white shirt and a dark blue tie. He also wore a bowler hat on his head. Usually he was in complete charge of any given situation. But not today.

'You've had enough warnings, Mrs Brown,' he said, doing his best to remain calm, 'and it won't wash any longer. Seven days and you pay in full or you and your whole family will be evicted.'

Martha Brown lost her patience. 'My husband is on short time at the foundry and this last four weeks is the first time in all the years that we've lived here that I haven't had my rent ready and waiting for you.' She stuck a finger within an inch of his face. Mr Smart-arse, as the locals had nicknamed him, gasped and took a step backwards. Martha wasn't finished, not by a long chalk. 'You might frighten some of the poor old souls round 'ere but you don't frighten me. I've told you, as soon as my man is set on full time again you'll get every penny that's owing. Meanwhile, if you dare t' threaten me again I'll go straight up to Ensign's offices and ask t' see the owner of these properties, 'cos

1

you're not the organ grinder by any means. You're only the employed monkey.' Martha's voice was set with emphasis. 'You wanna remember, two-thirds of these houses in all these three streets are occupied by my relatives and Ensign's know we've always been good tenants.'

The collector looked at her as if she were someone from the gutter. 'Yes . . . well, I'll be here as usual next Monday.'

Martha closed the door in his face and pressed her aching head against the solid wood. She closed her eyes and thought of her children, but mostly of Rose, her only daughter.

Her two sons, Lenny and Bernie, were good lads and she loved them both dearly. Lenny, nineteen years old, was the image of his father, and Sid Brown was a big man. In his stockinged feet he stood six foot one, though these days his back was no longer ramrod straight. From the day he'd left the East End of London where he had been born and bred to move south of the Thames, he'd held down an un-believably hard job at Merton Foundry, where massive furnaces were kept going day and night in order to separate metal from ore. Broad-shouldered and thick-set, he had grown tough over the years. It was said of him that he could fell a man with one blow from his huge fist. Lenny was quite content to walk in his father's shadow. He'd worked in Wandsworth Brewery since he was fourteen years old and was never happier than when rolling the huge barrels of beer down the ramps which led to the cellars of various pubs. His pride and joy were the enormous dray horses which he always groomed with the greatest of care.

Bernie was different. Just one year younger than his brother, he was always frustrated. He wanted so much more out of life than his parents had. He'd grown up with misery and poverty, and he yearned to be educated. Although he was not quite as tall or as muscular as his father and brother he was still well-built and strong – and the best-looking one of the family. His striking good looks would always be a powerful asset. He worked in Paines' firework factory and hated every minute that he had to spend there.

Third time lucky, Martha and Sid had said when their lovely daughter had been born. 'As beautiful as a rose, and well worth waiting for,' Sid had exclaimed. Martha had never known her husband to show such emotion and immediately decided that would be her baby's name. Rosie, with her blonde curly hair, pale skin and wide blue eyes, was the opposite of her brothers who both had dark hair and sharp brown eyes. Most definitely Rosie took after her side of the family.

Rose was a gentle child, endearing herself to people by smiling readily and chatting away nineteen to the dozen. It was said that she could charm the birds out of the trees. She'd learnt to twist her big brothers and her father around her little finger. Her cheeky, expressive face with those big, innocent-looking blue eyes always captivated them completely. Almost every Saturday one of them brought her something: a colouring book and crayons, a pretty hair slide, a bag of sweets, even a skipping rope with colourful painted handles. The fact that just lately she had changed so much was worrying Martha more than she would admit. At first she had supposed that turning thirteen and becoming a teenager a couple of weeks ago had made the difference. She'd changed so suddenly, one minute behaving as if she were afraid of something and the next, without warning, back-answering and acting too big for her boots. It was as if now there was a different side to her; she'd become deceitful, cunning and wilful.

Slowly Martha walked into her scullery, filled the tin kettle from the single cold tap at the brown-stone sink, struck a match and lit one of the four rings on the top of her enamel gas stove. Having placed the kettle over the flame she walked into the living room and sat down to wait for it to come to the boil. After that rumpus with that

3

pompous old git over the rent she badly needed a cup of strong tea.

She sighed heavily and murmured, 'Oh, Rosie, Rosie, Rosie. Why won't you talk to me?' Even a blind man would be able to tell there was something wrong and she was ninety per cent sure that she already knew what it was. If half of what she feared was true there was no way she could shift the blame. It would all fall on her shoulders and Sid would do his nut. She'd had a hard enough job persuading him to let their little girl do a favour for her Auntie Joan in the first place.

Joan was Martha's elder sister by two years. Despite being up at the crack of dawn every morning to catch the tram which would take her to the city where she cleaned offices, Joan had got herself an extra job making lampshades. It worked out very well because she could work from home. Trouble was she had to report to the factory twice a week between four and six o'clock in order to deliver her finished work and collect a fresh set of lampshade frames and material. Her mother-in law lived with Joan, had done from the day she'd been married, and Joan loved her dearly. Sadly, in the latter years, the old lady had become ill. Sick in the mind as much as bodily ill, but Joan cared for her to the best of her ability. Which was more than could be said of her son.

Daily Joan washed and fed the old lady, and if she had the time she would give her a blanket bath, dress her and get her settled in a chair by the front window to enable her to see folk passing by. She could never be left on her own, because her movements were jerky and disjointed and she often fell. Martha helped her sister as much as she could and many a good neighbour came in to sit with the old lady when Joan needed to go to the shops for a bit of shopping. But the evenings when she had to go to the lampshade factory were awkward. Martha had to have dinner ready on

4

the table for Sid and her own two sons when they came home from work and it was the same for most local women, and so she had agreed that Rosie would go round, only into the next street, for those couple of hours and sit with the old lady just to make sure she didn't get out of bed.

Poor Joan! Christ knows she needs the money. Martha shook her head in disgust. Married to Bill Baldwin, Joan had not found life a bed of roses. Lazy sod he was and always would be. Work was something other people did, not him.

Through the open door Martha saw that the kettle was steaming. She got to her feet, poured some water into the brown china teapot and swilled it round before throwing it into the sink. She would have liked to use two heaped teaspoons of leaves because she liked her tea hot and very strong, but it was the middle of the week and the way things were going there would only be the few shillings that her sons gave her coming into her purse this weekend, so she sighed and made do with just one level spoonful. 'Don't drown it,' she muttered as she poured on the boiling water.

Settled back in what was Sid's wooden armchair, she sipped at her tea. She'd bet her last penny that the way young Rosie was acting up was something to do with Bill Baldwin. Quite unexpectedly Martha felt tears sting the back of her eyes. She swallowed hard. She hadn't cried in years, but now memory had her mind jumping back far into the past.

She'd been fifteen and flattered that her big sister's boyfriend had paid her attention. Bill Baldwin had been twenty-one, six years older than herself and four years older than Joan. She had gone for a walk across Tooting Bec Common with him and he'd taken her into a pub, where he'd had a pint of beer and bought her a shandy. She shouldn't really have been in a public house because she wasn't old enough but the experience had made her feel very grown up. And Bill Baldwin had acted nice, holding her hand as they walked back across the common, but when they were almost home he'd tried it on.

'God forgive me,' she muttered beneath her breath. He'd almost got there. His kisses had been lovely to begin with and she hadn't given a thought to the fact that he was walking out regularly with Joan. It was only when he'd tried to get his hand up the leg of her knickers that she had come to her senses.

She'd kicked him in the shins and run like the devil, never once stopping until she reached the safety of their porch. Even then, for a good many minutes she hadn't been able to pull the string through the letter box which held the key to the front door. She'd had to get her breath back and straighten her clothing before she could face her mum and dad.

For months afterwards she'd been nervous whenever Bill Baldwin was in their house. She hadn't been able to tell anyone, her sister least of all, because only days after she'd gone for a walk with Bill he had given Joan a ring and they'd become engaged.

It had been an awful situation. Joan would be sitting snuggled up to him on the sofa and he'd look over the top of Joan's head and wink at her. Nothing had ever been said but the looks he gave her on the quiet made her flesh crawl.

But all that had been donkey's years ago. She and Sid had been married for almost twenty years. They'd had their ups and downs but they'd weathered them and, thank God, they had three healthy children. The same could not be said for her sister. Joan had had one hell of a life. Although it was Bill's mother whom Joan loved and cared for he never lifted a finger to help. Any money that did come his way went into either a publican's pocket or that of a bookmaker. Three times Joan had been pregnant and each time she had miscarried. No one could tell Martha that the cause of her sister's being unable to carry a baby to full term was not

6

down to that bugger of a husband of hers. She knew, when he had had too much to drink, or even when he hadn't, he would think nothing of using Joan as a punch bag.

'Why the hell does your sister stay with him?' Sid had often asked. Martha was sure she knew the answer. If Joan didn't take care of old Mrs Baldwin, then who the hell would?

Half the trouble was that Joan appeared to come from a different mould from the man she had chosen to marry. But in those long-ago days when a whole host of East-Enders had moved to South London because both houses and employment were more plentiful there, Joan had been deemed old enough to be put into service. Having had hardly any schooling she started at the bottom, but as it turned out that period of her life had been a blessing in disguise. Her employers had been taken with this girl who came from such a poor background. As a worker they thought of her as a little wonder. As to her looks, she was a beauty, even if it was an unusual sort of beauty. Quiet and peaceful was how the mistress described her. She was small and slight, with soft features, a gentle nature and long soft golden-brown hair which she mainly kept rolled up in a bun, which was a shame, Martha thought, because it caused her, at times, to look stern. She had given her name as Joanie, but that was not how they referred to her in that posh household. Always Joan. Her own way of speaking had soon altered, and not only that, she was taught manners and that there was a right way to do everything one was asked to do. After proving that she was willing to learn she rose from being a kitchen maid to a parlour maid, and finally she'd been promoted to the position of lady's maid. It was during that time she had learnt about clothes. Indeed she had. Even today Joan's handiwork with a needle was something to be admired.

Joan had quickly seen the vast difference between life at

Morley House and life for lower-class families. The pampered Morleys wanted for nothing, totally unaware of the harsh realities of the lives of their employees, especially when the man of the family was unable to find work even though he tramped endless miles searching for it, willing to do the meanest of jobs if he could only earn enough to keep his wife and children in the bare essentials of life. It hadn't taken her long to realise that money bought not only necessities, but so much more as well. How many times, Martha wondered, had Joan told her that her mother-in-law needed medicines and nourishing food, not to mention spare clean bedding. It was at such times that the pair of them had readily agreed that money is the answer to everything.

Martha decided that she was going to have to put some direct questions to Rosie. She had done her best to talk to her, and although her daughter always avoided giving straight answers, on one occasion she had blurted out that her Uncle Bill had been in the house when she was supposed to be on her own looking after Granny Baldwin.

Martha felt betwixt and between. Should she stop Rosie going round there? That would only be victimising Joan. Whatever was going on couldn't be Rosie's fault. What did she know at her age? She's always got on well with her Uncle Bill. He tickled her, made her laugh, and as far as Martha was concerned, up until now, there had not been any reason not to trust him. She decided, at least for the time being, she was going to have to keep her suspicions to herself. She couldn't bear to think that there might come a time when she would have to tell her husband, which would involve her two sons at the same time. Then God help us. Things might get out of hand.

Rose came down the stairs just as the front door opened and her father walked in. 'Daddy,' she shrieked, totally forgetting that her mum had allowed her to stay home from school because she'd pleaded an awful headache. She ran down the passage, her face wreathed in smiles.

Sid eased his great body towards her and swept her, the apple of his eye, up into his brawny arms, swung her round several times until the walls whirled before her eyes, and then held her tenderly as he carried her into the living room.

''Allo, my luv,' he said to his wife. 'I'm sure we've got the prettiest daughter in the world. But what I can't make out is why she's so small and dainty when our two boys are such great big louts.'

'I've told yer often enough. You've only got t' look in the mirror to see who Lenny and Bernie take after, while our Rosie looks a bit like me but much more like her Auntie Joan.'

Sid put Rosie down and walked over to Martha and took hold of her arm before planting a kiss on her cheek. 'You're nice an' plump 'cos you're 'appy an' well cared for whereas your sister, Gawd bless 'er, ain't nothing but skin an' bone 'cos she spends 'er entire life slogging away to keep that useless sod she married an' his mother.' When Martha didn't answer he looked intently into her eyes and asked very quietly, 'What's the matter, gal? Is something wrong?'

She didn't answer, but turned her face away.

'Why isn't Rosie at school? There is something wrong, isn't there?' he said again, more loudly, at the same time catching hold of her arm.

She shook his hand off. 'No, nuffin's wrong. She wasn't very perky this morning – said 'er 'ead ached, that's all.'

'But you look worried. An' yer jumped when I touched yer arm.'

'No I didn't. I was just surprised to see you 'ome so early.'

'There was nuffin' doing. They've even let two of the furnaces burn out an' I ain't ever seen that 'appen before.' He turned away, realising he wasn't going to get any answers

9

from her at the moment. He'd leave it for a bit. But for days there'd been a funny uneasy atmosphere. Why couldn't he put his finger on it? *Before this day is out I will, though*, he vowed to himself. *I'll get Martha on her own and I will find out what is going on.*

He wandered over to where Rose sat and, doing his best to be gentle, he sat down on the floor at her feet and looked up at her. 'Do you feel better now, luv?'

'Yes, Dad,' Rose said quietly.

'You would tell me if there was something troubling you, wouldn't you, babe?'

Martha held her breath.

'Course I would,' Rose murmured, hanging her head.

Her father got to his feet and took hold of both of her hands. 'Rosie, I know everything is not all right with you. Are you gonna tell me about it?'

She didn't raise her head, merely shook it and muttered, 'Ask Mum.'

It took a lot to make Sid Brown lose his temper but when he did, God help the person who had upset him. He took a very deep breath as he turned his gaze on to his wife and instinctively was aware that she knew more than she was letting on. This wasn't a bit like his Martha. Even when times had been really hard, with five mouths to feed, food and clothes to buy and money to be found for coal because the kitchen range was the only heating in the whole house and there was times when the weather was so cold that ice formed on the *inside* of the bedroom windows, his Martha had never let her feelings show. He couldn't remember when he'd come home and Martha hadn't had a smile on her face. He clenched his fists in frustration. No matter what he said or did he was being balked at every turn. He knew full well he wasn't going to get anything out of either of them just yet but he couldn't resist saying, 'Well, it'll take a bit more talking to convince me that something 'asn't 'appened to upset the apple cart in this family.'

Martha didn't like the way Sid was scowling. 'I've got to get the meal on. Let's leave it till the boys are 'ome an' we've all eaten, shall we, Sid?' She smiled, but there was no mistaking the note of pleading in her voice as she looked at her daughter and added kindly, 'You're all right now, aren't you, pet?'

Sid's face was set straight, no answering smile. 'All right,' he said gruffly, letting her know that nothing was settled until she had told him the truth.

There was no way out. Martha knew that she would have to voice her fears to her husband. He'd get the truth out of Rosie and he'd know what to do, he always did. But there was one point she was going to make. Joan mustn't know about this. Every time Bill Baldwin got himself in a bit of bother it was always left to Joan to sort it all out. What with looking after old Mrs Baldwin twenty-four hours of every day and trying to keep up with two jobs, Joan was almost at the end of her tether; certainly she was in no fit state to take on more worries. She had no children of her own and Rosie was the light of her life, and if she thought that her Bill had hurt the child in any way she would probably go berserk.

As Martha went towards the scullery, Sid stepped in front of her and said firmly, 'Remember what you've promised. As soon as we've eaten we're getting this matter sorted. No matter what it is. Do you hear me?'

She nodded.

The vegetables she was preparing for their evening meal were done in next to no time because as she peeled potatoes and scraped carrots she was venting her fury by muttering over and over again, 'Bloody Bill Baldwin.'

11

Chapter Two

'BUT, DAD, I LIKE sitting with Granny Baldwin. I tell her all about what we do at school and Auntie Joan always leaves us some sweets and an apple or an orange which we have half each of. You won't stop me going round there, will you?' Rosie's eyes were imploring.

Big Sid's face was creased with worry. He was sitting opposite his daughter, and now he stretched out his hand and took hold of hers and sighed deeply. Rosie was especially dear to him, as she was to all of them, and she would for ever be regarded as the baby of the family. Yet the relationship she had with Granny Baldwin was amazing. She had the ability to listen, to care, and to show kindness to the old lady – unlike the do-gooders who, when Joan had asked for their help, had only come up with the suggestion that Mrs Baldwin would be far better off in a council home. The last thing he wanted was to forbid Rosie to go and sit with the old lady. Besides, Martha would raise hell if he even suggested it. Martha was never one to mince words or hesitate to go where even angels would fear to tread. All the same, he knew he and his two sons had to sort something out, and soon. If it weren't for the fact that Joan was Martha's sister he wouldn't be hesitating: he'd be round to Baldwin's place and he'd make damn sure the bastard wouldn't be able to walk for weeks on end.

It was Bernie, the quietest of his two sons, who had gently got most of the story out of their Rosie.

'Just tell me why you've suddenly gone off yer Uncle Bill,' he had asked, his manner not accusing, just soft and soothing. He smiled at her and his sister had smiled back and looked at him with utter trust. 'Don't you like him any more?'

Rosie seemed to be struggling to find an answer. Then quietly she said with complete honesty, 'Not really, no. He gives me the creeps.'

'Get on with it,' Lenny chipped in irritatedly. 'I don't know why we don't just get round there an' knock the bloody 'ell out of him.'

Martha's faced paled. If this all blew up into a full scale fight it would be poor Joan who would come off worst in the end. 'Don't be so damned stupid, Lenny,' she snapped. 'We don't know the 'alf of it yet and we won't unless Rosie tells us the truth.'

Rosie wasn't daft. No different from most of the girls in her class at school. It was just that she had two elder brothers and her dad was a great big man and she knew exactly where she stood with them. If the three of them had their way they wouldn't let the wind blow on her. They were always questioning her as to where she was going and whom she was going with.

A lot of her friends plastered their faces with cheap make-up and some even smoked when they could cadge enough pennies to buy a packet of fags. Two girls she knew had big breasts and they boasted about how they let the boys touch them. She was probably the smallest girl in her class and her breasts were scarcely formed. She'd asked her mum to buy her a brassiere but she'd only laughed and told her to give herself a chance to have something to put into it first. For all that, she liked boys as much as the other girls did; they could be great fun at times. But this thing with her own uncle . . . well, it wasn't the same. It was nasty.

'I dunno why Uncle Bill keeps wanting to touch me.' She suddenly opened up. 'He always used to be out somewhere when I first started going to sit with Gran, but not now. He's always there. Granny Baldwin saw him come up behind me the other night when he pulled my dress up and put both his hands on my bottom. I yelled 'cos he made me jump and Granny said he was a dirty twisted git. I thought he was going to hit Gran and that's when I told him I was gonna tell Auntie Joan.'

'And did you?' her mother asked, cagily.

'No, I didn't, 'cos Auntie Joan 'as all sorts of things to worry about. She works all the time. She's always changing Gran's clothes 'cos sometimes she can't get to the lav quick enough an' she wets herself. And she dribbles an' drops her food down her jumper. She can't 'elp it, though – her hands shake. Loads of washing Auntie 'as t' do yet she still cooks lovely meals, but Uncle Bill moans and shouts at her all the time and . . .'

'*And what?*' Her father and her mother bawled the question simultaneously.

Rosie shrank back into her chair, wishing she didn't have to answer, but one look at her father's face told her she had to. 'Uncle Bill hits Auntie Joan,' she said, trying not to cry.

Martha shook her head sadly, thanking God that she had a good man and wondering how Joan managed to put up with the life she had to lead.

'I can't believe I'm hearing this.' Sid's anger was choking him. 'Come on, Lenny. You too, Bernie,' their father said, standing up and straightening his shoulders. 'It's about time we paid that relation of ours a visit and believe you me by the time I've finished with him he'll think he's been hung, drawn and quartered.

Bill Baldwin was feeling very proud of himself as he glanced in the mirror that hung over the fireplace. He'd used brilliantine to smooth down his thick mop of jet black hair and as he rolled down his shirt sleeves he was well pleased with his brawny arms which from wrist to elbow were covered in tattoos. He thought and acted tough and as he shrugged his jacket on he was thinking he was well able to take care of himself. He'd only had to give Joan a couple of slaps around the head and she'd opened her purse and given him a ten bob note. Why the hell hadn't she given it to him in the first place? She knew it was pointless arguing with him. He had to have a drink; any man was entitled to that and he hadn't got a penny to his name. He was whistling away, happy as a lark as he walked down the passage and opened the front door.

The flat of Sid Brown's hand was shoved straight into Bill's chest and he had no option but to stagger backwards down the passage. To say that he was dismayed to see this great brute of a man was to put it mildly, but when he looked beyond and saw Lenny and Bernie behind their father he knew he was in deep trouble and the colour drained away from his face. Already he was conscious that if he made a wrong move or uttered a wrong word these brothers and their father would beat him so badly it was quite possible that they might even kill him.

Sid was pleased to see Bill's scared expression. Grabbing his tie and glaring into his eyes he yelled, 'You're a sodding coward, yer pick on women, yer ignore the needs of yer own mother, yer've never done an 'ard day's work in yer life but my God you've gone too far when you start puttin' yer filthy 'ands on my Rosie.' By now Sid's fury had got the better

15

of him and without giving it a second thought he drew back his arm, clenched his fist and used brute force to land a punch square on Bill's face, breaking his nose and sending blood splashing all over the place.

He stepped aside and Lenny aimed his punches well, one in Bill's kidneys and one in his belly.

Bernie went for his legs, kicking his shins with his steel-toecapped boots. As Bill Baldwin hit the floor, Sid stood over him spattered with blood that was not his own.

Joan watched the commotion from her kitchen doorway. Bernie stared at her. She was wearing a thin cotton dress and an old cardigan. She looked a mess. Her face was a mass of bruises and the side of her head was streaked with blood.

'You all right, Aunt Joan?' Bernie really liked his aunt and tonight he felt especially sorry for her.

Joan had heard her husband scream once and now it seemed as if his loud moaning was coming from far away. She had no idea why her brother-in-law and his two sons were here, giving her Bill a right good going over by the looks of things. She thought it must be about money, although she knew of old that Sid was wise enough not to listen to her Bill's hard luck stories.

Then it came to her what these three men were threatening Bill with and her heart came into her mouth. Oh, no! She didn't want to believe what she was hearing. Lovely young Rosie! Christ almighty, she's his niece! She had good cause to know that her husband was selfish to the core, no good to man nor beast. But this! Even he couldn't have sunk so low. Could he?

It was Lenny who manhandled his uncle to his feet and dragged him outside into the street. Bill was in such a state that they had to let him slide down until he was sitting on the pavement with his back propped up against the front garden wall, head hanging limply, chin resting on his blood-splattered chest.

Sid waved his two sons aside. He was going to be the one to make sure that this lousy sod understood that what he was about to say was not empty threats or intimidation but that every word was for real. 'This won't be the end of the matter, Bill, you realise that, don't you?'

Bill was frightened and he didn't try to hide it.

'I can't think what possessed you to think you'd get away with mucking about with our Rosie.' Sid was in full steam now and he bent over and hollered, 'While we're about it we may as well sort a few more things out that should 'ave been dealt with years ago. Your wife works like a slave. She's a decent woman. A bloody kind woman. Too good for the likes of you. Where would your mother be if it weren't for Joan? You've never brought a wage packet home in yer whole life. You're no better than a scavenger. Left t' you she'd bloody starve, that's for sure, or even worse you'd 'ave shoved 'er away in some lousy institution. From now on me an' my boys will stop at nothing to see that you start pulling your weight. You get yerself a job, you bring yer wages 'ome every week an' you take care of Joan and your mother.'

As Bill tried his best to raise himself on to his elbows, Lenny pushed his father out of his way. 'My dad might be finished with you but I'm not.' By now quite a few neighbours had come out into the street and Lenny's booming voice took them all by surprise. 'What goes on in your married life is your own business but from now on there are a couple of things you'd do well t' remember. One, your wife is our relation, part an' parcel of our family, and two, you so much as lay a finger on our Rosie and you're a dead man. Don't even look at her. Got it? I'm not threatening you, matey, I am pure an' simply stating a fact an' you'd better believe it.'

Bill could hardly see through the blood that covered his face but he was well aware that the words spoken by Sid and his elder son were well and truly meant. He would have dearly loved to tell this bullying brother-in-law of his where to go but he knew better than to put on an act of bravado. So when he did manage to speak, his words came out very meekly.

'I've tried t' get a job, honest I 'ave, Sid. There just ain't any work about.'

'Try harder.' Sid taunted him. ''Cos this visit ain't a one off by any means. Me an' me boys are gonna pay you a weekly visit t' make sure Joan is getting regular housekeeping money and that your dear old mum is being well looked after. Oh, and by the way, our Rosie is still coming round to your 'ouse 'cos she loves Gran Baldwin; an' her auntie, but where will you be, Bill?' he asked sarcastically. 'You'll be at work. Won't you?' The last two words were hollered into Bill's ear.

Sid and his two boys backed off, watching as Bill slowly got himself up until he was kneeling on all fours. That was when Sid's booted foot kicked his backside and he fell flat on his face this time. Bernie bent so low his face was almost touching the back of his uncle's head. 'Don't forget,' he said mockingly. 'Mend yer ways, you spineless bastard!'

Sid and Lenny turned to go, but Bernie seemed to have an afterthought. Bending his knees and leaning close to make sure that Bill could hear his words he said, 'Oh, and by the way, we'll be round next week to see if you've learnt anything tonight or if you will be needing another lesson.'

Bill Baldwin stayed put. He listened to his neighbours moving away, heard their front doors closing. The ring of heavy footsteps as Sid and his two sons walked the pavement. At that moment he was wishing he could be miles away. There had never been a time when he had needed a drink more badly than he did right now. There was a boozer on the corner of the street but it might as well have been at

18

the furthest corner of the world because he couldn't even bloody well crawl there.

Let alone walk.

Chapter Three

JOAN WAS FEELING VERY THOUGHTFUL as she walked down Mitcham Road and turned right into Welford's Dairy. Her basket already held a warm cottage loaf, and now she was going to buy a half-pound of Welford's speciality, a really strong Cheddar cheese. Then she was going to get on the tram, only today she was not going straight home but calling in to see her sister. A crusty knobby off each end of the top half of the loaf, a lump of cheese and a couple of Martha's famous pickled onions washed down with a good hot strong cup of tea plus a good old natter would set them both up for the day.

Just lately she had felt she had much to be grateful for, and one of the many blessings she counted was having a little time to herself. And the way her life had changed for the better was all down to her sister's husband and his two sons.

Things wouldn't have altered if it weren't for the fact that the three of them had kept their word. She had to smile as she thought back to the first week after they had given her husband a beating. Bill had really kidded himself that the subject was over and done with. They had made their point and to him that had been the end of the matter.

20

Not so!

Sid and his sons had turned up that weekend and the first thing they saw as they stepped into her living room was Bill stretched out on the sofa, fag hanging from the side of his mouth, reading the *Racing News*.

In two strides Sid had crossed the room and was towering over Bill. 'Got a job then, 'ave you?' he had asked, his voice quiet but menacing.

It had certainly been a shock to Bill's system just to stare up at his brother-in-law, whom he'd freely admit he was terrified of. From the position he was in Sid Brown appeared to be even bigger in stature than he was because of the largeness of his frame, his broad shoulders and his powerful arms. He might be brawny and well built but there was no excess flesh on him. He was all muscle and sinew and Bill had had first-hand experience of his unbeatable strength.

Sid grabbed him by the hair, pulling him to a sitting position. Bill let out a piercing scream which scared his mother, whose bed was in the corner on the opposite side of the room.

'It's all right, Mrs Baldwin,' Bernie softly soothed her.

And it was. Bill hadn't made another sound because Lenny had stuffed his mouth with pages from the sporting paper he had been reading. They only gave him a few slaps around his face and head before saying, 'We'll see you same time next week an' if you 'aven't got a job by then, well, we'll just say no more warnings, shall we?'

Joan grinned to herself at the memory. That had been eight weeks ago and after a third visit from Sid and his boys Bill had shifted himself and got a job. Not much of a job, it had to be said, but Bill now knew better than to refuse it. He was night watchman at Young's Brewery which was situated in Wandsworth High Street. The few shillings he now gave her regularly every Friday had made a huge difference, especially where his mother was concerned. Poor

Granny Baldwin – she couldn't last out much longer. Worn out as she was by the struggle to survive, riddled with consumption, undernourished and constantly racked by a terrible chesty cough, she was beginning to fade. At least now Joan was able to buy new-laid eggs and fresh fruit with which to tempt the old lady. Strange, wasn't it, was Joan's daily thought, that she herself, related only by marriage, had come to love Gwen Baldwin so much, whilst her only son didn't give a hoot as to whether she lived or died.

Having finished her shopping, Joan boarded the tram at Tooting Broadway and sat smiling to herself as she thought of the welcome she would get from her sister.

'Cooee,' she called loudly as she opened the door, using the key that hung on the length of string behind the letter box. It was the first week in October and already there was a nip in the air, but the sight that met her as she opened the door to the living room was heartening. A fire was burning brightly and there was a smell of baking coming from the oven which was part and parcel of the kitchen range. 'Anyone in?' she called again, as she took off her coat and scarf and hung them on the hook on the back of the door.

There was a thump, thump of footsteps coming down the stairs and within seconds a beaming red face appeared round the door. 'I 'eard yer the first time,' Martha said. 'I was expecting you, anyway – that's why I've got an enormous bread pudding in the oven.'

Joan giggled at the sight of her sister but nevertheless she threw her arms round her bulky frame and hugged her close. Martha, in her late thirties, was two years younger than her sister Joan but the way she dressed and neglected her overweight body made her look much older. Joan was still giggling as she released her hold and stood back. 'Don't you ever wear anything different?' she asked, her voice full of laughter.

22

'Give a body a chance,' Martha snapped. 'I've been turning the boys' rooms out an' believe you me there ain't much room to turn round in there.'

Joan shook her head, doing her best to control her merriment. Martha was wearing a long grey dress over which she had tied a floral wrapround pinafore. Her hair was covered by a pink scarf tied to look like a turban and peeping out here and there was a mass of metal dinkie hair rollers.

'Ain't yer put the kettle on yet?' she demanded as she dumped an armful of dirty bedlinen down on to the floor. 'Don't yer want a cuppa? Christ knows, I could do with one.'

'Give us a chance. I've only just got 'ere. But I have bought a few bits in for our midday snack.'

'Good on yer, luv, that's what I like to 'ear. Got t' keep our strength up.'

It wasn't long before Joan had set two ploughmans down on the table and fetched two great breakfast cups filled with scalding tea from the scullery. 'Come on, Martha,' she yelled. 'Come and take the weight off yer feet and feed yer face.'

Her sister was out in the outhouse where a stone copper had been fitted. This makeshift building was next to the lavatory shed. Only cold water was connected and a fire had to be lit in the metal container which was fixed to the bottom of the copper in order to heat the water before the washing could be done.

'All right, luv,' she yelled back, 'just finishing poking these sheets in an' I'll be with you.'

The two sisters got on so well together, yet in a funny sort of way they were entirely different. Everyone took Martha to be the older of the two. She was always happy and contented and with three great men and one little girl to feed and take care of she was endlessly cooking and cleaning, so perhaps it wasn't unreasonable that she had let herself go a bit.

Joan had the harder life. Even now, with Bill working, who was to say how long it would last? Yet she appeared neat and tidy at all times. Most of her clothes she made herself. More often than not a dress or even a coat bought off a top barrow or at a jumble sale would be patiently taken to pieces and remodelled. Her most precious possession was her Singer treadle sewing machine. There had been times when Bill had sold almost everything of any value that they possessed, but even he knew it was more than his life was worth to touch her machine. Every piece of secondhand calico or linen that she came across Joan would haggle a price for in order to be able to run up spare nightdresses for Granny Baldwin and draw-sheets for her bed. If on the odd occasion her sister queried her devotion to her mother-in-law, Joan's reply would always be the same. 'I'll be old some day and perhaps need help myself.'

'Not from strangers if I'm still around,' Martha would reassure her aggressively.

When their plates were empty and their cups drained Martha could not hold back her curiosity any longer.

'So how's your Bill been getting on at Young's? Can't be that the work is too 'ard 'cos he's been there now, what, over two months, ain't it?'

Joan grinned. 'I wouldn't have laid bets on him staying there two weeks, not at first, that's for sure.' She shrugged her shoulders. 'Now, well, I wouldn't say he is over the moon but he's changed some, I have t' give him that much. He doesn't tell me a lot but then he never was much good at holding a conversation.'

'Except about racing.' Martha laughed loudly. 'The times he's told me he's been on to a dead certainty and the next day he'd be scratching around for someone t' lend him a couple of bob.'

'Tell me about it,' Joan muttered. 'He wore that one out with me years ago and yet still he'll try it on if he thinks he'll get away with it. Everyone seems t' know that there was a bit of trouble the first week my Bill started at Young's, but no one's ever told me the extent of it. I do get the feeling he doesn't like Mr Grant, who's the general manager, but on the other hand I'm pretty sure that Bill will do his best never to get on the wrong side of him.'

Martha giggled. 'My Lenny told me about Mr Grant. Said he's not over tall but by God he's got a head like a bull on his very thick neck and real broad shoulders. The saying goes he could fell an ox with his bare hands.'

'Well, I know for a fact that when Mr Grant is not around Bill doesn't think he has t' graft so hard, which sits well with him, but before he gets his head down for a snooze about midnight he tells me he has to groom the big dray cart horses, and yer know what? He went on an' on about how much he liked doing that job.'

'Must be a smattering of good in him somewhere,' Martha sneered, 'though I bet a blind man would be glad t' see it.'

The two sisters looked sadly at each other. Joan was the first to compose herself and with a note of sensitivity in her voice said, 'Well, if there is I've never seen sight nor sound of it, at least not since we've been married I haven't. I wouldn't mind so much for myself if only he would spare a thought now and again for his mother. It's such a shame. Honestly, Martha, you wouldn't believe some of the horrible things he says to her. Especially if she has an accident and messes her bed. There are times when I could cheerfully murder him. He leaves her in no doubt that she's nothing but a burden to him and anyway that's not true 'cos he does sod all for her. God forgive my language. I know it's not the best situation, her having to be in bed most of the time and the fact that her bed is in our living room, but there'll come a day when . . . oh, I don't know. I daren't leave her on her own with him, though.'

Joan was close to tears at that moment. She shook her

25

head fiercely, her temper rising, and her face was twisted with a mixture of loathing and deadly intent. Suddenly Martha felt afraid. More so when Joan said, 'He hasn't got a spark of humanity in him! His own mother!' Her limbs were shaking, and her face now showed confusion but also disgust.

'He really is a nasty bugger,' Martha agreed passionately, at the same time wondering to what lengths he would eventually drive her sister. The very thought that Bill Baldwin might hurt his mother and that Joan might retaliate and do something she would bitterly regret brought a sharp stab of pain to her heart. It took a moment or two for her to compose herself. Then she took a deep breath, moved to take hold of her sister's hand and say, 'It's all right, luv. God 'as a way of paying His debts without any money.' Then as an afterthought she added, 'Why don't Sid an' me come round one night and sit with Mrs Baldwin? You could take yerself off to the pictures or t' the Hippodrome. A night out might do yer all the good in the world.' Beneath her breath she muttered, 'Christ knows yer deserve a break.'

'No, thanks all the same, Martha. I appreciate yer offer, but I don't have the money to spare for one thing and another reason is Granny would get in a state if I weren't there t' take her to the lav. Mrs Bradshaw is with her now – brings her ironing over to do at my place and talks away to Gran and Gran don't mind her so much 'cos she's used to seeing her. There's nothing t' stop you and Sid coming round, though. We could have a game of cards.'

Martha gave her sister a thoughtful look. 'How about when our Rosie used to sit with her?'

'She's got a lot worse since then and I've given up that lampshade job since Bill started handing over a regular wage to me.' She grinned. 'Only 'cos he knows I'll tell your Sid if he don't.'

It was galling for Martha to see what was happening to

her sister. Poor Joan! What made it worse was the fact that Joan had seen both sides of the coin. Having been in service she knew there were other ways of living where one had lovely clothes to wear and really good food on the table at each and every mealtime. Now she was nothing more than a drudge. She led such a monotonous life, scrimping and scratching around to make every penny go a long way, and for what? Certainly no thanks or even a kind word from that rotter of a husband of hers. It wasn't as if she had any company, any children to lighten up the place, just day in day out she seemed to be at the beck and call of Mrs Baldwin with no help whatsoever from Bill.

'God knows how long it will last.' Joan muttered her thoughts aloud. 'Never in my wildest dreams did I think my Bill would have held down a job this long, and it's only down to your Sid that he has, but . . .'

'But what?' Martha cried quickly.

Joan sighed heavily, wishing she hadn't mentioned her doubts, but it was too late. Martha had cottoned on to the fact that not everything had changed for the better in her sister's life and she wouldn't rest until she got to the bottom of the matter. So Joan took a deep breath and blurted it all out.

'Bill's still drinking more than he should and he's gambling. Got in way over his head this time if what I've been told is true.'

'Oh yeah, an' who was the kind person who gave you that information?' Martha's voice was full of sarcasm.

'Well, if you must know it was Mabel Richards, and I believe her, Martha. Not that I want to, but I think she has got her facts straight and she sounded very convincing to me.'

Martha leant forward and looked quizzically at her. 'Mabel Richards? Ain't 'eard tell of 'er for some time, let alone seen 'er. She moved down to Tooting last I 'eard an' at the time there was more than a few of us remarked we'd 'ave t' buy the bloody local paper now she wasn't around to pass all the gossip on. Try telling me what she's told yer and see what my feelings are. Not that either of us should really be surprised. Like you say, if my Sid and my boys didn't keep a check on your Bill there's no way he would still be working at that brewery.'

Martha was like a dog with a bone. She wouldn't let it go until she'd got some answers. Sighing again, Joan sat on the edge of her chair and began.

'You know where the back end of Tooting Market comes out in Totterdown Street?'

Martha nodded her head, showing she was all ears.

'It appears Mabel's got herself a job there, on the very last stall, which faces the roadway. Greengrocery and fruit is mainly what they sell. Anyway, she gets to see everyone who comes and goes or is just passing, an' you know what? They've opened a club upstairs over the top of the market.'

'Oh, fer Christ's sake get t' the point, Joan,' Martha moaned. 'The way you're going on we'll both be 'ere t' the middle of next week.'

'It's not only a drinking club, it's a gambling club as well.'

The bitterness in her sister's voice was like a red rag to a bull where Martha was concerned. 'You don't 'ave t' say any more. I can guess. That's where your Bill 'as been spending his afternoons, isn't it?'

'Got it in one,' Joan muttered.

'You said he's over his 'ead in debt. Did he tell you that himself?'

'As if he would! Mabel Richards said she heard the Riley brothers talking an' everyone knows you don't mess with that lot.'

''Ave yer asked Bill about it?'

'Not likely. I do my best never t' wind him up. I just listen, if ever he talks to me, which is not very often. But

28

how he's going t' get out of this mess God only knows.' Joan's voice was low with fright.

Martha shook her head impatiently. 'That's his worry not yours. Your 'usband is a stupid ignorant fool an' he'll never change. Leave him t' get on with whatever mess he's in. After all, it's of his own making.'

'I know, but for all he's no good I don't want to see him really hurt. Those Riley brothers won't stop at a warning if he owes them a packet.'

Martha got to her feet and hugged her. 'Come on, cheer up. I'll put the kettle on an' we'll 'ave another cup of tea and a lump of hot bread pudding, 'ow does that sound?'

'Well, if it tastes as good as it smells I'm all for it.'

Martha was halfway to the scullery when she stopped and turned to face her sister. Her shoulders were heaving and her face was creased up with laughter.

'What the hell has tickled you?' Joan asked, sounding bewildered.

It was a job for Martha to get the words out but eventually she said, 'Don't know what we're doing worrying ourselves over your Bill. The devil takes care of his own, an' come t' think of it, if Bill Baldwin fell down a sewage drain he'd come up smelling of roses.' Martha let out a hearty chuckle and Joan couldn't help herself. She joined her.

Chapter Four

MARTHA STOOD AT THE FRONT DOOR and could not believe what she was hearing. Joan was screaming and shouting as if all hell had been let loose. Joan, the quiet one, the one who looked after her mother-in-law day and night and was never heard to grumble, the one who did all the cleaning and cooking and loads of washing and would bend over backwards to keep the peace.

Martha put her hand over her face to smother her smiles. If she was shocked she'd have loved to see her brother-in-law's face. Wondered how he was feeling knowing the worm had turned at last. She waited a few seconds before coughing loudly as she went down the passage and walking into the kitchen with a big smile on her face.

''Allo, everyone. Everything all right?'

Joan was white-faced with anger as she pointed her finger at her husband. 'He hit his mother! Can you believe it, Martha? He actually struck his mother, an' when I tried to reason with him he slapped me one and then kicked me.'

'You asked for it, you lying cow. You said you've got no money and I know for a fact you're lying through yer teeth.' Bill was red-faced and roaring with temper as he clenched his fist and stepped towards Joan.

Martha got between them. She was worried now. Her sister was not normally an aggressive person and in many ways that was more than half the trouble. She had let Bill get away with far too much. Allowed him to see that she was frightened of him. Whatever had set her off today it must have been serious and Martha would bet her last penny her sister was in the right.

Joan pushed herself past the pair of them and leant over the single bed where Granny Baldwin was lying. The poor old soul's face was so white she looked deathly. Her eyes were closed and there was a trickle of dark blood running down the side of her face.

'Oh, you didn't deserve that, you poor darling.' Joan was dabbing at the blood with a piece of white rag and she was nearly crying with frustration and anger.

'Oh, going to put on a show for yer sister now, are we?' Bill shouted. 'Playing for her sympathy? Well I'll tell yer this much, I've 'ad it up to my back teeth with the bloody pair of yer. You're a mean pair of bitches, you and me mother; all you do is make my life a misery. And you coming 'ere don't 'elp, Martha. If it weren't for your heavy-handed mob my life would be a damn sight more simple. Always were a nosy lot, you Browns.'

With an effort, Martha held her tongue between her teeth as she watched Bill shrug himself into his coat and storm out of the room. She didn't really need to ask what had started this shemozzle: the smell coming from the old lady's bed said it all.

'Take a few deep breaths, Joan, an' calm down,' Martha pleaded. 'I'll put the kettle on, get a nice bowl of hot water while you take Gran's nightie off, and between us we'll give her a good wash and a nice clean bed.'

'Ah, thanks, Martha, but you don't have to do it. I can manage,' said Joan, her voice still trembling.

'I know I don't *have* to, but I'm going to. I'm just glad I came round this morning. The way you were going on you might have done your old man a real mischief.'

'You're dead right, sis. I don't think I've ever felt so mad in my life before. Fancy, a son hitting his own mother! Bad enough if she were up and about on her own two legs, but lying there utterly defenceless— Only a spineless git like Bill would do such a thing.'

'Wanting money, was he?'

'Isn't he always?'

Martha nodded and they both sighed.

'Well, let's get cracking.' Joan took hold of her mother-in-law's hand. It felt very cold and lifeless. 'Mam, my sister Martha is here and between us we are going to clean you up and make you nice and warm and comfortable.'

Gwen Baldwin opened her eyes slowly, as if to lift her lids was too much effort. 'Thanks, Joan, luv,' she said weakly. She attempted to touch her daughter-in-law's face, but she was too exhausted and her hand dropped limply back down on to the bed.

The two sisters worked well together. They tenderly washed her from head to toe, powdered her bottom and slipped a clean nightdress over her head. Each guided a thin bony arm into a sleeve. Lastly, they gently sponged her thin white hair and softly ran a comb through it. At last, when a piece of white lint and a plaster covered the gash on her forehead and she was propped up by three pillows covered with snow-white cases, Joan whispered, 'Here's the final touch, Mum.' Showing her a bottle of Yardley's lavender water, she dabbed a spot of the scent behind each of Gwen's ears.

'Ah.' The old lady sighed deeply as her head rested back. 'That feels so lovely. Yer a good girl, Joan.' She paused, as if talking was too much of an exertion, but after a minute or two had passed she roused herself. 'Joan, when I go don't stay with my son. You deserve a much better life.'

32

Joan felt quite stunned, and she had to control her feelings before she was able to say, 'You're not going anywhere yet, and neither am I. I'm staying here and I shall look after you.' Tears rolled silently down her cheeks as she leaned forward and kissed her mother-in-law's forehead. 'Go to sleep now. I'll have a nice bowl of soup ready for when you wake up.'

Gwen Baldwin did wake up and she did manage to eat some of the soup which Joan had made. She also lived another three days.

It was the very early hours of the morning. It had not been a peaceful night. Joan had called the doctor the previous evening. He had been very sympathetic but as Joan had gone to the front door with him he had shaken his head and held her hand for longer than was necessary before saying, 'I know it is sad, but the poor woman has no fight left in her. She is very much weaker than when I last saw her.'

Joan had sat the rest of the night beside her bed and in the very early hours of the morning, when she saw Gwen stir, she asked if she fancied a cup of tea. Gwen struggled to sit up. 'No thank you, Joan dear, you've done enough for me. Nobody could have done more,' she said.

Her voice was so clear and so strong that Joan was startled. She caught her in her arms as she fell back. Gwen's eyes were wide open as she looked at her daughter-in-law. A loving smile briefly came to her lips and her bony hand came up and stroked Joan's cheek. She half smiled; sighed heavily.

And then she was still.

By the time Bill Baldwin returned from his shift at the brewery, he found his wife and sister-in-law just putting the finishing touches to laying his mother out.

'Yer mum died peacefully,' Martha told him.

He drew in his breath sharply and stared at her, then looked across the room to where his wife was kneeling beside his mother's bed. Joan raised her head and said quietly, 'I am so sorry you weren't here, Bill.' The look she gave him was full of sadness and her shoulders drooped.

'Oh my God!' he exclaimed as he took off his coat and threw it on to a chair. 'We ain't got t' live fer days now with nothing but gloom an' doom, 'ave we?' When neither his wife nor her sister answered he said, 'Why don't yer stop being a pair of hypocrites? She's a darn sight better off dead than lying there all day, ain't she? At least with 'er out of the way we might manage t' have a decent Christmas. By the way, 'ave yer looked for 'er insurance policy? I know she 'ad one an' all I hope is that it will pay out enough t' bury her.'

Joan was up and on her feet. Sadness, for the moment, had been swept away and she was seething with anger. Martha got in first. Shaking her head in disbelief she said, 'You're something else, you are, Bill. Your own mother is lying there an' you can't be bothered to cross the room and even look at her.'

'Leave him be, Martha. He's a cold-blooded sod. Never has had a decent bone in his body but I never realised until now just how callous he can be.'

'I don't 'ave t' take all this hassle from you two,' he bellowed, as his attitude changed and became threatening.

It was at that moment that a discreet cough was heard and a cautious voice called out, 'The door was open. Is it all right to come in?'

Joan had asked a neighbour to go for the local undertaker and he could not have arrived at a more opportune moment. He and his men went about the grave task of preparing to take the body of Gwen Baldwin to their chapel of rest, and her son sussed out that it was a good moment for him to scarper. Joan and Martha were left to surmise what evil they might have done to Bill if there had been no intervention.

'Perhaps it is just as well that Bill took himself off,' Joan said tersely when she and her sister were finally alone. They had both collapsed on to what had been Gwen's bed, each quietly crying, whether from sadness or temper they couldn't have said at that moment.

'Yer can't believe that 'ard-hearted bastard, can yer?' Martha muttered.

Joan sighed deeply. 'I really could have killed him today. I didn't realise how much I've come to hate him. When Gran's funeral is over I am going to get away from this place and from him. There must be more to life than this.'

Martha couldn't answer her. There was nothing to add. Joan had spoken the truth.

Chapter Five

MARTHA LOOKED AROUND her sister's neat living room and said admiringly, 'My, you must 'ave worked yer socks off. Made quite a difference, ain't yer?'

'Well, without Gran's bed it's given us a lot more room.' Joan sounded funny and Martha moved nearer and looked at her hard. She gasped, then stood white-faced and silent. It was only a few moments before she felt her temper rise and her face burn with rage.

'How the hell? When? Why?' Her questions poured out.

'Please, Martha, leave it. Go and put the kettle on and we'll have a cup of tea.'

'Plenty of time for tea later.' Martha's voice was trembling with anger. 'Sit down and tell me what 'appened 'cos I ain't moving from this spot till I get some answers.'

Joan stood still like a statue against the wall. Her eyebrow had been split open, and there was dark bruising and a huge discoloured patch that ran from below her ear to her jawline. Martha couldn't find words to say. That bugger must have given her a couple of really hard punches.

The next thing Joan was aware of was her sister pulling her across the room and pressing her down into an armchair.

'I'm going t' make that tea. I brought some doughnuts with me and when we've had that I'm off t' the chemist to see what he thinks we should put on your face.' Martha knew she was prattling, but the sight of her sister just sitting there utterly listless was heartbreaking. She walked through to the scullery and went through the motions of filling the kettle, lighting the gas and making a pot of tea.

Her mind was in a turmoil. If her bloody brother-in-law were here now she'd throw the whole kettle of boiling water over him and stand and watch as it scalded him. Only a bully would attack a defenceless woman. But why in the name of God did Joan never retaliate? *If he went for someone the likes of me it would be a different story. Christ knows he'd only ever do it the once. He'd never get a second chance.* Why was there so much difference between herself and Joan? Was it because Joan had been in service, learnt to live with the nobs? Surely not. Maybe the men in those big houses were gentlemen but they were still human beings so doubtless they lost their tempers sometimes. Did ladylike women learn to take it in silence? *God knows!* She answered her own question. Whatever, the kind of life Joan was leading couldn't be allowed to go on.

As Martha carried the tea tray through, her thoughts were muddled and fearful. Someday something terrible would happen. It was quite possible that blighter might end up killing Joan. It crossed her mind that if that happened there would be total disaster. The whole family would get involved. It would be the end of Bill Baldwin, that's for sure.

Joan only nibbled at her doughnut but she gratefully drank her cup of tea. Martha hesitated to ask questions but the need to know was great. Joan looked a shadow of her normal self and as she placed her cup down on the saucer Martha could see that her hands were shaking.

'What started him off this time, Joan?'

Joan sighed. 'What does it ever take?'

Martha drained her cup and kept silent, knowing Joan would tell her in her own good time.

A loud knocking on the door made both of them jump with fright. The look that passed between them was dreadful and the expression on Joan's face told Martha that she was terrified.

'Who do you think it is?'

'How do I know, Martha? It could be anyone. But one thing's for sure – they'll be after Bill for money, 'cos he owes left right and centre.'

The loud knocking was repeated.

'Come on, I'll come to the door with you.'

Opening the front door, Joan breathed a sigh of relief on seeing not more heavy-set thugs after her husband, but the owner of the funeral parlour. He had removed his tall hat and was twirling it nervously between his hands. However, his voice was firm as he said, 'Good morning, Mrs Baldwin. I should like a word with your husband if it is convenient, please.'

His tone of voice might have sounded firm but somehow he looked nervous as he stared at the two women standing side by side.

'I'm afraid he's not in,' Joan answered. It was just as she had thought. He might not be one of the great brutes who were after Bill for gambling debts and what have you, but he was still someone to whom Bill owed money. It wasn't fair. While she had been sitting at home worrying herself sick, he had been spending his mother's insurance money. Nevertheless, her conscience was bothering her. After all, this gentleman and the men who had acted as pall-bearers had given her mother-in-law a very respectable send-off, and he was entitled to have his fee paid. 'Has he not been in to your office to see you?' she asked timidly.

The poor man suddenly looked extremely embarrassed. Perhaps it was the sight of Joan's swollen, bruised face. He shook his head. 'No, I'm afraid he hasn't.'

She sighed then, a long weary sigh. 'I am sorry. I will talk to my husband as soon as he comes home and I will do my best to settle our account with you before the week is out.'

'I would be more than obliged, Mrs Baldwin.'

The two sisters watched as the somberly dressed gentleman walked away from the house. Back in the kitchen, Martha shook her head impatiently. 'Are you going to tell me what's going on?'

'I just don't understand how my Bill could act the way he is.'

The bitterness in her older sister's voice made Martha want to shake her, and she turned on her.

'You're covering up for Bill each and every way and what thanks 'ave yer got? All I can see is that he's given you a bloody good hiding and still you sit there and take it. The sad thing is, he's not worth it. All he's ever done is bully you an' cause yer heartache.'

'I know, I know,' Joan murmured, and Martha was amazed to see her eyes brim with tears. This was all she needed. She so much wanted to help her sister and yet at this moment she felt utterly useless.

'I suppose you're still waiting on him 'and foot an' finger even though you're still his favourite punch bag.'

Even Joan had to smile at that. 'Since his mum died he's been ten times worse. Hasn't been near nor by me for the last two days and whenever I have set eyes on him he's always been the worse for drink. I'm terrified by the blokes that have been here looking for him. You wouldn't believe what rough types they are.'

'I wouldn't worry about him, Joan,' Martha said. 'Whatever they are after him for he's brought it all on himself, and he'll 'ave t' learn that there's a price t' be paid for everything.' She leaned across the table and squeezed her sister's arm in a reassuring way.

Joan shook her head. 'He's so downright deceitful. Never

39

wants to discuss anything with me. You want to know something, Martha? He's never let on to me how much the Prudential paid out on his mum's insurance. It couldn't have been bad – I came in when he had the cheque in his hand and his face was wreathed in smiles. Shoved it in his pocket quick enough and was out of that front door like greased lightning.'

Martha sighed. She'd only popped in for a cuppa, and the conversation was beginning to irritate her. She threw her sister a furious glance, and said harshly, 'Leave it out, Joan. You never expected anything different, did yer? You've wasted enough of yer life worrying over that rotter. You did all yer could and more in looking after his mother, but now's the time to start thinking about yerself and what *you* are going to do.'

'Easier said than done,' Joan snapped.

Martha looked at her and sniffed. 'I expect it will be 'ard, but yer won't know till yer try, will yer?'

Joan looked startled, for it was unlike Martha to be so unkind, but before she could answer the kitchen door was thrown open with such a crash that it bashed against the dresser and caused the china it held to rattle.

'Tongues still wagging?' asked Bill, glaring at both women with open hostility. 'Pity yer ain't got nothing better t' do.'

Joan shivered involuntarily. She could smell the drink on her husband's breath from across the room. 'I'll get you something t' eat,' she said nervously.

'You'll do a bit more than that,' he shouted. 'I've got a job t' go to, so move, yer lazy cow, and get me a clean shirt. And I'd like some boiling water 'cos I'm going t' have a strip wash and a shave.' He turned and outstared Martha. 'And unless you want t' stay and watch the show yer can sling yer hook right now. Yer spend more time in my 'ouse than yer do in yer own.'

He was shouting and crashing about with such violence

that Martha was afraid to leave her sister alone with him. 'You're a selfish pig, you know that, Bill Baldwin? You think of nobody but yer bloody self. *And* you're a bully. Take a good look at my sister's face. Proud of yerself, are yer?'

Bill snarled. 'Go 'ome, Martha, before I do something you'll be sorry for. I ain't in the mood for your preaching today.' He shoved her hard in the chest and she almost lost her balance. She clenched her fists and was about to retaliate when she saw her sister was quietly crying.

'All right.' Her voice was harsh with hatred. 'I'm going, but just you remember all of this is only lent. I'll 'ave my day with you, you see if I don't.'

'Shut yer mouth. An' if you ain't gone in two minutes, I'll bash the pair of yer.'

Knowing he meant what he said, Martha rose quickly to her feet. She'd have her day with this bully, she vowed, but now was not the time. Joan fetched her coat and held it for her and together they walked down the passage to the front door.

'You going t' be all right, love?'

Joan half smiled and nodded her head. When Martha rumpled her hair and kissed her in her motherly fashion, Joan's thin arms went round Martha's neck and she nuzzled against her affectionately. 'Stop worrying about me.' She kissed her plump cheek. 'Thanks for always being there for me. I love you, Martha. Ever so much,' she whispered.

'I luv yer, too, Joan,' Martha answered, hugging her tightly. 'Think on what I said. I'll be back later when I've been to the chemist an' he's out of the way. Meanwhile you take care.'

'I will, I promise,' Joan said, watching until her sister stopped at the corner of the road and waved before she slowly closed the front door.

Joan cursed under her breath as she worked. She had laid

41

out clean underwear and a neatly ironed shirt on the double bed she shared with a man she had grown to dislike. From the top drawer of the chest of drawers she took out a pair of navy blue socks and a white handkerchief. Let him choose his own tie; whichever one she picked was bound to be wrong. Getting down on to her knees she pulled open the bottom drawer, which was twice the depth of the other five, and the minute her eyes rested on the two neat piles of jumpers and cardigans that lay side by side she felt tears prick at the back of her eyelids. Every article had been hand-knitted by Gwen Baldwin. Such intricate patterns! At the time of their making, when Gwen had been a lot younger and fitter, every stitch had probably been knitted with love. And how had that only son of hers repaid her? Certainly not with any show of appreciation. Martha was right. He hadn't got an ounce of love in him, except for himself.

She selected one of the heavier jumpers, for it was bitterly cold outside. During the previous night there had been a slight fall of snow followed by a really heavy frost. The pavements were slippery and the roads treacherous. Bill would have the luxury of a brazier with no lack of either coal or wood to burn but his duties did not permit him to sit by it all night. Whether or not he did was another matter. At least, since he'd bothered to come home today, she would send him off well wrapped up, with a good pile of sandwiches in his tin and a flask of hot tea which should see him through the night.

His overcoat was quite scruffy – even the edges of the sleeves were ragged – but apart from that he looked quite presentable as he settled his cap on his head, tucked his scarf round his neck, picked up the evening paper and the carrier bag which held what Joan had prepared for him and walked out of the door without so much as a goodbye, let alone a thank you. When he had gone, Joan stood stock still staring into space. She was a fool for putting up with the way he treated her. She needed no one to tell her that.

The sound of a faint, hollow voice came back to her, and she heard again the words her mother-in-law had said to her only a few days before she died. She remembered them so clearly.

'Don't stay with my son, Joan. You deserve better.'

Granny Baldwin had known a lot more about what went on than Bill gave her credit for, Joan thought. *She knew how unhappy I was.*

She gripped the edge of the table and closed her eyes. She shouldn't have to take this. She didn't feel that she could. There and then, she made a vow to herself that never again would she allow a man to use her, least of all a rotter like the man she had married.

Such high hopes she had had on her wedding day. If anyone had told her then that he would use his fists on her whenever he felt like it, keep her short of money and deny her children, she would never have believed them. But although she had never admitted it aloud before now, those three miscarriages hadn't come about naturally. He had had no respect for her at any time, and the months she had been pregnant had made no difference. If anything, he had treated her worse. She was the one who was out at five in the morning in all weathers, scubbing and polishing offices up in the West End, and ten to one Bill would still be lying in their warm bed when she came home at midday, expecting her to cook him a meal. And like a fool she always had.

Well, not any more. It was a dreadful thing to admit, but it was the truth: she had not only stopped loving her husband, she had come to loathe him.

She was going to have to leave him. Good. She was at least halfway towards making a decision. Then doubt crept in and she fell to wondering how she would manage on her own. What would she do? Where would she go? She didn't know, but at this moment she didn't care. She only knew beyond a shadow of doubt that very soon she was going to have to leave. If she stayed her life would not be worth living.

Later that night Bill Baldwin strolled across the cobbled brewery yard, a contented expression on his face. His luck had certainly changed for the better since the death of his mother. At least one good thing she had done for him: named him beneficiary of the few pounds there was to come from her long-term insurance policy. Two days running he'd had a good little earner. He'd won on the dogs at Wimbledon, and on the second day he had taken a chance on the gee-gees and placed a triple bet. It was a long shot, but it had paid off handsomely. He laughed to himself. Good job he'd used a betting shop in Wandsworth. If he'd placed the bet in the club at Tooting they'd never have paid out. They'd have hung on to his winnings against what he owed.

He hadn't given so much as half a thought to paying the undertakers for his mother's funeral, but there again he hadn't arranged for them to bury her. Joan had taken it upon herself to see to everything. Let her pay them. Even the collection the neighbours had contributed to, Joan had hung on to. She'd used part of that money to put flowers on the altar in the church so his mum's coffin could be near them. Did you ever hear of anything so bloody daft in all yer life? When you're dead you're dead. You can't see and you certainly can't smell. So why waste the money? According to him, he'd done what most men would have done. Had a drop of good whisky, toasted the old gal and hoped she'd gone to that wonderful heaven she was always talking about.

His thoughts stopped wandering when he reached the horses tethered in their stalls. He petted his favourite, big old Dobby, then continued along the line, stroking, petting and holding a knob of sugar in the flat palm of his hand for each of them. He enjoyed watching their big wet mouths and the saliva which dribbled from their long tongues because of their eager anticipation. These carthorses had become his best friends. He felt different when he was with these huge creatures and he felt it to be a privilege to have been put in charge of them. He took his time in grooming them, almost two hours. Not that he didn't stop every so often to make a roll-up and have a smoke, and of course every now and again he needed a swig from the half-bottle of Johnnie Walker which he had in his pocket.

In spite of the cold outside he was sweating and felt he needed a breath of fresh air. Walking to the end of the stables, he used all his strength to open the heavy wooden door a few inches. It was pitch dark and bitterly cold, and the strong wind was biting. He put one foot outside and heard the crackle as his heavy boot hit the ice on the frozen cobbles.

'Blow that for a lark,' he muttered, heaving hard with his shoulder in order to get the door closed again. 'I'm better off staying in here.'

He knew full well he should check on the warehouse, but more than likely his brazier would have burnt out, and in any case he didn't care. He'd had the presence of mind to bring his carrier bag over to the stables with him. He'd snuggle down between two bales of hay, eat the grub Joan had put up for him, have a cup of tea with maybe a drop of the hard stuff in it and read his paper, and he would be set for the night.

The whisky bottle lay empty at his side and Bill Baldwin was too far gone to notice the little whirls of smoke that were gathering speed as he slept. It was only when the horses began to whinny and stamp their great hoofs that he came to and smelt it. He sniffed hard, struggled to his feet and to his horror saw smoke wafting up towards the rafters. He caught his breath, suddenly aware of the heat. The dry straw on each side of him was smouldering and he crawled away to get clear.

It was pure instinct that made him run towards the main door. Fear was making him tremble as he began tugging at the latch. This way, that way. No matter which way he tried to wrench it, it would not budge. He swung round to go back and was met by the tremendous heat. Turning again, he continued his fumbling efforts to open the door and finally managed it.

Should he run? Whatever, he couldn't save all of the horses, but he'd have to try and big Dobby had to be first. At the far end of the stables bales of hay and bags of winter feed were stacked one on top of the other on wooden platforms. By now they were blazing furiously, one by one catching light in rapid succession.

Thank God Dobby was the nearest to the door. It seemed to Bill to take for ever to open his stall door, untie the rope which was restraining him and lead him towards the exit.

'Go, go, run,' he screamed, slapping Dobby hard on the rump. For a moment he stayed in the yard, yelling, 'Fire! Fire! Help, someone!'

For a split second he had the urge to run himself. His good sense said he must try to get the other horses out, but instinct was urging him to save himself. For a moment he hesitated, staring into the stables. He was scared stiff but for once he told himself he had no choice.

The next horse whinnied loudly and pranced like a mad thing, and Bill suffered a painful kick in the shin from the horse's hoof as he tried to free him. Bill wanted to drop where he stood. The heavy smoke was choking him, and his vision was blurred because his eyes were watering. With the rope freed he slapped the second horse's rump really hard and breathed a sigh of relief as it galloped towards the fresh air.

46

So far it was only the end of the building where Bill had been sleeping that was going up in flames, but sparks and embers were flying all over the place and the billowing smoke was getting more dense by the minute. He had to try to get at least one more horse out. He knew it would be the last no matter how hard he tried. He'd got the main door wide open but that had only made matters worse for the terrific wind coming in now was fanning the flames. Suddenly the heat was unbearable and the smoke overpowering. He could hear voices yelling, the clanging of the bells on the fire engines. Thank God! He spluttered. He was coughing harshly and could barely see through the thick smoke. But he made himself go forward. He flinched as the heat of the bolt on the third stall seared his hand but he held on, and managed to slide it open. The animal was terrified, wouldn't come forward, was not whinnying but whimpering plaintively. Bill got behind it and beat on its flank. He sighed thankfully when at last the horse ran like a bat out of hell through the smoke and out through the open door. He staggered after it. He could do no more.

At that moment one of the high platforms sagged, disintegrated and collapsed. Bill looked up in horror. Bales of burning hay were falling haphazardly. He saw one coming, bent over double and covered his face with his hands. One of the flaming bales landed on top of Bill's back, knocking him to the ground. The fire immediately ignited his clothes and his flesh began to burn. Heaving, twisting and kicking, he struggled hard to throw off the flaming bale. Pain tore through him. Choking on the smoke he had inhaled, he wanted to scream but no sound came. All he felt was excruciating pain, and then, mercifully, he lost consciousness.

Joan sat with Martha and Sid and their two sons, Lenny and Bernie. She could not have faced the inquest on her

47

own. A neighbour had kindly suggested that young Rosie remain at home with her and her children.

The coroner was a well-dressed, handsome, smooth-talking man who, on the surface, seemed cordial enough. Yet for reasons she could not fathom Joan had disliked him from the moment he opened the proceedings. Mr Grant, General Manager of Young's Brewery, was the only person to be questioned.

The coroner started by reading from the typed report he had been handed by the chief fire brigade officer, who had gathered evidence from the team of fire-fighters who had attended the blaze at the brewery.

'I'm given to understand that the bales of hay were already smouldering when Mr Baldwin opened the main door of the stables, and that the draught from the door obviously fanned the flames. May we ask your opinion as to how you think the fire was started?'

Mr Grant cleared his throat. His face was bright red and he could feel the sweat running from his armpits. His manner was very stern. 'Well, sir, I could hazard a guess.'

The coroner leant forward and stared at Mr Grant. 'Speak up, then. You've obviously given this matter some thought.'

Mr Grant scowled. 'Mr Baldwin, the man I took on as night watchman, had himself too much to drink, lit a cigarette, fell asleep and did not notice that the cigarette had fallen from his lips whilst still alight. The bales of hay were very dry; it would only have taken a spark to set . . .' He couldn't continue.

The coroner sighed, and took a sip from the glass of water that had been placed on the table in front of him. Then he looked Mr Grant squarely in the eye. 'Should Mr Baldwin have been in the stables in the early hours of the morning?'

Mr Grant hesitated. He knew damn well that Baldwin had caused that fire. In his mind he had been over and over the facts for hours on end. He felt he could say a great deal but he had to be cautious when voicing his opinion. He nervously cleared his throat again. 'No, sir, he should have been back at the warehouse. But, well, sir, if there was one thing that Mr Baldwin did exceptionally well it was seeing to the grooming of the horses. He took his time over them, liked being with them. Thinking back, it was a terrible night, and the stables would have been . . .' He had been about to say the warmest place to be, but decided it would not have been an appropriate turn of phrase.

The coroner looked thoughtful, reflecting on Grant's words. Then he said, 'Sadly, what you're saying is along the lines of the chief fire brigade officer's report.'

Mr Grant composed himself. Quietly, he asked if he might add something to what he had already said. The coroner drew himself up straight and looked very pompous.

'If you think it is relevant.'

Mr Grant did not shirk what he considered to be his duty to the dead man. He cleared his throat and spoke loudly. 'Mr Baldwin might have been a lot of things but it should be remembered that he stayed there in those stables and freed three horses. Because of that he lost his own life.'

Joan clutched Martha's hand. Tears were streaming down her cheeks. Very quietly, she said, 'Nice, that at the end somebody had something good to say about him, isn't it?'

Martha sighed as she nodded her head. Everything else was better left unsaid.

Chapter Six

MARCH 1927

JOAN WAS SITTING STARING into the fire, doing her best to convince herself that she was feeling better and knowing that she should be grateful to her sister and brother-in-law for having taken her into their home, and for all their kindness. But no matter how hard she tried she didn't seem able to come to terms with all that had happened during the past miserable months. She had had to give up her house because she had no means of keeping up with the rent, yet only last night Sid had told her that she would feel better given time, that she must put the past behind her because things could only get better for her. Then he had said that the only road open to her was forward.

Forward to where? It was a question she had asked herself over and over again. She hadn't a penny to her name, and nowhere to go.

It had stayed freezing all through January, and February too. Biting winds and even a week of snow. Try as she might, Joan couldn't feel optimistic about the future. She helped Martha with the housework, even did some of the cooking, but whatever she attempted held little interest. Even books could not hold her attention for long. The days dragged by and the hands on the clock seemed to move more slowly than usual. She couldn't be a burden on Martha and Sid for much longer.

'Can Auntie Joan stay here with us for ever?'

Oh, dear God. Joan wished young Rosie hadn't asked that question. Worse still, she saw a flicker of uncertainty in her sister's eyes.

'Come an' sit by me an' give yer old mum a cuddle,' Martha patted the horsehair sofa, 'and you, me and yer auntie'll 'ave a little talk.'

Rosie was as bright as a button. She might be only thirteen years old but there wasn't much going on that she missed. Joan's heart plummeted. She knew it wasn't a case of wearing out her welcome: there just wasn't room for her to stay in this house for much longer. Sid and Martha had Lenny and Bernie besides young Rosie to consider. Yes, there were three bedrooms, but one was only a boxroom, just about big enough to take a single bed, and it was normally used as Rose's bedroom. The two lads were grown men now but they still shared a room. Since Sid had been so kind-hearted and insisted that Joan stay with them until she got herself sorted, Rose had slept on a truckle bed in her parents' room and Joan had been occupying the boxroom. With no bathroom it was a scramble every morning for everyone to get washed and the men to shave, all at the stone sink in the scullery. On top of all that there wasn't enough money coming into the house to enable her sister to go on feeding her for ever. Deep down Joan knew she should have shifted herself a while ago, but her feelings were still mixed up and being with her family these last weeks had been so comforting.

Martha did her best to spell things out kindly to her daughter. 'Poor Auntie Joan wasn't feeling too well, what with one thing an' another, as you well know. Now, though, she's gonna pick herself up, get a nice job and start to live

51

her own life. She'll never be far away and you'll see ever such a lot of her still. When she gets a little flat or whatever, you'll even be able to go an' stay with her.'

'Is that true, Auntie Joan? Will I be able to stay with you? 'Cos otherwise you'll be ever so lonely.'

Joan forced herself to smile reassuringly. She didn't want to make any promises she wouldn't be able to keep. 'If it works out the way your mother says it will I'll buy a new bed just for you so you can stay whenever your dad says you may.'

Rosie broke free from her mother's arm, which was round her shoulders, and sat up straight. 'What do you mean *if* it works out? Why won't it?'

Martha gave her sister a tense look but Joan had her answer ready. 'I can't say what will happen for certain. You see, pet, it's hard for women to get work. Before I was married to your Uncle Bill I worked in a great big house where they had servants and I might have to consider doing something like that again.'

'Were you happy there?' Young Rosie's face was puckered with concern.

'Oh, Rosie, leave yer poor aunt alone,' her mother implored.

'It's all right, Martha.' Joan smiled. 'She's always been inquisitive, and that's a good thing. It broadens a child's mind.'

'I'm not a child. I'll be able to leave school next year,' Rosie protested loudly. 'But please, Auntie, tell me what you had t' do in the big house.'

'I'm going to put the kettle on an' leave you two to it,' Martha said, struggling to her feet.

Joan moved to sit in the place that Martha had quit and Rosie snuggled up to her. Rosie was the light of Joan's life. How often had she wished she had been able to have a little girl like her. Too late now. She would soon be forty-one.

52

Jesus, it didn't bear thinking about. Who in God's name was likely to offer her a job?

'Come on, Auntie, tell me some things before Mum comes back with the tea, 'cos she'll only grumble if I ask you a load of questions.'

Joan looked down at her niece. She was, as her father was fond of saying, 'as pretty as a picture', with her slender frame, golden-fair hair and skin that could be described as peaches and cream. And as for those wide blue eyes . . . There would come a time when this young lady would break a lot of young men's hearts.

'The family I worked for were very nice,' Joan began, 'but I hated every moment when I first went to work there. The place was so big and scary, and there was always so much to do.'

'Such as?' Rosie interrupted.

Joan laughed. 'Mountains of washing up for a start. Huge great saucepans to scrub and baking tins to clean and God help you if Cook found one that didn't shine.'

She paused, letting her mind wander back over the years.

'I had to be downstairs every morning at a quarter to six. Rake the fire out first then go down the steep stairs into the cellar and make sure the coal scuttles were full. That wasn't too bad, though your aprons did get dirty shovelling the coal. I was supposed to pin a clean sack round my waist but more often than not I forgot. It was the lugging of the filled coal scuttles back up the stairs that used to almost break my back.'

'That must 'ave been 'orrible,' Rosie murmured. Then, sounding indignant, she asked, 'What about the men that worked there? Weren't they supposed to do jobs like that?' Her solemn blue eyes regarded her aunt steadily as she waited to hear her reply.

Joan's voice was strong but cold as she said, 'The only men employed inside the house were the butler and . . .'

She laughed. 'Two cellar men, but before you ask they never went near the coal cellars. They were employed to take care of the wine cellars, which were vastly different. Outside of the house there were a number of male employees, men and boys.'

'And what did they do?'

'Some were grooms, who looked after the horses.' That thought brought Bill's untimely death to mind and she struggled for a moment before going on. 'Some were stable lads; they got all the dirty jobs. Others were known as groundsmen.'

'What does groundsmen mean?' inquisitive Rosie cut in again.

Joan chuckled. 'Posh word for the gardeners.'

Rosie giggled. 'You like posh words, don't yer, Auntie?

'It's what you get used to. It's a very long time ago that I lived like that, and anyway I think that the way we speak is all to do with surroundings. And before you ask, I mean that the people one lives with, the community, in all different parts of the country have their own way of talking. If you stay long enough in one place you are bound to pick up a certain amount. On the other hand I do think that you never lose the accent from the place where you were born and brought up.'

'I know what yer mean, Auntie Joan. Sometimes you let slip an' talk like me mum. An' there's a boy in my class who is a right laugh. When he first came to London none of us understood 'alf of what he was saying and even now if we make faces at him he goes all daft like an' says, "Cows chew grass, clouds bring rain, price of milk's gone up again."'

'I can see you like this boy,' said Joan.

'You've got funny eyesight, then,' said Rosie. 'But get on with telling me what you had t' do once yer'd got the fires alight.'

'Help Cook get everyone's breakfast, and once that was

over there was tons of vegetables to scrape, peel and chop. Then came polishing and dusting, then beds had to be made and chamber pots emptied.'

Rosie made a terrible face. 'Eeh, you didn't really have to empty other people's pots, did yer?'

'I certainly did. But the worst thing was the times the staff had to go up and down the great staircase. I'd be rich if I had ten shillings for every time I've dragged myself up those stairs, and loaded like a donkey most times.'

'Didn't you get any nice jobs? Not even one?'

Joan didn't have to stop and think. She let her mind wander back again and she dreamily said, 'Afternoon tea was lovely. I had to change my working uniform for a black dress, a white frilly apron and a white mobcap before I could go into the drawing room and serve the tea. Tiny sandwiches with all the crusts cut off the bread. Scones and strawberry jam, cake stands that had four and sometimes five tiers which held every assortment of dainty cakes and slices of the richest fruit cake you could imagine.'

'What's a drawing room?'

'A very posh front room.' Joan giggled at the thought and that set Rosie off.

'I thought you meant people had paper and coloured pencils and drew pictures in a special room.'

'Oh, Rosie, I love you.' Joan tickled her and when she wriggled she kissed the top of her head.

'Why did you stay there if it was so bad?' Rosie's bright blue eyes were sparkling with merriment. 'I mean, I do feel sorry that you had to work so hard, but couldn't you 'ave come 'ome t' yer mum?'

Joan shook her head. 'It wasn't like that in those days. My mother had two girls, your mother and me. I was the eldest and I had to be sent into service. We had three brothers, one, your Uncle Tom, who is in the Merchant Navy, I'm sure you remember him – it's not so long ago

55

that he came home. He's never married. Another brother died when he was only five years old and the last one died in a pit accident.'

'I know about that uncle. Dad told me. He worked down the coal mines in Kent, didn't he?'

Joan nodded her head and there was a pause before Rosie came up with her next question.

'You said you hated it when you first went into service. Does that mean that later on you got to like it?'

'That's quite right, Rosie. Thinking about it I'm very grateful that my mother sent me away into service. I learnt so much, especially after I got promotion, and got given a very nice little bedroom all to myself. At first there was four girls sleeping in one attic room.'

Rosie looked baffled for a moment. Then she laughed and it was a joy to hear her and watch as she tossed strands of her long blonde hair back from her face. 'What was the best thing you learnt?'

Joan thought hard for a moment. 'Being taught to sew, I think. I loved it. Took to it like a duck to water, and you know what, Rosie? You know my old sewing machine that is in your dad's shed at the moment?'

Rose nodded her head.

'Well, that is the machine that I first learnt on, and when I left to get married to your Uncle Bill, Mr and Mrs Morley, my employers, gave it to me as a wedding present.'

Rosie had the fidgets. She spun round until she was able to look up into her aunt's face. 'I know some more things you learnt by working in that big house.'

'Do you now? Well, let's hear them.'

'I already told yer. You talk different.'

'Do I? Different in what way?'

'You don't talk like what we do. Mum an' Dad an' Lenny an' Bernie, we all say ain't. You don't. My teacher at school is always telling us that there isn't any such word as ain't 'cos it ain't in the dictionary. And you dress different an' all, an' another thing, you always lay the table nice.'

Joan was saved from having to comment because Martha was pushing the door open with her hip. Joan nudged Rosie out of the way, got to her feet and cleared a space on the table for the heavy tray that her sister was carrying.

'Well, 'ave yer had yer natter?' Martha grinned at the pair of them.

'Yeah, we 'ave. Auntie Joan learnt to talk posh 'cos of when she was in service,' Rosie answered, her voice riddled with laughter. Then she looked at the laden tray and asked, 'What yer got t' eat, Mum?'

Martha whipped off the cloths that were covering two large plates. 'Victoria sponge, and I was gonna say rock cakes but perhaps I'd better think of another name. And seeing as we're going all posh you can move yerself, young lady, and go and fetch three small plates off the dresser, 'cos I ain't 'aving crumbs all over my best rug.'

Rosie and her aunt looked at each other. They each managed to keep a straight face, but when Martha looked at Rosie and asked, 'Well, are yer going for the plates or ain't yer?' they both had to smother their laughter. Fortunately, Martha had her back to them as she poured milk into the cups, and by the time she turned round again Joan had put her finger to her lips. Rosie went to fetch the plates without saying a word.

It rained solidly for the next two days and the horrible view of endless small grimy houses with a gigantic factory at the end of the road did nothing to make anyone feel cheerful, least of all Joan. But on Thursday morning the rain had stopped, and watery sunshine was doing its best to shine through the clouds. Joan had finished washing up the breakfast things and tidied the kitchen and scullery. Suddenly she made up her mind to walk to the Labour

Exchange and see if there were any jobs on offer which might be suitable for her. If she were going to get her own place to live she would have bills to pay besides buying food and other necessary commodities so she would need a decent wage. At this moment that seemed too much to ask for.

It was just after half-past ten when she stepped out into the street, looking businesslike in a navy blue straight skirt, the hem of which just reached her ankles. The knee-length jacket, made of the same heavy material, had a velvet collar and was nipped in at the waist, and her white blouse had a ruffled collar which stood high round her neck. All three articles she had made herself, albeit a very long time ago. She had also retrimmed the black felt hat she had worn for Bill's funeral, and she carried a small handbag. Her hands were warm and snug in hand-knitted white woollen gloves.

As she closed the gate her sister yelled, 'Good luck, gal.'

Joan knew she was certainly going to need it. Her thoughts were sombre as she walked and tried to weigh up her situation. On the plus side, she spoke well, could write a good hand and was intelligent if not well educated. Now for the minus side of things. Her clothes, although clean and well pressed, had seen a lot of wear and were hardly up to date. She looked down at her boots. Half an hour she'd spent polishing them, but the shine did not hide the fact that they were shabby and well worn. Looking as she did now she wasn't going to be offered the best of jobs if she was offered anything at all.

She was on a treadmill, and until she found a way of earning enough money to buy some decent clothes, or material to make them, she thought it highly unlikely that she would be able to get off it. She'd hit rock bottom and did not know which way to turn. Everyone had been so kind, but no one who lived around these parts had long pockets. Neighbours had given generously when Gwen Baldwin had died, and with a struggle and a bit of help Joan had managed to pay off the undertaker, for the old lady had been well liked and respected. The same could not be said of her son. Joan felt it was only because the local paper had made such a good story of the fact that Bill had lost his life because he had gone back into the burning stables and saved three horses that the owners of the brewery had paid for his quiet funeral.

She had reached the drab building that was known as the Labour Exchange. The inside walls were painted in two colours, the top half dark brown and the other half dark green, making the inside of the building no more welcoming than the outside. The far wall was divided into sections. A thin wooden partition between each booth allowed for some privacy.

Joan took a seat and soon cottoned on to the fact that whenever a clerk called out 'Next' a person went forward and everybody else moved up one seat in the row. She seemed to have been waiting for ages. Her hands felt sticky, and because she had washed her hair last night it was so soft it was falling loose from the pins she had used to put it up into what she had thought was a very neat long pleat. She took a minute or two to tuck up the stray strands beneath the rim of her hat. Her hair used to be her best feature. People thought her face was beautiful, and her brown hair with its golden glints framed it well. It was only these latter years, when her marriage had become so hard to cope with and she had had to manage alone with the failing health of her mother-in-law, that she had let herself go a bit. It wasn't laziness on her part. There just hadn't been the money to spend on herself, let alone have her hair done or buy new clothes.

What did she look like today? Passable, she supposed, but only just. She wondered if there were any lavatories in this place where she might go and tidy herself up, but she was afraid to ask.

'Next.' A nudge from the girl sitting next to her made Joan realise she was at the end of the line. She went forward and was surprised to be greeted with a smile from a sweet-faced young woman who looked about thirty. Joan gave her name and address and started to explain that she had come to enquire if there were any suitable vacancies on the books as she needed to find work.

'Whoa, not so fast,' the young woman cautioned. 'Is this your first application?'

'Yes. Yes, it is,' Joan stammered.

'In that case you have to see Mr Thompson. He will fill out a form with all your details.' Seeing the colour drain from Joan's face, she very quickly assured her, 'Mr Thompson is a very nice understanding gentleman.' She leant forward over the counter and whispered, 'He doesn't bite. Just go to the far end of the room. I'll let him know you are waiting and he will open the door for you.'

'Thank you,' Joan said, thinking what a kind, considerate person she was.

She was startled by the office she was led into. It was a lovely light room with just one big curtainless window, one enormous desk and two upright chairs, one standing in front of the desk and the second one behind it. She turned to look at the man who was closing the door behind her.

'I'm Mr Thompson,' he said, holding out his hand, 'and you are?'

Joan shook his hand and murmured, 'Mrs Baldwin.'

Mr Thompson was smartly dressed, aged about fifty, with stooped shoulders and a happy-looking face. He pointed to the nearest chair. 'Please sit down,' he said, going behind the desk and seating himself.

He was so courteous Joan forgot her appearance and her anxiety for a moment. He asked all the normal questions she had been expecting, and she began to relax and to feel extremely comfortable in his company. He told her how the

Exchange worked and that if they sent her after any position she would be given a green card to present to the employer. But he wasn't a know-all type, nor was he overly officious. He prompted her to speak about her own life, and why at her age she so badly needed to find work.

She told him how her husband and her mother-in-law had recently died. She even told him how she had nursed Gwen. Then there was the fact that she had had to give up her own house and was temporarily living with her sister and her brother-in-law.

'What kind of work have you done, say before you were married?' he asked.

'I was in service to a Mr and Mrs Morley.' She went on to tell him roughly what her duties had been.

The time flew by, and suddenly he looked very serious. 'So, what it boils down to, Mrs Baldwin, is that you need not only a job but somewhere to live.'

Joan's only thought was that Mr Thompson had summarised her situation very promptly. Mr Thompson, on the other hand, was afraid it would be a hard task to find a situation that would be suitable for this lady. As he continued to stare at her he guessed she was undernourished. Her neck was thin, her face looked peaky, and the costume she was wearing was shabby. But he also saw something else: her lady-like attitude, the proud way she held her head, her soft manner of speaking. She had known better days, of that he was certain. Lately? Well, his guess would be a life of drudgery and a lot of grief. Grief that still showed in her beautiful brown eyes.

Reluctantly he rose to his feet and quietly said, 'I am sorry that at the moment we do not have anything suitable on our books. However, Mrs Baldwin, you may rest assured that I shall do my best to find a position that will be entirely suitable for you.'

Joan smiled grimly to herself as she pulled on her gloves.

'We shall keep you informed,' he said as he held the office door open for her.

I'll believe it when it happens, she almost replied, but stopped herself in time.

She walked the streets slowly, in no hurry to go back to what was her sister's home but not hers. She had no home of her own. Mr Thompson had been discreet and attentive, but would he be able to find her employment? As she knew only too well, life in general was full of broken promises.

Chapter Seven

JOAN WAS AMAZED. She was actually window-shopping in the beautiful royal town of Tunbridge Wells.

She had been working at Mulborough House for two months and this was her first full day off. The first four weeks she had been on trial and only allowed two half-days.

Mr Thompson had come up trumps. Three days after her visit to the Labour Exchange a postcard had arrived requesting her to call in to see him as soon as possible, and within two hours of receiving it she was once again seated in that bare office.

Mr Thompson returned her gaze, smiling broadly. 'You did not expect to be seeing me again quite so soon, did you?'

Staring at his open, friendly face, Joan took in his warm smile and the somewhat mischievous glint in his eyes. Her hands were trembling, he noticed, and with quick sympathy he said, 'I think we may have come up with a solution to many of your problems.'

For the life of her Joan didn't know what to say, so she nodded her head and waited for him to go on.

'The kind of position that would be suitable for you, Mrs

Baldwin, is very rare in this neighbourhood, as you well know. However, my colleagues have been very helpful and here on my desk I have the details of a vacancy for a housemaid. With your past experience I thought it might be worth your while to go for an interview. The house is in Kent, at no great distance from Maidstone and Canterbury, but the address I have been given is Tunbridge Wells. The whole area has quite a history. Did you know, for instance, that those born west of the Medway are called Kentish Men, while the inhabitants of the eastern part are known as Men of Kent?' He smiled, doing his best to ease the tension, but Joan did not react. He looked uncertain as he lowered his gaze and silently reread the papers that lay in front of him. He decided honesty was the best policy.

'The lady of the house had been made aware of your age. Nevertheless, she has agreed to grant you an interview.' Seeing Joan's downcast eyes, the drooping of her mouth and the sad expression that swept across her face, he hastened to add, 'You've nothing to lose by going to apply for the job. It isn't too long a journey, only about thirty-five miles from London.'

Joan was speechless, and the colour had gone from her cheeks.

Mr Thompson guessed straight away what was troubling this quiet lady. Quickly, he added, 'Of course, it is entirely up to you to decide as to whether or not you go for this interview, but I should tell you that all expenses will be paid by this Exchange. You would be given cash to get you to the railway station, and a travel warrant for your return journey.'

He recognised the relief on Joan's face, and knew that his insight had been right. She hadn't the money to pay the fare to Kent herself.

Her job description was that of housemaid and while she

would be the very first to admit that she had fallen on her feet, not everything about her new life was wonderful. But then she shouldn't expect it to be so, she often chided herself. Mrs Hamilton was a real lady and had freely admitted at Joan's interview that she had expected the applicant for the position to be a much younger person. Joan hadn't held it against her because that very doubt had been uppermost in her own mind since Mr Thompson had broached the subject. Then this gracious lady had thought hard for a moment and said, 'Shall we give each other a trial period? After all, you won't want to be climbing out of windows and scampering off to meet young men late at night, will you?' They had smiled together at the thought.

At first sight, Joan had been overawed by the dignified splendour of Mulborough House and had almost turned away. She stood at the foot of the wide front steps, sure she would never find the courage to walk up them and ring the shiny brass bell beside the huge front door.

While she was wondering what to do a young man came round the side of the house wearing a green baize apron, his shirt sleeves rolled up above his elbows. He smiled and raised a hand in greeting to Joan, which certainly helped to settle her nerves.

'Come on, miss. Don't look so troubled. I'll take you round the back. Not many other than the family use the front entrance.'

Joan had followed the lad through an archway and she'd gazed in surprise at the beautiful green lawns and flower beds that seemed to stretch for miles. She wondered how he knew what she was there for. It hadn't taken much thought for the reason to hit her.

She wasn't exactly dressed as a visitor might be.

June had come in with a heat wave. The sunshine was brilliant and the sky clear and blue, and the clothes she was wearing were hardly appropriate. She had no decent summer dresses, but when she had started out from Merton early that morning her navy blue suit had seemed to be passable. Now it felt hot and cumbersome.

She might have entered Mulborough House through the back door but she certainly had not been disappointed. Even the rooms below stairs were enormous and airy. And the welcome she had received from the cook had been so unexpected that all she could do was mumble her thanks. She had also been very impressed by the size of the kitchen and the massive, coal-burning range with its two ovens. In fact, since she had started working there she had been stunned by everything she saw. There had been new surprises each and every day.

Mrs Hamilton, the mistress of the house, was kindly but firm, but her husband's behaviour baffled Joan. Cook had told her that he just had not been the same since he had returned from the war in 1918. It seemed to Joan that all the spirit had been knocked out of the poor man, because he was given to quiet, withdrawn moods. He would often sit for hours, never moving, not answering anyone who spoke to him, staring vacantly into space like a lost child. At other times he would erupt into sudden almost uncontrollable anger over the simplest of things. Sometimes she wished she could grab hold of him and take him for a walk in the grounds. She was too small to cope with him. He was a huge man with a strong body and she wished it were possible to make his life somehow more worthwhile.

It was such a pity.

Of all the people who constantly came and went Joan felt the best friend she had made since coming to Mulborough House was the cook, Kathleen O'Leary. Round, fat and jolly, just as a cook should be. There was happiness in every line of her face. She was a kind person who saw only good in everyone, and a marvellous cook to boot. During what little free time they did have, and always while drinking a cup of

66

Kathleen's strong brew, Joan had learnt that the cook was fifty-six years old and had been a widow for the past twelve years.

Joan had been wandering along the Pantiles, an avenue of very smart and different kinds of shops, and now the smell of freshly ground coffee was tempting her to enter a very luxurious-looking tearoom. Before she had become housemaid to Mrs Hamilton the only coffee she had ever tasted came from a bottle. Fresh coffee was something she had quickly learnt to enjoy very much.

Yes, Joan suddenly decided, she was going to splash out and treat herself to an iced bun and a cup of coffee. So before her confidence faded she opened the door, smiled as she heard a bell tinkle and made her way to a corner table that was not only covered by a white linen cloth but had a delicate lace one draped three-cornerways on top. A glass vase that held a few brightly coloured and highly perfumed sweet peas had been placed in the centre.

She removed her gloves, and gave her order to a friendly waitress who appeared to be a few years older than herself. Considering her fellow servants at Mulborough House, she wondered whether Tunbridge Wells favoured older employees. Certainly the housekeeper, Miss Reid, was elderly, nearer sixty than fifty. Janet, who only worked part-time as a chambermaid when the spare rooms were occupied by guests, was about thirty-five. Mr Farrant, the butler, wore an impeccably cut suit when he was above stairs, which helped to hide his big belly, and even his bald head gave him an air of distinction, but as to his age she wouldn't like to hazard a guess. All she really knew about him was that he lived with his wife in a cottage in the grounds, although to Joan he never seemed to go home, for whatever job she was doing Mr Farrant was always nearby. The only two youngsters who were employed inside the house were the kitchen maid, sixteen-year-old Mabel, and seventeen-year-old John, whom she had met when she came for her interview. John seemed to spend most of his time cleaning shoes and boots or polishing silverware – and God knows there was enough silver in that household.

Joan was well aware of just how good her life was now. But for all that she had landed on her feet, there was always something missing: her sister and her family.

To begin with the nights had been awful. Having one's own bedroom was nice but when it was dark outside she could hear all the strange sounds of the country. She missed the noise of the traffic, missed knowing that she had good neighbours next door and friendly folk close by. She even felt the loss of hearing men singing on their way home when the pubs turned out. Mostly, though, tears stung the backs of her eyes when her thoughts were of her dear sister Martha, and young Rosie. Oh, God, how she missed that girl. *She'll be all grown by the time I get to see her again.* Joan sighed to herself as she sipped her coffee from the dainty bone-china cup.

All her toughness and determination to get on with her new life dissolved when her thoughts turned that way. She found it particularly hard when she was helping to serve a meal to a room full of people, all related, each a member of a close-knit family. Then she felt bleak and lonely. If only she had some relatives living nearby. During the first few weeks, alone in her room, she had often shed tears of despair, afraid that she would never stick it. But whenever she was tempted to quit and take herself back to London she made herself stop and think. What had she to go back to? Where would she live? How would she live? She certainly couldn't plant herself on Martha and Sid again, though the thought of those small rooms and the crowded table as they'd eaten together, laughing and chatting . . . it didn't pay to look back. She should count herself lucky and count her blessings, she often chided herself. Then she would think of the freshness of the home-grown vegetables, newly laid eggs and farm produce that everyone in Mulborough House took for granted. Martha's eyes would pop out of her head if she saw some of the meals that Kathleen O'Leary was able to turn out.

The waitress came back and with a friendly smile asked Joan if she would like her cup refilled. The waitress was wearing a black dress and a frilly white apron, much like the ones Joan wore of an afternoon in the big house, though she'd be the first to admit the uniform fitted this waitress far better than the dress she had been given fitted her. She'd give a lot to be able to buy some decent material and make her own. Several reasons stopped her. For one thing, since the wages were paid once a month, she'd only been paid twice. She got twenty-five shillings a week and all found, and the first five pounds she had posted straight off to Martha and Sid. After all, although Sid was back on full time at the smelting works they owed a few bob here and there and some of their debts had to be because she had lived off them for a considerable time.

She smiled, remembering. Martha had written her such a lovely letter. Five pounds! Think you're lady bountiful, do yer? Rosie, too, had written to her. Her mum had given her and her friend the money to go to the Saturday morning pictures at the Central Hall in Tooting, and she'd told Rosie that her Auntie Joan had sent the money especially for her.

Joan finished her snack, paid her bill and gave the waitress a threepenny bit as a tip.

'Come in and see us again. We do lovely lunches,' the friendly waitress said as she opened the door for Joan.

Joan was tempted to say, So do we up at the house and I don't have to pay. Instead she nodded her head and said quietly, 'Thanks. Hope to see you soon. 'Bye for now.'

For a while Joan continued to walk round the shops. She looked at clothes and at beauty products, wishing there was a market here like the one in Whitechapel Road in the East End of London where she could buy remnants of really good material for next to nothing. However, even if that had been possible she didn't have her sewing machine, which was still lying in Sid's garden shed, more's the pity. Of course she could sew by hand and in the past had done, many a time, but that would take time and that was something she didn't have a lot of to spare.

In the end she decided there was nothing she needed to spend her money on. Everything was provided for her, even down to soap and tooth-cleaning powder. Time had certainly brought about some changes since she had been in service all those years ago. Her days were still long, and she still only got a half-day a week off and a whole day once a month, but the tasks she was asked to do were nowhere near so hard as they were in days gone by.

Joan looked at the big clock that was on a high plinth and decided it was time for her to catch the single-decker bus which would set her down within about half a mile of the house. By the time she'd strolled down between the leafy trees on each side of the lane she'd be hungry; she'd be more so when she smelt all the good things that Cook would have ready for the evening meal. Besides, Mr and Mrs Hamilton's two daughters were expected home from abroad today and their only son and his wife were due to arrive tomorrow. There had been talk about some kind of celebration but nothing definite had been settled yet. Joan had made up the beds for the daughters yesterday, hung big white fluffy towels each side of the washstands and made sure that toiletries were set out in the enormous bathroom. In her mind she knew that although it was her day off Cook would be more than pleased to see her. Ten to one there would be some job that she'd beg her to do before dinner. She wouldn't mind. Cook did her many a favour.

Joan's assumption wasn't wrong!

'Ah, lass, am I glad t' see thee, so I am,' was the greeting that met her as she stepped into the kitchen. Cook was red in the face and the starched white cap perched like a crown on top of her thick mop of hair bobbed about as she moved. 'I know it's yer day off, me darling, but I could surely use a hand. Would you mind seeing to the joint of beef I've got in the oven? It needs basting and I can't be leaving these egg whites I'm whisking.'

'Of course I'll be only too glad to help,' Joan cried as she ran across the kitchen, pulling off her jacket and hanging it over the back of a chair. With one of Cook's large aprons tied twice around her slim waist she was soon on her knees, thick sacking oven gloves protecting her hands as she pulled the baking tray towards her and slowly and carefully ladled the juices from the bottom of the tray over and over the joint. Cautiously she slid the tin towards the back of the oven once more and carefully closed the door.

'It's fine, Cook. Won't be long and it will be done to a tee.'

'Ah, I send thanks to the blessed saints for the day that you came here, Joan, so I do.'

'Get on with you.' Joan chuckled. 'You manage fine, but do you want to tell me what all the haste is about and why you are working yourself into a fine old lather?'

Cook's eyes flashed with indignation. 'At noon today I was informed that there would be eight for dinner tonight. Besides Mr and Mrs Hamilton and their daughters Fiona and Delia – who, by the way, have arrived – Bruce and his wife are coming from London today not tomorrow and they are bringing two friends with them. It's no wonder I'm in a devil of a mess.'

At that moment Miss Reid appeared. 'Ah, you're back, Joan. How very fortunate for us. I presume you will have no objection to stepping into the breach. It would be so helpful if first off you'd see that extra place settings are added to the table.'

Joan ignored this friendly greeting. Frosty-face was the nickname she had given to the housekeeper right from the word go. Trying hard not to let her embarrassment show, she said, 'I don't mind in the least doing the dining room, Miss Reid, but I cannot be in two places at the same time. Has anyone thought to tell Janet that extra guests are expected and that her services will be required today?'

'I thought you had made up the bedrooms yesterday,' the housekeeper replied starchily.

'Yes, Miss Reid, I had, for Mrs Hamilton's two daughters, but I was advised that young Mr and Mrs Hamilton were not arriving until tomorrow and that Janet would be here by then. No mention was made that two extra guests were accompanying them.'

Had Mr Farrant been eavesdropping? It would seem so.

He barged in quickly, pouring oil on troubled waters. 'I'll send young John off on his bicycle to inform Janet that she is needed for this evening.'

Miss Reid huffed, turned on her heel and left them to it.

Kathleen O'Leary was smiling to herself as she bustled around the stove, clattering pan lids, peering at the contents of her boiling pots. Miss Reid always irritated her, thought she was a cut above everyone else. She looked across at James Farrant and he rewarded her with a sly wink. They were both thinking the same thing. Glad that Joan Baldwin had found the guts to stand up to that one. After all, it was her very first day off and she hadn't uttered one word of complaint at being asked to work the minute she'd stepped into the kitchen.

Miraculously, everything in the kitchen was well under control, and although Cook was flushed and perspiring she was presiding over all the preparations and the dishing up with a certain amount of pride and a smile on her chubby, rosy face.

Joan rinsed her hands under the running cold tap and said, 'If you don't need me for anything else, Cook, I think I'd better go and get ready to wait table.'

'All right, Joan, me darling.' Cook beamed at her. 'Everything's fine here now. Thanks for your help, love. I hope it's plain sailing upstairs for you tonight, but you don't want to let them get away with forgetting that you are owed some free time. Ain't many as would have worked on their night off.'

Mabel, who was polishing some serving spoons that Joan had brought down from the dining room, looked up and grinned. 'When I've finished these I'm going to make a pot of tea for me an' Cook, so if you've time when you're dressed pop down an' have a cup. I'll put cosy on the pot t' keep it hot.'

Joan returned her smile. 'Thanks, Mabel. I'll see you later.'

She climbed the back stairs that led to the staff quarters, and smiled as she entered her room. It was a pretty sight with its single bed and the pale pink bedspread that matched the curtains. She stood at the small window for a few minutes, thinking how wonderful the view was. She could see the sparkle of the panes of glass in the greenhouses in the nearby kitchen gardens, and she told herself what a lovely summer's day it had been. Bet it was hot and dusty in London, she thought.

She moved to the marble-topped washstand, poured cold water from the enormous jug into the large floral-patterned bowl, and then quickly undressed and washed herself from head to toe, leaving her face until last. For this she cupped fresh water from the jug to splash her face, leaning over the bowl and rubbing her skin with her face flannel until it felt really fresh. She spent some time brushing her dark hair, then twisted it cleverly into a thick plait before winding it into a bun that sat at the nape of her neck.

She sighed as she laid out her dining room uniform. It

was supposed to be for the summer, but the material was a heavy crêpe and the dress had been made for someone considerably bigger than herself. She did her best to fold the sides of the dress into a pleat, hoping that if she tied the frilly white apron tight enough round her waist it would hold the surplus material in place. It often didn't. The white cotton collar looked very nice but as the sleeves of the dress were a couple of inches too long she had to fold them back, which made it hard to keep the separate white cuffs in place. Joan stared at her reflection in the mirror and was not at all pleased by what she saw. Sighing again, she picked up the white band of linen which was worn of an evening in place of the daytime mobcap, and secured it round her forehead. At least that fitted, and it kept the odd strand of hair from falling into her eyes. Finally, slipping her feet into her black shoes with their paper-thin soles, she promised herself that that was the first thing she was going to buy. A brand new pair of shoes.

She made her way down the main staircase. When she reached the hall she heard her name called and turned to see Miss Fiona and Miss Delia, who greeted her quite eagerly, she thought, considering she had only met them once before and then only briefly, when they had come down from London just for the day to see their parents. She was surprised at how well and suntanned they both looked, but then she remembered they had been on holiday abroad.

'How have you settled in, Joan?' asked the younger sister, Fiona.

'Very well, thank you, miss.'

'Good,' they both said in unison, but Delia gave Joan a funny look and added, 'Would you turn round, please, Joan?'

Joan did as she asked, feeling very awkward.

'Joan, is that the uniform my mother gave you?'

Joan felt her cheeks flush up and to her dismay she saw

that one of the folds she'd made in the sides of the dress had worked its way loose as she had come down the stairs and the extra cloth was hanging over the edge of her apron. Feeling very embarrassed, she answered, 'Yes, miss.'

'Well, don't look like that, Joan,' Delia said kindly. 'It's not your fault.' Then, turning to her sister, she said, 'I don't know what Mother could have been thinking of. Does she think one uniform fits all staff?'

Fiona had been studying Joan, and now she said, 'First thing in the morning we'll sort you out. Delia will take your measurements and she and I will go into Tunbridge Wells and have a good old forage around. One of the department stores must sell uniforms, surely.'

'If not, we'll go on to Maidstone,' Delia said forcefully.

Joan spoke up. It was something she had been dying to say ever since she had tried the first dress on. 'Excuse me, Miss Delia, and you, Miss Fiona, I could make my own uniforms, both sets, if I were given the material.'

The girls looked at each other and raised their eyebrows.

'Sorry if you think I'm speaking out of turn,' Joan mumbled self-consciously.

'Not at all.' Fiona hastened to reassure her. Then, almost as an afterthought, she asked, 'Have you ever used a sewing machine?'

'Yes, quite a lot,' Joan said quietly. 'Before now I have cut out a pattern from my own drawing and made up dresses for a few ladies on my own treadle sewing machine.' Hurriedly she added, 'They paid me for my work.'

The two sisters chuckled. 'Did they indeed? That's excellent. Did you know our old schoolroom at the top of the house was at one time used as a sewing room?'

Joan shook her head.

'We'll have a word with Mother later on,' Delia promised. Then, turning to Fiona, she asked, 'Is there a sewing machine up there still?'

'I haven't the faintest idea, but I'm sure Miss Reid would know.'

Joan's heart sank. She knew she was not the housekeeper's favourite person. Old Frosty-face wouldn't do anything to help the housemaid look smarter.

'Well, I'd better get on. Thank you both, very much.' She nodded her head and hurried across the hall to the dining room.

She did not see the look that passed between Fiona and Delia Hamilton, nor was she mindful of just how shabby she looked and how much sympathy she had aroused in those two young ladies. She was unaware that she had set in motion a chain of events that in the end would make a world of difference to her life.

Chapter Eight

THE NEXT DAY was one of the happiest that Joan had spent since arriving at Mulborough House. First thing after breakfast Miss Reid had asked Joan to follow her, saying she had orders to show her what had once been the sewing room. Undoubtedly, Miss Fiona and Miss Delia had discussed their conversation with their mother.

'Well, Joan, I've been given to understand that you are pretty good with a needle and are to be given free run of the old sewing room.' The housekeeper spoke over her shoulder to Joan as they climbed the back stairs. Her voice sounded friendly for once, even though she added, 'I hope you know what you are letting yourself in for.'

Walking behind her, Joan smiled to herself, and there was a flicker of satisfaction in her eyes.

Miss Reid opened the door to an attic room and stood back to allow Joan to enter before her. The first sight that met Joan's eyes was a collection of long forgotten toys: a doll's house and an assortment of dolls; a toy-sized perambulator; a huge rocking horse with a real leather saddle and silver stirrups. Against a side wall there was a complete set of drums and further along two well-worn desks, each with one drawer and a sloping top, and a child-sized chair tucked beneath it. It was only as she walked further into the room that she let out a peal of laughter. There, right at the end of the room, was everything that she could desire.

Joan felt they had discovered Aladdin's cave. Placed on a long trestle table was a sewing machine that one worked by turning a handle. Further along was an exact replica of her own treadle machine that was lying idle in her brother-in-law's garden shed. And, 'God above,' Joan cried, 'will you look at those? Two tailor's dummies.'

'The whole place will need a fair bit of cleaning,' Miss Reid said, sighing heavily, 'and as for those two stuffed dummies you're getting so excited about, they are so thick with dust the only place for them is on a bonfire.'

Joan concealed another smile. Over my dead body, she only just stopped herself from saying.

That evening, Joan knew without a doubt that her making known the fact that she could sew and being told she could have the run of the sewing room whenever she had any free time was as good as finding a gold mine.

'Miss Delia is asking for you, Joan.'

Joan looked up from laying the dining table in readiness for the evening meal to see Miss Reid standing in the open doorway.

'Go along, Joan, quickly. I'll finish laying up for you.'

Joan couldn't believe what she'd heard and had a job to stop herself from raising her eyebrows in complete surprise. As she climbed the stairs she was thinking that it was a nice change to have Miss Reid speak to her in a friendly tone. She couldn't help wondering why the housekeeper had appeared to regard her as the enemy almost from the day she arrived.

Miss Delia had worked herself into a fair old state and Joan had hardly set foot in her bedroom when she burst out, 'Joan, please, can you do anything with this dress? I thought it looked great in the shop this morning when I tried it on, but now . . . just look at it.'

'Please, stand still,' Joan said as she slowly walked round Delia. It was indeed a beautiful dress, calf length, the colour of rich port wine. She spotted the trouble straight away. The actual material of the dress itself was a soft, shimmering chiffon, and the slip lining was of heavy satin.

'You say you tried the dress on in the store, miss?'

'Yes, I did. It fitted perfectly. Fiona said it could have been made for me.'

'It won't take me a few minutes to set it right, if I can just pop upstairs and hopefully find a reel of silk thread that will be near enough a match. And I'll need a pair of sharp scissors. Will you carefully slip the dress off, please, miss.'

Minutes later Delia watched as Joan turned the dress inside out and snipped at a few stitches of the inner lining. Then, having threaded a needle with a length of dark Silko, she began to sew along the side hem of the heavy satin using tiny neat stitches.

'Are you sure you know what you're doing?' Delia asked nervously. 'What's wrong with the dress, anyway?'

'Hardly anything at all, Miss Delia, as you pulled the dress over your head when you were in the fitting room one of your rings probably caught the two materials together, and the chiffon being so much lighter in weight than the underslip they joined together and caused the whole side of the dress to ruck up.' Seeing the look on her young mistress's face she added quickly, 'Of course, it could have been the fault of the young lady assistant when she was packing the dress. Anyway, it's fine now.' She cut the thread, stood up and carefully turned the dress back to the right side, giving the whole garment a gentle shake. 'Hold both your arms straight up in the air and I will slip the dress over your head.' Joan spoke nervously, hoping against hope that she had cleared the problem to the satisfaction of her young mistress.

Seconds later Delia was smiling broadly, and as Joan held out the matching bolero for her to put her arms into she stared at her reflection in the long mirror and visibly brightened. Joan breathed a sigh of relief, just as Fiona burst into the room and let out a long, low, unladylike whistle.

'Wow, I told you that dress had been made for you, Delia.'

It was true. The rich dark colour accentuated the creaminess of her skin and the golden glints in her shoulder-length hair.

'Joan, you are a marvel.' Delia nodded appreciatively. 'I cannot thank you enough.'

'You're welcome, miss.'

Flying down the staircase to catch up on her duties Joan had the foresight to recognise that fate had been on her side this evening.

From little acorns great oak trees grow.

As time passed even Miss Reid had cause to be grateful for Joan's hidden talent. Accordingly, she made it possible for Joan to work in a more efficient and orderly manner. Some days she would even reduce her workload, and thus Joan was able on a few afternoons a week to retire to the sewing room and work on the household linen, some of which was badly in need of repair. She herself also looked a whole lot better in the well-fitting uniforms she had made for herself, and as a result she felt better.

She had been congratulated several times on having achieved such a skilful result.

It wasn't long before she was being asked to alter or repair clothes for Mrs Hamilton and both her daughters. Even Miss Reid had approached her, somewhat timidly it had to be said, but nevertheless she had brought some fine underwear to Joan, explaining that the petticoats were too long and showed below her dress, so she had never been able to wear them. Would Joan be so kind as to shorten them?

'Only too pleased to,' had been Joan's reply, and she had taken the time to hand-sew the delicate fabric using the finest of needles and making sure that each stitch was perfect. Joan felt she needed Miss Reid as a friend. After all, the housekeeper was responsible for how much free time Joan was allowed in order to pursue her sewing.

There came a time when even more progress was offered.

All the family were in the drawing room and Joan was serving afternoon tea. The French doors were wide open, for the summer was stretching out well. The lawns were an emerald green and the gardens were still a blaze of colour, with tall stone pots filled with great bushy geraniums spaced along the edges of the pathways. In the hearth of the white marble fireplace stood a lovely floral arrangement, the flowers filling the room with a soft perfume. That in itself was a bonus. All this lovely sunny weather meant no fires had to be lit and no grates had to be cleared of ashes every morning.

Even the old gentleman (as Joan always thought of Mr Hamilton) was brighter today and seemed to be listening with interest to the conversation. Joan had served everyone with a cup of tea and seen that everyone had a plate, a napkin and a cake fork before pushing the laiden tea trolley to the centre of the room where it would be within easy reach of every member of the family. She was about to leave the room when Mrs Hamilton asked her to stay.

'Joan, my daughters and I have a proposal which we would like to put to you. First, though, I must compliment you. Indeed I must. Not only are your uniforms a credit to you, Miss Reid tells me you have been through every article in the linen cupboard, hemming napkins, repairing torn pillow cases and sheets, and restitching the edges of frayed tablecloths. It would seem we have found a treasure in you. You certainly are a talented woman.'

Joan was delighted with the knowledge that her efforts had been successful, but she managed to conceal her smiles as Mrs Hamilton went on.

'It will be autumn soon, and Christmas won't be far behind, and we thought it would be wonderful if you would design and make at least one dress for each of us. During the winter months we attend many functions and it would delight us to know that we were wearing something different. A dress or a two-piece that one would not be able to purchase even in the London stores.'

Joan was flabbergasted.

Mrs Hamilton smiled at her. 'You're probably wondering how you would ever find the time to fit in this extra work alongside all your other tasks. We were of the same mind to begin with. However, we have hit on a solution. We will hire another girl, someone from the village who would not need to live in. If you are of a mind to take on this dressmaking we shall pay you separately for the work. I would insist on that.'

Joan's head was buzzing. It would be work she would relish *and* she would be able to save some money. Having a bit put by wouldn't be a bad thing, because the way things stood now if she were to lose this job tomorrow she would have nowhere to live and no savings to fall back on. Could she do it? Well enough to satisfy not only Mrs Hamilton but the very fashion-conscious Miss Delia and Miss Fiona? She could give it a go. After all, there were enough magazines coming into the house that she could get ideas from. Even more likely, the two girls would probably bring patterns down from London.

What if they did? She was a dab hand at cutting cloth. Not so long ago she had been making every stitch that young Rosie put on her back. Even her school uniform. And that was besides the dressmaking that she sometimes did for neighbours. Word had got around years ago that Mrs

Baldwin did alterations and repairs, from shortening or lengthening skirts and trousers to turning a well-worn shirt collar. But then nobody would have moaned at her had she messed up any article she was working on. God almighty! This chance was a very different kettle of fish!

'Are you going to stand there all night, Joan?' Fiona laughed as she asked the question. Delia was quick to urge her to agree.

'Please, Joan, think what fun it will be choosing all the lovely colours and the different materials.'

'And while you are busy making our outfits we'll scour the shops for shoes and evening bags to exactly match what we have chosen.' Fiona sounded excited and it was infectious. Soon even Mr Hamilton was smiling and nodding his head with approval.

'Please, Mrs Hamilton,' Joan begged, 'may I think about this? I wouldn't want any of you to go to the expense of buying material all at once. May we talk more tomorrow morning? I am honoured that you trust me so much, truly I am, but perhaps I should take it slowly. Make just one outfit, then you can be the judge of whether I should carry on or not.'

'That is an excellent idea, Joan. We shall talk again tomorrow. Meanwhile you are not to lose any sleep tonight worrying over this. You promise, now?'

'Yes, I promise, and thank you, ma'am,' Joan mumbled before she made what she hoped was a respectable retreat. The idea was so sudden and incredible. Could she pull it off?

As she lay in her bed that night Joan felt she was inadequate to tackle such a task. She felt that everything that was happening was slightly unreal, as though she was dreaming it all. It seemed ages since anything good had happened to her, and now that it had she couldn't make herself believe that she would be able to cope.

First thing next morning she was greeted enthusiastically by both Fiona and Delia. 'You are going to do it, aren't you?' Delia smiled.

Joan shook her head. 'I still haven't taken it in. It's very exciting but you two young ladies and your mother are in a position to buy your clothes from any of the great fashion houses. Why pick me to make an outfit for you?'

'Because we want to be different,' Fiona cried. 'I've seen some of the sketches you've left lying about in the kitchen. They are unusual, to say the least. We could put our heads together, you sketching and us commenting, and together we might come up with an exclusive design. Please, Joan, say you'll give it a try.'

'I can see it working just as well as my sister has described, but there is one thing I am afraid of,' Delia said, but her eyes were flashing mischievously. Seeing the smile fade from Joan's face, she said quickly, 'Hey, I was only joking. I was going to say that we'll be the belles of any ball that we get invited to. Ladies will plead with us to tell them where we bought our original dresses, and should we be so silly as to tell them word will get around and you'll be whipped off to Paris before you know what is happening and we shall lose you.'

'Oh, don't be so daft!' Joan's fingers flew to cover her mouth. For a moment she had forgotten who she was talking to.

At that moment Mrs Hamilton put her head round her bedroom door and looked amazed to see her daughters hugging each other and laughing fit to bust. 'What on earth?' their mother cried.

It was a minute or two before the girls were able to speak and by then Joan had taken herself off into the dining room.

'It's all right, Mother. We have not taken leave of our senses but we do believe we shall be able to persuade Joan to go along with our scheme.' Fiona nodded merrily at her sister and added, 'Right, Dee?'

'Dead cert, I'd say. Besides, Joan is a likeable and clever lady and she will be far happier using her talents than merely being a housemaid. Given different circumstances I believe she could have a different life, and what's more I believe she is the kind of person who deserves it.'

Their mother's eyes widened in admiration, and Delia was puzzled at the smile on her face. 'What is it – did I say something funny?'

'No, no,' said Mrs Hamilton hastily. 'I agree with both of you and it is nice to hear that you are willing to help someone who has not been so fortunate in life as you have.'

'Is *that* all?' Delia laughed and looked at her sister.

'So now we are being thought of as angels of mercy.' Fiona laughed back.

'Oh well. I guess we can live with that. Come on, let's go and have some breakfast.'

Everything had been set in motion.

Joan told herself time and time again how lucky she was. Oh, how she loved the room that had been transformed for her at the top of the house. The cleaning and oiling of both machines had given her no problems at all and there weren't many afternoons that the whirr of machinery couldn't be heard.

Two extra tables had been found and more often than not were filled to overflowing with paper patterns, reams of brown paper that Joan found useful to use when making the first cut-out pattern. Whether it be a blouse, skirt or dress it was always made up in stiff brown paper before she allowed herself to put scissors to cloth.

Best of all were her tailor's dummies. They were not a perfect fit for the three females she was making clothes for, but absolutely indispensable when the first stages of any garment were only held together by tacking stitches.

There was only three weeks to go until 25 December.

Mrs Hamilton had kept her word and had hired another girl, Mary, from the village, whom Miss Reid was doing her best to train as the between maid. This gave Joan more time to sew, and the domestic routine was kept running so smoothly that Joan thought at times it was all too good to be true. Each night she prayed that it would last. In the sewing room there now hung two evening dresses, and one two-piece for Mrs Hamilton that had a skirt that reached the floor. All three outfits needed just the finishing touches. It had been grim determination that had kept Joan Baldwin going as summer had turned into autumn and winter had not been far behind.

Mrs Hamilton was easy to please. Delia and Fiona changed their minds so many times as to how they wanted their very different dresses to hang, and what adornment they preferred, that some days Joan was tempted to throw her arms up in the air and suggest that they finished the work themselves.

If only her sister lived nearer. She so much missed being able to talk to her. Martha wrote regular letters which told her about the neighbours, what Lenny and Bernie were getting up to, how Sid always took her to the pub for a drink on a Saturday evening. Every letter ended by saying how Rosie was growing, how much she missed her Auntie Joan and how she was constantly asking when was she coming home for a visit. You'd think that Martha would be a bit more thoughtful. She didn't stop to think, that was her trouble. Surely she realised that Joan didn't work just a few miles away, and that she would dearly love to come home if she could.

Most of the time Joan felt happy enough, but at the back

of her mind was always the fact that she wasn't here by choice. After all, she was no spring chicken. By rights she should be happily married with children of her own to care for and love. Life wasn't fair. But come to think of it, who ever promised that it was going to be?

Chapter Nine

TOMORROW WOULD BE Christmas Eve.

Joan had spent all morning helping to put the finishing touches to the decorations in the hall and the dining room. For the past week a huge tree had stood at the far side of the drawing room shimmering with tinsel and exquisite glass ornaments. Whenever possible she had also lent a hand in the kitchen. Joan shook her head and grinned as she thought of Kathleen O'Leary. One could be forgiven for thinking that she had been asked to prepare enough food to feed an army. She certainly was an amazing woman. It was not only the quantity of the food that she was preparing, but the variety and the quality.

'Joan, be a dear and check this list that Miss Reid has given me.' Kathleen sounded flustered, which was unusual. Normally she took everything in her stride.

Joan took the sheet of paper and quickly ran her eyes down the list. 'It's just the numbers, including guests, who will be in the house over the holiday. It's no different from what we were told three weeks ago.'

'I know that, Joan, but first someone tells me one thing and then along comes someone else saying something different. With all the blessed saints on me side I don't get the same number no matter how many times I tally it up.'

Joan did her best not to laugh. 'Come on, Cook, we'll do it together.'

Kathleen, who already had a sheet of paper in front of her, slipped on her steel-rimmed glasses and, having licked the end of the pencil she was holding, looked across to Joan and said, 'Right.'

'Shall we start with the family?'

'Yes, that's a good idea,' Cook agreed.

'First off there is Mr and Mrs Hamilton – that's two. Bruce, their son, will be bringing his wife Pamela with him. They haven't any children, have they?'

'No, more's the pity,' Cook answered with a wry little smile.

'Well, that's another two.'

'Then there's Delia, and the youngest is Fiona. If you ask me, Joan, which I know you haven't, but all the same my opinion is that those two young ladies are very sweet and nice when they want to be but they are flibbertigibbets, the pair of 'em, an' I can't be seeing either one of them pushing a pram with a bairn of their own in it.'

'So that's another two,' Joan said cheerily, thinking it was always the best policy to let Cook have her say. She studied the list that had been handwritten by Miss Reid and commented, 'All that is written after the family names is "Six guests, i.e. three married couples". No names are given.'

'That's what I'm on about,' Cook answered abruptly. 'Preparing meals for folk with no names.'

Now Joan could not stop herself from laughing. 'What difference does it make? It adds up to twelve upstairs for the holiday, and Miss Reid will see to the names on the place cards.' But Joan just could not resist teasing Cook. She murmured softly, 'Of course, the family and their guests will be going to watch the hunt on Boxing Day, or so I've been told, which means God alone knows how many folk they might invite back for lunch.'

Cook was about to explode when the merriment in Joan's eyes caused her to pause. 'Get on with yer,' she said, playfully swiping Joan around the head. 'You've come out of your shell these past few weeks. Wouldn't have said boo to a goose when you first set foot in my kitchen.'

'Only teasing, my fair Kathleen. I wouldn't be hurting you 'cos I know you'd set the Irish little folk on to me, so you would.'

'Let me tell you, young lady, you're getting too saucy for your own good, and for your cheek you can put the kettle on and make me a pot of tea for a change.'

'Yes, ma'am.' Joan smiled and gave Cook a mock salute.

As she waited for the kettle to come to the boil she pondered on how a certain kind of comradeship had developed between Kathleen and herself in the last few months. Different as they were in background and age, they were curiously at ease with each other. Although they never talked about their previous lives, and no questions were asked, there was still a caring understanding. Without words being said they both knew the feeling of friendship was very real.

Joan had had her work cut out to make last-minute alterations and put finishing touches to the two evening dresses she had made, plus the evening suit which Mrs Hamilton insisted on saying was a work of art. It was with a sigh of relief that Joan tidied up the room, clearing the tables of reels of cotton, skeins of embroidery silk, scraps of material, and small tins and boxes which contained pins and needles of all shapes and sizes and several different-sized thimbles. Three different pairs of scissors and one pair of pinking shears were carefully wrapped separately in squares of white linen before she placed them in the huge wicker basket, overflowing with paper pattern and fashion magazines, that had served so faithfully as her sewing basket over the last few months.

Delia's dress could only be described as sophisticated. Black taffeta, it had a tight bodice with two wide shoulder straps, a very full skirt that fell in folds to the floor, and as the only decoration a small single red rose sewn into the right side of the waistband. To wear with it Delia had chosen red shoes with a small heel.

Fiona's dress was entirely different: a simple cream silk. Joan touched it tenderly. It was so elegant, and undoubtedly the one she was most proud of. It could easily pass as a wedding dress. The bodice was cut straight across in a wide band that fastened at the back with a row of silver buttons. There were no shoulder straps and no sleeves. The front of the dress was perfectly plain, while the back of the skirt was a mass of tiny pleats that fell skimming over the hips and falling in a straight line to the floor. Fiona's choice of accessories had been pale rose pumps and a small evening bag to match. To cover her bare shoulders Joan had made a long, wide stole of the same soft material and had edged the bottom of each side with a heavy rose-coloured silk fringe.

Mrs Hamilton's outfit was coffee and cream. Joan had copied the pattern from a sketch that Delia had drawn, and when their mother had had the final fitting both her daughters had declared that Joan had done so well it was perfection personified. The beige skirt was long and straight, with a slit in the centre of the back to make walking, even dancing, that much easier. The hip-length loose jacket was of the same heavy beige silk, with the collar, revers and wide turned-back cuffs all edged with a rich, dark brown velvet. The piping on the cuffs of the sleeves was embroidered with tiny pearl and crystal beads. Joan had also made a high-necked sleeveless vest to be worn beneath the jacket. Very plain but extremely smart, as befitted the lady of the house.

It was the kind of Christmas most people love to dream about, bitterly cold but bright and sunny. Earlier there had been a light fall of snow, then severe frost had covered the lawns, giving the grass a silver carpet. Icicles hung from the bare branches of the deciduous trees, whereas the evergreens were coated as if with white paint. From every window she looked out of Joan was enthralled by the view.

Everyone, including all the staff, enjoyed the magnificent dinner that Kathleen O'Leary had provided and drank wine from Mr Hamilton's vast cellar. During the evening the sounds of great merriment came from the drawing room as the family and their friends played charades, while downstairs in the huge kitchen four members of the indoors staff played cards: Cook, Miss Reid, Joan and Mr Farrant.

Just as they were about to start a hand of bridge, Mrs Farrant came to join her husband. 'Brr, it's cold out there,' she said, removing her gloves and rubbing her hands together.

Moving swiftly, Mr Farrant was on his feet, helping his wife to take her coat off. 'You said you weren't going to come over to the house, dear. I would have come for you if you had said.'

'I changed my mind, and it's only a few minutes' walk, and I knew the company would be good.' When an introduction had been made, Joan looked at the thin lady whose hand she was shaking. Mrs Farrant was very attractive. Pretty was not the right word. Dazzling would have been better, and Joan wondered how portly Mr Farrant had found himself such a beautiful wife.

'Please take my place, Mrs Farrant,' Joan said, moving hastily away from the table.

'Certainly not, my dear. I'm quite happy to sit and watch.' Even her voice was pleasant to listen to.

'You would be doing me a favour,' Joan insisted. 'I have never played bridge in my life, but as Cook said they needed two pairs of players I was going to give it a try. I'm really glad not to have to. Truly I am. I'll sit by the fire and maybe learn a thing or two.'

Mrs Farrant was gracious in her thanks as she took Joan's place at the table. Now Joan was seated in Cook's favourite armchair close to the fire and she began to try to convince herself just how lucky she was and what a happy Christmas Day it had been. There was a bowl of fruit in the centre of the table, as well as sweets and chocolates which had been given as presents to the staff. A huge fire burned halfway up the chimney, chestnuts roasted and popped on top of the range and there was plenty to drink. What more could anyone ask for?

All the same, Joan was relieved when the day was over and she was able to go to her own room and let her thoughts run freely. Taking off her clothes she slipped her nightdress over her head, washed her hands and face in cold water and got into bed. Why, oh, why did she feel she wanted to lie there and cry her eyes out? It had been a good Christmas, but even with the house full of people she had felt lonely. Who did she have to wish her a happy Christmas? Not one single person of her own. Here at Mulborough House she had had everything good that money could buy, but today she would so dearly have loved to be at Martha's. To sit round a crowded table, all of them wearing cheap but colourful paper hats. To know that she was among people who loved her. Wanted her, because she was family. True, she felt secure here. She wanted for nothing. But . . .

She missed her sister and the whole of Martha's family. She missed the children who lived in the same street. They'd have been knocking on her door this morning, bringing her small gifts, and she would have managed to wrap up a gift for each and every one of them. Most of all she missed

Rosie. What would she have given her if she'd been at home? Not toys any more, that's for sure.

She missed Sid and Lenny and Bernie. Their teasing, their warmth and their laughter. Maybe each of the lads had a girlfriend by now and big-hearted Martha would welcome them into her home, pleased that she would have even more folk around her to mother. Working here, she led almost a life of luxury. But what good did it do her? She had no one to share her day off with. Nowhere in particular to go to. Letters were her only link with her family. She read and reread them, only to find that they made her feel even more lonely. Almost unwanted. Always the odd one out.

Sometimes Martha wrote about having gone to the school to see Rosie acting in a play. If she'd been there she would probably have made the costumes for all the children. Was this how it would be for ever? No. Because soon she'd be too old to be a housemaid. Kind as the Hamiltons were, they weren't going to house and feed her if she wasn't able to do her work or became ill and needed medical attention. Were they?

She had thought it was really nice when first she had been given this bedroom with its glorious view of the gardens and the countryside beyond, but at this moment she would have given a lot to be back in her old house in London taking care of poor old Granny Baldwin, even though it had entailed a great deal of hard work and money had been so short. Why, oh, why had Bill been as he was? Why couldn't he have taken a little more care of his own mother? *And why couldn't he have loved me?* He had done once. When they had first met he had often told her that he adored her. So what went wrong? Folk were wont to say that when poverty came in through the window, love went out of the door. Not true. At least not in every case. God knows Sid Brown had had his share of hard times but he'd walk miles to earn a shilling before he'd let Martha and his three children starve.

The more she thought about London and the people she had left behind the more lonely she felt. She sighed, then speaking out loud she said, 'I never thought I would miss my folk as much as I do.' She was tired, too. Tired of hoping that one day everything would come right for her. She turned over and buried her head in the pillow and cried bitterly.

It was in the early hours of the morning, when she had no more tears left in her, that Joan came to a decision. She would let the remainder of the holiday go by but as soon as the guests had left the house and things were back on to a normal footing she was going to ask Mrs Hamilton to let her have a whole week off. She had put in a good many more hours than she was paid for, and in fact for the three weeks leading up to Christmas she had not even taken her half-day off. She had been too busy sewing. She had quite a nice little nest egg put away, what with her wages and the money she had received for making the three outfits. Mrs Hamilton had given her five guineas. She supposed that was for seeing to the linen as well as making her outfit. Miss Delia and Miss Fiona had each given her two pounds. She now had enough money for her train fare and to buy each member of her family a nice present. They'd have a party while she was there. Better still, she'd write and ask Martha if they could have another Christmas Day. One that she could share in, when she would feel wanted and be part of a family again.

With that final thought she felt happier and at last fell into an exhausted sleep.

Chapter Ten

JOAN STOOD STILL and stretched her arms above her head. The effort helped to ease the pain in her shoulders. Her legs ached and her feet were burning. What a New Year's Eve it had been. They had had to bring Mabel upstairs to take coats from what seemed like a never-ending stream of arriving guests. Mr Farrant and herself had struggled through the evening meal, when twenty people had sat down to dine. Even when Mr Bruce had suggested the diners retire to the drawing room, it was not all over. Time and time again Joan had climbed the stairs in Mr Farrant's wake as they carried up trays of tasty morsels, all prepared and decorated by Kathleen. Surely the family and their guests wouldn't want to go on eating all evening? Some of the elderly folk, including Mr Hamilton, had settled themselves in front of the fire. The younger ones, led by Delia and her brother Bruce, were dancing to the loud music coming from the gramophone. At the far end of the room Fiona and her sister-in-law, Pamela, were plotting with others as to how they would put on the very popular game of guessing the names of famous people, the participants having been given very few details. Mr Farrant had poured drinks for everyone and even now was replenishing glasses. At last, Mr Bruce took him aside and told him, in no uncertain terms, that he had done enough for one day and should retire downstairs. 'And take Joan with you. She looks fit to drop,' he added.

Mr Farrant placed the whisky bottle and soda syphon on a side table with the utmost care and thankfully murmured, 'Thank you, sir.'

In the kitchen the atmosphere was warm and friendly. Mr Farrant and John, being the only two male members of the party, had made sure all the females had a drink and plenty to eat. Mrs Farrant was there, Miss Reid, Joan, Cook, Mabel the kitchen maid, and Mary the in-between, who had written permission from her parents to stay the night at Mulborough House.

Kathleen took a good swig from her glass of Guinness, looked at the clock and called loudly, 'Open the door wide, Mr Farrant, there's only two minutes to go.'

Each of them got to their feet, glass in hand ready to be raised, and not a word was spoken until the sound of Big Ben striking midnight could be heard coming from the wireless in the upstairs drawing room.

'Happy New Year,' all the members of the staff chorused. Everyone hugged and kissed each other on the cheek. It was 1 January 1928.

A sudden thought struck Joan. There had been no tall dark man entering the house bringing a lump of coal. Perhaps this household did not believe in first-footing. After all, she said to herself, they aren't Londoners, are they? And they certainly aren't Scottish. Every house in Scotland would have a first-footing tonight.

The new year brought Joan some unexpected good luck.

It had taken the staff two days to set the house to rights.

Beds had been stripped and laundry hampers filled with dirty linen. That was one blessing about this house: only smalls were washed. Everything heavy was sent to the Sunlight Laundry or to one of those new-fangled dry-cleaning premises. Joan thought they were a godsend. Still, there was furniture to dust and polish, baths and wash bowls to be cleaned. The smallest of the carpets were carried out into the back yard by the gardeners and hung over the clothes lines, where Mabel or Mary beat the dust from them using a bamboo beater shaped like a large paddle.

It was on the third day after the holiday, when Joan was preparing afternoon tea in the drawing room, that Mrs Hamilton entered the room on her own and Joan managed to pluck up enough courage to speak to her.

'Please, ma'am, would you consider allowing me to take a week's holiday? I would dearly love to see my sister and her family,' she said wistfully.

After a moment's thought Mrs Hamilton asked, 'How would you intend to travel, Joan?'

'By train to London and then a tram to Wimbledon, ma'am. I can walk from there.'

'Hmm.' Mrs Hamilton looked thoughtful. 'Of course you may have a break, Joan. You have certainly proved your worth. As to travel arrangements, leave it with me for the moment and I will see what we can come up with.'

'Come up with?' Joan was puzzled, not having the least idea what her mistress was thinking of.

Long ago, Joan had come to the conclusion that she had been unlucky where men were concerned. God knows Bill had hurt her enough. Now, as she stood facing Mr Hamilton and listening to what he was saying, she could hardly believe her ears. It seemed odd, because Mr Hamilton, although always a gentleman and appreciative of anything that she did for him, hardly ever spoke more than a few words at any one time. At the moment, however, his speech was quite fluent.

'Please, Joan, don't feel that you are obliged to accept my son's offer, but be assured he would not be going out of his way. Unless, of course, you would prefer to travel by train.'

Bruce Hamilton was standing beside his father's chair. The first time Joan had set eyes on him she had thought him a handsome young man. His hair was thick and dark, as his father's must have been before it turned white. 'What's the matter, Joan? Don't you trust me?' he asked, but his brown eyes were smiling. 'As my father has told you, I shall be leaving here on Thursday, which will give you two days to get yourself ready, and I can drop you off at any point in London that you care to suggest.'

Still, Joan's mind was in a complete whirl. A lift in a motor car! All the way to London. And the offer being made by the son of the house.

Having studied Joan's face for a moment or two, quite suddenly Bruce burst out laughing. Bending to speak to his father, he said, 'The penny has just dropped. We haven't explained to Joan that Pamela will be travelling with me.'

Joan knew her face had flushed, because he had read her thoughts. She knew darn well housemaids did not travel in a car with the young master of the house. Not on their own they didn't!

'Oh, Joan, I am sorry. I really haven't made myself very clear.' The old gentleman sounded so conscience-stricken that had the circumstances been different she would have thrown her arms around him and given him a hug. She had to restrain herself. 'What I should have said in the first place was my son and his wife will be going home, and as they have no passengers you could travel in the back of their car in comfort.'

Bruce leapt in. 'Well, now all has been made clear, are you going to travel with my wife and me? Oh, by the way,

I must mention that we shall be leaving at six in the morning as I have an early appointment in town. Is that all right?'

More than all right. It's bloody marvellous, Joan felt like saying. What she did say was, 'Yes, thank you, sir, and I am very grateful.'

'No need for you to feel you are under any obligation, Joan. I assure you, what my father said is true. You will not be taking me out of my way. Not in the least.'

Joan had never been in a car before. Oh yes you have, she reminded herself. On the day that they had buried her husband. Mr Young from the brewery had paid for one car to follow the hearse and she, Martha, Sid, Lenny and Bernie had travelled to the church in a large black limousine.

She didn't want to remember that day. This was different. As she slipped into the back seat and Bruce closed the door her heart was beating nineteen to the dozen with excitement. The smell and feel of leather . . . it was going to be a real adventure.

Pamela Hamilton half turned from where she sat in the front passenger seat and asked, 'Are you comfortable, Joan? If you should feel cold there is a travelling rug on the seat beside you.'

'I'm fine, Mrs Hamilton, really I am, more than fine, thank you.'

At such an early hour there was not much traffic on the road. The only hold-up they were caught up in was when Bruce tried to manoeuvre his car round a herd of cows that a young farmer, with only the help of a long cane, was urging to move off the roadway and pass through an open gate and into a green field that lay beyond.

As they neared London, Bruce glanced into his mirror. Speaking to Joan's reflection, he asked, 'Joan, is there anywhere in particular you would like me to set you down?'

'Wherever suits you, sir. I know London quite well – I shan't get lost.'

Pamela laughed. 'Well spoken, Joan. From the few times we've met I've never had you down as a country bumpkin.'

'How about the Elephant and Castle, then?' Bruce asked, smiling.

'Spot on, sir. Thank you. That will suit me fine.'

Joan stood a moment or two on the pavement after she had waved to Pamela and watched Mr Bruce drive away. She took a huge breath. Even the air smelt different. It wasn't quite eight o'clock in the morning yet the streets were full of people. Looking about her, she felt she had entered another world. 'You'd think I'd been away for years instead of only months,' she muttered as she watched the costermongers set up the market and the young boys their barrows. Big brawny men, their strong powerful arms steadying the loaded boxes they were carrying either on their shoulders or on top of their heads.

'Out the way, luv.' 'Shove over, me darling,' they called cheekily as they shouldered their way through. This was London and it would never change. Joan smiled broadly as one strapping great man brazenly winked at her. She didn't mind; in fact she felt flattered. After all, it was not so far from here where I was born, she was thinking as she wandered along to the nearest bus stop. She only had a few minutes to wait for the bus and when it came she decided to climb the stairs. From the top of the double-decker she would be able to see so much more.

Through the city, already bustling with activity, past Lambeth Palace and its gatehouse, over the bridge, looking down the dear old River Thames and seeing the brightly painted barges and the dirty sooty freighters which had brought coal down from Newcastle. As the bus neared Victoria station she gripped her small attaché case and slipped the strap of her handbag over her wrist, descending the stairs her mind was going way back into the past.

101

When she was on the pavement once more, for a moment or two she could not move. She was lost in thought. How different Bill had been before they had been married.

There had been days when he had brought her to Kensington Gardens and shown her the statue of Peter Pan, and they had stood holding hands, gazing at Kensington Palace. Another day they had spent time in Hyde Park. Bill had hired a boat and taken her on the Serpentine. It had been there that he had asked her to marry him. She had been so happy and excited, believing that the world was her oyster and that they would both live happily ever after.

She shook herself. Why, oh why, was she trying to relive the past? It was gone. Done with. And life with Bill had not been the happy time her mind was picturing now. She was looking through rose-coloured glasses, that's what she was doing. She shuddered, suddenly aware of the biting wind, which was blowing straight through her thin coat, getting right into her bones. She tugged her hat down tighter over her ears and pulled her scarf more securely round her neck. Her teeth chattered and her eyes watered from the icy blasts and she couldn't get to Martha's warm kitchen quickly enough.

Rosie had been in and out of the house like a jack-in-the-box for the last half-hour, looking for her Auntie Joan. Martha came to the gate. 'Still no sign of her?' she asked her daughter.

'No, not yet.' Rosie crossed her arms over her chest and shivered.

'Well, come on in.' Her mother waved towards the house. 'You'll catch yer death if yer stand here much longer, 'sides letting all the cold air into the 'ouse. Come on now, inside.' She put her arm round Rosie's shoulders and edged her towards the open front door.

They were almost inside when Rosie turned her head,

broke away from her mother and yelled, 'She's here! She's just turned the corner!'

Never mind the cold, with the wind behind her Rosie went flying up the street. Joan put her case down and stood still with her arms wide open and Rosie flew into them. Martha, watching them hugging as if they would never let go of each other, felt tears sting the back of her eyes and she lifted the corner of her overall to wipe them away before she bellowed, 'Are yer mad, the pair of yer? It's cold enough to freeze the brass balls off the pawn shop. Come on, get yerselves in 'ere before I shut the door an' leave yer there.'

Still holding tightly on to each other, aunt and niece were stepping over the front doormat when a young voice called, 'Oi, Mrs Baldwin, yer left yer case up the road.'

Martha looked at her sister and, half laughing but still half crying, said, 'You 'aven't altered. Lose yer bloody 'ead if it weren't screwed on.'

Joan took her case from the lad, thanking him, then she hesitated. 'Are you Johnny Carter?'

'Course I am, Mrs Baldwin. You come 'ome now? Me mum was saying you'd been gone a long time.'

'I'm going to have a little holiday, Johnny. Tell your mum I'll pop in and see her tomorrow.'

'All right, missus. Ta-ta.'

'Can we shut the door now?' Martha asked sarcastically.

Joan and Rosie both burst out laughing and would have hugged again but Martha pushed her daughter out of the way. 'You've had your turn,' she said. Then, turning to her sister, she spoke softly. 'God alone knows 'ow much I've missed you. You're a sight for sore eyes. Come here.'

Joan went willingly into those fat wobbly arms, laid her head on Martha's ample bosom and burst into tears. Martha stood holding her and rocking her for a good few minutes before she said, 'We must be mad. I've got the fire burning 'alfway up the chimney and the kettle has boiled dry twice and there's us standing out 'ere in this drafty passage! We must be a right pair of lunatics.'

The pleasure of that afternoon would stay with Joan for the rest of her life. The warmth of that small but sparkling clean living room, the tasty shepherd's pie Martha had cooked for their midday meal, telling Joan that they'd all have their proper dinner tonight when Sid and the boys got home.

The difference Joan noticed in Rosie was unbelievable. How could she have changed so much in nine months? She would be fifteen this year, probably going to leave school come Easter. She was taller, still slim and fresh-faced, with a mop of the fairest curly hair you'd hardly ever see the like of. And she spoke nicely, which pleased Joan a great deal. Not that her thoughts were knocking Martha. To her there had never been another person in the world like her sister and there never would be.

They chatted non-stop and it was a miracle that dinner was ever produced at all. When the menfolk came home it was sheer pandemonium. How a room the size of Martha's living room could hold so many people Joan didn't know. Sid was first through the door. His massive hands went straight round Joan's waist and she was lifted up to his face level where he held her and kissed her over and over again. When he did let her feet touch the ground once more he held her at arm's length, looked into her eyes, and asked, 'You been all right gal? 'Cos if you ain't then yer looks don't pity yer. Fattened you up a little bit, ain't they? And there's a bit of colour in them cheeks. Must be the country air.'

'Something like that I suppose, Sid, but you'll never know what coming home to this house and such a welcome means to me.'

'Well, gal, I've said it before and I'll say it again, home is where the heart is an' as long as me an' Martha have got a roof over our 'eads then you've got a home.'

Joan couldn't answer, she was so choked up. She had known she would be made welcome but she hadn't anticipated anything like this.

Now Bernie and Lenny were standing facing her.

'Goodness me, what a pair of good-looking fellas.' Joan felt quite shy of her nephews.

'Yeah,' Sid said proudly. 'Right chips off the old block, wouldn't yer say?'

There was only a year between them but the difference was visible, at least to Joan. Lenny, twenty years old now, was tough-looking, well over six feet tall and broad-shouldered. Bernie was not quite so tall, still well-built and strong, but he had an eager studious look about him and there was no arguing that he was well and truly strikingly good-looking. Both lads had large brown eyes and at this moment they were twinkling with merriment as they watched their aunt sum them up.

'Well, Aunt Joan, do we pass muster?' Lenny grinned cheekily.

'You know darn well you do. You're only fishing for compliments,' Joan told them.

'If you've all finished telling each other how wonderful you all are, I've a dinner ready to put on the table, so wash yer 'ands and sit yerselves up,' Martha said, doing her best to sound stern, but her happiness showed through. She had all her family round the table tonight and that gave her the greatest of pleasure.

But no more than it did Joan.

How she'd dreamed of sitting round this large kitchen table, staring at the old black-leaded kitchen range that wasn't half the size of the one at Mulborough House. But in front of Martha's was a massive steel fender with a lidded box fitted to each end, and now Joan was remembering the times she had sat there toasting bread on the end of a long toasting fork. Oh, it was so good to be home.

Her heart was swelling with love as they all enjoyed a homely meal. Only when it came time to say good night did a little doubt creep in. This was not her home. She was sleeping in Rosie's little room. To be honest, whichever way you looked at it she would be forty-two years old this year and she had no home to call her own.

Chapter Eleven

THE HOUSE WAS STILL DARK when Joan woke up, dark and cold. She couldn't hear anyone moving about and she hadn't any idea of the time. Martha had put a box of matches on the chair beside her bed so that if she wanted to get up in the night she could light the gas mantle. She pulled the blankets and the eiderdown up to her neck and snuggled down again, deciding she would have a little extra time in bed seeing as how she was on holiday. She didn't go to sleep again, though, because the street was coming alive and it was bringing back so many memories. The clip-clop of the horses drawing the milk cart, followed by the clinking of milk bottles as the milkman stood them on folk's doorsteps. Joan grinned when she remembered how men who had allotments would be out with buckets and shovels before they went to work. That is if the horses had obliged and done their business in the middle of the road. The steaming dung never lay there for long. Next came the paper boy, whistling as he delivered the daily newspapers, and then the clang of letter boxes as the postman did his first round of the day.

Better get up now. Too late – her bedroom door was being

pushed open and a smiling Martha came in holding out a steaming cup of tea.

'Sit up. I thought I'd spoil you for a change. Bet you don't get tea in bed in that posh house where you work.'

No, Joan thought, it's me that takes it to other folk, but then she chided herself. *That's all part and parcel of what you get paid for.*

She wriggled herself up and Martha put the tea down on the chair and plumped her pillows behind her shoulders. Then she kissed her, gave her a hug and told her, 'Stay there till the men are out of the way. Rosie will be in to see you before she goes to school. Mind you, I'm 'aving a helluva job to make her go. Says she don't feel well!'

They both laughed, knowing full well the only thing wrong with Rosie was that she wanted to stay home with her aunt.

'Oh, Joan, you don't know what it meant t' me to wake up and know you were here.'

Joan shook her head. 'It cuts both ways, Martha. There has been times when I've been so lonely I've thought about chucking the job in and coming back to London.' Yet she knew they were both thinking the same thing.

What was there for her in London?

You count yer blessings, Martha wanted to say, because Joan had fallen on her feet when she got that job down in Kent. She would also have liked to add, Sufficient unto the day; let tomorrow take care of itself. Instead she playfully pushed her sister and said, 'Anyway, I've got the porridge all ready for Sid and the boys. I'm just going to rake the embers of the range. It never goes out, not this cold weather, but I'll get it built up and the fire roaring away by the time you're ready to come down.'

Rosie had won.

Her mother had had to agree. How long would it be before they set eyes on Joan again? Rosie sat back on her heels and pushed a strand of hair out of her eyes. She was sitting on the rug in front of the fire and had been making toast for her mother, her aunt and herself.

'That'll be enough for now,' Martha said. 'Come and sit up at the table, 'cos as soon as we've had our breakfast, had a quick dust round an' made the beds, we can be off down the market an' the rest of the day will be all ours.'

Never had toast and marmalade tasted better, Joan was thinking, but she knew it was mostly the company. Just looking at her niece made her heart jump for joy. She really was a beauty. Rosie would break many a young man's heart before she was much older.

Between mouthfuls of hot toast, Rosie said, 'I'll come upstairs with you, Aunt Joan, 'cos if we make the beds together it won't take us long.'

'All right,' her mother agreed, 'but no playing about else by the time we get out all the best things will be gone off the stalls.'

'Do they still have a stall that sells remnants?' Joan asked.

'Now why did I know that you were going t' ask me that question?' Martha grinned. 'Still beavering away with yer needle, are you?'

'Oh, there's much more to it than that,' Joan told her, sounding really enthusiastic. 'Leave it for now, but when we sit down tonight I've got a whole lot to tell you.'

'You always were one for planning things on the quiet.' Glad to see the smile on her sister's face, Martha went on, 'You wouldn't believe the people what still knock on this door asking where you are 'cos they want something altered. One woman even wanted to know if you'd make her daughter's wedding dress and when I told her you didn't live here no more she asked if I'd do it. I ask yer. Me with a needle? I couldn't mend a hole if yer paid me a pound a stitch.' Then Martha added, 'Our Rosie ain't bad, though. I always said she looks like you, an' when it comes to needlework she takes after you for that an' all.'

Deep thoughts began to run through Joan's mind. She might never be able to put them into practice but it didn't cost anything to dream.

Even on a bitter cold day like today Joan loved the street market, and although Martha kept saying how much warmer it would be in the indoor market Joan and Rosie would not be persuaded.

'You go inside and do your bits of shopping, and then sit in the café and have a cup of coffee and Rose and I will come and find you later,' Joan said, patting her sister's shoulder kindly.

'I 'ate coffee and I need t' buy some fresh veg an' it's much cheaper out here on the stalls,' Martha grumbled, but she walked away, throwing over her shoulder the sharp words, 'I know you two. Don't take all day. I'll see yer in the café.'

The barrow boys were cheekily shouting their wares, each one trying to outdo the other. Paraffin lamps were lit as well as the gas jets above the stalls, relieving the gloom of the damp dark January day. Joan watched with pleasure as Rosie bent over the haberdashery stall, fingering soft ribbons and strands of velvet, exclaiming over the cards of buttons, so many varieties, from ordinary shirt buttons to coloured glass ones, and even silver and gold ones, in all shapes and sizes. There was braid to match. Oh, what she couldn't do with just ten per cent of this marvellous stock.

'There it is, Aunt Joan. It's the same lady and gent that you used to buy from. Look, over there. It's your material stall.'

Joan walked slowly towards the stall, savouring the sight of the bolts of cloth and remnants in every colour you could name laid out for buyers' inspection. Martin and Marjorie Goldsmith. Joan felt a surge of happiness. It had been ages

110

since she bought material from them. As soon as Martin spotted her he came round from behind the stall. He looked just the same, tall and gangly, with his hair flying all over the place.

'Joan, me darling.' He grinned, kissing her cheek.

'Oh, Martin,' she gasped. 'It's so good to see you. How are you?'

'Doing very well.' He grinned again. 'And it looks as if you ain't doing too badly yerself.'

Marjorie had finished serving her customer and soon she too was kissing and hugging Joan. A lovely smart lady, was Marjorie, and she made every customer feel that their custom was important. A great dressmaker herself, she was always ready to offer advice, and Joan had brought many a problem to her when she had first started to sew for other people. 'I was sad to hear that you'd gone away into service, Joan,' she said now, still keeping her arm round Joan's shoulders.

'Needs must when the devil drives.' Joan smiled. 'But I'm on holiday for a week, staying with my sister Martha.'

Marjorie turned to Rosie. 'You used to come and tell me how your aunt was doing, but we haven't seen you for ages.' She looked back at Joan. 'My God, she's a beauty and no mistake. Make a wonderful model, she would.'

The kind words had Rosie blushing, but the very thought set Joan's mind working overtime. Plans. That's all she had at the moment, but if only!

Marjorie linked arms with Joan. 'You do know everyone round here is so proud of you,' she said. 'When we think of what you've been through and the fact that you literally lost everything and then had to go into service just t' put a roof over your head. It all seemed so unfair. We were all concerned for you and most of us still are.'

'Thanks, Marjorie. I don't know that I did the right thing, but at the time I hadn't any choice.'

'Martin and I had hoped you would come to us for help. We could have put many a sewing job your way. My main thought at the time was that there isn't a maternity stall here on the market. You know the kind of thing: cheap wrapround skirts and loose tops for mums-to-be, then maybe baby clothes and even pram covers.'

'That's the kind of thing I would love to do,' Joan confessed, 'but work was not the only problem. I had to find somewhere to live, somewhere with a rent that I could afford.'

'You could have gone on living with us,' Rosie chipped in. 'Me nor me mum wanted you to go away.'

'It wasn't fair to sponge off your mum and dad any longer,' said Joan regretfully as she turned swiftly to Rose and took her hand in hers.

Martin was busy measuring and cutting cloth and there were several customers waiting to be served. A middle-aged man, who sold ready-made dresses with his brother from a stall opposite the Goldsmiths', called, 'It's all right, Marge, you chat away with Joan. I'll give Martin a hand.'

'That's Jack Parker, isn't it? And his brother is Brian. They must have been on the market a few years by now,' Joan remarked thoughtfully.

'Yes, you're dead right, Joan. Thing is, stalls don't very often come up for rent, not on the open market at any rate. They get passed from one member of the family to another, hardly ever does a mother or father let one go.' Marjorie informed her. 'Still, I'll keep me eyes and ears open for both an opening and a decent flat, and I'll let your Martha know if anything comes up. You can always say no if you decide you've made the right decision, but I'll tell you this for nothing, love. Service wouldn't do for me. And with the talent you've got, well . . . but keep on with your sewing and if we can help at any time you have only to ask. You know that, don't you? Never could understand why you upped and disappeared so quickly.'

112

'You always were so good to me.' Joan hugged her.

'You won't have heard, but Martin has his own warehouse now and we have a shop in Balham, so any time you need some cloth you know where to come.' Marjorie laughed. 'Got a gorgeous length of white grosgrain there. Make a lovely wedding dress.'

'Oh yeah.' Both Rosie and Joan laughed.

'Course, I'll find something smashing for your aunt to make up if you're thinking of being her bridesmaid,' Marjorie teased Rosie, looking slyly at Joan, who grinned.

'I've got one answer for you, my dear friend: with me it's a case of once bitten twice shy. But I could do with some remnants today. I've a sewing machine at my disposal where I work and making a few bits for myself for a change wouldn't come amiss.'

'Since you've mentioned it, Joan, I'd say that coat you're wearing ain't exactly keeping the cold out.' Marjorie turned to nod at her husband and silently mouthed a few words. Martin dived underneath the stall and came up with a bulky brown paper parcel which he held out to Joan.

'What is it?' Joan asked, reluctantly taking hold of the parcel.

'You tell her, Martin. I've got t' go now, luv, customers waiting, but I meant every word I said and you know I did. We're here when you need to talk.' With that Marjorie leaned over and kissed young Rosie first and then Joan, holding on to Joan's hand for a long minute. Which said far more than words to Joan.

'Martin . . .' Joan was lost for words. She was clutching the bulky parcel to her chest and finally she managed to say, 'Please let me pay you for this.'

Martin grinned. 'You'd buy a pig in a poke, would you? Don't be so daft. It was a special order that we had to buy in and that piece was surplus to requirements. We are not a penny out of pocket so you are more than welcome to it.'

113

'Martin,' Joan said shyly, 'I stopped believing in the tooth fairy years ago. But thanks. Thanks a million.'

'Do me one favour,' he asked as she and Rosie turned to go.

'Anything.'

'Don't be a stranger. Come and see us more often – and we want to see that material made up and you wearing it. That's part of the deal.'

Rosie's eyes were wide with excitement as they made their way to the café to meet Martha. 'Wonder what sort of stuff it is? What colour?' she kept saying, once she had related every detail of what had happened to her mother.

'Well, you are going to have to wait until we get home to get the answers to all your questions.' Joan held out a ten shilling note and said, 'Be a dear and fetch me a cup of tea and a Bath bun and anything you fancy for yourself.'

'Ooh, ta,' Rosie answered, lapsing into the kind of speech that was going on around her.

'Wait a moment,' Joan called, having glanced at her sister's empty cup. 'Fetch a fresh tea for your mum and make it two Bath buns.'

It was darts night down at the local pub for Sid and his sons. With dinner all over and the chenille tablecloth covering the wooden top of the table, Joan and Rosie sat with a pad of plain paper and a pencil in front of them.

'Don't be giving me any of that,' Martha said from the comfort of her armchair besides the fire. 'I couldn't make a sketch of a tom-cat, never mind a winter coat. But I have to say I've never seen a finer piece of cloth in all me days.'

The parcel had been undone and the oohs and ahhs had shown how much the contents were appreciated. The colour of the cloth that Martin had given to Joan was beige according to Martha, biscuit according to Rosie and camel according to Joan.

'Let's leave 'em to it,' Sid had bellowed as the argument hotted up.

The opinion that the fabric was a very soft pure wool was unanimous. Martha had it in her lap, letting her fingers run slowly over the surface. How kind some people could be. She prayed with all her strength that Joan would be able to make herself a really decent coat from this unexpected gift. God knows she deserves it, she thought as she looked at her sister and Rosie with their heads together. A lump came to her throat. Why had her sister experienced so much bad luck? It never came to those who deserved it. Why did she have to be so far away all the time? In order to make a living, was the only answer she could come up with.

Joan softly cursed under her breath as she and Rosie discarded another drawing. 'We both have a good idea of the coat I would like to make,' she said as she watched Rosie throw her pencil down, 'but we are never going to be able to make our own pattern, never mind put scissors into that cloth, until we are absolutely sure that we know what we are doing.'

'You can buy patterns for coats, can't yer?' Martha's deep growl made them both jump.

Rosie sorted through the pages of paper that they had cast aside until she found the one she was looking for. 'This is the one we agreed we both liked the best, Aunt Joan, though each of us said we hadn't got it exactly right, didn't we?'

Joan took the drawing from Rosie's hand and studied it closely. It was one of Rosie's sketches. Wide collar, large revers, double breasted, two side pockets cut on the slant. 'No belt,' Joan murmured.

'I thought a half-belt at the back with two enormous buttons would look different,' Rosie said wearily.

'Oh, darling, it is cleverly drawn. It is along the lines of what I think is known as a reefer coat.' Joan raised her head

115

to look at her niece and said swiftly, 'Oh, I am sorry, pet. You look tired to death. Let's clear all this away and leave it for tonight. I'll make us all a cup of cocoa. Is that all right, Martha?'

'For God's sake,' Martha moaned. 'You don't 'ave t' ask. You know where everything is an' you making us all a hot drink is the best idea you've 'ad tonight.'

Rosie had just finished straightening out each drawing and was putting all the coloured pencils they had been using into a wooden pencil box when Joan came in with the tray. When they each had their drink Joan glanced at her sister.

'Fancy a trip to Croydon tomorrow? I take it Grants is still there.'

'Course it is,' Martha said, looking thoughtful. 'Bit posh, though, and very expensive.'

'I'm only think of buying a pattern and maybe some sateen for the lining,' Joan said gloomily.

'A pattern I agree. You won't get a decent one anywhere else, but you ain't spending good money buying lining from Grants. Not unless you've come into a bloody fortune.' Martha finished on a laugh. 'Besides, you ain't going back for days yet. We can still take another trip to the market. Oh, and that reminds me, Mrs Bradshaw called in when you were upstairs before dinner, said she couldn't stay but if you could spare a few minutes she'd love to see you. I told her you'd probably pop over early in the morning.'

'Mrs Bradshaw, eh? Course I'll go and see her. She was very good to me. Especially when I had that job making lampshades and had to go to the factory two evenings a week. She used to come over and sit with Granny Baldwin – though sit is probably not the right word. Such a busy lady, Mrs Bradshaw, always on the go. Used to bring a pile of ironing over to my house to do rather than just sit and twiddle her thumbs.'

'Yeah, well, when you were brought up like we were you

116

learnt to keep busy. Remember what Dad used to say? The devil finds work for idle hands.'

Joan smiled at Martha. 'And whenever we got given a job to do, such as cleaning those long brass stair-rods, Mum used to put that wooden motto in the middle of the table.' Rosie looked on in amazement as her mother and her aunt fell about laughing, both saying in a sing-song tone of voice, '*If a job is worth doing it is worth doing well.*'

'I'm going to bed,' Rosie said, her own lips curling with laughter as she hugged each of them in turn. 'Good night, God bless.'

Chapter Twelve

JOAN RAPPED ON THE DOOR with her knuckles. If she were still living in this area she would slip her hand through the letter box and pull out the length of string to find the door key that was always fastened on to the end. It seemed a bit of a liberty to let herself into Mrs Bradshaw's house when it was such a long time since they had met. The front door opened and Joan got quite a shock. Mrs Bradshaw had aged so much, and her face had such an unhealthy drawn look, that for a second Joan did not recognise her.

'Ah, it's you, Joan dear. Please come in.' The old lady smiled and stepped back to let Joan come inside.

Joan felt uncomfortable as she sat in the homely kitchen that she remembered so well from the time when they had been good neighbours. Mrs Bradshaw seemed to be staring strangely at her, and when at last she spoke her voice was not at all steady.

'Oh, Joan, I've got something to tell you, something I think you should know, and yet I am not at all sure that it would be right to open up old wounds.'

'Mrs Bradshaw, whatever is it? You look done in.' Joan put out a hand and patted her knee, but her own heart was thumping with apprehension. Whatever could have happened to affect this kind lady so much? 'I'll make you a strong cup of tea,' she offered. Receiving no reply, she took herself out into the scullery, found the teapot, ladled in two heaped spoons of tea and took the pot back into the living room, where a large black kettle was singing away on the back of the range. Having poured the boiling water on to the tea leaves she set the pot to stand in the hearth and fetched a cup and saucer from the dresser. She looked around but couldn't see any milk, and then it dawned on her that the bottle was probably standing outside the back door. It was certainly cold enough out there to stop the milk from turning sour.

She was right. There was half a bottle of milk with an upturned earthenware pot covering its top on the back doorstep.

Mrs Bradshaw accepted the tea gratefully and as she sipped it a little colour gradually came back into her cheeks. At last she began to speak, shaking her head from side to side. 'As I said, I have something to tell you. It will come as a shock, and I'm sorry.'

Joan was well and truly bewildered by now. She turned to look at Mrs Bradshaw, a slight frown on her face. 'Whatever it is, I think you had better tell me and be done with it. Come on, get this thing that's worrying you off your chest. You know what they say: a trouble shared is a trouble halved.'

Mrs Bradshaw took another sip of her tea. 'It's about my granddaughter. You must remember Linda? My daughter died when she was born and she lived with me all her life 'cos her father married again within six months and his new wife couldn't be bothered with another woman's baby.' She paused and tried to catch her breath. Meanwhile Joan was completely at sea.

'I well remember Linda. I watched her growing up. There

was a time when she used to come round to my place quite a lot. Kind girl, was Linda; she used to sit and talk to Granny Baldwin. Weren't many youngsters who would give a sick old lady the time of day.'

Mrs Bradshaw muttered something, but Joan didn't catch her words.

'Anyway, what about Linda?' Joan prompted. 'Something must be wrong. You look worried to death. I can see you're not yourself. Linda moved away some time ago, didn't she?'

'Yes, she did.' Mrs Bradshaw kept her head down and would not meet Joan's eyes. 'Just over two years ago she came t' me an' told me she was pregnant. She was only sixteen. The shock of it nearly killed me, I can tell yer.' Now she had actually got to the point, there was no stopping her. 'I wasn't 'aving my good name dragged through the mud. Folk 'ave a rotten name for a baby born out of wedlock and what they call the mother doesn't bear thinking about. Bad enough if we could 'ave 'ad a shotgun wedding. But oh no, the father was a slimy git, he got off scot free. My Fred only just stopped short of blaming me. Said I should 'ave kept an eye on her, but I didn't know she was carrying on with a married fella. Anyway, give the girl what's due to 'er, she up an' left this house, more for my sake than anything else. She kept in touch. I 'ad a few letters. Apparently her and a mate both got a job and a flat and they did shift work bringing the baby up between them. Then it became a case of be sure yer sins will find you out. Her friend got herself married and moved out, and then my Linda met a bloke who wanted to marry her and take 'er back to where he came from. New Zealand, would you believe.'

Joan remained silent while Mrs Bradshaw nervously cleared her throat before continuing. 'Talk about history repeating itself. This fella was keen enough to have my Linda, the baby was another matter altogether. He wanted nothing to do with the boy. Oh yeah. I didn't say, did I? It was a boy. He's about eighteen months old now.'

A white-faced Joan badly wanted to ask what all this had to do with her. A fearful expression had settled on her face. She could smell trouble brewing and to be honest she just wanted to get up and go. She couldn't bring herself to do it. This old lady had been kind to her in the past and more so to Granny Baldwin, yet fear was gripping her heart and she somehow knew she was going to be very sorry that she had walked into this house this morning.

'Better finish what I've started.' Mrs Bradshaw sighed. 'A month ago my Linda asked me to meet her on Victoria station and spend the afternoon with her. She told me she had put the child into care with a view to having it adopted and the very next day after we met she was off to New Zealand. Just like that. All cut and dried. Going to get married and live out there, so she said. Can't say I altogether blame 'er. Have to grab at what bit of 'appiness yer can get in this life. She'd done well in my opinion. At least she had tried to bring the child up on her own.'

Sitting there in the cosy living room Joan felt horrified, knowing she had to ask the vital question. Yet in her heart she already knew the answer, because there could be only one reason why Mrs Bradshaw was pouring the tale out to her now.

'So you've brought me here today to tell me who the father is? I am right, aren't I?'

Mrs Bradshaw really did look worried to death. Tears trickled down her cheeks and she began to cry. 'I loved my Linda from the day she was born. I was her mother in every sense of the word. What that bastard did to her wasn't right. She was only a slip of a girl.' She waved her hands at Joan as though trying to tell her to go.

'I'm sorry to see you so upset, and truly I do understand,

121

but please, Mrs Bradshaw, you asked me to come here this morning because you wanted to tell me something. Be honest. You haven't told me the main part, have you? You've only hinted, and I can't live with that. So please, find the courage and tell me who the man was who made your granddaughter pregnant.'

'Your husband. Bloody Bill Baldwin.'

Trembling with anger, Joan went to the sobbing woman and held her in her arms. Somehow she had to find words that might comfort this grandmother, but it would be one of the hardest things that she had ever had to do. What she really wanted to do was get out of this house. But she breathed in deeply and spoke with as much sympathy as she could manage.

'I can only hope and pray that you might feel relieved, even find a little comfort in the fact that you have been able to tell me this terrible, shameful secret, which came about because of the wrong my husband did. From now on you have to believe that Linda will be settled and happy in her new life.'

Mrs Bradshaw dabbed at her eyes and managed to smile at Joan. 'I've tried to tell myself all that, but what it really means is I shall never see my granddaughter again. At my age I'm never going to visit New Zealand. Nor will I set eyes on the baby who is rightfully my great-grandson.'

Joan could find no answer to that.

The silence between them hung heavy until Mrs Bradshaw timidly asked, 'Did I do right to tell you?'

Joan had to sniff hard. Again she couldn't bring herself to voice the whole truth. 'If telling me has made you feel better, then I am pleased that I was able to listen.' Feeling that she couldn't just walk out and leave the old lady suffering as she was, she added reluctantly, 'Perhaps you'll come over to Martha's and have a cup of tea with us before I have to return to Kent.'

'I can see I've upset you, but if you really mean it, thanks very much, Joan. I'd love to.'

Joan covered the short distance back to her sister's house very slowly. Should she tell Martha? She had to tell someone. If she kept mulling over and over this turn of events she'd end up going out of her mind. Bill Baldwin! Even dead and buried he was still intruding, upsetting her life, to say nothing of the poor young girl he had made pregnant.

Why hadn't she noticed anything wrong at the time? She knew the answer to that question only too well. For one thing, he had never told her where he was going or when he would be back. And another reason was that she had learnt the hard way not to ask questions. She needed no reminding that all she had ever got for her trouble was not a straight answer, just a slap round the head to begin with. Should she have been daft enough to persist, a jolly good beating would have followed.

The business with Linda, however, was a terrible shock. She had always known her Bill was a gambler, an out and out liar, and someone with a reputation for being a lady's man. But a young girl! Hardly out of school!

To say the least, that must have been his dirtiest trick ever.

Martha took one look at her sister's face and cried, '*Joan!* Gawd almighty, what's 'appened? What's wrong?'

Joan lowered her eyes. 'Oh, Martha. I just don't know where to start.'

'Sit down, do, Joan. Before yer fall down. And a good place t' start is always at the beginning.' Martha took hold of Joan's hand and found it icy cold. 'Oh my God, girl, you're like an iceberg!' She began to chafe her hands between her own. 'What in the world is the matter with you?'

Joan was trying to tell her, but it was hard. Her teeth

123

were chattering so that speech was difficult and the words, if they came out at all, were disjointed. And now for the first time helpless tears began to trickle down her cheeks.

'What did Mrs Bradshaw say to you that seems to 'ave turned your world upside down?' Martha pushed Joan down into an armchair and then perched herself on the edge of the chair opposite her. 'Come on then, out with it,' she commanded.

Still Joan hesitated, but she knew she had to share the sad story. The question was how to do it. Yet she didn't feel that she should be held responsible for Bill's misdeeds. She fiddled with the wedding ring she still wore, avoiding her sister's gaze. Then she took the bull by the horns, lowered her voice and, speaking slowly, did her best to repeat word for word the tale Mrs Bradshaw had told her.

When she had finished, Martha was biting her bottom lip and her cheeks were bright red, but so far she hadn't said a word.

'I suppose I'll have to seek legal advice.'

Joan had spoken with such sadness that Martha got quickly to her feet and moved to stand looking down on her. 'You ain't gonna bother about no advice, Joan, legal or otherwise. All of what Nellie Bradshaw has told you 'appened over two years ago. I reckon her Linda was a great kid. She took it on the chin and now, after having done her best for the baby, she's decided to cut an' run. *Her* decision. *Her* choice. She's done what she thinks is best for her child an' now she's gonna make a new life for 'erself, an' I fer one say darn good luck to her.'

'But what about Mrs Bradshaw? She's ever so upset,' Joan stammered.

'Nellie Bradshaw should count 'er blessings. Things might 'ave turned out a whole lot different if at the time Linda found she was pregnant her grandparents had said sod the neighbours, ignored all the gossip and stuck by Linda and let her keep the baby. Mind you, I ain't saying that would have been the right decision.'

Joan's face went bright red. It didn't bear thinking about. The entanglement that would have come about if two years ago Mr and Mrs Bradshaw had encouraged Linda to stay around and have the baby!

Martha gave her sister a wry grin. 'I can read your thoughts, yer know. I can tell exactly what's going through your mind. Would 'ave been a right old shemozzle, wouldn't it? I got ter say again, I admire that Linda.'

What Martha was also thinking was that it would have broken her sister's heart to see a young girl with a baby in her arms that had been fathered by her own husband. Best not voice those kinds of thoughts out loud, she scolded herself. Pulling the kettle near to the front of the range she said, 'It's on the point of boiling. We'll 'ave a cuppa an' I'll put a drop of the 'ard stuff in it. Do us both good.'

Soon they were both sipping the tea to which Martha had added a good drop of whisky, each busy with her own thoughts. Martha was the first to speak.

'It must 'ave took that young girl some courage to meet up with her grandma and tell 'er to her face that she's gonna live on the other side of the world. *And* to be honest enough t' tell her what arrangements she had made for the baby. There's some that would 'ave just gone off without saying a word an' Nellie wouldn't 'ave been any the wiser. No, say what yer like, that Linda's been a brave girl. Right from the start when she moved out, not leaving the mess on her gran's doorstep.'

Joan couldn't bring herself to believe how callous her sister was being. 'Martha, don't you care that little boy is my Bill's son?'

Martha assumed a measure of dignity. 'To be honest, Joan, no, I don't care. That child is better off without Bill Baldwin as his father. If I'm sorry at all it is because young

Linda's new boyfriend isn't willing to take him on. It would seem he asked Linda to make her choice and she has. She might live to regret it and she might not. But that's her business. You have to go along with it and leave it at that.'

Still Joan did not feel it was right. 'The little boy has been placed into care,' she protested.

'I'd bet my last tanner not for long.' Martha pressed her point. 'If he were ten or eleven I'd say he hadn't a chance in hell of being adopted, but a dear little boy, hardly more than a baby, there'll be couples lining up to give him a good home.'

'So I'm to sit back and do nothing.' This time Joan shouted at her sister.

'Actually,' Martha tried her best to soften her voice, 'that is exactly what you should do. Bill is dead. Nothing will alter that fact, and as I've already said, I reckon that Linda has sorted matters out very well, all things considered. After all, it's her life we're talking about. So it was up to her an' her alone to make the choice.'

Throughout the day Joan repeatedly told herself that Martha had given her a straight talking to. She almost came to believe that the suggestions she had offered were sound advice. One very sore point rankled, though, and it probably would for the rest of her life.

How she would loved to have had children. From the day she and Bill had been married it had been her dearest wish. Her arms ached when she thought of the three miscarriages she had suffered. But nearly's didn't count. She had never got to hold even one of her babies.

She would go to the ends of the earth to find this little boy if she thought she might be allowed to adopt him. To hold him in her arms. Be allowed to bring him up as her very own boy. Love him for always. However, common sense told her it would be as useless as banging her head against a brick wall. She was on her own. Adoption societies would be looking for two parents. Another point: she'd be considered too old. Anyway, what security could she offer a child? Where would she take him to live? How would she keep him fed and clothed? What education would she be able to offer him? Stop it. *Stop it!* Her head was going round and round, and the more she tried to convince herself that she should do something for her husband's son the more confused she became. At last she made herself acknowledge that she had to do what Martha had said she should do. Absolutely nothing.

All the same, she knew this was not the end of the matter. At the end of the day it would not be gone and forgotten. In the future there would be many a time when her mind would be full, wondering where that little boy was and whether he was happy. To think it could have been her and Bill's son. She must strive hard not to dwell on what she had been told, because the irony of it was enough to break her heart.

She closed her eyes, hating herself for the resentment she felt. If only things could have been different. If only . . . Best to let sleeping dogs lie.

Chapter Thirteen

THE DAYS THAT FOLLOWED went far too quickly. Martha and Joan had a day out on their own looking round the shops in Croydon. Of course their first stop had to be in Grants, where they had sat in armchairs and waded through endless pattern books. Spoilt for choice and undecided, they had been approached by a young lady dressed in the customary little black dress with a white collar, who asked politely, 'Would you two ladies like any help?'

Joan explained that she had been given a present of a length of cloth and was intending to make herself a winter coat. 'I was thinking of a double-breasted one with perhaps raglan sleeves.'

'I would be better able to advise on a pattern if Madam would say what type of cloth it is, and the colour would be helpful.'

'I've been told it is seventy per cent pure wool and thirty per cent cashmere.' Joan spoke hesitantly. 'And beige – or maybe you would call it camel.'

'Madam is not taking the material to a tailor?' The shop assistant sounded horrified. Joan realised that although the clothes she was wearing were neat and tidy they didn't send out the message that she could afford material made of such fine soft wool.

'It won't be the first coat I have made, nor yet the last I hope, but as the material was a present from a gentleman who owns a warehouse, I shall be extra careful when cutting the cloth.' Joan's answer was like an iron fist in a silk glove. The young lady's attitude changed immediately and she came as near to saying sorry as she could.

'We have a pattern for what is known as a reefing jacket. It can be made up to any length that Madam would wish.'

'That is kind of you. I would like to see it, if I may,' Joan said, smiling to herself, because she hadn't told the assistant that the gentleman also had a stall on the market. That bit of information she had thought it wise to keep to herself.

Martha smiled with pleasure and pride in Joan. She didn't know where her artistic talent sprang from but she knew from past experience that her sister's taste was always the best. She felt like telling this toffee-nosed shop girl that Joan was a natural genius when it came to sewing.

Joan knew instinctively that the pattern she was now looking at was exactly what she had been searching for. 'Thank you.' Joan looked up at the young lady, her blue eyes smiling sweetly as she said, 'That will be perfect.'

'If Madam would like to come this way I can show you a wide choice of linings and we could match up the sewing thread.'

'I'll just pay for the pattern, please,' said Joan as she rose from the comfortable chair that Grants provided for their customers.

Outside the shop the two sisters looked at each other and burst out laughing. Martha, still wobbling with merriment, said, 'Come on, let's find a café an' have a cup of tea.'

Joan went to the counter while Martha found two seats, and when Joan came back with two steaming teas and two plates that each held an enormous meat pie, Martha could not resist teasing Joan. 'I'll just pay for the pattern, please,' she mimicked. Then, in her own voice, she said, 'I noticed you didn't tell Miss Smarty-pants that Grants lining is three and eleven a yard and cotton is sixpence a reel, whereas on the market cotton is only tuppence a reel and lining starts off at a shilling a yard.'

'Course I didn't, yer daft ha'p'orth, but while I was waiting for my change I had the feeling that any minute now that's exactly what you were going to tell her.'

Martha let out a bellow of a laugh. 'I was sorely tempted, I'll tell yer. But you'd 'ave hit the roof and we both would 'ave got thrown out.'

'Eat your pie and shut up,' Joan pleaded. 'We'll go to the market and see Marjorie and Martin tomorrow. You can say what you like there without treading on anyone's toes.'

'What makes yer think I won't?' Martha was still giggling as she tried to drink her tea.

'Oh, Mum, please don't make me go to school today. I'll be leaving at Easter anyway.'

Rosie was pleading and Joan covered her mouth with her hand to hide her smile. She knew full well Rosie would win her mother over if she kept on long enough.

'It's not fair, Mum. You had Aunt Joan all to yourself yesterday when you went to Croydon. A few more days an' she'll be going back to Kent and how long before I'll get to see her again? I bet it will be ages and ages.' Rosie knew how to lay it on. Her beautiful big blue eyes were sparkling with tears.

'Oh, all right.' Martha gave in grudgingly. 'But we're going to the market first. Yer aunt needs to get a few things off Mr Goldsmith's stall.'

Rosie jumped up from the breakfast table, plonked a kiss on her mother's cheek, winked at her aunt and made a bolt for the door. Her voice was as sweet as honey as she called out, 'Shall I wear my Sunday coat and the new scarf that Aunt Joan bought for me?'

Both sisters shook with laughter. 'What would yer do with 'er?' Martha asked.

'Like you always do. Love her t' bits,' Joan answered, still laughing.

Joan was miles away as the three of them got off the tram and made their way to the lively market. She felt happy enough working at Mulborough House. True, when Christmas had passed she had sighed thankfully, relieved that it was all over. Even in a crowded room you could feel lonely if there was no one to call your own. These past days with her sister and her family had made her realise what she was truly missing. Her own home, and cheery companionship.

It would be almost February by the time she returned to Kent. The weather had not got any better; in fact they had announced on the wireless that all parts of Kent had suffered severe snow storms. That meant that even on her day off she would be unlikely to get outside the house. She had no friends or relations living locally whom she could go and visit. No, she said to herself, to be truthful I am not looking forward to going back to work.

'A bit quiet this morning, ain't yer, Joan?' Martha's expression was amused. 'You've got the feel of London again. Don't wanna go back t' be buried in the countryside, do yer?'

Joan shook her head. It was truly amazing how her sister could almost always read her thoughts.

They arrived at the Goldsmiths' stall and Martha related in detail to Martin and Marjorie what had taken place during her and Joan's visit to Grants. Jack and Brian Parker heard the laughter and walked across from their own stall. 'Can anyone join in?' Jack asked, smiling broadly.

Martha didn't need much persuasion to begin again at the beginning, exaggerating the details as it suited her until everybody was having a good old laugh.

'I'll cut you off enough lining now and throw in two reels of thread,' Martin said to Joan, 'though I think you should wait till you finish the coat before you decide how many buttons you are going to need.'

'You lot doing anything this afternoon?' Marjorie asked.

'Why? D'yer want us t' mind the stall for yer?' Martha giggled, staring at Martin.

'God forbid!' Martin cried. 'We'd have more customers demanding their money back tomorrow than we could deal with. Don't forget, Martha Brown, I've seen the way you slice a loaf of bread. What you would do let loose with a bolt of cloth and a pair of scissors don't bear thinking about.'

'Cheeky sod.' Martha grinned. 'You wait till you come to my 'ouse an' say you're 'ungry, I'll cut you a sandwich, you see if I don't.'

Marjorie butted in. 'If you lot have finished sparring I was going to suggest that you come home with me for the afternoon. It's not very busy here today. Martin can manage, can't you, love?'

'Do I have any choice in the matter?' He smirked.

'You do, actually. I could stay here with you all day and when we get home you'll get cheese on toast *or* I can sneak off now and have a really good dinner ready for you by the time you get home tonight.'

'Stewed steak and dumplings *and* the gravy thick with vegetables?'

'Yeah, all right then,' Marjorie agreed gleefully. To Martha, Joan and Rosie she said, 'Quick, jump in the van before he changes his mind.'

An excited gleam came to Joan's eyes as all four of them stood on the pavement in Balham outside a double-fronted shop which had a sign above it saying Goldsmith's Haberdashery. There were three people looking round inside the shop and two middle-aged ladies, both wearing long-sleeved black dresses, were serving. The first window was dressed to seem as if one were gazing into a lady's parlour. The backdrop had lace curtains in the centre, while a heavily embossed linen curtain was draped at each side, looped back and held by a silken rope from which hung long, heavy tassels.

Set out on various tables were bolts of cloth in all the beautiful colours of the rainbow. Cushions large and small were scattered on the floor, some plain, some braided, some with frilled edges, others with corner tassels. All could be colour-coordinated not only with the curtains but also with the lengths of material on display. There were also two amazingly beautiful standard lamps with huge lampshades so elaborately embroidered that Joan found herself longing to own one.

Moving across to stare into the second window even young Rosie let out a great 'Ah' on seeing the much lighter materials on show.

'Much more suitable for dressmaking,' Joan mumbled enviously to herself. There were a few rolls of suit-weight cloth, plus a great many bolts of both linen and cotton material, plain, patterned or floral. Again, it was no ordinary display, with a great variety of hats, gloves, shoes and handbags scattered loosely about, all compatible with the various shades of the draped cloth. Joan turned to Marjorie, her curiosity getting the better of her. 'Whatever gave you the idea of setting out such wonderful window displays?'

'It was Martin's idea in the first place, but who knows what made him think of it,' she answered with a shrug. 'All the backdrop framework – which is altered every now and again – is made for us by a man on the market, Jim Taylor.

I call him the bare wood man. Anyhow, it's freezing us all standing here. Come on upstairs and let's get into the warm.'

To Joan and Martha's surprise the flat above the shop was much larger and a great deal grander than they had expected. The kitchen was large and homely but the sitting room was something else, more like two rooms in one. A large sofa and several comfortable armchairs, a sideboard and two small occasional tables were set round a huge marble fireplace at one end of the room, while at the other stood the most beautiful mahogany table surrounded by six matching chairs. The carpet was attractively patterned and of a good quality. Within a very short time they had removed their coats and Marjorie was pushing a well-laden tea trolley into the room. The tea was hot and strong, the cakes absolutely delicious.

Joan couldn't take her eyes off Marjorie. Up until now she had mostly seen her behind the stall on the market, buttoned up to the neck in a heavy coat and wearing a scarf and a velvet hat. Even during the summer months she was never what Joan considered well dressed. Now she looked entirely different. She was wearing a sage green woollen dress which had a long straight skirt and long sleeves with wide cuffs decorated by a row of glittering buttons. The same ornamental buttons were sewn round the neck of the dress to form a collar. Joan was impressed. Marjorie looked immaculate. Before, her hair had been hidden; now the sheen of her wavy auburn hair was a joy to behold.

Rosie had found a jigsaw and was sitting on the floor quite happily finding pieces to fit the spaces. Martha thought she was in heaven. Big cosy armchair, feet up on a foot stool, nothing to do but glance through the glossy magazines that Marjorie had placed on the floor beside her. Weren't many lazy afternoons like this, not for her at least. Martha sighed contentedly.

For her part, Joan wanted to ask numerous questions and

Marjorie had detected as much. Apart from the fact that it was obvious that these two sisters loved each other dearly, there was no comparison. Martha had a heart of gold, was never discontented with her way of life, and her attitude was always take each day as it comes. Joan was intelligent besides being beautiful in a strange sort of way. She had the clearest of blue eyes, dark hair that had golden glints and a refined look about her even though she was not dressed as well as she might be. But my God, Marjorie was thinking, Joan Baldwin would pay for dressing. She could easily be a model, for she had a figure that most young women would die for. But she wasn't a young woman. Looking at her now and thinking of all the years she had known her, Marjorie came to the conclusion that Joan had never been given a chance. Worse than that, she had had a really rough deal.

'First question?'

Joan was startled. 'How do you know I wanted to ask questions? Everybody seems to be able to read my mind today.'

'Don't dilly-dally. Ask away.' Marjorie laughed. 'I won't be in the least offended.'

'Well . . .' Joan hesitated. 'The man you said made the backdrop for the window dressings, Jim Taylor, I think you said his name was.'

Marjorie looked surprised. 'That's not at all the kind of thing I thought you were going to ask me about. Why him?'

'Because you called him the bare wood man.'

'Oh, I see.' Now Marjorie threw back her head and laughed. 'I didn't mean he stood bare in the market.'

'I never thought you did,' Joan said, laughing at the thought, 'but I still can't fathom out how he came to be given that name.'

'Easy. He works with every different kind of wood he can lay his hands on. As a carpenter he ranks with the best but no matter what he makes, be it a plain pine shelf or a

135

mahogany table, he never gives it the finishing touches. He has a deal with a well-known firm that do the polishing and fix the handles. On his stall in the market he sells mostly cheap white wood things – clothes horses, stools, boxes of all shapes and sizes or anything you fancy he'll make to order. But tell me, Joan, why the sudden interest in Jim?'

'I did see a nicely shaped wooden stool in the market this morning. Didn't give it another thought until I saw the display in your shop downstairs.'

Marjorie frowned. 'I don't get the connection.'

'I don't know that I do exactly. But my thoughts were that maybe, only maybe mind, I might be able to teach myself to pad and cover the seat of a stool, kind of make it into a dressing-table stool, probably to match a pair of curtains or even a bedspread.'

Marjorie was suddenly intrigued, as she always was by new ideas. 'Jesus, gal, I'll have to get you talking to my Martin. You're wasted being a ruddy servant. You should have yer own shop. There's no limit to what you can do with a needle. I know that of old, and customers still ask after you. And as for the upholstery, you could get a book on that. Probably got several in the library.'

Joan was so surprised that Marjorie had taken her seriously that she was almost speechless. At last she found her voice. 'Oh yeah, I could reach for the stars but I'd never get them. Where would I get the money from to rent a shop, even if I found somewhere up here to live?'

'When are you going back to Kent?'

'Day after tomorrow.'

Marjorie glanced at her. 'Don't give up before you've even started. Take your time. Give a whole lot of thought to what we've talked about. You'd be more than halfway there as regards cloth and suchlike. Martin would see to all that for you, you know he would, and he'd give you credit till you got on your feet.'

Marjorie was talking so enthusiastically that Joan was halfway to believing it might all come about. Big ideas were rolling round in her head but still disbelief showed in her eyes. It would not be easy, Joan was well aware of that, but the seeds of ambition had been planted. Perhaps all she needed was determination. On the other hand, a great deal of dedication wouldn't come amiss either. That would only leave the question of how and where she was going to be able to come up with enough working capital to start her own commercial business. Her next thought brought her sharply down to earth with a bump. Suppose she did manage to convince a bank to lend her just enough money to start her off, where on earth would she find suitable premises?

'Lot to think about when you get back to Kent,' Marjorie said encouragingly. 'But you'll do it. I know you will. Just keep telling yourself, nothing ventured, nothing gained.'

Joan smiled at the dear friend who was going out of her way to help her, but she didn't answer her. She really didn't know what to say. Dreams come cheap. Reality was a different matter altogether.

Chapter Fourteen

JOAN'S THOUGHTFUL MOOD stayed with her for the rest of the afternoon and well into the evening. She was glad when their dinner was over and Bernie got out a pack of cards. Sid poured the drinks and they settled themselves round the table. Joan was grateful to Lenny and Bernie for staying at home this evening. They were only doing it because her holiday was almost over and they knew it might be some time before they all met up again.

'Listen, all of you,' she announced abruptly. 'There's something I would like to talk to you about.'

Martha looked at her sister closely, frowning. 'You sound serious, luv. I knew there was something wrong. You've been dead quiet ever since we left Marjorie's. If you don't tell us what's wrong 'ow the hell can we 'elp you?'

Joan hesitated, and cleared her throat. 'There's nothing wrong, honestly. It's just that Martin started the ball rolling by giving me that lovely material and then Marjorie came up with some ideas that got me thinking. She suggests that if I want to come back to live near all of you I should find an empty shop to rent, preferably one that has living quarters above it. She also said that she and Martin had spoken about me and that Martin was all for it, recommending I start up slowly at first, taking in sewing repair jobs, then progressing to making various things to sell.'

Sid's face turned red. 'I guessed you weren't all that 'appy, stuck away down there in Kent, and watching you these past few days all my fears 'ave been confirmed. I don't want you rushing into something you might be sorry for. Getting up to yer ears in debt. Don't be too 'asty. But if you're not 'appy then don't go back. I've told yer time an' time again, as long as Martha an' me 'ave a roof over our 'eads there will always be a 'ome here for you with us.'

'Please stay, Auntie. I know you don't want to go back,' Rosie pleaded tearfully.

'Oh, dear. None of you have understood what I was trying to say. I didn't mean to upset any of you. Of course I am going back to my job. I would never leave Mr and Mrs Hamilton in the lurch. What I will admit is that there are times when I feel really lonely. Though I know full well how lucky I was to be offered this job, and I really am treated very well, I'm not young and I have to say that the future worries me.'

'Good 'eavens, Joan, we wouldn't see you with nowhere to go.' Martha leant across the table and grasped her sister's hand.

Bernie, who was sitting next to her, put his arm round his aunt's shoulder and for a horrible moment he thought she was going to cry. 'Come on, Aunt Joan, buck up. You haven't finished telling us what it is you're thinking about doing, have you?'

'No, I haven't,' Joan said, looking thoughtful. 'I have loved being here and I do appreciate how you all care for me. It has made me realise just how much I do miss my family. All the same, I am going back to Mulborough House. It wouldn't be right not to. In the meantime,' she paused and looked at each of her dear ones in turn, 'I'd like you all to keep your eyes and ears open for a property that you think might be suitable, and if, and God knows it's a great big if, I can find enough money to start me off I would like to own my own business.'

There was a stunned silence, broken by a very excited Rosie. 'Cor, can I come and work for you, Auntie?'

Everyone laughed. Sid Brown found it especially funny. 'Well there you are, gal. Staff already pleading for a job. Just goes to show that yer niece has faith in yer.'

'Yes,' Joan said emotionally. She moved towards Rosie, who got to her feet straight away, and the two of them stood in front of the fire silently hugging each other tight. One middle-aged woman, and one young girl just starting out on the road of life, each of them letting her imagination run riot, building castles in the air.

The whole family had helped to persuade Joan to stay until the Sunday and take the midday train to Tunbridge Wells. Now, on this brilliantly sunny but bitterly cold February afternoon, she walked along the long drive that led to Mulborough House. She was lost in thought as she put her hand on the latch of the back door, but was suddenly startled back to the present by Kathleen O'Leary's voice as the cook came towards her with her arms outstretched.

'Ah, there ye are, me darling. Am I glad to see you.'

Joan went into Kathleen's arms, lowered her head, and kissed her affectionately on the cheek. She was unable to keep the worry out of her voice when she asked, 'Why, what's wrong?'

'Ah, Joan, I don't know where to start. I'll make us a pot of tea, you sit yerself down and while the kettle comes to the boil I'll begin at the beginning.'

Joan watched as the dumpy, lovable woman pulled the kettle to the front of the enormous range. Her hands were shaking and her head was nodding non-stop, and despite her words she seemed reluctant to begin her story. Joan pushed her attaché case across the floor with her foot until it rested against the wall out of the way, then returned to the table and laid out two cups and saucers. She wished to God Cook would tell her what had happened while she had been in London. She knew that sooner or later she would hear all the news, down to the very last detail, but not before Kathleen was good and ready. Yet having poured the boiling water on to the tea leaves the cook was stirring the tea round and round in the pot until Joan was on the point of asking her to stop. When at last the two of them were seated, each with a cup of tea in front of her, Joan could stand the silence no longer.

'Well, Kathleen, are you going to tell me what's been going on while I've been away? Because I don't have to be psychic to know that all is not well in this house at the moment, do I?' Joan demanded.

Kathleen looked upset. At last, she sighed and said, 'To start off Mr Hamilton had a stroke, only the day after you left. Mrs Hamilton wouldn't hear of him being taken into hospital so we've had nurses living in, day and night, an' by golly they want more waiting on than I should think the Queen herself does.'

Joan took her hand gently. 'I'm so sorry. How bad was the stroke, and how is Mr Hamilton now?'

'I haven't seen him, but the missus tells me he is in a very bad way. I gather all the right side of his body is affected, even his face. His mouth is so twisted he can hardly speak, and apparently his right arm is useless. When you go in to see him you should be prepared for quite a change in his appearance. He can only drink through a straw or a special feeding cup Mr Bruce brought down from London. I prepare special meals for him – have to mince or mash everything up – and the nurse feeds him, though she moans about the mess, says more food dribbles out than goes into him. Real

141

uppity those nurses are. Both the day and the night nurse think I'm here to wait on them.'

Joan could sense how worried and tired Kathleen was. She lifted her shoulders helplessly. 'This would have to happen when I was away. You must have had so much put on your shoulders.'

'You ain't heard the 'alf of it yet,' Cook said sharply.

'Well, whatever more there is to tell it can hardly be worse,' Joan said glumly.

'Can't it?' Cook looked at her reproachfully. 'Just listen to this. Miss Reid took a jug of coffee upstairs for the night nurse and was bringing that lazy beggar's dinner tray down when she tripped and fell from the top of the stairs to the bottom. We just couldn't move her. Had to send for the ambulance an' she's been in hospital ever since. Broke her hip, and her arm, would you believe.'

Joan sat back, placed her teacup down on its saucer and stared at her in astonishment.

'And before you ask if that's all, Mr Farrant's wife has been taken ill. Don't know what's wrong with her. Only know he comes up to the house each morning for about an hour and we don't see him again for the rest of the day.'

Joan could hardly believe that all these disasters had taken place in the short time that she had been away.

'Well, say something,' Cook demanded impatiently.

Joan shook her head sadly. 'I can't think of anything to say. So much worry for everyone.'

'You know what they say, everything comes in threes,' Cook said, leaning towards Joan and studying her face carefully. 'Worked out yet what this is going to mean for you, Joan?'

Those few words hit Joan almost as if lightning had struck. They had a far deeper meaning than Kathleen O'Leary could imagine. For, while Joan had thought that she had come to a decision regarding her future, she found that what she had just heard had changed everything. Now she really would have to make a choice!

She took the cups and saucers to the sink, rinsed them under the running tap and set them upside down on the wooden draining board. Then, feeling very far from confident, she turned to face Cook. 'I'm going up to my room to change and put my uniform on, and then I suppose I'd better go and speak to Mrs Hamilton.'

'Madam will be lying down. She needs her afternoon rest. Miss Delia and Miss Fiona have been here for about four days but they left on Friday. Mr Bruce and his wife are both in the drawing room. I think it would be best for you to have a word with them. They seem very capable and I for one will be eternally grateful that they turned up so quickly when they got the news about his father.'

While Joan changed her clothes, her thoughts were going round in circles. She had come back to Mulborough House fully convinced that she was going to hand in a month's notice. So much had been offered to her. Wouldn't she be doing the right thing, branching out on her own? If everything worked out as planned she would not only be earning a living but once again have a home to call her own.

On the other hand, what if everything failed? She had made up her mind to put that thought to the back of her mind. At least she would have tried.

Martha had confessed that she had thought Joan's idea of opening a shop very foolish at first, but later, having listened to Marjorie, she said she was beginning to think it might turn out for the best. At least it would bring her sister back to London and she'd see a darn sight more of her.

Sid had been very supportive. 'Go for it, gal. In this life if you're given the chance to achieve something it's best t' grab it with both 'ands, 'cos opportunity don't knock twice. With Marjorie and Martin backing yer I'd say yer can't lose.'

The offers from Martin and Marjorie had been amazingly generous. They had even asked if she'd like to work on their stall in the market until a suitable property could be found. 'Your expertise in sewing would be invaluable, especially with some of our more dodgy customers,' Martin had said laughingly. He had also reassured her that he was more than pleased to do as Marjorie had suggested. 'Unlimited credit until yer on yer feet, my darling. I'd not lose a wink of sleep 'cos with you I know I'd be backing a winner.'

Where else would she find such support and so many friends?

Jack and Brian Parker had urged her to take up the offer, telling her she would be an asset to the market. And she'd had a long talk with Jim Taylor, the bare wood man. She smiled to herself, thinking of the name that Marjorie had given him. When she had told him about her idea for padding and upholstering a dressing stool, he had suggested he make her one with a curved surface. 'Much easier on the ladies' bums,' he had joked. Joan had felt he was a thoroughly nice, middle-aged man, and if Martin said he was honest and reliable she felt sure he was right.

All these plans! Come to nothing now, wouldn't they? Not that any of them had materialised yet, but there had been a chance. A slim one, perhaps, but at least it had given her hope that maybe she could go back and live with her own kind. Somewhere where she knew people, could knock on several doors and always be sure of a cuppa and a chat. And the thought of owning her own little business had been a great ambition. Now what? She knew what she would like to do but she hadn't the heart. It would be like deserting a sinking ship.

She did her best to walk briskly down the stairs and tap lightly on the door of the drawing room.

'Come in.' Bruce's voice sounded firm. His pleasant face

144

lightened as Joan walked into the room. Both he and Pamela walked towards her, hands outstretched. 'Very pleased to have you back,' Bruce said as they shook hands.

'I am so sorry to hear your father is ill,' Joan said politely.

'Thank you, Joan. Please come and sit down. My wife and I have something to ask you.' Joan remained silent.

Bruce took a deep breath and said hesitantly, 'We'd like to offer you the position of housekeeper here in my parents' house.'

Joan spoke without thinking. 'You must be mad! Me, housekeeper! I wouldn't have a clue about the household books – and a good many other things besides.'

Bruce regarded her intently. She was direct and honest, there was no doubt about that. Her spirit was refreshing and his apprehension about her ability was rapidly diminishing.

Pamela spoke up. 'I take it Mrs O'Leary has given you the facts of the predicament we find ourselves in?'

'Yes, Cook did outline what has happened, but I have only just arrived back and am not sure of all the details.'

Bruce nodded. 'Of course, we could call a domestic staff agency. I am sure there must be one in Tunbridge Wells. However, my mother is not herself, and does not want too many strangers in the house. She is finding it hard to cope with the nurses, who are an unavoidable necessity, whereas she is familiar with you. Fond of you, I'd say. And of course your wages would be increased considerably.'

Joan hesitated. 'I don't really know what to say.'

Conscious that she was wavering, Pamela spoke up again. 'Joan, we wouldn't expect you to do the impossible. My husband and I have to be back in London by Tuesday and on Thursday we are due to go to Italy. We cannot allow our business to slide. Competition is always so great. We would feel so much better if we knew Mother had you here with her. Say you will give the job a try, if only temporarily.'

Pamela Hamilton was a nice person, but she thought she could always get her own way. Both Fiona and Delia asked favours from time to time, but their approach was much softer. Still, Mr Bruce had said her wages would be increased, and young Mrs Hamilton had said it could be a temporary arrangement. She could save the extra money towards a deposit for when she found premises in London. But how long was temporary?

Pamela leaned forward and touched her arm gently. 'Your duties wouldn't be that much different from what you have been doing. You have made yourself useful in so many ways, and if you need help with the heavier tasks we can ask the gardener to let you have one of his lads for a couple of hours each day.'

Joan shivered as another thought struck her. 'Cook said Mr Farrant wasn't able to be in the house on a regular basis now. Is that right?'

Bruce and his wife exchanged regretful glances. 'That unfortunately is true,' Bruce admitted. 'We aren't exactly sure just how ill Mrs Farrant is.' He sighed heavily. 'It seems to be true that troubles never come singly.'

A heavy silence hung between them. Joan felt she had to get out of the room before she committed herself to something she might later regret. She stood up and said, 'Please may I have a short while to think about this? I also feel I shouldn't make a decision until after I have spoken to Mrs Hamilton.'

'Quite right, my dear,' Bruce hastily agreed. 'My mother will be able to put you more in the picture as to my father's health, and the extra work all this trouble will entail for you.'

Joan quietly closed the drawing room door behind her, leant her back against the solid wood and let all her breath out in one great gasp. Talk about being betwixt and between! Would she have come back to Mulborough House if she had known the confusion that would be facing her? However,

146

it was too late to be asking herself such a question. She was here and she'd have to refrain from giving the family her answer until she'd had time to consider very carefully what she would be letting herself in for.

She went about her business, doing all the jobs she normally would have done. Tackling the dining room first she suddenly stopped short. How many should she set places for? Thank God for young Mabel, who came through the door beaming with pleasure and hugged her, telling her how glad she was that she was back.

'Only three places, Mr Bruce, Mrs Bruce and Mrs Hamilton.' Mabel told her, adding, 'Course, Madam would prefer to have her dinner on a tray and sit beside the poor master, but that day nurse terrifies her. She frightens the life out of me an' all. Still, as Mr Bruce keeps saying, it does his mother good to come downstairs and eat with them – not that she eats enough to keep a fly alive these days.'

'Thanks, Mabel.' Joan smiled. 'Can you tell me where Mrs Hamilton spends most of her time now?'

'I can tell you where she'd like t' be, day an' night, an' that's beside her husband, but the nurses won't hear of it. She stays in the small back sitting room staring out over the garden most of the time. She's only allowed to go in and see Mr Hamilton when the nurse says she may and even then she's not allowed to stay in the big bedroom for long. By the way, does she know you're back?'

'I'm not sure. I haven't seen her yet.'

'Well I'm just about to take her up a jug of cordial. Would it be all right if I tell her?'

Joan laughed. Mabel was like an excited child. Joan supposed that she must feel relieved there was someone else in the house now to take on some of the responsibility. Poor kid – she must have been run off her feet this last week.

'It would be fine, Mabel. Just let Mrs Hamilton know I

shall be waiting table for tonight's dinner and if she feels up to it I would like to have a chat with her this evening.'

'Oh, miss, she'll be over the moon. The times she's said to me that she'd feel happier when you came back.'

Joan had to keep a tight rein on her thoughts as she responded to Mrs Hamilton's greeting and watched as her son seated his mother at the head of the table.

She looked so fragile. The delicate features that had contributed so much to her beauty were now drawn and tired-looking. Her honey-coloured hair had turned almost white and her hazel eyes were filled with sadness. Joan watched her toy with each course, and as she removed each plate, the food hardly touched, she thought, I can't leave this woman. She offered me work and shelter when I had neither. I have to stay in this house for as long as she needs me.

It was eight o'clock before Joan tapped softly on the sitting room door and went in. She had always loved this room. It was small but neat, and not at all cluttered. The heavy blue velvet curtains at the window were drawn, but she well knew the glorious view of the gardens that lay beyond. The pieces of furniture that she had polished so regularly were dark mahogany.

Mrs Hamilton was sitting in one of two armchairs drawn up to a roaring fire. Gesturing to Joan to take the other, she said, 'I'm so happy to have you back, Joan.'

Joan felt she had to say, 'I am happy to be back, Mrs Hamilton.'

'You will stay even if you won't accept the position of housekeeper, won't you? Please say you will.'

The request was uttered so softly and so kindly that it brought a lump to Joan's throat. Then, speaking gravely, Mrs Hamilton gave Joan the precise details of the stroke her husband had suffered, and the consequences he was having to endure in the aftermath. Joan's blood ran cold as she listened. Mrs Hamilton's bearing and clothes were still immaculate, but by God she had aged. Joan shuddered, and her heart ached as she imagined the torment this poor woman must be going through as she watched her husband change from a normal man into a damaged invalid.

'Of course I will stay, and I will undertake as many of Miss Reid's duties as I can,' she said.

'I can't begin to thank you, Joan. My children lead such busy lives one cannot expect them to be here all the time. I shall see that not too much work is put on your shoulders.' Mrs Hamilton put out a slender hand and as Joan shook it gently Mrs Hamilton smiled and whispered, 'You won't regret your decision.'

Joan sighed as she stared into the fire. Beneath her breath she mumbled, 'I hope you're right. Believe me I do.'

Chapter Fifteen

Joan found settling back into a much more harassed way of life at Mulborough House more difficult than she had imagined. To begin with she was on the go from morning till night, and try as she would, she could not get used to taking orders from the four nurses who between them looked after Mr Hamilton. Without Miss Reid and Mr Farrant the atmosphere was totally different. Cook kept saying that they must take it all in their stride. But there didn't seem to be any time for joking or laughing. Hardly any time for the odd cup of tea.

Each of the nurses was harsh and demanding. Rigid discipline reigned. The only member of staff allowed to enter the sick room was Joan. She hated the smell of the oil with which the nurses continually rubbed Mr Hamilton's withered limbs. Her heart did lift when she dusted near to the bed or changed his water carafe and he recognised her and managed a twisted smile. The bedroom was enormous, light and airy, but to the old gentleman lying there it was still a prison. Why didn't they get him out of bed? Let him sit in a chair near the window? Of all the rooms in the house this one had the most breathtaking view of the garden and the fields beyond. If he wasn't able to sit in a chair, surely they could at least have moved the bed nearer to the window.

Four months had slipped by since she had come back from London, months that had seen the coming of spring with all the buds on the trees bursting into new life, and great clumps of daffodils, jonquils and tulips making a glorious blaze of colour while the air was heavy with their scent. Soon it would be high summer, and Joan found herself once again longing for a week's holiday. Two of the nurses had left, but their replacements seemed to Joan to be just as hard-hearted as their predecessors had been. Miss Reid had never been fit enough to return to Mulborough House and Mrs Farrant had died. Mr Farrant had somewhat reluctantly resumed his duties but he was not the bright soul that he had been and Joan often wondered whether, if it wasn't for the fact that the cottage in the grounds in which he lived was owned by the Hamiltons, he would have returned at all.

Mrs Hamilton was a considerate employer, satisfied as long as the household was running smoothly and there were no problems she was expected to deal with personally. Mr Bruce and his wife came down every other weekend, but they only stayed the one night. Mr Bruce would spend at least a couple of hours each day with his father. Mrs Bruce just about managed to put her head round the door of the bedroom where the dear old man still lay.

Miss Fiona and Miss Delia came down from time to time, always unannounced and always with requests that Joan sew up a torn hem of a dress or secure loose buttons on their blouses. They breezed into their father's room but never stayed long. One good thing the two daughters always did was take their mother out for a nice long lunch. It was a treat that Mrs Hamilton always enjoyed, praising her girls for being so thoughtful. Joan kept her own thoughts to herself.

She never had a spare moment, and as for her sewing, let alone tackling the lovely material that Martin had so kindly given her, that had all been shelved. Maybe by next winter she would get round to making herself the gorgeous coat she had dreamed about. For she was still determined to better herself someday. She tried to reassure herself that her chance would come sometime. And when it did she would seize it with both hands. What scared her most was that she had overheard Mr Bruce telling his mother that sooner or later his father would have to be taken into a nursing home. And then what?

Her worst fears were realised when Mr Bruce came to the house on a weekday, bringing a solicitor with him. The two of them were closeted in Mr Hamilton's bedroom for some length of time. Later, as Mr Farrant opened the front door to let him out, the lawyer shook hands with Mr Bruce and said, 'I'll have the papers ready for your father's signature in three days' time.' When Joan related this piece of news to Kathleen, she folded her arms across her ample bosom, nodded her head wisely and gave her opinion.

'They're making sure that the old man's affairs are all in good order. Trust Mr Bruce to see everything is done legally and above board.'

'Well, isn't that better than leaving things to chance?' Joan asked.

'Better for Mr Bruce, I'd stake me life on that. After all, poor Mr Hamilton is in no state to make his own decisions, is he?'

Joan thought the best policy was to keep quiet. She nodded her head, but her thoughts were running along different lines. Mr Hamilton might be unable to do much for himself, but there was nothing wrong with his brain. His speech was by no means perfect, even after all this time, but Joan had not only got to know the old gentleman quite well but also become very fond of him, and there was no way anybody could convince her that he wasn't fully aware of what was going on around him.

As time passed the house began to feel different. The dining room was hardly used. Guests for dinner were a thing of the past. Occasionally Joan would stand in the huge room and daydream amid the two cabinets holding glittering crystal glasses and fine china, the thick soft Chinese carpets and the floor-length velvet curtains. Just looking at the sheer luxury of it all made her feel so sad.

John still collected and cleaned the silverware. There certainly weren't any boots for him to clean these days, though he was invaluable in so many other ways.

If some different arrangement were to be made for Mr Hamilton, his wife would not want to stay on in this large house, would she? She'd rattle around like a pea on a drum. And where would that leave me, Joan asked herself.

She had, just once, taken the bit between her teeth and asked Mr Bruce what would become of the staff if things turned out as she suspected they would. He had merely stared at her and Joan had burned with humiliation until he had finally said, 'We'll all have to wait and see.' In other words, the inevitable would happen sooner or later.

She still received long newsy letters from Rosie and short but more to the point notes from her sister Martha. She even had a letter from Marjorie telling her not to lose hope. Yet not one of them mentioned that they were still keen on her coming home or that they were still searching for a suitable property for her. She did her best to keep cheerful but she was only human and there were days when the thought of where she might end up in the future filled her with foreboding.

For the moment, she was content to remain at Mulborough House and do all she could to make life easier for Mrs Hamilton during this awful time. One thing that helped keep her going was her relationship with Kathleen O'Leary, which had developed from a working arrangement into friendship. A cuppa and a good old chat in the vast kitchen always boosted Joan's spirits. Nevertheless, constantly at the back of her mind was the hope that one day things might finally start going her way.

Whenever she thought about Martha and Sid and their lovely family she felt envious, and that in turn made her feel guilty. She'd had her chance. The fact that she had chosen to marry a man who had turned out to be no good was neither here nor there now. She had been grateful to have been given this job and she had done the best she could to be loyal to the family, but the thought persisted that she was letting life pass her by. Living in the country hadn't altered her allegiances. In her heart she was still a Londoner. A cockney born and bred.

Summer had come. The trees around Mulborough House were green, their branches covered with foliage, and heavily scented white and mauve lilac sprays dangled from the great bushes in the garden. Mr Hamilton's health had slightly improved. Only a night nurse was now in attendance, from eight in the evening until eight o'clock next morning, and this had made life a great deal pleasanter for both the inside and the outside staff. It had become a habit for Joan to sit with Mr Hamilton during the afternoon. Sometimes she would read to him. He showed an interest in passages from the daily newspaper, seeming to enjoy keeping up with day to day happenings. His speech had improved, though he found certain words difficult to pronounce and at times became so frustrated that the remaining words blurred and ran together. However, being a good listener, Joan had learned a lot about the early life of Edward Hamilton. He had been a captain in the army

154

and had been awarded the Victoria Cross for 'bravery above and beyond the call of duty'. Over the weeks Joan had come to admire his patience and the fact that he never grumbled when God above knew he had enough cause to. He could manage to feed himself with his left hand provided the food was cut into small pieces for him, and with help he would leave his bed of a morning and sit in an armchair which Joan herself had positioned near to the big window in his room. She often wished that she could put him in a wheelchair and take him for a walk around the gardens, in the sunshine she felt would do him so much good. Time was passing quickly and soon autumn would be here.

It was the first of October. Joan was sitting quietly sewing beside Mr Hamilton who, propped up by four pillows, had dozed off.

The doorbell rang, echoing through the silent house. Knowing that Mrs Hamilton had been driven into Tunbridge Wells by Mr Farrant, to have her hair washed and set, Joan rose and went out on to the landing. She looked over the banisters but there was no sign of Cook or Mabel. The bell rang for a second time so she went quickly down the stairs. She opened the front door and the smile on her face faded. A young policeman was standing there, his helmet tucked beneath his arm.

'Good afternoon, miss,' he said respectfully. 'I'm sorry to be the bearer of bad news, but the station officer said you needed to be informed that Mrs Hamilton has been taken into hospital.'

'Oh my goodness.' She stared blankly at him, her lips trembling. Eventually she managed to ask, 'Can you tell me what has happened to her? Has she been involved in an accident?'

'Not that I'm aware of, miss. All I've been told is that

the lady was taken ill while in the hairdressers and the proprietor thought it best to call an ambulance.'

At that moment the family car turned into the drive and Joan and the police officer stood silently until the car was brought to a halt at the foot of the entrance steps and Mr Farrant got out from the driver's seat. When he came quickly up the steps carrying his cap, looking extremely upset, the policeman turned to face him, but before the young man was able to say anything Mr Farrant let him know that he was in charge of the situation.

'It's all right, constable, I know what has happened. I was hoping to arrive back here before our housekeeper became aware that our mistress has been taken into hospital.'

'In that case, sir, I'll leave the lady in your good hands.' The constable put his helmet on, touched the brim of it with two fingers and said, 'Good afternoon, sir, miss,' and ran down the steps.

Joan stepped back, watching Mr Farrant as he stepped inside and closed the front door. 'Thank God,' she murmured beneath her breath, at the same time heaving a sigh of relief. At least Mr Farrant could take over now. If he hadn't turned up she wouldn't have had the slightest idea of what she was supposed to do.

'Mr Hamilton was asleep when the door bell rang,' she told him, then quickly she added, 'I'll just pop up and see he's all right and then I'll come down and make us all a strong pot of tea.' She almost took the stairs two at a time, thanking her lucky stars that the butler was going to be the one to break the news to Cook and Mabel.

Mrs Hamilton hadn't been herself for some time. Only to be expected, really; it was a wonder she hadn't been struck down before this, what with all the worry and stress she'd had forced on her. But by golly, this was going to create a good many more problems! Still, the reins were in Mr Farrant's hands now. He was the one who would have to notify the Hamiltons' son and daughters, and they'd have the biggest decision of all to make.

What was going to happen to their parents?

It was ten o'clock that night before Mr Bruce and his two sisters arrived at the house. All three had travelled from London and gone straight to the hospital. Thankfully the news was not too bad. The doctors feared Mrs Hamilton had suffered a heart attack, no doubt brought on by months of worry. They had admitted her to the cardiac care unit, where a close watch would be kept on her for the next twenty-four hours, and then, if she was fit enough, several tests were to be carried out to determine what medication should be prescribed. For the time being, the heart specialist who had spoken to Bruce had said absolute rest was the best remedy.

Cook had plates of sandwiches all ready and for once everybody gathered in the kitchen, drinking hot cocoa. As Joan looked around it didn't seem strange to see the family sitting round the wooden-topped table. The fire was still alight, even though the night was warm, and the glow from the range made the big room seem very comforting. Bruce and his sisters seemed to be lost in contemplation. And who could blame them? It would take a wise man to sort this household out from now on.

Bruce was the first to rise. 'I am going up to see Father; better I tell him straight away. He must be wondering already why Mother hasn't been in to see him.'

Delia looked at Fiona and it was apparent what each was thinking: rather you than me.

Mr Farrant coughed. 'Excuse me, Mr Bruce, but might it not be a good idea if the night nurse gave Mr Hamilton a sleeping draught?'

Bruce looked tired and apprehensive as he said, 'I will mention it, thanks.' I expect Father is given one every night, he thought.

The lights were lowered and the fire was banked down, and as everyone prepared to go to bed Mr Farrant said he would stay in the house in case he was needed during the night.

It seemed to Joan that she had barely closed her eyes when she heard a tapping on her bedroom door and the voice of the night nurse calling urgently, 'Mrs Baldwin.' The nurse opened the door a crack, allowing the light from the landing to shine into Joan's room, and called again, 'Mrs Baldwin.'

Joan was shocked. She looked at the small clock that stood on her bedside table and saw that it was five minutes past three. She needed no telling that the nurse was the bearer of bad news. Why else would she be calling her in the early hours of the morning? She was out of her bed and across the room in seconds.

Poor woman, was Joan's first thought as she faced the nurse. She looked petrified, and when Joan put a hand on her shoulder she jumped nervously and she began to shake. Joan took hold of her firmly, attempting to calm her. 'Please, nurse, calm down and tell me what has happened.'

'It's serious, Mrs Baldwin,' she answered sadly. 'It's Mr Hamilton. I thought you were the best person to come to.'

'Had a bad turn, has he? I'll see about contacting the doctor straight away. He'll be here very . . .'

'I think he's died,' the nurse interrupted mournfully.

'Dead!' Joan took an involuntary step backward. She felt as if the world was falling round her ears. She could feel the colour draining from her face and her legs trembled. For a split second the two of them stood staring at each other as if they had lost the power of further speech.

Joan was the first to recover. She realised she must go and tell Mr Bruce, but at that moment the butler appeared at the top of the stairs. Joan stared at him, her face registering utter relief. Had he had a premonition that something was going to happen during the night when he had offered to stay in the house rather than returning to his own home? He was wearing his black trousers and black butler's coat, as if he had not got undressed. He leant on the upright post at the top of the stair rail and pushed his hand over his forehead in a futile gesture.

'It's the master, isn't it?' he said quietly. It was a statement rather than a question. He turned to the nurse. 'Is he dead?'

The nurse felt more composed now. She looked Mr Farrant straight in the eye and as calmly as she was able she said, 'Mr Hamilton spoke to me for a while after his son had told him that his wife was in hospital. He seemed agitated but he would not accept the sleeping pill I offered him. He merely asked me for a glass of water. Some time later I heard him coughing and went to his bedside. I managed to prop him higher on his pillows and then I sat beside him. Not long after that he turned a little blue and then I think . . .' She couldn't go on.

Mr Farrant noticed that Joan was shivering and suddenly he was very apologetic. 'I'm so sorry, Joan. Please get yourself dressed, or at least put your dressing gown on. I will see to everything that has to be done, and while we wait for the doctor I think hot tea and a good-sized brandy would be in order for each of us. So come downstairs when you're ready.'

The silence in the sun-filled kitchen was heavy, broken only by the soft crying of Kathleen O'Leary. John was holding Mabel's hand and Joan had her elbows on the table with her head resting in her cupped palms. After a while Mr Farrant emerged from his pantry and said bluntly, 'All this sorrow won't bring him back, you know, and if you want my opinion it is a happy release for the poor master. It was odds on that he was going to be placed in a nursing home sooner or later. If the mistress is going to be poorly it would have become a certainty. None of us would have wished that on him, would we?' He cleared his throat. 'Miss Fiona, Miss Delia and Mr Bruce are talking to Dr Simmons in the drawing room. I will tell you the arrangements as soon as I know them myself. Meanwhile, let's get a move on down here. For a start, one of you make a pot of strong tea for all of us, and would you, Joan, please lay a tray and take it into the drawing room. Better add a few savouries. I don't suppose any of them feel like eating but it won't hurt to offer.'

Joan nodded, and hurried to do as he had asked.

Mr Farrant spoke to Cook in a louder voice. 'Pull yourself together, Kathleen. Please, there's a lot to be done and everyone will be here for dinner tonight.'

Cook lifted her tear-stained face and wiped it with her overall. Her big bosom was still heaving, but her crying had stopped. Nodding her head, she pushed herself up out of the chair, picked up her massive white apron and tied it round her waist. 'Let me have a cup of tea and then I'll start on lunch and dinner. Not that I think anybody will want to eat much.' Turning to Mabel, she said, 'You can make a start on the vegetables,' and then to John she added, 'And you can go round the house and draw all the curtains. We must show proper respect for the dead.'

Joan laid a large doily on a silver tray, set four cups and saucers, milk jug and sugar basin, then followed Cook into the larder to discuss what eats she should take up for the doctor, Mr Bruce and his sisters. As she worked there were two questions running through her mind and it didn't take much imagination to know that one of them was also troubling Kathleen O'Leary.

With the master dead and the missus ill, where did that leave them? For each of them this was not only a job but the place where they lived and laid their heads down at night. For Kathleen it had been so for a good number of years and Joan felt immense pity for her. And what about Mr Hamilton. When told that his loving wife would not be coming in to say goodnight to him, had he felt lonely, perhaps even abandoned? Joan felt she could easily imagine his misery. And then to die alone. Without one member of his family at his side. It seemed so unfair.

Joan found herself crying softly for the loss of this decent man, and for Mrs Hamilton, who had not been given a chance to hold his hand as he died or even to say her goodbyes. She prayed that Mrs Hamilton might be comforted by many good memories of the life they had shared together.

Chapter Sixteen

THERE CERTAINLY WAS a lot to do and yet the days seemed
long and the weeks dragged by. Joan was aware that all the
staff were unsettled because they knew they would soon be
leaving Mulborough House, but in her own case it couldn't
come quickly enough. Not now.

Mr Hamilton's funeral had been a well attended and
dignified affair. Mrs Hamilton was back living at home but
rarely left the house. She looked like a lost sheep and no
one could blame her for that. Mr Bruce had been more
than fair. He had held a meeting in the dining room to
which every member of the staff had been invited, from Mr
Farrant down to the stable lads. The house and grounds
were to be sold and it was his and his sisters' intention to
take their mother to live in Kensington. The apartment they
had bought for her would be near enough both to himself
and to Delia and Fiona to enable them to visit her frequently.
They intended to employ a companion for her, too.

Joan was flabbergasted. Poor Mrs Hamilton, to have to
leave this beautiful house and the wonderful grounds that
surrounded it, to go to London and live in an apartment.

Mr Bruce asked the staff to stay on until the sale of the

house was complete. He had many business matters to see to but he promised that all would be finalised before Christmas. He added that his father had remembered them in his will and left a token bequest to each member of his staff according to the length of time they had been in his employment.

Mrs Hamilton had made her choice of which articles and pieces of furniture she wanted to take with her. It had torn Joan apart to watch the sad lady run her fingers over several objects and murmur, 'Bruce will say this is far too big for the apartment.' What decisions! What memories she would be leaving behind!

Some curtains had been taken down and sent to the dry cleaners; others so heavy that only professionals would be able to remove them had been left hanging at the windows. Dust sheets now covered most of the furniture that was to be sold with the property. Joan had just finished wrapping several delicate pieces of bone china in tissue paper. The set was a twelve-piece tea service and because it was so exceptionally fine she found herself wondering if it had been a wedding present to the Hamiltons all those years ago. She put the lid on the box and leant her head against the window pane, closing her eyes. In a few weeks' time it would be Christmas again and this time she would be back in London herself. Was she sorry that she had come to work at Mulborough House? She could answer quite truthfully that she wasn't.

It had been an experience. Some days she had thought it not unlike the time when her mother had first put her into service, only then she had been a mere slip of a girl. Now she was a middle-aged woman. She was glad she was going to spend Christmas at Martha's, but what then? As Mr Bruce had said weeks ago, one had to wait and see. Well, since the death of Edward Hamilton she seemed to have done a lot of waiting.

She took Martha's last letter out of her pocket and read it again. Short and to the point, it reminded her that she would always have a home with her and Sid and how much all the family and the neighbours were looking forward to seeing her. She smiled to herself as she remembered that Rosie had informed her that she had a boyfriend and that he was dying to meet her Auntie Joan.

She was going to enjoy every minute of the Christmas holiday. But as soon as the holiday was over she wasn't going to waste much time. She had saved nearly all of her wages: there had never been very much to spend the money on. And she was to receive two hundred guineas from Mr Hamilton's estate. The amount seemed like a fortune to her. Probably it would be cold and icy as soon as January came in but that wouldn't bother her. She was determined to walk her feet off, read every property advertisement and visit every estate agency. Surely somewhere there was a small shop standing empty with a couple of rooms over the top. Who knows, if Sid would get her sewing machine out of the shed and Martha could spare the space, she would go to work like mad to make herself that long promised winter coat.

On 4 December Mr Farrant drove Joan to the railway station. She couldn't say she was sorry to go, because the atmosphere in Mulborough House had become very morbid, only Kathleen O'Leary suddenly becoming like a bird that had just been set free from its cage. A cousin of hers had written and invited her to return to Ireland and share her house with her.

'Sure and hasn't St Anthony turned up trumps for me,' she cried joyfully to Joan. Seeing the look of bewilderment on Joan's face she had enlightened her by saying, 'St Anthony is the patron saint of lost things. And wasn't I lost, and half out of me mind not knowing where it would be that I'd end up. And then there was Molly, owning a house but having no company. So St Anthony has set us both up proud.'

Joan tried hard not to laugh at Kathleen's reasoning but it didn't take a minute before the pair of them were laughing fit to bust. Their parting, however, had been a tearful one, each saying the other must come and visit, both knowing they would probably never meet again. But they promised to keep in touch by letter, because it had been grand working together, and they both knew they had formed a special kind of friendship.

To begin with, the house in Blackshaw Crescent felt cramped and inconvenient after Mulborough House. Here there was no countryside, the small terraced houses had shiny slate roofs and smoky chimneys, and try as she would Joan could not get used to having no running hot water. The shock hit hard when she remembered that the only lavatory was outside in the back yard. Martha still seemed to take all this in her stride. Both she and Sid had urged her to forget about looking for work.

'For God's sake give yerself a break. Just enjoy being with us for a change, instead of being at the beck an' call of rich folk all the time,' was Martha's advice.

'Time enough after Christmas for you to think about setting up yer own business if you're still of the same mind.' Sid smiled down at her.

'Thank you, both of you. You're so good to me,' Joan answered with a sob in her voice.

'Are you all right, Joan?' Martha poured her a cup of tea. 'You look as if you ain't 'ad a good night's sleep for ages.'

Joan sighed and leant forward in her chair, holding her hands out to the blazing fire. The gaslight was dim but it still showed up the deep hollows beneath her cheekbones, and Martha knew darn well that her sister had not been happy these last few months, stuck away down there in Kent.

'Tell yer what,' Martha said, doing her best to sound merry, 'tomorrow you can spend the whole morning in bed. By lunch time I'll have the big bath ready for you in front of the fire. Everyone will be out except us two, and you can have a good soak. Then we'll go down the market. I 'aven't told Martin and Marjorie that you've finished at that job. Be a nice surprise for them.'

Joan was so taken aback that she didn't know what to say, but she quickly found her voice. 'Why, thanks, Martha, that'll be great.' To herself she was thinking, I'd almost forgotten. I used to think nothing of having a bath in front of the fire in an old tin bath when I lived round the corner and I always used to get down on my knees to scrub Bill's back. Like living in two different worlds! Still, don't suppose it will take me long to get back into the old ways. It has to be a case of needs must when the devil drives.

The market was alive and doing great business. The buying and selling, especially at this time of year, went on from early morning until as late as ten at night, when huge paraffin flares would light up the stalls and kids would scavenge under them hoping to find pieces of fruit and vegetables that were still eatable. Each and every stall was decorated in the true Christmas spirit.

An excited gleam came to Martin's eyes as he spotted the two sisters. 'Marjorie, look! Joan is back.'

While Marjorie finished serving her customer Joan took the time to look over their stock. She was surprised at the variety and quality of the gifts on show, and even more so when she read several large printed cards stating which articles were hand-made. To think Marjorie had done all this. The very thought left her speechless.

When at last they had a spare moment Martin kissed Joan on each cheek and Marjorie put her arms round her and together they did a little dance, Marjorie chanting, 'Free at last. Free at last.' Other stallholders were not going to be left out. Their greetings to Joan were loud and saucy but Joan gladly went along with this bawdy reception.

Nellie Rogers, the local flower seller, looked exactly the same, almost as if she hadn't moved since Joan's last visit. Her humpy shoulders were wound very tight in a black shawl, a flat battered old hat that hid her wispy hair was secured with a large hatpin, and her face was wrinkled and weather-beaten, for she plied her trade in all weathers.

''Allo, Joanie, gal. 'Ow are yer?' Nellie Rogers called, her voice sounding much stronger than one would have imagined. Joan walked the few steps to where the old lady sat, bent down and kissed her withered cheek.

'I'm very well, thank you, Nellie. But how about you, aren't you cold?'

'Nar, take more than this gusty wind t' kill me off.' She held up her hands, showing Joan her thick woollen mittens. 'See these? Great, ain't they? Me granddaughter made them for me at school, doing a darn sight better than I ever did. I couldn't learn t' knit t' save me life.'

'They are really nice,' Joan said admiringly, thinking how little it had taken to please the old lady. 'I'll see you later, Nellie.'

'All right, Joanie. I'll be 'ere any time yer feel like a chat.'

Martin chuckled as Joan came back to join her sister. 'Go on, Marge, take them both over t' the café an' get yerselves a big mug of tea, 'cos we're not going to take much money with you lot just standing around kissing an' hugging each other.'

It was Martha who said, 'Thanks, Martin. It's a long time since I've seen my sister look so 'appy.'

'Get on with yer. Her eyes are brimming with tears,' Martin teased her.

'Yeah, they are, an' you an' I know why. 'Cos she's back among her own kind an' she knows she can't do better than that.'

Martin came to the end of his stall and hugged her tight. 'You've missed her, 'aven't you, Martha?'

'Yeah I 'ave, an' you're all 'eart, Martin, letting Marge slip away to 'ave a cuppa with us.'

'Go on then, before I change me mind,' he said, giving her a frisky shove. And as the three of them pushed through the crowds he shouted after them, 'And don't forget to bring back a large tea for me.'

'Us an' all,' the two Parker brothers called. 'And you can give a hand on our stall any time you feel like it, Joanie dear.'

'In yer dreams,' Joan shouted back, and Martha slyly said to Marjorie, 'Ain't taken 'er long to realise where 'er roots lie, 'as it?'

The market café was large, warm and steamy, and furnished with numerous tables, each surrounded by six chairs. Reg and Hilda Kennedy were the proprietors, and had been for as long as Joan could remember. Hilda was behind the counter dressed in a long-sleeved black dress and a crisp white apron. She nodded her head and smiled broadly as the three of them came through the door. She couldn't return their wave because both hands were needed to hold the enormous teapot from which she was filling a line of six big mugs.

'You two sit down and catch up on the news,' Martha ordered Joan and Marjorie. 'I'll fetch the teas.'

Within minutes she returned with three large mugs on a tray. She handed one to each of them. 'That'll put 'airs on yer chest. Hilda is bringing over a plate of hot toast as soon as she gets a free minute.' She kicked her shopping bag under the table and struggled to get her backside down on to a chair.

It was Reg who brought the toast to the table. 'Haven't yer got any staff on today, Reg?' Marjorie sounded concerned.

'Neither of the sods turned up this morning,' said Reg. 'An' this time I ain't 'aving them back. Bleeding good riddance. I've stood all I'm gonna stand from that pair of saucy bitches. I was going to boot them out soon anyway, an' Hilda's already put the word out. We'll take on a couple of older women this time, more reliable types, I 'ope.'

'Would you like me to give you a hand, just for today?' Joan asked timidly.

Reg let out a roar of a laugh. 'Thanks, luv, but we'll get by. You just enjoy being back 'ome with yer sister.'

'He thinks your posh voice will frighten his customers away.' Martha grinned.

'You're taking the mickey out of me,' Joan said crossly. She sounded as if a deep melancholy had come over her and Martha realised that it was a long time since her sister had been amongst market folk.

'Course I'm not,' she cried, passing the bowl of sugar to her sister. 'It's worrying you that you ain't got a job, I know it is, but when we get 'ome you can tell me all your troubles, Joan. I've burdened you often enough with mine.'

Joan was well aware that her sister meant well, and what was more had hit the nail on the head. She was back where she had been when Bill had died. Living with Martha and Sid, with no home of her own, and although she had savings now, how long would they last?

Marjorie looked at her sympathetically. No two sisters had ever been closer and she understood the tension that lay beneath Joan's tetchiness. God knows she had been through the mill these last few years. Martha was a rough diamond, but Marjorie knew that beneath that rough exterior she had a heart that was bursting with love for her only sister and all she wanted was what was best for her. 'Get Christmas over, Joan, and we'll have you sorted in no time,' she declared.

Joan smiled, sorry she had snapped at her sister. She

sipped her tea and immediately muttered, 'Dear God.' It was sweet and hot, but that didn't account for the way it burnt her throat like blazes.

Martha had been watching Joan's face and she had to laugh. 'Reg put a drop of whisky in it, said to say welcome 'ome.' Marjorie started the ball rolling, leaning across the table and taking hold of Joan's hand. 'You can make as many plans as you like, but try and be patient. Nothing's going to happen this side of Christmas, is it? So why not make up your mind to enjoy the holiday?'

'You're right, Marjorie, and I've just decided, I intend to make a start on my coat.'

'Martha has kept us up on all the news. We know you haven't had any time to yourself, but leave the matter of your making that coat for the moment. Would you like a job for the next three weeks?'

Joan felt her cheeks redden, wondering if Marjorie thought she was short of money. 'You mean working for you, don't you?'

'Course I do. You'd be a godsend.'

'Marjorie, it is ever so kind of you but I couldn't, really I couldn't.'

''Cos you think it's charity we're offering. That's it, isn't it?' Marjorie said bluntly. Then, without giving Joan a minute to think of an answer, she went on, 'Well you're wrong. Dead wrong. What with the shop, the warehouse and the stall we're rushed off our feet. Don't get me wrong – I am not complaining. What we earn in the run-up to Christmas has to last a while. January and February half our customers won't have two pennies t' rub together. We do need another pair of hands and we need someone we can trust. We want to sell gifts, not give them away.'

Martha nudged her sister and they both burst out laughing.

At that moment Hilda came to the table bringing another

170

plate piled high with thick slices of toast that were dripping with butter. 'Get that down yer,' she said as she set the plate in the middle of the table. Turning to Joan, she put her arm round her shoulders and said, 'By Jesus, you need fattening up. Looks like they've been starving you down in Kent.'

Reg was going by carrying a tray loaded with dirty plates, but he stopped and grinned at Joan. 'You tell 'em, luv. Can't fatten a thoroughbred. An' another thing – I've aways found the nearer the bone the sweeter the meat.'

Martha was the nearest to him and she playfully swiped his arm. 'Saucy sod, ain't yer? Been at the bottle yerself, 'ave yer?'

'Sorry, Martha. Honest, darling, when I look at you I know just how lucky your Sid is, 'cos yer can't 'ave too much of a good thing.' And with that he went on out to the kitchen, the sound of his laughter bellowing back to them.

'That man will trip himself up one day,' Hilda said, wiping the tears of laughter from her eyes. 'He always believes in running with the hare and the hounds. That way he covers himself on all sides.'

Chapter Seventeen

FOR THE NEXT THREE WEEKS Joan really did live in a different world and she enjoyed every minute of it. Working on Martin's stall was a joy to her. And the thing that really put a smile on her face was that most mornings her young niece Rosie came to work with her. The fact that amazed her most was just how much Rosie had altered. Her skin, her hair and her eyes glowed with health. Her body had rounded out in all the right places. She had taken notice of what Joan had said about her speech and the way she now spoke really pleased her aunt. Her natural cockney tones had faded almost completely. But not quite. She could still hold her own with the costermongers if needs be.

Joan was anxious to do well on the stall and prove her worth to Martin and Marjorie. Besides, she liked the way the other stallholders treated her. They kept an eye on her, especially the Parker brothers, who were forever calling out, 'All right, Joanie? Say when yer want us to fetch yer a hot drink.'

Jim Taylor had also become a real friend, even though he was a quiet man, thin and serious-looking with glasses and not very much to say for himself, though he had a warm smile when he chose to show it and a good head of dark brown hair. He hadn't forgotten their previous conversations and one morning very early, before most of the stalls had their goods out on show, he had come to Joan with a charming dressing stool, its curved seat ideal for padding and covering. Joan had stared at it, delight shining in her eyes, her thoughts running wild.

'Oh, Jim, that must have taken you ages to make. I really want to buy it, and after Christmas perhaps I can see about upholstering it.' She spoke with such eagerness that Jim had to smile.

'Martin has told me a bit about your hopes for owning your own business and I've actually made three stools and a tea trolley,' he sheepishly told her. Before she could think of an answer he added quickly, 'I've used good wood and I can varnish the legs of the stool and do whatever you think best with the trolley, paint it or varnish it.'

Joan was taken aback. 'But Jim,' she stammered, 'I can't afford to buy all those pieces right now, although I would love to. For one thing, I don't have any storage space.'

'Please don't upset youself, Joan. I didn't mean you should buy any of my work. Martin suggested I made things for you on a sale or return agreement – that is, of course, if you think my work is good enough for you to put on display.'

Joan found herself smiling. 'I think we're both jumping the gun a bit here, Jim. I would be proud to put your work on show but I don't own a business yet, let alone have any suitable premises in mind.'

'Oh, you will,' Jim assured her. 'Meanwhile, I have two sheds besides the place I use as my workshop, so if you think of any other item you would like I would always be willing to have a go at making it for you, and then I could store it until you were ready.'

'Jim . . . I don't know what to say. I am grateful, and if and when I ever do get started up on my own I would appreciate your co-operation very much.'

'That will do me for now,' he said softly. 'If at any time you want to take a look at my workshop I'd be happy to show you. Would you like to keep the stool for now?'

Joan frowned. 'There's nothing I would like better, but I just don't have any room to store anything. I feel I am imposing on my sister and her husband as it is.'

'I'm sure they don't feel that way.' He smiled. 'Anyway, I'll hold on to it for the time being and we'll talk again after Christmas, shall we?'

'I shall look forward to it,' Joan told him. And she meant it.

The house was usually in an uproar of a weekend. Len and Bernie went to play football, Sid took himself off to the pub for a game of darts, and Martha caught up with her chores, sweeping and dusting and – weather permitting – getting all the men's working clothes washed and hung out on the line in the back yard.

The Saturday before Christmas, both Rosie and Joan were going like the clappers, selling boxes of initialled hankerchiefs, embroidered pillow cases, gorgeous cushion covers and dozens of paper tablecloths that were adorned with Father Christmases, holly and golden bells. They must have sold more than fifty celluloid fairy dolls for the tops of folk's Christmas trees. At a shilling each, they were good value. Each doll had a pair of wings attached to her back and a tinsel-wrapped wand in one hand. They had almost sold out of red and gold candles. Paper chains and rolls of tinsel were unavailable now unless Martin turned up with a fresh supply.

The noise going on around them was almost deafening. The fruit and vegetable sellers, the butchers with their rows of poultry, the hot chestnut man, the lads selling clockwork toys, none of them suffered from lung disease, that was for sure. At one time Joan thought they were all endeavouring to outdo each other by seeing who could shout the loudest.

Never before had she been wished 'Happy Christmas' by so many folk. And Rosie wasn't shy at playing to the crowd. Looking as sweet and pretty as ever, she smiled at the lads as they winked at her.

Joan woke to the sound of bells pealing out from the church in the next road.

It was Christmas Day.

On the bottom of her narrow bed lay a full stocking. She hadn't heard anyone come into the room, but then the whole family including herself, plus more than half the street, had gone to the pub last night and they had all had a few drinks and sung carols and songs of yesteryear that brought tears to the older folk's eyes.

Crawling down to the end of her bed, she grabbed her stocking. Dear, dear, Martha! She had put in a tangerine, some nuts, a sugar mouse, a bar of Nestlé's chocolate and a brand-new shiny penny. What a start to what was going to be a wonderful day. Already the smells rising up the stairs from the kitchen below told her that the turkey and a half-leg of pork that Sid had brought home yesterday morning were slowly roasting in the oven, together with the gorgeous bowl of stuffing that Joan had watched her sister make last night before they went out. Joan laughed to herself. Good job she had. Martha wasn't in any state to make anything when they'd come home, and all she had had to drink was three glasses of port wine and lemonade.

Still, it never took much to make Martha merry. Bless her.

At two o'clock Martha said they could all come and sit up at the table. The boys had put planks of wood along what chairs they owned, placing cushions on top to make enough seating for ten people. There were the six of them, plus Ivy and George Martin who lived next door, and Nellie and Fred Bradshaw. Since having been told that Linda had

had her baby adopted and taken herself off to New Zealand, Joan had not felt at ease on the odd occasion that she had met Nellie Bradshaw, but today was Christmas and Martha had opened up her heart and invited them. A cracker and a paper hat lay by everyone's knife and fork. On an enormous china dish set at the head of the table the turkey lay browned and basted to a turn, ready for Sid to carve and just waiting to be eaten. Dishes containing every kind of vegetable, roast potatoes, stuffing and apple sauce and two jugs of gravy ran the length of the table, and in front of each person was a hot dinner plate on which had been placed two thick slices of roast pork and a glistening piece of crackling.

Sid held the bird steady with a long-handled fork and started to carve while Martha, grinning from ear to ear, loudly ordered, 'Come on, everyone get stuck in an' 'elp yerselves. We don't want our Christmas dinner going cold, do we?'

To say it was a jovial meal would be to put it mildly. The noise was at its height by the time Martha carried in the Christmas pudding, blue flames burning merrily on top thanks to the generous amount of brandy Sid had poured over the pudding and then set light to.

By five o'clock presents had been exchanged and opened. The inevitable cups of tea and hot mince pies appeared, and by half past six Lenny and Bernie had gone off to visit their girlfriends, taking Rosie with them as far as the corner of the street where Elsie Jones, a schoolmate of Rosie's, lived. The Jones family had five children, three of them girls, and it was only natural that Rosie should fancy being with her young friends for a couple of hours.

Ivy and George Martin followed them out of the front door and Sid watched until they were safely in their own house. They had both assured Martha that they had spent a marvellous day, but now they were tired, which was to be expected since both of them were turned eighty. Then Sid and Martha took themselves off to the kitchen to sort out drinks for everyone, leaving Joan alone with Nellie and Fred Bradshaw.

During the day Joan had got the feeling that everyone was skirting the subject of their granddaughter. After all, the two families had been neighbours for years, and Martha had been a tower of strength to Nellie when her daughter had died. The sudden silence in the room was unbearable and Joan decided to take the plunge. 'Does Linda write regularly?' she asked Nellie.

'She used to, luv, when she first went to New Zealand. We answered every letter straight away, didn't we, Fred?'

'Yeah, we did.' Nellie's husband never had much to say for himself but now he added, 'I always wrote a few lines on the bottom of Nellie's letters.'

Nellie gave a sad little sigh. 'The gap between Linda's letters got longer each time and now . . . well, August it was when we last 'eard from 'er. Not even a Christmas card this year.'

Their obvious sadness made Joan's heart ache and she said the first thing that came into her head. 'They do say no news is good news. I'm pretty sure you will hear from Linda again soon. After all, you were mother and father to her and she is not going to forget you just like that. If you think about it, you know she really loves you and she must have a good reason not to be writing.'

'I suppose so,' Nellie said reluctantly.

'You got to stop worrying over 'er,' said Fred, a trifle irritably. 'If she don't wanna write no more there ain't much we can do about it.'

At that moment Sid pushed the door to the front room open with his bottom. He was carrying a scuttle full of coal and in the crook of his other arm he had tucked half a dozen logs. 'Just been out to the coal shed,' he muttered. 'It's so damn cold out there it's enough to freeze yer t' death.' That said, he placed two logs on the glowing embers of the fire and then tipped the lid of the scuttle, allowing several great knobs of coal to settle on the top.

Martha followed him into the room carrying a tray which held several bottles and five glasses. 'Let's 'ope that on a night like this there aren't any poor devils who can't afford coal,' she said quietly.

Sid poured whisky into each glass and added a drop of ginger wine. Fred accepted his drink but said gruffly, 'We'd better get 'ome after we've drunk this.'

Nellie did her best to smile. 'Been a smashing day, an' we can't thank yer enough. It was ever so good of you to 'ave us both.'

'Our pleasure,' Martha assured them.

'I'll get your coats an' me own,' Sid insisted. 'I'll walk you round. Don't want yer slipping over, do we?'

'Well, this'll be a great end t' the day,' Nellie laughed. 'Two men, one on each arm, to take me 'ome. Maybe me luck will change with the new year.'

When they were alone the two sisters looked at each other. 'They had nowhere else to go, did they? They'd have had a rotten Christmas if it weren't for you and Sid,' said Joan very quietly.

'Oh, Christ, Joan, you're as big a mug as me,' Martha said. 'Come on, get on yer feet an' make us a cup of tea, I'm parched. That blooming whisky has dried me throat up.'

'I think maybe you deserve one,' Joan told her, thinking what a kind person her sister was. She smiled as she put the kettle on. It really had been a great day. And it had taught her one thing: there were hundreds of people far worse off than she was. At least she had a loving family.

Joan was very restless that night. She couldn't get the thought of Nellie Bradshaw's young granddaughter out of her mind. What on earth could have happened to Linda that would prevent her from keeping in contact with her grandparents? Her mother had died giving birth to her, and had it not been for them Linda could easily have grown up feeling she had been completely abandoned. But Nellie and Fred Bradshaw had done even more than was asked of them. They had loved that child. Had the fellow that Linda had gone off to New Zealand with ever married her? Was she happy? It must have torn at the young girl's heartstrings to put her baby into a home and sign adoption papers, then go off to the other side of the world, to live among people where she did not know a single soul. Joan herself had never had to give a living child away, but no one knew better than she did what it was like to carry a baby within your own body only to lose it before it had taken a breath.

Joan felt herself getting really agitated. Her own husband had been the father of Linda's child. It was his brutal treatment that had caused her own childlessness, yet he had been callous enough to get a young girl pregnant. If anyone had asked her at this moment whether she was sorry that her husband had died, the answer would have to be no. He didn't deserve to die the way he had. But then neither herself nor young Linda had deserved to be so ill treated by him.

She prayed silently that the Bradshaws might hear from Linda soon.

Chapter Eighteen

IT WAS A TYPICAL BOXING DAY. No one rose early and when Sid came back indoors from picking up the two quart bottles of milk off the doorstep he yelled loudly, 'It's too bloody cold for snow.'

'He's probably right for once,' Lenny remarked to his brother. 'That flipping wind bites right through yer. Just listen to it howling.'

'How would you know? You ain't been out, 'ave yer?'

'Only to the paper shop t' get some fags. I got twenty for you as well. Didn't think you'd be wanting 'alf an ounce of Old Holborn today.'

'Oh, thanks, Len. Are there any papers today?'

'Well if there are they're not in yet. Did yer want t' see if there was any racing on anywhere?'

'I did think you an' me might slope off somewhere after breakfast. Bound to 'ave 'alf the street popping in an' out t'day an' we don't wanna be sitting around listening to old wives' tales, do we?'

Lenny stared at Bernie and burst out laughing. 'Breakfast? You've got some 'opes. Mum an' Aunt Joan are out there getting the dinner ready.'

'But we always 'ave our dinner at night-time,' Bernie protested.

'Not on Christmas Day, nor on Boxing Day. Call it lunch if yer like, but you're getting it soon anyway.'

'But I'm starving now,' Bernie declared.

'In that case you shouldn't 'ave stayed out until the early hours of the morning an' then you might 'ave got up in time for a bit of breakfast.'

It was true. Martha had announced that she wasn't going to spend the whole day slaving over a hot stove. Joan had agreed with her. There were tons of cold vegetables left over from yesterday and Joan had tipped them all into a large mixing bowl, added two eggs, and mixed it all up. Now she began to pat portions of the mixture into shape and fry bubble and squeak. Martha had peeled a load of potatoes and already the big black saucepan was on the gas stove. She dipped her hand into the brown earthenware jar and came out with a half-handful of salt which she added to the now bubbling water, turned the gas down lower, placed the lid on the saucepan and said, 'I'll mash them later with plenty of butter and there are about four different jars of pickles and out in the shed there's salad, with plenty of beetroots. We can do some hard-boiled eggs if yer like but there's loads of turkey and pork so if they don't like it they can lump it today.' Joan was prevented from answering her sister by an excited call from Rosie, who was still upstairs.

'Mum, Mum, a car's just pulled up outside our house.'

Martha pretended not to have heard, and Joan looked at her suspiciously. There wasn't one person in a hundred who owned a car round these parts. 'You expecting anyone?'

'Not really,' Martha said, keeping her face turned away from Joan.

The boys had been quick to open the front door and the pleasure was plain in their voices as they both shouted, 'Mum, it's Marjorie and Martin.'

181

'Did you know they were coming?' Joan asked.

Martha just shook her head and moved past Joan to go and welcome her visitors, who wore beaming smiles and were loaded with fancily wrapped parcels. The fire was roaring halfway up the chimney, and Rosie took their coats upstairs to lay on one of the beds. Sid made sure that everyone had a drink in their hand before he proposed a toast. 'Good health and prosperity. Lovely to see you, Marge, an' you, Martin.'

'Plenty of grub t' go round, but it won't be ready just yet,' Martha told them. Again Joan gave her sister a funny look. It was as if she had been expecting Martin and Marjorie, yet she hadn't said a word to her.

Rosie dragged parcels from under the tree and handed them to the Goldsmiths and they in turn handed out a parcel to every member of the family. Finally, Martin offered a small, neatly wrapped package to Joan. Before she could take it, however, he drew his hand back. 'I forgot. This present was to go with the coat you were going to make for yourself, but you never got around to doing it, did you?'

Joan felt her face flush up. Martin made her feel ungrateful, and she stammered something about what a busy year she'd had and how she had worked every day on the stall with him since she had been home.

'Never mind, Joan.' He patted her shoulder. 'But what did you do with the material?'

Again Joan wished the floor would open up and swallow her. 'It's upstairs, underneath my bed.'

'Well, just pop up and fetch it down and we'll see if this present does tone in with the colour. Marjorie said it would.'

The silence in the room was awful and Joan felt like a naughty child. She felt even worse when she got down on her hands and knees, moved her old suitcase backwards and forwards but could find no sign of the brown paper parcel. She attempted to crawl beneath the bed but all she

182

managed to do was bang her head twice. The parcel was not there.

The thought entered her head that she could climb out of the window and run away. She moved the short lace curtain to one side. It was a fair old way down to the pavement and the drainpipe looked very icy.

There was nothing else she could do. She had to go downstairs and ask Martha if she had put the parcel somewhere safe.

The door to the front room was firmly closed and she stood in the passageway and listened. She couldn't hear a sound. Slowly, she opened the door and the sight that met her eyes would stay with her for the rest of her life. It fair took her breath away and she didn't know whether to laugh or to burst into tears.

The whole family, including Martin, had joined hands and formed a circle. In the centre of the circle Marjorie was standing on a chair. Her right arm was held high. She was holding a wooden coat-hanger aloft and buttoned up on the hanger was the smartest double-breasted camel coat anyone could wish to see.

Joan's hands flew to cover her mouth, and that was the signal for Martin to help his wife step down and for the family to start cheering as he unbuttoned the coat and held it for Joan to try on. It fitted perfectly. Joan turned this way and that, turned up the collar, put her hands in the pockets and strutted up and down while everyone clapped their hands. With tears pricking the backs of her eyes she asked, 'How . . . when . . . who made it?'

Everyone in the room was laughing fit to bust. Rosie even more than her brothers. Joan turned to Martha and Sid first. 'You knew about this, didn't you?'

'Course we did,' Sid told her. 'The way you were going on, Martha said the moths would have eaten 'alf the cloth away before you got round to making it into a coat.'

'It were Marge's idea to have a tailor do it,' Martha admitted, 'and it were easy enough t' find the parcel, but I turned that little bedroom out at least 'alf a dozen times before I come across the place where you'd put the pattern. Time and time again I was on the verge of asking you what you'd done with it but that would have given the game away. Smashing Christmas present, ain't it?'

Joan was still wearing the coat but for the life of her she didn't know what to say. She accepted the handkerchief that her sister was laughingly holding out to her, brushed the tears away from her eyes and took a minute to calm herself down. Never before in her whole life had she been on the receiving end of such a lovely surprise. Then she flung her arms wide, gathering Marjorie and Martin together so that she could hug them both at the same time. 'How can I ever thank you?' she whispered.

'By wearing it often and keeping yourself warm,' Martin told her as Marjorie reached for the small package and said, 'You can open this one now.'

Slowly Joan tore open the pretty paper to find a pair of leather fur-lined gloves. She held them to her nose and sniffed at the luxurious smell of real leather. The rich deep brown colour would go well with the beige of the coat. Martha rounded the moment off for her by saying softly, 'Always remember, my luv, you're as rich as the number of friends you've got.'

Chapter Nineteen

TWO DAYS AFTER BOXING DAY the snow fell in bucketfuls, and it seemed as if it was never going to stop. By New Year's Eve deep mounds of the stuff had frozen and made the pavements treacherous to walk on. No one went out unless they had to, and beyond the windows all was frosty, white, silent and still. Rosie was anxious. If she didn't meet her friends that night to wish them all a happy new year it would turn out to be a very unlucky year. And the local publicans weren't too happy either. They took more money over the bar on New Year's Eve than at any other time of the year.

The thought of spending the evening stuck indoors drove Lenny and Bernie into action. 'Shut that damn door,' Sid shouted as the two of them made it down the back yard and into their father's old shed. It was about twenty minutes before they returned and it was hard to say which member of the family was the most staggered.

'What *do* you look like?' cried Martha.

Rosie was the only one who thought it funny. She stopped laughing only long enough to say, 'You're not going out like that! Are you?'

Lenny had on an old overcoat of his father's, what looked

like two woollen scarves round his neck, and a flat cap on his head. Bernie had found a pair of dungarees, covered in old paint, over which he had struggled into a padded mackintosh which was so large it must have at one time belonged to his mother and a woolly bobble hat that came well down over his ears. Each of them had dirty wellington boots on his feet and their hands were covered by very thick gardening gloves.

'We're just popping up t' the pub,' Len declared.

'They must 'ave come up with some kind of idea to get customers into the pub tonight. New Year's Eve without a sing-song an' a knees-up! The old regulars will go mad if they can't 'ave their do on this one night of the year,' Sid remarked.

'Well, yes, it would be sad for the old 'uns,' Martha said sympathetically, 'but I fail to see that you two dressing up like blooming tramps is going t' help a lot.'

'We'll see,' Lenny said, firmly walking up the passage and opening the front door.

'Give 'em credit,' said Sid, as he watched his two boys and four other young men knock on doors and call out, 'Are yer ready?' The six of them had already been round all the houses and explained that anyone who wanted to come to the New Year's Eve party which was being held in the local pub would be fetched and brought back home safely soon after the new year had been seen in. Horses and carts had been the answer.

The rag and bone man had generously offered his one cart and two horses. Dunnett's the coal merchants had offered two carts and horses, nobly doing their best to clear some of the coal dust from the carts and finding something to line the floor so that folk would not get their clothes too dirty. Several people had offered to lend blankets to wrap the passengers in, even though it would only be a short trip to the pub. Carrying the old folk from their houses across the slippery pavement and raising them up on to the carts had proved hilarious. Each time there was a new arrival in the bars, cheers from the customers rang out loud and clear. The landlord and his missus were of the opinion that where there's a will there's always a way. Cockney traders had brought their wives and young men their girlfriends, and the young mums and dads had brought their children because the landlord had set aside his own sitting room for them to play in. Parents took it in turn to stay with the kiddies and lemonade, Smith's crisps and arrowroot biscuits kept them happy as they showed off the toys they had received for Christmas.

After being cooped up indoors for days on end because of the weather, everyone was determined to enjoy the party. The drinks flowed freely, the music got louder and people had to shout to be heard above the din. Joan was amazed at the goings-on, especially when six women she did not know came into the bar. The older people present, herself included, looked at them curiously, taking in the different artificial shades of their coloured hair and the outrageously short skirts they were wearing. As for their jewellery, Joan had never seen the like: long dangling earrings, bangles, chokers, and rings on almost every finger. The married men heeded the warning looks their wives were giving out, but the young lads were eyeing them eagerly, asking what they would like to drink, though Martha said in a voice loud enough for her boys to hear, 'Underneath all that war paint they're probably as old as me.'

'You wish,' murmured Lenny, but made sure his mother hadn't heard.

'Bit cold fer them out there t'night,' Bernie offered by way of explanation, and his words made the penny drop for Joan.

'Are they what I think they are?' Joan had leant nearer

to Martha and whispered the question into her sister's ear.

'Are you dim or what?' Martha looked at her sister in disbelief. 'Suppose they've got t' earn their living in the only way they know. More than likely got 'alf a dozen kids between them an' I'd lay my money that they take bloody good care of 'em an' all. But for the next hour or so they're going to be in the warm an' 'ave a darn good time. You watch them. Two or three drinks an' they'll be goofy gigglers.'

It turned out that the newcomers actually made the night. The entertainment they put on was exceptional. One, wearing a very long curly wig and looking quite attractive, at least from a distance, turned out to have a beautiful voice. After at least four gins, she sang haunting songs about bonny Scotland, very fitting for New Year's Eve, and Joan felt sad for her, thinking that she was probably far away from her own kith and kin.

Five minutes before midnight the landlord was doing his best to quieten some of his customers down. He placed a wireless set on the counter and switched it on. The loud singing tailed off as they listened to the sound of Big Ben striking twelve. Everyone rose to their feet and formed three circles, crossing their arms and holding their neighbours' hands. It went without saying that the woman who looked like a tart but sang like a songbird led the singing of 'Auld Lang Syne'. As the last notes died away there were not many women who were dry-eyed.

Joan wondered what it was about New Year's Eve that made everyone so emotional. She was blinking quite hard herself when she looked up and saw her two nephews bearing down on her.

'Happy New Year, Aunt Joan!' They each hugged her warmly, and when they saw the tears in her eyes they both laughed.

'Now, none of that,' Len said, as he bent his head and kissed her cheek. 'It doesn't pay to look back. It's 1929 and

I predict that you are going to become a very good business woman before this new year is out.'

If only Lenny's prediction were to come true, Joan was thinking as her brother-in-law helped her into her coat. Any effort would be worthwhile if she could achieve that.

Chapter Twenty

JANUARY WAS A HORRIBLE MONTH, full of cold dreary days which were dark by four o'clock, and long, long evenings. Joan did her best to keep herself occupied but she wished she had something permanent to do. She made several trips to the library and took out books on upholstery. One such book was of great value because the illustrations showed step by step exactly how to set about tackling small objects.

There were days of indecision when the family argued as to where, how, and when Joan should start looking for premises that would not only be suitable for business but also provide her with living accommodation. Her two nephews were of the opinion that she should go upmarket. 'Go where the money is and some of it is sure to rub off on you,' said Lenny in his outspoken way. His father disagreed.

'She's got to learn t' walk before she can run. Besides, poor folk need alterations to their clothes, sometimes curtains made an' such like, don't they?'

'Who said she was only going to do needlework?' Martha was quick to add her twopennyworth. 'According to Marjorie she's hoping to get our Joan set up in a variety of other things.'

'Now, now, Rosie laughed. 'No squabbling. Auntie Joan knows what she's doing, she's just feeling a bit down because things aren't happening quick enough.'

A wise head on young shoulders, had Rosie! Sid Brown had never been a great talker but that was not to say that he didn't do a great deal of thinking. He looked steadily at his sister-in-law and said quietly, 'Why don't yer get on t' Martin, ask him if you can spend a few days in his Balham shop? I'm sure you could make yerself useful in a good many ways. You could also look and learn. See the difference in customers, for one thing. Some like to be waited on hand, foot and finger, others just want to browse and take their time before they part with their cash. I bet Monday is a quiet day, though as things stand at the moment I suppose most days are quiet when you're in trade.'

'Sid, that's a marvellous idea,' replied Joan gratefully. 'But don't you think it would be a bit cheeky to ask Martin?'

'Well, it's up to you,' replied Sid placidly. 'But did I ever guide you wrong? It's something you need to do, get a bit of experience. I promise you, luv, you'll find a great deal of difference working in a shop rather than on a stall in the market. And, who knows, you might even find a rich backer. Martin will show you the ropes and probably take you to a few warehouses with him, teach you to be selective about what stock you buy.'

'You might even find a rich husband out there,' Len said cheekily.

'Oh, shut up!' cried Joan, blushing madly.

Eventually everyone agreed that Joan should stop dithering and go for it. Bernie set out a pack of cards and they began to play. So, by the end of the evening, Joan had stopped wavering and promised she would get in touch with Martin in the morning.

*   *   *

191

Marjorie and Martin had been all for it and Joan now worked four days a week at the Balham shop. The job kept her occupied from nine in the morning until six on Mondays and Tuesdays, and on Fridays and Saturdays she stayed until seven. She enjoyed the work, and had done so since the first day. Her way of life had changed, and so had her image. Early every morning she washed herself from head to toe, set her hair, put on the smart black dress she had made for herself and her new camel coat, and set off to catch the tram with a smile on her face. It gave her great satisfaction to know that she was working and learning, preparing the way for when she would become her own boss. It was strange how different she felt. Her timid approach to life, even the feeling that she would end up a complete failure, seemed to have entirely disappeared. For a whole month now Martin had employed her and had insisted on giving her a weekly wage. Even after she had paid Martha for her keep she still had money over.

During her lunch hour she wandered around the big stores because it was warm in there and there were so many nice things to look at, but she seldom bought anything unless it was a small gift for her sister or for young Rosie. She had not touched the money she had saved while she had been at Mulborough House, or the sum she had inherited from Mr Hamilton. The thriftiness of a lifetime was still with her.

Martha was thrilled with the change in her sister and one Wednesday when they were out together she suddenly remarked, 'I wonder why you are so much shorter than me?'

Joan smiled. 'I guess God patted me on the head when I was born.'

'Well, if that's the case he must have dragged me up by my hair,' Martha replied huffily, scrutinising her sister closely. 'I must say, you look a lot taller than you used to. You are walking more upright now. Before, you used to

192

wander around with your shoulders hunched and you tended to lean forward all the time.'

'I'm glad you approve of the change in me,' said Joan with a gentle smile.

'Oh, I do. I hated it when you were always so down-trodden. You led such a rotten life one way an' another. Bill was never a good 'usband and you took on the job of caring for his mother right up until the day she died. You were always so sad when you lost yer babies and in the end you lost yer 'ome as well. I'd say you were about due for some luck, and I pray that good times will come for you before too long.'

'Thank you, Martha. You've always been there for me, and even though what you say is true, you have only to look around you to see that there are a good many folk who have been forced to lead lives far worse than mine has been.'

'True,' Martha said thoughtfully, then grinned. 'I'll tell yer something else while I'm about it. You're much more relaxed these days an' you look a good ten years younger.'

'I think you've flattered me enough for one day.' Joan chuckled. 'Come on, we'll go into the ABC and I'll buy us a pot of tea and we'll have a buttered bun.'

'Does it 'ave t' be the ABC?' Martha grumbled. 'The complicated self-service system drives me mad. Can't we go to the café in the market?'

'No, we are going to have a nice change. You can sit yourself down and I shall line up and carry the tray.'

'Oh, all right.' Martha sighed, giving in gracefully. 'I was only thinking of you really. It costs less up the market an' you're gonna need every penny when you find a place of yer own.'

'I know you were, Martha,' said Joan, kissing her. 'Nobody ever had a better sister than you, but I do wish you wouldn't worry quite so much over me. I'm doing fine, thanks mainly to you and Sid, and the future for me is looking good. The bad part of my life is all over now.'

As they walked towards the ABC they met Nellie and Fred Bradshaw. Martha asked if they were both all right.

'Not too bad. Jogging along,' replied Fred with a deep sigh.

'Have you had any news of Linda yet?' Joan asked.

Nellie shrugged and said sadly, 'Not a word.'

Joan hugged her affectionately. 'Would you both like to come and have a cup of tea with us? We're going into the ABC.'

Nellie gave her husband a doubtful look and he quickly said, 'No, thanks all the same, Joan, but we're on our way to the market. We always have a cuppa in there, don't we, gal?'

'Yeah, we do. It's cheaper down there.'

Martha was grinning cockily and Joan only just stopped herself from saying that it would be her treat. Martha saved the day by saying, 'Come on. We'll all go to the market café, and since Joan is a working gal now she's going to pay today.'

If it were possible, Joan loved her sister even more than usual at that moment. For such a big, rough and ready woman she certainly knew how to be tactful. Martha's care for others ensured that she was always mindful of their feelings.

It was true what folk said. Martha Brown had a heart of gold!

Chapter Twenty-one

QUITE BY CHANCE, Marjorie Goldsmith was up very early. At seven o'clock she decided to take a run up to Brixton, watch the market stallholders setting out their gear. You were never too old to learn new tricks and it paid to keep abreast of what was for sale. Actually, she was missing Martin. He had been gone three days now, touring the cotton warehouses in Manchester, and it seemed much longer.

It was as she walked back to where she had parked her car that Marjorie saw it. *The shop!* The shop that just might be suitable for Joan Baldwin. It was on the opposite of the road, near the Brixton Empress.

Marjorie stopped dead in her tracks, staring across at it in utter disbelief. It was the end one of six that fronted on to the high street. The other five shops looked fairly prosperous. This vacant one was filthy. The large window had been whitewashed, but by the look of it now, that must have been ages ago. She walked briskly across the road, stood well back on the edge of the pavement and stared upwards. Yes! She screamed the word inside her head. Above the shop were two sets of windows facing the road still hung with greyish-looking torn lace curtains.

The name plate had been removed from the front, but there was no sign to say that the premises were 'To Let' nor any indication as to where one might contact the landlord. However, Marjorie was not deterred. She was prepared to go to any lengths to find out why such premises had been left to go to the dogs. And where better to start than in the local pubs?

Marjorie was very familiar with Brixton but she did not know it as well as Martin did. She knew how much he liked the Prince of Wales and remembered what good times they had enjoyed there in their younger days. It was a massive pub, a Free House, at the corner of Brixton Road and Atlantic Avenue. More than once she and Martin had been invited to a party there. The first occasion had been a family wedding where the reception had been held upstairs and as Marjorie recalled that day she found herself laughing out loud as she walked.

Besides several bars and function rooms downstairs, 'the Prince' boasted more than 20 rooms upstairs and the *kitchen*! well, one guest had remarked that one of the three ovens was large enough to roast a cow!

That pub had been in the hands of the same family for donkey's years, according to the tales that folk had to tell about the place. The present landlord and his wife, Les and Annie Jackson, had been there for as long as Marjorie could remember. She made a spur of the moment decision. If anyone would know about the empty property she'd just spotted she felt sure Les Jackson would. Besides, her tummy was rumbling. She hadn't had any breakfast yet, and the Prince was known for the good homemade food it served. That was one of the main reasons Martin liked to go there.

Marjorie wondered if the district would be suitable for Joan. She couldn't see why not. Brixton was a district of south-west London, in the borough of Lambeth, about four miles from the city. It was a friendly place. Like most it had its poorer areas, but there were also plenty of good-quality detached houses. Lambeth Town Hall had always been known as a showpiece, and the Empress Theatre put on some marvellous old time musical shows. Marjorie chuckled as she remembered her parents making her and her brothers climb up all the stairs to The Gallery, known as The Gods, because the tickets to sit up there were only a tanner and it was half price for the kids. The place used to get packed on Friday and Saturday nights.

Having made her decision, Marjorie hadn't too far to walk. The Prince of Wales stood right opposite the Town Hall and as it came into view she couldn't help thinking what enormous, grand, old-fashioned buildings both the pub and the Town Hall were. She looked at her watch. Shame. It was still barely nine o'clock, and none of the bars would be open until eleven. However, luck was still with her. The Prince of Wales was getting a delivery.

Two, big wooden doors had been folded back, one to the left and one to the right, to lie flat on the pavement, and the draymen were rolling barrels of beer deep into the cellar below street level by means of a wide wooden plank which they used as a slide.

'Mind where yer going, darling.' A burly, bald-headed man wearing a heavy leather apron grinned at Marjorie as she approached. She stepped off the pavement and into the road, and walked past the cart, which still held several barrels, enjoying the sight of the great dray horses nibbling from their nosebags. She slowed her pace, and as she approached the door marked in gold lettering 'Saloon Bar' she heard the sound of bolts being drawn back. A tall, very sturdily built youngish man appeared. He was fair-haired, almost pure blond, with large blue eyes. He was in his shirt sleeves and his handsome face broke into a smile as he saw Marjorie standing there.

'Well, this is a surprise. Been out on the tiles all night, have you, Marjorie darling?' he joked.

Marjorie stared up at him, surprised to see Jeffrey Harper. Yet she had to smile as he came towards her, took hold of both her hands and gently kissed her on each cheek. Jeff was still running true to form.

'Is Martin with you?' he asked. When she shook her head, he pretended to look hurt. 'Nevertheless, my darling, you will sweeten my morning by coming inside and having breakfast with me and Mark.'

Marjorie stood still, her mind in a whirl. Breakfast sounded good, but what on earth was Jeffrey Harper doing there? She watched as he signed the drayman's waybill, and slipped a folded note to each of them. ''Bye,' he called, 'nice meeting you.' Then, his arm round Marjorie's shoulders, he led her into the pub.

Inside were three women cleaners, each wearing a floral wrapround overall. Two had their hair tied up in headscarves, while the other one wore a man's flat cap on her head. One was washing tabletops, another was cleaning the massive mirror which hung over the bar, and the third was on her hands and knees polishing the brass foot rail that ran the full length of the long counter. Behind the bar two brawny barmen were bottling up the shelves. In the distance she could hear the hum of what might be a Goblin cleaner, and the thought of the wage bill that Les Jackson must have to fork out every week had her cringing.

'What the hell are you doing here?' cried Marjorie at last, as Jeff walked her towards the staircase. 'Don't tell me Les has given you the job of manager. I wouldn't have thought working in a pub was your cup of tea.'

'As if, sweetie. Can you see me working seven days a week?' Jeff swiped the air with his hand as if to indicate that Marjorie had taken leave of her senses. 'One of Les's customers offered him the use of a flat he owns in Barcelona and poor old Annie needed a break. Come to that they both did. So Mark and I said we'd step into the breach, kind-hearted souls that we are.'

'Bet that gave some of the customers a bit of a surprise.' Marjorie could hardly contain her laughter. She had known Jeff and all his family since she was a young girl. He really was a lovely man, but a publican he was not and never would be. She'd lay a pound to a penny there would be a lot more young ladies using this pub while Jeff and his companion were here, but they'd be wasting their time. Although he would treat them really nicely and certainly admire their clothes if they were well dressed, he wasn't into affairs with girls.

She and Martin had known Jeff Harper and Mark Townsend for a very long time and counted them as their friends. As to their lifestyle, her and Martin's thoughts on the subject had always been live and let live. They weren't young lads; they were well into their forties, although from the smart way they dressed and the way they kept themselves so fit they could easily be taken for much younger.

'Come on, let's go upstairs,' Jeff said, leading the way.

Mark had been watching from the window and he greeted Marjorie warmly. 'It's great to see you, Marjorie,' he said, and hardly pausing for breath he added, 'You'll eat with us? Scrambled eggs and smoked salmon sound all right? Jeff will make us loads of toast.'

'More than all right,' Marjorie said politely, inwardly wondering how all this had come about.

It would be an understatement to say that she enjoyed her meal. Everything was perfect. Even the coffee was beyond reproach: served black by Jeff as Mark hovered waiting to add a measure of Irish whiskey and pour cream slowly over the back of a silver spoon to complete the concoction. The companionship of the two good-looking fellows was remarkable and Marjorie felt totally at ease as they chatted about friends the three of them had in common. Jeff's pure blond head, his handsome face and kind-looking eyes made her think, what a waste! Then in her next breath she was saying to herself, 'As long as they are happy, it's their lives, bless them.'

Suddenly Jeff looked serious and turning to face Marjorie he asked, 'Why don't you tell us the real reason why you are wandering the streets of this district so early in the morning?' he said. 'Can we help in any way?'

Marjorie felt her cheeks flush. Not knowing quite where to start, she looked round the room. She almost grimaced as her eyes took in the over-stuffed furniture – not that it wasn't good furniture, she thought. There was just too much of it. And in her mind's eye she pictured the glorious flat where these two men lived on the other side of the river. She and Martin had been invited to an evening do at their place and she remembered how everything had seemed so smart yet so simple. She recalled thinking at the time that money talked in all kinds of voices and that neither Mark nor Jeff gave the impression of being short of a bob or two.

'Why am I here? To be honest, it began this morning merely as a whim to get out and about, mainly because I was missing Martin and was fed up with my own company. But now . . .' Marjorie paused for a second and then took the plunge. 'I have an irresistible temptation to tell you about a lady who has, so far, had a rough deal from life. I would give a great deal to be able to give her a helping hand.'

'Is it money she needs?' Mark asked quietly.

Marjorie's eyebrows shot up. 'Oh no,' she answered sharply, 'I'm not on the scrounge. If anything, all I would like from you two is information. The lady in question is strong-willed and does her best to stand on her own two feet. Given the chance she would seize it with both hands, because life has taught her that opportunity does not come knocking on the same door twice in a lifetime.'

It was a very thoughtful Jeff that got up from the table to fetch fresh coffee for each of them, and as he passed Mark he placed his hand on Mark's shoulder using a certain amount of pressure. Mark knew it was a signal.

'Marjorie,' he spoke softly, 'Why don't you tell us the lady's name and just what you have in mind for her?'

Marjorie remained thoughtful as she watched Jeff refill their cups.

'Begin at the beginning, tell us how you came to know so much about this lady,' urged Mark encouragingly. 'And are we allowed to know her name?'

'All right. All right.' Marjorie grinned nervously but she decided to take a gamble and started the story of Joan Baldwin right from the early days when Joan had been unfortunate enough to be married to a right loser. She was downright in her speech, as she related how Joan had worked two jobs and still cared for Granny Baldwin right up until the day she had died. How Joan had carried three babies and lost them all because of the way Baldwin had bashed her about.

By now, both men were seething with rage as they listened to Marjorie.

Then smiles came to Jeff and Mark's faces as she related how Joan's brother-in-law and his two sons had given Joan's husband a right seeing to and forced him to take a job as nightwatchman in a Wandsworth Brewery. After a short pause she gave them an account of the fire in the stables and consequently the many interviews with the police. With her husband and her mother-in-law both dead, Marjorie went on to explain how Joan had lost her home and owned nothing but what she stood up in. However, Marjorie was quick to assure them, Joan had not lain down and bemoaned the fact that nothing good ever came her way. The Labour Exchange had found her a job in service. It was a good job, and Joan had proved her worth. The only trouble was that it was miles away in Kent, she knew no one in the area and often did not take her day off because she knew of nowhere she could pop in and be made welcome.

Marjorie paused and then thoughtfully muttered, 'I suppose it was really a case of once a Londoner always a Londoner.'

They looked from one to the other and all three burst out laughing, which eased the tension for a while.

Marjorie carried on, telling the men how Joan had been working for Martin and herself on the stalls over Christmas and that at present she did four days a week in their Balham shop.

'Hang on a minute, Marge, I think you've jumped the gun a bit here.' Mark said cheerfully. 'If she's working in a household down in Kent how come she's been working for you?'

Marjorie's smile was sad as she said, 'Yeah, I've missed out quite a lot, haven't I? But I don't want to take up too much more of your time.'

The two men grinned. 'Handsome bleeders we are, decorative, not the run of the mill. Our motto is never do what you pay your employees to do for you,' Mark joked, 'so go on, finish what you were saying and then maybe we'll get to the point as to why you are here so early in the morning.'

'Not that we're not thrilled to see you,' Jeff hastened to add.

Marjorie sighed, it all sounded so unbelievable in the cold light of day, but she carried on. 'Last year when Joan got leave from this Mulborough House, Martin remarked at how sad she looked and Joan admitted she was lonely, she missed her neighbours and her family. Martin and I persuaded her to give her employers a month's notice when she returned and we promised that we would help set her up in a little business of her own. Any premises we did come across had to have living accommodation over the shop because more than anything Joan wanted a home of her own.

'Sadly, as always, it must have seemed to Joan, that fate was still not on her side. She never did hand her notice in because the household was in uproar when she got back. The master had suffered a stroke and her mistress was very ill. Never one to desert a sinking ship, Joan stayed on another year until the master died. She did inherit a small legacy, from Mr Hamilton, he was her employer, plus she had saved almost all of her wages, and since her return she has been living with her sister and brother-in-law. They have two sons and a young daughter. They really are a nice family and I'm sure they love Joan dearly, they do their utmost to make her feel welcome but she feels as if she's intruding too much now because the house is very small and cramped.

'Martin, myself, and all of her friends have been looking for suitable premises for her. We've none of us had any luck until this morning when I saw this shop. An empty shop! With what looked liked spacious living quarters up above it. It was filthy, mind, but nothing that a bucket of soapy water and some elbow grease couldn't cure.' Marjorie had spoken these two last sentences with great emphasis and her eyes were half closed as if she could already visualise Joan's dream coming true.

'At last!' Mark punched Jeff playfully. 'We have finally got to the crunch of the matter.'

Jeff winked back at him before saying, 'In a nutshell, Marjorie, you want to rent or buy the property, even though you haven't set foot inside the door yet.'

'Well, I suppose we do have to give the premises the once-over first, always providing we can find the owner, but other than that, Jeff, you've got it in one.'

'Who's we?' Mark asked, smiling.

'Daft question,' Jeff rebuked him. 'Marjorie needs our

help, and isn't it ironic that we two know all there is to know about that shop?'

'I was only joking,' Mark hastened to assure her. 'And I do think it's a marvellous case of us all being in the right place at the right time.'

'Really?' Marjorie's voice was full of disbelief. 'How long has the place been empty? And why has nobody rented it? Can you get in touch with the owner?'

'Whoa, hold your horses, Marge.' Mark took a snow-white handkerchief out of his pocket and made an exaggerated show of wiping his brow. 'Slow down and we'll answer your questions one at a time.'

Jeff leant forward and took one of Marjorie's hands and held it between both of his own. His lovely blue eyes, full of emotion, were staring straight at her. 'We know all there is to know about that shop and the gent who owns the whole caboodle and if your friend doesn't end up as the new tenant then I promise you, Marge, it won't be for the want of us trying.'

Marjorie sank back in her chair and silently sent up a prayer of thanks. The two men got up slowly from their seats and Jeff said, 'We're just going down to the bar. Make yourself comfortable, Marge. We won't be long.' When they had left, Marjorie let out a long drawn-out sigh. If only everything would turn out as easy as Mark and Jeff seemed to think.

Within the hour Marjorie was in a taxi with Jeff and Mark. There was no conversation between them until the cab drew to a halt outside a tall house set back from the embankment on the other side of Albert Bridge and fronted by massive iron gates which automatically opened as the taxi driver sounded his horn. Marjorie's nerves were jangling and she swallowed deeply as she walked up the steps to the front door. They were obviously expected because the door was open and standing in the hall was an immaculately dressed grey-haired man who was very tall with a military bearing.

'Come in.' It was an order rather than an invitation. He stepped aside and allowed them to pass and then followed them down the hall and into the sitting room.

'How about a drink?' he asked gruffly. 'Tea, coffee, whisky?'

Marjorie shook her head. 'No thank you, nothing for me.'

Jeff and Mark both said, 'Scotch will be fine.'

'Forgot yer manners, 'ave yer? I thought better of you two than that. No drinks until you have introduced the lady.' The man smiled but it didn't reach his eyes. Jeff crossed the room quickly.

'Marjorie, this is Edward Tyler, a big businessman in our manor.' Then, turning to their host, he said, 'Teddy, this is Marjorie Goldsmith. I know you have met her husband Martin on many an occasion, but . . .'

'I've never had the pleasure,' Teddy Tyler cut in. 'No one could forget having met this beautiful young lady.' He bent low, took her hand and brushed his lips lightly over the back of it.

Marjorie was always elegantly dressed but the brown suit she was wearing today was far more expensive than most of her other outfits. The beige colouring of her neat blouse matched up well and the two colours suited her. Her shoulder-length dark hair gleamed like spun silk. Her high heels made her seem taller than she was and she looked closer to forty than her real age of fifty-three.

'Very pleased to meet you, Mr Tyler,' Marjorie said, feeling intimidated by this tall, strange man.

Edward straightened up to his full height. 'I'm aware that this is our first contact, but I hope you will find it in your heart to call me Teddy. I loathe the name Edward.' He grinned widely, walked over to a drinks table and poured two measures of whisky. 'Help yourselves to soda,' he said as he handed Jeffrey and Mark their drinks. He then took a bottle of white wine from an ice bucket, poured some into a tall, slender glass and offered it to Marjorie. 'Relax,' he said. 'Nothing like a glass of wine to give you a bit of Dutch courage when you're seeking to do a business deal.'

'Thank you.' Marjorie suddenly felt more at ease with this unusual man. She took a sip and found the wine to be excellent. It was certainly not a cheap bottle of plonk. She sipped it appreciatively.

Suddenly Teddy Tyler became businesslike. 'The lads here have given me the gist of why you want to rent the Brixton shop. They told me on the blower that your Martin is away. Can't it wait till he gets back?'

'Is there a reason not to do business with a woman?' Marjorie said, sounding far more confident than she actually felt.

'Ooh, you answer a question with a question. Right Londoner's trick. Born within the sound of Bow Bells, were you?'

'Well, in North London,' said Marjorie, 'a place known as the Nile.'

'I know it well,' he said. 'Used to play around there when I was a boy. I was born in Ludgate, you know, Whitechapel Road area. Don't know about you, but we used to play out in the streets till it was dark, and there wasn't much we wouldn't 'ave done to earn a penny.'

While this bit of banter was going on, Jeff and Mark had made themselves comfortable and behind Teddy's back they both gave Marjorie the thumbs-up sign.

'Ever 'eard of Jimmy Erlock?' Teddy flung the question at her.

'Can't say that I have,' Marjorie answered seriously.

'You ain't missed much. Nasty piece of work. He was the last tenant of the Brixton shop. I did a deal with him in good faith but he used my premises to set up a scam and no one gets away with tucking me up.' He turned to the two men. 'Top yet drinks up, lads,' he ordered, and let out a great belly laugh. 'Jimmy Erlock is getting free board and lodging at the moment, compliments of His Majesty.'

Both the lads laughed but it was Jeff who said, 'Anything been heard of his bird?'

'No, but I'm in no hurry. Remember how she was always going on about sex and violence? Especially when she'd had too much to drink.'

Jeff nodded. 'Bit of a simpleton, we both thought.'

'Not too silly to have scarpered with most of the dosh.' Mark's remark touched a sore point with Teddy and he turned and glared at him.

'Yeah well, let's hope she's making the most of it 'cos it's only lent. When my lads do catch up with her, and they will, she'll be screaming about violence all right.'

Having listened to the men talking Marjorie was feeling a bit apprehensive and she decided she'd rather have Teddy Tyler as a friend than an enemy. Teddy gave her a kind but critical stare. 'You're convinced this Mrs Baldwin is on the level? Deserving of your 'elp?'

'Definitely. One hundred per cent, Mr Tyler.'

Teddy was looking very thoughtful. 'Known her long, 'ave you?'

Marjorie nodded. 'Yes, since she was a young girl. Why?'

'Just wondered,' Teddy replied. He walked over to the window to avoid the necessity of explaining himself, or being accused of going soft. Although he had only been given a sketchy outline of Joan Baldwin's circumstances, he found himself fully understanding her frustration at having no home of her own. If Martin Goldsmith's wife thought so much of her he felt she must be worth helping. He turned from the window and said quietly to Marjorie, 'I've a proposition to put to you. Your friend can have the shop in Brixton high street and the rooms above, rent free for three months, in return for cleaning the place up from top to bottom.'

'She'll jump at the chance, Mr Tyler, I just know she will.'

'In that case the lads can 'ave the keys and take yer to see over the place. But I'll set up the long-term details with Martin when he gets back. Right?'

Marjorie was tongue-tied. She just nodded her head and smiled happily and stammered, 'Thanks, Mr Tyler.'

'I don't want no thanks, but could yer try an' remember I'm Teddy to me friends. Edward makes me flesh crawl and Mr Tyler is a bit stuffed shirt. I keep that for those that owe me.'

'Sorry, Teddy,' Marjorie said sheepishly.

Jeff and Mark drained their glasses and got to their feet, and Mark caught the bunch of keys that Teddy threw at them.

Marjorie was thinking she could come to like this old man and she was so happy that at last she might be able to tell Joan she was to be given a new start in life.

Teddy held out his hand and Marjorie shook it gratefully. 'If you do come to an agreement with Martin, I promise you, Teddy, Mrs Baldwin will be a good tenant.'

Teddy Tyler looked into her eyes and said flatly, 'If she isn't, Marjorie, you will be the first to know.'

Chapter Twenty-two

It was Wednesday morning and Joan was having a lie-in. Outside it was still a cold winter's day and the windows were frosted up. The men had all gone to work and Rosie to the office job she had got in the paper mills. It didn't seem possible that Rosie would soon be sixteen. Snuggling deeper down in the bed Joan smiled because she knew that very soon now Martha would come upstairs bringing her a cup of tea. Suddenly the sound of the door knocker going rat-a-tat-tat made her sit up straight. When she heard Martha open the front door and scream 'Oh my Gawd, it's a blinking telegram' she flung back the bedclothes and ran to the top of the stairs. Telegrams always meant bad news – at least to people in this area they did.

Martha leant against the wall, her chest heaving. Having read the typed words on the front of the envelope she sighed and looked up at Joan. 'It's addressed to you, luv.' She didn't hand it up to her sister, instead she said thoughtfully, 'Go and put your dressing gown on and come downstairs. I was just about to make a fresh pot of tea. You can read your telegram down 'ere in the warm – I've got a roaring fire going.'

Martha knew she was talking too much but her thoughts were all for her sister. What if it were really bad news? She didn't want her falling down the stairs. Who the ruddy hell would be sending Joan a telegram anyway? She looked up and saw that Joan had gone back into her bedroom and she was half tempted to slit the envelope open and read the message for herself. However, she didn't let her curiosity get the better of her, but went into the warm kitchen, laid the yellow envelope down on the table and busied herself by lifting the big black kettle off the hob and pouring the boiling water over the tea leaves she had spooned into the large brown teapot. Bad news or good news they still needed a good strong cup of tea. Seeing the telegram boy standing on her doorstep and his red bicycle propped up against her front gate had half frightened the life out of her.

She heard Joan coming down the stairs, and as the kitchen door opened Martha forced herself to smile. Nodding to where she had placed the telegram she said, 'Sit yourself down, luv, before you open that.'

Joan did as she was told and for a minute she sat bolt upright in the chair and clutched the arms. 'I can't think of a single soul who would want to get in touch with me by sending a telegram,' she cried, her eyes flaring with apprehension.

Conscious of her sister's feelings, Martha picked up the envelope and said gently, 'It won't take you a minute to find out.' Thrusting it towards Joan she urged, 'Go on, open the ruddy thing. The suspense is killing me.'

Joan took a deep breath to steady herself, took the telegram from Martha and slit the flap open with her thumbnail. In no time at all Joan's face lit up. 'It's all right, it's all right,' she cried, her voice rising to a shriek.

'Then for Christ's sake put me out of my bloody misery and read the damn thing to me, or at least tell me who it's from.' Martha had been so afraid that it was some sort of bad news that by now her temper was smouldering.

'It's from Marjorie,' Joan said, and grinning from ear to ear she silently reread the short message, hardly able to take it in. 'Get a cab. Come to shop. Good news. Marjorie.'

Joan read the message aloud this time, then jumped to her feet, crossed the room and threw her arms round her sister.

Martha was moved to tears as they hugged each other tightly. 'Wasn't it only the other day that I said you were about due for some good luck,' she murmured when at last they separated. 'Sit yer down and I'll pour the tea out. I don't care what you say, you are not leaving this house until you've got some food inside you.'

'Oh, Martha, I am so excited. What do you think Marjorie means by good news?'

'Oh, 'ere we go. Supposing this that an' the other ain't gonna get you anywhere. Just drink yer tea and then while you're getting washed and dressed I'll cook yer a bit of breakfast an' then you can be off.'

The two sisters sat facing each other as they sipped at the strong, scalding tea. They weren't talking for the simple reason they were both lost in thought. Whatever the good news turned out to be, Martha was truly thrilled. For more years than she cared to remember Joan had been the main worry of her life. She knew for a fact that Joan wouldn't rest until she had got herself regular work and, more to the point, her own place to live. She was well aware that her sister's main aim in life was to be independent. She was also sure that never again would she allow a man to treat her in the awful way that bleeding Bill Baldwin had. She might even end up being well off, because she'd succeed no matter what she took on.

But at what cost? Martha asked herself. Look at her now. She's as thin as a rake. I thought her idea of having a shop was really daft when she first started going on about it, but now I am beginning to think it might be the best thing that could happen to her. But only if it puts a roof over her head.

Joan had finished drinking her cup of tea, yet she stayed perfectly still. Her heart was beating rapidly and a tingling excitement surged through her veins. For the life of her she couldn't put into words the way she was feeling. Suddenly she sprang to her feet. 'I'm going to have a wash and get dressed,' she cried.

'All right.' Martha laughed. 'And while you're getting ready I'll cook you that breakfast.'

'All right, Martha. Thanks, dear, but please don't do me a huge fry-up. May I just have some toast?'

'With a boiled egg and some soldiers?' Martha kept a straight face as she teased her sister.

Joan could give tit-for-tat when the occasion arose and she saucily answered, 'I'm not very keen on soldiers. Please may I have ladies' fingers and gentlemen's thumbs?'

'I'll 'ave less of yer cheek,' said Martha, swiping Joan with the tea cloth she had in her hand. 'You'll eat what I set in front of you.' Joan was still laughing to herself as she walked slowly up the stairs.

Martha cut two thick slices of bread and took the toasting fork down from where it hung on a nail in the wall beside the cooking range. While she prepared the light breakfast for her sister, she murmured, 'Please, let this turn out to be the break that Joan has been waiting for. Dear God, you know she deserves a chance if anyone ever did.'

As Joan stepped into the taxi there was a look of resolve on her face. She leant back against the soft leather and looked down at herself. The beige skirt in strong, twilled fabric and the long hound's-tooth check jacket in brown and white were the best she'd ever made. Martin had given her the two remnants and while she was sewing them she had kept

212

telling herself how lucky she was. They weren't for some lady, they were for herself. She had debated as to whether or not she would wear a hat today; finally decided against. Instead she had wound her long, soft brown hair into a French pleat and had pinned a few strands of hair into curls and set them just above her forehead, which made her look at least a little taller than she was.

It seemed to take ages for the taxi to reach Balham. Finally the cab drew to a halt outside Goldsmith's Haberdashery and Marjorie and Martin were rushing from the shop to greet her. While Martin paid the cab driver Marjorie wrapped her arms round Joan and whispered in her ear, 'I think I have found just the place for you.'

These few hurried words set Joan's heart beating rapidly and a tingling excitement surged through her veins.

'Break it up, you two.' Martin laughed. Joan went to him and he lovingly kissed her cheek.

'What are we standing about outside on the pavement for?' he asked. 'Take Joan upstairs, Marjorie. The side door is open and I'll be up myself in about ten minutes.'

A few minutes later, as Joan walked into Marjorie's beautifully furnished front room, she got a surprise. Standing in the middle of the room was a tall man. Marjorie quickly made the introductions. 'Joan, this is Mr Edward Tyler, the owner of the property we are going to take you to view. Teddy, this is our good friend Joan Baldwin.'

Mr Tyler was, without doubt, impressive. Easily over six foot tall, he was large, but not fat. There was a lot of heavy muscle in the shoulders of his immaculate dark suit. Thick, grey wavy hair spilled over the collar of his jacket.

'Pleased to meet you, Mr Tyler,' Joan said, holding out her hand.

He shook it, immediately thinking how cold it felt through the thin gloves she was wearing. 'Bit on the small side, aren't you?' he remarked, then added, 'And before we go any

213

further, as I told Marjorie, I'm Teddy to my friends, I loathe the name Edward and Mr Tyler is useful only for business and those that owe me.' His accent was pure London, powerful and positive.

'Yes, I am small,' Joan answered, 'but my mother always insisted that good things come in small parcels.' The minute the words left her mouth she wished she hadn't been so flippant.

'Well, Miss Baldwin, I've heard quite a bit about you and I understand you would like to rent a shop from me, is that right?'

Joan was saved from answering straight away because Marjorie came back into the room carrying a tray which held four cups of coffee. Martin joined them at the same time, and straight off he said, 'Why on earth are you standing up? For goodness' sake sit yourselves down and be comfortable.'

Joan sipped her hot coffee gratefully. She felt a bit intimidated by this big man. Mr Tyler seemed to suddenly sense just how ill at ease Joan was and in a much softer voice he turned to her and said, 'Miss Baldwin, you haven't answered my question.'

Just as quietly she replied, 'Yes, I would like to rent a shop and start up my own business, but shall we start again? I am Mrs Baldwin, not Miss. However, since you asked me to call you Teddy, you may call me Joan.'

He actually laughed, a great belly laugh. 'Well, Joan, that gets us off on a better footing. What experience do you have of retailing?'

The question surprised Joan and she wondered why he wanted to know. It wasn't as if he was interviewing her for a job. However, the last thing she wanted to do was rub him up the wrong way. So she said, 'I have a great deal of experience of working for myself. For many years I have been doing dressmaking, alterations and curtain-making.

'Whilst I was in service I made two ball gowns and a silk two-piece suit for the ladies of the house. If only I had the space I feel I could build up a trade with good, steady customers. Besides, I have Martin and Marjorie to guide me. They won't let me buy shoddy stock and when it comes to material Martin is an expert.'

'Oh,' said Teddy, dumbfounded. He shook his head. 'Got it all worked out, 'ave you? You think yer could earn a living and pay a rent just by doing needlework?' He sounded unimpressed.

'More coffee, anyone?' Marjorie asked cheerfully, feeling things were getting a bit tense. Martin also thought that Teddy was being a bit forceful. He wanted to say why the hell don't you give us the keys and let us take Joan to see the place. But one didn't argue with Teddy Taylor.

Joan grabbed the moment to drive her point home. 'Not just needlework. I do have other things in mind.'

''Ave yer now. Such as?'

Joan sighed. 'Well, I can't decide until I know how big the premises are. And then there is the living accommodation. I can't afford to rent if I can't live there.'

'Oh, you could live there all right. I've been told you're a lady on yer own. Well, the living quarters are good. There are two big rooms in the front, a very large kitchen, a flush toilet but no bathroom. Oh, an' there's a huge cellar for storage.'

Martin had had enough. 'For God's sake, Teddy, you aren't offering her bloody Buckingham Palace. From what Marjorie has told me it's you that's getting a good deal if she's got to clean it from top to bottom.'

Teddy was taken aback and it showed. He glanced at Marjorie. 'Did you think it was that bad?'

'Disgusting would be an apt description,' Marjorie quietly informed him. 'Mark and Jeff considered you'd need to put an army of cleaners in there. But I really don't know why we're sitting around like this. Why the hell don't you just

215

give me the keys and let me take Joan to see the place? After all, it's her decision.'

Martin glanced at the clock. It was ten minutes to eleven. 'Come on, Teddy. Pubs will be open by the time we get there. Let's leave the girls to it. They can catch up with us later and we'll all have a bit of lunch.'

Teddy didn't say a word. He stood up, shrugged himself into his black overcoat and took a small bunch of keys from the pocket and handed them to Marjorie. Martin kissed Joan first, then his wife. 'Make it the Prince, shall we? About one o'clock?'

Teddy Tyler merely nodded at the two women as he followed Martin out of the room. Marjorie and Joan heard Martin whistling as he went downstairs and they each breathed a sigh of relief.

'Come on,' Marjorie said, 'put your jacket on. My car is just round the corner. Let's go and see what you're letting yourself in for.'

Chapter Twenty-three

MARJORIE PARKED HER CAR in the road behind the shop and Joan couldn't get out quickly enough, keen to see not only the inside of the shop but the living accommodation. The very thought of having her own home had her quivering with excitement. They walked side by side for a few yards until Marjorie stopped and pushed open a gate and they went into an untidy, neglected back yard, past a water tap, a coal shed and what appeared to be a washhouse. Then, selecting a key from the bunch that Teddy Tyler had given her, Marjorie turned the key in the lock and they went through into what might have once been a downstairs kitchen. There was an iron stove with a flat top on one side and an oven on the other. Joan thought that it must have been many a long day since that stove had seen any blacklead. There was also a shallow brown sink fixed beneath a small window so dirty one couldn't possibly see out of it.

'Would you like to go through to the shop first or go upstairs?' asked Marjorie. Smiling, she added, 'You'll probably have a fit whichever way we start.'

'No doubt,' said Joan, 'but then I'm not expecting anything special.'

Marjorie shrugged. 'Come on then, follow me.'

They went down a narrow corridor and into a large shop at the far end, and although it was in a filthy state it made Joan's heart sing. Double fronted, it had two huge windows with a door in the centre leading out into the main road. The premises had at some time been an estate agent's and was still partly furnished as an office, but by God the whole place smelt awful, there was rubbish and litter all over the floor and Joan could have written her name in the dust.

'I did try to prepare you.' Marjorie sighed. 'If you think this front shop is awful wait until you see the side room, and the upstairs looks as if the last occupants lived like pigs. And as to the cellar, the Lord only knows for what purpose they used that.'

'This room is not so bad,' Joan exclaimed, looking at the shelves that were fixed along the full length of one wall and held an array of books and papers. There were also several tin boxes, all bearing labels. A wall safe was set into the far corner, its wide-open door showing that it was completely empty.

Marjorie sighed once again as they both stared at that empty space. 'In some ways I can't help feeling sorry for Jimmy Erlock. He's inside. Teddy's lost a lot of money on the place, I gather, but he's more upset that the man he trusted did the dirty on him.' When Joan made no answer Marjorie went on almost as if she were talking to herself. 'That Rita Thomas is something else. Beautiful, mind you, and always dressed as if she's just stepped out of a bandbox, but selfish, pompous and vain are only a few of the words I can think of to describe her. Oh, I've thought of one more. Greedy. Oh yes, very greedy. And if I told you the whole truth about her you'd have every right to ask, "Why is it that only dogs are called bitches?"'

Joan was still looking around with interest. On the other side of the large room there was a long, narrow trestle-type table which would be very useful if and when she came to laying out patterns and cutting cloth. Also, a drawing board had been set up and pinned to it lay a map of the local district.

'Stop daydreaming,' Marjorie ordered, pointing a finger to a grubby-looking door. 'Through there is a small kitchenette, a washroom and a toilet. Downstairs is an enormous basement and most importantly, the flooring and the walls show no signs of dampness. I'm not sure about lighting – we'd have to get someone in to check on that but Jeff and Mark and I thought it might make a great workshop. Room down there for several people to work without getting in each other's way.'

Joan gasped. 'Getting a bit ahead of yourself, aren't you, Marjorie? According to you I shall have staff working here with me and yet I haven't taken the place yet. Who knows if I'll even be able to afford the rent.'

'Oh, don't be such a pessimist. If you want this place you've got three months free of rent. I know it will take a lot of elbow grease to get the premises looking shipshape, but try looking on the bright side. Three months is a long time – it will give you breathing space. Do you want to go upstairs or have you given up on the idea?'

'Of course I haven't given up, but the way you talk about me going into business seems hopelessly optimistic.'

'Oh, you're impossible. Have some faith in yourself, girl. Anyway, before we start another discussion, let's go and take a look at the living quarters. I know it's in a terrible state but for all that the accommodation is really good. Ever so spacious.'

Joan couldn't help smiling. Marjorie was such a good friend, and her bubbling enthusiasm so great it was impossible not to be carried along with it. Suddenly they both stood still. They could hear footsteps coming along the passageway. Then the door opened and Martin was standing there.

'Well, well, well,' Marjorie said, and from the happy look on her face one would never have guessed that these two people had been married for more than thirty years. As Joan watched Martin hug his wife she couldn't help thinking what a pity it was that this loving couple had never been blessed with children of their own. Though she was aware they had quite a few nieces and nephews whom they saw quite regularly. They certainly made a handsome couple. Martin also had a good head of thick dark hair and he was quite a few inches taller than Marjorie even though she was wearing high heels. Marjorie's shining auburn shoulder-length hair, and big, dark brown eyes made her attractive but she was also an expert when it came to make-up, her natural unblemished skin had been given a matt porcelain powdering, her lips lightly outlined with a dark red lipstick. The expensive black suit she was wearing and her manicured, red-nailed hands had her looking years younger than she really was.

He let go of his wife and kissed Joan on the cheek. 'Teddy couldn't stay, so I decided not to hang around in the Prince. All set up for business, are we?'

'We haven't been here very long,' Marjorie answered. 'We were just about to go upstairs.' She winked at her husband and nodded towards Joan. 'I rather fancy this is going to be the deciding factor.'

'Make or break, eh?' Martin wagged a finger at Joan. 'Nothing ventured, nothing gained.'

Joan was smiling nervously. 'I don't care how dirty the rooms are, I can soon sort that out. As long as it gives me a place to call my own home and I can afford to pay the rent I will be more than happy.' Her words were honestly said and with spirit.

'Well, view the rooms first and then we'll talk about finances later,' Martin said encouragingly.

At the top of the stairs Marjorie and Martin hung back, thinking it best to let Joan inspect the rooms on her own.

She stepped past them into what appeared a very narrow hallway and pushed open a door that was already ajar. Then she gasped in surprise. Never had she imagined any of the rooms would be as big as this one was. She walked around it, smiling, her eyes roaming from side to side. Her imagination had never led her to even think the accommodation might be anything like this. The main feature of the room was the fireplace, it was huge and Joan thought how lovely it would be to sit there if a log fire was burning in the open grate. She was quick to notice that the surround was probably made of marble. The mantelshelf had a velvet cover with a deep fringed edging. She thought the colour might be a rich dark green but there was no way she could be sure because from end to end it was thick with dust and in places cobwebs joined it to the wall. There were two big armchairs set one each side of the large fireplace, neither of which was any good, both being tattered and torn, with the springs showing through the seats. A few other pieces of furniture had been left behind, most of which would also have to be taken to the council dump. The carpet was rotten, so threadbare that in places she could see the floorboards showing through. Against the far wall there was a huge sofa which might have been bright red at one time but now, like the rest of the room, it had seen better days. However, although faded, it did not appear to have been badly treated and already Joan was imagining how good it would look if she set to and made a loose cover for it. Slowly, she walked to the window. She lifted the dirty lace curtain and felt it crumble between her fingers. She was surprised to find that she was now looking down on to the main road and that the area appeared to be thriving.

Martin's voice made her jump. 'Are you going to stay in here all day or would you like to see the other rooms?'

Joan smiled broadly. 'It's remarkable, it really is.'

'The walls and ceiling are filthy. Take some getting off

will all this old embossed wallpaper,' Martin told her wisely.

'Oh, I'd get Martha's boys and their mates up here. They'd soon scrape these walls.'

Martin threw back his head and let out a big belly laugh and to his wife he called, 'Our Joan has it all worked out. She's going to be the queen and get all her slaves working to make this place fit to be her palace.'

Joan was just as thrilled with the next room. It was almost identical, except the fireplace was much smaller. There were only two items of furniture left in here, one a marble-topped washstand on top of which stood a huge china bowl and a large jug to match. She itched to get the china into hot soapy water, for she suspected that beneath the dirt lay a charming floral design which, years ago, had probably been hand painted. The other piece was a coiled-spring double bed. It held no mattress. A tall, brass head rail with knobs at each end adorned the top of the bedstead, and a shorter version was placed at the tail end. The floor was just bare boards, and they were certainly in need of a jolly good scrub.

The third room was smaller and completely empty. A quick glance through the bare window told her this back bedroom looked down on to the grubby back yard, but already she was telling herself that she would soon have that area ablaze with colour by planting up lots of pots and dotting them about as soon as the spring plants were available.

The kitchen was an unbelievable mess. The sink was so badly stained it smelt rotten, and the wooden draining board was covered in what at some time might have been vegetables, now rotting and slimy. More than half the floor space seemed to be cluttered up with broken china. At one point Joan smiled broadly. She was gazing at a black, cast-iron *gas* stove, which even had a grill beneath the four burners. What a wonder! A closer look showed that the stove was thick with grease and as she pulled the grill pan out she wrinkled her nose in disgust. That at least would have to go straight into the dustbin. How on earth could anybody leave a place as lovely as this in such an awful mess, Joan thought, seething with annoyance.

'Oh, Marjorie, Martin, I never in my wildest dreams imagined the living quarters would be anything like this.' She was blinking tears away, yet she smiled as she said, 'What a great size the rooms are. And when I've finished with it you won't know this kitchen.'

The indoor toilet was the jewel in the crown. To flush it there hung a knotted piece of rope for one to pull. Already Joan's mind had jumped to the day when she would visit an ironmonger's and choose a chain, perhaps with a shiny white enamel handle to dangle from the end. Martin and Marjorie watched the different expressions flit across her face and softly Marjorie murmured, 'Poor Joan. She has so much charm and talent, yet the whole of her life has been dogged by tragedy and sadness.'

Martin suddenly looked very thoughtful. 'You're right, my love. Joan deserves a successful future and we can help her with that.' He grinned, and almost as an afterthought he added, 'let's hope Mr Right might pop up along the way and that she'll find someone to really love and care for her.'

'Eeh . . . you're still an old softie, Martin Goldsmith. Didn't know you had it in you to be a match-maker,' Marjorie said smiling.

Back downstairs, Martin insisted that he take them both to a nearby café and that no one should speak about their plans until they had a pot of tea in front of them and the meal of their choice was being prepared.

Marjorie said she would be mother and Joan drank her cup of tea gratefully while they waited for the homemade steak and kidney pie that Martin had assured them would be extremely good. She was thinking of her dear sister Martha and her good husband Sid. If things did work out

223

well for herself she was going to make sure that she repaid those two for all the kindness they had shown her. Rosie was almost certainly going to come and work for her. The travelling distance wasn't too far: a tube train from Colliers Wood to Stockwell and a penny tram ride would bring her almost to the shop. As she ate her pie her mind was jumping miles ahead. That back room would make a lovely bedroom and she was sure Martha would let Rosie stay with her sometimes. Oh, she would make it look so pretty. Rosie would be over the moon with it.

Everything had been so much better at Martha's house since Sid was back working full time and both Lenny and Bernie were doing well, but she still felt that they hadn't much space in their little house at the best of times and it would be so good for her to be able to get out from under their feet. Not that she wouldn't be a constant visitor. Martha's Sunday dinners were always great.

When they had eaten their fill, which included apple dumplings and custard, and Marjorie had poured them all a second cup of tea, it was Martin who leant back in his chair and said, 'Come on then, Joan, talk away. Are you impressed enough with what's on offer or do you think it is a no go?'

Joan hesitated. 'Surely you both know how much I would like to have that place. But I will feel a whole lot better when Mr Tyler tells me what the rent is going to be.'

'Are you really that worried?' Marjorie asked, frowning deeply.

'Of course I am,' Joan answered crossly, which was unusual for her. 'I know Mr Tyler is allowing me three months free of rent but I think the situation should be on a solid basis before I commit myself.' Seeing the look that passed between her friends she hastened to explain. 'Supposing I scrub and clean the place, which I am more than willing to do, and pay my nephews and their mates to scrape

224

walls. Even if I only give the place a clean coat of whitewash for now, it will still cost me money, and what if when it's all done Mr Tyler quotes a rent that is more than I can afford?'

'It won't be like that,' Martin promised. 'I will have a chat with Teddy, and whatever we work out we'll make sure he does the deal with you all fair and square and above board.

'And we'll come to the solicitors with you,' Marjorie added.

Martin was thinking hard. 'Joan, would you like to tell us what your financial situation is? It's not that I want to be nosy, but it will help us to help you more if we know your circumstances from the beginning. Do you mind?'

'Not in the least,' Joan was quick to assure him. Looking from one to the other she said, 'I thought I was nicely placed when I left Mulborough House, but now with so much to do and stock to buy I am not so sure. While I was working I hardly spent a penny, especially when I was helping to look after Mr Hamilton, because I never left the house for weeks. So I have quite a bit of money saved, and also the two hundred guineas which Mr Hamilton left me in his will.'

The silence that followed her statement was hard for Joan to bear and she spoke again. 'This is quite a posh area, isn't it? All the other businesses seem to be doing well and Mr Tyler has already lost money on those premises, so he's not going to let them go for a song, is he?'

Marjorie looked across at her husband and nodded her head, which meant nothing to Joan but to Martin it was a signal. He leant forward and patted Joan's hand. 'Just you listen to me. With your ability and organisational skills you'll be earning in no time. Meanwhile, Marjorie and myself would like to invest in your new business, that is, if you will have us.'

Joan lifted her head and glanced at Martin apprehensively. Then she asked, 'Why are you both being so good to me? If you had just offered to continue to employ me on your market stall I would have been grateful, though where I would live would be a problem.'

Marjorie gave her a puzzled smile. 'I don't know what you're on about. We struck oil finding those premises. You deserve your own business. You don't want to be stuck out on the market in all weathers. Think about the living accommodation you've just looked at and then tell me you don't want it.'

'Oh, Marjorie, I know I would simply love to live and work there. But . . .'

'No buts,' Martin cut in. Then, smiling gently he said, 'I'll set up another meeting with Teddy. Let him know that Marjorie and myself will be standing as guarantors.' Then, smiling again he said, 'The hardest thing you have to do is come up with a catchy name for your new business and stop worrying about finance. You'll be fine. Given time you'll end up really rich.'

'I'd like to think so,' Joan answered. But it was said without conviction.

Chapter Twenty-four

TEDDY TYLER'S VOICE was full of barely suppressed irritation as he pointed a finger at Joan and said, 'For God's sake look a bit more cheerful, woman!'

Joan was sitting on the settee in the Goldsmiths' front room with Marjorie beside her. Inwardly Joan was trembling, but not Marjorie. She purposely allowed her skirt to wriggle up to just above her knees, crossed her legs, and swung one foot from the ankle. Her long legs, pure silk stockings and high-heeled black court shoes were enough to catch Teddy's eye. He grinned, and Marjorie realised that he looked smug. Smug and very sure of himself.

'Lay off her, Teddy. I've told you Martin won't be long. He's bringing the cash, then everything will be sorted. I'll get you a drink,' Marjorie offered quickly.

'Best idea you've had this morning,' Teddy replied, his features relaxing as he watched Marjorie pour brandy into one of their cut-glass goblets.

Joan felt she owed so much to Martin. He had been slowly teaching her the ropes over the last three months, taking her to factories and warehouses, until now, the first week in May, she was finally feeling more confident of all the different aspects of the business. After today, when money changed hands, she would be the tenant of the premises, now to be known as 'Distinctive Designs'. The tenancy agreement had been drawn up for a period of five years.

God, it seemed a lifetime!

When it had come to the signing of the lease Joan had prayed that she would be able to work up enough business to last that long.

There had been a great deal of argument over the finding of a name for Joan's shop. In the end it had been Jim Taylor, the bare wood man, who had come up with the idea of naming the premises 'Distinctive Designs'. Martha had immediately begun to refer to the business as D&D and the shortened version had quickly caught on.

As the days and weeks had rushed busily by and the date set for the opening of her shop had grown closer, life for Joan had grown more and more hectic. There had been no time to brood on whether or not she was doing the right thing or to speculate about the future and Joan was thankful for that. Every member of her family had helped in various ways and friends she never even knew she had, mainly stallholders from the market, had thrown their weight in and offered whatever assistance they could.

Bernie, Lenny and four of their mates had given up their evenings and weekends to decorate the place throughout. Mind you, all six young men had become damn good customers of the Prince of Wales! Somehow Martin had acquired three fairly good sewing machines, Teddy Tyler had set a glazier on to put two windows into the walls of the part of the basement that was not entirely underground, and electricity was working now through the whole of the building. Joan had sewn until her fingers were sore, yet she still enjoyed listening to the burring of the machines and nothing pleased her more at the end of the day than to neatly fold and lay embroidered articles between sheets of tissue paper or to place all the finished garments on coat-hangers. More·often than not she was too tired to think of what tomorrow might bring.

Martin had also sent two of his own needle-women over to help Joan, and for the time being he was paying their wages.

Upstairs was nothing short of a transformation. The whole place smelt of paint and both walls and ceilings were now pure white. Sid had told his boys the place looked like a ruddy hospital, but that did not deter Joan. Time enough for expensive wallpaper and carpets when she was earning money. She would be glad, though, when she could afford to have lino or cheap carpet on the stairs. The bare boards irritated her.

Today she would officially take up residence. For the past two weeks she had been camping out in the big front bedroom. If it weren't for the fact that she couldn't help worrying whether or not she was going to be able to make a success of this great venture she would gladly admit it was exciting to be setting up a new home. Martha and herself had visited several second-hand furniture shops and had, or so they had thought at the time, bought quite a few useful items at bargain prices, which they'd agreed would make the place homely, at least for the time being.

It was in the middle of a Sunday afternoon that Jim Taylor had turned up, driving a large van. When Joan went downstairs to answer the ring of the doorbell, Jim had opened the double doors at the back of the van and invited her to jump up and inspect the contents.

'Anything that takes your fancy, just name it and it's yours.' He beamed at her. Joan had a job to believe what she was seeing. A complete home and more was tidily stacked from front to back of the vehicle.

'I couldn't possible accept any of this wonderful furniture,

Jim. Where on earth has it come from? It looks as if the bailiffs have raided someone's home. All these cardboard boxes look to me to be full of cooking utensils.'

'Joan, it is nothing as bad as that, I promise you,' Jim answered quietly. 'There's a mate I do a lot of work with and his grandmother has been taken into an old folk's home. Sad really, because her daughter had been caring for her, but unfortunately the daughter has died first. My mate, Doug Morgan, had to empty the house out quickly because he couldn't afford to go on paying the rent. He offered me a business deal. I thought I'd be a fool not to take it up.'

'Oh, Jim! It's wonderful. The rooms upstairs are so big I thought it would be donkey's years before I would be able to furnish them all.' Suddenly she pulled a face. 'I'm jumping the gun a bit here, aren't I? You haven't told me how much any of this will cost me.'

'Oh, huh.' He wagged a finger at her. 'There's no question of you not being able to afford it. Just let me help you sort out what you can use and the rest I know full well I can sell on and I won't be a penny out of pocket.'

'I couldn't accept things without paying a penny.' Joan sounded outraged.

Jim let out a long sigh, then said as though by way of an explanation, 'I've done Doug many a favour and he's done the same for me. He did get one dealer in, who offered to clear the house for forty pounds. The cheek of the man – he would have stood to make a small fortune. If you must know, we settled on sixty-five pounds.'

Joan stood silent for a minute or two, weighing up in her mind how useful several of these items would be to her. It was the chance of a lifetime, but she wouldn't accept charity. She wasn't sure how Jim was placed financially, but in any case she wouldn't want him to be out of pocket because of her. She looked the length of the van again, her mind working busily. In fact it had already turned a few somersaults.

There was a single bed and a pretty little dressing table which would go beautifully in the small room she already thought of as Rosie's room. And an old-fashioned dining room table and chairs which she would dearly love to own. 'I can manage forty pounds,' she murmured, naming the items she had been thinking about.

'There is a single wardrobe tucked away at the back that goes with that single set,' Jim told her, smiling broadly. He guessed she had her niece Rosie in mind and it made him feel happy to think that the young girl might come to stay with her aunt from time to time. 'I'll take thirty pounds and throw in the contents all those cardboard boxes. It would be a job to get rid of the odd assortments of junk, but I will make money on those larger pieces of furniture, don't you worry.'

She glanced gratefully at him, knowing full well those boxes did not contain junk. 'You know, Jim, looking back, ever since I got married my life has been a bit complicated. Now suddenly even strangers are going out of their way to help me, and as for friends – they seem to be going to the ends of the earth to make sure that I have a decent place to live. I'll never be able to thank all of you.' They were smiling at each other now. 'You have surprised me today, Jim.'

'Oh Joan, not as much as you have surprised me on many an occasion, not nearly as much. Anyway, I'll garage the van at my place tonight and Doug and I will come back tomorrow and unload all the items you select.'

Suddenly, without stopping to think, she asked, 'Do you have to go now? What about coming upstairs and having Sunday tea with me?'

Jim didn't hesitate. 'No, I don't have to rush off and yes I would like that. I *would* like that.'

Joan gave him the Sunday newspaper to read and saw him settled on the big sofa, which she thankfully reflected looked rather good since she had made a jade green cover for it and four cushions, which she had covered in beige linen and piped the edges with strips of the jade green material. It was about twenty minutes before she came back from the kitchen carrying a heavy tray. Jim was on his feet in an instant, took the tray from her and looked around for a table on which to place it. Of course there wasn't one.

'Sorry. We'll have to put it down on the floor.' Joan felt really embarrassed, and explained hastily, 'I haven't eaten in this room yet. I've been eating in the kitchen.'

Jim badly wanted her to relax. 'We'll manage. Tomorrow you'll have your dining room set, and there is a small nest of coffee tables that will be handy for in here. Or there is always that tea trolley I made for you ages ago.'

Joan's voice was subdued as she said, 'I know I keep saying it but it's true. I'll never be able to thank you enough.'

They sat side by side and ate egg and cress sandwiches, and Joan got down on the floor to pour them each a cup of tea and to cut into portions a coffee and walnut cake she had bought the previous day from Fuller's.

'Tell me about your friend Doug. Does he know that you are letting me have some of his gran's furniture?'

'Oh yes, he does. He's a good man. We've known each other since our schooldays. He's good with his hands, does similar work to what I do. He's an intelligent fellow when you get to know him. Most likely he won't open his mouth when he first meets you tomorrow but once he gets used to you he'll be fine.'

Joan leant over and placed her empty teacup on the saucer. Then, raising her head, she stared intently at him and said, 'It's going to be a different life for me, Jim. Quite a new life.'

He held back from saying, 'For me too,' for he might have said it too eagerly. Not only did he need company to fill the great hole of loneliness he had felt in the years since his

232

wife had gone off with another man, but in a strange way he knew he needed her, her in particular, and had done ever since Marjorie and Martin Goldsmith had introduced her to him. He couldn't help the way he felt, even knowing that the very thought was ridiculous and far-fetched.

Joan Baldwin had an outgoing personality, was small and beautiful, and her long soft golden-brown hair that she mostly wore twisted up into a bun had him longing to release it from the pins that held it in place and run his fingers through the long silky strands. If she gave him any thought at all she probably considered him to be quiet and serious, and the fact that he wore glasses didn't help. However, he had proved he could be useful to her and perhaps there would be many more opportunities when he could be of help to her.

But regarding anything more than that, he was well aware, he stood no chance. Still, having Joan as a friend was a bonus.

Chapter Twenty-five

JOAN PUSHED OPEN the back gate and smiled broadly. What a transformation!

The yard looked entirely different. There was no longer a mass of dirt and decay and no sign of the empty beer bottles and other debris that had been strewn around on her first visit. In one corner rotting refuse had been piled high; now in that same corner stood a wooden tub filled with compost and planted with high green plants at the back and a variety of brightly coloured flowers at the front. All round the edges were trailing petunias. In addition, several large stone pots had been scattered around and each one planted with a flowering shrub.

This was all down to Martha, bless her. Martha loved gardening. An image of herself and her sister sitting out here drinking a cup of tea on a nice sunny day came to Joan's mind. Then she shook her head, and laughingly reminded herself she'd have to find the time first. Her days were going to be really busy from now on. She spent another few minutes admiring her sister's handiwork, but now the time had come.

She had chosen to come here on her own today and yet

as she turned the key in the lock and stepped into what was now her own home *and* business she really felt lonely. So much had happened so fast, she had never dreamed she would feel the way she felt at this moment. All the same, she smiled. Here she was on her own facing the future and the results, whatever they might be, of her first major decision. She freely admitted to herself she was feeling very far from confident.

Where should she go first? Along the corridor and into the shop, or upstairs? Business first, she decided.

Joan stood in the middle of the floor and surveyed her own and Martin and Marjorie's handiwork with a great deal of satisfaction. Without a doubt everything looked wonderful, and had been well worth the hard work and long hours. She was longing to pull the cord and raise the blinds, but she had to resist the temptation. Tomorrow was to be the official opening.

If everybody that had promised to attend the opening were to turn up, well, what the outcome would be she had no idea.

Under Martin's watchful eye Marjorie and she had created special displays in both windows. They had taken notice of every word of advice he had given and the results were fantastic. Easter had come and gone so they had lost the chance to have small yellow chicks as a theme. However, the coming weekend was to be the Whitsuntide bank holiday and they had agreed to go for springtime.

Her keen eyes took in every item that was laid out in the left-hand window. One wax female model held centre position, wearing a flimsy ankle-length dress in the palest shade of green. The white silk lining was faintly visible. The waist sash was also white, and the wig that had been placed on the head of the model was shoulder length and pale blonde. One arm hung to the side while the other hand was positioned to hold a pretty wicker basket filled with moss

235

into which had been bedded several primulas, all one colour, a deep rich golden yellow. On the model's feet were sea green strappy sandals.

There was muslin draped along one wall. Three summery hats, three raffia handbags and three pairs of crocheted gloves were secured to the muslin with gay red ribbon. Laid out across the floor to the front of the display was a simple but very elegant navy blue silk dress. To the side had been placed a scarf and a pair of plain court shoes, both the exact same shade of deep old rose.

'Perfect,' Joan murmured as she walked to the other side of the shop. This window was entirely different. Joan, assisted by Martin's two employees, had spent endless hours making not only useful things for the home but decorative cushion covers, table runners, chair-backs and tablecloths. On the floor, bolts of cloth had been set out in a ring, making a colourful clock face. Textures varied, as did prices: some extremely cheap, others for the more wealthy ladies who could afford to indulge their taste. The original shelves which ran along one side wall had come in handy. Joan had made elaborate covers for them, finishing them off with dangling gold tassels, and then spread along them everything in the haberdashery line that one would need to do home dressmaking.

Jim had made two small wooden wheelbarrows and painted them green. It had been Marjorie's idea to fill them with fresh fruit. This had been done with much laughter and teasing as a pineapple and two grapefruit were placed in the bottom, apples, oranges and pears followed while jars of crystallised fruit and bunches of grapes were added until each wheelbarrow was filled to overflowing.

Martin had insisted that she bought a great deal of stock, and she was hoping and praying that they might do a brisk business in the first few days. Rosie had pleaded to be given a job straight away but both her mother and her aunt had insisted she remain where she was until Joan saw just how much trade the shop was going to attract. However, because Rosie had really implored, they had given in and told her she could take one day off and come to the opening of Distinctive Designs.

Joan gave the shop a final glance, her eyes lighting up at the difference they had made to this place. Between them they had made two sample pairs of curtains, one expensive, one much cheaper. Each set had been draped to great advantage. The more costly pair was tied back with contrasting silk cords, beneath a very full eight-inch frill. For the cheaper pair Jim had made a plain wooden pelmet board which the girls had padded and covered with the same material as the curtains, sewing a fringe along this valance. The idea for this pair of curtains had started out to be cheap and cheerful, and the end product was simple but very striking.

Along the two back walls Jim had made and fixed innumerable shelves which soared up to the ceiling. These now held bolts of cloth in every colour of the rainbow. There was even wall to wall carpet throughout the whole of the double-fronted shop which Bernie had insisted was surplus to requirements when some of his mates were fitting out one of the big London stores. When Joan had made it clear that she distrusted what Bernie was telling her because the asking price was so low, Bernie had been quick to say, 'Never look a gift horse in the mouth.'

His father told Joan it had probably fallen off the back of a lorry and Bernie's mates had picked it up from the middle of the road to prevent it causing an accident. Martha's comment had been, 'And if you believe that then you'll believe that some men can walk on water.'

Joan took the stairs slowly. The treads were still only bare boards, and she reminded herself yet again that she had to walk before she could run.

She stood in the doorway of the front room, placed her arms crossways around her body and hugged herself. Just looking at what was part of her new home gave her so much pleasure. As the transformation had taken place there had been times when she was afraid to go to sleep in case she woke up and found it to be all a dream. She was particularly pleased with the big old sofa which had been left behind. Self praise is no recommendation, she smiled to herself, but she knew very well that no matter what anyone else's opinion might be she had made a darn good job of covering it.

There was an armchair placed near to the open fireplace, which Jim had taken off the van and said was a present from him. Nearby stood the nest of coffee tables he had included in her purchase. The mahogany dining table and six chairs at the far end of the room almost took her breath away. She had polished that table top until she could see her face in it. She had many folk to be grateful to, but none more than Jim Taylor. As Martha said, 'Jim's a good man. Help anybody, he would, providing they were worthy like.'

Joan walked out on to the landing. Everywhere was spotlessly clean. The small bedroom was neatly furnished with the pieces she had got from Jim. The single mattress, like the double flock one for the iron bedstead which had been left in the larger of the two bedrooms, was brand new, and Martha had added the finishing touches by giving her a chair and two rugs, one for each side of the bed. They had already worked it out that if Sid and Martha wanted to come up for the weekend, she, herself, could easily sleep on the huge settee and Sid and Martha could have her double bedroom.

Suddenly Joan laughed out loud and the happy sound rang out loudly in the high-ceilinged flat. She was thinking back to when Martha had told her that Bon Marché, Brixton's largest department store, was having a white sale. The two of them had joined the queue at eight o'clock even though the store did not open until nine. They had brought a flask of tea with them and Martha had nipped across the road to the fantastic Yiddish bakery and bought hot bagels and pretzels. Then, rushing from counter to counter, they had spent thirty shillings! Joan had felt very proud as she had made up the two beds with new sheets and pulled snow white pillow cases on to plump new pillows.

As she looked now she vowed that the minute she got some spare time she was going to make a really pretty bedspread for Rosie's bed. She knew time would be precious. If things went well every minute would have to be made to count. She would work all the hours that God sent, seven days a week if necessary, to make a success of the opportunity that had been given to her.

Tomorrow was going to be her big day. She felt quite sure people would come. Martin had placed a large advertisement in the local paper inviting folk to look round and partake of free refreshments. But would they turn up just out of curiosity or would most of them become customers?

She hoped against hope for the latter. For there were only two routes open to her: survive or go bust!

Chapter Twenty-six

JOAN WAS AT A LOSS for words. Distinctive Designs had been open for almost three hours and still folk were coming in. She watched as Martha smoothed the fresh white cloth on the table which had been set up in the far corner of the shop. Martha must have spent hours baking all the little titbits. Marjorie had borrowed the small side plates, cups and saucers from the local café and Rosie was doing a good job of making tea and coffee. Part of one shelf had been cleared and now held wine glasses and bottles. Martin was offering wine to the commercial travellers who had called in, insisting that a little hospitality didn't cost much but paid enormous dividends.

The biggest surprise was that Teddy Tyler himself had turned up and with him were Jeffrey Harper and Mark Townsend. Jeff and Mark were immaculately dressed in dark double-breasted suits and were going out of their way to be charming to the ladies.

'Joan, do you have a moment?' Jeff smiled at her and she saw a hint of a saucy wink. 'I'd like to introduce you to Mrs Johnson. She and her husband own the local newsagent's.'

'I am so pleased to meet you, Mrs Baldwin. The way this

property has been improved will do so much good for the neighbourhood,' Mrs Johnson gushed as she accepted a glass of wine from Martin.

'Thank you, Mrs Johnson,' Joan answered. 'The place had been run down but hopefully things will run smoothly from now on and I shall be over to make a regular order for my paper and magazines to be delivered.'

Mrs Johnson's eyes roved over the shelves behind Joan. 'You certainly have a wide choice of material. Marion James, the wife of our local butcher, told me that she came in earlier and one of the girls you have serving behind the counter told her you are going to stock paper patterns and will make up dresses or even suits to order.'

'That's quite true. There will be three fittings for each garment, to be sure that at every stage we have the right cut and the right fit. We have a workroom downstairs and as soon as the workmen are free we hope to have a fitting room installed.'

A few minutes later, Jeff's face showed concern as he said, 'Joan, this is Mrs Bates. She would like to ask you a question.'

The lady was extremely large yet she seemed timid. Her face was pleasant and Joan couldn't have said why but she felt sorry for her. 'How can I help you?' she asked, smiling to put the woman at ease.

'Oh, please, don't bother. You are busy enough without me troubling you.'

'It's no trouble, Mrs Bates,' Joan assured her.

'If you don't mind I really wanted to ask if you were thinking of doing alterations. The ready made clothes I buy never seem to fit properly.'

Do I do alterations! Joan's mind jumped back to the days when she had sat at Granny Baldwin's bedside and shortened skirts, turned worn-out collars on men's shirts and put new pockets in many a pair of old trousers. The

241

payment had never been more than a bob or two. She shook her head to clear it, then, smiling brightly, she said, 'We would be more than happy to oblige. Come in any time, Mrs Bates, and we'll discuss the best way to alter whatever garment you don't feel comfortable in.'

Another buxom woman was having a right old laugh with Teddy Tyler, and although they had each been given a cup of coffee by Rosie Joan would have bet a pound to a penny that Teddy had well laced their cups with brandy from the hip flask that he always carried.

'Joan, this is Molly Worsfold, the landlady of the public house known as the Beehive.' Teddy's voice as he made the introduction was full of joviality.

Joan's first thought was, well, that's not hard to believe, because the lady looked every inch the part. She was small in height, had a big bosom and bottle-blonde hair, and was wearing a brilliant red suit, sheer black silk stockings, and black patent court shoes with four-inch heels. Her nails were painted the same colour as her suit and her lipstick also was an exact match.

''Allo, darlin'.' Molly grinned. 'Gonna work for yer living, aren't yer? Wouldn't catch me within a mile of a sewing machine. I like t' mix business with pleasure, an' yer can't get much more pleasure than a load of blokes coming in to see yer every night all wanting to buy yer drinks.'

Teddy let out a great belly laugh. 'And you ain't ever been known t' say no, 'ave yer, petal?'

Joan wasn't sorry when it was six o'clock and time to close the shop. She had certainly had a far better day than she had expected. They hadn't sold much in what she now referred to as the made to measure half of the shop, but there had been a great number of enquiries from ladies who liked the idea of having a dress for a special occasion made to order in material of their own choosing. The haberdashery side, however, had exceeded all expectations. They had sold all but two of the embroidered cushion covers and a great many table runners and chair-backs. Trade had also been brisk in small items such as needles, reels of cotton and silk thread, buttons, tape and elastic.

As Joan walked into her sitting room, followed by Mark and Jeff, her sister handed her a steaming cup of tea. 'Here. For Christ's sake sit yerself down and drink that. You've been on yer pins the whole day long,' Martha said, sounding really concerned. Mark suggested that they all had a drink and relaxed for a while, and about eight o'clock he and Jeff would take them out for a meal.

'May I come too?' Rosie asked.

'Of course you can,' both men answered straight away and Jeff added, 'You've been a proper little gem today, keeping the drinks flowing and doing the washing up.'

'Hang on a minute,' Martha said sternly. 'Your father is coming t' take us home about seven and we said we'd get fish an' chips for our supper.' Everyone saw the funny side of Martha's objections and they had a hard job to smother their smiles.

'Give over, Martha,' said Joan. 'Even your Sid won't say no to a decent meal out for a change. He can have fish an' chips any day of the week.'

'Oh no he can't, Joan, you know full well I cook him a decent dinner every night. Very rarely do we 'ave fish an' chips 'cos they ain't cheap. A tuppenny and a pennyworth ain't enough for my Sid.'

'All the more reason for Sid to join us,' Jeff said. 'Anyway we'll ask him as soon as he gets here.'

It was almost half-past seven before Sid arrived and nobody was more surprised than his wife at the way he was dressed. Introductions were made, because this was the first time that he had set eyes on Mark and Jeff. They both shook hands with him and Mark explained that they were planning

243

to take them all out for a meal. 'Is that all right with you, Sid?'

'Yes, mate, fine, just so long as it ain't in one of those posh places where all the money is spent on the furnishings and when yer dinner comes there's not much on the plate. Good job I went 'ome and washed and changed before coming 'ere, wasn't it?'

Jeff grinned. 'You do look well turned out, Sid. I like the whistle.'

Martha piped up. 'He only wears it for funerals and weddings.'

Rosie stared first at her father and then at Jeff, a very puzzled look on her face. 'What whistle? Dad's not wearing any whistle.'

Even Joan looked a little confused but Martha looked at Mark and Jeff and the three of them roared with laughter. Sid glanced down at himself before he self-consciously smiled at his wife. It was Martha who calmed down enough to say, 'You can see my sister has only rubbed shoulders with the nobs. And as for my Rosie, she ain't ever lived in the East End.'

'What's that got to do with it?' Rosie asked crossly.

Jeff straightened his face and very gently explained to Rosie that Mark had been using cockney rhyming slang. 'It goes like this, Rosie: "whistle" short for "whistle an' flute", meaning suit.'

'Oh,' she muttered, still looking bewildered. 'Are there any more such sayings?'

'Hundreds,' he told her. 'More than Mark and I know.'

'Tell me a few more,' she pleaded.

'OK, how about "china" meaning "china plate", mate or friend. "Cat" meaning "cat and mouse", house; "lean" meaning "lean and lurch", church . . . and so on. Once you get the idea, much of the rhyming slang can be worked out by using your common sense.'

'Ever been in the Prince of Wales, Sid?' asked Mark, while Rosie thought over what Jeff had said.

'Yeah, a few times when me an' Martha 'ave come up to Brixton to go to the Empress.'

'Have you ever had a meal there?'

'No. Can't say that we 'ave.'

'Well, Les and Annie Jackson serve up some of the greatest grub this side of the Thames. How about we all go there?'

'What d'you think, Martha?' Sid asked doubtfully.

Both Mark and Jeff could see that this kind-hearted working man was thinking about the cost of the meal, and they quickly did their best to put him at ease. Jeff spoke first. 'It's a very special day for Joan, and we've already promised Martin and Marjorie to bring her to the Prince as a kind of celebration.'

'It was Marjorie's idea to ask Joan's family to join us 'cos you've all done your bit to help her. I wouldn't be a bit surprised, Sid, to see your two boys and their mates there. After all, those young men not only decorated this place from top to bottom, they've become damn good customers at the pub, so Les tells us,' Mark added.

That settled the matter.

They had a great meal and a great night.

Once back at Joan's flat, Martha looked at the large clock on the wall. It was a quarter to one in the morning. 'Before we all go to bed, can I make a drink for anyone? Tea? Coffee?' she asked.

Joan smiled, 'Coffee would be great.'

Sid plonked himself down beside Joan on the settee. 'You've done a blinder today, gal,' he said, patting her knee. 'Nothing can stop you now.'

Joan grinned. 'Bit early off the mark for congratulations, wouldn't you say Sid?'

'Course not. You're up and running. No stopping you now, luv.'

Joan was dead tired but so happy. She leant towards him, resting her head on his shoulder and said, 'Let's hope so, Sid. Let's hope so.'

Chapter Twenty-seven

JULY 1930

THE PAST TWELVE MONTHS had been a real eye-opener for
Joan.

She had made a few mistakes but she had also learnt a
lot. Looking back, she knew darn well that with Marjorie
and Martin Goldsmith as her backers she could hardly have
gone wrong. Martin had taken her to Lancashire and
Yorkshire to visit warehouses where she had seen such a
huge variety of beautiful woven material that she had found
herself gasping with envy. She hadn't known such mills and
warehouses existed. With so much cloth to choose from it
had been hard for Joan to decide which would be the most
suitable for her type of work, and the best value for money.
But with Martin on hand to negotiate on her behalf she was
able to secure deals that meant she could make outfits for
her customers at very competitive prices.

During these visits she had also become aware that in the
north of England poverty was an even bigger problem than
it was in the south. It was on a day when Martin had taken
her to Jarrow that she had been shocked by the slum housing
and the ragged children. According to Martin, it was a case
of one half of the world not knowing how the other half lived.

'There had been a time,' he said, 'when the river port of Durham, on the Tyne, only four miles away, had two chief industries, shipbuilding and iron smelting. It had been a slap in the face to those hard-working independent men when their shipyards closed. There had been offers of help for even the poorest family but those proud men had said very bluntly that they didn't want charity, they wanted work.'

She also owed a debt of gratitude to Jim Taylor and to a lesser degree to his mate Doug Morgan. She had learnt that Jim played his cards very close to his chest. It had taken a while before she had discovered that he was employed by several auction rooms on a freelance basis. Jim never boasted. It was only by chance that she had come to know that he was an expert restorer and had done work for several well-known cabinet makers from time to time. On one occasion she had asked him why he still had a stall on the market and sold white wood furniture.

'Even folk who are not so well off need useful items in their homes,' had been his cagey answer. But then he had opened up and told her he liked meeting folk and appreciated the good fellowship and comradeship that existed between the stallholders. She had got the impression that his short spells on the market were probably the only bit of socialising that he did.

Over a period of time she had learnt quite a bit about this quiet man.

He was forty-nine years old, five years older than herself, and he didn't want to be fully employed by anyone. He liked being freelance where work was concerned. Since his wife had gone off with a younger man he'd never wanted a permanent arrangement. As there had been no children from the marriage he felt he had no one to answer to and so had become a free man in every sense of the term.

Joan and Jim had come to a mutually satisfactory

agreement. When it suited him, Jim would work downstairs in a partitioned-off part of the basement of Distinctive Designs, making useful items for selling on the market but also slowly and painstakingly restoring damaged and neglected items of antique furniture to their former beauty.

It had taken time for Jim to pluck up enough courage to ask Joan if she would like to accompany him to an auction sale. She had been very eager, and now whenever a large sale was taking place it had become accepted that they would go together. He taught her what to look for in various articles and how to assess their value. To his surprise, she quickly became an expert bidder, often getting valuable pieces that at first sight looked worthless for knock-down prices. On the other hand she was clever enough not to let herself be drawn in above her head. She was always quick to withdraw from the bidding if she felt the offers were going too high. House sales were her favourite. She loved to see how the upper classes lived.

She was now in a position to leave her premises in safe hands when she needed to visit warehouses with Martin or attend auctions with Jim, due to the fact that she was able to employ two loyal shop assistants: her niece Rosie, now seventeen, and Josephine Pattison, affectionately known as Jody, who was twenty years old. Despite the age gap the two young ladies had soon discovered that they had much in common, although they were as different as chalk from cheese in looks. They had liked each other on sight.

Rosie was small and dainty, with white-blonde hair, pale skin and wide blue eyes, still as pretty as any picture and still loved t' bits by her Auntie Joan. Jody was the reverse, tall and slender with shoulder-length thick dark hair that bounced as she moved her head. They both loved clothes and always wanted to stay after work if Joan declared that she was going to spend the evening drawing designs for costumes which would then be made up in her workroom where she employed three full-time machinists. Such garments were always advertised as being exclusive to Distinctive Designs.

Luck had also been on Joan's side the day that Mark Townsend had introduced her to Freda Preston, a tall, slim, extremely smart lady with threads of grey in her brown hair, sixty-one years old but wearing her age so well she could have passed anywhere for fifty.

Freda had worked as what was known as a selective buyer for a very well established fashion house in the West End of London. Customers would let the store know when they needed an outfit for a particular occasion and most would ask that Mrs Preston, personally, be allowed to bring a selection of appropriate garments out to their private residence. Extremely competent at measuring and fitting each individual, she had gained the reputation of having the ability to produce the desired result. Nevertheless, the store said they had to dispense with her services as soon as she reached the age of sixty.

Freda had been married, but after only five years of wedded bliss her husband had died of consumption at the age of thirty-one. Never having remarried, Freda had made her job her life. She had very much enjoyed visiting the homes of those she referred to as *well off*. Joan had listened spellbound to the tales that Freda had to tell.

At the time of their first meeting Joan felt they had hit it off from the word go. She had never taken to any other woman so quickly, or liked her so much, as Freda Preston. There was one fact of which she was sure: Freda was a lonely lady. Joan had explained that her establishment was very small, and nothing they made or sold could compare with the merchandise that Freda's old firm handled. 'Besides,' she had added, 'even if I could afford to pay you a suitable wage you would be dealing with a very different kind of clientele. This is Brixton, remember?'

The elegant lady had burst out laughing, and what she said next had Joan staring open-mouthed.

'God love yer, Mrs Baldwin, I was born just round the corner from 'ere an' I still live there. I can leave my posh voice behind whenever it suits me. For one thing, luv, how d'you think Mark Townsend came to recommend me to you? I'll tell yer. 'Cos Mark and Jeff have been good friends to me over the years and I often have a drink with them in the Prince of Wales. They know I'm not hard up – I get a pension from my old firm and I've savings. Some of my customers were very generous to me, though I never let on because we were not supposed to accept gratuities. Still, as I always maintained, the money was given voluntarily and what the bosses didn't know they didn't have to worry about. To be honest, I'd come here four or five days a week for next to nothing. It's company I need more than money, and to be able to keep in touch with the rag trade would be a bonus.'

'In that case,' Joan had said, with enthusiasm, 'let's start by calling each other by our Christian names. Then I think it's time you met the other members of my staff and gave our lowly premises the once-over.'

From the day Freda had joined Distinctive Designs Joan knew she had never made a better decision. To have an older member of staff to keep the shop and the workroom running smoothly meant that Joan herself could spend more time travelling with Martin and attending auction rooms with Jim. In fact, there were days when Joan worried because things were going *too* well. Over the months the business had slowly but surely changed from what had started out as a little business, which would provide her with a much-needed income and a roof over her head, into a small but thriving fashion establishment. However, Joan made sure that the haberdashery side of the shop – her bread and butter trade as she referred to it in her own head – was never neglected. The stock varied considerably depending mostly on what she and Jim managed to buy at auction sales, and sometimes she was utterly amazed by what Jim could do with what some would regard as an old relic. His better objects were used as part of the window displays and a discreet notice would be placed stating that such artefacts were for sale. They always carried a good supply of the everyday requirements needed by housewives who were interested in knitting, sewing and embroidery. In addition, they were careful to cater for the needs of the poorer families and word soon got around that although the new shop had a posh side there was always a bargain to be had.

Joan saw to it that not a scrap of material was wasted. When a machinist happened to be having a quiet day Joan encouraged her to run up such items as workaday dresses, petticoats, nightdresses, blouses, aprons, and even clothes-peg bags, using pieces of material that were surplus from other jobs and so could be sold quite cheaply.

Martha had laughed her head off when two huge cardboard cartons had been delivered to the shop on a day when she was there. 'Where the 'ell 'ave they come from?' she asked, staring at them, her curiosity getting the better of her.

'Manchester,' Joan told her. 'You can open them up if you like,' she added, hiding a smile with her handkerchief by pretending to blow her nose.

Martha needed no second bidding, and looked round for something to cut the string.

'Don't you dare use those,' Joan screamed. 'They are my precious cutting scissors; they cost a fortune. Fetch a small knife from the kitchen.'

Martha did as she was told and soon had the string cut on both cartons. As she delved into the contents thrifty Joan carefully wound the long lengths of string into a ball to be saved and used again some other time.

'Socks! 'Undreds of pairs of bloody socks! What the 'ell d'you think you're going to do with them, for Christ's sake? You'll never sell them.'

'I will, yer know,' Joan insisted, lapsing into her sister's vocabulary. 'A girl in the warehouse office made a mistake and duplicated the order. Mr Morrison's such a nice man he didn't go mad even when he found out that the manufacturers wouldn't take the second lot back. He offered them to me for just what they cost him.'

'Who is this bloke?' asked Martha.

'The owner of a warehouse where Martin does a lot of business, but in the short time that I have been dealing with him he's become a friend.'

'Oh, come off it, luv. How many times have I 'eard folk say there ain't no friends when it comes to business?'

'Martha, don't be so cynical. There's an exception to every rule.'

Not being used to being chastised, Martha remained silent for a moment. Then, holding several pairs of white cotton ankle socks in her hand, she said thoughtfully, 'I must admit, they look jolly good quality, and the coloured tops on these little girls' ankle socks are ever so pretty. I'll give yer the benefit of the doubt and we'll wait an' see, shall we?' Martha suggested.

'Yes, we'll see. By the way, do you know what the going rate for socks of this quality is, on the market?'

'Fivepence or sixpence a pair, I'd say.'

'Well, I've done my sums and I could sell them for half that price and still double what I've laid out.'

'Crikey. Pity you ain't got any little girls of your own, ain't it?'

'Yes, it is,' Joan answered sadly. For a moment there had been an embarrassed silence in the shop, as they both thought about the children Joan might have had if her husband hadn't bashed her about so much when she was pregnant. Martha had held her arms open and without a word being said by either of them had held her sister and comforted her. After a few minutes, Martha reminded her of the person who was still the apple of her eye.

'No matter what else,' she said, 'you know you'll always 'ave a share in Rosie. And there's another thing you don't need no telling: there ain't much my two boys wouldn't do fer you. Them an' their father would go to the end of the earth fer you.'

'Yes, I know.' Joan smiled again as she added, 'I just don't know what I'd do without you or your family.'

That memory had lingered. As each day passed she counted her blessings. Her family, her friends and the fact that her business was a success. On top of all that she also had a very comfortable home of her own now.

One way and another she was doing just fine.

Chapter Twenty-eight

IT HAD BECOME a regular habit for Joan's sister and brother-in-law to come up to Brixton almost every Saturday night. It had started because for one thing young Rosie was living with her aunt now, only going home on her days off, so naturally Sid and Martha frequently came to Brixton to visit. Another reason was that Joan and Martha loved to go to a show at the Empress while Sid and his sons had taken a shine to the Prince of Wales. They all declared they liked the pub so much because of the food that Les and Annie Jackson served. In their opinion it could not be beaten near or far. Another point, probably of even more importance to them, was that Les kept a good cellar. The pipes were cleaned regularly and the glasses shone, thereby assuring that Les served a jolly good pint.

Rosie and Jody would do their own thing as long as they said where they were going and promised not to be home too late. More often than not, with her parents' permission, Jody stayed the night, sharing Rosie's bedroom. Martha and Joan would go to the first house at the Empress, which started at seven o'clock and finished at nine, and then make their way to the Prince of Wales where they would meet up with Sid, and nine times out of ten Lenny, Bernie and several of their mates would be there. Some evenings the goings-on in the pub would be so entertaining that Martha, having laughed till she cried, would wipe the tears from her eyes and remark to her sister, 'I don't know why we bother going t' the Empress. There's more real life drama going on in this 'ere pub than any bugger could put on a stage.'

'You're dead right,' Joan would agree, digging her fork into a huge plate of steaming shepherd's pie, golden brown on top because Annie made sure her cook always grated a load of strong cheese on to the top of each plateful and shoved it under a really hot grill.

Les Jackson had always been a good landlord. He knew his customers and they knew him. He was a hard man but tolerant and fair in so far as he knew what most of his regulars got up to, but as long as they did not overstep the mark and jeopardise his licence his motto was live and let live. Most would say that he was a big fish in a little pond and they would be right, but if he overheard such a statement he would always say, 'Yeah, but the difference is that me and my Annie own this little pond! This 'appen's t' be a Free 'Ouse. My missus and meself don't work fer some big brewery, we work for ourselves.'

Joan, and indeed all of her family, had begun to look forward to Saturday nights which now were almost always spent in the Prince of Wales. Many colourful characters came into the pub and if Les knew them and knew their behaviour would be tolerable to his other customers then they were more than welcome. If some of the street ladies were vulgar prostitutes touting for business then their feet didn't touch the ground as either he or one of his barmen showed them the door. Given aggravation, Les could be as hard as the next man, and ultimately people respected him for it.

However, there was one exception to Les's rule. 'Lulu', known fondly as a 'tart with a heart'.

It was said you could set your watch by her. She would come in every day at noon, order an orange juice for herself and collect a bag of stale bread from Annie Jackson, then with great regularity, come rain or shine, she would walk to the small grassed area outside Brixton Library where she would sit and feed the birds. She would reappear in the pub at ten o'clock most evenings, half an hour before Les called time, and buy herself a whisky and dry ginger. The only time she deviated from this routine was on a Saturday night when the pub stayed open until eleven o'clock. Then Lulu would have two whiskies, but Mark and Jeff, and occasionally Les, were the only men she ever allowed to buy her a drink.

The first time that Joan's two nephews set eyes on Lulu was a Saturday night that Joan would never forget if she lived to be a hundred. The Prince was packed to the gills. Men were standing three or four deep at the bar and there were three barmen, besides Les himself, serving as fast as they could pull a pint. One of the reasons the pub was so busy was because it had been well advertised that several bouts of wrestling would be taking place that evening in Vassall Road, and the Prince of Wales, being the nearest public house to the hall where the events were taking place, was reaping the benefits. Both organisers and wrestlers had met in the pub at lunch time, for a meeting ground and to partake of some jolly good pub grub. By the looks of it they and a good many more men had decided it wasn't a bad place in which to pass the remaining hours of Saturday night.

Joan, Martha and Freda Preston were sitting on a long padded bench set up against the far wall, well away from the bar. Standing huddled in a bunch nearby were Sid Brown and his two sons, Lenny and Bernie, each with a pint glass in his hand. Within the last few minutes Jeff Harper and Mark Townsend had approached the three ladies and placed

257

a drink for each of them down on the table in front of them before joining their men nearby.

On the stroke of ten the double doors to the saloon bar swung open and Lulu walked in, dressed up to the nines. There wasn't a man in the pub who did not have his eyes glued on her. Conversations had ceased and eyes were bulging.

Jeff was the first to move and as Joan watched the customers stand aside to make a path for him she could not help but admire him. That he was not interested in ladies was a well known fact but there wasn't a man in the place who would face either him or Mark and question their morality. Their height was extraordinary, and one look at their broad shoulders, wide chests and hands that when clenched were as big as any you would ever see, would soon have you agreeing that you would rather have these two men as friends rather than as enemies. Besides, in Joan's eyes, they were not only real gentlemen, they were good friends.

Lulu had only moved a few paces from the door. Jeff offered her his arm and together they walked towards where Joan and Martha were sitting. Freda hunched up to make room for Lulu to sit down and Mark said, 'I'll fetch you a drink, Lulu.'

'Thank you, Mark,' she replied quietly.

It was all very civilised and very good-mannered. No more and no less. Sid and his boys looked at each other but their tongues could not form the words to describe what they were feeling.

Jeff, having rejoined them, grinned broadly. 'Something else, our Lulu, isn't she?' he asked.

Lenny, eyes still popping, said, 'You can say that again.'

Bernie was more outspoken. 'Blimey, I've seen some dames in me time but by God she leaves them all standing. She looks as if she's been poured into that dress!'

Freda, Martha and Joan would have agreed with him one hundred per cent.

From top to toe Lulu looked flawless. Her hair had been cut, coloured and arranged by a specialist, her face made up by an expert. The dress she wore was made from the finest cream-coloured lace interwoven with gold lamé threads and was lined with pure silk. The length of the dress was such that it reached to her ankles, allowing her gold strappy high-heeled shoes to peep from below. The *top* of this gorgeous dress, however, was extremely low cut!

Loosely draped round her shoulders was a stole the like of which Joan had never set eyes on before, and she had helped dress many a rich lady in her time. This one was entirely woven from gold and silver lamé threads.

Even Freda remarked that she could not recall having seen such an outfit before. She murmured beneath her breath, 'She's one hell of a lady, always has been. Easy to tell she works from home.'

Joan just about caught Freda's comment, but the implication of her words was lost on her. However, both Mark and Jeff had heard and they both grinned and leaning towards Joan, Mark whispered, 'You should see her flat!'

That was when the penny had dropped for Joan.

Chapter Twenty-nine

THE TELEPHONE WAS RINGING as Joan came downstairs into the shop. As usual, its demanding tone made her jump. She felt she would never get used to this new-fangled instrument that Martin had insisted she have installed. Marjorie was the one who had persuaded her, by saying it was a necessary evil of the modern times.

'Good morning, Distinctive Designs,' she said into the mouthpiece.

'Joan, I'm not going to be able to make it this morning, I'm afraid. You'll have to keep our appointment with Eric Roussel without me.'

'Oh no, Martin,' Joan gasped, gripping the phone very tightly. 'I've never even met the man and you've gone on and on about how important and rich he is.'

'So he is, and that's the reason you have to go. He won't bite.' She could hear Martin laughing at the other end of the line and that made her cross.

'How will I recognise him?'

'You know we were to meet him at the Strand Palace Hotel, so just take a cab and ask for him at the reception desk. I am going to ring him now and make my apologies.

I'll tell him you will be alone and he will be watching out for you.'

'Do I have to go? Can't you postpone the meeting until another day?'

'Now you are being silly, Joan. Eric has been a good friend to me over the years and he's only in London for a few days. You'll like him. Just look for a middle-aged, well-dressed man, listen to what he has to say but whatever you do don't sign anything. Oh, and remember Eric is a true socialite. See you tomorrow. Have a good lunch.' The line went dead and Joan stood there feeling an odd sense of adventure. It was only later, when she went upstairs to change, that she panicked.

Lunch with a stranger! A middle-aged businessman, Martin had said, and in a West End hotel! What should she wear? She shook her head and said aloud, 'I won't go.' But she knew she had to. Martin had done so much for her, it wasn't much for him to ask of her. She opened the wardrobe door, and flicked through the clothes that were hanging there. The last few days had been warm and sunny, showing that summer was well into its stride. She didn't want to wear a dress that looked too summery. Definitely a suit, she decided; after all, it was a business meeting. Not black: too hot. Finally she chose a beige linen suit, a dark brown blouse and a pair of brown court shoes with a beige toe-cap.

Eric Roussel stood to the front of the foyer of the Strand Palace Hotel, looking extremely smart and very cool in a silver grey suit with which he was wearing a crisp white shirt and a navy blue tie. Outside all the hustle and bustle of London was going on and taxis were drawing up to the entrance of the hotel every few minutes. The minute one slowed down and he spotted the single lady occupant he knew at once it was Joan Baldwin. In a trice he was out there, beating the doorman, he had the cab door open and was assisting Joan to step down on to the pavement. 'Excuse me just one moment,' he murmured, and turned to pay the cab driver the fare to which he added a generous tip. Turning back to Joan, he took her elbow but he did not speak again until they were inside the entrance hall of the hotel. Then he let go his hold on her, held out his hand and said, 'Eric Roussel. I feel I know you rather well. Both Martin and his wife have told me so much about you.'

Joan felt the colour rush to her cheeks. 'Joan Baldwin, pleased to meet you,' she whispered.

'Oh my goodness, have I blotted my copy-book already?' Eric hastily did his best to make amends. 'I assure you our friends have told me nothing but good about you. Shall we start again?' Not waiting for her reply he said, 'I'm Eric and you are Joan and we've plenty of time before lunch to get acquainted over a drink, so shall we make our way to the bar?'

Joan had to smile as she nodded her head. She had already decided that Eric Roussel was a real gentleman, courteous and kind. Look at the way he had rushed out to meet her, paid her cab fare, was opening the door to the bar. He was older than she had expected, late fifties or even early sixties she imagined, but everything about him suggested a man of taste. He wasn't over-tall, about five foot ten. His face was attractive and tanned. In fact he didn't look English. His silver grey hair had been styled very short which added to his clean-cut appearance.

'What would you like to drink?' he asked as soon as they were seated.

Joan hesitated. She wasn't used to drinking alcohol at midday.

'How about white wine? Nice and cool and not too heavy before we eat.'

'That would be nice,' Joan answered shyly. She watched as he summoned a waiter and gave his order, naming the exact bottle of wine he preferred, and again Joan came to the conclusion that his world spun round smart hotels and good restaurants.

'Cheers,' they said as they touched glasses. He smiled down at her. He had already noted how softly spoken she was. Now he had time to study her and found she was small but beautiful in a really unassuming way. She didn't use thick layers of paint and powder, just enough to give her complexion a truly natural look. He was thinking that her thick golden-brown hair must be quite long because she had put it up in an intricate style and he couldn't help but wonder what it would look like hanging down over her shoulders. She also had the most beautiful clear blue eyes.

Joan could feel that he was studying her and she lowered her eyes and sipped her wine. It was very pleasant. After a few more sips she felt easier.

'Tell me about your business,' he said. 'Martin tells me you're making a great success of it.'

She smiled at him. 'I've had a great deal of help from Marjorie and Martin and they tell me you import a wonderful variety of cloth from many different countries.'

'Yes, I do. My main supply, though, comes from Italy.' He went on making small talk, telling her how he had started in the business. He found himself wondering what had driven such an obviously intelligent woman, who spoke so well, to work on a market stall before Martin Goldsmith had helped to set her up in a business of her own.

The restaurant of the Strand Palace Hotel was vast and as a waiter pulled out a chair and helped Joan to be seated she felt very intimidated. There were a great many businessmen lunching there, but at the next table was a family with three teenaged children and that took the edge off Joan's fear – until she was presented with the menu, which was so huge she could only stare in bewilderment.

'Shall I order for you? Melon to start with and roast beef to follow, perhaps?'

'That would be very nice, thank you, Mr Roussel.'

'I thought we had decided on Christian names. You can't call me Mr Roussel all the time if we are to be friends. If I tell you a bit about myself maybe you will find it easier to call me Eric.'

'All right.' She smiled.

'I was born in Malta, so naturally I am a Roman Catholic. I shall be sixty this year, which I am sure makes me old enough to be your father.'

'Now you are flattering me,' said Joan.

He ignored that remark and continued. 'You could say I am jack of all trades but master of none. I went to a church school on the island of Gozo, did very well according to the priests, but I never thought of getting a proper job or joining any of the professions, which is what my parents would have preferred. I came to London, studied art, even found a job in an art gallery. Then my father died and left a lot of money so my mother and my sister and myself were well taken care of. So you see I've never had to face up to the real world. I could lead my life as I saw fit.'

'Did you get married?' something prompted Joan to ask.

'No,' he said thoughtfully. 'I have to admit I love the companionship of beautiful women, but I also love to travel. I've never felt the urge to settle down in one place for any length of time.'

They had finished their melon, and as the waiter carved their roast beef at the table the wine waiter was pouring a little red wine for Eric to sample. He took a minute, then nodded his approval. The waiter wiped the neck of the bottle with a white cloth before filling Joan's glass. She had never tasted red wine before. Mr Farrant used to drink it when she had worked at Mulborough House, but she herself had never fancied it.

'Does your sister have a family?' she asked.

'Yes, she does. She married quite young and has five children.'

'Well, that must be a blessing for you, especially at holiday times and most of all at Christmas.'

'I hardly ever hear from them, let alone see them,' he answered jovially, but Joan couldn't help wondering whether it was all bravado. She put her hand over the top of her glass to prevent him from refilling it and watched as he refilled his own. 'Your turn now,' he said.

If she hadn't already drunk both white and red wine, Joan might not have been able to tell a virtual stranger as much of her life story as she did. She started by telling him how she had come to work on the market stall for Martin and Marjorie, then suddenly she had gone back in time and all her bottled-up feelings came pouring out. Her disastrous marriage, the jobs she had taken on to enable herself to look after Granny Baldwin. The three times she had been pregnant and the beatings that had been the cause of her losing her babies. How wonderful her sister Martha, her husband Sid and their two sons Lenny and Bernie had been to her, and how these three men had given her Bill a jolly good hiding and made sure that he had got himself a job.

'Whoa, whoa. Take a deep breath and I insist that you have at least half a glass of wine before you go on.' His concern for her was real. How could anyone pick themselves up time and time again when their life had been so cruel?

Joan did slowly sip her wine before she told Eric how Bill's death had come about. She didn't leave out the fact that he had bravely brought three of the horses through the fire to safety.

Then she related the story of her going into service because she had nowhere to live. The benefits weren't left out. The dress-making for Miss Fiona and Miss Delia. The legacy that Mr Hamilton had left to her in his will. Then last but by no means least, how Marjorie had found her premises which had great living accommodation up above.

As she described her landlord, Teddy Tyler, Eric Roussel was smiling broadly. 'I think we'd better retire to the lounge and have some strong coffee, don't you?' he finally said.

It was late afternoon before Eric looked at his wristwatch. They hadn't even mentioned business but he didn't give a toss about that. He had never before met such a regular normal woman whom he really felt was a genuine, honest, sweet lady. There weren't many of them about, as he knew to his cost.

He stood up, held out both his hands and lifted her to her feet. 'Joan,' he said quietly, 'it *has* been a pleasure to meet you. I'll give Martin a ring tonight, set up another meeting with him. But look,' he stammered, 'may we stay friends? Would you come to the theatre with me one evening?'

'Are you asking me just to be polite?' Joan asked in her own straightforward way.

'I never say or promise anything that I don't mean. I really would like us to meet again.'

'In that case, I would very much like to.'

'So we part as friends, even if we didn't get down to discussing any business, yes?'

'Certainly. One can never have too many friends,' Joan replied.

'Does a friend get a kiss, then?' He smiled.

For a moment Joan hung back. Suddenly she found herself acutely aware of Eric Roussel as a man, not just someone Martin had asked her to have a business lunch with.

He looked at her serious face, leant forward and gently placed his lips on hers.

'Thank you for lunch,' she stammered.

It seemed natural then for his arms to go round her and

for her to respond to his hug. That they were two very different people from two very different worlds didn't seem to matter one iota.

Just two people, meeting for the first time and finding that they liked each other.

Chapter Thirty

THERE WASN'T MUCH THAT Martha Brown missed. Not when it concerned her sister's well-being. What Joan had just told her had her worried and her voice was raised as she said, 'You had lunch with this foreign bloke, on yer own, and after that one meeting he wants to take you out to dinner and to the theatre afterwards? What did yer say his name was?'

'Eric Roussel, and he's not that much of a foreigner. He was born in Malta.'

Martha threw back her head and let out a great belly laugh. It was ages since her sister had found the time to come and visit her. It was usually the other way round. Now they were sitting opposite each other in her kitchen drinking a cup of strong tea, and she couldn't believe that her sister who was normally so sensible was acting so foolishly.

'Course he's foreign if he weren't born in this country. My Sid always says 'alf the Mafia live in Malta an' the other 'alf live in Sicily.'

Now it was Joan's turn to laugh. 'Since when was Sid an authority on the Mafia? I've never even heard him mention such a thing.'

Martha grinned. 'Don't suppose he knows sod all about them really. It's just that his dad died when him and his brothers and sisters were all small and he left behind a load of gambling debts. His poor old mum had a helluva job convincing them bookies that he'd left her stony broke. My Sid always declared that the bookmakers that pestered the life out of his mother were part an' parcel of the Mafia.'

Joan giggled at her sister's reasoning. 'Martin has known Mr Roussel for years. They do a great deal of business with each other and I'm quite sure it does not involve gambling or bookmaking. Besides, I liked him. He was a real gentleman.' Joan stated firmly.

'How can yer tell? You've only met him the once.' Martha looked carefully at her sister. She had certainly altered a helluva lot since she had opened her own business. These days she was an entirely different person compared with how she used to look and act when she lived just round the corner and was married to that brute of a bloke Bill Baldwin. In those days she was frightened to open her mouth for fear of getting a bashing. And as for her clothes, if it weren't for the fact that she was damn good with a needle she would have been walking about in rags. Today her clothes were fashionable, her skin was clear and her brown hair gleamed like a polished chestnut when the light caught it. And she wasn't that old. Forty-four was a good age for a woman to find the right man if he still had plenty of life left in him.

'How old was this Maltese bloke then? And is he married?' she was bold enough to ask.

'He's sixty and no, he's never been married. Though why you want to know all about him beats me.'

'Hmm. You've only got his word for both those statements when yer come to think about it.'

'It wasn't a pack of lies he told me,' Joan insisted. 'I believed him.'

'That still doesn't alter the fact that he's sixteen years older than you are.'

'What difference does that make? I only met him because Martin asked me to. We had a very nice lunch and that was that. Now please may I have another cup of tea and may we change the subject?'

Martha had a sly smile on her face as she got to her feet, picked up the teapot and made for the scullery to make a fresh brew. As she tipped the cold tea leaves down the sink she was saying to herself, she's smitten with this fellow! She can say what she likes but the truth is staring me in the face. 'Let's hope t' God that he sees you all right,' she said, coming back into the kitchen and setting a fresh jug of milk down on the table.

'Hold on a minute.' Joan didn't know whether to laugh or lose her temper. 'You're reading far too much into this. It's not the way you think.'

Martha grinned. 'If you say so. Of course if he were married that would be an entirely different kettle of fish. But if Martin vouches for him I suppose it's all right. Let him take you out an' about if you're so sure he's on the up an' up. Grab the chance while you can. God knows you deserve it.'

'Martha, will you stop it,' Joan pleaded. 'I don't for one moment think he meant it when he said he'd like to take me out one evening. He was just being polite, that's all.'

'By the sound of him, he's well off, footloose and fancy-free. So why don't yer start thinking about what a good time he could give you? You like him, you said he's good-looking, well mannered and easy to talk to. What more do you want?'

Joan thought hard for a moment. Her sister had just put a very difficult question to her. She thought she knew exactly what she wanted out of life, but to put it into words that Martha would understand was beyond her. She actually would like to have what her sister had. A good steady husband, the security of knowing that she was loved day in and day out. And above all else, children of her own.

Now she was being envious, she chided herself. Nobody had everything in this life. Not so long ago she had been praying for a roof over her head and a way to earn her living without having to go back into service. Now she had both, thanks to her many friends. I'm happy enough, she insisted to herself, though in her heart she felt it would be nice to have a man in her life.

Martin had told her that he had met up with Eric Roussel and that they had done a deal which if all went well would be very profitable for both of them. He had also added the fact that Eric had been very impressed with Joan and had sent her his good wishes.

In Brixton the shops had Wednesday half-day closing while in Wandsworth they closed half day on a Thursday, which meant the shops there were open when Joan had time off. Quite often she took advantage of this as she had today. It was almost five o'clock when she staggered up the stairs with bags of shopping, put the bags down, put her key into the lock, turned it and pushed the door shut behind her with one foot.

As she staggered down the hallway, Rosie appeared from the kitchen. 'Oh, Auntie, you're absolutely loaded. Here, let me take some of those bags. I've got the kettle on. You go into the front room and sit yourself down and I'll bring you in a cup of tea straight away.'

Joan passed the bags over and heaved a sigh of relief, then she lifted her hands and cupped her niece's face. 'You're a little treasure,' she said.

Rosie laughed. 'I've laid the table and I've made a salad. It's far too hot to eat anything else, isn't it?'

'Oh, Rosie, what would I do without you?'

'Drink your tea and stop being so daft,' Rosie ordered.

'I've put some new potatoes on to boil – they won't be long – and we've got tinned salmon and grated cheese to have with the salad. By the way, a letter came for you by the second post. I've put it up there, behind the clock. It looks personal, nothing to do with the business I wouldn't think.'

Joan drained her cup, stood up and looked behind her. Rosie was such a good girl. She had set the dining table so prettily, even put two roses into a slender vase and placed them in the centre of the table. She turned and walked to the fireplace, took down her letter, slit it open, glanced at the signature and felt the colour rush to her cheeks.

It was a short note written on thick hotel paper from Manchester.

Dear Joan,
   I will be back in London for the August bank holiday weekend. I will ring you on the Saturday morning. Hope you don't have anything planned for the Sunday and Monday.
Eric

Thursday and Friday dragged by and every time the telephone rang on Saturday morning it took all Joan's courage to pick up the receiver. Finally she heard his voice say, 'Joan?'

'Yes,' was all she managed to say.

'How early can you meet me tomorrow?' he asked, then not waiting for an answer he suggested, 'How about ten thirty at the Strand Palace again. We can have coffee and decide where you would like to have lunch and plan the rest of the day.'

Joan could not believe her ears. He sounded so masterful. 'All right,' she stammered.

As the taxi approached the hotel Joan again had butterflies

in her stomach and her heart was banging against her ribs. It was the liveried doorman this time who opened the cab door and she paid the taxi driver herself. She had to take a deep breath before she could face walking through the big doors.

Eric had said he would be waiting in reception, but at first she couldn't see him. When she did spot him she breathed out. He came quickly towards her, smiling, then caught hold of her hands and kissed her cheek.

'It's so good to see you again. I've thought about you a lot.' He could tell that she was flustered and said quickly, 'Come and have coffee.' Taking hold of her hand, he led her towards the lounge.

He looked very distinguished in his dark suit and striped tie. His face still had that healthy tanned look and she dropped her eyes so that he wouldn't think she was staring at him.

'You look very smart,' he told her as they sat down. 'Nice and cool. This August has turned out to be a scorcher, hasn't it?'

'It has indeed.' She smiled, thankful that she had chosen to wear a navy blue linen suit, the jacket being edged with white.

Over coffee, Eric told her a little about the deal he had struck with Martin.

'Seems I am to benefit too.' Joan smiled. 'Martin said you had a few bales of winter-weight cloth that he selected for me – ideal for skirts, apparently.'

Eric reached across the table and put his hand over hers. 'I am so pleased your business is doing so well. What about the living accommodation? Are you sure you are comfortable?'

'It couldn't be better,' she said, and went on to describe how her nephews and their mates had decorated the flat throughout and how Jim Taylor and his mate Doug had provided her with some really good furniture. 'It really is a nice home, and more so since my young niece, Rosie, has moved in with me.'

'Well, good for you. I wish you continued success, you really are a determined lady.'

Later he took her to a really lovely restaurant in Knightsbridge and over a leisurely meal he told her about all the countries he'd been to. 'My visits usually turn out to be quite profitable.' He laughed. 'Keeps me in the way I have become accustomed to and keeps the bank manager happy.'

Joan studied his face as he was speaking. She noticed the way he hesitated sometimes and didn't say what he had been going to. Was he wary of her knowing too much about him? He was a clear-cut example of a prosperous businessman, everything about him was immaculate, and yet there was a tiny feeling in her head that warned her he was overdoing the good life just a bit. Martha's words about him being older and the fact that she had no way of knowing if he were telling her the truth about his prosperity were niggling her. Was he laying it on a bit thick?

When they had finished their meal, Eric ordered two brandies to come with their coffee. 'Promise me something, Joan,' he suddenly said. 'That you won't make your business your whole life. Try not to do that. I know how it will be for you if you aren't careful.' He spoke gently. 'If you will let me I can show you how to have fun, even be irresponsible at times. It would do you a world of good.'

'What's wrong with being independent, earning one's own living?' she asked.

'Nothing at all.' He squeezed her hand. 'But you know the old saying, all work and no play. Tell you what, tomorrow I'll pick you up in my car and we'll head for the coast. None of the popular resorts, they'll all be too crowded with it being a bank holiday. I shall think of a nice quiet spot. What do you say?' Despite her age, Eric was thinking that Joan looked like a frightened rabbit. She had never really lived. 'Come on,' he urged, 'be daring.'

Joan could hardly believe what he was saying. A whole day in his company! She thought she ought to say no, but she liked the idea of a car ride and a day by the sea. She hesitated.

'I'll pick you up at your place about eight o'clock, get an early start. We'll have a lovely day and I'll bring you home safely in the evening.' Joan was torn two ways. She stirred her coffee and took a gulp of her brandy to cover her confusion, before saying, 'Thank you, Eric. I would love to spend the day with you.'

There was no need for Martha to know, she decided. It would only be a one-off. Besides, what the eye doesn't see, the heart doesn't grieve over. As Eric had said, it was about time she learned to live a little.

Chapter Thirty-one

JOAN WRIGGLED BACK COMFORTABLY in the front passenger seat of Eric's car. It couldn't have been a better day. There wasn't a cloud in the sky and the sun was already shining brightly even though it was only nine-thirty. There were green fields on either side of the road they were travelling and in every field a great number of sheep were grazing.

'Where are we?' she asked.

'We're into Kent.' Eric smiled faintly. 'We are actually crossing the Romney Marshes. We'll stop in Romney village and have coffee, then we'll go on to Greatstone where there is a beautiful long stretch of sandy beach.'

Joan turned her head towards him. Today he was much more casually dressed, in fawn trousers, a dark brown open-necked shirt and a beige pullover with a V-neckline. On his feet he still wore brown lace-up shoes of the finest leather. For the first time she noticed that despite his tanned skin his eyes were an astonishingly light and clear blue.

'What are you thinking about?' she asked.

'About today, how I have you all to myself and what to show you first. Have you ever been in this part of the world before?'

'No, I haven't. I was in service, as you know, in Tunbridge Wells but I never got to go out and about much because I didn't have friends or relatives in the area to visit.'

Eric parked the car and they found tearooms that served coffee and hot doughnuts. They looked at each other and laughed and Eric said to the elderly waitress, 'Who could possibly resist such a tempting offer?'

The coffee was served with thick fresh cream and the doughnuts were so warm and sugary that they found themselves not only thoroughly enjoying this unexpected treat but licking their fingers into the bargain.

Back in the car they drove down one very long road and came to the beach. There were folk walking their dogs, children running in and out of the sea, and adults either sitting in deckchairs or lounging on the grass. Greatstone not only boasted the most wonderful sands but acres of grass verge which was sprinkled with every type of wild flower it was possible to imagine. The beach was so long and so wide that it did not appear even remotely crowded.

Eric had come prepared. He had brought swimming trunks with him and changed in the back of the car. Joan walked to the sea edge with him, removed her sandals and stepped into the warm shallow water.

'I won't be long,' he called as she watched him wade in to deeper water. She was finding it hard to believe that all this was actually happening to her. Bank holiday Monday would usually be spent with Martha and Sid on Tooting Bec Common or Ravensbury Park, and the day would more than likely have finished up with them having a drink in the nearest pub. Now she was looking at Eric's tanned back, his broad shoulders and strong arms. Suddenly he dived beneath the waves and arm over arm he struck out, swimming strongly against the tide. She continued to paddle, walking up and down, kicking at the waves as they swept over her ankles.

277

Eric was out of sight now. Joan walked back up across the wide beach to the car, fetched two towels which Eric had told her she would find in the boot, and spread them out on the grass. Some time passed before she saw him striding towards her, droplets of salt water glistening on his tanned body.

'That was great,' he shouted, as Joan flung him the larger of the two towels which he straight away wrapped round his middle, using the smaller towel to rub his limbs and to dry his mass of grey hair.

'Right,' he called later when he emerged fully dressed from the rear of the car. 'Now we're going to Dungeness.'

'Why, what's there?' Joan was eager to know.

Eric laughed loudly. 'Well, there's a lighthouse and a coastguard station and the whole area is a haven for wild birds, but the main reason we are going there is because I am very hungry and there is a very old pub there which serves the freshest fish you've ever eaten.'

'With chips?' Joan playfully asked.

'Oh, Joan, promise me you are not going to demand chips.'

'I'll do my best not to, but the idea is very tempting,' Joan said, smiling affectionately as she handed him a comb because his towel-dried hair was sticking up all over his head.

Dungeness turned out to be like nothing Joan had ever seen before. The first word that came to her mind was ramshackle.

One side appeared to be efficient and very well managed, with both the lighthouse and the coastguard station standing out on the sky-line as the tide swept along easily and swiftly, forming a white foam as it lapped the sand.

The other side of the bay was totally different.

The homes, they could hardly be called houses, for in the main they were wooden contraptions, were so badly constructed and disorganised that Joan wondered if people

278

really did live in them. However, long lines of washing blowing in the breeze proved that family life really existed in this quaint place. There were fishing boats everywhere, some bobbing out to sea, others drawn up on to the beach. Several men were sitting in groups repairing their nets. As Joan looked round she was glad that Eric had persuaded her to come, for it was a perfect day, with a nice cool breeze that smelt salty. Besides it was good to see how the other half lived.

Just five minutes' walk and they came to a long, low wooden building that Eric told her was the one and only public house the area had, and that it was suitably named the Pilot. Joan was smiling even before they actually reached it, for she could see and hear that the atmosphere was jovial as a bank holiday should be. It was also a sight to behold.

A whole row of hanging baskets decorated the front of the Pilot, each packed tight with pink and purple fuchsias which dangled down like miniature ballerinas. The place was very busy. Apart from the fishermen leaning up against the bar in what Eric said was known as the snug, there was a long wide bar with many tables, the far wall of which was mainly glass so that diners could look straight out over the glorious sandy beach to the sea beyond whilst eating their meal.

Eric ordered a lager for himself and Joan chose to have a sweet sherry. They had to wait twenty minutes before a table was available, but it was well worth the wait. The menu itself was enormous, bristling with the names of fish that Joan had never heard of. The choice of shellfish included oysters, scallops, mussels, prawns, cockles, whelks and even winkles and shrimps.

After much deliberation they both settled for a grilled Dover sole, new potatoes and asparagus tips. When the food came Joan couldn't stop herself from letting out a gasp of surprise. Their meal was served on platters that were so large they would have held a roast turkey! The new potatoes were well buttered and sprinkled with freshly chopped parsley, and wedges of lemon lined the big fish. There were crusty rolls in a basket, a dish of butter and a jug of a creamy sauce so delicious that Joan felt she would die to have the recipe and be able to make it at home. Eric beamed at Joan's reaction as he watched her take her first forkful of a perfect Dover sole.

They rounded off their meal with ice cream, followed by coffee, and then walked slowly back to the car, holding hands.

The next place they visited was Rye, with its cobbled hilly streets. Joan was much more at ease with Eric now, but though she admired everything about him she was finding him baffling – especially when, just after nine o'clock that night, he drew the car to a halt outside Distinctive Designs.

'Thank you, Eric, for a truly lovely day,' she said, leaning towards him meaning to kiss his cheek. He turned his head away, got out of the car and came round to her side to hold the door open for her.

'My pleasure,' he told her. Then he did brush her cheek with his lips but so lightly she scarcely felt it. 'I will be in touch soon,' he called as he got back into the car.

As she put the key in the lock of her side door she was telling herself to be grateful for having been taken out for the whole day and for having been given such a wonderful time. But instead she felt like crying. Why hadn't Eric kissed her properly? Had he tired of her already or had he discovered that he didn't find her attractive?

August had given way to September. The weather was holding well and autumn still seemed a long way away. Life was good, the business was doing well, and Joan had decided to have a sale, reducing the price of nearly all the summer items they still had in stock to make way for the winter designs. It had been a great success. The cloth that Martin had ordered from Eric had arrived and it was excellent, even better than she had anticipated. Already her machinists were busy making up samples using the sketches that she herself had drawn.

Socially, though, her days seemed humdrum. August bank holiday had given her a glimpse of another life, allowing her to realise there was a big world out there and all work and no play did not have to be the way one lived. Yet from that day to this she had not heard a word from Eric Roussel, except when Martin mentioned him during the course of business. Actions speak louder than words and Joan had drawn the conclusion that Eric had not enjoyed her company.

One evening she felt so low that she stripped off her grey suit, and stood for a moment in front of the wardrobe mirror wearing only her underwear, looking herself over from top to toe. She was forty-four, but her body was still as good as when she had been thirty. Her breasts were firm, her waist was slim, she had curvy hips and really good-shaped legs. She sighed. She knew she was doing well, but there was no trace of smugness in her face and certainly no one special person in her life, she admitted sadly.

The family still came over on a Saturday evening and they always had a jolly good time at the Prince of Wales. Recently Jim Taylor and his mate Doug Morgan had joined the party. It was good to end the week together. The women talked non-stop about anything and everything and the men didn't do so badly either. There was no getting away from it, Les and Annie Jackson ran a lively pub and the food they provided continued to be really good. Martha and Sid were thrilled that Lenny had found himself a young lady, Janet Marshal, and they had decided to get married early in the new year. It seemed natural that they had already asked Les if they could book their wedding reception at the Prince, so that was something for them all to look forward to.

Joan felt a little guilty when she thought about Jim Taylor. He was always there when she needed to talk, and when it came to the day-to-day repairs of the building he took a lot of responsibility off her shoulders. She had built up a trade in smart ready-to-wear clothes which sold at affordable prices. She also had a list of better-off customers who regularly asked her to design and make an outfit when they needed to look good for a special occasion. However, the small items that Jim secured at house sales also brought in a good income and the antiques he renovated so lovingly were always a good talking point when used as part of a window display. For some time now she had been thinking of a way in which she could show him her appreciation. And when he suggested that she accompany him to a very large house sale that was to be held in Richmond she thought it would be a golden opportunity to talk to him.

It was only nine o'clock when they arrived in Richmond and the sale did not start until ten. Jim had visited the salerooms two days ago and bought a programme on which he had marked off several items that would be of interest to them both. With an hour to spare Jim took her to a small restaurant near the river. He was more smartly dressed than she had expected, in a lightweight suit and a tie. They agreed that a fried breakfast and some hot toast would go down very well. When Joan watched Jim glance up at the young waitress and almost plead, 'Would it be possible for us to have a pot of tea right now, please? I'm parched,' that everyday saying endeared him to her because she felt exactly the same way.

They each had the devil of a job securing the items that Jim had marked off on their programme, and three they had to let go because the bidding was so brisk. On the other hand, there were four additional articles that caught Joan's eye and she managed to bid successfully for all of them.

The sale wasn't over and when it was there would be a long queue of folk waiting to pay for their purchases. 'Let's go and sit in Richmond Park,' Jim suggested. Joan was all for it. The air in the saleroom had become hot and stuffy.

'There was once a royal residence in Richmond Park,' Jim remarked, doing his best to make conversation as they walked along by the River Thames, because he thought Joan was miles away. When she made no answer, he added, 'It is still crown property.'

Joan shook her head. 'I'm sorry, Jim. Do you mind if we sit down?'

'Not at all,' he said straight away, pointing to a vacant bench beneath a sprawling leafy tree.

It was now or never, Joan decided once they were seated. 'I have a proposal to put to you, Jim,' she said.

'Really?' Jim sounded surprised. 'What do you have in mind?'

'You and me becoming partners.' She saw his face stiffen and hurried on. 'Please, Jim, don't dismiss the idea out of hand. This isn't a sudden suggestion. I have given the matter a great deal of thought. You do so much for me, give most of your time to making sure that my business runs smoothly. I think we've reached the point when sharing the load legally would be more fitting.'

'*No.*' He reached out and took her hand between both of his. 'I can't thank you enough for the offer, but it is your business, you've worked your socks off to make a go of it and for the first time in your life you are an independent lady.'

Joan slid along the bench to be a little closer to him. 'I am not going to take no for an answer. If it weren't for you starting me off, even furnishing my flat, I probably would never have got the business up and running.'

'You're being too generous with your praise,' he said gently, wondering what would be the outcome if he agreed.

'I am not,' she declared. 'If you would only agree I wouldn't have half the headaches.'

Jim's face wore a guarded expression. 'I'll think about it.'

Joan's face broke into a wide grin. 'I'm not asking you to put any money into the business. I don't want an investor, I just want us to carry on as we are but on a much firmer footing. We could go together to a solicitor and have him draw up an agreement.'

'I've said I will think about it.' He smiled sheepishly at her.

Joan flung her arms around him and hugged him.

She would never know how much he wanted to respond in the same manner. Instead he said, 'We'd better go and make arrangements for our purchases to be delivered and then get back to the shop before Freda begins to think she's the one in charge.'

He would dearly love to become Joan's partner, in more ways than one. However, he knew only too well that what she was offering was a purely business deal and before he made a decision on that he would have a great deal of soul-searching to do.

Chapter Thirty-two

FREDA PRESTON WAS the last of the staff to leave. She pulled up the collar of her coat and opened her umbrella. 'Filthy rotten night,' she said. 'Like me, I don't suppose you'll be going out tonight.'

'No, cosy night in, put my feet up,' Joan answered. 'I do miss Rosie.'

'I expect you do. It seems such a shame that the weather has turned so bad just when you'd given her a week's holiday. Anyway, see you in the morning. Good night, Joan.'

'Good night, Freda. Glad you haven't got far to go.'

Joan stood in the open doorway of the shop for a few minutes watching the rain lashing down. Then she stepped back, shot the three bolts on the front door and pushed the latches up on the two Yale locks.

It was well over two months since Eric Roussel had taken her out for the day and she had not heard a word from him in all that time. These last few days the weather had been as miserable as she'd felt, strong winds and heavy rain warning that winter was almost here.

'Lovely,' she muttered sarcastically. Such a lot to look forward to, short gloomy days, dark evenings. Sundays visiting Martha and Sid or staying home on her own hugging the fire and doing endless sewing, while continually thinking of Eric. Maybe he preferred younger women? Did he think she wasn't sophisticated enough for him? However many excuses she thought of, it didn't make her feel any the less rejected. It was a shame, really, because during that day something amazing had happened. When Eric had held her hand it had been like a sudden charge of electricity passing between them, taking her totally by surprise. At the time an uncanny instinct had told her that the attraction was the same for him as it was for her. How wrong she must have been!

In the short time she had known him he had held out a dream to her. Companionship at the very least. Someone to share her old age with. Marjorie and Martin had lunched with him two days after their trip into Kent and they had told her that Eric hadn't stopped talking about her. 'Really smitten with you, is Eric,' was how Marjorie had put it. If that were true then he had a funny way of showing it.

One minute she was sad because he had held so much hope out to her, the next she was angry and bitter. As she walked down the passage towards the stairs she was giving herself a good talking to. *You've got far more here than you ever thought was possible, a well-established business, good friends. You don't need a man in your life, certainly not like the one you were daft enough to marry when you were only a slip of a girl.*

Yes, that was true, and over the years since Bill's death while she had concentrated on earning her own living the fact that there hadn't been a man in her life hadn't worried her too much. At times it had actually been a relief. Then Eric Roussel had come along and altered her whole way of thinking. He had shown her there was more to life than just work, in fact, he had started her dreaming of maybe living a more interesting life.

The days passed quickly enough though. They were busy in the shop, a fact that Joan thanked God for every day, for she had never imagined that running her own business would bring so many bills through her letter box. Teddy Tyler had raised the rent, the electricity bill had arrived and as sure as eggs were eggs the gas and phone bills wouldn't be far behind. Jim hadn't yet taken her up on her offer of a partnership, but had quietly told her that he was still giving the matter a lot of thought. Joan half smiled to herself. Jim was not a man who would rush blindly into anything.

With only herself to cater for she couldn't be bothered to cook a dinner. Cheese on toast, she decided.

Her foot was only on the first tread of the stairs when she heard an urgent rapping on the front door of the shop. She hesitated. She made it a rule never to open the door after dark to anyone when she was alone in the building. No, she was going to ignore whoever it was, she decided, and although the rapping continued she carried on up to her living quarters, closing the door at the top of the stairs very firmly. She went into the kitchen, half filled the kettle, placed it on the stove and lit the gas ring beneath it, then set about laying a tray ready for her evening meal. She had decided that for once she would be lazy, take the tray into the lounge, put some records on the radiogram and eat her meal off the tray balanced on her lap.

She was just pouring boiling water on to the tea leaves she had spooned into the pot when the telephone rang. She picked up the receiver, but before she had time to even say hello an oh so familiar voice said, 'Oh, Joan dear, please come down and open the door. I'm getting soaked to the skin.'

'Eric!' she shrieked. 'Go to the side door.' She banged the phone down, all trace of tiredness now vanished, and her feet scarcely touched the treads as she flew down the stairs. She fumbled to unlock the door but at last she had it open and Eric was standing there. He must have run all the way back from the phone box on the corner. He held open his arms and Joan flung hers round him.

'What a lovely surprise. I'd begun to think I would never see you again.'

He didn't answer, just held her close. She could feel how wet his thick overcoat was.

'Never mind explanations now. Come on upstairs and let's get that wet coat off you.'

Over a cup of tea, which Joan had laced with whisky, he gave her a number of plausible reasons as to why he hadn't been in touch before now, none of which Joan felt she could wholeheartedly believe. His face looked thinner and his skin did not have that healthy glow. She was almost sure that he had lost quite a bit of weight.

'What is it, Eric?' she asked anxiously. Just the sound of his voice had brought back happy memories of the short times she had spent with him, but he was acting very strangely.

'You seem as glad to see me as I am to see you, and yet you are not being straight with me.' She said, wanting so much to be reassured.

'You wouldn't like it if I were to tell you the truth.'

'Try me. We are at least friends, aren't we?'

'I've been in prison,' he blurted out.

Joan was lost for words. There was much she wanted to ask, but all she could do was stare at him.

'I got three months and I've served two.' The silence hung heavy between them until Eric asked, 'Why have you got tears in your eyes? Not feeling sorry for me, are you?'

'No, it's because I'm so pleased to see you again and I want to know what you've been up to,' she said, with a funny smile. Then very quickly she asked, 'Am I allowed to hug you?'

Eric carefully laid his cup and saucer down on a side table and got to his feet. She felt his arms go round her waist and her head was soon nestling against his shoulder. They stayed locked together for some time until Eric led her to the sofa and they sat down side by side.

'You know, you are something else,' Eric told her, smiling broadly. 'You haven't even asked why the police picked me up or why I was given a prison sentence.'

'You'll tell me in your own good time,' she answered with confidence. 'Meanwhile you can make that fire up while I get us something to eat and then we can talk as much as we like.'

Joan changed her mind and laid the table. She still did cheese on toast but with more pleasure as it was now for two. While it was under the grill she quickly chopped up a large salad, tossing it into a glass bowl she sprinkled in olive oil and spooned mayonnaise into a dish and potato salad from a tin into another dish. It was a bit of a scratch meal but the best she could manage, not having had any warning that she might be having a visitor.

There was no deep conversation while they were eating. Eric was certainly not at ease. There was sweat on his brow and several times Joan watched as he wiped the palms of his hands on his napkin. They finished eating and Joan got up and cleared the table. Minutes later she was back with a tray that held a pot of coffee, two cups and saucers and a jug of cream. Tucked beneath her arm was a bottle of brandy. She left the coffee to steep and poured two generous measures of brandy into cut-glass goblets. 'I shouldn't,' Eric protested as she handed one to him. 'My car is parked round the corner and I have to drive back to my hotel.'

'If you drove here how come your coat was so wet?'

'Because I was walking up and down outside waiting until your staff had left before I could screw up enough courage to come in and face you.'

'You don't have to drive anywhere tonight if you don't want to,' she told him quietly.

He gave a low whistle.

She knew exactly what he meant. She was being far too trusting. Asking for trouble, actually, but she had come this far and she did not want to turn back. Naturally she wanted to know why he had been in prison. Truth to tell there was a whole lot more she would have liked to know about Eric Roussel, but she was throwing caution to the wind. She hadn't felt like this since she was about sixteen years old and that was a very long time ago. Almost a waste of a lifetime.

'I want you to stay, Eric.' Her voice was low.

He pulled her closer to his side, slid an arm along her shoulders and, lowering his head, placed his lips over hers.

Joan felt her insides turn to jelly. His kisses became stronger and his tongue flicked in and out of her mouth. His non-committal attitude towards her had gone. He was no longer treating her as if she would break, and certainly not as a mere friend.

'Oh, Joan,' he finally gasped, 'I've dreamt of kissing you like that every day for the past two months. In fact I've wanted to do that from the first moment I met you.'

She raised her eyebrows. 'Then why didn't you?'

'Because you were . . .' Joan could sense him searching for a word and wondered what he would come up with. 'Unworldly,' he finally said. 'I didn't want to take advantage of you, mostly because I am so much older than you are.'

'Unworldly? That's a funny word to use.'

'It is entirely appropriate where you are concerned, Joan. You haven't even asked me why I was sent to prison. You know nothing about me and yet you trust me.'

Joan smiled. 'It was my good friends Marjorie and Martin who first sent me to meet you on my own, and if you were their friend that was good enough for me.'

290

Eric sighed heavily. 'The Goldsmiths and I have known each other for many years and we do a great deal of business together, one way and another, but it is a wise man who treads carefully during any business transaction.'

Joan felt her heart sink. 'You wouldn't do the dirty on Martin, would you?'

Then to her amazement Eric actually grinned and winked at her saucily. 'I'd not pass up the chance to get one over on him if he were daft enough to let me.'

Joan moved back along the sofa and sat up straight. Doubts had crept into her mind. 'Eric, perhaps you had better tell me why the police arrested you.'

They sat for a while in silence before Eric said, 'You're a funny one, Joan, and no mistake. You invite me to stay the night with you and then suddenly you decide you had better find out why I was sent to prison.'

Joan saw his point and started to giggle. Eric chuckled with her and soon they were both helpless with laughter. When they calmed down Eric stretched his hand across the space between them and took hold of Joan's. Squeezing it tightly, he said, 'I owed a fellow a lot of money and the bank returned the cheque I gave him marked "insufficient funds".'

'When you wrote the cheque weren't you aware that you didn't have the means to cover it?' Her voice sounded sceptical.

'I don't expect you to believe me, the judge didn't, but the answer is I should have had ample funds in my account.' He took a gulp of his brandy. He needed a stiff drink in order to convince Joan that he was telling her the truth and to let her know what he intended to do. The thought that if things did not go right for him he might well end up back in prison, and for a very much longer time, had his heart hammering against his ribs.

'I have to go home to Malta,' he said bluntly. 'I need to see a few men who have made the mistake of double-crossing me. I sent their goods in good faith and they accepted them, but they have been slow to pay and consequently it was like a rack of dominoes. One falls they all fall. Only this time it was me that fell the hardest. It has never happened before and I shall make damn sure it never ever happens again.' As he looked at Joan he saw only her lovely trusting face. 'I'm sorry . . .' His voice trailed off. He felt so bad he could not meet her eyes.

'Will you be able to sort it out?' Her voice sounded small and hurt.

He laughed bitterly. 'Oh, yes.' The two words held a great deal of confidence. Suddenly he sat up straight, looking at Joan. He thought she looked frightened. It was then that an idea came to him and he wasn't going to take no for an answer. 'Come home with me, Joan. It will only be for a short time, and we could go at the weekend.' He looked really pleased with himself as he added, 'Please, Joan, say you will come. I can see about our tickets tomorrow.'

Joan's face was full of concern and her hands were fluttering.

'You all right, love?' Eric asked quickly.

She gave him a small smile. 'No, actually I'm confused. You asked me to go home with you. Where exactly is home?'

Eric was stunned. 'I've told you I come from Malta. You'll be made so welcome. My father is dead but my mother and all my family will love to meet you. It will give you a chance to meet my family and see something of the island at the same time.'

Thoughts were flying round in her head. How badly she wanted to say yes, let's go. She had never in her whole life been offered such an opportunity and yet all she was asking herself was, what am I going to do? Her mind was racing from one question to another. 'I can't just walk off and leave the shop.' Her voice was shocked.

'Why not?' Eric was now full of good cheer. 'You've plenty

of good staff, and friends who will keep an eye on them. We need only stay in Malta a few days as long as two of the days are when the banks are open. My accounts both here in England and in Malta need to be replenished and believe you me, Joan, they will be. I unconditionally promise you that our journey will be well worth while.'

Joan found herself believing him. His enthusiasm was infectious. 'How would we get there?'

Eric smothered his laughter. 'It is some years since I went home so I'll have to check the travel arrangements but I'm pretty sure that P&O have not gone broke. I think we can safely assume that they are still running their liners.'

'But I've never been on a ship before.'

'Well, you'll have a couple of days to think about getting your sea legs,' he teased her.

Much later Joan asked, 'Shall we go to bed?' Her voice was childlike.

He put his arms round her, moved her long hair to one side and kissed her neck several times. 'You are amazing! And I love you, Joan. More than you think.'

She smiled at him. She hoped that what he said was true because she was about to commit herself to something from which there would be no turning back.

Chapter Thirty-three

ERIC WAS STILL SOUND ASLEEP, lying on his stomach, his head resting on one curled-up arm.

Joan was also still in bed but wide awake, sitting up beside him, staring at his brown body, broad back, firm buttocks and slender legs. She was actually finding it hard to believe that last night had really happened. The longing had started within her the minute he ran his fingers over her bare flesh. Never in her wildest dreams had she thought that lovemaking could take place with such sensitivity. Eric had been so gentle from the first moment that their lips met. Starting with her forehead he had gently kissed her body from top to toe. Then he parted her legs and his kisses were growing stronger.

No longer was she able to lie still and passively let him do anything he wanted to. She realised that her own feelings had been pent up for far too long, mainly because sex in her mind had always been associated with brutality. Bill hadn't known how to treat a woman with care. According to him she was his wife and there for him to use whenever he felt the need. He had never been interested in satisfying her.

As Eric had kissed her again and again, Joan had felt her own emotion matching his. Suddenly her body was arching up towards him and within seconds wanting had become fierce desire.

A long time after that, when they were lying contented, he with his right hand cupping her breast, he had murmured, 'Oh, Joan, my darling, you make me feel really young again.'

Their ages were immaterial now.

Time to wake him up. Bending over him, she put her lips to his ear and whispered, 'Good morning, my darling.'

Eric opened his eyes, turned over to lie on his back, put his arms round and held her tightly, his face burrowing into her neck. 'Are you all right, Joan? I watched you for ages last night before I fell asleep, wondering if you would have any regrets when you woke up.'

'Oh, Eric, I'm . . .' She hesitated, searching for the right words, because it had become very important to let him know exactly how she was feeling. 'I had no idea lovemaking could be so meaningful. For me it was like being loved for the very first time in my life.'

'So, my love, are you going to come to Malta with me?'

A silence fell between them. He was waiting for her reply.

She wriggled out of his arms and sat up. 'It's a big decision, Eric,' she said at last.

'I know. You must have time to think about it. How would it be if we got ourselves washed and dressed, had something to eat and talked the matter over in a bit more detail?'

To Joan's utter surprise he insisted on beating up eggs and chopping up some ham and then made two light fluffy omelettes while she made a pot of coffee and some toast and laid the table. They ate their breakfast in the kitchen, and afterwards Eric said it was time he went because he had a number of things to do and Joan had to think about opening the shop.

They stood in the open doorway and Eric kissed her gently on each cheek. She still hadn't given him a straight answer as to whether or nor she would travel to Malta with him.

Suddenly Eric said, 'I may not be able to get back here tonight but I will phone you sometime during the day.'

Joan, who had been feeling on top of the world, watched him walk away, a well-dressed, efficient man-about-town, briefcase in one hand, car keys in the other, and found herself trembling with panic. Was that the last she was going to see of him?

The day seemed endless. Twice Freda asked if there was something troubling her. The telephone only rang a few times and Joan asked Jody to take the calls. Her instinct told her it would not be Eric on the end of the line.

Two days went by without a word from him and Joan asked herself how she could have been such a fool. The evenings were long and she was thankful that Rosie was not here to see the state she had worked herself up into. Nevertheless, with time to consider her actions, she came to the conclusion that she wasn't sorry she had allowed Eric to spend the night with her. Everyone was entitled to some joy in their life and for those few hours she had felt loved and wanted. She smiled ruefully as she murmured to herself, 'At least I have been given a glimpse of what life could be like.'

As the third day drew to a close Freda drew Joan to one side. 'I want to talk to you and I'm going to make sure that you listen to every word I say. Understood?'

Joan looked at Freda Preston and knew that she wasn't going to be able to give any excuses. She sighed and said, 'Well, let's go through to the back room.'

They didn't sit down but stood facing each other. The older woman came straight to the point. 'You can tell me to mind my own business but it won't do you a scrap of good because I'm gonna talk straight. Something has happened and it has knocked you for six. My guess would normally be a man was at the root of the trouble but you never go out anywhere socially except to the Prince on a Saturday night. There's plenty of men there who think you're a really nice lady but you never give any one of them the time of day. A few months ago your sister Martha and I thought you were finally going to live a little when you had a few meals and a couple of days out with that foreign bloke who Martin deals with on and off, but as he's not been around we presumed that had fizzled out.'

Joan had thought of herself as too old to cry, and certainly too old to fall in love, but by now her eyes were brimming with tears.

'Right, here's what we are going to do,' Freda said forcefully. 'We will close the shop on the dot of six, go upstairs and freshen ourselves up, and then you and I are going to the Prince of Wales. We'll have a meal, and a few drinks, and if they loosen your tongue you'll find I'm a good listener. If not, at least we'll drown your sorrows together.'

As Annie Jackson placed a loaded dinner plate in front of Joan, and another one in front of Freda, she said, 'There's treacle pud or spotted dick for afters when you're ready.'

Joan looked at her plate. Toad in the hole, Brussels sprouts, carrots, mashed swede and at least five roast potatoes. 'Good God,' she said, 'I'll never get through half of this.'

'Take a good swig from your glass of lager and I'll call Les to bring us a bottle of wine. That will help wash it down,' Freda said, signalling to Les to come over to where they were sitting.

Les grinned broadly at the pair of them as Freda asked him for a bottle of wine. 'Oh yeah! And who let you two out on the loose tonight? Special occasion, is it, gals?'

'More like drowning our sorrows,' Freda said mournfully, taking the mickey out of Joan. 'Drastic measures are needed sometimes, yer know.'

'Well get stuck into that plateful an' I'll be back in a few minutes.' Les was shaking his head as he walked back to the bar. He'd send Annie over with the bottle; she'd be the one to find out what was wrong with Joan. Obviously something was, because she had a face like a wet weekend and that wasn't like the Joan they all knew and loved. On the other hand, he decided, if Annie sat down with those two he wouldn't get another stroke of work out of her tonight.

Joan and Freda managed to clear their plates despite the fact that Joan had said it was far too much. 'Can't manage a pudding though, can we?' Freda asked as she filled their wine glasses for the third time.

'Oh, no!' Joan muttered, patting her tummy. 'I couldn't eat another morsel.'

There had been a lot of cheering every now and again, coming from the very end of the long bar where a darts match was in progress. Suddenly there was complete silence and both Freda and Joan turned their heads to see what was going on. Four Salvation Army girls, working in pairs, were going round the bars rattling their tins and selling copies of their paper, *War Cry*, to raise funds to enable the Army to continue its good work.

'Some of those "Ally Looya Lassies" are strikingly pretty,' Freda remarked as she and Joan fished in their purses for coppers to put in their tins. Joan fully agreed. These four wore dark cloaks which had stand-up collars embroidered with the initials SA in gold thread. From beneath their black Victorian bonnets peeped their lovely curly hair and the big bows of black ribbon which were sewn on to the left hand sides of the bonnets helped to make the girls look very young and vulnerable.

'How brave they are to go into public houses, some of which must be very rough,' Joan remarked.

'Yes, you've got a point there, but even the roughest of men respect them. God help a man who so much as laid a finger on any one of those lassies. No matter whether you believe in their religion or not they do some marvellous work, especially amongst the poor.' That was quite a speech coming from Freda.

Joan smiled, for the first time since they had sat down. 'It always amazes me how happy every member of the Salvation Army always seems to be. When I was in service in Kent their band used to march past the gates every Sunday morning and even Cook would start singing the well known hymns they played.'

Freda straightened herself up and looked Joan straight in the eye. 'Well, are you still going to keep your troubles to yourself? I promise I am not a gossip. Whatever you choose to tell me would go no further and who knows, I might even be able to help.'

Joan felt the need to talk to someone and the wine had certainly loosened her tongue as Freda had said it would. From their first meeting, Joan had been impressed by Freda. When it suited her to influence a client she could be quite snobbish, but most of the time she was a very down-to-earth kind of person. A good worker and a good friend to Martha as well as herself. Saturdays when they all went out together Freda had bothered to show both sisters how to use make-up effectively and she had persuaded Martha to have her hair cut into a smart but easy to manage style.

'All right.' She heaved a sigh. 'I suppose sooner or later you will find out anyway.' She proceeded to tell Freda how successful her outings with Eric Roussel had been and how disappointed she was when he hadn't turned up for over two months.

'And now?' Freda prompted.

'He came to visit me three days ago. Remember when I saw you off and it was raining cats and dogs? Well, he was outside then.'

Freda didn't need a picture drawn for her. She grinned and shook her head. Joan felt the colour rising in her cheeks but then the thought came to her that she was a grown woman, not a silly lovesick teenager. She returned Freda's look and they both laughed.

'All right.' Joan grinned. 'So I let him stay the night.'

'Good for you, Joan. You've no one to answer to and if he's halfway as dishy as you make out then you did right.'

Joan felt a bit guilty. She hadn't told Freda that Eric had been in prison or that there was something devious about him that she couldn't quite put out of her mind.

'When was he supposed to be seeing you again?' Freda felt compelled to ask.

'He said maybe he wouldn't be able to get back that same day but that he would phone me.'

'Hmm, and he hasn't or you wouldn't have been walking about looking like a lost sheep.'

In for a penny in for a pound, Joan decided. She blurted out, 'Eric said he was going to make arrangements for me to travel home with him. I told him I wouldn't be able to leave the shop and he said I had a gem in you and from what I had told him about you he thought you were more than capable of running the business. He also said that Martin and Marjorie would keep an eye on the place.'

'Hey, hang on a minute! Couldn't get a word out of you for days and now you're running on like a steam train. When he said travel home with him, where exactly was he talking about?'

'Malta,' Joan told her. 'Apparently he still has quite a big family living there but he hasn't been home for years.'

'Did you say you would go?' Freda was all ears by now.

Joan dodged the question. 'Not exactly.'

300

Freda rested her elbows on the table, cupped her hands round her face and said, 'I don't believe you! I just wish I were your age an' a bloke asked me to go abroad with him. I'd have been up to the travel agent's with him before the office opened.'

She had spoken so loudly that everyone near them stopped talking and looked at her. 'Don't be ridiculous,' Joan said huffily.

'You can't turn an offer like that down,' Freda went on, undeterred. 'I've lived a long time and I've come to know that it's best to grab any gift that comes your way 'cos you get no second chances. Sometimes of course it's risky, but taking a risk just adds to the spice of life. You'd be mad not to go. Wish he'd ask me.' She gave another roar of laughter.

I didn't say I definitely wouldn't go. Joan kept this snippet of information to herself. For all she knew she might never set eyes on Eric again and she didn't want to be made a laughing stock.

They were both a little unsteady on their feet as they made to put their arms into the sleeves of their coats. Les came across to them, smiling broadly. 'This is one time when I really wish that Jeff and Mark had been in the bar tonight. They could each have taken one of you home. Still, I've called a cab and he can drop Joan off first as she's nearest and then see you to your front door, Freda.'

'No need,' Freda declared haughtily. 'We are quite capable of getting ourselves home.'

'You think so, do yer? Well for once, ladies, you're doing as I tell you,' Les said, grabbing an arm of each of them. 'Got yer handbags, 'ave yer?' He propelled them through the open doors to where the cab was already waiting at the kerbside. Kissing them each in turn, he helped settle them both on the back seat and then had a few words with the cab driver, who let out a belly laugh and said, 'OK, Les, they'll be all right with me. I'll see yer later.'

It was only when Joan opened her front door that a feeling of melancholy came over her. The flat felt so empty. And for all she had opened up her heart to Freda she was still no wiser as to when or even *if* she would see Eric again.

The thought that she might not did not do much for her self-esteem.

Chapter Thirty-four

It was six thirty by the time Joan had cashed up and filled in the ledgers, one for each side of the business. She had just reached the foot of the stairs when there was a knocking on the side door. Slowly she turned and made her way back through the dark shop. If you had any sense at all, she was saying to herself, you would ignore the knocking and not open the door. Every instinct told her Eric was standing on the other side and it would only lead to more heartache if she were to let him in again. Hadn't he proved beyond any doubt that he was not to be trusted?

She ignored her warning thoughts, and opened the door.

'Oh, Eric.' For a ridiculous moment, Joan felt a bit weepy, but instead she took a deep breath, put her arms round him and hugged him tightly. He stepped inside and Joan closed the door and before she could protest he was kissing her, long lingering kisses that melted her heart.

'May we leave explanations until later?' he pleaded when at last he let go his hold on her. 'At a guess I would say you need reassuring and cheering up. Well, I'm back, and with a whole lot of good news, so let's celebrate. How long will it take you to get ready? We'll go to any restaurant or hotel of your choosing and have a slap-up meal, a bottle of bubbly, and drink to our holiday in Malta.'

'You've made all the arrangements?' Joan sounded flabbergasted.

'Of course. Didn't I say I would?'

It was almost ten thirty. Not being familiar with fancy restaurants Joan had left the choice to Eric. She had tried to persuade him to stay in and talk to her. There were still a lot of unanswered questions where Eric was concerned and she felt she would never get open and honest answers while having a meal in a public place. He would have none of it. They had much to celebrate, he insisted.

Joan changed into what she called her glad rags and went along with his wishes, but she did so reluctantly, and it was just as bad as she had feared, with too many people talking loudly and much noisy laughter. Not the right place in which to make important decisions. It had been a very good meal but now she was tired. She found herself staring at Eric, her hands clamped round her coffee cup, while he tossed down another brandy.

'Now,' he said as he set his glass down, 'have you decided if you are coming home with me? Yes or no.'

Joan leaned back in her chair and smiled. 'When we get home and you give me the full details as to how and when you suggest we are going to travel to Malta, then I'll decide.'

It was dark and very cold when Eric parked the car and they walked the few remaining yards to the shop. Once upstairs he stayed silent for a moment. 'Shall we leave all the details until the morning?' he asked finally. 'Let's go to bed.'

'I think so.' Joan wished she could tell him that she felt she couldn't trust him, but her pride wouldn't let her. Much as she wanted him to hold her and make love to her again she felt irritated that he hadn't bothered to tell her why he hadn't even telephoned.

'You only think so?' He smiled, the lines on his tanned face seeming deeper than she remembered. 'Let's make tonight something special.' He took her in his arms, and as his lips met hers all the longing came flooding back and her doubts were wiped away. Much later, as she lay content in the curve of his arm, she felt she would have to agree. It had been very special.

Eric was as good as his word. He had made good use of the days that he had stayed away. He had used his contacts, his keen mind and his powers of organisation to make sure that they travelled to Malta in the utmost comfort possible. As he explained the journey, step by step, Joan began to see how Eric Roussel had become so successful. He had the ability to motivate others. Whether his intentions and actions were always completely honest remained to be seen.

He teased Joan unmercifully by making her wait until they had eaten breakfast before laying out two Malta guidebooks and some pamphlets for her to look at. Eric had marked the relevant pages and Joan smiled as she studied them. There were two P&O steamers to choose from, the Peninsular or the Oriental line. The advertisement stated that an all-sea route leaving London every other Friday and arriving every other Sunday was a nine-day trip, first-class fare from twenty pounds, second class from fourteen pounds. P&O also ran a service across the English Channel and down to Marseilles, from where one travelled on by mail boat to Malta. That journey only took three and a half days, first-class fare from eighteen pounds and sixteen shillings, second class from twelve pounds and sixteen shillings. Or there was an all-sea route going by the Commonwealth line. This was a six-day trip, one class only, a return fare costing eighteen pounds, but that ship only made the journey once a month.

Joan looked up, both surprise and joy showing on her

face. 'You said you've already bought the tickets, so please, Eric, which way are we travelling and when are we supposed to be going?'

'No suppose about it, my darling,' he said, producing a large paper wallet from the inside pocket of his jacket. 'We are going on a nine-day, first-class cruise.'

'Oh, Eric!' Joan was stunned. Doubt, fright and excitement were all mixed up in her mind. Should she be going off to a place that she had hardly ever heard of before? With a fellow she hardly knew? She began to argue with herself. *You know him well enough to have spent practically two whole nights making love with him.* Besides, on the plus side, he was introduced to her by Martin and Marjorie Goldsmith and you couldn't find two more reliable people than them.

But nine days to get there! How long would they stay in Malta? Then another nine days for the return journey. God almighty! She'd be away the best part of a month! How could she leave her business for that long? Then there was her sister Martha. What in heaven's name would she have to say about all of this?

Then another thought struck her. Eric had said his term in prison had been because he had written cheques without sufficient cash in the bank to meet them. If that were so, where on earth had he found the cash that he was flashing around now? Their meal at the restaurant had cost a pretty penny, which Eric had paid in cash. Then there was these first-class tickets, and he had not given her any real explanation of why he needed to go to Malta so badly. Was she mad to be even considering going with him?

Eric watched the different emotions flicker across Joan's face and he could have made a very good guess at what she was thinking, but he was used to getting his own way and this time wasn't going to be any different. There wasn't any problem that he couldn't iron out, given time. The length of the trip, nine days, had set him a problem to begin with, but he had found a way to turn that to his advantage. A few phone calls and a few owed favours called in would help to give him the advantage of surprise when he did arrive in Valletta. Then he certainly meant to repay those who had sought to cross him. He would live to have his day!

'What about my business, Eric? It's taken me all my life to get as far as I have. I've worked hard to get it up to standard.'

'Joan, that is one of the reasons why you deserve a break. Have you never thought that it was about time you began to have some fun?'

Every member of Joan's staff and each member of her family urged her to take the break that was being offered her.

In the end she convinced herself that she would regret it for ever more if she didn't grab this once in a lifetime offer. But settling business matters, and sorting out what clothes to take, was more traumatic than she had even dreamed it would be. There was so much for her to do.

Eric was very understanding. He booked them into an hotel in London the day before they were due to board the P&O liner, and held her in his arms for most of the night. When she awoke and realised that this was the day when she was setting out on the high seas to a destination unknown to her, and to whatever else was anybody's guess, she was suddenly filled with a wonderful sense of well-being and vitality, and it was at that moment that she made a resolution. She was leaving all her cares and worries behind her. She was going cruising in the Mediterranean. Who would have thought that she, Joan Baldwin, would be travelling on a P&O liner, first class at that!

She took her time to have a bath and dress in what was an entirely brand new outfit.

At the sight of her Eric let out a long, low whistle of

admiration, which gave her an exhilarating sensation of carefree happiness.

They were welcomed aboard by two extremely smart uniformed officers. A young sailor, dressed from head to toe in white, showed them to their outside state room and informed them that their luggage would be delivered quite soon. Joan's eyes nearly popped out of her head. This was luxury personified. Their cabin had everything that one could wish for and more. And that was only the beginning.

'One does not dress for dinner, not on the first evening,' Eric informed her. Then he went into the bathroom and came back holding out a large white box tied with silver ribbons. Even to Joan the name of the firm which was printed on the lid was familiar. Swears & Wells, dealers in quality furs.

'You will have to wait until tomorrow to wear it, my darling, but open the box and give me a private showing now, please,' he implored her.

Joan did as he bid and as she removed the lid she exclaimed, 'Good gracious!' Gently she lifted a honey-coloured fur stole from the layers of tissue paper, held it up to her face and buried her cheeks in its softness.

Eric took the stole from her and lovingly draped it round her shoulders. She absolutely loved it, but the thought of how much money this gorgeous fur must have cost him frightened her half to death. Thank God she had brought two new long evening dresses as well as the three she had made herself.

Before the second day was over Joan was telling herself that this had to be the best thing that had ever happened to her in her entire life. Eric was there to hold her hand, pay attention to her all day, and then be there in the same bed with her for the whole night long.

She could not begin to describe the ship. To her it was a floating palace. The passengers had freedom of movement and could indulge in all kinds of sport, most of which Eric excelled in. There was a theatre, a hairdressing salon and shops which sold exquisite gifts. Eric's opinion was that the cuisine served on the liner was equal to that of a really first-class hotel. By the time the steamer docked at Malta, Joan wholeheartedly believed that her trip in the Mediterranean had given her the holiday of a lifetime and left her with a sensation of carefree happiness. Yet as they took their leave of the captain and stepped on to the long gangplank, she couldn't stop herself from wondering.

What next?

Chapter Thirty-five

'GOOD TO SEE YOU, Emmanuel.'

Three men greeted Eric, each in turn hugging him and patting his back. They were identically dressed in black suits, crisp white shirts, and black ties. All of them were dark-skinned, but while two had a good head of dark hair, the third man was completely bald. Joan guessed that each was in his late thirties or early forties. All much younger than Eric.

Eric introduced them, stating only their Christian names. 'Nicholas, Gerard and Anthony, this is Madam Joan Baldwin.' Each in turn lifted her right hand and lightly brushed the back of it with his lips, and then the five of them got into a very large black car that looked to Joan as if it had taken a bit of a battering at some time.

She felt most uncomfortable. Eric, who had suddenly become Emmanuel, got into the front seat beside Nicholas, who was the driver, while she was squeezed between the bald-headed Anthony and the good-looking Gerard, who informed her he was the brother of Nicholas. The conversation between the men was non-stop yet Joan was unable to understand one word because none of them, including Eric, was speaking in English. She was puzzled, because while they had been standing on the quayside they had spoken in English.

Soon Eric rested his arm on the top of his seat and turned his head to face her. Smiling, he said, 'We are lucky indeed. We are being allowed the use of a property at Spinola Bay for the duration of our stay.'

For all Joan knew he might just as well have said Timbuctoo but she was relieved to hear that they would not be staying with a Maltese family. At least, she gathered as much from the little that Eric had said.

In less than thirty minutes they had passed through the town and a couple of villages, and the car was slowing down as they approached a narrow road that held a bar, two or three shops with goods displayed out on the pavement under shady blinds, and what looked like a small restaurant. Set back from the street was a church and to the side of it Joan could see an ancient graveyard.

At the end of the road Joan caught a glimpse of a small harbour and a rocky beach. There were few people about, and when she remarked on this fact Gerard replied, 'It's siesta time. You'll get used to it.'

Moments later the car turned off to the right down an old country lane as Eric said, 'This is Spinola Bay.'

Joan was pleasantly surprised as the car turned into a paved courtyard and Nicholas turned the engine off. As she got out of the car, she was looking at what seemed to be a very old stone cottage such as a farm labourer might have been allocated in England.

She felt ridiculously excited. This holiday was turning out to be quite an adventure. She had never in her wildest dreams even thought that something like this might happen to her. Especially at her age! When she had opened Distinctive Designs she had been amazed and relieved that at last she had her own home and a means of earning her own living. She had thanked her lucky stars, thinking she had reached the top of the tree, and had been thoroughly content.

Well, mostly. At times when she was alone she did still feel lonely because everyone else of her age seemed to have children, or at least a partner.

Then Eric Roussel had come into her life, and now here she was, having crossed the Mediterranean, contemplating a holiday in this stone house with Eric, who had suddenly become Emmanuel!

She went inside the house, loosened the buttons on her coat and hung it on a hook behind the door. There were two very large rooms, one apparently a family kitchen with a huge fireplace in which a fire was laid, an oven set in the wall, a deep sink and a wooden draining board. An enormous dresser covered almost the whole of one wall and there appeared to be a plentiful supply of china. Copper-bottomed pans hung from a bar which stretched across the ceiling. The centre of this room was taken up by a large table, the top of which was covered by a heavily fringed chenille tablecloth, surrounded by six high-backed chairs.

To the back of the house was a sitting room, sparsely furnished but comfortable. Three small windows set into the far wall looked out over farmland, though no animals or buildings were in sight. At each end of this room a huge lantern-type lamp had been placed, so Joan assumed that there was no electricity. She hoped that at least there might be running water.

She decided that she would wait until the three men had gone before she explored the upstairs. She hadn't long to wait. While their luggage was carried in, the men continued to talk non-stop, all the time making frantic gestures with their hands to emphasise what they were saying. Joan had the feeling that tempers were becoming a little frayed and she was right because suddenly Eric thumped the table with his fist and very loudly and aggressively spat out a whole string of words.

Joan's face turned scarlet. Whatever had she let herself in for? Tears of frustration burned at the back of her eyes and she stood staring at Eric while she wondered what to do. He ignored her. Anthony, the bald-headed one, opened a wooden door which was set into the stone wall and took out a bottle of Scotch whisky and four glasses. Having poured generous measures he handed the glasses round. The men raised their glasses high and in unison they loudly proposed a toast. Whom or what they were toasting Joan had no idea. Although she would have refused a drink of whisky if it had been offered she was a bit piqued at being totally disregarded.

In one gulp the drink was swallowed, the glasses placed down on the table and all three men in turn shook Eric's hand. To Joan they merely nodded. Eric went outside with them, and as she didn't hear the car start up Joan went up the stone steps that led to the first floor. Going straight to the window of the room that looked out over the front of the house, she found she could look over the strip of lace curtain and down to where the men were standing around the car in the courtyard. She was in time to see Nicholas open the driver's door, reach down, and pull out a leather briefcase from beneath the seat. He placed the case on the bonnet of the car, snapped open the lock and took out a sheaf of papers and a bulky manilla envelope, both of which he offered to Eric. Eric grinned broadly, and said something which was obviously amusing because all three men laughed heartily.

Before accepting the papers and the envelope Eric slapped Nicholas on the back and then shook his hand. Then stepping back a few paces he watched as the three men got into the car. Joan noticed that as the car moved off it was still Nicholas who was driving, while Gerard and Anthony were sitting together in the back.

Hurriedly, Joan went from the front bedroom into the back room. She couldn't for the life of her have said why but she knew it wouldn't have done for Eric to find out that she had been looking down on him from above.

The bedrooms were identical, each furnished with a large double bed which had brass rails at the head and foot. Both beds were made up ready for use, covered by a pure white lacy bedspread, and placed at the head of each bed were four large white cotton-covered pillows. Each pillow case had an edging of the most beautiful heavy lace that Joan had ever seen, and each strip of lace was at least four inches wide. Later she was to learn that lace-making was one of the main industries on the island.

Everything smelt sweetly clean. A rug was placed on the stone floor on either side of both beds. Two very ornate but shabby armchairs, a pine chest of drawers and a marble-topped washstand on which was placed a large jug and bowl completed the furnishing of both rooms. Each washbowl and jug was decorated with a bright floral design, and beside each washstand was a free-standing wooden clothes horse, from which hung a large white fluffy towel and a huckaback hand towel. There go my hopes for running water in the house, at least upstairs, Joan said to herself. After the luxury of the P&O liner it was only natural that she felt a bit let down.

Eric was calling her and as she came downstairs she was taken aback to see a quantity of provisions laid out on the table.

'Where on earth have they come from?' She sounded as surprised as she felt. There was fresh milk, a very unusual-shaped loaf of bread, several lovely brown eggs, a whole cheese, a dish of butter and a great deal of assorted salad including the biggest ripe tomatoes she had ever seen.

Laughing, Eric took hold of her hand and led her through a back door into what appeared to be half garden and half courtyard. The stone-paved area was shaded by a huge awning beneath which stood many large earthen pots, each with its own heavy lid.

'This is where all perishable goods are kept. A cooling space. Every house has one.' Then, pointing a finger, he said, 'Look up.' On top of the end of the far brick wall were pumpkins, marrows and tomato vines. 'Summer is over now but there is still enough produce to last a few more weeks,' he told her as they went back inside the house.

After a refreshing salad and a glass of cool creamy milk, Eric carried their cases up the stairs. He placed his belongings in the back bedroom and Joan's in the front, yet he smiled at her in such a saucy way as he told her he was going to hang his clothes up that she needed no reminding that come night time they would be using only one of the double beds. A warm glow of anticipation came over her as she thought of what might lie ahead that evening.

'If you've finished unpacking, would you like to go for a walk?' Eric called to her from the back bedroom.

'Yes, that would be nice,' she answered. 'I won't be a few minutes.' She had changed from her suit into a linen dress that had a jacket to match, and her shoes for a pair of sandals. Eric had told her that with Christmas not too far away the evenings would be drawing in, but the weather would stay warm for a few more weeks yet. If today was anything to go by he was right. The ship had docked in brilliant sunshine and it was still quite warm.

As they left the house they were holding hands, a fact that had Joan smiling to herself. There were open fields on each side as they wandered down the lane. What few houses they did pass had a lot of character about them. All were made of stone, and had small windows with shutters, and open courtyards. Some even had external staircases leading up to a garden terrace.

When they reached the bay, Eric gave a happy shout.

'Couldn't have timed it better,' he called, dragging her down the beach to stand at the edge of the sea, where the waves were breaking against the rocky beach sending salty spray up into the air. Joan sniffed. The air was fantastic.

Although they had been at sea for nine days, it hadn't felt like this. With luxury all around, it hadn't seemed like the real world. She slipped her sandals off and ventured into the water, wriggling her toes and murmuring, 'Free! No customers, deliveries, or accounts to deal with. I still can't take in how all this has come about!' Just then three seagulls swooped low and she laughed, thinking to herself, yes, I am as free as you are, at least for the time being.

'Look.' Eric excitedly pointed a finger. 'It's years since even I have seen this.'

Not too far from the shore several fishing boats had anchored. Men wearing rubber aprons, knee-high boots and waterproof leggings were leaning over the sides of their vessels hauling in their nets. 'Looks like they've had a good catch,' Eric remarked as loads of fish were tipped into boxes, some left to lie on the deck while others were hand-lifted from cradle-like pots and tipped into big water containers. 'That last lot will be going on to St Julian's Bay. Crabs and lobsters for the restaurants and a couple of hotels. Tomorrow we'll go into St Julian's for our evening meal. Would you like that, Joan?'

'Very much so, please.' She smiled.

'I thought tonight we can just laze around, or maybe wander down to the local taverna.' He grinned broadly. 'Might as well let the locals get a good look at you because there isn't a man or woman in the village who hasn't heard already that you have arrived.'

It was nine thirty before they walked down the main street. It was dark, but there were two street lights and doors were open, and old people were sitting on chairs placed along the outside walls. Eric held the beaded curtain up out of the way to enable Joan to enter through the doorway of what looked to her very much like a homely café, because all the tables had red-checked linen tablecloths. She sat herself down on a chair at the nearest table. Eric did not follow suit. He remained standing just inside the doorway, and as Joan gazed at him, his appearance tonight seemed suddenly to be totally out of place. Very smart. Black suit, white silk shirt, open at the neck to reveal a heavy gold cross and chain, gold watch on his wrist and three heavy gold rings on the fingers of his right hand.

Joan was no fool. Eric had planned this. As she watched she had to smother the urge to laugh. There were three other woman besides herself, but the majority of the customers were men. She had sensed the masculine interest, seen the glances and the heads turn her way as she had sat down, but now it was as if Eric was on a stage and playing to the crowds. Seconds ticked by and the silence was not broken until at the back of the tavern a door opened and a gorgeous-looking man came forward leading a tall, white-haired, elderly gentleman. Joan thought the younger man to be about forty and quite the best-looking fellow she had ever seen.

The older man squinted his eyes, took two more steps towards Eric and then flung his arms wide. Eric went into them and the two men stood holding on to each other and rocking on the spot, one saying, 'Oh, my dear Emmanuel. Manny, my boy,' and Eric saying, 'Isidore, Isidore, we have left it too long.'

When at last they broke free and came to sit at the table with Joan she could see that each man had tears sparkling in his eyes. Introductions were made, and the younger man, whose name was Stephan, went away and came back with a bottle of red wine which he deftly opened. 'Do you wish to taste it, Grandfather?' he asked.

The elderly gentleman shook his head. Four glasses were

filled, and the bottle was placed on the table. When the three men raised their glasses to their lips Joan did the same and found the wine to be delicious. Eric and Isidore began to speak in low tones and the language was not English, and Joan was more than pleased when Stephan asked, 'Would you like to come and sit with my cousin and her husband? We can leave these two to catch up on old times.'

Stephan introduced his cousin as Anastasia, but quickly added, 'We mostly call her Anna, and her husband is good old plain John.'

John jumped to his feet and gently shook Joan's hand before playfully punching Stephan's shoulder. 'Joan and John are good solid names given to saints in years gone by,' he said knowledgeably.

'If you say so.' Stephan grinned.

Joan was thankful that all three of them were speaking to her in English. She learnt that this couple lived on Gozo, and were here to visit members of the family who were too frail to come to their home. 'I will ask that Emmanuel bring you to meet our family,' Anna said, sounding sincere. 'We don't often see friends from England and you would be sure of a welcome.'

Stephan looked thoughtful. 'I don't know what Emmanuel's plans are but a visit to Gozo for all of us is long overdue. We'll see if we can persuade Grandfather to come with us.'

Anna clapped her hands, tossed her sleek black hair over one shoulder and smiled at Joan. 'I shall look forward to it, as will John. You'll see. The visit will happen.' Anna's big dark brown eyes and well-tanned skin made her beautiful, and she was a lovely person. In fact Joan was thinking she was the kind of young woman she could easily be friends with.

It was after midnight, and four empty wine bottles stood on the table at which Joan had been sitting with her new-found friends, when Eric placed his hand on her shoulder.

'Hello,' she giggled. 'Where have you been?'

'I know where you are going,' Eric said, grinning widely. 'You've obviously found you like Isidore's stock of wine.'

Joan made to rise, but sat down again quickly with a bump.

With Stephan on one side and Eric on the other, they slowly walked Joan the few yards down the lane to where they were staying. All the while Joan was protesting, 'You didn't give me time to say goodnight to Anna an' John.'

'You will see them again tomorrow,' Eric repeatedly assured her.

'Shall I give you a hand to get Joan upstairs?' Stephan asked as he held her upright while Eric opened the front door.

'I'm sure I can manage,' Eric said as he took her weight from Stephan and placed her bodily across his shoulder. Her hair was loose, her head pointing downwards and her legs were dangling across Eric's chest, held secure by his strong arms.

Stephan went on his way, whistling to himself, while Eric negotiated the stone stairs with care. In the front bedroom he laid Joan across the foot of the bed, removed her sandals, and undid the two top buttons of her dress. She must have taken the jacket off and it had been left behind in the taverna. He folded the lace bedspread back and then half pushed and half pulled Joan's body until she was lying between the sheets, her head resting on two pillows. She was out like a light. Dead to the world.

For a long time he stood smiling down at her, then shaking his head he went slowly into the back bedroom where he undressed and got into bed. His last wakeful thought was, this night had not gone according to plan!

Next morning Joan woke up with the mother of all headaches. She too cast her mind back to the previous evening. She should have acted a lot more wisely than she had done. She had drunk far too much wine and as far as she could tell Eric must have slept on his own in the other bedroom. 'Oh well!' she sighed sleepily, as she closed her eyes again. Too late now to think about how differently the night had turned out from what she had been anticipating.

Chapter Thirty-six

JOAN OPENED ONE EYE to see Eric standing there fully dressed, washed and shaved. She tried to raise her head from the pillow but failed miserably.

He was smiling as he set down a small tray which held a steaming cup of tea. Placing one arm beneath her shoulder blades he dragged all four pillows into a heap and helped to prop her up against them. 'Good morning, my darling. I won't bother to ask how you are feeling.' He grinned. Then he handed her a glass that held a small amount of colourless liquid. 'Here, drink this, and then you may have your tea.'

Gingerly she took the glass from his hand and sniffed the contents. 'Ugh, it smells terrible,' she moaned.

'I know it does, and it won't taste good either, but you *will* drink it.'

Joan squinted up at him, gaining the impression that she had better do as he said. She tightened her hold on the glass, tossed the liquid to the back of her throat and shuddered as she swallowed. It tasted utterly foul. She grabbed the cup that Eric was holding out to her and gratefully took a gulp, not caring that the tea was hot. Then she took another before she sighed and said, 'Oh, thank you. That's much better.'

Eric sat on the edge of the bed and waited until she had drained the cup. 'Did you have a good time last night?' he asked finally.

Joan thought for a minute before forming an answer. 'Yes, yes I did. That is, what I remember of it. I liked Anna – she was such a nice person. It wasn't until I made to stand up that everything went wrong. I am sorry.'

Eric soothed her tangled hair away from her face. 'I am to blame for the state you were in and it is me that should be apologising to you.'

'How did you work that out?' Joan muttered. Her tongue felt as if it was made of dried cotton wool.

'You were given too much wine to drink. I should have warned Stephan that you were not used to it. I met Isidore and we stayed longer than we had intended.'

'Please, may I have another cup of tea?' Joan begged.

'Of course, my darling, and then I will bring you up two pitchers of hot water so that you may get washed and dressed. I am so sorry that the accommodation does not run to a bathroom. There is a shower rigged up in the outside courtyard but the supply of water is only cold.'

Joan shivered. 'I'll manage,' she said, longing for him to go so that she could at least use the chamber pot and then clean her teeth.

Whatever the foul drink was that Eric had given her, the effect it had had on Joan was like a shot in the arm. Her head had cleared in no time.

They had skipped breakfast but over lunch they talked of all manner of things including their proposed visit to Gozo, which Eric promised would take place at the weekend. Joan drank three glasses of clear water and when she emerged from the kitchen, after clearing the meal away and washing up their plates and dishes, she found Eric waiting for her, already dressed in his overcoat and looking very different from yesterday. Today his image was more businesslike and the fact that he was impatiently leaning against the doorframe, with his hands resting on the bone handle of a very posh walking stick, was very puzzling. She had never known him to use a stick before. She didn't even know that he owned one. Come to think of it, there was a lot she didn't know about Eric Roussel.

'Let's be off then, and I promise we shall have a slap-up meal tonight.'

'You'll have to give me a few minutes, till I finish dressing and change my shoes.'

'Get a move on then. It is imperative that I meet up with a couple of men and I am late already. No, wait. I've had a better idea. I can't be doing without a car for the length of our stay. You stay, take your time, I'll get off, attend to my business and while I'm in the city I'll hire a car and come back for you later. Stephan will drive me in now.' He crossed the room, gave her a quick kiss, and then was out of the door like a bat out of hell.

It was after five o'clock before he came back, driving a dark saloon car, the first decent vehicle that Joan had seen since she set foot on the island. He offered no explanation as to where he had been and Joan did not ask. He did seem immensely pleased with himself as he set a bottle of Scotch on the table and threw his arms round Joan's neck, kissing her on both cheeks.

'Oh, my darling, I have everything sorted out. I am taking you out tonight and we are really going to celebrate.'

Eric was humming to himself as he drove and as they passed a sign which pointed the way to St Julian's Bay Joan felt compelled to ask, 'Weren't we supposed to be going to St Julian's tonight?'

'How observant you are.' Eric laughed. 'We were indeed, but during the course of a business meeting this morning I met some friends, one of whom owns a restaurant up in the north part of the island, and we, my darling, are invited to dine there tonight.'

'Eric,' Joan said cautiously, 'may I ask you a question?'

'Of course. Fire away.'

'How is it you know so many people and have so many friends here when you told me that you haven't been back to Malta for years? And just where are we going now?'

Eric took his eyes off the road for a second and smiled at her. 'That, my darling, is two questions. First, I was born here, and what I said was, I have not *lived* here since I was a lad. That's not to say I haven't made flying visits from time to time. When one is in business it pays to keep in contact with one's business partners and to strike without warning never does any harm. Can't let it be thought that I am getting too old to cope. My motto is, the older you are the wiser you are, and during this visit I promise you there are some fellows who are going to be brought up sharply to my way of thinking. I have already settled my account with two men who thought they could outwit me.'

'Hmm.' Joan was busy with her own thoughts. Eric's mind was like a deep well. Hard to get to the bottom of. 'You still haven't told me where we are going.'

'We are heading for the north of the island, to a place called Marfa. Wait till you see it. I guarantee you will remember this visit for the rest of your life.'

Eric was right.

The building itself was not much to write home about but the setting was what Joan could only describe as paradise. They were high up and the whole area seemed to be planted with exotic trees, shrubs and wild flowers, while the scented air was bracing. They were seated at a table which was set outside the café in what appeared to be a built-on annexe. Three walls were of plain wood, the fourth was sheer glass. It was a glorious evening, with the sound of waves breaking on the beach far below and the flimsy curtains stirring at the open window.

'It's a pity it has got dark so early,' Eric said. 'If we have time I must bring you back here during the day, because looking out across the water from up here one can see the islands of Comino and Gozo.'

Not only was the eating of the meal a delight, but the preparing and the cooking of the food was a joy to watch. Out on the hillside great flares were lit and in a deep hole that had cemented sides a fire was kindled. Iron grids were laid crossways over the top once the embers were red and glowing. Healthy, tanned young men skinned and filleted huge flat fish which they brushed with melted butter and sprinkled with a variety of mixed herbs and then grilled to perfection. The fish was served with tiny boiled potatoes, dishes of pasta, rice and salad, and hot crusty bread. Also placed on the table was a tray that held six round china dishes, each one containing a different delicious-tasting homemade sauce. Several different kinds of wine were liberally poured, but Joan had learnt her lesson last night.

She suddenly smiled to herself as her thoughts flew back to England and her sister Martha. In the Prince of Wales she had often sailed near the wind but never had she been so drunk that she couldn't remember how she had got home and into her bed. The last thing she remembered about last night was trying to stand up and failing miserably. She smiled again, hearing in her head Martha's voice loud and clear saying, 'You were as pissed as a pudding!'

With the first course over, glasses were refilled, and the taste of the sweet that followed had Joan smacking her lips: big succulent strawberries surrounded by brandy-flavoured ice cream.

'Strawberries, at this time of the year?' she exclaimed to Eric. 'And I have never tasted such sweet ones.'

'This is Malta,' he reminded her. 'Here everything is different.'

'You can say that again,' Joan said as she looked towards the inside of the café. It was by now almost ten o'clock at night but scores of people were still dining and gorgeous, healthy-looking children sat with their parents or on the floor. Nearly every child had a mop of thick curly hair and their skin was in the main the lovely colour of milk chocolate.

It was one o'clock in the morning when they finally left Marfa. For the last hour they had drunk nothing but very strong black coffee. The farewells they received were affectionate and warm, every man in sight hugging Eric and giving him what seemed the obligatory pats on the back.

It really was a lovely night, or early morning, the sky dark but twinkling with more stars than Joan remembered having seen before. Eric drove slowly and Joan had the window on the passenger side of the car wound down. Coming down from the hills she could at times hear the sea lapping against the shore. She had been wined and dined to perfection, and this evening she was well aware of where she was and what she was doing as she snuggled up against Eric's shoulder.

Only one bedroom was occupied that night and Joan's last thought before she fell asleep was that Eric was like no other man who had been in her life. Would his lovemaking, his wealth and his wisdom be enough to sustain their future together? One little point still niggled at the back of her mind as she lay naked in the crook of his arm.

There was still an awful lot that she did not know about Eric Roussel.

Chapter Thirty-seven

IT WAS WITH A horrible sinking feeling in the pit of her stomach that Joan watched from the bedroom window as a big black car drove into the courtyard, and it did not make her feel any better to see two men whom, at first glance, she would describe as thugs get out of the car and stride towards the house.

There definitely was something sinister about both of them. Tall and heavily built, they had very broad shoulders, their arms rippled with muscles and their hands were enormous. Unusually for Maltese men, they wore no jackets, and their shirt sleeves were rolled up to beyond their elbows.

Joan came quietly down the stairs in time to see one of the men pass an envelope to Eric. His fingers were trembling slightly as he unfolded the single sheet of paper he had withdrawn from the envelope. Then, having read the words, he exploded with rage. His cheeks turned blood red as he thumped his fist on the table top, and he screamed what Joan feared had to be a whole string of offensive words at the two messengers. He looked furious when he glanced up and saw Joan standing on the bottom step of the stone staircase.

'Put your coat on and go for a walk,' he shouted.

Joan had no option but to do as he said. It was not a suggestion, it was an order. The silence hung heavy in the room as she took down her coat from the hook behind the door. Without waiting to put it on, she walked out of the house, hearing the door being slammed behind her as she walked away.

In the lane she hesitated. To say the least, she was frightened. No, that word did not describe her feelings. She was terrified! Should she turn left and go to the taverna? Maybe tell Stephan that she felt something was wrong? Or should she turn right and head for Spinola Bay?

Better to mind your own business. Eric is more than capable of taking care of himself. Normally that would be the case, but this morning she was not so sure. If those two men calling on Eric were friendly then she would hate to be around when his enemies made an appearance.

Sighing heavily, she decided her best course was to take a walk, give herself time to calm down. At the moment her heart was still beating nineteen to the dozen and her stomach was churning. She walked slowly towards the bay, her mind playing tricks all the time. Eric had been well pleased with himself when he came back from Valletta yesterday and on the way to Marfa last night he had said that he had settled his account with two men. From his choice of words, she had judged the outcome to have been to Eric's benefit. But now what?

There was no one in the cove with the exception of one fisherman sitting on the rocks. Joan stood watching him for a while as his fingers weaved in and out repairing his nets with an instrument that looked like a cross between a knitting needle and a crochet hook. Looking up and seeing Joan, he called a cheery greeting and beckoned her over. By the time she reached his side he had laid aside the nets and

328

was slicing into a fat juicy melon. He patted the rock beside him and gestured for Joan to sit beside him. She did so gladly and accepted a huge slice of his melon. He fished in a bag that lay at his feet, brought out a small bundle of white cloth and tore off a wide strip. 'Napkin,' he said, laughing loudly, and Joan laughed with him as she held the piece of cloth beneath her chin to catch the juice that was running from the ripe fruit. How kind and generous these local people were.

This man had a wrinkled weather-beaten face, though he was not that old; about the same age as herself, she guessed. Both his trousers and his thick, heavy, navy blue jersey had seen better days, yet he was as happy as a lark. The ordinary Maltese folk certainly seemed to live an entirely different life from Londoners. The other men, always dressed in black suits, whom Eric associated with were a different breed entirely from her companion, who was now offering to roll her a cigarette.

Soon the fisherman took up his nets again and Joan watched with admiration as his knobbly fingers flew in and out. It wasn't long before he was joined by another man, similar in size and dress to himself. The two men spoke a few words and they seemed to be in agreement, for they turned to Joan, smiling broadly and making gestures with their hands towards a boat that lay bobbing at the edge of the sea. Joan frowned. It took a couple of minutes before it dawned on her that they were inviting her to join them on a boat trip.

'Please, miss, you enjoy,' the second man said, and then as if it had only just dawned on him he pointed to his mate, saying. 'He Tamara,' then stabbing his own chest with his forefinger added, 'me Zack.' Then he pointed to the sky. 'Nice day, you enjoy.'

Joan repeated each of their names, smiled, and holding out her hand said, 'My name is Joan.'

'Please, Joan, you come,' said Tamara.

A trip out to sea with two men she didn't know from Adam? On the other hand it was certainly an attractive proposition. Joan suddenly laughed aloud, stood up and said, 'Why not?'

The two men grinned at each other and began to walk towards the boat. Joan followed and smiled in appreciation as Zack placed a cushion on the bare seat of the boat and Tamara steadied her as she climbed aboard. She was thinking that it was a godsend meeting these fishermen this morning. Her head had been full of dreadful thoughts as she had left Eric in the house with those two brutes. But if she had gone against Eric's orders and stayed, what could she have done? She hadn't got the slightest idea as to what they had come to the house for. Eric had certainly not been pleased to see them!

She hadn't been able to understand a word they were rattling on about, but it didn't take much deduction to realise that the argument that was raging when she left had hardly been a friendly one. No, she had done the right thing. She was well out of it.

The purr of the boat's engine was reassuring and the further out to sea they got the easier Joan began to feel. The sight of the sparkling, brilliant sea for as far as she could see went a long way towards calming her feelings. When Zack cut the engine and the two men prepared to haul their lobster pots aboard, he motioned to Joan to stand up and lift up the top of the seat on which she was sitting. She did so, and smiled. At her feet was a deep cupboard which held a few thick china mugs and two thermos flasks which must have stood the battering of time for they bore the marks of a few dents. She needed no further instructions.

Setting three mugs in a line, she unscrewed the cap of one flask and found it to contain boiling hot strong black coffee. Delving further into the cupboard, she wasn't in the least surprised to find a jar of sugar and a bottle, which had a spring-like buckled top, containing a thick yellow creamy liquid that Tamara later told her was goat's milk. Whatever, the brew they eventually sat slowly sipping as the boat rocked gently was one of the best drinks of coffee that Joan had ever tasted.

The companionable atmosphere was to Joan like no other that she had ever experienced. It was as if she had known these two middle-aged men all her life and that they had always been friends. When they were back at the bay and she was being half lifted from the boat by their four strong arms she was almost reluctant to leave them. Three times she paused as she walked up the beach and turned to wave at her new friends, who were still standing watching her.

It had been a unique experience. To others, the telling might sound like just an ordinary boat trip out with two fishermen to bring in their lobster pots. To Joan it had been a delightful change. A soothing time that she would remember for the rest of her life.

Now she had to go back. To what? Her thoughts shied away from forming an answer to that question.

She lingered in the courtyard, unable to believe her ears. The sounds of revelry coming from inside the house were enough to give anyone the impression that a party was going on. Gingerly, she opened the door and the sight that met her eyes amazed her. There were at least a half a dozen men, all holding glasses in their hands. But there was no sign of the two men who had been with Eric when she had left. Whatever had transpired, there was no mistaking the overall happiness. Never could Joan remember being so pleased to see anyone as when Anna broke free from the back of the room and came smiling towards her.

'Where ever have you been?' Anna asked, as she hugged Joan tightly. 'Manny has been afraid for you.'

Joan looked to where Eric was standing, surrounded by men and looking extremely pleased with himself. As yet he hadn't even noticed that she was back.

Anna steered Joan into the back sitting room, closing the door behind the two of them. 'You deserve an explanation,' she said. 'You must have been frightened this morning, but you should have come straight down to us, not wandered off on your own.'

Joan didn't know what to say. She still hadn't the slightest idea of what was going on.

'Nothing happens on the island that Isidore does not get to know about, and Stephan and some other relatives were ready for Emmanuel's visitors this morning.' Anna was quick to reassure her. 'All is well now. So smile, Joan, and try to remember that Manny has more friends than enemies. There is not a village on Malta where the inhabitants do not have great respect for the Roussel family.'

If her speech was supposed to make Joan feel better and clear the air it hadn't worked. It hadn't been an explanation that Joan could understand, but she knew by now that it was not her place to ask questions.

'Only one more day and the whole family is off to Gozo,' Anna said breezily. 'Once there you will meet Manny's closest family and we shall all have a great time. But come now and have a drink. There is plenty to eat and much to celebrate.'

To say that Joan was bewildered would be putting it mildly. However, she put on a brave face and followed Anna.

The minute Eric saw her he set down his drink and reached out his hands. 'Come here.'

Joan went to him. He pulled her straight into his arms and kissed her, very gently and tenderly. It was a while before he drew away from her and stood smiling down into her clear blue eyes. 'I almost wish,' he told her, 'that I hadn't promised we would go and eat with Isidore this evening.'

332

'We'll still have the whole night to ourselves,' she told him.

The answering squeeze that he gave her wiped away all of her misgivings. At least for the moment.

That night it was cold as Joan climbed in between the linen sheets, and she tucked her feet up into the bottom of her satin nightdress.

Eric came and flung the bedclothes off her, laughing as he did so. 'You won't be cold for long, that much I promise you.'

She was freezing, but his touch was warm and she snuggled up close to his body. They were together now and she felt safe. Her face was pressed into his bare shoulder, his fingers twined in her long hair and they kissed liked young lovers who had only recently met.

Tonight was different again. There were no problems. England was far away; this was their time with nobody to disapprove. Eric was the only person in the world that she wanted to be with.

Much, much later she lay on her side, Eric's arms still holding her close. 'Oh, Eric . . .' It was a whisper, because she wasn't capable of putting into words what she was feeling.

Eric smiled and said, 'I love you.' He kissed the top of her head. 'I love you,' he repeated. 'I think I've been in love with you since the first moment I set eyes on you, when you were terrified because Martin had sent you to have lunch with me on your own. You feared I might turn out to be an ogre, didn't you?'

'Well, I didn't know what to expect.'

'And I let you down so many times by not turning up. Why did you let me come back into your life each time?'

Joan answered without thinking. 'I couldn't get you out of my mind. And looking back I don't think I tried very

333

hard. I only knew that everything about my life changed when you walked through the door.'

'And, my darling, do you still feel the same way?'

'Oh, Eric, how could I not? Look what you've done for me! Taken me places, shown me a whole different life. Before now I could never have imagined that I would do the things that I have with you. My previous life was dull and dreary compared to what it is now.'

'I like the bit about doing things with me.'

'Now you're teasing me rotten.' But she laughed as she said the words.

'Well, if you make us each a nice cup of coffee we might be able to start all over again and the rest of the night might even turn out to be better than it has been so far.'

'Oh, Eric.' She sighed, but it was a happy sigh. 'I never knew. I never even guessed that lovemaking could be . . .' She couldn't go on.

'You are a wonderful lady, Joan. Until now you haven't really done anything with your life except look after other people. In future you must keep reminding yourself each and every day that you will not just *get by*, or just *exist*. Life is for living and we should all of us live it to the full.'

What Eric was saying was exciting but a little bit scary, and she felt compelled to ask, 'Don't you ever give a thought to tomorrow?'

'Tomorrow may never come, sweetheart.' He grinned. 'I've told you things can get even better. Who knows?'

Joan looked into his twinkling eyes and she began to laugh and that was when he tried to kiss her. But her mouth was wide open, laughing with sheer joy. So he took her into his arms and words were no longer necessary.

Chapter Thirty-eight

WHAT A HAPPY GATHERING.

Judging by the number of people, half the residents of Malta must have relatives living on the tiny island of Gozo, Joan was thinking to herself as she watched several small craft ferry their way along the quayside. All around her were families; young children, their parents, grandparents and even great grandparents. The waterfront seemed to be humming with the same excited expectancy that she was feeling. She could hear a hubbub of voices as people formed orderly queues to board one of the boats. It was Sunday morning: blue skies and weak sunshine, a typical autumn morning. Joan felt like a child going on a Sunday school outing. She was excited at the thought of crossing the water to visit another island and at the same time a little fearful at the thought of meeting Eric's family.

Three horse-drawn carriages had brought Eric, herself and the rest of the relations and friends down to the dock. Stephan, Eric and John were helping the older folk along the quayside and assisting them to board one of the largest boats. Anna was standing beside Joan, waiting until everyone else was safely settled. Suddenly Anna asked, 'Joan, is something bothering you?'

'No, not really.'

'What do you mean, not really? Either there is something wrong or there isn't, but the look on your face tells me you're a bit bewildered.'

Joan gave a small sigh. 'To tell you the truth, Anna, I am, but I don't think I should be talking about it.'

'Don't be silly. Is it something one of my aunts said or did?'

'No, honestly. Besides, it isn't only your family – it's almost everyone who is stepping into the boats.'

Anna looked mystified, so Joan told her what she had seen.

'Adults and even children all touch their foreheads and then their chests. Left to right, making the sign of the cross. Some are even fingering small gold medals hanging round their necks, while their lips are moving all the while as if they are praying.'

'They are praying. To St Christopher, the patron saint of travellers. The medallions they are wearing are figures of St Christopher.'

'What? You mean they are afraid of crossing this stretch of water?'

'Not exactly. Most folk do it when they travel no matter by what means. Everyone wants a safe journey.'

'Oh, I see,' said Joan, not sure that she really did.

John held his arms out and lifted Anna down into the boat and Eric did the same for Joan. She let out a great sigh of pleasure as the mooring rope was freed and they set out on their short crossing.

A small edition of an ancient coach was waiting for the family when they arrived at the landing stage. The driver was treated as an old friend by all the men, who put their arms round him, kissed his weather-beaten cheeks and patted his back. Not at all the way the men acted towards one another in England. The arrival of the women he totally ignored. Joan thought she wouldn't care to guess his age but she couldn't help but notice that his clothes hung on him as though he had shrunk.

On the bus Eric came to sit beside her. He was looking exceptionally smart this morning, as though he had been dressed by an expensive tailor, and smelling good too. As they drove along, he held her hand between both of his. They did not talk, as Joan was too busy looking at the countryside. Her first impression of Gozo was that it was even greener, quieter and more unspoilt than Malta was. They passed a couple of picturesque fishing villages, clusters of stone-built houses and a fair number of churches. Then the coach began to climb and Eric explained that his family all lived in a farmhouse on the outskirts of the village of Xaghra. Joan did her best to repeat the name, but although Eric slowly spelt it out for her she was unable to get her tongue round such a difficult word.

'Never mind,' Eric sympathised. 'Enough for you to know that it is on high ground, a very rural area, breathtaking scenery, but a slow way of life.'

He was right. The driver brought the coach to a halt and Joan got her first glimpse of country folk living on a small island. It was like stepping into another world.

There were about five or six houses set almost into a semicircle yet leaving plenty of space between each rustic building. The large open courtyard in which they stood also boasted a watermill which actually worked, and Joan was fascinated as she watched the wooden paddles being driven by the clear sparkling water. There seemed to be animals of every description roaming over the cobbles, yet there was still a feeling of peacefulness, almost as if time did not exist in this place.

'Come,' Eric said. 'Meet my mother and the rest of the ladies.'

The elderly female members of the family sat together in

a line, their backs ramrod straight against the stone wall. Each was dressed in black, with a beautiful lace mantilla draped over her grey hair. All of them were working. And what an art! Knitting needles flew as some produced chunky jerseys from thick oily wool, the type that fishermen wore. Others were making lace, bringing forth articles so exquisite they resembled cobwebs. As Eric and Joan approached the work was dropped on to their chairs and they all got to their feet, crying, 'He's come. He's come. It really is our Manny.'

They rushed to put their arms about him to the extent that he was almost smothered. Younger women ran to join the throng, every one of them eager to embrace him. Joan stood to one side, feeling left out.

Finally Eric broke free, took Joan's hand and began to introduce her. 'This is my mother, Nadia Roussel. Isidore whom you have met is her brother-in-law.'

The elegant but frail little lady was smiling sweetly at Joan. Joan almost felt she should curtsey, but instead she held out her hand and said, 'I am very pleased to meet you, Madam Roussel.'

'I am more than pleased that my son has brought you to join our party.'

Party? By now Joan had got the jitters. Was it some special occasion? Should she have brought a present? She hadn't time for more reflections, Eric was taking her along the line, names running off his tongue: Bianca, Chole, Fiona, Ingrid. Two maiden aunts had come to swell the family, and even more cousins, though it appeared that Nadia was the only one who spoke any English. Suddenly Anna was at her elbow, speaking to her relatives in their own language. Whatever she said to them it must have been something nice, for all the ladies were smiling and nodding their heads in approval.

'Halfway there,' Anna laughed. 'Now you get to meet the men.' Leaving Eric surrounded by the women, she took Joan by the elbow and led her across the courtyard to where a bar had been set up. All talking and laughter ceased as the two young women approached. The men moved sideways to make a pathway for them and at once Joan could see that two large wicker chairs had been placed at one end of the bar. Isidore was seated in one, and the other was occupied by someone who was introduced to Joan as Theodore. She needed no telling that they were related because they were as alike as two peas in a pod.

Isidore smilingly kissed the back of her hand and in perfect English asked if she had enjoyed her short trip over to Gozo. This was a bit of a shock, because in the taverna she had been under the impression that he did not speak English. She would have to watch her step, she warned herself.

Theodore got to his feet and he, too, gallantly took her hand and kissed it, saying, 'Welcome to the home of the Kramer and Roussel families.' Then he looked towards the group of men and issued a curt order in his own language. It seemed it was to be left to Anna to make the introductions this time. Dark, swarthy-looking young men, older men who had the same grace and elegance as oozed from Eric. 'Claude, Boris, Luke, John my husband you already know and Stephan my cousin, Marcus, Ezra.'

Joan's jaw ached with smiling and she almost pleaded with Anna to stop, but she was saved the embarrassment. Several young women were clapping their hands and pointing to where several trestle tables had been joined and set up as one very long table. It was time to eat. As if from nowhere, hordes of laughing children appeared and were seated at a table of their own which ran parallel to that where their parents would be eating.

Joan could not remember having seen so much food laid out at any one time. Dishes lined the table from one end to the other, and every morsel looked superb. Good food was taken very seriously in Malta and it would appear to be no different on this wonderful little island where time seemed to stand still.

Before they started to eat, while the wine was being poured, Eric disappeared for a few minutes and came back bearing a sack of gaily wrapped presents. He knew each child by name. They were beautiful children, beautifully dressed and well mannered. A chubby little girl aged about four tore the wrapping off her present and found a doll which she immediately cradled in her arms, murmuring, 'Thank you, Uncle Manny.' The young boy sitting next to her, obviously her brother but slightly older, had received a clockwork lorry and the expression on his face as he wound the key was a joy to watch. No child had been forgotten, and all of them were agog with excitement as boys set out toy soldiers and girls discovered all kinds of pretty things according to their age. Joan couldn't fathom Eric. He was so kind and thoughtful most of the time, but remembering the morning when those two thugs had come to Spinola Bay she knew only too well that there was a darker side to him.

Everyone was in a happy mood. Men came up from the village to play for them. Some had fiddles, one even had a banjo, another an accordion, and as the music started Nadia gave the order and everyone began to eat.

Between courses local girls danced for them. Then the band changed their instruments and began to play waltzes. Eric roared with laughter as couples got to their feet and attempted to dance on the flagstones of the courtyard, but Stephan wiped the smile from Eric's face when he came and asked Joan if she would dance with him. Tall and slim, light on his feet, Stephan was the perfect partner. Joan hadn't danced in years and yet with Stephan's arm around her, his hand in the small of her back, she never put a foot wrong. It felt as if she was gliding in time to the music. Stephan lowered his head and deliberately let their cheeks touch, and every now and again he would murmur in her ear, 'Good to be able to show old Manny just how lucky he is. He's too old to be able to move like this.'

'I bet you wouldn't say that to his face,' she teased.

Stephan wouldn't let her go when the tune ended, but kept her out in the open ready for the next dance. She felt like a young girl when finally, holding hands and stifling their laughter, they made their way back to the table. To her utter surprise Eric had stood up, and as she reached his side, to her great embarrassment, he took her in his arms and kissed her long and lovingly.

She couldn't meet the look in Stephan's eyes as he thanked her for dancing with him and turned and walked over to the bar. They both knew that Eric's kiss had been his way of staking his claim to her. It made her feel extremely special, but at the same time she knew that every eye had been on her. She mustn't drink any more wine, she told herself, she was getting too cocksure of herself. But then, when in her life had two men paid her so much attention in one day? Or even *one* man, come to that!

No sooner was she seated than Eric took off his jacket, unknotted his tie, loosened it and undid the top button of his shirt. Then he pulled her to her feet and laughingly said, 'My turn now.' He made hand signals to the musicians, and the couples who were already dancing stopped and formed a circle. The music changed to catchy tunes, the beat now loud and fast, but that was all right because Joan and Eric had their arms round each other and were moving as one. Every now and then Eric would kiss her on the lips, whispering outrageous suggestions as their friends and relations clapped their hands and egged Eric on. Joan knew why he was entering into the spirit of it all. He was determined to show that anything Stephan could do he could do better, even if he were a good few years older.

The breeze had strengthened and several older folk

proposed that they cleared the tables and go into the house. However, Nadia Roussel had other ideas. She called Anna and Eric to her side and issued instructions. Eric stayed by his mother, talking softly to her, while Anna came back over to where Joan was sitting.

'Aunt Nadia says you cannot visit Gozo without going into at least one of our churches. There are two nearby. They are entirely different, yet both are beautiful in their own way. Manny is going to ask Joseph, the coach driver, to take those of us who wish to go to visit both churches. Would you care to come with us, Joan?'

Joan didn't hesitate. 'Of course. It would be a privilege.'

'Well, let's go inside and freshen ourselves up first, shall we?'

As the coach came to a halt the men got off first, and as Eric handed Joan down he looked very serious. She felt something was wrong.

Eric nodded to where three of the older men and Stephan were standing apart. 'Bit of business to attend to,' he said vaguely. 'If we're not back by the time you have visited both churches we'll meet up again at the farmhouse.' He planted a hasty kiss on her cheek and moved away, leaving only four women besides Anna and Joan to go viewing.

The church they were standing outside looked to be very old and desperately in need of repair and yet it somehow gave off a graceful appearance, mainly because the structure was tall and narrow. Near to the top of the stonework there were four round empty spaces, one on each side of the building. Joan thought they might at one time have held the face of a clock. Similar to London's Big Ben. Not that the spire of this church was anywhere near as impressive as London's world famous clock.

As one of the aunts pushed open the door to the church, Anna held Joan back and from her bag she produced two

342

black mantillas. 'We cannot enter unless we cover our heads,' she explained as she demonstrated how Joan should twist one into shape to cover her hair.

The outside of the church had given Joan the impression of an ordinary place of worship for a working-class farming community. She couldn't have been more wrong. One look at the beautiful interior had her gasping in surprise.

The sun had gone down, but the stained glass windows shone with so many colours that Joan was transfixed. The women dipped their fingers into a bowl of holy water and made the sign of the cross on their foreheads, Anna also performed this act on Joan, then they toured the small interior of the church walking in single file.

Above the altar was a mighty display of Christ's crucifixion but dominating the whole scene was the figure of the Virgin Mary. Her facial beauty and the glorious simple robes in which she was adorned was enough to bring tears to Joan's eyes. But that was *not* what amazed her. If someone had related to her the sight she was now looking at she knew she would have found it hard to believe. Pinned to the robes of the Virgin Mary were many treasury notes in several different currencies and dominations. That was not all. There was also jewellery in different shapes and forms, including wedding rings. Anna had to nudge her to move on, so spellbound was Joan by this unusual sight.

The second church they visited, only a short walk away, was beyond description. In London this church would be referred to as a cathedral. It was on a par with St Paul's with its golden dome which was a landmark wherever one was in London. This was indeed a rich Catholic church. Its beauty beyond belief.

Joseph took them back to the farmhouse, where a hot meal of braised kidneys and rice was waiting for them. Although Joan didn't think her stomach would hold much more food she had to admit to Anna that she had thoroughly enjoyed the unusual meal. It was now getting dark and the men had still not returned. Joan could only tell that the older women were getting anxious by the tone of their voices and the agitated glances they kept casting at each other. Anna translated some of the comments for her, but she knew full well she wasn't being told the whole story. Even Anna herself was showing signs of becoming uneasy.

When at last the men did return there was a rush to get everyone on to the coach. Anna explained to Joan that they would miss the last boat if they did not leave immediately. Hurried, affectionate goodbyes were said, and Anna explained that the women were urging Joan to come back and spend Christmas with them. Joan smiled, but gave non-committal answers. She had had a lovely time, but Christmas was for families, and Martha and Sid would never forgive her if she were not sitting at their dinner table on that one day of the year.

They were in the boat before Joan noticed that Eric was clutching a small leather attaché case. Its corners were reinforced with steel studs, and besides the main lock there was a heavy padlocked chain which ran beneath the handle and round the whole of the case. He never once released his hold on that handle, not even when they were back in Malta and he stood on the quay to assist her to climb up beside him. The horse-drawn carriages were waiting for them, and Eric and Joan were the first to get off. Joan hugged Anna lovingly, and Eric promised to bring her down to the taverna the next day. Then, arm in arm, they turned off down into the lane that would take them to what had almost become home to Joan. The attaché case was still held fast in Eric's right hand and he swung it jauntily as they walked. Joan would be lying to herself if she said she didn't wonder what the case contained. On the other hand, she was wise enough to understand that what she didn't know she couldn't worry about.

Once in bed, safe and content in Eric's arms, Joan found her thoughts were mixed. Despite her anxieties regarding Eric, there was no denying that she was living, and thoroughly enjoying herself, in a totally different world. She needed no reminder that soon it had to come to an end and she would have to return to reality. However, today had been an absolutely wonderful day, and now she had even more memories to add to her fast growing list.

Chapter Thirty-nine

NEXT MORNING JOAN WOKE to find that she was in bed on her own. Eric usually made a great play of waking her up, sometimes by bringing her a cup of tea but mostly by kissing her and indulging in love play. He must have crept out of bed today, because she hadn't heard a sound.

Hastily she washed, using the jug of cold water from the washstand, thinking she would get Eric to carry hot water upstairs for her later in the day. Then she dressed and did her hair. Halfway down the staircase she hesitated. There was no hand rail or side to these stone steps and she could see right down into the main living room.

Eric was sitting at the table, on which was the leather case he had brought back from Gozo. The lid of the case was up and the contents were visible. Stacked neatly in piles were wads of notes. A few of these bundles of money were lying on the table beside the open case.

Joan lowered her head, and forced herself to cough as she came slowly down the rest of the stairs. She sensed, rather than saw, Eric gather up the bundles of notes, and it wasn't until she heard the lock click, confirming that Eric had closed the case, that she gaily called out, 'My, you're an early bird this morning.'

Treading the last steps slowly she could see that the case had been removed from the table. Thank God for that. At least she hadn't embarrassed him. On the contrary, Eric was full of the joys of spring as he came forward and kissed her good morning. 'Scrambled eggs OK by you, darling?' he asked.

'Lovely. I'll make the toast and coffee.' Joan could hear the tremor in her voice and tried to control it. That was no small amount of money that Eric had in that case. They ate their breakfast, each making small talk, but it wouldn't have taken someone with a crystal ball to realise that both of them were edgy.

As Joan began to clear the table Eric looked pointedly at his watch. 'I have to go into Valletta this morning and book our passage back to London. We'll travel Khedivial mail line this time. It only takes three to four days.'

'Sudden decision, isn't it?' He had taken Joan by surprise.

Eric sighed heavily. It was unusual to see him so straight-faced. 'Needs must when the devil drives. The quicker I'm back in London the safer I shall feel.'

Joan jumped on that word. 'Safer? Are you in trouble, Eric? Why do you not feel safe here?'

Eric laughed, but it was a hollow sound. 'Slip of the tongue, Joan. I didn't mean personal safety, only that I have a business deal going on and I don't want to lose it.' He was talking for the sake of talking, Joan thought, but better that she kept her own counsel. They had had a marvellous time and now it was time to go home.

'All right.' Making a great effort, she smiled. 'I'll do our packing while you are out.'

Eric shrugged himself into his coat, pulled the case out from beneath the table, and kissed her goodbye. As soon as she was alone, Joan sat down again. She didn't need to be

347

told that whatever Eric was dabbling in, he was up to his ears in trouble.

'Oh well,' she muttered as she went upstairs to pack. 'Good times don't last for ever.'

How right she was.

They spent their last evening at the taverna. Joan and Anna sat together at the back of the large room. A huge round table was littered with food, glasses and bottles, and the double swing doors were propped open wide to cope with the cigar smoke. Joan had never seen Eric look so happy, and for that she was grateful.

Isidore was silently watching everyone with a wary eye and finally he asked a question. 'So what's going to happen, Manny, when you get back to London?'

Eric shot Joan a warning look before saying, 'I'll settle everything. Those entitled to it will get their share of the profits.' He had tried hard to speak in a jocular way, but Joan had heard the seriousness in his voice. It sobered her up immediately.

'Will you deal with the main business and be back here for Christmas?' Isidore sounded stern.

'I can't honestly answer that question,' Manny said. 'I will do my best, but I have no idea where everyone is or what the situation is at that end.'

There were quite a few men in the taverna tonight whom Joan had never seen before. They were all watching closely.

'All right, Manny.' Isidore stared at him, his old eyes never wavering. 'If you can't make it by Christmas, so be it, but New Year's Eve is the deadline.'

Joan felt very sorry for Eric. He knew he had the eyes of everyone in the room on him. 'I'll do the best I can, Isidore, you know that.'

The old man shook his head sadly. 'Manny, my boy, this

time you had better make quite sure that your best is good enough.'

There was a quiet discussion going on amongst the men until Stephan broke away and came to tell Joan that he and John were going to walk her home because Manny had some papers to sign for Isidore.

Joan felt sorrow right down to the pit of her stomach as she said goodbye to Anna. There was so much going on on this island it would take a month of Sundays for her to understand it all, and she wasn't at all sure that Anna didn't feel exactly the same way. It was a sad and lingering farewell, for they had become such good friends.

John and Stephan saw her safely into the house, then each in turn caught her fingers and raised them to their lips. So gallant. 'God go with you,' they called out as they closed the front door behind them.

Joan lay in bed listening for Eric's footsteps. Somehow tonight she didn't feel safe in this house on her own. She shook up her pillows in an attempt to get comfortable. She wondered what Eric was doing and tried not to care. It really was none of her business. She closed her eyes tightly and tried to stop her mind from imagining all sorts of horrors. Instead, she began to wonder what it would be like to be back home.

What had been happening while she had been away? Had Jody stayed over with Rosie? Had Freda kept an eye on them both and on the rest of the staff? Had Martha and Sid been over to the Prince of Wales and were Jeff and Mark still about?

It didn't work. She still couldn't sleep.

In spite of the good time Eric had shown her she wouldn't be sorry to set foot on that mail boat tomorrow. To be able see London and her family and friends again suddenly seemed a very attractive idea.

*   *   *

The return journey was nowhere near as romantic as their outward voyage had been. For one thing, the mail boat wasn't half as luxurious as the P&O liner had been and in future if anyone were to tell her that surroundings didn't make any difference she would certainly set them straight on that point.

Eric was still attentive to her but at times she wished she were able to read his mind. She was aware that his thoughts were often a long way away.

In what seemed like no time at all they were steering into London Docks, and that was where Joan got her biggest shock.

The stewards carried their luggage down the gangway and saluted Eric as he generously tipped each man. There was no sign of the leather attaché case, and Joan could only conclude that Eric had packed it inside of one of his large suitcases, amongst his clothes.

'Darling, I'll put you in a taxi. You'll be all right the other end. There will be plenty of folk to help you with your luggage.' Then he walked off and left her standing there surrounded by their luggage.

Joan was absolutely stunned. He hadn't given her a moment even to ask why he wasn't coming to Brixton with her. Was he dumping her?

It was only a couple of minutes before Eric was back with two black cabs. He was a passenger in the first one, and both drivers got out with him and began to pick up their suitcases.

Eric hastily drew her into his arms, kissed her long and hard, then let her go. 'I'll take the first cab. I have given the second driver your address, and I've paid him and tipped him well so you'll be all right.'

Joan had to bite her tongue to stop herself from saying, 'Bloody generous to the last,' but he sensed she wasn't too pleased.

'I will be in touch, my darling,' he whispered, 'but I do have quite a few things to do.' With that, he jumped into the back of the first cab, leant out of the window, waved and blew her a kiss.

Joan stood stock still. She was absolutely astounded.

But it was no good standing there like some stuffed dummy. Joan stared after the now disappearing Eric and muttered, 'Well, I won't hold my breath.'

The driver had finished loading her luggage and turning to her he said, 'Brixton is it then, ma'am?'

'Yes, please.' Joan settled back in her seat. Already everything appeared so different from Malta. For one thing, the weather was drab, and it was very cold. The driver seemed to be holding the middle of the road, hurtling towards the oncoming traffic. Just when Joan was bracing herself for the inevitable crash, the driver jerked to the left and slid past a lorry with only inches to spare. She let her head fall back against the upholstery and closed her eyes for a moment.

London! So familiar, and yet Joan found herself making comparisons. The pace of life was so much faster. The peace and quiet of Malta seemed a whole world away.

Already the area was teeming with life. Pedestrians jostled between the traffic to cross the road and one could almost have walked on people's heads, the pavements were so crowded. Everybody was in a hurry. Horns honked, bicycle bells rang continually, barrow boys shouted their wares: the noise was dreadful. Joan was relieved when the driver drew the cab to a halt outside her premises. She stepped down and stood on the pavement and looked upward to the sign *Distinctive Designs*, and found that mingled with her relief to be home was a real feeling of pride.

The cab driver tipped his cap to her and drove off, leaving her standing on the pavement surrounded by her luggage.

The windows were her first priority. The one on the left-hand side was crowded with as many goods as possible. Joan gazed critically at an array of bolts of cloth, all in lovely autumn shades. Paper patterns were laid in a semicircle on the floor. A whole row of fine wool jumpers and cardigans was accompanied by balls of wool, knitting patterns and knitting needles. Two very heavy jumpers, one in the palest shade of blue and the other one cream, were attractively laid out on a chair, one spread across the seat and the other draped over the back. That was good thinking, anticipating the coming winter. Finally, near the front of the window, someone had arranged a dazzling selection of reels of sewing thread and row upon row of cards of buttons, ribbons and tape, all giving encouragement to women who liked to knit and sew.

Joan moved along to look at the second window and found herself gasping with surprise. This display would catch any fashionable lady's imagination. There were only two models, one wearing a winter white coat with a huge dark fur collar and a small hat made out of the same fur. Gloves, high-heeled shoes and handbag were all of the finest, softest leather. *Since when did we sell shoes?* Was one question she was asking herself. Then she remembered that Freda Preston was well known and trusted in the trade. She had more than likely begged Jones's, the exclusive shoe shop, to loan her the shoes when planning the display.

Her eyes roamed quickly to the second model, placed slightly to the fore on the other side of the window. It was certainly aimed at the business type of woman. The outfit looked fantastic: the long black skirt in pure wool was slim and elegant, while the tight-waisted jacket had a velvet collar. Several leather handbags and pairs of gloves were arranged in sets on the carpet. The only other item on show was a magnificent carved mahogany writing desk on which had been placed a tall slender vase holding just one white rose and a spray of green fern.

One thought hammered inside Joan's head. *Jim Taylor*. No one else could have restored that desk to all its original beauty. To think that in her days on the market stall he was only referred to as the bare wood man!

For the umpteenth time, she thanked God for the staff who worked for her. Each and every one of them was loyal, capable of coming up with original ideas, never afraid to try something new.

She was just about to pick up some of her luggage when the main entrance door flew open and Rosie, screaming with delight, threw herself at her. Before Joan could catch her breath she was surrounded by Jody, Freda and even one or two of her machinists. For a moment she was overcome by the feeling of coming home, the slightly guilty pleasure of having been missed and now the thrill of actually being wanted.

Freda took charge. 'Calm down, everyone. Each of you pick up a bag or a case and let's get Joan inside. We're making a right show of ourselves out here on the pavement.' Everyone laughed but they immediately did as Freda had ordered.

Joan stood in the middle of the shop and gazed round in delight. The whole place had an inviting look, laid out in such a way that you could feast your eyes on all the colours of the rainbow. The display of drapery and such like was overwhelming. Moving over to what, in her mind, she still referred to as the posh side of the shop she couldn't help but notice that the floor was covered by a Chinese carpet which looked both beautiful and expensive. The soft thickness of the pile and the brilliant vibrant colours were a joy to behold.

She hadn't uttered a word, yet although the words were spoken softly from behind her, she clearly heard them. 'Gorgeous, isn't it?'

She spoke his name even before she turned round to face him. 'Jim!' Automatically she opened her arms, and so did he, and the two stood silently in a tight embrace. To an onlooker it could easily have appeared that these were two lovers who had been parted for a very long time.

Freda broke the silence. 'Come on, girls, back to work. You'll have a chance to talk to Joan later on.'

Recalled to a sense of his surroundings, Jim Taylor kept his eyes lowered as he picked up two cases and said, 'You go on upstairs, Joan, and put the kettle on. Bet you're gasping for a cup of tea. I'll bring your luggage up.'

'I can take some, otherwise you will have to make two journeys,' Joan protested.

Jim laughed. 'Get yerself away. Have you forgotten that I'm Superman?'

Joan still lingered. Jim Taylor looked different. He had put a bit of weight on and it suited him. His dark hair had been cut in a much better style and he was no longer wearing those awful steel-rimmed glasses. The new pair had a tortoiseshell frame which broadened his face and gave him a distinguished look.

'I can see you like the carpet,' he said softly.

'Yes I do, Jim, very much. Must have cost a bomb, though.'

'Now, Joan, you know me better than that. I picked it up in a house sale. At first sight it was a bit of a mess, but I took a chance. It took ages to clean and five days to dry out. Only laid it down the day before yesterday, after Freda had done the window.'

'Ah, the window. It looks great, but where on earth did that beautiful desk come from? I'll lay a pound to a penny it wasn't in that condition when you acquired it.'

'You don't remember us bidding for that? Even the auctioneer remarked that this piece was in a really bad state and would need a great deal of restoration. But because it was of such an early period I knew it would be worth the labour. It's a collector's piece now, and besides, it savours of bygone times, don't you think?'

'I do indeed. You have excelled yourself. But, Jim, I have to ask you something . . .' She hesitated.

'Well out with it then, because we can't stand here talking all morning. You should get yourself upstairs, get settled in.'

'All right.' Joan dropped her voice. 'It's just that on the other side of the shop I noticed there are still quite a few articles made by you for sale. Small things that when we were on the market you used to call white wood goods.'

'So?'

'Well, why do you bother now when we are doing so well with other things?'

It was a moment or two before he answered. When he did, he looked into Joan's eyes and spoke quietly. 'To remind me not to get above myself, and more importantly to remember that it is your business.'

'Oh, Jim!' Joan felt a lump rise in her throat. Some time ago she had suggested that he become her partner, but then Eric had swept her off her feet and she had disregarded the feelings of this kind man who from the very beginning had always been there for her. However, this was not the time nor the place for her to raise the subject, so she put on a smile and said, 'Thank you. Now I am going to take your advice and go upstairs and put the kettle on.'

Rosie was serving a customer as Joan made for the stairs but she called out, 'It's great to have you home, Aunt Joan.'

Joan smiled and continued up the stairs. In her front room, everything was sparklingly clean. The dining table was covered with the plush chenille cloth and a huge potted azalea had been placed in a glass bowl and set in the centre of the table. The brass fire irons were shining brightly in the hearth. A fire had been laid in the grate, needing only a match to set it burning.

She sighed happily to herself. It was great to be home.

Chapter Forty

JOAN COULD SCARCELY BELIEVE that she had been home for five days, they had sped by so quickly. Now it was Saturday and every member of her staff, herself included, had been on the go from the moment they had opened the shop doors at nine o'clock. Everything and everybody seemed geared up for Christmas.

Tonight Martha and Sid and their two sons were coming over and all of them were to meet up in the Prince of Wales. As the day wore on Joan had to scold herself for feeling that she would much rather spend the evening indoors by the fire with her feet up. She knew it wasn't possible. This was such a friendly, caring community, and folk had gone out of their way to help her in so many ways. Besides, she hadn't seen any member of her family since she had been back, with the exception of Rosie.

Come to that she hadn't set eyes on Eric, nor heard a word from him, although to be honest she wasn't altogether surprised. Eric would turn up again when it suited him. He played things so close to his chest that it was a wonder he knew himself whether he was coming or going half the time.

Rosie was an absolute darling. She had sat on the rug in front of the fire every evening after they had eaten their meal, her back leaning against her aunt's legs, and asked question after question, really interested in hearing about Malta. Joan had stared into the flames and relived some of the days she had spent there. She hadn't found the words to describe to Rosie, the calmness, the beauty and the slow pace at which life was lived on the island but she had done her best. Rosie thought the story of how her aunt had put to sea with two fishermen she had never set eyes on before an absolute gem.

'Mum's got something to tell you,' she had blurted out last night.

'Oh, and what's that? Nice or nasty?'

'Mum made me promise not to tell you, but you'll be very surprised.' Rosie grinned impishly. 'She said we're all going to eat at the pub tomorrow night and that's when she's going to tell you.'

Several times during the day Joan had looked up to see Rosie gazing at her, and she couldn't help wondering what it was that her niece and her sister knew and as yet she did not.

That evening at seven o'clock, Joan was being hugged tightly by both Annie and Les Jackson, while several of the customers were shouting, 'Welcome home, Joan.'

'You'd think I'd been away for months instead of a couple of weeks,' Joan murmured as she found herself staring at a table laid for twelve people. After so many enthusiastic greetings she was flustered as she took her seat and looked at all the smiling faces. Rosie, Freda and Jim, Martha and Sid with Lenny and Bernie. Lenny had brought his fiancée, Janet Marshal, while Bernie had a gorgeous-looking girlfriend with him whom he introduced by merely saying, 'Aunt Joan, this is Linda.' And of course a celebration meal at the Prince would not be complete without those two dear gentlemen, Jeff and Mark.

When the first course of thick vegetable soup served with hunks of crusty bread had been eaten and the plates cleared away, there was no shortage of conversation while they waited for the main course. Jeff and Mark started the men off on the topic of football, while Rosie was engrossed in telling Freda that she and Jody would be going to Tooting Bec Common tomorrow hoping to find some holly that had plenty of red berries. They also intended to gather some long strands of dark green ivy from the wall that ran the length of the avenue, because Joan had promised that come Monday morning they could start to decorate the shop.

Martha was sitting on Joan's right-hand side. Leaning nearer, she whispered to her sister, 'What d'yer make of our Bernie's girlfriend?'

'She's lovely,' Joan answered, looking down the length of the table to where her two nephews and their girlfriends were sitting. 'How long has Bernie been taking her out?'

'Your guess is as good as mine. He's only been bringing her to our house for about the last six weeks.'

'Rosie said you had something to tell me. Is this it? Bernie and his lady friend?'

'Our Rosie's mouth will get her into trouble one of these days.' Martha grinned. 'Sid always said she had eyes and ears out the back of her 'ead. While you were away Rosie popped over to see us on her 'alf-day and she listened in to me an' her dad having a conversation that 'ad nothing t' do with 'er. Still, it will be common knowledge soon. I'll tell you the whole story later on.' For the moment Joan had to be content with that because the main course was being placed in front of everybody.

It was well turned nine by the time all twelve of them left the dining area and retreated to the saloon bar.

Everything here was much the same as Joan remembered it. The Ally Looya Lassies were still wandering amongst the crowd selling copies of *War Cry*. The men managed to find an empty table and gathered enough chairs to. allow the women to sit down. Martha looked across to where her husband was leaning against the bar, with both his sons and Mark and Jeff.

'Funny, ain't it?' Martha remarked.

'What is?' Joan looked puzzled.

'To see my old man out with our boys is great, but the fact that he would stand up to anyone and state that Mark and Jeff were two of his best mates, even part of our family if yer like, still wants some getting used to.'

'Why, Martha? Are you saying because Mark and Jeff live together men like your Sid shouldn't give them the time of day?'

'Course not, love. Didn't mean nothing of the sort. Sorry if it came out all wrong. But be 'onest, luv, before you opened your shop 'ere in Brixton, you wouldn't have seen that lot socialising, now would yer?'

Joan could hardly stifle her laughter, and to make matters worse, dead on the stroke of ten, the double doors swung open and there, in all her finery, stood Lulu.

Seeing Joan, she made a beeline for their table, said good evening to Freda, Janet and Rosie and nodded her head towards Linda, before embracing Joan and telling her it seemed that she had been away for ages.

'That young lady is Linda, my Bernie's friend,' Martha explained, and Lulu held out her hand and said graciously, 'I'm very pleased to meet you, Linda.'

Joan felt uncomfortable. Martha and even Bernie only referred to the girl as Linda, no surname. That in itself wasn't strange, but the fact that Martha had said she would tell her the whole story later was puzzling.

Jeff and Mark came over with refill drinks for the women

and a fresh double whisky and a bottle of ginger ale for Lulu. Placing all the glasses down on the table, the two men in turn bent low and placed a kiss on Lulu's cheek. Joan felt very tempted to say to her sister, how about that, then? Before I lived in Brixton you would have huffed and puffed at such goings-on. Instead she reminded herself that it was a big world and everyone must live their life as they saw fit.

Les Jackson called time dead on eleven, but by the time all the goodbyes were said and they had walked home, seeing Freda safely inside her house on the way, it was closer to midnight. The youngsters went their own way, but Sid and Martha decided to stay the night with Joan and Rosie.

On Sunday morning Sid did the honours by bringing a cup of tea to Martha in bed and to Joan where she was snuggled on the big old sofa in the living room. They agreed to let Rosie sleep late, as she was up early all the other days of the week. It was a companionable breakfast, Martha and Joan settling for toast and marmalade but Sid asking for his normal Sunday morning fry-up.

'And make it two eggs, please,' he called to Joan.

The morning was great. Sid took himself off to buy shellfish for their tea – or so he said, but as the shrimps, winkles and prawns were sold from a stall set up on the forecourt of the Prince of Wales it was a dead cert that he would be having a pint or two. The sisters didn't mind one bit. By the time Jody arrived to go to the common, Rosie was up and dressed and the girls left with a warning ringing in their ears that dinner would be on the table by half-past two. Most women had found from experience that there was no point in being ready any earlier because the pubs didn't close until two.

Martha was peeling the parsnips while Joan did the

sprouts. A nice rib of beef on the bone was slowly roasting in the oven and a huge bowl of batter, into which Martha had beaten four eggs, sat on the draining board. 'Before I start on the carrots, d'you fancy a cuppa?' Joan asked.

'Yeah, why not? By the way, how many are you expecting for dinner?'

'Don't know exactly. Freda and Jim were only too pleased to accept – well, it's natural, isn't it? They both live on their own. Doesn't matter if we do too much veg. Rosie and I can always have bubble and squeak tomorrow.'

'Are Jeff an' Mark coming?'

'Well, if they meet up with your Sid he's bound to bring them back with him. I never mind them coming, though. They are so generous in so many ways.'

'Sit down and take the weight off yer feet,' Martha ordered as Joan set two steaming cups of tea down on the table.

Joan did as she was told. She took a couple of sips of her tea, set the cup back down on the saucer, looked Martha straight in the eye and said, 'Don't you think it's about time you brought me up to date with what is going on with your Bernie and that new girlfriend of his?'

'I thought you might have worked it out for yourself by now.' Martha looked serious.

'Well, I haven't, so why all the mystery?'

'Doesn't the name Linda ring any bells?'

Joan thought hard for a moment and then she felt the colour drain from her cheeks. No! It couldn't be! But she still had to ask. 'The only Linda I've ever known was Nellie Bradshaw's granddaughter.'

'You've hit the nail right on the head.' Martha knew she didn't have to say any more.

'She really is Linda Bradshaw?'

Martha sighed. 'Well, what her real surname is now no one knows. Nellie Bradshaw brought her up and she took her gran's name right from the day that her mother died and her father rejected her.'

'How come I never recognised her?' Joan murmured thoughtfully.

'None of us did first off,' Martha reassured her. 'She's certainly altered her looks and dyed her hair, and she can't have been much more than a slip of a girl when she used to come round to your place and sit with Granny Baldwin.'

Joan was well and truly upset by now. She looked at her sister and there was a plea in her voice as she asked, 'Has there been any mention of the little boy?'

'Not that me or my Sid have heard, an' Bernie hasn't brought the subject up. Suppose he must remember what 'appened, but my Sid warned me not to poke me nose in or to ask any questions.'

'I dare say he's right. Your Sid usually is. From what I recall Linda tried hard to bring that baby up by herself in the beginning. Then she met a fella who wanted to marry her but the baby was another matter altogether. I think the man came from New Zealand. He's supposed to have told Linda that if she'd put the baby up for adoption he would take her home with him and that they would get married out there.

'Sounds all cut an' dried but I'd bet my last shilling things didn't work out so well for Linda. She wouldn't be back in London if life in New Zealand had been good. Is she staying with her grandparents?'

Martha crossed her arms over her chest and heaved her bosom up. 'So our Bernie said.'

'How old is she?'

'I should think you'd know better than me. About the same age as our Bernie, I would guess.'

'All I know is she was sixteen when she found out she was pregnant and she disappeared soon after to save her grandparents having to face the shame. That's a few years ago.'

'Did you know about it at the time?' Martha asked quietly.

'No, I didn't.' Joan sighed heavily, she hated the past being dragged up again. She took a deep breath before she raised her head and looked at her sister. 'Two years had gone by before Nellie Bradshaw felt she wanted me to know that her grandaughter had had a baby and that my husband had been the father of that child. If you work it out, my Bill was dead and buried before Linda left the neighbourhood so I suppose at the time they didn't see any point in bringing it all out in the open.'

'I remember now. You were working down in Kent, had worked all over the Christmas, and that Mrs Hamilton had let you come home for the New Year. You were staying with Sid and me when Nellie Bradshaw asked to see you. Christ, it gives me the shivers still to this day the way you looked when you came back and said she'd told you about your Bill making 'er Linda pregnant.'

'Could we please change the subject,' Joan begged. 'What good will it do raking over the coals after all this time?'

'No good whatsoever, I shouldn't think, but the truth is the girl has turned up again like a bad penny.' Martha leant across the table and took her sister's hand between both of her own. 'Seems t' me it's nobody's business except my Bernie's. If Linda has told him, well, he's a grown man and she's not a slip of a girl any longer so they can make their own decisions.'

In spite of wanting to change the subject Joan heard herself saying, 'Can't help wondering what became of the little boy.'

'Well stop wondering, luv. Be best all round if everybody were to let sleeping dogs lie.'

Joan was well aware that that was good advice, but . . .

Martha struggled to her feet. 'Come on, let's get a move on. The vegetables won't cook themselves.'

Joan did as she was bid, but her mind was telling her that none of them had heard the end of this story.

Not by a long chalk they hadn't.

Chapter Forty-one

IT WAS CHRISTMAS EVE, and the run-up had been exciting. Folk had money in their pockets because almost every pub in England ran a weekly money club which paid out two weeks before 25th December. Even so, the trade they were doing in Distinctive Designs was unbelievable and everything was going well until the moment when Joan looked up and saw Eric Roussel standing at the back of the shop. In one hand he was clutching a dozen red roses and in the other was the largest box of chocolates she had ever seen. His grin, as he watched her, spread from ear to ear. Joan told herself she wouldn't be human if she didn't feel a flash of excitement.

But today of all days, his turning up was a nightmare!

Still, she had to admit he looked superb. His taste in clothes was extraordinary, even if it was a little daring. His navy blue overcoat had a velvet collar of rich burgundy. Unbuttoned, it allowed the observer a glimpse of his dark grey single-breasted suit, worn with a crisp white shirt as always, complemented today by a silk tie the exact shade of burgundy as the collar of his overcoat. His iron-grey hair had been smoothed back, probably with brilliantine, because it had a habit of curling round his ears and Eric did not take kindly to being teased because of his curly hair. Handsome, clean cut and smart, he certainly stood out in any crowd.

Joan finished serving her customer, wished her a Merry Christmas and gave her a prettily wrapped parcel which contained a tablet of Yardley's lavender toilet soap.

'Oh, thank you, Mrs Baldwin, how kind of you,' the customer murmured.

'Just a little show of appreciation to our customers.' Joan beamed in reply. Then, coming round from behind the counter, she walked to where Eric stood, still smiling. 'Not today, Eric, please,' she whispered. 'You can see how busy we are.'

Eric lowered his head until his face was level with her own. 'Ten minutes, please, my darling?'

'No. I cannot spare the time.' Joan was trying to sound cross but really she was thinking how romantic he was. Unreliable but certainly romantic.

'Sorry, but it is extremely important. I cannot move from here until you have listened to what I have to say.'

'No, Eric. Go away,' Joan said as firmly as she could. But by the time she had again taken up her station behind the counter, Eric had placed the flowers and chocolates on a shelf and was lighting a small cigar. Oh no, Joan thought to herself. Those cigars had such a strong smell.

Eric took the cigar from his mouth and held up the five fingers of his other hand, mouthing, 'Five, I promise.'

His air of assurance didn't help. Sighing heavily, she called to Jody, 'I am going upstairs for ten minutes.' She knew whatever he had to say wouldn't be said in five. Eric picked up the roses and the chocolates, winked at Jody, and followed Joan towards the stairs.

Inside her front room they stood facing each other and suddenly they were both laughing. Joan tried to string words together but before she could get them out she was in Eric's arms and his lips were gently kissing hers. 'Oh, darling, I have missed you,' he whispered softly.

She almost said, me too, but stopped short and changed it to, 'Not enough to pick up the telephone.'

'To hear your voice and not to be able to reach out and touch you would have been too much to bear,' he murmured, his lips against her ear.

Reluctantly, Joan wriggled free from his arms. 'You really lay it on with a trowel. Now honestly, Eric, glad as I am to see you, today is *not* a good time.'

'All right.' He held up both hands in a gesture of surrender. 'I'll say what I have to say as quickly as possible.' His hand delved into his inside pocket and drew out two envelopes. 'All arranged and paid for, and as promised we shall see the New Year in together in Malta.'

You could have knocked Joan down with a feather. She didn't believe she was hearing right.

Her face did not leave Eric in any doubt. She would need some convincing before she agreed to go with him. So, smooth talker that he was, he vowed he would persuade her. 'Joan, my love, you will have all of the Christmas holiday period with your family. I do so want to see the New Year in with mine.'

'Nobody is stopping you. Go for Christmas and stay on.' Joan's short and sweet solution did not please Eric at all.

'We told my family we would be back for the New Year.'

'No, *you* told them. I did not promise anything.'

'Joan, my dear, you should be there. I want you there. It will only be a short visit and I promise there will be no business taking up my time. Last time, I admit, there were several matters that required my attention. Places I just had to go to. But this time it will be different, this time will be for *us*.' Judging by the softer look on Joan's face he thought she might be wavering, so he pressed home his advantage.

'Please come with me, Joan. We will stay at a first-class hotel, and have great celebrations with all of my family. It will be a joyous time that would not be the same if you weren't with me.'

Changing tack again, he took Joan into his arms, kissed the top of her head, then her forehead, then the tip of her nose, and finally placed his lips hard over hers. He was getting reckless, allowing himself to fondle her breasts, which were still high and firm. He could feel her gently rounded thighs and still flat stomach as he held her in his arms. When he did loosen his hold he was asking himself why he had ever let her go. Why hadn't he left her in Malta? Come to London, settled his affairs and then gone back to her.

It was astonishing how much this woman had affected him. He had made such plans since he had met Joan. To lose her now did not bear thinking about. One last try, he decided.

'Surely, my darling, after all we have come to mean to each other I deserve to have you to myself for this short time?'

Joan sighed softly. His hands running over her body had brought back to life the memory of the nights she had lain in bed with this handsome man. No one had ever said such sweet things to her. She hadn't known that lovemaking could be as thrilling for a woman as it was for a man. Eric had shown her a whole new way of life. Treated her as if she was someone very special. She raised her head until she could look directly into his eyes. If she were to refuse him now she might never get another chance. Could she refuse him?

Eric knew she was wavering but he was an old hand at this game. He sighed heavily before saying, 'I understand, Joan. I have taken too much for granted. Of course you want to see the New Year in with your own folk, but I had to try. Better go now and let you get back to your business, busiest day of the year and all that.' He kissed her gently. 'Happy Christmas, my darling. I shall be thinking of you every minute.' Pulling his gloves from the pocket of his overcoat, he turned to go.

'Eric.' Joan put out a hand and touched his arm. 'I am really sorry. It isn't that I don't want to come with you, but you have sprung this on me. You've given me no time to make arrangements. You say we would only stay a short time, but with the journey both ways I doubt we would be back in time for the January sales.'

Inwardly Eric was smiling, but he sighed again, softly this time. 'I'm not only thoughtless, I am selfish. Let me ask you to do one thing. During the day, will you give the matter some thought? Talk it over with your staff if you get the chance – or even ask them to stay behind for a few minutes after you close the shop. Ask them if they think they could cope again without you. I'll phone you, but not until about nine o'clock, and if you still feel you have to turn me down . . .' He shrugged his shoulders, turned again, and this time he left her.

Joan was thankful that for the rest of the day she didn't have much time to dwell on Eric's plans. The thought of returning to that lovely island and being with him again, this time staying in a real hotel, was never far from her mind, but customers came non-stop. The atmosphere was festive. Each one received a small gift and the regulars were offered a hot mince pie and a glass of sherry.

It was six thirty by the time the shop had closed and Martha and Sid had arrived – because where else would all of them spend the evening of Christmas Eve if not in the Prince of Wales? Not that they would be getting there until about nine thirty, but Les had applied for an extension of his licence which allowed him to remain open until midnight.

The team that Joan employed as machinists were so good.

She only had to give them sketches, explain in detail such points as seam length and trimmings and her women got on with the job. They had not worked today or yesterday. Joan had given them their wages plus a bonus two days ago, together with a present from her to each of them. She knew she could rely on them to help Freda at the start of the January sales should she decide to go with Eric.

For the rest of the staff, a few friends and her family she had arranged a small party in her flat upstairs. She stood in the middle of her front room and looked around her with a smile of satisfaction. Eric had not even remarked on the decorations, though Rosie and Jody had done a good job, with no small amount of help from Jim Taylor. Everything looked beautiful, she decided. And the food, which had been sent in by the local delicatessen, looked marvellous.

Martin and Marjorie Goldsmith arrived hot on the heels of Martha and Sid, bringing Teddy Tyler with them. He still looked and acted larger than life and still would not answer to the name of Edward. Jim had asked if his work mate Doug Morgan might be invited and Joan had not hesitated, well aware that she owed quite a lot in her lovely home to the generosity of Doug. A ring at the bell sent Jim down to open the door and she heard the voices of two of her favourite friends, Jeff and Mark. Since Lenny and Bernie had other plans – although they would be in the Prince with Janet and Linda at about half-past ten – the party was therefore complete.

When everyone's plate was full, Joan paused in offering food and stood for a moment staring into the fire. She had a problem. She had put it to the back of her mind all day but now she had to deal with it. She badly wanted to discuss Eric and his plans with her sister and her husband, but also with Freda because if – and it was still only an *if*, she told herself – she were to take up Eric's offer it would mean asking Freda if she would mind taking charge of the business and the staff once again. She also felt that were she to ask Freda she would have to be truthful and warn her that she wouldn't be here for the start of the January sales, which were a great opportunity to clear out old stock and make way for the spring collection. But how could she get those three people on their own?

It was Jim, without knowing it, who came to her rescue. 'Listen up, folks,' he called, then having waited a few minutes to get everyone's attention he said, 'Taxi cabs are at a premium tonight. I've done the best I can and got two for eight o'clock, but I couldn't book another until nine thirty. Sorry to split the party up, but . . .'

'No, no, Jim, don't apologise. We should have booked cabs days ago,' Joan interrupted him. 'Sort out how many you can take. I'll stay behind; it'll give me a chance to tidy up.'

The gods were on Joan's side. 'I'll stay with you,' Martha offered.

'I better stay as well,' Sid said, 'otherwise I'll only 'ave Martha on at me the whole 'oliday about how I went off an' left 'er.'

'Won't hurt me to stay here awhile either, put me feet up,' Freda said.

'I have to be off anyway,' Teddy announced. 'I've a lady friend I promised to see at eight o'clock.'

'Running true to form, eh, Teddy?' Marjorie teased him.

Martin was doing a head count. 'I make that thirteen of us here, minus Teddy leaves twelve, four have offered to stay behind and wait for the later cab, that leaves eight. What do you reckon, Jim, eight of us all right in two cabs?'

'Fine, if everyone is happy.'

Joan was not only happy, she was really relieved.

It was an uncanny silence that reigned while the three women covered what food was left, carried china out into the kitchen and picked up bits and pieces from the floor.

Sid busied himself with the dirty glasses, putting tops on wine and spirit bottles, and throwing away the empty beer bottles. Martha knew her sister too well not to be aware that there was something bothering her, and after a while she just blurted out, 'Right, that's about it. Come on, let's all sit down an' Joan can tell us what is on her mind.' She stared straight at her sister and added, 'If you tell me there's nothing going on in that 'ead of yours I'll eat my ruddy hat.'

'All right, all right.' Joan smiled. 'Eric came to see me this morning.'

Freda laughed. 'I didn't need any telling it was down to him. I saw you both go upstairs and then come down. You weren't up there long.'

Joan looked to her brother-in-law for help. There had always been a close bond between them. Even when she was married to Bill Baldwin, Sid had always known when things got out of hand and he and his two boys had always rushed to help her. It was no different now. 'Come on, luv, get it off yer chest,' he ordered.

So, as accurately as she could remember, Joan set out the facts of what Eric had said. She had hardly finished speaking before Martha was loudly offering advice.

'For Christ's sake stop dithering an' make up yer mind. Go with the bloke. He treated yer all right last time, didn't he?'

Joan nodded her head.

'Well, answer me this. How many times has Lady Luck knocked on your door, Joan? I know you and Eric are not man and wife, but according to my Sid you never will be 'cos that man ain't the marrying kind.'

Joan turned her head to glance at Sid, who looked sheepishly down at his feet. They must have been discussing me quite a lot, Joan thought, and that surprised her. Martha and Sid never interfered. For one thing, Sid never had a lot to say, really. Over the years she had come to believe they were a wise and well-matched couple.

'Sid, why do you say Eric is not the type to get married?' she asked quietly.

'Oh my Gawd, do you really have to ask that question?' Sid sounded dismayed. 'How old is he? Fifteen, sixteen years older than you are. OK, he sounds a nice enough fella and from all accounts he's worn bloody well but you're not going t' tell me you're the first woman in his life.' Shaking his head, Sid muttered, 'Not by any means.'

'I'm not that daft,' Joan retorted, sounding unusually angry. 'Anyone only has to look at him to tell he's a lady's man, probably always has been, but he treats me well.'

'It's your life,' Sid answered abruptly. Then he half smiled. 'I'll always be here to soften the blow, you know that.'

Joan felt sorry for having snapped at Sid. As he said, no matter what, she could always rely on his being there for her.

'Opportunities such as this hardly ever come along. Certainly not twice, take it from me.' Freda brought herself quietly into the conversation. Receiving no answer, she felt it was all right to carry on. 'Just watching the two of you it is easy to tell that Eric adores you, Joan. I'll give you my advice, even though you haven't asked for it. Go back to Malta, see the New Year in. You work so hard. Live a little for a change.'

'Damned good advice,' Martha muttered.

'But Freda, it would mean I wouldn't be back for the January sales. It doesn't seem fair to go off again and leave everything to you.'

'Did I do so badly last time?'

'No, of course you didn't. You managed extremely well.'

'And you paid me a good bonus. Now listen, Joan, things between you and me cut both ways. I love to work, especially doing something for which I have been well trained. Up west, the big stores don't want to know me any more. I'm too old. I was grateful when you took me on and I still am.

You treat me as if I were family and that means a lot when one lives on one's own.'

'There you are then, one problem solved.' Martha couldn't keep quiet any longer. 'Joan, grab at the chance, go back to Malta, but just don't look at that man through rose-coloured glasses. From what you've told us I'd bet that underneath all that gloss and charm he's as deep as the ocean. In the short time that you've known him, luv, how many times 'as he disappeared? Not turned up when he promised he would? And more to the point, what does he get up to?'

'I know all that,' Joan admitted. 'But . . .'

'I know, luv, you've never been treated so well in yer life. He makes yer feel good and there's nothing wrong with that. Gawd above knows there ain't been a lot of spoiling in your life. Work from the day you left school – before that, even, because you were only seven when our dad died. I remember when our mum used t' take you with 'er up to the big 'ouses and if she were doing the washing you 'ad to turn the 'andle of the mangle while Mum fed the sheets an' things through the rollers. Eric has come late in yer life, 'cos let's face it, you ain't no spring chicken yerself, so that's all the more reason you should grab every minute of 'appiness he offers you.'

'Even if you really got to know Eric, you wouldn't like him, would you, Martha?' Joan shot the question to her sister.

Martha hesitated. 'Probably be hard not to, but . . .'

'Go on, please.'

'You want it straight?'

'Course I do, Martha. Don't I always come to you with my problems?'

'Right. Well, there has t' be another side to that man.'

'You think so?'

'Yes, I do. So do you, Sid, don't you?'

'Have t' say yes, Joan. I don't think you've scratched the surface of that man. I'd go so far as to say he's more than likely been involved in more dodgy deals than you, my girl, 'ave 'ad hot dinners.' That was a long speech for Sid.

Suddenly, Joan burst out laughing. In no time at all, all four of them were holding their sides. When they'd settled down, Joan spoke again.

'Sid, both you and my sister are something else. One minute you're telling me to live life to the full with Eric, and in the next breath you're telling me he is more than likely an out and out scoundrel.'

Martha grinned widely. 'Joan, remember there was a time when you said you envied me, married to a safe, secure, reliable man like my Sid. Well, my luv, I'm only human and while I do know how lucky I am and I wouldn't change Sid and our family for the world, that doesn't stop me from envying you some days. What woman wouldn't? This Eric, be what he may, 'as given you a great time: sea voyages, a chance to visit a foreign country. I'm telling you, luv, make the most of it while it lasts.' To herself Martha was saying, as sure as eggs are eggs it won't last, but that was all the more reason why her sister should go back to Malta. See the New Year in with gusto. At least when the bubble did burst she'd have some good memories to look back on.

Sid had had enough. He got to his feet. 'Nearly time that cab was 'ere. We're wasting good drinking time sitting around here.'

When the phone rang everybody looked at Joan and grinned as she left the room to answer it. She was only gone a short while. All three pairs of eyes were on her as she came back and stood in the doorway.

Eyebrows raised, it was Sid who asked the vital question. 'Well, are you going with him or not?'

Joan felt like a small child as she said, 'Yes, I am going

to Malta on the day after Boxing Day. Eric is picking me up here at three o'clock in the afternoon.'

'Good, that's settled at last,' Sid blustered, and grinned at his wife.

Martha, standing well behind her sister, held up two fingers which were tightly crossed. Freda, smiling, nodded her agreement. To her way of thinking Joan was doing the right thing, at least she hoped that was true anyway.

Chapter Forty-two

AT SEVEN THIRTY on Boxing Day morning Joan came downstairs in Martha's house to find her sister already unlocking the front door to bring the milk in. They smiled at each other as they went through to the kitchen, where Joan opened the window a chink to let the fresh air in and the smell of food and drink out. 'Some Christmas, eh?' she groaned, putting her hand to her forehead.

'One to remember I'd say.' Martha grinned. 'And the weather is running true to form. It always seems to save the worst until Christmas Day has come an' gone.'

'It looks great out there,' Joan said, 'though I think snow would have been better than this heavy frost. Look at the icicles hanging from the gutters of the houses opposite.'

'Too cold for snow, though it won't be many days off. You put the kettle on, Joan, an' I'll get the fire going. You an' me will 'ave a cup of tea on our own before we disturb the others.' Martha suddenly stopped talking and gave her sister a queer look.

'Something wrong?' Joan asked.

'Only that I haven't got a clue who slept in this house last night.'

378

Joan laughed. 'Well, I can tell you that neither Lenny nor Bernie did. They went off with their lady friends.'

'Well, folk were in an' out of here all day yesterday and during the evening I thought the walls of my front room were going to burst. I do remember you going out to the scullery with Linda Bradshaw and when you came back you were a lot quieter all of a sudden. Did she say anything to upset you?'

Joan shivered, glad that her sister was down on her knees holding a lighted quill to the newspaper and wood that she had arranged on top of the ashes in the grate.

'Well did she?' Martha turned her head to look up at Joan as she repeated the question.

'Not really,' Joan muttered.

'Oh for Christ's sake, Joan, either she did or she didn't.'

'Well, if you must know she asked me to pop over this morning and have a word with her and her grandma.'

'But her grandparents were both 'ere last night. Why didn't they say whatever it was they wanted to say to you then?'

'Suppose they didn't think it was the right time. Anyway, I couldn't have heard what they were saying. Most of the time we were all singing.'

'That were Jim Taylor's fault. As soon as one carol was finished he led us all into another one. Gotta say, though, Jim's got a ruddy good voice and it wasn't the beer egging him on because he didn't drink 'alf as much as my lads did.'

'I think a good time was had by one and all. But now, sister dear, are you going to stay on your knees all day, 'cos if you are all I can say is you are not as badly in need of this cup of tea as I am.' With that, Joan plumped herself down at the table and gratefully began to sip from one of the teacups she had filled from the big brown pot. It took a while for Martha to get back on her feet.

'Too much Christmas pudding,' she moaned.

'Washed down with too many glasses of port, you mean.'

'Hey you, you didn't do so badly yourself.'

'No, nobody did. Thanks to you, Martha, a lot of people had a great Christmas. Jim said it were the best Christmas he had spent since his wife walked out on him.'

'It wasn't all down t' me by a long chalk. We all did our bit. Anyway, are you going to go over to see Nellie Bradshaw?'

'Doesn't seem like I've got much choice. But it won't be for a while yet; got to get my head clear first.'

'How about a nice fry-up?'

'Oh, Martha, don't be so wicked.' Joan made a horrible face. 'Piece of dry toast is about all I'll be able to manage.'

'You and everyone else right now, but come midday an' they'll all be here for cold turkey, ham, bubble an' squeak and pickles. You'll see.' Martha drained her cup and pushing it towards her sister said, 'Be a dear an' pour me another one.' She went to the range and opened the vent to stop the heat from going up the chimney before putting another shovelful of coal on to the glowing embers. 'There. That's all set for the time being and for once in my life I'm gonna put me feet up and have a lazy day.'

By ten thirty Joan was getting edgy. Better go and get it over and done with, she told herself. In the passageway, she took her thick coat down from its peg and pulled it on, then slung a woollen scarf round her neck, tugged her velour hat down tight over her ears and stepped into her ankle-length boots. She went back into the kitchen and picked up the pair of fur-lined gloves that Rosie had bought her for Christmas. Sid, Martha and Freda were in the front room, where Sid had got a log fire roaring away. She popped her head round the door. 'Won't be too long. 'Bye.'

Making sure that she had closed the front door tight Joan walked down the front path and into the cold, frosty biting wind of the December morning. All the time, as she walked, she couldn't help but wonder just what it was that Linda and her grandmother had to say to her. She was in no doubt that the one subject she had fought so hard to erase from her memory would be the main topic of the conversation. No doubt whatsoever.

Nellie Bradshaw opened the front door in answer to her knock. 'Come in, Joan, you're more than welcome. Everyone had a great time over at your sister's house last night, didn't they? Found it slippery walking round here, did you? Ice everywhere, isn't there? Would you like some hot ginger wine or a glass of port or maybe just a cup of tea and a piece of me Christmas cake? I did make it myself.'

God! The woman hardly stopped talking long enough to draw breath.

'Please, Mrs Bradshaw, I don't need anything. I'm fine. Is Linda in?'

'Yes.' She seemed to have run out of steam at last.

'Well, please may we get down to what it is you want to talk to me about?'

'All right.' The old lady sighed heavily and led the way into her front room.

Not much had changed since Joan was last here. Everything was spotlessly clean, there were antimacassars in place on the back of each armchair, family photographs stood on the sideboard and the brass fire irons had been polished until they shone.

Linda had her legs curled up under her as she sat on the sofa, but as soon as Joan walked into the room she came to her feet. 'Hello, Mrs Baldwin. I hope you didn't mind me asking you to call round here, did you?'

'Rather depends on what you want to talk to me about, Linda,' Joan answered, sitting down in the chair that Mrs Bradshaw had drawn up opposite the sofa.

When all three of them were settled, Linda's grandmother

said, 'Well, if she has as much to say to you as she has to her grandfather and myself, you won't be here for long, Joan.'

'Gran, I'm sorry, I really am. You and Pops have made me so welcome since I've been back and I know it's quite a few months now and I still haven't told you where I've been or what I've done. To begin with I didn't seem able to get up the nerve to spill it all out, and then I met Bernie and after he'd taken me out a few times I realised that he was Mrs Baldwin's nephew. I couldn't face meeting her or Bernie's mother at first. I thought it would be bound to cause trouble, be like opening up a can of old worms.'

Joan was intrigued. 'Why did you want me to be present when you spoke to your gran?'

'I thought I owed you that much. Bit late in the day, I know, but better we talked head on than you heard a load of the rumours that have naturally been flying around amongst the neighbours since I turned up.'

'All right.' Her gran spoke up. 'Whatever you have to say, Linda, won't alter my feelings for you one little bit. It was an answer to my prayers when you walked through that door. I'd almost come to accept the fact that I would die before I set eyes on you again.'

Linda was on her feet like a shot, kneeling down in front of her gran, clutching hold of both of her hands. 'You were the one person I never wanted to hurt. The only reason I went away was because Pops was laying the blame on you for me being pregnant. That and all the shame, it wasn't fair. Besides, you had done your duty and more. When my mother died giving birth to me you took me on. I've always thought of you as my mother, not as my gran. I couldn't ask you to take on my illegitimate baby and start all over again.'

The silence was heavy, each of them reluctant to break it. Joan was first. 'I still can't work out why you want me to be here,' she said, looking Linda straight in the face.

Linda sighed, got up from the floor and sat on the sofa again. 'I want to apologise, Mrs Baldwin. For ever having listened to the smooth talking that your husband was capable of dishing out. For using make-up as soon as I was out of this house. For wearing tarty clothes so as to catch Bill's eye. He was a very good-looking man, a man of the world to a starry-eyed fourteen-year-old girl, 'cos that was what I was when he first started buying me sweets and taking me to the pictures. He even took me to see the dog racing, which made me feel really grown up.' She hesitated. 'I know I'm making feeble excuses. The truth is I have met Bernie, about the only straight guy I've had anything to do with in my life, and things started to get serious between us before I found out that he was related to you. He has to be told that my baby was fathered by your husband. That is not something I feel proud about. I've done nothing but put off the day when it will all have to be brought out into the open.'

Nellie Bradshaw was wiping a tear from her eye as she turned to her granddaughter. 'Linda, do you remember the day you asked me to meet you in London?'

'Course I do, Gran. That's when I told you I had put my baby up for adoption and was going to New Zealand.'

'To be married, you said.'

'Yes, I know. Wish I had known then what I know now.'

'Can't put old heads on young shoulders. Have you heard enough, Joan? Do you want to get going? It is still Christmas.' Nellie sighed.

'No, I'm all right for a bit.' Turning to Linda, Joan asked, 'Would you like to tell us a bit about what happened to you?'

'I'll tell you the bare bones and that is all. No good comes of raking up things I can't alter. I gave birth to a little boy, set up home with a friend, and between us we did our best. Got ourselves shift work so that someone was there with him all the time. Even had him christened. Called him David. Fine until Penny, my friend, met her fella, got married, and I was on my own again.'

A lump of coal moved in the fire sending out a few sparks, which made them all jump. They laughed, but it was a weak kind of laughter.

'Then I met a lovely young man, Tony. He offered me everything. New life in New Zealand. Marriage as soon as we got there. Only one fly in the ointment. Just as my father's new wife refused to take on me, Tony said he wanted nothing to do with another man's son.' Linda closed her eyes and choked back the lump that had risen in her throat. 'I made a decision. A bad one, as it turned out, but God knows I've paid for it. It wasn't until we arrived in New Zealand that I realised Tony wasn't prepared to share his life totally with any one person, and I don't think he ever will be. I was too young and naive to realise it at the time.'

There was a long pause before Linda started to talk again and when she did, emotions between the two that were listening were running high.

She went on to tell them about the guilt she felt for having abandoned her baby. How Tony was in danger of becoming an alcoholic and when drunk became very violent towards her. She knew no one in New Zealand, had no one to seek advice from. Quietly she admitted she herself had declined into bitterness and alcoholism. 'My life would have been finished if a Catholic priest hadn't found me slumped in a doorway. He got me into a home, found people to help me dry out and finally paid my fare home.'

There was a long silence, broken only by the soft crying of Nellie Bradshaw. Eventually, she dried her eyes and said, 'Linda, love, perhaps it would have been better if you hadn't told Joan any of this.'

'Gran, I had been back in this country for five months before I contacted you. I got myself a bed-sitting room and found myself a good job, the same one I am still holding down today. The truth is I longed to see you and Pops. I was so lonely. And then you both welcomed me with open arms and neither of you asked any questions.'

'So why tell us now?' Joan felt compelled to ask.

Linda gave a wry smile. 'I met your Bernie and that wasn't on the cards.' She paused. 'I couldn't just go on seeing him without him knowing. Someday, someone might find out and tell him, and then . . . who knows.'

'Telling us won't make any difference,' her gran said. 'What's done's done, I suppose, and it was all a long time ago.'

'Linda, you're thinking of telling Bernie yourself, aren't you?' Joan asked quietly.

'I didn't want to, but if I want to go on seeing him I have to. I will tell Bernie the whole story, but, Mrs Baldwin, I think it would be better if his mother told him about the baby being fathered by your husband.'

For a moment Joan looked very uncomfortable, then she had second thoughts. Hearing the truth from his mother would give Bernie time to digest the terrible facts, allow him to let off steam or not according to how he took the news. 'All right,' she said finally. 'I can't promise that our Martha will agree, but if she does she'll tell it fair and square. There's nobody more straightforward than my sister.'

Boxing Day, or what was left of it after everyone had eaten their fill, was every bit as festive as Christmas Day had been. It was getting on for midnight before Joan got a chance to have a word on the quiet with Martha. Having listened to what her sister had to tell her, Martha simply said, 'I'll sleep on it.' And for the time being Joan had to be content with that.

She kissed her sister good night and wearily climbed the stairs to go to bed. She had just reached the top landing when she suddenly realised that it was tomorrow that she was supposed to be going back to Malta with Eric. Oh well, she'd just have to get up early, get home and get a case packed. I'll take a cab, she promised herself. Her last thought as she scrambled into bed was that her life had suddenly taken an interesting turn. She certainly could no longer describe it as humdrum.

Chapter Forty-three

Joan heard the honk of the cab's horn just as she looked at the clock. It still wanted five minutes to three o'clock. Eric was eager today. She ran lightly down the stairs, opened the door and practically fell into Eric's arms.

He held her close and asked, 'Are you looking forward to returning to Malta?'

'Oh yes, I am, Eric. It will be lovely for us both to be able to see the New Year in with your family.'

He held her at arm's length and looked lovingly at her small face. 'I am not having the family wanting to take you here there and everywhere. This is going to be just as I promised, *our* time.' He smiled reassuringly and kissed her before asking, 'And where is your luggage?'

'I've only packed one suitcase, it's at the top of the stairs.'

'All right, you get into the cab and I'll run up and get it. Give me your keys and I'll lock the front door.'

Joan was bubbling with excitement. Then, just as she was about to step into the taxi, she happened to look at the back of the cab and to her amazement saw that two huge cabin trunks were secured to the rack. How much luggage did one require for a short stay? She couldn't say why, but her

387

immediate thought was, Eric isn't going to come back, he's planning to stay in Malta!

'Come on, slowcoach, we don't want the ship sailing without us, do we?' Eric had come up behind her and was almost lifting her into the taxi. 'Shift along,' he said laughingly, as he first handed her case to the driver and then planted himself beside her on the long, leather-covered seat. The cab had hardly drawn away from the kerbside before Eric had her in his arms. Joan responded immediately. It felt wonderful to be held by him again. He smelt as if he had come straight from the barber's, and the soft touch of his cashmere overcoat was heavenly as she buried her face into his shoulder. What a marvellous opportunity it was, to be taken again to that lovely island. How could she have hesitated for a moment over whether or not she should accept Eric's invitation?

He suddenly grinned and winked at her. 'My darling, we are going to have the time of our lives, you'll see. Nothing but the best on this trip.'

'Have you come into a fortune then, Eric?'

'Not exactly,' he answered, still grinning, 'but I have been thinking, what's the point of having money if you don't get any pleasure from it? So I'm aiming to spend it. That's what it's for.' He placed his lips softly over hers and when he lifted his head he spoke seriously. 'I aim to buy you everything your heart desires, Joan. You have become an inspiration in my life, like a really fresh breeze blowing away the cobwebs.'

Joan regarded him soberly. Mostly when she thought of money it was in terms of the necessities of life. Having at times not known where her next shilling was going to come from she was cautious. Like most women she enjoyed having nice clothes to wear, good food and enough heat in the house, but above all those things came the bills. The bills and the rent always had to come first.

'Joan dear, don't look so serious,' Eric pleaded. 'Aren't you pleased to know that businesswise I am doing very well?'

'Yes. Yes, I am,' she said slowly. 'As long as you aren't going to squander it all.'

He threw back his head and roared with laughter, until tears were trickling out of the corners of his eyes. 'My, but you're the careful one,' he gasped. He took a handkerchief from the pocket of his coat and wiped his eyes. Then squeezing her hand tightly he murmured, 'Oh, Joan, you baffle me. If I didn't know that there are times when you can and do throw caution to the wind and become totally uninhibited, wanton even, I'd say there was no hope for you.'

'Eric!' Feeling the blood rush to her cheeks, Joan punched his shoulder and turned her face away to look out of the window. She was more than relieved when she saw the signpost directing traffic to King George V docks.

Eric leaned across the seat and showed their tickets to the cab driver, who glanced at them and said, 'That's fine, mate. I've already dropped one fare at that dock today. If I'm lucky I'll be able to pull right by their landing stage. You jump out and find yerself a porter.'

Joan just stood there, taking in the different smells from the cargoes that were being swung aboard ships to be carried to distant destinations, savouring the noise, the hustle and the bustle of this busy dock. She watched Eric walk swiftly along the quay. He looked so dapper, so well dressed. There were several ships lined up in the inner harbour and Joan couldn't help but feel how lucky she was to be making this second journey to Malta on one of them. She did have a few misgivings. It had been such a good Christmas, and now she was leaving her staff to cope with her business and Martha, Sid and their family to see the New Year in without her. On the other hand, it was Freda, Martha and even Sid who had urged her to go with Eric.

She smiled to herself, admitting that she hadn't needed very much persuasion.

It was quite some time before Eric came back, a hefty-looking porter walking beside him pushing an upright trolley. The cab driver undid the straps that held Eric's two trunks and with what looked like ease the porter lugged them off and placed one on top of the other on the metal trolley. Meanwhile Eric was paying the cab fare and he must have tipped well for the driver touched the tip of his cap and said, 'Gawd bless yer, sir. You an' the lady 'ave a good time.'

Then, so suddenly that it seemed to Joan that they had appeared from nowhere, two police constables and another man dressed in a heavy dark overcoat came up to her and Eric.

'PC Christie,' one of the uniformed bobbies said as he laid a hand on Eric's arm.

PC Harris, the other constable, identified himself, looked at the crowd of onlookers that had gathered, and bellowed, 'All right, all right, there's nothing to see, so move on, please.'

The plain-clothes officer produced his warrant card. 'DI Mitchell.'

Eric looked grave-faced and muttered aggressively, 'Fucking hell.'

Joan couldn't believe that Eric had said that. She watched him close his eyes, doing his damnedest to control his temper.

'Going on a cruise, were you, Roussel?' DI Mitchell said snidely.

Joan stood rooted to the spot, her legs shaking. She was suddenly freezing cold; the icy temperature of the concrete she was standing on was penetrating right through the soles of her boots. She heard the inspector speaking to Eric but his voice seemed to be coming from a long way away. Suddenly he turned to her. 'Afraid you won't be going on any sea voyage today, ma'am. At least not with this gentleman.' He smiled

390

slowly. 'Though I suppose there is nothing to stop you going on your own if you wish.' Swinging back to Eric, he said, 'You must have been barmy, Roussel, if you really thought you could get away with it. Anyhow, you'll have plenty of time down at the station to tell us what your plans were.'

Eric was ignoring him. He was trying frantically to make Joan understand that she should leave. PC Christie intervened. 'Your luggage hasn't been taken on board, ma'am. I suggest you take your case and go back home. Shame you got caught up with this . . .' He glimpsed the stern look on the detective inspector's face and let the end of the sentence remain unsaid.

PC Harris was worried. Every bit of colour had drained from Joan's face and she wasn't at all steady on her pins. He put out a hand towards her and asked, 'Are you sure you can handle this?'

She swayed a little but managed to answer him quite forcefully. 'Doesn't look as if I've got much choice, does it?'

'My trunks have been taken aboard.' Eric drew himself up to his full height as he protested, but the inspector's voice was like thunder as he answered.

'Well, *sir*, you won't be following them.' Then, with a smirk, he added, 'It's a dead cert you won't need all those fine clothes where you're likely to be going.'

Deliberately, Eric took a packet of his small cigars from his overcoat pocket, extracted one, placed it between his lips, set a match to it and inhaled deeply. 'Stop making assumptions, Inspector, and try acting like a gentleman. Call a cab for Mrs Baldwin and allow her to return home as your constable has already suggested.' His voice was as loud and aggressive as the DI's and everyone nearby stopped what they were doing to stare openly at the group. When he turned to face Joan, however, all the fight seemed to go out of him, though he did his best to smile as he said, 'Sorry, my darling. Please go now.'

Joan picked up her case and walked stiffly to the high boundary wall, where she stood with her back against the cold stone for about twenty minutes. Not once did she look to see what was happening to Eric. Her head was going round and round and her mind was screaming, how could I have been so gullible? It isn't as if I was born yesterday.

At last, she picked up her case and began to walk again, but nearly jumped out of her skin when she felt a hand laid on her shoulder from behind. Dropping her case, she turned quickly and the relief of seeing Jim Taylor was so great that the tears that had been burning at the back of her eyelids spilled over and trickled down her cheeks.

'Oh, Jim!' She let go her case. 'You gave me such a fright . . . I thought I was being arrested!'

'Come on, Joan, we'll find a café and get you a cup of hot sweet tea. It will make you feel better. It's the best thing for shock and I'm damn sure you have had a very big one of those.'

Joan looked up at this kindly, reliable man and blinked away her tears, but all she could think of saying was, 'Jim, you know I never take sugar.'

'Never say never.' He grinned as he bent and picked up her case.

'Hey, wait a minute,' Joan protested. 'How did you get here? How did you know where to find me, and why would you have wanted to?'

'I came here in my van. The rest of your questions I will answer one at a time when we get inside the café.'

Sure enough, there was the usual café to be found in the dockland area. Christmas made not the slightest difference; ships came into dock and others put to sea on the crest of the tide. Dockers and seamen all had to be fed.

Jim led the way down an alleyway. Joan could smell cooking and she made for a doorway but was pulled back by Jim. 'Come on. The café we want is about three doors down.'

Once seated inside a steamy room where the air was still filled with the smell of frying sausages and bacon even at this time in the afternoon, Joan asked, 'What was wrong with the other tea rooms?'

'Nothing at all, Joan, but it might not have been what you were expecting. It's a Jewish café, so I suppose you could have had a pretzel and lemon tea.'

'Oh,' was all that Joan could manage.

Jim left her staring into space and soon came back with two big thick mugs filled with a strong hot brew. Watching Joan slowly sip the dark brown liquid his heart ached for her. She was so smartly dressed, but her face showed how distressed she was and her hands were shaking as she placed the mug back down on the table. In a very quiet voice he asked, 'Would you like me to answer your questions now?'

Joan didn't even look up, just stared at the table top and nodded her head.

'Right, I'll start at the beginning. When you were in Malta, the police came into the Prince of Wales and showed Les Jackson a photograph and asked if he had ever seen this man in his pub. Les shook his head, and as I was standing at the bar having a drink with Les at the time the policeman shoved the photo towards me. I shook my head too and asked what the man had done. The two officers weren't that forthcoming, but one of them did say he had been released from prison when he shouldn't have been because there was another warrant pending against him.'

There was a faraway look in Joan's eyes as she asked, 'Did you recognise the man in the photo?'

Jim pushed his lips together and nodded yes.

'Was it Eric?'

'Um, I'm afraid so. Couldn't mistake him. Last bank holiday Monday I came to ask you to come out with me for the day but just as I got out of my van I saw you leaving your place with him.' It was a sad silence that followed and Jim badly wanted to take her in his arms and comfort her. He didn't, though. As always, he kept his distance.

'You haven't told me how you knew where to find me.' Joan sounded so miserable even Jim felt a lump in his throat.

'Easy. Everyone knew you were going back to Malta the day after Boxing Day and so in the course of conversation I said to your brother-in-law I wonder what docks they are going from? Sid came straight out and told me – King George the fifth London docks did the Malta run.'

'That would have been easy enough to find out from a good many places, or you could have just asked me. But why did you want to know?'

'Joan, I honestly can't tell you. Right from the minute you started seeing him, I had the feeling that he wasn't all he made himself out to be. All day yesterday I had you on my mind, and this morning . . . well, I was jealous, if you want the truth. I thought I'd just come and see you off, though if all had been well I wouldn't have thrown a spanner into the works, truly. I wouldn't have said a word.'

Joan was staring at him, disbelief written all over her face. 'You said you were jealous.'

Jim looked a bit sheepish. 'We were getting on so well, going to auctions and so on. You even wanted to make me your business partner . . .' He hesitated, then said slowly, sounding disappointed, 'It hasn't been the same since Eric came on the scene.'

'Oh, Jim, nothing will ever alter between you and me,' Joan said sincerely.

'We'll see.' That was not the way he really wanted to answer her but it would have to do for now. 'Joan,' he began again, 'I didn't get here in time to see you walk away but one of the coppers did me a favour, said he'd felt sorry for you and had watched where you went. He pointed down the docks, said you were leaning against a wall down there. I came after you as quick as I could, saw you just before you started to leave.'

Joan had both hands cupped round her mug and didn't make any comment. Jim leant across the table until his face was nearer to hers. 'Don't you want to hear what else the copper told me?'

Joan shrugged her shoulders.

'All right, I'll tell you anyway. They will be keeping Eric at Leman Street police station for questioning before taking him to be rearrested. He said if we gave them time to take him from the harbourmaster's office we could call in at the station an' maybe, only maybe, the duty officer would allow you to have a few minutes with him. Do you want to do that or shall I take you straight home?' Endless time seemed to slip by without Joan's saying a word. She sat there, both hands clasped round the warm mug. 'Only you can decide.'

'Dear Jesus, if ever I needed help, I need it now.' It was a groan rather than a request.

Recently, Jim had been of the opinion that Joan would walk over red-hot coals for Eric Roussel. Now his heart went out to her and he said, 'You're still in shock.'

Joan continued to hang her head. Reluctantly Jim knew he had to take the lead. 'We can't sit here much longer. Only you can decide what you want to do, Joan. Either walk away now and put the man out of your thoughts and out of your life, or . . .' He couldn't go on because he couldn't find an alternative to offer her. Well, not one that she would even consider at this point.

It was still some time before Joan lifted her head and looked Jim in the face. 'You shouldn't be here with me. You should be at Martha's; I know she invited you for tea tonight. She'll be worried about you.'

Jim just had to laugh. 'If your sister knew the half of

what's been going on it wouldn't be me she'd be worried about, you know darn well it would be you.'

Even Joan managed half a smile. 'I know, I know,' she said, reaching out to take hold of his hand. 'I think I want to go and see Eric. It may not be the wisest thing to do but I owe myself that much.'

Jim was stunned. 'Are you sure?'

Joan nodded. 'Yes, Jim, I'm sure.'

Inwardly Jim was cursing himself for having mentioned that there might be a chance that she'd be able to see and speak to Eric. Still, he had to accept the fact that that was what she wanted and the sooner he got her to the police station and then took her home, the better it would be for all of them.

Chapter Forty-four

'DON'T YOU WORRY about anything.' Jim took Joan's arm as they walked towards the entrance of the police station.

A siren blared out suddenly, making Joan jump, and a second police car came to a halt beside the one that was already there. Joan shuddered, suddenly aware of where she was and what she was about to do. 'Who would have thought I would get myself mixed up in something like this?' she muttered, more to herself than to Jim.

Three steps up, Jim thrust his arm out and held the big heavy oak door wide open. Once inside the front office, Joan looked to her left and saw an endless corridor with many doors leading off it. Jim tugged at her arm and led her forward to a huge desk. Standing to one side was Detective Inspector Mitchell, and Joan smiled weakly at him, glad to see a face she recognised. Behind the desk stood a lanky young constable whom Joan immediately thought must be too young to be in the police force.

Jim spoke up. 'This is Mrs Baldwin,' he said, addressing the constable. 'If possible she would like to see Mr Roussel.'

The lad was given no time to reply. DI Mitchell stepped forward. 'Are you all right, Mrs Baldwin?'

Jim had to hold his temper in check, because he was capable of telling this bloke that no, she wasn't all right. He forced himself to remain silent.

Joan didn't answer the DI's enquiry. Instead, she said, 'Please may I see Eric, just for a few minutes?'

'Yes, Mrs Baldwin, I'll take you to him myself.' He nodded his head towards Jim. 'There's a chair behind you, you'll not have a long wait.' Then, taking hold of Joan's arm, the DI gave her a sympathetic smile. 'You had a nasty shock. I am sorry if I sounded a bit brusque with you out there at the docks.' He stopped walking suddenly, swung a chain from his belt which had a large bunch of keys dangling from it, selected one and opened a door.

Joan hadn't known what to expect, but it certainly wasn't this. She looked horror-struck. It was a bare cell, with just a long narrow bench attached to the far wall, on which Eric was sitting.

The DI looked down at Joan and said quietly, 'Five minutes, no longer.' His voice held a note of pity and that was something Joan felt she could do without. She was as much to blame as Eric for this unholy mess. He had got into whatever it was from choice and, when it came down to the nitty-gritty, so had she.

Eric rose to his feet, stunned. He hadn't expected to see her, and he didn't know whether he was pleased or not. For once in his life he was at a loss to find words to say. He clasped both of Joan's hands and they sat down beside each other on the bench.

'Oh, Eric.' The backs of her eyelids were prickling with unshed tears. Like Eric, she couldn't find anything to say, but she squeezed his hands tightly. He was immaculate as ever: snow white shirt cuffs, gold links, smooth light brown skin, well-manicured nails, onyx and gold signet ring on his little finger. 'You'll never alter will you?' she said, and Eric heard the sob in her voice. He couldn't bear her to see him like this and he really was sorry to have caused her such pain. But the devilish manner that Eric Roussel always showed to the world would not lie dormant and so he began to tease her.

'A few weeks ago you wouldn't have wanted me to, would you?' Seeing her smile, he withdrew one hand from her grasp and placed his arm round her shoulders. 'Now you listen to me, my darling. You've done nothing wrong. Nothing at all. You've just lived a little. Learnt that life doesn't have to be all sweat and toil. I made you realise that there is another side to life, didn't I?'

Choking back her tears, Joan murmured, 'You certainly did that!'

'Good, well you just remember the good times and only the good ones. Nothing ever came of constantly looking backwards. Try living your own life to the full. Will you promise me that much, Joan?'

'I'll try,' she whispered. 'But what will happen to you?'

He found himself thinking he really did love this woman. If only . . . but if onlys didn't figure in his life and he had to make a joke of it all even now. 'Joan, that is not your worry. Besides, if the gods are on my side I might get transported back to Malta. Can you imagine my family? Strings would be pulled and action would be taken. Who knows, one day you might even come and visit me.'

At that moment the young constable appeared in the open doorway. My, my, he said to himself, who'd have thought it? The posh old guy had that middle-aged woman in his arms and was kissing her! Not just peck on the cheek kisses, either, but long lingering ones. *Christ, they say there's many a good tune played on an old fiddle, and this guy could certainly teach me a thing or two.*

Discreetly, he coughed. 'Time t' go, missus,' he called, feeling a rotter for breaking the parting up.

It would have been hard to tell whether Eric was more upset than Joan as they drew apart and whispered goodbye! As Joan reached the doorway she heard Eric call out, 'I will always love you, Joan.' She couldn't bring herself to turn round and look at him.

She took a few steps, then leant against the cold wall of the corridor and handkerchief to her face she sobbed. Then, pulling herself together, she made straight for where Jim had parked his van, leaving him to jump to his feet and follow her. Outside in the cold air she blew her nose and wiped her eyes. Stony silence reigned during the ride back to Brixton.

Outside Distinctive Designs Jim pulled his van up to the kerb and turned off the engine. 'Shall I come upstairs with you?' he asked, leaning forward to look at her face.

'No, I'll be fine. But Jim,' she slowly put out a hand and placed it on his arm, 'thank you for coming to my rescue. You really are a good friend.'

He got out, went round to the passenger side and almost lifted her down on to the pavement. Holding out his hand he said, 'Give me the keys. I'll unlock the door and put your suitcase at the foot of the stairs, if you're sure you will be all right.'

'Yes, I will be fine. Thank you again, Jim.'

He got back into the van and drove off, cursing himself for not being more masterful. There was so much he could have said to her and done for her. Her big rooms would be cold, and she would be there all on her own. Rosie was still at her parents' house. If nothing else, he could have lit the fire. Why hadn't he insisted he stayed with her, if only for a while?

''Cos you're a loser, Jim Taylor. You've let so many opportunities slip past you.'

He was still upbraiding himself when he pulled up outside Martha and Sid's house. All he had to do now was tell them what had happened.

It was a task he was not looking forward to one little bit.

Chapter Forty-five

THERE WAS UPROAR in Martha's house.

Jim had just given them a rundown of the afternoon's events. He could see Martha out of the corner of his eye, her mouth hanging open in shock.

Suddenly everyone was talking at once.

Why did everyone have to be at home today, Jim was asking himself. Telling Martha and Sid would have been bad enough, but now he was getting an ear-bashing from both Lenny and Bernie, and there was young Rosie, the colour quite gone from her cheeks, repeating, 'Poor Auntie Joan, poor Auntie Joan.'

'Be quiet the lot of you!' Sid bellowed. 'Jim, I can't think why you didn't tell us where you were off to. You must have had some idea that things might go wrong for our Joan.'

'Yeah, I did,' Jim was quick to reply, 'but don't tell me that none of you had the slightest idea that Roussel wasn't all he cracked himself up to be.'

Sid had the grace to look sheepish. 'You're right, lad. I'd go so far as t' say yer could lay a lot of the blame on me and Martha, 'cos we egged our Joan on to going with the bloke.'

Martha found her voice. 'Hang on a minute, we did it from the best intentions and Freda was in agreement an' all. All we wanted for our Joan was a bit of spice in her life for a change. Didn't for a moment think it would turn out the way it 'as.'

'Why didn't you bring my auntie back here?' Rosie asked in tearful voice.

'I think she wanted a bit of time on her own, Rosie, to think about things.'

'Had enough on her plate on Boxing Day when old coals were raked over.' Lenny put his twopennyworth in.

'That's enough.' Bernie turned on him. 'Linda and our aunt have agreed to put the past behind them and that's good enough for me, so leave Linda and what happened with that rotter Bill Baldwin out of this.'

Martha shook her head, utterly bewildered by all the different turns of events that had taken place over this Christmas holiday. She couldn't believe the change in her youngest son. Blessed with striking good looks, he had always yearned to do well in life, but at the same time he'd played the field where girls were concerned. Mostly it had been young blonde ladies that he'd brought home before Linda Bradshaw turned up again. Seemed serious, her and him. Ah well, it was his life. To be fair to Linda she'd only been a slip of a girl when she'd found herself pregnant, and it seemed she'd been prepared to hold on to her little boy until what she thought was love had come along. What did any of us know about love when we were only sixteen years old? By God, from all accounts, she'd paid dearly for her mistakes. If Bernie thought she was the one for him then the least they could do was give them a chance.

Jim felt he was betwixt and between when Rosie asked if they could go and visit her aunt.

'No, love,' Sid said in his blunt way, 'we'll leave 'er be for tonight. Your aunt has a lot of thinking to do. Still, there's

402

one good thing t' come out of all this. She'll be with us for New Year's Eve.'

Jim wholeheartedly agreed with that.

Two days had passed since Jim had brought Joan home and there were still two days to go before it would be 31 December. He just couldn't settle to any job no matter what he tried. He wanted to see Joan. There was so much that he wanted to say to her. You're mad, he kept telling himself. They talked about everything else, business, her family, even discussed what they ate, so why couldn't he put his feelings towards her into words?

'I love you' wouldn't cover it. He needed her, wanted to take care of her, wanted to wake up every morning with her beside him. How could he explain his feelings without getting everything wrong? What would he do if she rejected him? Well, he decided at last, there is only one way to find out.

He wasn't brave enough to call on her unannounced. He made a quick telephone call. Yes, she was on her own, and yes, she would be pleased to see him.

Dependable as ever, Jim arrived within twenty-five minutes of making the call. Joan opened the side door and together they went upstairs to her flat. He couldn't believe how downcast she looked.

'Not downstairs working then?' Joan gave him a funny look and he quickly added, 'Silly question.'

'Sit down, Jim,' she said, smiling, 'No, Freda is managing fine, tells me the sales have been even better than expected so I thought I wouldn't show my face. Not just yet. But I'm OK,' she insisted.

'Don't be daft,' he said firmly, holding out a Fuller's coffee and walnut cake that he had stopped to buy. 'You've had a tremendous shock; what happened was bound to affect you. You sit down, Joan, while I make us some tea.'

She had no choice but to sit still until he brought in the tea, then the coffee cake laid out on a glass plate with a knife beside it and two small side plates. Setting everything out on a small table he asked, 'Where do you keep the serviettes?'

'Second drawer on the left past the cooker,' she told him.

Maybe Jim thought she was suffering from delayed shock and in a way that was true. But not entirely so. In fact, her thoughts were centred on him. She watched him pour out the tea, then cut two wedges of the cake, expertly sliding each piece off the knife and on to one of the side plates. It was as he bent over to put her slice in front of her that she put out her hand and gently pulled his head down so that she was able to kiss his cheek.

'Thank you, Jim,' she said. 'Thank you for being there, whenever I need you.'

He caught hold of her hand and lifted it to his cheek, pressing it hard with his, and his eyes told her more than words ever could. Love shone in them. Nothing like the look she'd had from Eric. He came round from behind the table and sat down next to her. Slowly he took her into his arms.

Joan didn't move away. She couldn't. When she lifted her face, he lowered his head and gently placed his lips over hers. It was some while before he let her go and when he did he said, 'God alone knows how long I have wanted to do that.'

His kiss had been hesitant, as if he didn't believe this was any more than gratitude. But it was Joan who took the initiative now as she slid her arms round his neck to draw him closer still. Emotions that he had kept hidden for a long time stirred inside Jim. Nothing mattered other than that at last she was in his arms. The warmth of her lips was wonderful. Nothing existed at this moment other than the need to hold her and never let her go.

It was Joan that moved away first. 'What is it?' he asked.

Then, feeling her sigh deeply, he said, 'You're afraid it is too soon?' Without waiting for an answer he took her head in his hands, lifting it up so she could look at him. If she'd had any doubts before, they flew away.

'Tell me,' she said, knowing, but needing to hear him say it.

'I love you,' he whispered, his voice muffled on her neck.

Joan knew without any doubt that what he said was true. However mixed up everything else had become, this time and this man were right.

She had admired him for years, ever since she first met him on the market. Admired him for his talents, his patience, his intelligence. He had become first her workmate and then her loyal friend. Now they had both seen the light and she knew it was meant to be.

'You don't think I am taking advantage?' He smiled down at her. 'Because, Joan, I can't wait to ask you. Please will you marry me? Please, Joan, will you be my wife?'

Joan was a long time answering so Jim pressed his point. 'I mean it,' he said. 'You do believe me, don't you?'

She wanted to say yes but she was a little scared now. After a while she whispered, 'I do believe you, Jim. I'd be proud to marry you, but only on one condition.'

'And that is?' he asked, his heart in his mouth.

'Oh, Jim.' She leant against him, reaching for his hand. 'It is something we should have done a long time ago. Become business partners.'

Jim quietly considered her offer before answering. When he did speak, the words came from his heart. 'Joan dear, we neither of us are spring chickens, but to spend the rest of our lives together is all that I'm asking.'

'Only if we are partners in everything.' Now it was Joan's turn to push her point. And while she waited for his answer she smiled, really smiled, for the first time in days.

'Partners in everything,' Jim finally agreed, then added,

'I seem to have waited years for you and I would have gone on waiting, but it has been such a long, horrible couple of days and I couldn't bear to see you so upset. The times I have imagined myself proposing to you – but it was always over a wonderful meal and a bottle of champagne. Now I feel mean. I haven't even got a ring to give you.'

'Plenty of time,' Joan said.

'Oh no there isn't. There's no going back. I want a ring on your finger when we open a bottle and tell all your family on New Year's Eve. How does that sound to you?' He pointed to the cups of tea that had gone cold and the cake that hadn't been touched. 'If I make a fresh pot of tea, will this do till then?'

Joan reached up and kissed him. 'Very well indeed,' she whispered.